Robyn

Hiya . . .

Have you ever wanted to change the world? Coco Tanberry reckons she might just be able to do it, armed only with an old violin, a fluffy panda hat, a rucksack full of cupcakes and a LOT of determination. Sadly, she has reckoned without surly loner Lawrie Marshall, who seems to think everything she does is ridiculous. When the two of them find themselves working together to rescue some ill-treated ponies, there's bound to be trouble . . .

Coco is a tomboy with big plans and bucketfuls of enthusiasm. She cares so much about so many things and wants to fix them all, but she's impulsive – she doesn't always think before she acts. While she's busy trying to save the world, her own family is falling to pieces – but Coco can't help the big sister she loves without drawing attention to herself and the tangle of lies and deceit she has woven to hide the dangerous risks she is taking.

Coco reminds me a lot of myself back at the age of twelve. I am still crazy about animals and hate injustice of any kind . . . and like Coco, if I thought I could save the world with cake, I'd definitely give it my best shot!

Coco Caramel is the fourth book in the Chocolate Box Girls series . . . a story of growing up and finding the courage to do the right thing, even if the 'right thing' turns out to be a little different from what you first imagined. Curl up with a cool chocolate milkshake and let the adventure begin . . .

Cathy Cassidy, xxx

the
chocolate box
girls

PUFFIN

PUFFIN BOOKS

Published by the Penguin Group
Penguin Books Ltd, 80 Strand, London WC2R ORL, England
Penguin Group (USA) Inc., 375 Hudson Street, New York, New York 10014, USA
Penguin Group (Canada), 90 Eglinton Avenue East, Suite 700, Toronto, Ontario, Canada M4P 2Y3
(a division of Pearson Penguin Canada Inc.)
Penguin Ireland, 25 St Stephen's Green, Dublin 2, Ireland (a division of Penguin Books Ltd)
Penguin Group (Australia), 707 Collins Street, Melbourne, Victoria 3008, Australia
(a division of Pearson Australia Group Pty Ltd)
Penguin Books India Pvt Ltd, 11 Community Centre, Panchsheel Park, New Delhi – 110 017, India
Penguin Group (NZ), 67 Apollo Drive, Rosedale, Auckland 0632, New Zealand
(a division of Pearson New Zealand Ltd)
Penguin Books (South Africa) (Pty) Ltd, Block D, Rosebank Office Park, 181 Jan Smuts Avenue,
Parktown North, Gauteng 2193, South Africa

Penguin Books Ltd, Registered Offices: 80 Strand, London WC2R ORL, England

puffinbooks.com

First published 2013
001

Text copyright © Cathy Cassidy, 2013
Illustrations copyright © Puffin Books, 2013
Illustrations by Sara Chadwick-Holmes

The moral right of the author and illustrator has been asserted

Set in 13.25/19.25 pt Baskerville MT Std by Palimpsest Book Production Ltd, Falkirk, Stirlingshire
Printed in Great Britain by Clays Ltd, St Ives plc

British Library Cataloguing in Publication Data
A CIP catalogue record for this book is available from the British Library

HARDBACK
ISBN: 978-0-141-34157-6

TRADE PAPERBACK
ISBN: 978-0-141-34158-3

www.greenpenguin.co.uk

Penguin Books is committed to a sustainable
future for our business, our readers and our planet.
This book is made from Forest Stewardship
Council™ certified paper.

ALWAYS LEARNING **PEARSON**

Thanks . . .

To Liam, Cal and Caitlin for being generally awesome, and to Mum, Joan, Andy, Lori and all of my fab family. Thanks to Helen, Sheena, Fiona, Jessie, Lal and Maggi for the hugs, the chocolate and the pep talks, and to all of my lovely friends for putting up with me.

Thanks to Ruth my ever-patient PA, to maths-guru Martyn and to my brilliant agent Darley and his team. Hugs to Alex, my editor, and Amanda too; also to Sara for the stunning artwork. Huge thanks to Adele, Jayde, Julia, Emily, Samantha, Helen and all of the creative, clever team at Puffin.

Special thanks to Roy and Jean for letting me borrow their names for the story. Jean ran the riding school I went to back when I was nine; I had zero talent at riding, but Roy and Jean have been much loved family friends all these years. Last but not least, thanks to all my lovely, loyal readers – YOU make all the hard work worthwhile!

1

They say that families are like chocolate – mostly sweet, with a few nuts. More than a few, in my family's case . . . and they say that I'm the crazy one? Yeah, right.

They also say that life is like a box of chocolates, and that you can't expect every one you pick to be exactly the way you'd like it to be. This seems a little ridiculous to me – and as my mum and my stepdad Paddy run a chocolate business, well . . . I think I should know. Better just to pick out your favourites, even if they don't come in a fancy box. With a little planning, you can get what you want, with no nasty surprises. Simple.

I lean back against the tree trunk and rest my violin across my lap.

I have just finished my practice. I have only been playing

❀❀❀❀❀❀❀❀❀❀❀❀❀❀❀❀❀❀❀❀❀❀❀

for a year and because my family is not especially musical and not especially tolerant of beginner violinists, I am banned from playing indoors.

Our house, Tanglewood, is a B&B, and Mum says that my playing might disturb the guests, and that she cannot afford to lose custom because of it. This shows you the kind of thing I have to put up with because only one or two guests actually complained, and that was *ages* ago, when I was just starting out. These days I am lots better and my playing sounds nothing at all like cats being strangled.

The B&B business is winding down a little lately now that the chocolate business is taking off, so why anyone cares about losing one or two guests who are probably tone-deaf anyway is quite beyond me. Still, I am banished from the house and so I have to practise outside, perched in my favourite climbing tree, an oak. It is quite a comfortable tree because there is a wide branch that meets the main trunk almost at a right angle. I have added a cushion from one of the garden chairs, and if you want to you can pull your legs up and lean back as if you are sitting in a lumpy old armchair.

✿✿✿✿✿✿✿✿✿✿✿✿✿✿✿✿✿✿✿✿✿✿✿✿✿✿

Or you can let your legs dangle, the way I am right now, and look down through the oak leaves at the ground below. It is October, the end of the half-term break, and the leaves are a hundred shades of gold and burnt orange and crimson. There is a definite chill in the air, and I am wearing a scarf, a jumper and a beanie hat. It's not quite cold enough yet for gloves, but it will be soon. If you have ever tried playing a violin wearing red and black striped woolly gloves, you will know that this is not good.

You'd think my family would take pity on me and let me practise indoors, but there's no chance of that. Sometimes I think they are philistines.

My friends at school think my family is cool, but they don't know the half of it. Mum and Paddy are always hassled and busy, juggling B&B stuff with chocolate orders and new truffle ideas and designs for the handpainted boxes. As for having four sisters . . . well, that can be seriously hard work, especially when you are the youngest.

Like I said, my family is mostly nuts.

Honey, my eldest sister, is definitely more sour than sweet – she looks cute on the outside, but inside she's pure rebel. It's like she has no limits, no rules. She

3

❀❀❀❀❀❀❀❀❀❀❀❀❀❀❀❀❀❀❀❀❀❀❀❀❀❀

accidentally caused a fire back in the summer and tried to run away; a few weeks after, she stayed out all night and skipped the first day of school. Everyone thought she'd run away again and the police and social services got involved. Scary stuff. Honey seems to have quietened down again now, but for how long?

My stepsister Cherry is cool, but when she first arrived last year, she had a few problems sorting fact from fiction. She also had a problem staying away from Honey's boyfriend, and now the two of them are an item. This is great for Cherry, but not so great for Honey – since Shay ditched Honey she has dated practically every boy in Somerset, the more unsuitable the better. Cherry and Shay broke up recently for a week, and rumour had it that Honey was responsible . . . but they're back together now and stronger than ever. Don't get me wrong, I like Cherry a lot, but still, I can't help wishing she hadn't fallen for Shay Fletcher.

So. My sister Skye likes to dress in dead girls' dresses, or 'vintage' as she calls it. Last year she had a crush on some imaginary ghost boy; this year she has a long-distance boyfriend up in London, and they are always

4

writing and texting and emailing. If you want my opinion, I think she should have stuck with the ghost boy.

As for Summer, Skye's twin – I used to think she had it all; looks, talent, popularity, big dreams, determination. She had a scholarship for a boarding ballet school this term . . . but she threw it all away, cracked under the pressure. Her dream turned into a nightmare, and she is still struggling to break free of it. These days, Summer is like a shadow girl, frail, fragile, lost. She picks at her food as if she thinks it could be poisoned, and we have to creep around her pretending nothing is wrong when we all know that things are very wrong indeed.

Summer hangs out the whole time with Alfie Anderson, who is a million miles from cool, the kind of boy who puts salt instead of sugar in your hot chocolate and thinks it's funny. I really don't, and I have no idea what Summer sees in him.

Boys are nothing but trouble – if they vanished off the face of the earth right now, Honey, Cherry, Skye and Summer would probably be a whole lot happier and much more fun. Personally, I think animals are far more reliable and rewarding.

5

✿✿✿✿✿✿✿✿✿✿✿✿✿✿✿✿✿✿✿✿✿✿✿✿

I peer down through the leaves at Fred the dog, who is waiting patiently at the foot of the tree, while Humbug my pet sheep munches grass nearby. You see? Animals are loyal. They don't care if you play a few dud notes when practising the violin. They never judge you, and they don't let you down.

People can learn a lot from animals. I know that my sisters are not perfect, but I love them and I am loyal to them. If someone else says anything at all against them, I will defend them to my last breath.

The problem with being the youngest is that people don't take you seriously. You are stuck forever as the baby of the family, which can be very annoying indeed. I'll show them, though. I have my life all planned out and I am pretty sure it's going to be *amazing*.

I want to work with animals – I will do voluntary work and save endangered species. I have started on this task already because let's face it, time is running out. I am having a cake sale at school on Monday, in aid of endangered pandas, and before half-term I started a petition to save the white rhino. I collected 233 signatures, and sent them all off to the government with a first-class stamp.

✿✿✿✿✿✿✿✿✿✿✿✿✿✿✿✿✿✿✿✿✿✿✿✿✿✿✿✿

Once I have saved the panda, the white rhino and a bunch of other threatened animals, I will train to be a vet and eventually I will live in a big house by the sea (a bit like Tanglewood) and have my own horses and play the violin whenever I like. Indoors and out.

I know what I want, and it doesn't seem too much to ask.

If life is a box of chocolates, I will just make sure that I pick carefully. Why waste time on nougat and jaw-breaking toffee brittle when you can have something you really love instead? I like most of the truffles that my stepdad Paddy makes for his business, The Chocolate Box, but the caramel truffle he invented for me back on my twelfth birthday a while ago is without a doubt the best of all.

If my life is going to be a box of chocolates, I will plan ahead and make sure I choose caramel, rich and smooth and sweet, every time.

2

I set up a table in the foyer of Exmoor Park Middle School, cover it with a red and white checked cloth and drape my handpainted banner, *Save the Giant Panda*, across the front of it. Then I set out the plates and arrange my home-baked cupcakes, which I have iced with little black and white panda faces. Who could resist?

'They look better than the whale ones you made last time,' my friend Sarah comments. 'These ones are actually quite cute. What are we charging? Ten pence? Twenty pence?'

'Thirty pence, or two for fifty pence,' I decide. 'It's for charity, isn't it?'

It is the first day back after the October holiday and Sarah and I have been allowed out of history ten minutes early to set up our stall, so that we can make the most of the breaktime rush once the bell goes.

Sarah unpacks a plastic box of chocolate fridge cake and I set out a slightly dented Victoria sponge, a tin of chocolate crispy cakes and a tub of rock buns that are a little too rock-like for comfort. My friends always rally round at times like this and manage to contribute something. I arrange my handmade leaflets, explaining why the giant panda is endangered and needs our help. I have learnt the hard way that my fellow pupils are rarely impressed by my efforts to raise funds with sponsored walks or silences. They are much more likely to part with their cash if cake is involved.

'OK,' Sarah says. 'Thirty seconds and counting. Watch out for those Year Six boys, I'm sure they nicked my flapjacks last time!'

'Nobody will dare swipe so much as a crumb while I'm watching,' I promise.

I pull on my fake-fur panda hat with the sticky-up ears and square my shoulders, ready to do battle.

'Here we go,' I say to Sarah. 'For the pandas!'

The bell rings and the foyer floods with kids. They can scent cake, and they swarm round the stall, grabbing panda cupcakes and wedges of Victoria sponge, shoving warm, sticky coins into the collection tin.

One cute little Year Five girl buys up the whole tin of chocolate crispy cakes for £5 because it's her mum's birthday. Then I spot a weaselly Year Six boy trying to pocket a couple of chunks of chocolate fridge cake and grab his wrist firmly. 'Fifty pence, please,' I say sweetly. 'All proceeds go to help the giant panda!'

'Help it do what?' he asks, reluctantly handing over his cash.

'Survive,' I explain patiently. 'They are almost extinct because bamboo forests are being cut down and pandas eat mainly bamboo shoots.'

'Why don't they eat something different then?' the kid asks. 'Fish 'n' chips. Big Macs. Chocolate fridge cake.'

I roll my eyes. 'They can't,' I explain. 'They are *pandas*, not people. They are supposed to eat bamboo shoots, and people are destroying their habitat. It's up to us to save them!'

The boy's face hardens. 'If that's true, you really shouldn't wear a panda hat,' he says. 'That's just sick.' He walks away, scoffing fridge cake.

❀❀❀❀❀❀❀❀❀❀❀❀❀❀❀❀❀❀❀❀❀❀❀

Boys really are infuriating and dim, especially Year Six boys.

And Year Eight boys are not much better. Lawrie Marshall has edged his way to the front of the crowd and is reading my panda leaflet with a sneery, disgusted look on his face.

Lawrie is the scratchiest, surliest boy I've ever met. He's a loner, radiating waves of simmering anger that keep both kids and teachers at arm's length. If he were a chocolate truffle, he'd be one of Paddy's disastrous experiments – dark chocolate filled with gherkins and liquorice, or something equally horrific.

He must have a sweet tooth, though, because he always turns up at my cake sales.

'How come you think you can change the world with cake?' he snarls, bundling four cupcakes into a paper bag and handing over a pound coin.

'I just do,' I say. 'I care about the pandas, and anything I can do to raise awareness and raise money has got to help.'

'Huh,' Lawrie says. 'What's the black and white icing supposed to be, anyway? Badgers?'

'Panda faces,' I say through gritted teeth. 'Obviously.'

'Right,' he grunts. 'Don't give up the day job, OK?'

I roll my eyes.

'Like the hat,' Lawrie sneers, stalking away. I resist the temptation to throw a rock bun at the back of his head – but only just.

'Ignore him,' Sarah says. 'He has a chip on his shoulder.'

'A what?'

'You know,' she shrugs. 'It's just one of those things that people say. He's angry at the world. Snippy with everyone. Don't take it personally.'

The teachers drift over, buying the last few cakes for the staffroom, and I hand out the remaining leaflets to anyone who will take one.

'There has to be twenty quid in there, at least,' Sarah says, grinning at the collection tin, and suddenly I feel doubtful, disappointed. Twenty quid isn't a whole lot really, especially considering all the flour and eggs and sugar and food colouring I've forked out for to make my cupcakes. It's not enough to save the giant panda, I am pretty sure. Looking around the table, I notice half a dozen discarded panda leaflets lying on the ground, and my spirits dip still further.

Saving the world with cake may actually be harder than I thought.

I glare at Lawrie Marshall as he stomps away along the corridor. I don't think he has a chip on his shoulder so much as a whole plateful of the things, drenched in vinegar.

3

Once we've counted it up properly it turns out that we have made almost £30 from the cake sale, so my mood has recovered a little by the time the last bell rings. When I get home, I will ask Mum to make a cheque out to the panda charity, and it will make a difference, I know it will. I expect £30 could plant a whole load of bamboo.

There's a steady drizzle falling as I walk down to the bus stop, but when I reach into my rucksack for my panda hat it isn't there. Maybe I left it in my locker? Once I get off the school bus in Kitnor, it's quite a long walk up to Tanglewood, and without my hat I will get wet.

'I'm going to run back and get my hat,' I tell Sarah. She lives in town, so she walks home, and at my words she just pulls up her jacket hood and shrugs.

'See you then!' she says.

I am sprinting back up to the school, dodging the crowds of kids going the other way, when I catch sight of something very odd fluttering from the school flagpole in the breeze.

My panda hat! I am outraged. Who would do such a thing?

I frown as a memory surfaces.

'Like the panda hat,' Lawrie Marshall had said at breaktime. And what he meant was that he *didn't* like the panda hat – the curl of his lip and the tone of his voice made that very clear.

I don't think he likes me and I definitely do not like him, but still, he wouldn't do something like this – would he? He seems too gloomy, too sour – I am not sure that practical jokes are his style. Then again, he sits right across the aisle from me in science, and if the hat had been at the top of my rucksack he could have swiped it easily.

I take a deep breath and storm across to the flagpole.

It takes forever to work out how to control the lines that hoist things up and down, and by then my hair is frizzy from the rain and I am very cross indeed. Eventually I manage to haul down the hat and untie it, and even though it is dripping wet I pull it on because at least that way I won't lose it again.

Seriously, if I find out that Lawrie Marshall is responsible for this I will make sure he is an endangered species himself. I leg it across the grass towards the bus stop, but as I run through the playground I have a bad feeling, a very bad feeling. It is too quiet, too empty. There are no clumps of kids, no waiting school buses, just a few stray students hurrying away, umbrellas angled against the rain. I must have been messing around with that stupid flagpole for longer than I thought because I've gone and missed the bus.

Great.

I slow to a walk. Once upon a time Skye and Summer would have made sure the bus waited for me, but they are at the high school now. My friends from junior school, Amy and Jayde, usually save me a seat, but I can't blame them for not getting the driver to hang on – they probably thought I was doing something after school.

❁❁❁❁❁❁❁❁❁❁❁❁❁❁❁❁❁❁❁❁❁❁❁❁

I have riding lessons on Fridays, at the stables on the edge of town, and on Tuesdays I have Save the Animals Club, which I invented and which usually consists of me, Sarah, Amy and Jayde talking about pandas/whales/tigers to assorted Year Five and Six kids. Lately, our numbers have dwindled and the week before half-term even Sarah made an excuse not to come, so it was just me, sitting alone in the science room after 3.30, looking at my home-made endangered species leaflets and wondering if I was the only one who actually cared. Sometimes I skip the school bus anyway, and walk up to meet Skye, Summer and Cherry at the high school, and we go into town and drink smoothies and mooch around the shops and catch the town bus home at half five.

It looks like I'll be catching that bus today. I trudge out of the school gates and turn the corner, my panda hat dripping, and walk right into a nightmare.

Lawrie Marshall is in the shady walkway next to the school gym. He is locked in battle with a small, scrawny kid, holding him by the jacket, shaking him, growling something angry right into his face.

The kid looks terrified, his eyes wide with fear, and I recognize the weaselly Year Six kid from earlier, the one who thought that pandas should branch out a bit and eat Big Macs and chocolate fridge cake.

My heart thuds. I hate bullying of any kind, and this is not name-calling or teasing, it is full-on aggression. Lawrie shoves the little kid up against the gym wall, and the kid winces. He wriggles helplessly, trying to get away, but Lawrie is two years older, six inches taller and a whole lot angrier. The little kid is going to be mincemeat.

'Let him go!' I scream, and two pairs of startled eyes swivel to look at me.

'Push off, panda girl,' Lawrie snarls. 'This is none of your business!'

That does it. I think of my hat, fluttering from the flagpole, a dozen nasty, snide remarks Lawrie Marshall has made in the year since he joined our school. I look at the Year Six kid, squirming as he struggles, and I see red.

I fling myself at Lawrie Marshall, grabbing his arms, pulling him backwards, away from the boy. His victim slithers free, grabs his abandoned sports bag and sprints

❀❀❀❀❀❀❀❀❀❀❀❀❀❀❀❀❀❀❀❀❀❀❀❀❀

off along the walkway, and Lawrie Marshall rounds on me, his face dark with fury.

'You idiot!' he yells. 'Now look what you've done!'

'Idiot? Me?' I yell back at him. 'You should be ashamed of yourself! You're loads bigger than that little kid, and old enough to know better . . . bullying sucks! Only losers have to threaten those who are weaker than themselves to feel good. D'you think it makes you tough? D'you think it makes you hard? It doesn't, it just makes you a lousy, rotten bully!'

Lawrie Marshall looks disgusted. His lip curls, his eyes flash and his nostrils flare dangerously. His fists are clenched and trembling, as if fighting the urge to lash out at me. Suddenly I'm scared, aware that I have just broken up a fight, yelled at a bully, shouted insults at the school misfit. Here I am on a shady walkway tucked away from the road with a psychopathic schoolboy, and trust me, he is not happy.

'Idiot,' he says again, his voice thick with scorn. 'You really think you're something, don't you? You reckon you can save the world, rescue the panda and wipe out bullying all in one day, then go home and eat your stupid little cakes. You don't have a clue about the real world! You don't know what you're talking about!'

Lawrie Marshall strides away, leaving me alone in the rain.

4

I spot the scrawny Year Six kid in the school corridor on Friday and corner him, concerned. 'Are you OK?' I ask. 'He hasn't bothered you again, has he?'

'Er . . . no,' the boy says shiftily. 'And yes, thanks, I'm fine. No hassle. No worries.'

His friends hover nearby, smirking. I can sense that the kid just wants to escape, but I grab his sleeve and haul him back and he rolls his eyes and tells his mates he'll catch up with them. You'd think he might be at least a little bit grateful that I saved him from being mashed to a pulp, but I guess that's boys for you.

'Have you told the teachers?' I push. 'Bullying is out of order, you know. Only lowlifes and losers pick on little kids. If that creep can do it to you, he can do it to others too, so speaking out really is the only way to stop it. Do you want me to say something to your guidance tutor?'

'No!' the kid gulps. 'No, honestly, don't say anything, I don't want a fuss . . . I've sorted it now. It won't happen again, I'm pretty sure of that. But thanks for looking out for me the other day. You saved my skin, and I appreciate that.'

I smile. 'Well . . . as long as you're sure everything's OK now?'

'I'm sure,' he says. 'And . . . look . . . I'm sorry about the hat.'

He races off along the corridor like a mad thing, bashing into a couple of Year Fives as he goes.

Boys. I will never understand them. And what did he mean about my hat?

'That was the kid Lawrie Marshall had a hold of the other day?' Sarah enquires.

'Yup. Poor thing.'

Sarah frowns. 'He doesn't look like a victim,' she says. 'More of a troublemaker. And what did he mean about your hat? Perhaps he hoisted it up the flagpole!'

'No, that had to be Lawrie,' I frown. 'He hates me,

❀❀❀❀❀❀❀❀❀❀❀❀❀❀❀❀❀❀❀❀❀❀❀

and he hates the hat. And he sits across from me in science, so . . .'

'So what?' Sarah shrugs. 'That proves nothing. You could have dropped the hat, or the Year Six kid could have taken it out of your locker . . .'

'Nah, I don't think so,' I frown. 'But whoever pulled the stunt with my hat, it doesn't change things. Lawrie Marshall is a bully, pure and simple.'

'He's definitely a loner,' Sarah says. 'He never seems to have any friends around. Maybe that's because of his temper?'

'Probably,' I agree.

'He'd be quite nice-looking if he ever smiled,' Sarah considers. 'In theory, of course. He never DOES smile – he is the sulkiest boy I know.'

'He never smiles because he is a horrible, bad-tempered bully,' I say. 'You should have seen him the other day, Sarah, it was horrible! He practically had that little kid by the throat!'

'Maybe the kid deserved it?' Sarah suggests.

'Nobody deserves that. Trust me, Lawrie Marshall is bad news.'

❀❀❀❀❀❀❀❀❀❀❀❀❀❀❀❀❀❀❀❀❀❀❀❀

As I finish speaking, the boy in question appears in the distance and stalks along the corridor towards us. As usual, he treats me to his best glare.

'Idiot!' he snarls as he passes.

My eyes widen in shock and my cheeks burn with embarrassment as I try to dredge up a reply.

'Oh boy.' Sarah blinks. 'I see what you mean!'

'Loser,' I mutter, but it's too little, too late, of course.

Lawrie Marshall has long gone.

I am out of sorts all day after that, but I have a riding lesson after school and that is the one thing that is pretty much guaranteed to put the smile back on my face. My lesson isn't until four, so I have lots of time to walk down to the stables on the edge of town. With every step the day's irritations loosen and lift away.

I have been learning to ride since Christmas, and although I know I still have a lot to learn, I love it. I love the smell of the stable yard, all fresh hay and ponies and leather. I love the paddock exercises my instructor teaches us for balance and confidence, scissors and frogs and round-the-world turns and riding with no stirrups. I love hacking

✿✿✿✿✿✿✿✿✿✿✿✿✿✿✿✿✿✿✿✿✿✿✿✿

through the countryside or riding along the beach, trotting or cantering with the wind in my face and the feeling that I'm free, soaring, that anything at all is possible.

Most of all, though, I love a pony called Caramel.

I liked her first of all because of her name – caramel, as you know, is my favourite sweet treat. Then I fell for her looks because Caramel is possibly the most beautiful pony in the world. She is a pure-bred Exmoor pony, twelve hands high and a beautiful dark bay colour, rich as caramel. Around her eyes and muzzle are pangaré markings, mealy-cream, and her mane and tail are thick and coarse and wild. She looks timeless, noble, magical, as though she could have ridden out of the Dark Ages, been the pony of a princess warrior or a Celtic queen from thousands of years ago.

She is my perfect pony, but I have never ridden her because unlike most Exmoors, who are steady and calm and trustworthy, Caramel can be hard to handle. The bosses at the riding school, Jean and Roy, think she was ill-treated in the past – she can be jumpy, unpredictable, flighty. There have been a couple of unpleasant incidents with Caramel this year, and Jean and Roy are wary. They make sure that only older, more experienced riders take her out these days.

It's the story of my life – everybody thinks I am too young for everything. They don't take me seriously at all.

For example, a couple of weeks ago there was a part-time job advertised at the stables for someone to help with mucking out and grooming, just a few hours for a couple of days a week after school. When Mum picked me up after my lesson that day, I was full of it – how I could spend more time with Caramel, get more experience with horses, cover the cost of my lessons and bring a little cash in on top of that. I thought she'd go for the idea for sure, but I was wrong.

Surprise, surprise, she said I was too young.

'You're only twelve,' she'd said on the drive home, as if I might have forgotten this vital fact. 'They probably wouldn't consider you for the job at that age, and besides, there's no need to start thinking about part-time jobs just yet! Just focus on your friends and your animals and your studies!'

'But . . .'

'No buts,' Mum insisted. 'Don't be in too much of a

❀❀❀❀❀❀❀❀❀❀❀❀❀❀❀❀❀❀❀❀❀❀❀❀

hurry to grow up, Coco. Enjoy your freedom while you can! If it's the money you're thinking about, I'll have a word with Paddy – now that the chocolate business is starting to take off, we might be able to give you a bit more pocket money.'

Pocket money? Honestly, I felt about five years old. As far as my family is concerned I might as well be – it's as if there is one rule for my sisters and another for me.

OK, I'm twelve. So what? At twelve Summer had been a regular student helper at the dance school for years. By the time she was thirteen she worked a whole week there in the summer holidays in exchange for extra lessons, and Skye was thirteen when she helped out with the costumes on the TV film they made in Kitnor a few months back. The twins aren't all that much older than me, but they get to do what they want.

As for Honey, she may not have had a job at twelve but she had way more freedom than any of us. She was a pre-teen drama queen – she didn't bother to ask permission for the things she wanted to do, she just went ahead and did them anyway. She still does. Maybe I should take a leaf out of her book?

❁❁❁❁❁❁❁❁❁❁❁❁❁❁❁❁❁❁❁❁❁❁❁❁

I push through the gates of the Woodlands Riding School, breathing in the smell of fresh hay and happiness. I am a little early, but I like it that way. I wave at Kelly, one of the teenage instructors who sometimes takes the paddock classes or leads the treks, then step into the warm office building, stash my rucksack in a locker and nip to the loos to change into my riding gear. Folding away my school uniform and replacing it with outsize jumper, jodhpurs and waterproof, I am the happiest I have felt all day. I leave my uniform in the locker and scoop up my riding hat, pulling it on as I wander back out into the stable yard.

Then I see a familiar figure in the doorway of one stall, gruff and grim in wellies and muddy jeans, forking manure into a wheelbarrow.

Lawrie Marshall looks up at me and his face registers surprise and then disgust. I am pretty sure my face mirrors those emotions too, and then some.

5

'What are you doing here?' Lawrie Marshall asks, and I swear I am so cross at this comment that if I could I would tip that barrowload of manure right over his head, then jab him with his own pitchfork, just for good measure.

'I am here for my riding lesson,' I tell him. 'The same as I have been every week since January. And I have never seen you at Woodlands before, so I think I could ask what *you* are doing here!'

Lawrie curls his lip. 'I work here,' he says icily. 'Started this week, three forty-five till six, Tuesdays and Fridays. If I'd known they gave lessons to fruitcakes like you, I might have had second thoughts . . .'

Fruitcake? Me? I am pretty sure this is an insult and not a reference to my baking abilities. And worse, it looks like Lawrie Marshall has *my* job. He is the same age as me, twelve years old . . . is that fair? Is that right? No, it is not.

'Oh . . . fruitcake to you too!' I snap.

As comebacks go, it isn't the best. You might even say it is lame and laughable, and Lawrie seems to think so because his lips twitch into a sour kind of smile and he starts shovelling manure again, a little carelessly. A clump of something deeply unpleasant lands sloppily on my boots, and I am pretty certain it wasn't an accident.

Words fail me. I turn on my heel and march over to Caramel's stall, seething inwardly. I reach up and stroke her face, press my cheek against the roughness of her through-a-hedge-backwards mane, inhaling her smell which is like dust and hay and sweet molasses all mixed up together.

'I do not like that boy,' I whisper so that only Caramel can hear. 'I do not like him at all.' She nuzzles me gently and I slide my arms around her neck, letting my anger dissolve. A few minutes later I am smiling again, feeding Caramel slices of apple from my palm.

'She likes you,' Kelly says, behind me. 'Caramel. You're

❀❀❀❀❀❀❀❀❀❀❀❀❀❀❀❀❀❀❀❀❀❀❀

good with her, Coco . . . not many people are. Come on, let's get you saddled up. Jean and Roy aren't here today, so I thought we'd do some exercises in the paddock . . . who would you like to ride, Bailey or Jojo?'

I frown. I like Bailey and I like Jojo, but the pony I most want to ride is Caramel. I am pretty certain she would behave well for me. She likes me – even Kelly can see that. And Jean and Roy are not here today, so maybe we can bend the rules a little?

'Can't I ride Caramel?' I plead. 'Jean said I was getting much better, much more confident. She said I would be ready to take Caramel out . . .'

She did say this, but she didn't specify when. I have the feeling the date Jean had in mind was several years ahead, but Kelly doesn't need to know this.

'I don't think so,' Kelly frowns. 'Not today. Caramel can be pretty tricky. Jean and Roy aren't even sure she's the right kind of pony for us – a riding school horse has to earn its keep, and Caramel can be unpredictable . . .'

I bite my lip. This doesn't sound good. If Jean and Roy aren't sure about the little Exmoor pony, she may be coming to the end of her time at the Woodlands

31

Riding School. Unless I can prove once and for all that she can behave well?

'Jean said I could!' I argue, aware that I am stretching the truth more than a little. 'She says I have a connection with Caramel, that I'm a natural with her! Please let me try, Kelly? It's only in the paddock. What could go wrong?'

'Plenty,' Kelly says, but I can tell that she's weakening. 'Maybe if Jean was here . . .'

'She isn't, though!' I sigh. 'Please, Kelly? I've been looking forward to this all week!'

Kelly rolls her eyes. 'Oh, go on then,' she says. 'But if it all goes pear-shaped . . .'

'It won't!' I grin.

'Lawrie?' she yells across the yard. 'Can you get Caramel saddled up, please? For Coco here.'

Lawrie raises an eyebrow. 'I thought you said only experienced riders could take Caramel?' he questions, and I can tell Kelly feels hassled by the comment. Now that the decision is made, she doesn't want to go back on it.

'Jean said it would be OK,' she tells Lawrie, walking

❀❀❀❀❀❀❀❀❀❀❀❀❀❀❀❀❀❀❀❀❀❀❀❀

away to help the other students get mounted. There are six of us today, but the other five are younger than me and need more support. They wait patiently as Kelly matches them with their ponies.

'I am an experienced rider, you know,' I say, as Lawrie saddles up Caramel and adjusts the stirrups. 'I know what I'm doing.'

'I doubt that somehow,' Lawrie says. 'Caramel is easily scared, OK? Go easy with her.'

'She likes me!'

'That makes one of us, I suppose,' he mutters, leading the pony out into the yard and holding her while I climb on. Luckily, Caramel stands as quiet and still as a mouse and I manage it smoothly. I collect the reins and press my heels gently into the pony's sides, and we walk forward across the yard to join Kelly and the other kids.

Caramel really does like me, I can tell. She seems calm and steady and settled as we walk down to the paddock and circle round, and when Kelly asks us to follow a figure-of-eight pattern and then negotiate a basic obstacle course, she takes it all in her stride. Nobody would ever guess she was a 'problem' pony.

✿✿✿✿✿✿✿✿✿✿✿✿✿✿✿✿✿✿✿✿✿✿✿✿✿✿✿✿

Kelly looks less anxious now, more confident. She has taken a risk letting me ride Caramel – I am not about to let her down. I plan to show her that I am a good rider, and more than that, that Caramel really can be trusted. All she needs is to be treated gently.

'Rising trot,' Kelly calls out, and I ease the pony forward smoothly. She trots beautifully, and when Kelly suggests that three of us try a canter, I know she is really starting to trust me. Caramel speeds up and I lean forward, exhilarated, enjoying every moment. This is without a doubt the best riding lesson I've ever had – it's as though the pony is a part of me, or I am part of her. We understand each other, and I know that she is loving this as much as I am.

Maybe Caramel was born of feral stock, the ponies living wild on the moors; maybe she was treated roughly at some point in her past; maybe, but I know she trusts me and I know she has it in her to be the best pony ever.

'Excellent, Coco!' Kelly calls as we slow to a walk again, and I can feel myself glowing with pride. 'Great, all of you. Right, folks, we'll cool down with some control

❀❀❀❀❀❀❀❀❀❀❀❀❀❀❀❀❀❀❀❀❀❀❀

exercises. Let's start off with "Round the World". If you're not sure, kids, watch Coco, she does this one really well . . .'

My cheeks glow pink with pleasure at the compliment, but I've been doing the paddock exercises for ages now, and I know I am good at them. 'Round the World' is all about teaching the rider balance and control – you have to scissor one leg over the pony's neck, so that you are balanced sideways on the saddle; then scissor again until you are sitting backwards in the saddle; again so that you are riding sideways to the other side; and once more until you are finally facing front again.

This exercise is always a little chaotic, with riders slipping and slithering about in a very undignified way, but I have it down to a fine art. To start with, you do it while your pony is standing still, then work up to doing it on the move. I am pretty good at both. I squeeze my heels gently inwards so that Caramel walks forward, then slide my feet out of the stirrups. Aware of the younger kids watching me, I shift my balance and scissor my leg up over Caramel's neck and down again.

My leg is still hovering in mid-air when the pony lurches

✿✿✿✿✿✿✿✿✿✿✿✿✿✿✿✿✿✿✿✿✿✿✿✿✿

forward into a sprint, then jolts to an abrupt stop. Caramel rears up, whinnying, and suddenly I am flying through the air. There's a thump as I land in a heap on the grass, my head hitting the edge of one of the obstacle course markers, my jaw hitting the gravel path. For a moment, I am seeing stars.

'Coco?' Kelly is saying, on her knees beside me. 'Coco, are you all right?'

I try to sit up and fall back again instantly. My head feels like it has been sliced open with an axe.

'*Ouchheee* . . .'

Kelly stands up and yells at the top of her voice for the first-aid kit, and I scrunch my eyes tightly closed and wish the ground would open up and swallow me. It doesn't, of course, and even with my eyes closed I know that five little kids watched my fall from grace with shock and horror. Oh, the shame of it . . .

Caramel, how could you do this to me? I thought we had an understanding . . .

A damp cloth smelling of witch hazel is pressed to my chin and my eyes snap open abruptly.

'There, that should help,' Kelly says, and over her

36

shoulder I see Lawrie Marshall with the first-aid box and the witch hazel, his face dark and disapproving.

I think I will survive the bump, but the wound to my pride may be fatal. This is the most humiliating moment of my life.

6

Sadly, it is not just my pride that has taken a battering. It would have been a lot worse without the riding hat, but still, there is a purple-red graze along my jaw and a whole constellation of bruises all over my bum and legs. Great.

'What did you *do*?' Skye demands as I hobble into the kitchen at Tanglewood, the cloth soaked in witch hazel pressed to my jaw. 'You look awful!'

'Thanks,' I sigh. 'You're a real comfort, Skye. I had an argument with my favourite pony . . . she got tired of behaving beautifully and decided to throw me off.'

'Seriously?' Summer chimes in. 'She threw you? What kind of psycho horses do they have at that place? It's supposed to be a riding school, not a rodeo!'

'Don't,' I say. 'It's taken me the whole drive home to convince Mum not to make a complaint.'

'I didn't want to complain, exactly,' Mum sighs. 'I just wanted to say . . . well, that pony really shouldn't be part of a riding school. She's too high-spirited, too nervy!'

'Mum,' I argue, 'I told you – it was all my own fault.'

'How come?' Cherry demands.

A dark blush seeps across my cheeks. I don't want to come clean, but if Caramel's future is in question I can't stay quiet.

'I didn't have permission to ride Caramel,' I admit. 'She's a bit unpredictable. Hard to handle. Jean and Roy only let the really confident riders take her out, but she's my favourite pony and they were away today. So I managed to convince one of the assistants to let me ride Caramel . . . I kind of pretended I'd been told I could.'

'But you hadn't,' Skye says. 'Boy, will you be in trouble!'

'I don't expect Jean and Roy will be impressed,' Mum comments, making teas and hot chocolates all round.

'Well, I agree with Mum,' Summer frowns. 'This Caramel doesn't sound like the kind of horse that should be around kids at all. She sounds dangerous.'

39

I put a hand to my aching head. Suppose Jean and Roy think that too? I wanted to help Caramel, but maybe I've made things worse for her. Whatever my sisters think, I know that Caramel did everything perfectly. It was only when I started shifting about that she lost the plot . . . she freaked out when I scissored my leg up over her neck. Maybe she doesn't like unexpected things, or things she can't see properly. Perhaps she thought I was going to hurt her?

If I could find out what was happening the other times she's behaved badly, maybe I could work out what's upsetting her and solve the problem, and then surely Jean and Roy won't even think about getting rid of her.

'Good job you had your hard hat on, baby sister,' Summer grins. 'You might have done some real damage!'

'I am not a baby,' I scowl. 'C'mon, you're only seventeen months older than me!'

'Maybe, but you'll always be the baby of the family to us,' Skye teases. 'We worry about you!'

'Well, don't!' I huff. 'I am very grown-up and independent, and you know it!'

'Now, now,' Mum says. 'Don't tease your sister, girls!'

That makes me feel like a three-year-old in the middle of a squabble.

Mum sets down hot drinks and a plate of home-baked chocolate chip cookies, scooping up a couple along with a mug of tea to take out to the workshop because Paddy is working late on a special sample order for some big department store. It has to be finished and sent off by Special Delivery to arrive on Monday, but apparently it will be worth all the hard work and long hours if they land the contract.

As soon as Mum has gone, Skye leans forward. 'It's not *you* I'm worrying about really, Coco,' she says in a whisper. 'It's Honey. I honestly thought she was trying harder after the mix-up at the start of term when we thought she'd gone missing, and all that stirring it with Shay. Well, it doesn't look like it. My art teacher asked me today when Honey would be back at school – she must have been skipping lessons. The teachers seem to think she's ill, so maybe she's sent in a forged note or something?'

'No way!' I gasp.

'She gets the school bus with us every day, the same as

always,' Cherry says. 'None of us had a clue she was skiving!'

'She may be on the bus, but she obviously isn't making it past the gates,' Skye shrugs. 'I know she likes to hang around by the wall at the front before the bell goes, but it looks like that's as far as she's getting. Wait till Mum finds out – she'll go nuts!'

'She will,' Summer says softly. 'Mum has enough on her plate already, with the B&B and the chocolate business and . . . well, stuff.'

Nobody comments, but we all know that Summer's illness is the part of the 'stuff' that is bothering Mum just now. A few months back, Summer put herself under so much pressure to succeed she just about unravelled in the process. For a while it seemed like she was trying to starve herself, and now she has to go to twice-weekly meetings at an eating-disorders clinic at the hospital in Exeter.

She had to give up her dance school place and watch her friend Jodie take it instead. Summer still goes to ballet class in Minehead, but she must think about the scholarship place she let slip through her fingers. We don't really

❀❀❀❀❀❀❀❀❀❀❀❀❀❀❀❀❀❀❀❀❀❀❀❀❀

talk about that and we don't mention her eating disorder either – we just tiptoe around her, scared to upset her, scared to say something that might make her feel bad. Although she has put a little weight back on, Summer is still fragile, brittle, with pale skin and blue shadows beneath her beautiful eyes. You get the feeling that if you held her too hard she might snap, crumble.

Mum says that time is a great healer, that we need to be patient and positive and kind, but I know that she worries about Summer – we all do. The last thing any of us needs is for Honey to go off the rails again on top of that.

Summer frowns. 'It's like Honey just can't help it, you know? She tries to get her act together, but she can't keep it up . . .'

I think that Honey can help it, actually. Ever since Dad left a few years ago, my big sister has been lurching from one disaster to the next. It's kind of exhausting to live with, and these days my patience is wearing thin.

'D'you think we should keep quiet about this?' Skye asks. 'Pretend we don't know? Or . . . should we tell? Not to get Honey into trouble, obviously, but . . . well, to stop her from getting into more trouble than she is in already, if that makes sense?'

'We can't,' Summer says. 'Sisters stick together, right?'

I bite my lip. The family rule that we don't tell tales is unshakeable, but I can't help wishing someone would speak out about Honey. It's no fun watching your big sister mess her life up.

'Maybe we should tell?' I venture.

'But . . . she'd never forgive us,' Summer points out.

There's a silence as we think about the fallout if we did dare tell. More than once, Mum has threatened Honey with boarding school, and this could just be the last straw. None of us wants to be responsible for that.

'The high school reports are out next Wednesday,' Cherry says. 'I guess Charlotte will find out then. No use stirring things up when we know it's going to come out anyway, right?'

'Right,' we agree.

The kitchen door swings open and Mum comes in again with an empty tray, humming some old tune from the Dark Ages. 'Nobody hungry?' she asks, scanning the untouched plate of cookies. 'That makes a change!'

❀❀❀❀❀❀❀❀❀❀❀❀❀❀❀❀❀❀❀❀❀❀❀❀

We all reach for the biscuits and bite into them guiltily, except for Summer who just breaks hers in half and feeds fragments slowly to Fred the dog.

Let's just say I am not looking forward to Wednesday.

7

By the time Wednesday rolls around my graze is healing, but the bruises on my legs have mellowed to rainbow shades of blue, purple and greenish-yellow. They look especially attractive with my gym shorts, and I have to recount the story of how the unpredictable, half-wild Exmoor pony at Woodlands got startled by something and threw me off.

'You have to get used to these things when you move on to riding more challenging horses,' I say. 'But they're the most rewarding ones, of course . . .'

I am not sure how many of my friends totally believe this version of events, but they say nothing.

I have been trying to steer clear of Lawrie Marshall. He wasn't in science on Monday – there was a football match apparently – but we have science again last lesson today and I am not looking forward to that. Should I blank him? Or smile sweetly and thank him for his help on Friday in the hope that he chokes on his own self-righteousness? He was as grumpy as ever when he handed over the first-aid kit, but while I was getting my bearings again I watched him catch Caramel and calm and coax her back up to the stable yard. Lawrie Marshall has zero charm with human beings, but I have to admit he's good with horses.

I have almost decided to swallow my pride and let bygones be bygones when Lawrie walks into class, throws his bag down across the aisle and shoots me the kind of look that could curdle milk.

'Pleased with yourself, are you?' he says coldly.

'Pleased?' I frown. 'What d'you mean?'

'You don't even know?' he asks, shaking his head slowly. 'You don't even care?'

'About what?' I frown, but Lawrie Marshall just glares and turns his back on me. Mr Harper starts the lesson and I have to sit there for fifty whole minutes gritting my teeth and wondering why I ever thought that saying thank

✿✿✿✿✿✿✿✿✿✿✿✿✿✿✿✿✿✿✿✿✿✿✿

you to the Year Eight bully was a good plan. He is sourer than stewed rhubarb without the sugar, bitter as aspirin.

What a loser. How come he always manages to make *me* feel like I'm the one who's done something wrong?

His comments get under my skin and bug me all lesson, and by the time the bell goes I decide to confront him. I tell Sarah I want to talk to Mr Harper about endangered antelopes because she may be my best friend, but she has a one-track mind when it comes to boys. Lately, she is much more interested in who fancies who than the plight of the white rhino and the blue whale, and if she made some quip about me and Lawrie Marshall I would not be amused. The minute she's gone I pack my things and run; I catch up with Lawrie on the playground, and my temper boils over.

'Hey!' I yell. 'I want to talk to you!'

He turns round, raising one eyebrow. 'I don't want to talk to you, so tough luck,' he snaps.

'What is your problem?' I demand. 'No wonder you don't have any friends! No wonder everyone thinks you're weird. You're just a spiteful, horrible bully!'

Lawrie Marshall flinches as if I've slapped him.

❀❀❀❀❀❀❀❀❀❀❀❀❀❀❀❀❀❀❀❀❀❀❀

'Shut up,' he scowls. 'You don't know what you're talking about.'

'I know exactly what I'm talking about,' I tell him. 'But you – you just spout rubbish! What did you mean earlier, about me feeling pleased with myself, and not even caring?'

He shakes his head. 'You are probably the most spoilt, selfish girl I have ever met,' he says. 'You lied about being allowed to ride Caramel, didn't you?'

'No, I –'

'You lied, and it all went wrong, and Kelly was in trouble.'

'What about me?' I protest. 'I was the one who got hurt!'

'You deserved it,' he shrugs. 'And after all that, you didn't even bother to apologize or call the stables to find out what was happening.'

A flicker of unease stirs within me.

'So . . . what is happening?' I ask.

'Plenty,' he snarls. 'The stables are selling Caramel. So, yeah, like I said, I hope you're pleased with yourself. It's all your fault.'

✿✿✿✿✿✿✿✿✿✿✿✿✿✿✿✿✿✿✿✿✿✿✿✿

He turns on his heel and walks away. Me, I stand very still in the playground, letting the waves of shame and guilt slide over me.

Then the school bus toots and starts its engine, and I run down to the gates and scramble aboard, just in time.

I am still upset when I arrive home. We finish a little ahead of the high school, so I'm usually home before my sisters and I'm planning to ask Mum if we can call the stables and ask them to hang on to Caramel. It's a long shot, but it has to be worth a try. When I walk into the kitchen, though, I find Mum and Paddy dancing around with champagne glasses in their hands. Fred the dog is leaping madly round their feet, and even Humbug my pet sheep has made her way into the kitchen and is curled up on an armchair in the corner.

The sight of this is enough to put a smile back on my face, briefly at any rate.

'So this is what you get up to when we're at school then?' I tease.

'Oh, Coco, love, we're celebrating!' Mum laughs. 'You'll never guess what's happened!'

✿✿✿✿✿✿✿✿✿✿✿✿✿✿✿✿✿✿✿✿✿✿✿

'Don't tell me – your three-month wedding anniversary?' I suggest. 'A lottery win?'

'As good as,' Paddy says in his cool Glaswegian accent. 'We've only gone and landed a major order from the Miller-Brown chain of department stores! They received my samples on Monday, and they really loved them. They've offered us the chance to supply fifty of their top stores with the option to expand into all of them if our chocolates do well . . .'

'And they will do well,' Mum laughs, taking another champagne glass from the cupboard, filling it up with pink lemonade from the fridge and handing it to me. 'They will do brilliantly because they are the best truffles in the entire universe and now everyone will get the chance to know that!'

I clink my glass against theirs. 'Was my truffle in the box of samples?' I want to know. 'The one named after me?'

'Well, of course,' Paddy says. 'All the chocolates you girls have inspired were in the box. Marshmallow Skye and Summer's Dream and Cherry Crush and Coco Caramel. There's even one called Sweet Honey, although your big sister says she doesn't like chocolate . . .'

I'm not so sure about that. My big sister likes chocolate all right, she just doesn't like Paddy.

'The buyers at Miller-Brown loved them, though,' he continues. 'The whole concept – the taste, the names, the packaging, the fair-trade angle . . . all of it. This order is *big*. It could take us off the breadline and into profit! It's epic!'

I blink. I wonder just how much profit a big order like that could bring in? The seed of an idea forms in my mind, growing quickly.

Caramel is for sale. Well, OK, that's my fault, kind of – but maybe, just maybe, if we could actually buy her, the story might still have a happy ending. It's not such a crazy thought, surely?

The possibilities bubble up inside me, sweeter than pink lemonade.

8

I bite my lip. 'Are we going to be rich?' I ask. 'Will we have lots of money?'

'Rich? Well, I wouldn't go that far,' Paddy says. 'We should be able to pay off our business loans, at any rate.'

Ah. Business loans. I had forgotten about them.

'We might just have enough to stretch as far as a takeaway curry,' Mum teases. 'By way of celebration. And perhaps we can let the B&B run down a little and turn Tanglewood back into a real family home.'

'Right,' I check. 'That's great. But . . . not enough to buy a pony, say?'

'A pony?'

'Mum, the stables are selling Caramel!' I explain. 'It's all my fault, and I thought that if we could just buy her . . .'

Mum holds her hands up. 'Whoa, whoa, a minute,' she says. 'Three things, Coco. First of all, if that pony is sold on it won't be your fault – she was clearly not suited to be a riding school horse. Second, no, I'm really sorry, but we won't have that kind of money – we don't have any money yet; we have to send the orders out first! Third . . . well, if we did have the cash to buy a pony, I certainly wouldn't choose Caramel. She's already thrown you once. I don't think she's trustworthy!'

'She is!' I wail. 'She is the best pony in the whole world, and if we could just save her . . . Mum, I want this more than anything! It could be all my birthday and Christmas presents from now right up until I die, I swear! Please!'

'Coco, listen –'

'Will you think about it? Please?' I beg. 'Just consider it? Maybe we could pay Jean and Roy in instalments? You know I've always wanted a pony, and I love Caramel, I really do! I will never, ever ask for anything again, truly.'

A look passes between Mum and Paddy, a quiet, thoughtful look that sets my heart racing. Maybe they really will consider it?

'We'll talk about it later,' Mum says. 'It's a huge

decision, and there are all kinds of reasons why now is not the right time for it, and really, you know yourself that Caramel is not the kind of pony I'd choose. So we'll think about it, yes; we'll talk about it; but that's all. Don't get your hopes up, Coco, I am not promising anything.'

I grin. 'Thank you, Mum!' I whoop. 'Thank you, Paddy!'

I clink glasses with them again, cranking up the volume on Mum's iPod, so happy I think I might burst. OK, Mum hasn't said yes . . . but she hasn't said no either. All is not lost!

Mum starts to dance again, taking me by the hand and dragging me up as well. The three of us are strutting our stuff to Abba's 'Dancing Queen' when Cherry, Summer, Skye and Honey come in from school. Their faces are serious, and they are all clutching big brown envelopes.

I remember what Cherry said about the high school reports being out today, and I have a strong feeling that the happy mood is about to crash.

Mum and Paddy launch into the story of the big order again, pouring more pink lemonade, failing to notice the serious faces. My sisters go along with it all, asking about

❀❀❀❀❀❀❀❀❀❀❀❀❀❀❀❀❀❀❀❀❀❀❀❀

the order, congratulating Paddy, talking of fame and fortune and chocolate-flavoured world domination.

Only Honey is silent. She waits for as long as she can bear, then flings her report down on the tabletop as if throwing down a challenge.

'Look,' she says. 'Better get it over with. It's report day – I mean, I know it won't be good, but I have been trying a lot harder, so . . .'

Mum and Paddy are serious suddenly, sitting down at the table, slicing open the envelope. Skye is chewing her lip, Summer is studying the ceiling and Cherry looks like she'd rather be anywhere, anywhere at all, than here.

Honey seems more relaxed than any of us, perched on the kitchen table, helping herself to an apple from the fruit dish as if she hasn't a care in the world. I can't help admiring her confidence.

To be honest, I am a little surprised she has shown her face at all because she must know exactly what's in that school report. Perhaps it's like she says, and she just wants to get the whole thing over with?

Mum frowns as she scans the first page, leafing through,

✿✿✿✿✿✿✿✿✿✿✿✿✿✿✿✿✿✿✿✿✿✿✿✿✿

studying each sheet in turn. Paddy is reading too, and finally, after the longest few minutes in the history of the world, Mum shakes her head and puts the report booklet down.

'Well . . . what can I say?'

'Is it OK?' Honey asks, still crunching apple. 'Have I improved?' Her jaw-length blonde hair falls across her face and her eyes look anxious, hopeful.

Mum laughs. 'Honey, it's more than OK,' she says. 'It's . . . well, it's an excellent report! The best report you've brought home since primary school. Well done! I am so pleased – I knew you could do it!'

Skye catches my gaze, a flicker of confusion in her eyes. Something doesn't feel quite right here.

'*Much improved attitude*,' Paddy reads out. '*Working hard to make up for lost time; bright, helpful, a pleasure to have in class* . . . this is terrific, Honey!'

My big sister shrugs and slides off the tabletop. 'Well, that's me off the hook then,' she laughs. 'How about you guys? Time to face the music?'

As Skye, Summer and Cherry hand over their school reports, I cannot help myself – I lean across and look at

❀❀❀❀❀❀❀❀❀❀❀❀❀❀❀❀❀❀❀❀❀❀❀

the top page of Honey's report because I seriously don't believe what I am hearing.

And there it is in black and white, printed out and signed by the school principal; *Attendance: 100 per cent.*

Skye, Summer and Cherry have all brought home reasonable reports, and mine came home before the October break and that was OK too. There is no doubt about it, though – Honey's report steals the show. My off-the-rails sister has turned model pupil overnight, just in time for her GCSE year.

'Looks like I got it wrong,' Skye whispers as I collect my violin, pull on my panda hat and slip outside to practise. 'Maybe my art teacher had Honey mixed up with someone else?'

I shrug, but personally, I cannot see how. Art is the only subject Honey actually enjoys, so the art teachers know her better than most – and let's face it, whatever else she may be, my big sister is not forgettable. Still, you cannot argue with a school report, can you?

I sit in my oak tree, leaning back against the trunk, playing jiggy tunes on my old violin. The branches are

❀❀❀❀❀❀❀❀❀❀❀❀❀❀❀❀❀❀❀❀❀❀❀❀

getting bare now, so I can see the blue sky darkening to velvet black. Paddy has rung down to the village for a takeaway curry feast, and everyone is hopeful because Summer said she really fancied pakoras and mango chutney, and maybe that is a sign that things are getting back to normal for her too.

Really, it's a night for celebration. A big order from a nationwide department store – that could mean real success for Mum and Paddy's business. And maybe Honey really is getting her act together and will scoop a whole bunch of A* grades at GCSE? Who knows.

I'll believe it when I see it.

All I can think about is the chance of putting things right for Caramel and actually, finally, having a pony of my own. Mum and Paddy might be talking about it right now, Mum setting the kitchen table, pouring more champagne and pink lemonade. They will want to know more about Caramel, of course. They will want to know whether she can be trained, trusted, relied upon. They will want to talk to Jean and Roy about prices and check with the farmer who owns the land next to us if we can rent one of the fields for grazing.

Still, all of that could happen.

I imagine shopping for saddles and bridles and horse blankets, wonder whether Humbug the sheep will be willing to share stable space. By the time the first stars come out between the branches and the little blue van from the Bengal Rose Takeaway chugs into the driveway to deliver our celebration feast, I am fizzing with happiness, with hope.

9

I manage to steer clear of Lawrie Marshall for the rest of the week at school. OK, so he thinks I'm spoilt and selfish and to blame for Caramel being sold. So what? Why should I care what he thinks? Maybe he is upset about Caramel, but he's still a lowlife bully.

Besides, I am hopeful that Mum and Paddy will make a decision about Caramel soon. I've been nagging Mum to ring the riding stables, but she says it's not something that can be decided overnight, and that she'd need to be reassured that it would be possible to train Caramel to be calmer, less jumpy.

Still, the fact that she is actually considering it is good enough for me. I plan to apologize to Jean and Roy about what happened last week, then let them know that we are interested in buying Caramel. Hopefully, they will talk to Mum about it when she comes to pick me up after class – once she actually meets Caramel I am pretty sure she will be as smitten as I am.

I am early as usual on Friday, and luckily there is no sign of Lawrie Marshall, although a big, shiny, silver four-wheel drive with a horsebox hitched to it is parked right across the yard. I head in towards the loos to get changed, and as I pass the office I notice a tall, sharp-faced man in a tweedy brown suit is in there talking to Jean and Roy. He looks kind of posh in a country land-owner kind of way, but there is a cold, no-nonsense look about him. He is probably some kind of country vet or a salesman selling saddles and horse blankets.

As I pass, his eyes skim over me then slide away, unim-pressed.

When I emerge five minutes later to stack my rucksack and school clothes in a locker, the tweedy guy is still there. This is very annoying because I need to apologize and tell Jean and Roy that we might be able to buy Caramel, as long as they don't need to sell her in a hurry. Whatever they are talking about must be important. Still, I suppose

✿✿✿✿✿✿✿✿✿✿✿✿✿✿✿✿✿✿✿✿✿✿✿

it delays the dreaded moment of having to say sorry for pulling the wool over Kelly's eyes and trying to convince the stable's bosses that I should be Caramel's new owner. I'll have to explain after my ride.

Out in the yard, there is still no sign of Lawrie and I allow myself to wonder if he has switched his days at the stable to avoid me. Better still, maybe he's been sacked?

Kelly has saddled Bailey, a quiet strawberry roan, for me. Bailey is the slowest, stodgiest pony at Woodlands – you could send your ninety-three-year-old great-granny out for a ride on him and she'd probably complain he was too dull. Still, I know better than to argue this time as Kelly hands me the reins.

'Have you seen Lawrie?' she asks me as I swing up into the saddle.

'Sorry, no . . .'

'Oh, for goodness' sake,' Kelly frowns. 'He could at least have called in if he wasn't going to turn up for work. He seemed so keen, but . . . obviously not.'

Not sacked then. Yet.

Kelly leads out Strider, one of the bigger ponies,

✿✿✿✿✿✿✿✿✿✿✿✿✿✿✿✿✿✿✿✿✿✿✿✿✿✿✿

mounting neatly before nudging him forward so she can unhook the gate.

'Jean and Roy wanted Lawrie to bring Caramel down to the paddock, but I expect they'll manage themselves,' Kelly sighs. 'Let's go. It's just us today – the Dempsey kids have chickenpox, Jake's at the dentist and Courtney and Jenna are at a party, so . . . nice and quiet! I thought we'd take a hack through the woods.'

'I can take Caramel down to the paddock if you like,' I offer. 'I don't mind! I could fill in for Lawrie if you need me to, instead of a lesson. Or, if Lawrie's quit –'

'Not a chance,' my instructor says firmly, waiting for me to walk Bailey through the gate before closing it behind me. 'Lawrie will turn up at some point, and your mum has paid for this lesson so a lesson is what you'll get. Jean and Roy have made it clear they don't want you anywhere near Caramel – you weren't exactly truthful with me last week about being allowed to ride her, were you?'

I hang my head.

Kelly leads us down into the woods, Strider picking his way.

✿✿✿✿✿✿✿✿✿✿✿✿✿✿✿✿✿✿✿✿✿✿✿✿

'I'm sorry,' I say, falling into place behind her. 'About last week. I really didn't mean to get you into trouble – I was trying to help Caramel, show that she could be good and quiet and steady. She's my favourite pony – we have this special bond, you know? I was trying to make sure she stayed at Woodlands.'

'Things didn't quite work out then, did they?' Kelly sighs.

'Don't,' I groan. 'Caramel is up for sale, and it's all my fault!'

'Don't be too hard on yourself,' Kelly shrugs. 'It probably would have happened anyway. She's always been a "problem" pony, and there's no room for difficult horses in a riding school. Jean and Roy just can't take the risk.'

'Well, I've got a plan,' I say, reining Bailey into step alongside her. 'I've asked my mum, and guess what? I think we'll probably be buying Caramel!'

Kelly looks surprised. 'Seriously? Your mum said that?'

I bite my lip. 'Not exactly,' I hedge. 'She said she'd think about it. Possibly. Maybe . . .'

❀❀❀❀❀❀❀❀❀❀❀❀❀❀❀❀❀❀❀❀❀❀❀❀

Kelly rolls her eyes, and in that moment she reminds me of my big sisters. I know she's laughing at me.

'Possibly?' she echoes. 'Maybe? That doesn't sound too definite!'

'It will be,' I protest as the ponies move steadily through the trees, hooves crunching down on twigs and dried leaves beneath. 'I'm working on her. I am pretty sure I can talk her round.'

'This is a pony we're talking about, Coco, not a new computer game!' Kelly says. 'You can't just nag your mum and hope she gives in. It's a huge undertaking, a real commitment.'

'I know!' I insist. 'Of course! I am a hundred per cent committed!'

Kelly looks at me, and her eyes reveal a mixture of sadness and pity and exasperation. I know what she's thinking – it's what people always think. That I'm too young, too silly; not to be taken seriously.

'I honestly don't think it'll happen,' Kelly says kindly. 'For all kinds of reasons. Caramel is a challenging pony – I know you love her, and you do have a good connection with her, but you've seen yourself how unpredictable she

66

can be. She needs an experienced owner. Jean and Roy would never sell her to a novice rider, even if your mum really did want to buy her.'

'I'll talk to them,' I argue. 'I'll apologize, explain. I might not be the best rider in the world, but . . . Caramel deserves a home where she'll be loved. They have to give me a chance, Kelly!'

'Coco, I hate to tell you, but I think you're too late,' she says. 'It's already sorted – that bloke in the office is almost certainly going to buy her.'

A sharp pang of grief shoots through me, dulling to a sad, heavy ache. I'm too late. Caramel is being sold.

'Is there anything I can do or say to stop it?' I plead.

'Doubtful,' Kelly sighs. 'It's probably for the best, you know. Mr Seddon has trained horses before, and he knows what he's taking on – he'll get her settled down. He's rich – he's got a big house with paddocks and stables out Hartshill way. Don't worry, she'll have a good life.'

I'm not so sure. I didn't like the look of the posh, tweedy bloke – he seemed too sharp, too cold, his lips a thin, hard line. Besides, if he buys Caramel, I will never see her again.

❀❀❀❀❀❀❀❀❀❀❀❀❀❀❀❀❀❀❀❀❀❀❀❀

My eyes well with tears and Kelly, panicking, distracts me with a sharp burst of rising trot and a long canter across the meadows that edge the woods. Later, as we trek back through the trees towards the stable-yard gate, we see the shiny, silver four-wheel drive move out slowly, towing the horsebox.

I'm too late even to say goodbye.

10

As I walk Bailey back to his stable, a figure steps out of the shadows.

'Well done, Coco,' Lawrie Marshall says coldly. 'Thanks to you, Caramel belongs to that thug Seddon now. Great stuff. Just great.'

'Thug?' I echo uneasily. 'Kelly says he's rich and knows loads about horses. She says Caramel will have a good life with him.'

'She obviously doesn't know him,' Lawrie says.

He turns away, stepping into Caramel's empty stable.

'What d'you mean, he's a thug?' I demand. 'You can't just make accusations like that! How do you even know?'

'I just know, all right?' he scowls, shovelling dirty straw. 'You don't like bullies, do you?'

'Who does?'

'Well, a bully is exactly what Seddon is,' Lawrie mutters. 'With animals, with people, with everyone.'

'Where were you earlier then?' I accuse. 'If it's true, you could have said something, stopped it all! Jean and Roy would never knowingly sell one of their ponies to someone like that!'

'Something came up,' he huffs. 'I'll make up the time, not that it's any of your business.'

'Have you told Jean and Roy what you know about Seddon?' I repeat.

'What's the point?' he shrugs. 'It's a done deal now. People like Seddon always get their way.'

He kicks the stable door closed, leaving me speechless.

I try to get the sharp face and cold eyes of the posh tweedy guy out of my mind, but I can't. Is he a rich guy who loves horses, like Kelly said, or a thug and a bully? I imagine him riding Caramel, tugging hard on the reins, digging his heels in, losing his temper if she is skittish.

Is he really bad news, or is Lawrie trying to wind me up? If so, it's working. I can't concentrate on anything. I have to trust Jean and Roy and Kelly. They would never let anyone dodgy buy Caramel, I am certain of that. Then again . . . what if Lawrie knows something that they don't?

'Maybe you could just ring Jean and Roy, explain that we're still interested in Caramel?' I ask Mum. 'In case things go wrong with her new home.'

Mum shakes her head. 'Coco, love, nothing will go wrong. I'd love for you to have a pony one day . . . in theory. But not the pony that threw you. And not right now. We are gearing up for the biggest order The Chocolate Box has ever had, and we need to focus on that for a while. Unless we do, there'll be no money for food and bills, let alone ponies!'

On Saturday morning I watch as endless deliveries of raw cocoa, sugar and flavourings arrive. One of the guest bedrooms is given over to towering piles of flat-packed boxes, ready to be assembled and filled. Paddy has enlisted extra help from Harry, the retired bloke from the village who helped out for three weeks back in the summer when Mum and Paddy went on their honeymoon. There is talk of a couple of part-timers being roped in, too, until this mammoth order has been filled.

My sisters don't seem bothered by the chaos. Cherry is making her own magazine for an English project at school, spreading sketches and photos and chunks of printed-out writing across the kitchen table. Summer is practising barre exercises against the Aga and Skye is sitting in the armchair, sewing a 1920s-style dress from an old velvet curtain. Honey, needless to say, is still in bed.

Normally, I would be a part of it all, drafting out a petition about saving the Siberian white tiger or painting a banner to protest about testing make-up on animals, but today I haven't the heart for anything at all. All I can think about is Caramel, my mind racing with fears and worries and confusion.

Nobody notices that I'm upset. Nobody notices me at all – I am practically invisible.

On impulse, I grab the phone book and look up 'Seddon'. There is only one entry, a listing for J. Seddon at Blue Downs House, Hartshill. I take the old Ordnance Survey map from the living-room shelf and find the place, not far from Hartshill and maybe five or six miles from here. So near and yet so far.

❀ ❀

In the cold light of day, I am pretty sure that Caramel is fine. I am pretty sure that Lawrie Marshall is just a nasty, bitter kid who is trying to make me feel bad because I happened to find him bullying a Year Six boy. I try to forget Seddon's thin-lipped scowl, his ice-blue eyes.

I can't imagine Mr Seddon riding a small, stocky, half-wild Exmoor pony, though. Perhaps he has bought Caramel for one of his children? I picture Caramel being petted by a little boy with a face full of freckles, a cute grin. He would bring her carrots and peppermints and fresh hay, but would he know that apple slices are her favourite? Probably not.

And what if Caramel throws that cute, imaginary boy? What then?

'I'm going out,' I tell Mum. 'I might cycle up to town to see Sarah. I won't be late.'

I pull on my fluffy panda hat and slip out of the kitchen, wheel my bike out of the shed and start to cycle. I am not going to Sarah's house, though. It's a bright, crisp autumn day and I soon warm up as I ride down through the village and out again, taking the road to Hartshill.

❁❁❁❁❁❁❁❁❁❁❁❁❁❁❁❁❁❁❁❁❁❁❁❁❁❁

I have no clear idea of what I will do when I get there, but I know I have to find Blue Downs House and see Caramel one last time, if only to say goodbye. Once I have seen her, I'll be able to let go, move on.

Maybe.

11

I take a right fork at the crossroads a mile before the village and head out towards the moorland. The cycling is harder now, and I have to get off and push the bike up some of the slopes. Cresting one windswept hill, I see a big whitewashed farmhouse in the valley below, a cobbled yard and some outbuildings and a paddock, flanked by woodland. Apart from a terrace of four pretty cottages further up the hill, the house is alone in the landscape, imposing and slightly forbidding.

I freewheel down the slope a little, skidding to a halt as I notice figures and a pony moving across the paddock in the distance. I step into the woodland, hiding my bike behind a mossy, tumbledown wall.

It's cold in the woods, and I move as quietly as I can,

twigs crackling and snapping underfoot, creeping forward until I can hear voices close by. Peering out from the fringe of trees, I see Mr Seddon standing in the centre of the paddock, a girl of seven or eight beside him. He is running Caramel on a long lunge line, turning slowly so that she trots in a circle round him.

I remember Kelly explaining that Mr Seddon has trained horses before, so I guess he is putting her through her paces, getting to know her. Caramel is trotting smoothly, but she looks tired, as if the training has been going on for a long time. The little girl's face looks grey and anxious, her lips quivering.

Suddenly a loud crack splits the air, and Caramel rears up, whinnying in distress. The sound rings out again, and I see that Seddon has a bullwhip, a huge, long-tailed whip that he is lashing out towards Caramel, who bucks to the side, trying to pull away. Seddon reels her in, then cracks his whip again, and this time the whiplash catches her flanks and I see the whites of her eyes as she struggles against the lunge line, terrified.

I want to run forward, into the paddock, grab the whip from Seddon and shove him away from Caramel, leave him sprawled on the ground in a puddle, red-faced and helpless. I want to wrench the lunge line from him and lead Caramel out of there, but fear and reason hold me back. I am twelve years old and all of five foot two inches tall. I don't honestly think I can fight some big, fierce bloke with a whip, no matter how much I want to.

I must not panic. I have to stay calm, think clearly, but it's easier said than done. I feel sick. Why would anyone deliberately frighten an already jumpy horse, then hit her when she flinches and bucks? My heart hammers so loudly I swear the world can hear it, but I force myself to be still, shielded by the trees.

'Stop it!' a voice appeals, and I see the little girl tugging at Seddon's sleeve. 'Please! Leave her alone!'

'She has to learn,' he snaps, shaking the child off. 'She's an animal, a wilful animal. She needs discipline!'

'You're hurting her!' the child argues. 'She's scared!'

'You wanted a pony, didn't you?' Seddon snaps.

'Yes, but –'

'But nothing,' he growls, cracking the whip again as Caramel trots forward, her eyes wild and frightened. 'This

✿✿✿✿✿✿✿✿✿✿✿✿✿✿✿✿✿✿✿✿✿✿✿✿✿

is how it works, Jasmine. Animals need to know who is master, and I am master here. Trust me, she will learn that. Sooner or later, she will learn.'

The child is crying now, trembling, her face streaked with tears. Seddon takes no notice, even when she sinks down to the ground, burying her face in her hands. He just goes on turning, stony-faced, running Caramel on her lunge line, on and on until I think she will fall to the ground too, exhausted.

At last, more than an hour later when the light begins to fade, Seddon stops. He pulls Caramel towards him, catching hold of her halter, and drags the little girl to her feet. I watch the three of them walk away, up towards the house, the stable yard.

Whatever I imagined when I tried to picture Caramel's new life, it wasn't this. There is no laughing, freckle-faced boy, no carrot treats or apple slices. And Seddon is exactly as Lawrie Marshall described him – a horrible, horrible bully. Well, it takes one to know one, I suppose.

I lean against a tree, trying to gather my wits. Should I call the RSPCA? Would they believe me? Would they think it was serious enough to take Caramel away from

❀❀❀❀❀❀❀❀❀❀❀❀❀❀❀❀❀❀❀❀❀❀❀

here, or would they just give Seddon a warning? What if he told them it was all lies?

Maybe ringing Jean and Roy at Woodlands would be better. They would hate to think that Caramel was being badly treated – maybe they could take her back again? I frown. Seddon has paid good money for Caramel, so I don't imagine he would be willing to let her go.

I can't risk leaving Caramel here – I have to get her out, no matter what.

A plan begins to unfurl in my mind. I sink down on to a fallen log, taking the little mobile I was given for my twelfth birthday and clicking on to Cherry's number. After three rings, my stepsister answers.

'It's me – Coco,' I say, huddling into my jacket. 'Are you alone? Can you talk? Because I need a favour. And it has to be a secret!'

'Coco? Yes, I'm in my room, but . . . what d'you mean? Where are you? What secret? And . . . why me?'

I roll my eyes. 'You're the only one who takes me seriously in this family,' I explain. 'Look . . . I need you to cover for me. I wouldn't ask, but it's *really* important. Life and death.'

❀❀❀❀❀❀❀❀❀❀❀❀❀❀❀❀❀❀❀❀❀❀❀

'*What?*' Cherry gasps.

'Chill out,' I say. 'I'm fine. But I need you to tell Mum and Paddy that I rang, and that I'm staying over with Sarah.'

'Aren't you with her?'

'Obviously not,' I say. 'Look, if you can just tell Mum –'

'What is going on? Where *are* you? And where are you staying tonight, if you're not coming home and you're not with Sarah?'

'I will be coming home,' I sigh. 'I promise. But it will be very late, and I don't want Mum to worry. I'll sleep in the gypsy caravan. I will explain everything when I see you. You have to trust me, Cherry, OK?'

'Oh, Coco!' she says. 'Are you in trouble?'

'No, no, I'm fine,' I insist. 'Honestly. I'll explain everything tomorrow. Will you cover for me, Cherry, please?'

There is a silence, and then I hear her sigh.

'Do you promise me you're not in any kind of trouble?' she asks.

'I'm fine,' I insist. 'It's no big deal, honestly, and I really will explain everything when I see you . . . please, Cherry?'

✿✿✿✿✿✿✿✿✿✿✿✿✿✿✿✿✿✿✿✿✿✿✿

I can just picture my stepsister's face, trying to balance concern with sisterly support and failing miserably.

'OK,' she says reluctantly. 'I'll tell Dad and Charlotte that you're staying with Sarah tonight. But . . . Coco? Whatever you're up to, be careful. OK?'

'I will,' I promise. 'Thanks, Cherry!'

I click to disconnect the call, then ring Sarah to make sure she will cover for me too if Mum should call her place to check. That's unlikely – Sarah and I often sleep over at each other's houses, so it's no big deal – but I need to be sure. I tell her I am on a secret mission against animal cruelty, and that I will explain everything at school on Monday. Sarah offers to come and help, and I am tempted to let her, but then she remembers that her bike has a flat tyre.

'I could ask Dad for a lift?' she suggests. I tell her to forget it – asking for lifts after dark to the middle of nowhere would be way too suspicious.

'Sure?' she presses. 'I could bring a flask of soup. And blankets. And torches!'

I wish I had all of those things. I wish I had a friend to sit beside me in the woods as the night sky darkens and the cold seeps into my bones, but it looks like I am on my own with this.

'I'll be OK,' I say gruffly. 'No problem.'

After I ring off, Sarah and I text back and forth for a while, until she is called down for dinner and a DVD. I imagine my sisters, gathered round the table at Tanglewood, talking, laughing, eating, warm from the Aga. I imagine them stretched out on the squashy blue sofas, watching TV, squabbling about who should make the hot chocolates, whether it's time for bed.

An owl swoops by silently overhead, white wings beating as it navigates the trees, making me jump. I wish I was at home with my sisters, not huddled into my jacket, leaning against a tree, in the woods miles from home, waiting for midnight.

12

In the end, I don't make it quite that long. I doze a little and wake with a crick in my neck and an imprint of beech bark along my cheek, so cold I think I may be frozen to the spot. If I don't move soon the search parties will find me, a few days from now, a huddled figure in a panda hat, dead from the cold and lack of hot chocolate. I stand up and rub my hands together to get the circulation moving, stamp my feet on the litter of fallen leaves and broken twigs.

My mobile says it is ten forty-five, but I can still see lights in the windows of Blue Downs House. Surely they'll be getting ready for bed soon?

I make my way out of the woods and walk alongside the paddock, creeping closer to the house. Everything is quiet. I stand for a while at the stable-yard gate, listening, watching. Inside the house, someone draws the upstairs curtains, switches off a light. I see the silhouette of a woman pass one of the downstairs windows, carrying two glasses.

A dog, tied up in the yard, sniffs the air and looks towards me, straining at its rope. *Don't bark,* I tell the dog, silently. *Please, don't bark . . .*

I think I hear a movement somewhere near the stables, but although I listen hard for more sounds and stare into the darkness for any sign of movement, there is nothing. Probably just Caramel shifting around in her stall.

I open the gate carefully, leave it ajar and walk slowly, quietly, across the yard. The dog, a thin, bedraggled mongrel, watches my progress keenly. It yaps once, but quietens when I begin talking to it in a low whisper, gently. Dogs are quite like people. If you come across an angry one, you can sometimes calm it down by acting cool and confident yourself – although this dog doesn't seem angry, just thin and lonely and perhaps a little scared.

I cross the yard and peep into the first stable, but it's empty, as is the second. Approaching the third, I inhale the sweet hay-and-treacle smell of pony.

'Caramel?' I whisper, pushing open the stable door.

A tall shadow looms at me in the dark and I am so shocked and scared I lose the plot completely, jumping back against the stable door.

'Whaaat the – urgghhh!' I yelp, and a hand clamps down across my mouth so that the last word dies a muffled death.

'Shut up!' a gruff voice tells me. 'You'll wake the whole place up!'

'Mnnnhh?' I grunt, wriggling free and turning on my captor. My eyes open wide.

'Lawrie Marshall?'

'You again!' he mutters. 'Unreal. Are you stalking me or something?'

Indignation just about chokes me.

'Stalk *you*?' I hiss. 'Get a life, Lawrie – are you crazy? I'm here for Caramel, obviously. What are *you* doing here?'

Lawrie sighs, and I look past him into the darkness to where Caramel is eating from a bucket of grain. I'm pretty sure Seddon didn't give her that . . . I guess Lawrie cares about the pony too.

✿✿✿✿✿✿✿✿✿✿✿✿✿✿✿✿✿✿✿✿✿✿✿✿✿

'You were right about Seddon,' I admit. 'I was watching him earlier, running Caramel in the paddock. He's horrible! Do you think we should ring the RSPCA?'

'That would only make things worse,' Lawrie says. 'You have no idea how powerful Seddon is. He owns a lot of land around here, knows all the right people. He's clever too, and he gets away with murder. He hasn't left a mark on Caramel, so it would be our word against his. Who do you think they'd believe? There's not much we can actually do except make sure she's fed properly . . . she was really hungry.'

Caramel lifts her head and mooches over to greet me, nuzzling her head against my cheek. I put my arms round her and hold her close, hoping she knows just how sorry I am. I think of her earlier, eyes wide with fear, and I know I cannot walk away and leave her here.

'Not much we can do?' I challenge Lawrie. 'I think there's plenty, actually. We can get Caramel out – ride her out of here, rescue her. Are you going to help?'

'Rescue?' he repeats. 'Steal, you mean! Are you serious?'

'Why not? Seddon may have paid for her, but he bought

Caramel under false pretences – Jean and Roy would never have let her go if they'd known what a creep he is. We can't leave her here, Lawrie!'

He frowns. 'Seddon really is bad news, y'know,' he tells me. 'He runs pheasant shoots for groups of toffs from the city, so he has a gun. Stealing something of his is not a good idea.'

'Do you have a better one?'

Lawrie laughs, and for a moment, in the shadowy stable, I catch a glimpse of the boy he could be if he wasn't always cross and scowling. His whole face lights up – it's kind of surprising.

'So . . . we're doing this?' he checks.

'I'm doing it,' I shrug. 'You can please yourself.'

I saddle Caramel quickly, then take her head collar and lead her forward, out into the yard. The dog stares at us, forlorn, but Lawrie talks to it in a low whisper and it makes no attempt to bark as we latch the stable-yard gate behind us and make for the woods.

'What now?' Lawrie asks as we step into the safety of the trees. 'Do you have a plan?'

'I'm going to hide Caramel in the stables at home,' I

reply. 'Our pet sheep Humbug lives there at the moment, but I am pretty sure she won't mind sharing.'

'What will you tell your parents?'

'I'm not sure yet,' I admit. 'This is a spur of the moment thing, I haven't had a chance to plan out the details . . .'

'Not going to work,' he says. 'Trust me, Seddon will go crazy once he discovers Caramel is gone. He'll get the police involved, the newspapers, you name it. Your parents would know exactly what had happened, and I bet they'd hand Caramel straight back. Even if they didn't want to, the police would probably make them. No, if we're going to help Caramel, we need to hide her – somewhere nobody will find her.'

'Where, though?' I ask. 'A pony is pretty hard to hide!'

Lawrie frowns, thoughtful.

'I know a place. But if we're really doing this . . . well, there's something else you should see.'

'What do you mean?'

Lawrie ties Caramel's reins to a branch and grabs my hand in the darkness. Shock and annoyance flood through me, but before I can argue or swat him away he pulls me out of the trees and into the farmyard, dropping my

✿✿✿✿✿✿✿✿✿✿✿✿✿✿✿✿✿✿✿✿✿✿✿

hand again and pushing open the door of the fourth stable. In the darkness, I breathe in the warm, slightly treacly smell of horse mixed with the sour ammoniac reek of wet straw.

'Another horse?' I whisper.

Lawrie flicks on a torch, lighting up a bedraggled dapple-grey pony cowering in the far corner of the stall. Her belly is round as a barrel, and her eyes flare with fear as she begins skittering, jostling, trying to back away.

'She's terrified!' I say.

'And she's in foal,' Lawrie points out. 'Seddon bought her cheap, and he's totally neglected her.'

I look at the startled pony and bite my lip. Rescuing one pony or rescuing two . . . what's the difference?

'Lawrie,' I say, 'we'll have to take her too. We can't leave her here!'

'Thought you'd say that,' he huffs, and I can't tell whether he is pleased or irritated by my decision. 'Suppose we might as well be hung for a sheep as a lamb . . .'

He moves forward slowly, talking softly to the pony, offering her grain, clipping a leading rein on to her head collar. Jumpy and afraid, she still allows Lawrie to lead

❀❀❀❀❀❀❀❀❀❀❀❀❀❀❀❀❀❀❀❀❀❀❀❀❀

her out of the stable and into the woods. I wonder just how this boy can be so good with horses and yet so awkward with people?

Half an hour later Lawrie is riding Caramel uphill through moonlit fields while I trudge along behind with the dapple-grey mare. Lawrie Marshall has not only hijacked my plan but taken charge of it – he really is the most annoying boy I know.

'You're good,' I tell him grudgingly, as I guide the frightened grey forward. 'Have you worked with horses before?'

'Loads,' he shrugs. 'Up until I came to Somerset, anyhow.'

'Where are we going?'

'You'll see . . .'

We go on, cross-country in the moonlight for a mile or so, until we are high up on the moors, scrunching through heather and bracken, listening to the drumming cry of grouse and the soft huffing of the ponies' breath as they climb. Just when I am losing the will to live, the dark shape of a house appears in the distance, and Lawrie swings down from the saddle.

❀❀❀❀❀❀❀❀❀❀❀❀❀❀❀❀❀❀❀❀❀❀

'They should be OK here,' he says. 'This place was a smallholding once, but it's been derelict for years – there's no proper road to it, you see. The ponies can go in the walled garden – it's all closed in and overgrown. Nobody would think of looking there – it's miles from the roads and there aren't any paths or tracks nearby, so hikers and tourists don't really bother with it. I'll bring them some grain and stuff tomorrow.'

'We will,' I correct him. 'This rescue was my idea, remember?'

'How could I forget?' Lawrie sighs. 'OK. Can you be here for half two-ish, d'you think?'

'I suppose,' I say, shivering a little in the moonlight. 'This place is spooky.'

'It's safe,' Lawrie shrugs. 'That's what matters, isn't it?'

For once in his life, I guess Lawrie is right.

13

I wake late, shivering under the quilt in the gypsy caravan with Fred the dog burrowed underneath the duvet. When the door opens and Cherry comes in with French toast and hot chocolate I think I've died and gone to heaven.

'You're awake,' she grins. 'I peeped in earlier, and you were still out for the count.'

I have no idea what time I finally made it home last night. By the time I'd trekked back over the moors to retrieve my bike from Blue Downs House and pedalled home in the moonlight, I was exhausted. I crept into the gypsy caravan, crawled under the covers and slept. I dreamt of Caramel and the dapple-grey mare galloping free across the moors, and then the dream turned into a nightmare and I was running through the darkness, lost, alone, being chased by horrible Mr Seddon and his shotgun.

Not good. I push the thought away.

'You are officially the best stepsister I have ever had,' I say to Cherry, reaching for the hot chocolate. 'Thank you!'

'I'm the *only* stepsister you've ever had,' she laughs. 'And I'm glad you slept well because I didn't – I was worried sick! Tell me what you were doing, Coco, please?'

'Promise you won't say anything to anyone?' I check. 'Seriously – you have to keep it secret. Sisters don't tell, right?'

Cherry frowns. 'I guess,' she shrugs. 'But . . . it's nothing awful, is it? Illegal?'

I tell Cherry the story of Caramel's rescue and her eyes open wide.

'It is illegal,' she whispers, horrified. 'But I can see exactly why you did it. Poor Caramel!'

I sip my hot chocolate. 'Actually, it wasn't just Caramel. There was another pony too – a pregnant mare. We couldn't leave her behind!'

✿✿✿✿✿✿✿✿✿✿✿✿✿✿✿✿✿✿✿✿✿✿✿

Cherry frowns. 'Two ponies? Be careful, Coco. That Seddon bloke sounds like a total creep. I think you should tell Dad and Charlotte!'

'But Seddon will report the theft and get the police involved,' I argue. 'And Mum and Paddy would make me give the ponies back. Adults always stick together!'

'Dad and Charlotte would understand, if you explained it properly,' Cherry says. 'They'd know what to do.'

I bite my lip. 'I can't,' I say. 'I promised Lawrie.'

Cherry frowns. 'So who is this Lawrie person?' she asks. 'Do I know him?'

'I don't think so,' I frown. 'He joined the middle school last year – moved from up north, I think, judging by his accent. He's a bit of a mystery boy.'

'They're the ones to watch out for,' Cherry says darkly. 'Tread carefully, Coco. This stunt with the horses is serious stuff – I bet you anything it will make the papers, cause a big fuss with the police. You could get into a whole heap of trouble. I mean, it's OK to like a boy, have a crush even, but don't let him lead you astray.'

I just about choke on my hot chocolate.

'Er, *no way* do I fancy Lawrie Marshall,' I snort. 'He is

✿✿✿✿✿✿✿✿✿✿✿✿✿✿✿✿✿✿✿✿✿✿✿

the most obnoxious, irritating boy in the world. Horrible and arrogant and rude.'

Cherry looks unconvinced.

'I mean it,' I argue. 'Not. Interested. End of story. Besides, Lawrie is *not* leading me astray – the rescue was all my idea. I agree with him about keeping it quiet, though. We can't let Seddon get his hands on Caramel again. As for the other pony, she was terrified – I can't let them go back there. We have to keep them hidden, for now at least – I'll make sure they're fed and groomed. I'll think of a better plan soon, but right now this has to stay secret. You won't give me away, will you?'

My stepsister bites her lip. 'I suppose not,' she promises. 'But I don't like this, Coco. Technically, it's stealing, and if anyone finds out you were involved . . .'

'They won't.'

Cherry sighs. 'You've rescued the ponies, and that's great, but . . . I think you should tell the authorities now. Caramel isn't your responsibility, and the other one definitely isn't – you shouldn't get in too deep!'

But I am already in too deep, and there is no turning back.

*

By the time I'm up and dressed, Tanglewood is in chaos. As usual, my sisters are so wrapped up in their own lives they barely notice me at all, and Mum and Paddy are interviewing people from the village to help them fill the big chocolate order. Even if I did want to confide in them, I doubt if they'd have time to listen. They either fuss over me as if I am three years old or else barely notice I'm alive. Right now, though, all this is working to my advantage – nobody except Cherry has the slightest idea I've been up to anything.

The interviews are all done by midday, and we gather round the kitchen table for a healthy brunch. Even Honey has made an effort and put in an appearance, smiling and helpful, doing her best impression of the perfect daughter.

We feast on fresh fruit and yoghurt, then Mum's special eggs Florentine, a poached egg, spinach and mushroom combo that everybody loves. Our meals are extra healthy these days because of Summer's eating disorder – although she doesn't eat very much of anything, just picks at her fruit and manages a few forkfuls of poached egg. We are

96

not allowed to mention this in case it makes her feel bad and makes her eat even less, but trust me, it is not easy watching your beautiful sister surviving on strawberries and fresh air. Apparently the twice-a-week day clinic is helping her get back into healthier eating patterns, but I can't see an awful lot of progress myself. Mum says that battling an eating disorder takes time.

Sometimes I wonder what would have happened if nobody had noticed what Summer was doing, if she'd packed her bags and headed off to dance school this September as she was supposed to. Even the thought of it scares me half to death.

'We need you girls to be patient, these next few weeks,' Paddy is saying, helping himself to a slice of toast. 'Charlotte and I will be working flat out to get this chocolate order sorted, so things could be hectic. We'll need you all to bear with us.'

'Don't worry,' Skye says. 'We'll all help.'

'Just tell us what needs doing,' Summer agrees, and I have to bite my tongue to stop myself from pointing out the irony of my anorexic sister offering to help out with the chocolate business. It's kind of sick.

Mum pours more orange juice. 'I think we have the production side of things pretty much covered,' she says. 'We've signed up enough part-time workers to do three shifts a day, morning, afternoon and evening. If things go according to plan we should be able to meet the order in time and get those chocolates on the shelves by the end of the month. Paddy and I will be busier than usual, but there are no B&B bookings over the next couple of weeks, and we won't take any more until all this is over, so . . .'

'So it's just us,' Cherry states. 'Don't worry, we'll manage fine. We were OK while you two were on honeymoon, weren't we?'

That's not strictly true – Grandma Kate came over to keep an eye on us back then. Besides, Summer's freaky food phobia started while Mum and Paddy were away in August, and Honey used their absence as an excuse to go off the rails again. She almost burnt the stable block down one night and Summer had to go to hospital with smoke inhalation, although they did find out about her eating disorder while she was there so it wasn't all bad.

Still, I am not sure the honeymoon is a good example of us managing on our own.

❀❀❀❀❀❀❀❀❀❀❀❀❀❀❀❀❀❀❀❀❀❀❀

Mum seems to agree. 'Well,' she frowns, 'it won't be quite like that. Paddy and I will be busy, but we're right here if you need us. I'll be running Summer to and from Exeter to the clinic as usual. You girls come first!'

Her eyes flicker over Summer, who is cutting a grilled tomato into careful quarters, spearing a few swirls of spinach but not actually eating anything.

'We'll be fine, Mum,' Summer says quietly.

'Sure you will,' she says brightly. 'I've stocked up the freezer, but you might have to keep a check that you've got clean clothes for school and shout out if you need anything. We'll all muddle through. Right?'

'Right,' Honey says. 'Don't stress, Mum. It's only for a couple of weeks – no hassle! The place will run like clockwork, I'll see to that.'

Mum smiles. 'I know you will, Honey,' she says. 'We're so pleased with your report – just look what you can achieve when you try! I'm so proud of you!'

'Whatever,' my big sister says, her cheeks flushing pink, either with modesty or guilt. 'I just want you to know you can rely on us to cope with stuff here. OK, you lot?'

❀❀❀❀❀❀❀❀❀❀❀❀❀❀❀❀❀❀❀❀❀❀❀❀

'OK,' I chime in with my sisters. 'No worries.'

Honey, Cherry and Skye look unconcerned, but I notice that Summer's eyes are shadowed with uncertainty. Me, I can't help thinking that dealing with two rescued ponies will be a whole lot easier while Mum and Paddy are run off their feet. The busier they are, the less likely they are to notice my comings and goings.

I take a deep breath.

'I'm going down to the village in a bit,' I say casually. 'To see Jayde and Amy. Is that OK?'

Cherry shoots me a questioning look, but I avoid her eyes and Mum just nods and tells me to make sure I'm not too late back, to call if I need a lift. I promise I will, but of course I won't need a lift because I'm not going to see my friends, I'm going up to the derelict cottage. I have already hidden my bike down behind the gypsy caravan, my rucksack dangling from the handlebars, stuffed with hay and apples.

I am not sure when I got to be so good at lying. It's like I am turning into a mini version of my big sister, only with save-the-whale tendencies and flatter shoes. Honey is turning over a new leaf, while I am flinging

✿✿✿✿✿✿✿✿✿✿✿✿✿✿✿✿✿✿✿✿✿✿✿✿

myself headlong into a whole lot of trouble. I have never been afraid to stand up for animals, but even I know stealing ponies is serious. It makes baking cakes to raise money for the pandas look like kid's stuff.

After brunch, I curl up in the oak tree to play my violin, but I can't concentrate; my mind is full of stolen ponies, angry landowners, surly boys. I check my watch, killing time until I can set off for the derelict cottage. I am kicking at the red-gold foliage, anxious, edgy, when Honey walks across the grass wearing a cute print minidress, mustard-coloured tights and high-heeled, lace-up boots. She leans up against the tree trunk, and takes a compact mirror out of her bag to paint on scarlet lipstick and shimmery gold eyeshadow.

Watching all this through the branches, I can't help thinking she is taking an awful lot of trouble to look cool and pretty for a girl who is grounded until Christmas.

Maybe I was wrong about the new-leaf thing?

'Going somewhere nice?' I ask, and Honey yelps, dropping her eyeshadow into the grass.

'Coco, you are such a freak,' she huffs, scooping it up and stuffing it into her handbag. 'What is it with you and trees? Are you actually part monkey?'

'Stop changing the subject,' I say. 'I thought you were grounded?'

'I'm just going down to Anthony's,' she tells me. 'Mum knows, and she says it's fine. He's helping me with my calculus homework, OK? I want to get good grades.'

I frown. Anthony is Kitnor's only teen maths and computer genius, one of those slightly eccentric boys who still lets his mum cut his hair in a little-boy bowl haircut and never seems to notice that his shirt tails are hanging. I think he has a bit of a crush on Honey, but it's definitely a one-way thing.

Besides, Honey doesn't look like she's dressed to walk down to the village to study calculus.

'Is Anthony your boyfriend now then?' I ask, swinging my legs just above her head.

'That's sick!' she squeals, outraged. 'Of course he isn't. I'm just studying, OK? Nothing else.'

She picks her way across the grass and I hear the gate creak as she steps out on to the lane, the clack-clack of her high-heeled boots on tarmac. As I listen, a car draws up blaring music and voices call out, laughing, telling

❀❀❀❀❀❀❀❀❀❀❀❀❀❀❀❀❀❀❀❀❀❀❀❀

Honey to jump in. 'Shhh!' I hear her hiss. 'My little sister is lurking about – keep the noise down! I'm grounded, remember!'

A door slams and the car accelerates away, and I am left with a sinking feeling. New leaf? Honey? That'll be the day.

14

It's eerily quiet as I cycle along the lanes towards the moors. It's not such a long ride as yesterday – according to Lawrie, the derelict farm is almost halfway between Hartshill and Kitnor as the crow flies, so I take the route Lawrie has suggested, staying well away from Blue Downs House. Once I reach the uplands I hide my bike in a coppice of hazel trees he told me to look for and find a tiny stream that is supposed to lead right up to the derelict cottage.

I leave the lane behind and begin to trek upwards, following the silver ribbon of stream as it cuts through the heather and bracken. Each step feels like freedom, like leaving the chaos of the big chocolate order and Summer's illness and Honey's latest rule-breaking all behind me. There is nobody else around, and all I can hear is the distant buzz of a car down below, the screech of geese flying overhead, the rhythm of my footsteps as I walk.

At one point I glimpse a herd of wild Exmoor ponies in the distance, their dark manes ruffled by the breeze as they watch me pass. If all else fails, maybe I could set Caramel loose on the moors and hope that she finds them? It would break my heart, but at least she'd be safe. That wouldn't work for the grey, of course – she's not an Exmoor, and her colour would mark her out from the herd instantly.

I am just beginning to worry that I'm following the wrong stream when the tumbledown smallholding appears in the distance. In the daylight I can see a rectangle of drystone wall enclosing an overgrown field and tall, ivy-covered walls shielding the garden. When I get closer, I notice a tatty red sign that reads *Danger: Unsafe Building* tied to the cast-iron gate.

As I duck through the gate a tangle of starry white jasmine flowers brushes against my face, the remnants of a long-forgotten garden now running wild. The air smells heady, musky, sweet, and everything seems peaceful in the fading sun – it's the kind of place where time stands still.

Walking along the overgrown path, I see another sign, fixed above the broken doorway, faded, the paint peeling. *Jasmine Cottage.* I think again of the little girl with Seddon yesterday, her pale face stained with tears. He called her Jasmine.

Who lived here, long ago? Was there a family, kids playing in the stream, parents tending the vegetable garden, a couple of cows and sheep in the field, ducks and chickens perhaps? What became of them? Perhaps the children grew up and headed for the city, leaving their parents to grow old alone, their home falling into disrepair around them.

What would they think of our kidnap, the hidden ponies?

'Hello?' I call, and Caramel comes trotting towards me through the tangle of undergrowth, pushing her nose against my shoulder and making soft, whickering sounds as I stroke her neck.

'Oh, Caramel,' I whisper into her mane. 'I'm so, so sorry . . .'

❀❀❀❀❀❀❀❀❀❀❀❀❀❀❀❀❀❀❀❀❀❀❀❀

After a while I step back, taking an apple from my rucksack and cutting it into slices to feed to her.

The dapple-grey mare appears behind Caramel, shy and jittery. She seems too nervous to approach, but I stay still and quiet, my arm outstretched, the juicy apple slices on my open palm, tempting her. I have learnt that when an animal is frightened, the best way forward is to let it come to you; after a while she edges close enough to take the apple, her nose like warm velvet against my skin, her breath soft and warm.

'Nice job,' a voice says behind me, and I turn to see Lawrie Marshall sitting on the window sill of the derelict cottage. 'That one's really wary of people . . . with good cause, obviously. We'll probably never know her real story.'

'At least now we know it has a happy ending,' I comment.

'Well, maybe,' Lawrie says. 'Having a mare in foal really complicates things. She's not in great condition and I've no idea when she's due to foal. What if we're lumped with delivering it?'

'We'd manage,' I say bravely, although I am starting to feel a little out of my depth.

'Maybe,' Lawrie says. 'Right now, anything we can do to rebuild her trust has to help. You've got patience – maybe even a way with animals. I suppose everyone has at least *some* good points.'

'Even me?' I huff. 'Careful. You almost said something nice then. Are you feeling ill or something?'

'Funny,' Lawrie says. 'Look, I didn't ask to be in this mess with you, you know. I can manage fine on my own if there's something else you'd rather be doing.'

'That's rich!' I splutter. 'Whose idea was this rescue? Mine, Lawrie Marshall, OK? If it wasn't for me, they'd still be stuck with that creep Seddon, half-starved and treated like dirt, so don't you tell me to push off and go and do something else –'

'Calm down,' he says. 'I didn't say that. Look . . . can we try to get along? For the sake of the horses? I don't much like you and I know you don't like me –'

'That's the understatement of the year,' I snap.

'Fine,' Lawrie shrugs. 'Forget about getting along. Let's just work out what needs to be done. I've brought up a net of hay and some grain, plus buckets for water and feed . . .'

I look around, taking in the feed buckets and the hay. My own effort – a rucksack filled with hay and apples – looks childish by comparison.

'Seddon must have noticed by now,' I say. 'He's bound to go to the police. Is it really safe to leave the ponies here?'

Lawrie shrugs. 'I think so. I've been up here tons of times over the summer and never seen another soul. Walkers usually stick to the pathways and the house is pretty much a wreck – dangerous too, most of it. The garden's secure and the wall is too high for anyone to notice the ponies from a distance, so I reckon they should be safe enough for now.'

'Won't Seddon search?' I frown. 'The police too?'

'They might,' Lawrie says. 'I just don't think they'd look here. They'll assume whoever stole the horses is planning to sell them on, profit from them somehow . . . not hide them out on the moors. Moving them both now would be a big risk, but if we sit tight and keep them here, they should be safe. Trust me.'

'Do I have a choice?'

Lawrie rolls his eyes. 'If you have a better plan, go

ahead and tell me,' he says. 'As long as it doesn't involve petitions or cupcakes iced with panda faces. And be careful what you tell your friends about this – one careless word could endanger these horses.'

'As if!' I protest. 'I'd never do anything to put them in danger.'

'If you do say anything about it, leave me out,' he adds. 'I don't want to be part of the gossip. This isn't a game, Coco . . . it's serious, or haven't you noticed?'

'Of course I've noticed,' I scowl. 'Don't worry, I won't exactly be spreading the word that you're involved. I did tell my stepsister Cherry, but she won't tell anyone – she promised.'

Lawrie curls his lip, as if he doesn't believe in promises, or in me for that matter.

'So, do we make a rota for coming up to feed and check on them?' I ask. 'Only it's getting dark quite early now that the clock's gone back, and school doesn't finish till half three, so . . .'

'Scared of the dark, are you?' Lawrie shakes his head. 'Don't worry, I'll bring up lanterns and candles, and you should carry a torch, obviously. How long did it take you

❁❁❁❁❁❁❁❁❁❁❁❁❁❁❁❁❁❁❁❁❁❁❁❁

to cycle to the hazel copse? We can meet down there most days at maybe half four, if you're too chicken to come on your own. I'll come up on my own on Tuesdays and Fridays, after work. Those can be your days off, and maybe you can do Saturdays for me in return? I have to take my little sister to dance class in Minehead on Saturday mornings.'

'No problem,' I say. 'I can do Sundays too, obviously, to keep it fair.'

'We can take turns,' he shrugs. 'Whatever.'

I bite my lip, glad to know I don't have to hike across the moors in the dark, alone – even if my companion happens to be the scratchiest, spikiest boy in Somerset.

'I didn't know you had a little sister,' I say, wondering how she puts up with him.

'There's a lot you don't know about me,' he replies. 'She's eight. I buy your cakes for her sometimes. She likes them, even the ridiculous panda-face ones.'

'You say the sweetest things,' I huff. 'There was me thinking you cared about the plight of the giant panda. Another illusion shattered.'

Lawrie gets to his feet, gazing into the dusk at the two

ponies grazing the knee-high grass. 'It's these two I'm bothered about right now,' he tells me. 'We may have got them away from Seddon, but we have to keep them safe and work out what to do with them. I don't suppose your plan goes that far?'

'Not yet,' I admit. 'I'm working on it.'

'Work fast then,' he says. 'These two ponies are trouble. One of them is unpredictable, unrideable; the other run-down, neglected, terrified of humans and in foal. They don't stand much chance of finding a happy-ever-after home if you ask me. That's the trouble with bullies like Seddon – the damage they do goes on and on.'

I raise an eyebrow. 'Not keen on bullies, all of a sudden?' I ask.

'Not keen on them, ever,' he says. 'I know you think I am one, but you couldn't be more wrong. That day you found me scrapping with Darren Holmes from Year Six . . . well, I'd just stopped him nicking a tinful of crispy cakes from some Year Five girl. He's the bully, and for the record, he's the one who hoisted your panda hat up the school flagpole too –'

'Hang on!' I interrupt. 'That kid you had by the collar –
he was the bully?'

'That's right,' Lawrie says. 'OK, I probably shouldn't
have grabbed him like that. I know I shouldn't. Makes
me no better than Seddon, I guess. But . . . sometimes
you just see red. I saw that Year Five girl and I thought,
y'know, she could have been my sister – I couldn't let
him get away with it!'

Shame floods me as I remember wading in to drag
Lawrie away from the weaselly Year Six boy. How did I
get it so wrong? Instead of stopping a bully, I helped one
escape.

'But . . . why didn't you tell me?' I stammer. 'You let
me say all kinds of stuff – I feel awful now! I remember
the little girl too. She was buying the cakes for her mum's
birthday.'

'Most of them ended up in a puddle,' he shrugs. 'I
didn't tell you because . . . well, you wouldn't have listened,
would you? People like you never do. For the record, I
hate bullies just as much as you do. More, actually. I can
guarantee that. OK?'

I blink. What does that even mean? I look at Lawrie,

taking in the proud set of his shoulders, the defiant tilt of his chin, the way his fringe flops down over his face, shadowing his eyes and giving him a distant, stay-away vibe. The look I mistook for surly aggression – could it be more about self-defence? He is still quite new at Exmoor Park Middle School, and nobody seems to know much about him. Perhaps he has been bullied himself?

Guilt lodges itself in my throat, awkward, embarrassing.

'Look, I'm sorry if I got it all wrong, I really didn't mean . . .'

Lawrie brushes off my apology. 'It's over now. Forget it. The ponies are fed and watered and safe. It's getting dark; we should head down to the road.'

How do you say sorry to someone who thinks you're annoying, who won't let anyone get close?

I duck out through the rusty iron gate, stopping to pick a tangle of jasmine flowers as I go. Their rich scent wraps itself around me as I follow Lawrie Marshall slowly across the dark moor, keeping the silver-glinting stream to our right. When we reach the road, I shove the bunch of starry white flowers at him, grabbing my bike.

'For your sister,' I blurt. 'She might like them.'

✿✿✿✿✿✿✿✿✿✿✿✿✿✿✿✿✿✿✿✿✿✿✿✿

I think of another little girl, scared and crying, watching her dad training Caramel to the point of exhaustion, and I pedal hard all the way home, dynamo lights flickering in the moonlight.

15

On Monday lunchtime, I call an emergency meeting of the Save the Animals Club. I drag Sarah, Amy and Jayde down to the edge of the playing fields and into the woods that skirt the school boundary.

'Why here?' Amy is complaining, her Ugg boots sinking into wet leaves. 'Why not the school canteen, or a corner of Mr Wolfe's classroom? This is crazy!'

'And cold,' Sarah grumbles as we settle ourselves on to fallen logs and huddle into our coats. 'Plus, we are breaking school rules – we're not allowed in the woods outside of PE cross-country lessons, Coco, you know that!'

'Which means it should be safe,' I point out. 'This is important!'

'It had better be,' Jayde huffs, snuggling into her scarf.

'If you've brought us out here to start telling us about the plight of the South American great crested newt or the Siberian mongoose, I will not be happy!'

I wish my friends were a bit more supportive sometimes. They used to care about endangered wildlife and animal cruelty as much as I did, or almost; but over the last year they have totally lost the plot. Lately, they spend more time giggling about boys or flicking through the pages of the latest teen mags, discussing music videos or fashion or glittery nail varnish. I despair of them sometimes.

I watch, exasperated, as Jayde takes out a dog-eared romance paperback and Amy flicks open a compact mirror to apply a slick of lipgloss. At least Sarah is listening, for now.

'I'm not actually sure there are great crested newts in South America, but anyway, it's nothing like that,' I say. 'This is much closer to home. It's big news – I happen to know that local animal rights activists rescued two ill-treated ponies from Blue Downs House this weekend.'

Jayde drops her paperback into the fallen leaves.

'Wow,' she breathes. 'Really?'

'Blue Downs?' Amy echoes, snapping shut her compact mirror. 'That's near Hartshill, I think.'

Sarah doesn't say anything, but her eyes narrow – I know that she is remembering Saturday's phone call and texts, when I told her I was on a secret mission.

'These local animal rights activists,' she says. 'Let's see. They would be . . . *you*, Coco, right?'

'Well . . . sort of!'

My three friends sit up straight, eyes wide. They are looking at me with a kind of admiration, which feels weird but nice.

'No way,' Jayde gasps. 'You rescued two ponies? By yourself?'

I bite my lip. It feels wrong taking all the credit, but Lawrie was very definite about not wanting to be mentioned.

'I had to,' I say. 'They were being ill-treated – anyone would have done the same. They are in a safe place for now, obviously, but this has to stay secret. I can trust you, right?'

'Of course,' Amy says. 'We won't breathe a word! Wow, Coco, I just can't believe you did that, all by yourself!'

'Safest way,' I shrug, feeling guilty at the lie but pleased to have their attention again. Of course, if they knew Lawrie was involved in the rescue, I'd have their attention all right – but not in a good way. I give my friends an edited version of the kidnap, and they promise to keep my secret, offering to chip in with apples, carrots and alibis in case I need to come up with excuses for Mum and Paddy.

'If the police come asking, we'll say you were with us,' Sarah offers. 'A sleepover, or something. Maybe we could say we were up till midnight, and that we looked out of the window and saw a big horsebox driving past. That would put them off the scent. They'd assume the ponies were long gone then!'

'Maybe,' I say, but I know that an alibi like that would never hold water, not for long. 'Hopefully, the police won't actually question us.'

Distant shouts ring through the woods, and the sound of breaking twigs jolts us to our feet. 'Running club,' Jayde says, picking up her abandoned paperback. 'They practise on Monday lunchtimes. We'd better go.'

As we crunch back towards the school playing fields,

✿✿✿✿✿✿✿✿✿✿✿✿✿✿✿✿✿✿✿✿✿✿✿✿✿

we pass a couple of kids in running kit, red-faced and sweating, staggering in the opposite direction. 'Cross-country running ought to carry a government health warning,' Sarah muses. 'Look how red-faced and sweaty they get. And all that jiggling about can't be good for your insides!'

A lone figure crashes through the undergrowth and lopes towards us, long limbs pounding the muddy path. Lawrie Marshall doesn't look red-faced or sweaty, just predictably grim, dark wavy hair flopping across his face, blue eyes guarded. He spots me and shoots me a disgusted look, the kind that could shrivel an oak tree, which I think is a bit harsh after our adventures this weekend. He could at least be polite – I tilt my chin and refuse to be frozen out.

'Hello, Lawrie,' I say.

'All right,' he mutters, and thunders past, splattering me with mud from a nearby puddle. Typical.

'He spoke to you!' Amy whispers the minute Lawrie has gone. 'And you spoke to him. What's going on? I thought you couldn't stand him!'

'I can't,' I say. 'He drives me nuts. But I have decided

not to let him get to me. If he scowls at me, I will smile. If he sneers, I will say hello. Why should I let him wind me up?'

'Right,' Jayde says. 'A new tactic – save the world with smiles. I like it!'

'Not sure it will work with loner-boy, though,' Sarah muses. 'Although he is quite good-looking, in a smouldering kind of way. Dark and brooding. Sort of wild!'

'What?' I frown. 'Lawrie Marshall? Are you mad?'

'The hero in this book is exactly the same,' Sarah tells me, waving her paperback in front of my nose. 'Moody and mysterious, but with hidden depths. Maybe Lawrie will ask you out. If he does, would you say yes?'

I will be spending most afternoons for the foreseeable future trudging across the moors with him, but Sarah doesn't need to know that.

'Of course not!' I scoff. 'Really, he's not interested – and nor am I. No way. I promise you, if Lawrie Marshall has hidden depths they are so well hidden that a whole team of archaeologists couldn't unearth them. Or whatever. Although personally, I am not sure he has any hidden depths at all . . .'

✿✿✿✿✿✿✿✿✿✿✿✿✿✿✿✿✿✿✿✿✿✿✿✿

I trail off into silence, aware that Sarah, Amy and Jayde are watching me keenly.

'You like him,' Amy says teasingly. 'I can tell!'

Instantly, the pony rescue is old news, replaced by a frenzied fascination for whether I am crushing on Lawrie Marshall. Why is everyone obsessed with boys all of a sudden? It's like the minute we all turned twelve, that's all anyone can think of. I am not totally immune to boys – I am only human, after all – but I am not about to let hormones rule my life. I have too many things to do to let boys get in the way. I have to save the whale and the tiger and the giant panda, then qualify as a vet, become a famous violinist and maybe start up my own sanctuary for ill-treated ponies as well. That doesn't leave a lot of time for romance.

Which is just as well, if Lawrie Marshall is the best candidate my friends can come up with.

'He's a mystery boy,' Sarah says thoughtfully, as we trudge back up to school across the playing fields. 'I mean, what do we actually know about him? Not much. He came here a year ago . . . didn't somebody say he was from the Lake District?'

'He used to look kind of scruffy,' Jayde adds. 'But these

days he wears quite nice stuff. I think he's probably quite well off.'

'Don't know about that,' I say. 'He told me he's working at the stables because he needs the money.'

Amy grins. 'So you do talk to him! I knew it! And you have loads in common, like your shared love of horses . . .'

'We don't talk,' I correct her. 'He just snaps at me from time to time. That's not a conversation!'

But yesterday evening we managed at least two minutes of chat without descending back into sniping. Does that count?

'I see him getting out of a very posh four-wheel drive some mornings,' Sarah comments. 'So he can't exactly be poor.'

Lawrie Marshall is a mystery boy all right. Is he angry at the world or just trying to be invisible? Is he rich or poor, cruel or kind, secretive or just plain rude? He doesn't make it easy for anyone to get to know him and he's definitely not the friendliest boy I've ever met, but does that make him a bad person?

I cannot work it out.

'He fancies you, definitely,' Amy smirks. 'I can tell!'

❀❀❀❀❀❀❀❀❀❀❀❀❀❀❀❀❀❀❀❀❀❀❀

Sometimes I wonder if I am the only sane one on this whole planet, I swear.

Lawrie Marshall is waiting in the copse of hazel trees beneath the moor at half four, doing some maths homework. When he sees me he closes his exercise book and stuffs it into a rucksack, watching while I hide my bike in a clump of bushes. He falls into step beside me, following the stream across the moor.

'So,' he says, as if the whole day at school hasn't even happened, 'I hear Seddon's been to the police. They're making enquiries, planning a search.'

'They mustn't find them,' I protest. 'They just mustn't, Lawrie!'

He shrugs. 'They probably won't – I think they're safe enough, for now. But we can't keep them hidden forever, can we?'

'Not forever,' I agree. 'But I am working on a plan, don't worry. A way to get them out of there.'

'OK,' he says. 'But I'm worried about the dapple-grey mare. She's been neglected and she's quite run-down. She could be closer to foaling than we think.'

❀❀❀❀❀❀❀❀❀❀❀❀❀❀❀❀❀❀❀❀❀❀❀❀

'Don't worry about that,' I say briskly. 'I'm going to be a vet, remember? Delivering a foal would be no problem at all.'

I promise myself I'll find out on the Internet how to help a pony foal. I have watched a sheep give birth, on the farm next door to Tanglewood, but I'm not sure that makes me an expert in animal midwifery.

'Let's just hope she doesn't foal too soon,' Lawrie grumbles. 'She's not really strong enough yet and if we need veterinary help this whole kidnap thing could back-fire on us, big style.'

'It won't,' I say. 'Don't be so defeatist!'

Lawrie laughs, but there is no warmth, no humour in the sound of it.

'When are you going to learn, Coco?' he says with a sigh. 'Wake up, will you, and open your eyes. Not every-thing in life has a happy ending. Not everything that's broken can be fixed. What if we've made everything worse for Caramel and the mare? If they're found now they either go back to Seddon, or . . . they have no future at all.'

'What do you mean?'

❀❀❀❀❀❀❀❀❀❀❀❀❀❀❀❀❀❀❀❀❀❀

'Think about it,' he says. 'What happens to ponies that can't be ridden, ponies that nobody wants? C'mon. You know all the answers, don't you?'

I shake my head, a feeling of dread inside me.

'They go to the knacker,' Lawries says flatly. 'They're put to sleep. Some of them even end up as *dog food*, OK? Or cheap burgers. Is that what you want for your precious Caramel?'

'No!' I whisper. 'No, of course not!'

I bite my lip until I can taste blood.

16

We stay up at Jasmine Cottage until past seven. We prop open the creaky back door of the cottage, allowing the ponies access to what was once a stone-floored kitchen. A couple of candle lanterns hang from the ceiling, giving out a thin, yellow light; an armchair with the springs and stuffing hanging out of it sits forlornly beside a rusted iron fireplace. If this place was Lawrie's summer hideout, he hasn't done much to make the place comfortable.

The two of us bicker endlessly over everything from names for the mare to how to provide the ponies with food. Lawrie wants to 'borrow' grain from the riding school, but that feels dishonest to me and neither of us has spare cash to pay. Both ponies have bridles and leading reins and Caramel has a saddle, but that's all we have – no grooming kit, no blankets to keep them warm and dry once the weather turns really cold.

My head is already working on ways to raise cash to cover the costs. It's time somebody took charge and got organized around here. I take out a notepad and begin making a list.

But Lawrie is right – if the mare foals early, we are in trouble. Big trouble . . .

By Tuesday night, the list has filled most of the notebook. I have packed a big travel bag with bright cushions, blankets and a few strings of solar-powered fairy lights – Mum and Paddy bought loads of them for the wedding party in June, and a whole bundle got boxed up and put away in the shed. I chuck in last year's fluffy boots, a pair of leggings and an old fisherman's sweater of Dad's I've had hidden at the back of my wardrobe ever since he left us.

It still smells of him, a little bit, and in a good way. There was a time when I used to snuggle up with it whenever I was sad because it made me think of Dad and fooled me into feeling he was still around, for a moment

❀❀❀❀❀❀❀❀❀❀❀❀❀❀❀❀❀❀❀❀❀❀❀❀

at least. These days I am much less easily fooled – it's just a ratty old jumper he used to wear when he worked in the garden, and it will keep me warm up at the derelict cottage.

I have packed a rucksack with biscuits and chocolate and apples, and after school tomorrow I will make a flask of hot chocolate to bring.

It looks a little like I am leaving home, but Mum and Paddy are too busy in the workshop to notice. Tanglewood is buzzing. Paddy's stable-block chocolate factory is working flat out, the B&B's breakfast room transformed into a packing room. At four o'clock the afternoon shift leaves and the evening shift arrives, and in the middle of it all Mum is making phone calls and signing for deliveries and making a tray of tea and biscuits for the workers. Paddy hasn't taken a break since breakfast time, but he can't stop grinning and his eyes shine like some modern-day Willie Wonka. This is his dream, his big chance to let The Chocolate Box grow into a well-known brand.

I am very happy for Mum and Paddy, but let's face it, Honey, Skye, Summer, Cherry and I could probably paint ourselves blue, dress in grass skirts and party until dawn

❀❀❀❀❀❀❀❀❀❀❀❀❀❀❀❀❀❀❀❀❀❀❀

with assorted wild boy-band lads right now, and they wouldn't even notice. Not that we'd want to, obviously. Or I wouldn't, anyhow. I am just glad that in all the madness nobody asks awkward questions about why I am taking bags of blankets and cushions out of the house.

I hide my supplies in the gypsy caravan, then head back to the kitchen and whisk up a double batch of cupcakes. I fill four trays and slide them into the oven, then rinse the mixing bowl and start work on a big carrot cake. If the ponies need cash for food, I will get it for them, and experience has taught me that cakes are the surest way to do it. Sarah, Amy and Jayde have promised to make traybakes and rocky road and scones for tomorrow too.

When the cupcakes are cool, I slice off the tops, scoop a little sponge out and spoon in thick, sweet caramel to create a cupcake version of Paddy's Coco Caramel truffles. I am pretty sure my secret ingredient will have the kids at school lining up for more, and surely it will bring luck to the real-life Caramel?

'What are the cakes for?' Skye queries, padding through to the kitchen to make hot chocolate. 'Giant panda? Siberian tiger? Blue whale?'

'Local pony sanctuary,' I lie, as confidently as I can. 'You probably won't have heard of it. But if you want to lend a hand . . .'

'Sure,' Skye shrugs. 'I'll rope in Summer and Cherry too!'

Skye and Cherry help me to ice the cupcakes with buttercream and piped horseshoe motifs. Summer whips up cream-cheese frosting for the carrot cake, not taking even the tiniest taste for herself. She loves to bake and cook, especially lately – she just doesn't eat any of what she makes, and she thinks we don't notice.

'How's the day clinic thing going?' I ask.

Summer blinks. 'It's OK, I suppose – I like the doctor running it. I just don't know if I need to be there. I know I was a little bit stressed a while back, but I'm fine now, really.'

'Eating normally?' I dare to ask, and Skye shoots me a warning glance.

'Well, not like before,' Summer admits. 'But normal for me now. The doctor says that something like this can't be fixed overnight, but . . . I put on another kilo this week – that's good, isn't it?'

'Brilliant,' I say, although to me Summer still looks almost as skinny and fragile as she did back in August. Still, at least she is eating with us these days, even if she has the kind of portions that would leave a mouse asking for more.

'Oh – I know someone whose little sister goes to the dance school in Minehead,' I say, thinking of Lawrie. 'She's eight. I don't know her name, though . . .'

'I probably know her,' Summer shrugs. 'I worked with a lot of the little ones at the summer dance classes. It's the best age, really. Everything seems so easy when you're eight . . .'

She looks wistful, thinking back to a time when Dad still lived here, when baking was all about scraping the mixing bowl clean and sampling the cakes while they were still warm from the oven. She wasn't scared of anything back then.

I hate the way things change.

While the twins pack the cakes into tins for me, Cherry helps me to chop up an old sheet (a new sheet, actually, but Mum will never notice) and paint *Exmoor Pony Sanctuary* on it in giant rainbow-coloured letters.

'Where's it based, this Exmoor Pony Sanctuary?' Skye asks, running a finger round the bowl that had held the buttercream icing and licking it before dumping the bowl into the sink. 'Is it new?'

'Quite new,' I say vaguely, exchanging glances with Cherry. 'It's up on the moors somewhere, I think. They're just a small set-up, but they do some amazing work, and they really need the money.'

'Good luck to them,' Summer says. 'They should be careful, though. My French teacher Miss Craven said two horses were stolen from a new trekking centre near Hartshill at the weekend. Some people will do anything for money!'

'A trekking centre?' Cherry asks, puzzled. 'I heard it was just a farm.'

'No, the horses were valuable, apparently,' Summer says. 'The owner is really upset. Who would steal animals, seriously?'

'No idea,' I say, but my voice seems to wobble as I speak. 'Awful.'

'By the way,' Skye chips in. 'Miss Craven gave me some worksheets for Honey too. She asked if she was feeling any better – I didn't know what to say. Something very

❀❀❀❀❀❀❀❀❀❀❀❀❀❀❀❀❀❀❀❀❀❀

dodgy is going on, I'm sure of it – no matter what Honey's school report says.'

Dismay curdles in my stomach, cold and uncomfortable. What is going on?

'She's skipping school again, or French lessons at least,' I say. 'Did you confront her?'

'She was on the bus as usual, so I just handed over the work,' Skye shrugged. 'I told her Miss Craven was asking after her. She laughed and said the teacher must be mixing her up with someone else. I don't believe her, though. That school report was perfect, but does Honey strike you as a reformed character?'

'No way,' Cherry says. 'Something fishy's going on.'

'Have the teachers said anything to you?' I ask.

My stepsister shrugs. 'Not exactly. But I did overhear a couple of them talking about Honey the other day. How she'd clearly given up, and how Dad and Charlotte don't seem to be bothered.'

'Not bothered?' I say, outraged. 'They've done everything possible to support Honey! And if her school report says everything is fine, then why should they be worried anyway?'

❁❁❁❁❁❁❁❁❁❁❁❁❁❁❁❁❁❁❁❁❁❁

Summer frowns. 'I don't know. Something's wrong, isn't it?'

'Definitely,' Skye agrees. 'I haven't seen Honey in school for ages. Should we say something? Forget that pact we made when we were little – some things shouldn't stay secret.'

Cherry shoots me a knowing look, and I avoid her gaze.

'We can't tell,' I argue. 'What would we say? After that report, it would just look like we were stirring up trouble.'

'But if we're right, and we don't speak out, isn't that worse?' Summer worries.

'Could we talk to Honey?' Cherry suggests sensibly. 'She's not going to listen to me, obviously, but perhaps one of you could speak to her?'

The twins exchange anxious looks.

'It'll look like we don't trust her,' Summer says.

'Like we're calling her a liar,' Skye echoes. 'Could you do it, Coco? You're the youngest, she won't get so cross with you.'

'Maybe,' I say, chewing my lip. 'If I get the chance . . .'

But digging up Honey's secrets is not top of my to-do

❀❀❀❀❀❀❀❀❀❀❀❀❀❀❀❀❀❀❀❀❀❀❀

list right now; it would feel kind of hypocritical, when I am keeping so many of my own.

By midnight, I am alone in the kitchen. My sisters have gone to bed, the evening chocolate factory shift has long since finished and Mum and Paddy have headed upstairs with hot chocolates and bleary smiles. I am sitting at the kitchen table, a riot of felt pens all around me, drawing posters for the imaginary Exmoor Pony Sanctuary and eating one of the reject cupcakes, with Fred curled up at my feet, when the back door creaks open and Honey sneaks in. If she is startled to see me, she doesn't show it.

'Colouring in, little sister?' she asks, kicking her shoes off beside the door. 'Cute.'

'Fund-raising,' I correct her. 'How about you? Late night with the long division? Or was Anthony explaining some fascinating chemical equations? You're such a geek-girl these days, Honey. Not.'

'Funny,' she says. 'I *was* studying – sort of – to begin with, at least. But . . . not with Anthony.'

I sigh, taking in the slightly smudged lipstick, the rumpled hair. 'I don't think I'll ask *what* you were studying . . .'

'Don't,' Honey advises. 'And don't tell on me, OK?'

136

❀❀❀❀❀❀❀❀❀❀❀❀❀❀❀❀❀❀❀❀❀❀❀

This is the perfect moment to challenge Honey about her school attendance, ask whether she's hiding something. Who knows, she might even tell me – but what then? I don't want to betray Honey's trust any more than I want Cherry to betray mine. Perhaps it's better not to know.

'I won't give you away,' I promise, although I think that someone probably needs to tell on Honey, for her own sake. And soon.

It just won't be me.

17

Some days I feel so full of energy I think I could conquer the world. My sisters would say it's sugar overload, but I disagree. I spring out of bed after just six hours' sleep, feeling like anything is possible; I have a list, I have cakes, I have bucketloads of determination – what's to stop me?

Mum and Paddy are sitting at the kitchen table eating porridge with raisins and cinnamon, and I help myself to a bowlful as I come in. My sisters are already there, talking about the bonfire party down in the village – Mum and Paddy are planning to work through the weekend, so we won't be having our usual beach bonfire party.

'I've been invited by some friends,' Honey says sweetly. 'If I'm allowed to go, that is? It's the girls from my lunchtime history club. We were going to look at the origins of Guy Fawkes night, have some food . . .'

Mum and Paddy exchange glances. 'Don't forget you're still grounded, Honey,' Mum points out. 'I know this is a study group, but . . .'

'Maybe we can bend the rules, just this once,' Paddy says. 'I think you should go, Honey. It sounds quite educational.'

It sounds quite unlikely to me, but who am I to say?

'Thank you, Paddy,' Honey says through gritted teeth.

'We're going to the village bonfire too,' Skye chips in. 'Want to tag along, Coco?'

That stings. Why am I never included properly? Why am I the tag-along, the one nobody ever takes seriously?

'I'm already going out,' I say coldly. 'With Jayde and Amy and Sarah. We are having an important fund-raising meeting for the pony sanctuary first, and planning a protest, because fireworks are actually quite distressing for pets, and there's really no need to have rockets and the ones that make those shrieking noises . . .'

'Saint Coco,' Honey says. 'Are you going to ban fun too?'

✿✿✿✿✿✿✿✿✿✿✿✿✿✿✿✿✿✿✿✿✿✿✿✿✿✿✿✿

I stick my tongue out at my big sister. I am about to tell her that Saturday is Sarah's birthday and that we are all going to the big firework display in Minehead and then on to the funfair, when there is a loud knock on the door. Paddy answers; there are two policemen on the doorstep.

I drop my spoon, splattering porridge all over my school trousers.

'Just a courtesy call, sir,' one of the officers says. 'We're asking locals to keep an eye out for any suspicious characters, especially where there are horses close by. We're investigating the theft of two ponies at the weekend, and it's possible there may be more incidents if the thieves are still in the area. We'll catch them, it's just a matter of time, but until we do . . .'

My face is so warm I am pretty sure you could toast a bagel on it, but Cherry is the only one looking at me. Her eyes are wide, terrified, as if she expects the policemen to snap handcuffs on me and bundle me into a nearby prison cell. I suppose it could happen.

'We'll let you know if we see or hear of anything unusual,' Paddy says. 'It's actually a very friendly community, so if anything happens we'll probably hear of it. We don't have

❀❀❀❀❀❀❀❀❀❀❀❀❀❀❀❀❀❀❀❀❀❀❀❀

horses ourselves, though – just ducks, a dog and a very badly behaved sheep . . .'

As he trails away into silence, Humbug the sheep trots in from outside and helps herself to a reject scone from last night that has found its way into Fred's feeding dish. The policemen laugh and ask us all to be vigilant, and then they're gone.

The five of us walk down to the village bus stop together, my sisters helping to carry the bags and tins of cupcakes and traybakes. My conquer-the-world feeling has evaporated, replaced by a heavy, guilty heart. It's not like I have actually done anything wrong, of course; not *morally* wrong. I am pretty sure any judge in the land would understand that.

Maybe.

'Will you visit me in prison?' I ask Cherry in a whisper.

'You betcha,' she says.

'Another cake sale?' Mr Wolfe asks at break, raising an eyebrow. 'That's the fourth one since September, Coco. First it was to save the tiger, then the elephant, then the giant panda . . . now you're raising cash for some local pony sanctuary? The dinner ladies have been complaining that nobody buys puddings on the days you sell cakes, and the food science department is grumbling about healthy eating. It's wonderful that you try so hard to help, but I would make this one the last cake sale for now if I were you. Mrs Gregg is not happy.'

Mrs Gregg is the head teacher, and she is actually never happy. As far as I can see, this has nothing to do with cakes and more to do with the stresses of running a large middle school, but I don't say this. Cakes make people happy, not unhappy – it's a well-known fact. As for healthy eating, surely a home-made caramel cupcake is better than the crisps, fizzy pop and chocolate bars on sale in the canteen vending machines? And the reason people don't buy school puddings is because they are always pure stodge, like treacle tart or bread-and-butter pudding or rhubarb pie, and come with generous helpings of lukewarm, lumpy custard. If I were the food science department, I would focus my attentions on the dinner ladies, seriously.

I am lucky that Mr Wolfe is so used to my animal charity fund-raising that he doesn't question the imaginary pony sanctuary, though.

❀❀❀❀❀❀❀❀❀❀❀❀❀❀❀❀❀❀❀❀❀❀

'I probably won't be doing too many more sales before Christmas,' I explain, waving politely at Lawrie who is glaring at me from across the lobby. 'It's just that there are so many endangered species out there – they need our help. And this time I wanted to raise money for a new pony sanctuary. It's important, Sir, life and death really . . .'

I look across the busy cake-sale queue for Lawrie, but he has vanished, taking his own personal raincloud with him. You'd think he would at least support the cause. I wrap a couple of the prettiest caramel cupcakes in foil to give to him later – why should his little sister miss out just because Lawrie is too sour and stingy to cough up his cash?

'Can I interest you in a cupcake, Sir?' I ask Mr Wolfe. 'Caramel Surprise. You won't regret it!'

'I probably will,' he sighs. 'I'll take one, though – and one for Mrs Gregg. It might sweeten her up, though I think she means it about the cake-sale ban, Coco. Time to give other kids and other charities a chance. OK?'

This seems a bit mean. I can't remember any other student fund-raising attempts, except for the time Summer and Skye did a sponsored three-legged day for Children in Need two years ago. You would think Mrs Gregg would be happy to have caring, charitable pupils raising funds and awareness in her school, but no, clearly not.

'OK,' I agree, my shoulders slumping. 'I guess. I don't suppose you can donate a horse blanket or a bale of hay to the sanctuary, can you? Or an unwanted saddle or curry comb?'

'Funnily enough, no,' Mr Wolfe says, paying for his cupcakes. 'Good luck, Coco.'

Sarah and I have almost sold out by the time the weaselly Year Six boy sidles up, offering five pence for a slightly lopsided piece of rocky road.

'No discounts,' Sarah tells him firmly. 'It's for charity.'

He prods it a few times until it cracks right down the middle. 'You'll have to sell it to me now,' he says. 'I've touched it. And besides, it's broken. You should give it to me for free.'

'Not a chance,' Sarah says. 'You broke it, now you'd better pay for it. Full price.'

'Can't,' the kid says, smirking. 'No money.'

This is the boy Lawrie found trying to steal crispy cakes

❁❁❁❁❁❁❁❁❁❁❁❁❁❁❁❁❁❁❁❁❁❁❁❁

from a Year Five girl, though I can't remember his name. His sticky little hand pushes down on the last remaining scone, reducing it to a mess of crumbs and jam. I start to get angry.

'This is a charity sale,' I point out. 'Where's your compassion?'

'Lost it,' the kid quips. 'Careless, me . . .'

'Just push off,' Sarah says crossly. 'Loser!'

I pick up the broken rocky road and hold it out to the Year Six boy. 'Want it?' I offer. 'You can have it, I guess. Why not?'

'Don't,' Sarah frowns. 'He doesn't deserve it.'

'Oh, but he does,' I say. 'He really, really does. What's your name, anyhow?'

The boy looks uncertain. 'Look,' he says, 'I don't really want your stupid cake. It was just a joke.'

'Your name?' I repeat, grabbing hold of his sleeve so he can't run away. 'Don't be shy, you can tell me.'

'Darren,' he mutters. 'Let me go!'

'You were the one who hoisted my panda hat up the school flagpole, weren't you?' I ask him. 'And the one who tried to steal a tin of crispy cakes from a Year Five

❀❀❀❀❀❀❀❀❀❀❀❀❀❀❀❀❀❀❀❀❀❀❀❀

kid, until Lawrie Marshall stopped you. I guess you deserve that cake because you're so *big* and so *brave*, right?'

I wave the rocky road slice in front of his nose, and he jerks his head away.

'Don't you want it any more?' I tease. 'You seemed so sure a minute ago. And it's not like we can sell it, not now you've put your sticky paws all over it.'

'Get off!' he snarls, and as he opens his mouth I shove a corner of cake in. It breaks and leaves a smear of chocolate across his face. He squirms away from me but I hang on to his sleeve, unshakeable. I may be smaller than this boy by a couple of inches, but I am stronger than I look.

'Not hungry?' I persist. 'Or have you changed your mind? Would you rather have a scone?'

'Gerroff me!' he yells. 'You've got the wrong person, OK? It was a misunderstanding. She offered me a crispy cake, and that Lawrie kid got the wrong idea. Mnnnnfff!'

I score a direct hit with the mashed-up scone. A shower of crumbs falls to the floor and Darren wipes his face, leaving a trail of strawberry jam across one cheek.

❀❀❀❀❀❀❀❀❀❀❀❀❀❀❀❀❀❀❀❀❀❀

'Leave the little kids alone from now on,' I tell him. 'Nobody likes a bully. OK?'

'OK . . .'

'Quick,' Sarah hisses. 'It's Wolfie!'

Mr Wolfe cuts his way through the crowd just as Darren ducks free at last, wriggling out of his blazer completely and leaving me holding the sleeve.

'Everything all right here?' the history teacher asks.

'Fine,' Darren splutters through a mouthful of cake. 'Mnnnfff. Perfect, Sir.'

'Coco?' Mr Wolfe presses. 'Darren not bothering you, is he?'

'Not at all,' I say sweetly, handing back the crumb-speckled blazer. 'Not at all.'

18

'Are you crazy?' Lawrie demands when I bring my bike to a wobbling halt beside the hazel trees at the moor's edge. 'You're taking all those bags up to the cottage? Seriously?'

I roll my eyes and refuse to answer.

'Are you moving in?' he goes on. 'Got your favourite knick-knacks and fluffy floor rugs? Did you pack a kitchen sink and a mattress, just in case? And more to the point, are you expecting me to help you carry all that junk?'

'No,' I tell him, wheeling my bicycle through the trees. 'Hoping, yes; expecting, no . . .'

'I worry about you,' Lawrie growls. 'We are in the middle of a very serious situation, and you spend your time carting great bags of stuff around and baking cupcakes for some imaginary pony sanctuary.'

✿✿✿✿✿✿✿✿✿✿✿✿✿✿✿✿✿✿✿✿✿✿✿✿

I grit my teeth and fish out the cake-sale cash from my shoulder bag, stuffing it into Lawrie's pocket. 'Thirty-seven pounds, almost,' I tell him. 'The caramel cupcakes were a big hit. Enough to buy feed for the ponies for a week or two, anyway. Unless you already found the money some place else . . .'

'No,' Lawrie admits. 'Well, OK. That's good then. Thank you.'

'Hurt to say that, didn't it?' I ask.

'A bit,' he grins, and I think again that Lawrie could be a whole lot nicer to be around if he just smiled more.

He takes the bicycle handlebars from me and begins pushing slowly uphill. 'The easiest way to carry it is to leave it all strapped to the bike,' he says. 'I did it yesterday, bringing up more hay from the stables after work.'

'All I'm doing is trying to help too, you know,' I say.

'I know,' Lawrie admits. 'I suppose we just go about things differently. I've been trying to make the place a bit more liveable as well. And the money will be useful. I'm just worried about those ponies, that's all.'

'You and me both,' I tell him. 'The police came to our house this morning, warning us that horse thieves were

❀❀❀❀❀❀❀❀❀❀❀❀❀❀❀❀❀❀❀❀❀❀❀

in the area – I swear, I nearly fainted with terror. I didn't think they would actually make a big thing of it – I mean, it's not exactly a murder or a gang war, is it? I suppose that's what happens when you live in a place where nothing ever happens.'

'Maybe,' Lawrie says. 'Seddon was always going to make a fuss, that's just the kind of bloke he is. You don't make an enemy of a thug like him.'

'Well, I have,' I say briskly. 'And I don't care. Besides, I've been thinking about the ponies, and I reckon I've come up with a plan . . .'

I tell Lawrie my ideas as we hike upstream together in the fading light, the wind ruffling our hair and pinching our cheeks raw. With Caramel, the plan is simple; I want to keep her. If I really work on Mum and Paddy – and if the chocolate order comes good and the cash starts rolling in – there's a chance it could happen. I would just have to wait a while, then set up a fake ad for an easy-going bay pony. I could say I'd seen it on the riding school noticeboard – who would ever know? If the price was right, Mum might just go for it.

'Caramel's not exactly easy-going, though, is she?'

Lawrie points out. 'And your mum was dead against you buying her, so . . .'

'That's the point,' I explain. 'She won't know it's her – she's never actually met Caramel, only heard about her. We'll make up a new name – I was thinking maybe "Cupcake".'

'No surprises there,' Lawrie says.

'Then we invent a new history for her . . . reluctant sale, child's pony, now outgrown . . . needs loving home. Simple but brilliant!'

'I think you've forgotten something,' he says. 'Half of Somerset is looking for Caramel. You can't just move her into Tanglewood – people will put two and two together!'

'I don't think so,' I reply. 'Sometimes, the best place to hide something is in full view, right under everyone's noses. It's all about confidence. Nobody's going to expect her to turn up just down the road, and it's not as if Seddon knows my family or anything. The police were warning us to look out for thieves, not searching for missing horses. If we give Caramel a new identity, it'll stick, I'm sure of it!'

'You're going to ask your mum to pay money for her?' Lawrie checks.

'Yes, it has to be plausible. If I was suggesting we take in a pony for free, that would be way more suspicious!'

'So . . . how do we arrange the actual sale?' he wants to know. 'Your mum will want to talk to Caramel's "old owners". She won't just give you the cash and wait for you to come home with a horse, will she? She'll want to meet the owners, do it properly.'

I adjust my rucksack, stopping for a moment to catch my breath. 'That's where you can help,' I tell him. 'Mum doesn't know you, or your family. I thought maybe you could get your mum or dad to pretend to be Caramel's owners?'

'You thought wrong,' Lawrie snaps. 'Forget it!'

We walk on in silence for a few moments, following the stream, and even in the dusk I can see Lawrie's lips are tight, his knuckles white on the bicycle handlebars. I know better than to argue – something has upset him, something I've said. Talking to him is like walking through a minefield – put the slightest foot wrong and everything blows up in your face.

✿✿✿✿✿✿✿✿✿✿✿✿✿✿✿✿✿✿✿✿✿✿✿✿✿✿

'Dad left us,' he says into the silence eventually. 'Couple of years ago. We haven't heard from him since – no phone calls, no maintenance, nothing. So no, I can't ask him to help out with your little scheme, Coco. And my mum can't help either, OK? She has enough problems of her own right now.'

'OK,' I tell him. 'I'm sorry.'

There is no sound except for our footfalls through the heather, the whirr of dynamo lights on my bike in the falling light.

'My dad left too,' I whisper. 'Sucks, right?'

'Just a bit.'

'Mine lives in Australia now,' I explain. 'Like London wasn't far enough – he had to go and move to the other side of the world. Makes you feel really wanted, y'know? Mum got married again in June, though, and I have a new stepdad now. Paddy – he's nice.'

I am surprised at how easy it is to say all this out loud – talking about Dad has always been off-limits for me, except with my sisters. Maybe it's the darkness closing around us, the cold wind, the fact that Lawrie's face is hidden beneath a fall of dark wavy hair, his eyes facing forward as he pushes the overloaded bike. Maybe it's because I think, crazy though it may seem, that the prickliest boy in the school might just understand.

Or not.

'Look, Coco, I can't talk about this,' he mutters. 'Not right now. I'm glad things are getting better for you, but – sheesh – what's in all these bags? Bricks?'

I roll my eyes. 'That's right. Thought we could rebuild the tumbledown walls and maybe install a ski-lift at the same time, make it easier to get up and down . . .'

'Ha,' he says. 'I knew you'd get fed up with it.'

'Did I complain?' I argue. 'I did not. But we both know this hiding place is only temporary – we need to move the ponies to safety. If we can't get any adults to pretend to be selling Caramel . . . OK, change of plan; you can pretend to be the son of the owners. Mum's never met you, so it could work.'

'She'll never take any notice of a kid!'

'Got a better idea?'

He sighs. 'OK. Supposing – just supposing – things work out with Caramel. What about the dapple-grey?'

'That's where it gets clever. We use the money from

✿✿✿✿✿✿✿✿✿✿✿✿✿✿✿✿✿✿✿✿✿✿✿

the "sale" of Caramel to hire a horsebox and driver and get her taken out of Somerset – to a real pony sanctuary. I've googled one in Wiltshire that takes in unwanted ponies and then rehomes them – they homecheck the new owners to be certain they're OK. Our grey could have her foal safely and then both she and the baby would have a fresh start, a new life. We'll have to invent a convincing backstory for her – perhaps say her owner died suddenly . . .'

'Do you think they'll take her?' Lawrie asks.

'No idea, but we have time to work on that, don't we?'

'Might work,' he concedes. 'As long as the sanctuary hasn't heard about the theft. At least you didn't suggest painting her brown and setting her loose on the moors.'

'That was my Plan B,' I grin. 'Let's hope it doesn't come to that. We'd have to use poster paint, and it rains a lot in Somerset . . .'

Images of a paint-streaked pony, rainbow-bright and round as a barrel, flash across my mind. I think Lawrie may be thinking something similar because he starts to grin, and by the time we reach the ruined cottage, the two of us are laughing.

❀❀❀❀❀❀❀❀❀❀❀❀❀❀❀❀❀❀❀❀❀❀❀❀

We work together in the twilight, feeding the ponies and grooming them as best we can. While I focus on Caramel, I notice that Lawrie is stroking the dapple-grey pony and feeding her grain from his palm . . . her trust is growing day by day, as if she knows that we mean her no harm.

'She's definitely not so frightened,' Lawrie says. 'Now that she's putting on a little weight, though, I'm sure she's nearer to foaling than we think.'

Disquiet settles inside me, and I shake it off, briskly.

'We need a name for her,' I say, changing the subject. 'We can't just keep calling her "the grey". Something positive, hopeful. Any ideas?'

'We'll never agree,' Lawrie says. 'Not a chance. You'll want to call her something sickly, like Sugar or . . . I dunno, Shortcake.'

'We'll pull names out of a hat,' I tell him. 'Compromise.'

'You? Compromise?' he teases. 'That'll be the day.'

An hour later, we are huddled in the kitchen drinking hot chocolate from the flask, a fire made of fallen branches roaring in the grate, candle lanterns that give out yellow pools of light hanging from the ceiling. A worn Indian rug covers the cold flagstones, cushions and blankets scattered across it. It's still cold because half the door is missing, and Caramel is leaning over what is left of it, her brown eyes glinting in the darkness.

'Any more suggestions?' I ask, scribbling names on scraps of paper and folding them before dropping them into the fluffy panda hat positioned between us.

'Shadow?' he offers. 'Misty? Swift? Whisper?'

'Good ones,' I say, scribbling them down and adding them to the lucky dip. 'OK. New name, new start . . . I'll mix them up and you pick.'

I stick my hand into the fun-fur hat to stir up the folded papers at exactly the same time as Lawrie goes to fish out a name, and both of us jump and mutter 'sorry' and pull our hands away as if we've been burnt.

Awkward.

'Did you pick?' I ask, watching him unfold his piece of paper.

'Spirit,' he reads. 'OK . . . that kind of suits her. Sorted then.'

Lawrie grins in the half-light, chinking his tin mug of hot chocolate against mine. 'So . . . do you want to come

✿✿✿✿✿✿✿✿✿✿✿✿✿✿✿✿✿✿✿✿✿✿✿✿✿

up on Saturday for a while?' he asks. 'If you're not busy, that is?'

'Don't you have to do something with your little sister?' I recall.

He shrugs. 'She has a ballet class at ten, but Mum can take her just this once. We could meet at ten or eleven, spend the whole day if you want to. It'd be nice to work with the ponies in daylight for a change. Or I could just come by myself . . .'

'No,' I tell him. 'I'll come. I have to go out later because it's Sarah's birthday and we're all going to the firework display in Minehead and on to the fair, but that won't be until evening, obviously, so I can still be here. Hey, I meant to ask, what's your sister's name? My big sister Summer goes to the dance school – she might know her. She often works with the little ones.'

'She hasn't been there long,' Lawrie says vaguely. 'She's not a great dancer, it's more a way of getting her out of the house, having her involved in something, y'know?'

I don't know, but Lawrie isn't giving any more away. His family, even his little sister, seems to be strictly off-limits. I fish the foil-wrapped cupcakes from earlier out of my rucksack. 'You didn't buy any cakes today, but I thought your little sister might like some anyway,' I tell him. 'I saved her some – you said she liked them.'

Lawrie smiles. 'She'll love them,' he says. 'Thanks, Coco. What is it with girls and cake?'

'True love,' I tell him. 'Cake never lets you down.'

19

I've been dreading Friday's riding lesson. I'm worried that everyone will be talking about the pony rustlers and that I'll somehow give myself away – and I haven't managed to apologize yet about riding Caramel without permission.

Besides, I'd much rather be up on the moors with Caramel and Spirit.

As predicted, my lesson is not the same without Caramel. An hour of hacking through the woods on Bailey with Kelly telling me about 'poor Mr Seddon' just about kills me. 'He won't let a bunch of horse thieves stop him,' Kelly insists. 'He wants to open a trekking centre – Jean and Roy reckon he's been asking around, trying to get new ponies. I think they're sorry they sold him Caramel now, what with the horse thieves and everything. And it's a bit cheeky to start up a trekking business so close to the stables. It would take custom from Jean and Roy, wouldn't it? Still, I do feel sorry for Seddon, losing two lovely horses to lowlife thieves . . .'

I open my mouth to tell Kelly exactly what I think of Seddon, then close it again. I would only incriminate myself. I realize then that no matter what Lawrie and I have done to get Caramel and Spirit to safety, we can't stop Seddon – he has money, status, power. It is all very depressing.

'I don't think I can face any more riding lessons right now,' I tell Lawrie afterwards, leading Bailey back to his stable. 'It's all spoilt. I don't want to be here now that Caramel's gone, and if Kelly tells me one more time what a shame it is for that rat Seddon I might lose the plot and tell her what a loser he really is.'

'Don't do that,' he says, lifting Bailey's saddle off and brushing him down. 'She'll start to wonder why you think so, and there's no way you can tell her without setting off alarm bells. Seddon's respected around here – nobody'd believe you, and it'd put the ponies in danger.'

I sigh. 'Well, if I stick around here I will put my foot in it for sure. I love riding, obviously, but . . . I think I'll

❀❀❀❀❀❀❀❀❀❀❀❀❀❀❀❀❀❀❀❀❀❀❀

take a break from lessons for now. Caramel and Spirit need me.'

'What will you tell your parents?' Lawrie asks. 'If you just stop, it might look suspicious!'

I shrug. 'I won't tell them. I'll find something else to do on Fridays – the school orchestra practise that day and Miss Noble is running auditions for new members. Paddy's taught me a few tunes and I practise every day, so they'd probably snap me up.'

'Modest, aren't you?' Lawrie asks.

'Just confident,' I shrug. 'And hopeful.'

Lawrie rolls his eyes. 'It's like you just naturally expect things to work out for you. As if you can pass every exam, get to uni, be a vet or whatever it is you want to do and then play in some orchestra in your spare time . . .'

'Don't forget about saving the whale, the tiger and the giant panda,' I grin. 'And setting up my own animal sanctuary. You've got to dream, haven't you? And it's no fun at all unless you believe that you can make it happen. It's hardly going to happen if you *don't* believe it, is it?'

'You make it sound so easy!'

❀❀❀❀❀❀❀❀❀❀❀❀❀❀❀❀❀❀❀❀❀❀❀

'Not easy, exactly, but . . . well, I don't see why it can't happen. Some of it, anyway. What about you? What would you like to be doing in ten years' time?'

'I'll still be shovelling wet straw, cleaning out stables,' Lawrie says gloomily. 'Not that I mind, exactly – I love working with horses. But I'm not like you, Coco. School stuff isn't easy for me.'

'It isn't easy for anyone, you just have to be organized and put in the work –'

'Not that simple,' he interrupts. 'Trust me.'

'But –'

'But nothing, OK? Just leave it!'

Lawrie ruffles Bailey's mane and walks out of the stable, leaving me pink-cheeked and open-mouthed. I hate the way that boy can switch from friendly to furious in the blink of an eye.

Some people are just plain impossible.

With ponies, you have to be patient, gentle, kind. You need to build up a trust. It's the same with any animal, really – Grandma Kate once had an old rescue dog called Gigi who would growl like crazy if you ever tried to take anything away from her. I found that out the hard way on one visit – Gigi had run off with one of my new red sandals and was trying to shred it, and I yelled and made a grab for it and ended up with grazed knuckles where she'd snapped at me.

Grandma Kate explained that rescue dogs have had a tough past, coping with things we can barely imagine – Gigi had been abandoned and lived on the streets for months, foraging and fighting for food. That was why she was so possessive about things now. Grandma Kate showed me how to talk softly to Gigi, calming her, stroking her, and when I finally took the chewed-up sandal away she barely even noticed. Minutes later, the grumpy old mongrel was rolling on her back, sighing with contentment while I tickled her tummy and scratched her ears. It was like being given a secret – instead of reacting with anger or exasperation, show animals kindness and most of the time they will do pretty much anything you want.

Lawrie's approach to the ponies is the same; he is calm, firm, gentle. It's like watching a completely different boy from the mean, moody middle-school version. Animals bring out the best in him, I can see that.

✿✿✿✿✿✿✿✿✿✿✿✿✿✿✿✿✿✿✿✿✿✿✿✿

I wonder if the calm, gentle approach works with people too?

I have already decided to tame Lawrie Marshall with smiles and kind words, but progress is painfully slow. He is worse than Spirit – he edges towards friendliness, then backs away, bucking and rearing. Well, not actually bucking and rearing, but you know what I mean. He is wild and angry and totally closed off.

If he were a pony I would offer him food, stroke his ears and scratch his neck; but he curls his lip at the idea of cake and I am seriously not going to stroke him. That would be just gross.

In spite of it all, the two of us have found a way to work together. By Saturday afternoon, Jasmine Cottage is starting to feel less like a ruin in the middle of nowhere and more like a den, a hideout. We've hauled more firewood into the murky kitchen, hung up extra lanterns and covered the wrecked armchair with an old quilt so it looks almost inviting, even if it is still wobbly to sit on. Outside, we have draped solar lights around the bushes to help when we're up there after dark and cleared the path that winds through the overgrown garden to the broken-down front door.

'It's a bit of a giveaway if the police come looking,' Lawrie frowns. 'You may not be able to see anything from the moors, but once they're inside the gate they'd suss something was up.'

'If they came through the gate the ponies would definitely give the game away,' I point out. 'They're much less jumpy now. Caramel's really relaxed and even Spirit is much less shy than she was – the minute they hear the gate creak they trot over, looking for a treat or a cuddle. Face it, if the police find Jasmine Cottage, we've had it – we just have to hope they won't look here.'

'They won't,' he says firmly. 'I hope.'

As if on cue, Spirit appears, nudging me, looking for carrots and hugs. In just a couple of days she has transformed from a nervous, neglected mare into a bright-eyed pony with tons of personality. This morning I groomed and petted her while Lawrie mixed up the feed, and if I wasn't already in love with Caramel I am pretty sure I'd be falling for Spirit.

'She's much calmer,' Lawrie comments. 'It's like she's shrugging off the past six weeks, letting go of it all.'

❀❀❀❀❀❀❀❀❀❀❀❀❀❀❀❀❀❀❀❀❀❀❀❀

'Six weeks?' I question. 'Is that how long Seddon had her? How d'you know?'

He shrugs. 'I don't, obviously,' he says gruffly. 'Just guessing. What I mean is, she seems to have a good, steady temperament in spite of what she's been through, and she's young enough to learn to trust again. If we can just get her to that rescue place you talked about before she foals . . .'

'Not such a crazy idea after all then?'

'Sometimes the crazy ideas are the best,' he says.

'OK, so here's another – can I ride Caramel?' I ask, an arm slung around her neck, my face pressed against hers. 'Outside the garden, I mean? On the moors? Would it be safe?'

Lawrie frowns. 'It's just the risk of somebody seeing, but the moors really do seem deserted today . . .'

'So . . . ?'

He pulls a face. 'Knowing you, you'll do something stupid and she'll throw you, and I'll have to leg it to the road and flag down a passing ambulance.'

'Funny,' I say. 'I am pretty sure it was the scissors exercise that spooked her that day, and Kelly told me the last time Caramel reared the rider had been waving – she gets scared by anything happening behind her head. Maybe she's been hit or startled by something coming at her from behind?'

Lawrie narrows his eyes. 'I think you might be right,' he says. 'In any case, I think that with time and under-standing she will overcome her fears. She just needs to learn to trust.'

'Like Spirit,' I say.

Like all of us, really, I think. *Lawrie, Honey, Summer . . . maybe even me.*

'I won't do anything to spook her,' I promise. 'I just think she needs the run.'

Lawrie shrugs. 'Well . . . up here I reckon we'd see people coming from miles away. I'll turn Spirit loose in the walled field, it'll do her good. Yeah . . . let's give it a try.'

I saddle Caramel, mount and ride her out along the crooked path and through the rickety iron gate. Starry white jasmine brushes my hair as I duck through, Lawrie leading Spirit behind me. He unlatches the gate of the enclosed field and lets the grey mare free. She hesitates for a moment, as if it's been way too long since she's had a taste of freedom, then begins to prance and play, finally bursting into a trot, her mane and tail flying.

'Will she come back, d'you think?' I ask.

'I reckon so,' Lawrie says. 'The field's all walled in, and she's getting to know us now. She'll come back, don't worry.'

I scan the moors around me, a patchwork of rough grass, purple heather and rust-brown bracken. Far below us in the distance the road snakes through the landscape, a dull grey thread occasionally brightened by the buzz of a car. There are no walkers, no birdwatchers, no tourists at all to worry about. Apart from a couple of rabbits mooching about in the distance, I cannot see another living creature anywhere. It feels like being on top of the world.

Caramel shakes her head, nostrils flared, and a shiver of excitement runs through her body. This is her habitat, her element; she fits into the wild landscape as if she was born to be here.

'Careful,' Lawrie tells me. 'Go easy. No riding hat and all that . . .'

'What are you, my mother?' I ask. 'I'll be fine.'

❀❀❀❀❀❀❀❀❀❀❀❀❀❀❀❀❀❀❀❀❀❀❀❀

'Sure. But Caramel can be a handful, you know that. Keep it slow, remember what happened last time.'

'Who's doing this?' I challenge, irritated. 'You or me?'

'There's no telling some people,' Lawrie grumbles, and before I can work out what he's doing, he takes Caramel's halter, leads her over to the field wall, clambers up over the mossy stones and slides into the saddle behind me. His arms close round me, warm hands covering mine, gathering up the reins.

'Lawrie, what the —'

My protests are lost in the wind as Caramel bursts forward into a trot, and as I struggle to adjust she moves seamlessly into a canter that lifts my hair and blows it back into his face.

'I don't need you or anyone else looking out for me,' I argue, but my protests are lost on the wind. 'I'm not some little kid, I —'

I swallow my words abruptly as Caramel lunges into a gallop that takes the breath from my body. I have never actually progressed as far as galloping, and suddenly I am terrified, clinging on for dear life.

'Relax,' Lawrie says into my ear. 'Let yourself be part

of the movement – lift yourself up out of the saddle, stand up in the stirrups . . .'

As I rise up in the stirrups, shakily, I am aware of Lawrie's body behind me, lean and muscled, and I can feel his warm breath against my neck, the roughness of the green Aran sweater he's wearing. Slowly, fear turns into exhilaration and I surrender to the hammering of my heart, the thud of hoofbeats on moorland. I have never felt so alive, not ever.

Moments later, Caramel slows again to a canter, then a trot and finally a walk, and I allow myself to slump back against Lawrie. I can feel the thumping of his heart as clearly as I can feel my own.

'What did you do that for?' I gasp, as soon as I can speak again. 'I thought you told me to go easy?'

'She wanted to gallop,' he says into my hair. 'I could have stopped her, but she's been cooped up all week – like you said, she needed the run. I didn't mean to scare you – you should have told me you'd never galloped before!'

'I have!' I scoff, but I'm not sure who I'm fooling. 'I've done it loads of times.'

Except that I haven't, and I am pretty sure it was obvious. As for riding double with a boy, I have never done that, never even dreamt of it. I want to be angry, want to lash out and yell at Lawrie for treating me like a child, but I don't feel like a child right now. I am flushed and breathless and I like the feeling of a boy's arms wrapped round me, holding me close.

'She coped great,' Lawrie is saying. 'A flighty horse would have put her ears back and tried to throw us off, but Caramel took it all in her stride.'

'We weren't too heavy for her?' I ask.

'Doubt it. Neither of us weighs much – you're just a titch, and Exmoors were used as pit ponies once, y'know. She wouldn't have galloped like that if she'd been unhappy.'

Back at the cottage gate, we dismount awkwardly, suddenly shy. I lead Caramel forward and Lawrie calls Spirit over; she comes to him quietly, curious yet calm, as if she's known him forever. I watch him take her halter and realize that whatever his connection with animals, it goes way beyond being gentle and patient. He has something special, something magical.

✿✿✿✿✿✿✿✿✿✿✿✿✿✿✿✿✿✿✿✿✿✿✿✿

Back inside the walled garden we unsaddle Caramel and set her loose, then sit for a moment in the crisp afternoon sunshine sharing apples and chocolate bars; as far as my theories on training go, this is kind of like offering grain to the ponies. Lawrie eats and smiles and pushes a tangle of hair out of his eyes, but I cannot tell any more who is taming who.

Everything is the same as it was before, the garden cold and sunny and still, the scent of late jasmine drifting on the air, the cry of a buzzard circling overhead; but somehow, for me, everything is different.

20

I am baffled; I don't know what to make of Lawrie Marshall at all. One minute he is sour and moody, a scowling boy with an attitude problem the size of Exmoor; the next he is a hero, standing up for a bullied kid, taming two nervous, ill-treated horses, vaulting up into the saddle behind me to hold me tight as we gallop across the moors.

Sarah, Jayde and Amy would have a field day if they knew that last bit, but I am not about to tell them. I would never hear the last of it.

I pitch up at Sarah's house at six with a birthday card and prezzie, a fluffy tiger toy which is very cute and also very cool because when you buy it £2 gets donated to a tiger charity. The others are already there, eating pizza slices as they get ready for the firework display. Sarah seems to like my prezzie, but I can't help noticing that once she's thanked me she leaves it in a corner and goes back to experimenting with the glittery nail polishes and shimmery eye colours Jayde and Amy have given her.

It is very strange; Sarah never used to be a glittery kind of girl. She used to say that make-up was silly and pointless, but now she is giggling and posing in front of a mirror and trying on different combinations of clothes to wear to the firework display. I do not like the way growing up seems to be brainwashing my friends, wiping away their interests and turning them all into giggling boy-mad fashionistas.

'So, are we going to make some placards to take to the firework display?' I ask, trying to drag my friends away from the make-up. 'I thought we could campaign to end the sale of fireworks except for use in big displays . . . kids like that awful Darren are fiddling about with rockets and screamers for weeks in the run-up to November the fifth. Most pets get really freaked out by it all!'

Sarah, Amy and Jayde exchange glances.

'Is there any point?' Amy asks. 'It's a public firework display anyway. It's the shops that sell fireworks to the public you should be talking to, Coco. Or you could just leave it, try enjoying yourself instead. Why does everything have to be some kind of campaign?'

'It's Sarah's birthday,' Jayde reminds me. 'Let's just have fun!'

I sigh. There is only so long you can go on trying to change the world when nobody else is interested. It is a big task for just one person, and my friends seem to have switched allegiance lately. They still care about animals, I know – they just find other things much more pressing.

I bite into a slice of pizza and try not to wish I'd stayed up at the ruined cottage with Lawrie.

'Aren't you going to change, Coco?' Amy wants to know. 'I brought a couple of different skirts along if you want to borrow something, and Sarah's got a sparkly top that would really suit you.'

'I'm not wearing a skirt to a firework display,' I grumble. 'It's freezing! I've wrapped up warm specially, and besides, these are my best jeans!'

'You are such a tomboy,' Jayde says disapprovingly. 'Will you let me do your make-up? You could look *so*

❀❀❀❀❀❀❀❀❀❀❀❀❀❀❀❀❀❀❀❀❀❀❀

much more grown-up if you just used the teeniest bit of eyeliner and shadow . . .'

'I don't want to look grown-up,' I huff. 'I like looking like *me*!'

After an hour of fussing about in Sarah's bedroom, we escape out into the darkness, making our way down to the seafront where the firework display will be held. I have managed to escape unscathed apart from a slick of lipgloss and a little glitter across my cheekbones, but even so I am glad it is dark; I feel awkward, over-decorated, like one of those OTT houses all decked out in cheesy Christmas decorations that fascinate and appal at the same time.

The fireworks begin as we make our way across the beach, feet sinking into the gritty sand. We buy hot soup and huddle together as plume after plume of rainbow colour unfurls across the dark sky, squealing and laughing as the fireworks shoot and soar and shatter into tiny sparks and shards.

Fireworks are exciting, exhilarating; they wake you up, make your heart thump, shock and scare you with their drama, their chaos, their spectacle. There is a point where you have to give in, stop wishing you had a placard to wave and start letting yourself feel the celebration.

'Fun?' Sarah asks, linking my arm with hers as the explosive finale dies away. 'I know you don't really approve, but . . .'

'I loved it,' I tell her. 'Sorry if I was a bit grumpy earlier – I get a bit obsessed sometimes. It's just that I have a lot on my mind right now.'

'The horses?' she checks. 'I am so proud of you for rescuing them, Coco, I hope you know that. It's like you are actually doing things, changing things, when the rest of us just think about it – you're so brave!'

'I don't know about that . . .'

Any chance of a heart-to-heart evaporates as Jayde and Amy appear, herding us off towards the funfair. Open all season for tourists and holidaymakers, the fair tradition-ally closes down for the winter after the bonfire night display, so it's a last chance to celebrate, a perfect way to make the bonfire night fun stretch a little further.

We follow the crowds along the seafront towards the bright flashing lights and the smell of hot doughnuts and toffee apples, the loud music of the fair. It's ages since I've been, but I'm still a sucker for the thrill of it, the squash of people, the sense that something special is happening. I remember coming here when I was little with Mum and Dad, throwing ping-pong balls into glass bowls to win a teddy bear, getting candyfloss stuck to my face, flying round and round on the carousel horses and wishing they were real. More recently I've been with Mum and Paddy, or with Sarah's parents, but I have never been without a watchful adult hovering in the background.

An extra prickle of excitement slides down my spine.

'Let's go on the waltzers,' Amy is saying, tugging us forward. 'You should see the boys that work on it – they are so fit!'

'I think I just saw Aaron Jones from the high school,' Jayde chips in. 'Didn't he go out with Summer for a while? Maybe we should say hello?'

'Don't bother,' I say. 'He was a loser. A creep.'

'Good-looking, though,' Amy comments. 'Just wait till you see this lad at the waltzers! If he still works there . . . there are two of them, and the one I like is just soooo cool. Wait till you see!'

I roll my eyes and allow myself to be led through the

knots of people to the waltzers, just in time to join the end of the queue as the ride comes to an end. One of the fairground workers is taking the money, another working on the ride itself, swinging back the safety bars and helping people out.

'That's him!' she whispers, breathless and pink-cheeked. 'Isn't he A-mazing?'

The legendary fairground boy is skinny and tanned with laughing eyes and darkly inked tattoos peeking out from the cuffs of his leather jacket. He's much older than us, and there's a rough edge to him that has my friends swooning.

He spots us waiting and waves us over to an empty waltzer, settles us in and pulls down the safety bar. 'Ready for the time of your life, girls?' he asks, confident and flirty. 'I'll make sure you have a good time!'

'He is SO good-looking!' Jayde whispers as soon as he moves on to the next waltzer. 'Like someone from a movie . . .'

'Way too old for us,' I point out. 'He must be at least seventeen or eighteen.'

'So what?' Amy shrugs. 'I'm not going to marry him, am I?'

✿✿✿✿✿✿✿✿✿✿✿✿✿✿✿✿✿✿✿✿✿✿✿

'Did you see his tattoos?' Sarah giggles.

'I saw him without his leather jacket, in the summer,' Amy says. 'The tattoos go right up his arms. Just imagine those arms round you!'

'Fairground boys are bad boys,' Jayde chips in. 'They smoke, they drink, they swear . . .'

'Who cares?' Amy giggles. 'They *flirt* as well!'

The music begins to build up again and the floor sways beneath us, the brightly painted waltzer car swaying with it. Squashed in between my friends, I hang on to the safety bar as we whirl round, slowly at first, then faster, faster. I am deafened by the music, the crash of the waltzers as they plunge and thunder round and round, clattering across the undulating floor, screams of laughter from all around us.

'All right, girls?' Tattoo Boy asks, stepping on to the back of our waltzer. 'Fast enough for you? Or would you like to see some real action?'

Laughing, he spins the waltzer round and all four of us yell like crazy, loving it, hating it, high as the moon. And then before we know it the ride is slowing, the music fading, the waltzers lurching to a halt.

❀❀❀❀❀❀❀❀❀❀❀❀❀❀❀❀❀❀❀❀❀❀❀❀❀

'There you go, sweethearts,' Tattoo Boy says, releasing the safety bar and setting us free. 'Come back again if you're after more thrills, OK?'

'We will!' Amy promises.

'Everything's spinning,' I complain, getting to my feet and flopping right back down again. 'Whoa!'

'I'm all dizzy,' Jayde yelps. 'I don't know if it was the ride or the flirting . . .'

'Fairground boys are mad, bad and dangerous to know,' Sarah proclaims as we cling together, making our way slowly across the undulating wooden floor. 'This has been the best birthday ever!'

We're staggering down the steps, still a little seasick from the ride, when Jayde tugs my sleeve. 'Hey, Coco,' she says. 'Isn't that your sister?'

I follow her gaze to where Tattoo Boy is leaning on the painted railings that edge the ride, talking to a pretty girl with jaw-length blonde waves, a green crochet hat, a wool jacket and the shortest skirt I have seen in quite some time.

My heart thumps.

'Honey?' I frown, shaking off my friends and running forward. 'Honey? What are you doing here?'

She looks at me, her gaze registering annoyance, then resignation, while Tattoo Boy watches, amused.

'I could ask you the same thing,' she snaps.

'It's Sarah's birthday, remember?' I say. 'We went to the firework display, then on here. Mum knows all about it.'

'Good for her,' Honey says, without missing a beat. 'Well, I'm at history club, remember? I am with the girls . . .'

She gestures towards a couple of hard-faced teenage girls in tight jeans and spike-heeled boots, leaning against the railing sharing a cigarette. They don't look like school-girls, or history geeks for that matter.

Tattoo Boy gives me an appraising look, then turns back to Honey. 'See you later,' he says, and goes back to the waltzers.

'What does he mean, "see you later"?' I demand. 'Don't tell me he's in your history club too? I may only be twelve years old, Honey, but I am not stupid!'

Honey rolls her eyes. 'OK, OK, I'll come clean,' she says. 'But you have to stay quiet about it, Coco, yeah? Because I am supposed to be grounded, as you know,

❀❀❀❀❀❀❀❀❀❀❀❀❀❀❀❀❀❀❀❀❀❀❀

and Mum and Paddy would go nuts if they knew I was here. But it's not what you think. I am working on a project for school . . .'

I blink. 'What project?'

Honey pulls a little camera from her pocket, pressing the buttons to display past photographs.

'It's for my art portfolio,' she explains. 'I've been studying the fairground. I didn't think Mum would understand, but art is actually the only subject I really care about and I want my portfolio to be as good as I can make it.'

She flicks through some of the images; there are grainy shots of Tattoo Boy leaning up against the painted fairground backboards, of the hard-faced girls, the man taking the money, of little kids laughing as they queue at the hot dog stand. They are good, as far as I can tell, and relief floods through me.

'You see?' Honey says. 'It's an art project – I'm researching for a painting. Nothing to worry about, and no need to say anything to Mum and Paddy, right? They might not understand, but you will, Coco, I know. I may be grounded, but I don't want my art project to suffer.'

184

✿✿✿✿✿✿✿✿✿✿✿✿✿✿✿✿✿✿✿✿✿✿✿✿✿✿

'I guess not . . .'

Honey hugs me, tousling my hair beneath the panda hat, and I run off to rejoin Sarah and the others.

I believe Honey – we all know how much she loves art – but I can't help feeling uneasy, all the same.

EXMOOR GAZETTE

p100

REWARD OFFERED
FOR STOLEN PONIES

OWNERS URGED TO BE VIGILANT

21

I take a leaf out of Lawrie's book and start bringing my school work up to the cottage; now we curl up with our homework most afternoons. Lawrie turns out to be smarter than he thinks; he helps me with maths and CDT and I help him with English and French. It works both ways and it makes the homework fun.

I wonder if that's why Honey likes studying with Anthony? If she actually does study, that is. She can pick his brain and pull her grades up, and he can hang out with the girl he's had a crush on since forever. There is no crushing going on between Lawrie and me, obviously, although sometimes I catch him watching me in a way that makes my cheeks burn. It's probably just my own stupid imagination; as far as I can tell, Lawrie finds me

❀❀❀❀❀❀❀❀❀❀❀❀❀❀❀❀❀❀❀❀❀❀❀❀

every bit as exasperating as he always did. He is just getting better at hiding it.

Sometimes, anyway.

'This is just about the only time I get for homework lately,' I say, writing out maths problems by lantern light. 'I'm always up here, and things are kind of crazy at home just now because of the big chocolate order. How do you manage, with this and your job at the stables?'

'I don't,' Lawrie says, glancing up from an English essay. 'Not usually. I haven't handed in a piece of homework on time for ages – Mr Wolfe almost fainted yesterday when I handed in that history assignment.'

'How come you got the stables job, anyway?' I press. 'I wanted to try out for it and they said I was too young, but you're twelve too, right?'

'I told them I was fourteen,' he shrugs. 'I needed the money.'

'How come?'

'Never mind,' he says.

'So . . . how come you don't study at home?' I ask.

'I just don't,' he says. 'You don't know what it's like at home for me. I'm too busy to study. Other things to do.'

❀❀❀❀❀❀❀❀❀❀❀❀❀❀❀❀❀❀❀❀❀❀❀❀❀

Lawrie is sending me back-off messages, loud and clear, but right now I don't want to take the hint.

'Like what?' I ask.

'Like looking out for my mum and my sister, helping around the place, that sort of stuff,' he growls. 'You're very nosy, aren't you?'

'You're very secretive,' I counter. 'What are you, some kind of pre-teen spy? You don't make it easy for anyone to get to know you.'

'Good,' Lawrie says. 'I'm not looking for friends. I had them once and I had to leave them all behind, so what's the point in making more? I hate it here. Move to the country, start over, Mum said – it's been a disaster from start to finish.'

I watch him in the half-light, leaning back against the broken-down armchair, his face unreadable. It's like he has forgotten I'm here.

'The only good thing about the countryside is the animals,' he goes on, gruffly. 'The people are rotten. They pretend to care, but they just gossip and gawp and never actually do anything at all, and the bullies get to call all the shots. How come some people think they can do whatever they want, treat everyone around them like dirt? There's no way out, and you can't even help the people you care about. I hate it!'

I blink. I have no idea what Lawrie is talking about, but it seems like more than just Darren Holmes nicking crispy cakes outside the school.

'Lawrie?' I whisper. 'I don't know what's going on, but if you ever want to talk –'

'I don't,' he snaps, jumping up, moving away into the shadows. 'I don't want to talk, not to you, not to anyone. Back off, Coco, OK? I am not one of your charity projects. Like I said, you can't fix everything that's broken – let go of it and leave me alone!'

Lawrie shoves his way out of the kitchen, but not before I see the glint of tears on his cheeks in the flickering lamplight. That shocks me more than anything because boys like Lawrie just don't cry.

It takes him half an hour to calm down, half an hour of clattering about in the dark, filling buckets with fresh water from the stream, chopping back overgrown branches with a pair of secateurs. Well, at least he doesn't storm off down to the road without me.

189

❀❀❀❀❀❀❀❀❀❀❀❀❀❀❀❀❀❀❀❀❀❀❀❀

I stay put, ploughing through my maths homework, hoping that if I am patient he will cool off and bluff his way forward as though the outburst never happened. 'Least said, soonest mended,' Grandma Kate used to say, and it's good advice. I have learnt the hard way that with a boy like Lawrie, patience heals a whole lot faster than panic ever can.

'You coming then?' Lawrie asks a while later. 'It's getting late; they'll be sending out a search party for you.'

'Some people will do anything to get out of doing an English essay,' I quip, packing up my rucksack. 'Moonlit gardening, huh?'

'Don't recommend it,' he says. 'I almost pruned Caramel in the dark there. She could have ended up with a topiary tail . . .'

We walk down across the moors in silence, but when we reach the hazel copse Lawrie turns to me, his face shadowed beneath the bare tree branches.

'I don't understand you,' he says. 'I don't understand why you stick around. You keep coming back, keep asking awkward questions and making me say stuff I really don't

❀❀❀❀❀❀❀❀❀❀❀❀❀❀❀❀❀❀❀❀❀❀❀❀

want to talk about. You drive me nuts and I think I drive you nuts too, but . . .'

His breath huffs out in a cloud of white, hovering in the icy air, and his brows draw together in a frown. 'I just don't get it!'

I sigh, wheeling my bike out on to the lane, hook a foot over one pedal.

'We're friends,' I tell him, pushing off into the darkness.

I think it's true.

At school, Lawrie mostly acts as though I don't exist, though if I pass him in the corridor or see him in the lunch hall he drags up a grudging 'hello'. He is a loner, dark wavy hair falling across his face, mouth unsmiling, blue eyes guarded. Sometimes I think he'd like to be invisible, but he's not, not to me.

On Thursday morning, Sarah, Jayde and Amy corner me at break.

'Did you see the newspaper?' Sarah asks, spreading a copy of the *Exmoor Gazette* out across the table. 'There's a big piece about the missing ponies. You're famous! Or infamous, maybe . . .'

'Shhh!' I hiss. 'Keep your voice down!'

I look at the headline – *Reward Offered for Stolen Ponies: Horse Owners Urged to be Vigilant* – and my heart begins to pound.

'*Ten days ago near Hartshill, heartless thieves stole a small girl's birthday pony, leaving her inconsolable,*' I read out. '*The much-loved family pet was taken, along with another valuable trekking pony in foal, in a well-planned midnight raid. Local landowner James Seddon is offering a cash reward for information leading to the return of the horses, and police fear the thugs may strike again . . .*'

'Are you sure they were being ill-treated?' Amy asks.

'Of course I'm sure!' I splutter. 'That article is rubbish! Trekking ponies? Spirit's only half-broken, and she was so petrified when we – I – first took her that I didn't think she'd ever calm down. And it's a miracle she is still in foal, after the way she's been neglected. As for the little girl, she looked as scared of Seddon as the ponies were. Honestly, I wish the newspaper knew what was really going on.'

'Offering a reward is bad news,' Jayde points out. 'People will be watching out for those ponies now. You shouldn't trust anyone.'

❀❀❀❀❀❀❀❀❀❀❀❀❀❀❀❀❀❀❀❀❀❀

'Especially not Jayde,' Amy grins, nudging her friend with an elbow. 'She talks too much. Walls have ears, right?'

'Huh?' Jayde asks. 'What walls? What are you talking about?'

'She's telling you to keep your voice down,' Sarah says, stuffing the paper into my schoolbag before anyone can see what we were reading, and glancing around furtively. 'We have to be extra careful now. Coco, are the . . . um . . . refugees definitely in a safe place?'

I blink. '*Refugees?*'

Sarah lowers her voice. 'You know what I mean! I don't want to say the word "horse". People might be listening!'

'Nobody's listening,' I tell her. 'I think they're safe, but . . . well, it's impossible to be sure, isn't it?'

'Better step up security then,' Sarah warns. 'Or you'll make the headlines again, as the youngest horse-thief in Britain.'

My day goes from bad to worse.

Mr Wolfe springs a spot-test on us in history, and I barely scrape through. In art I spend an hour making a carefully coiled clay pot and then drop it on the floor,

❀❀❀❀❀❀❀❀❀❀❀❀❀❀❀❀❀❀❀❀❀❀❀

squashing it flat; and in science I can't concentrate at all and almost set Sarah's hair on fire with a Bunsen burner. Sarah screams and Lawrie rolls his eyes at me across the lab and I end up with a punishment exercise to write out the legend *I must learn to respect laboratory equipment* one hundred times. Great.

'What about respecting my hair?' Sarah wants to know, but to be honest she has frazzled it more herself with excessive use of straighteners, so one small singed bit is not going to matter. Much.

I think the stresses of being the youngest horse-thief in Britain are beginning to tell.

After the bell, Lawrie corners me by the lockers.

'What's up with you?' he demands. 'You've been jumpy all day. Something wrong?'

'This is wrong,' I say, showing him the newspaper. 'We're in big trouble.'

'Don't panic,' Lawrie says, scanning the *Gazette*. 'Seddon was always likely to go to the press, always going to lie. We have to stay calm. It doesn't change anything.'

I bite my lip. 'I know. I do – it's just hard not to worry.'

Lawrie frowns. 'Tell me about it,' he says. 'I heard some

✿✿✿✿✿✿✿✿✿✿✿✿✿✿✿✿✿✿✿✿✿✿✿✿✿

bad news myself today. Seddon's bought two more horses. They're not in foal and they don't need breaking, but . . .'

My heart sinks. It feels like the final straw.

'Can we rescue them?' I ask. 'Get them out of there?'

'Don't even think about it, Coco,' he tells me. 'We may have got away with one rescue – so far – but trying another would be madness. The police think it's opportunist horse thieves at the moment – target the same place again and it's going to look very different. We can't risk it – it would put Caramel and Spirit in danger, blow the whole thing!'

'I hate him,' I huff, kicking at the wall in frustration. 'I really, really hate him.'

'You and me both,' Lawrie says. 'Look, we'll talk about this later . . .'

Sarah appears at my side and Lawrie gives her a dark look before striding away.

'What did *he* want?' she whispers.

'Just making some snarky comment about me burning the school down if I don't pay more attention,' I lie. 'He's such a charmer.'

'He fancies you,' Sarah says. 'I've seen the way he looks at you. All dark and smouldering.'

'That's the way he looks at everyone,' I tell her.

'Maybe,' Sarah says, watching Lawrie disappear into the scrum of kids heading for the school gate. 'Maybe not. He likes you. Mark my words.'

I worry about that all the way home.

22

Back at Tanglewood, the little chocolate factory is silent and for the first time in almost a fortnight there is no aroma of melted chocolate drifting on the air. I head for the kitchen to make a flask of hot chocolate to take up to the cottage as usual, but the moment I step inside I can see that something is very wrong. Mum and Paddy are sitting at the big pine table, their faces grim.

'Everything OK?' I ask. 'Things going to plan with the order?'

'Factory's running like clockwork,' Paddy says. 'Thank goodness. We should have everything shipped off by the end of next week, but I've had to let the workers go early today, obviously . . .'

'I've been a fool,' Mum states flatly. 'I've been kidding

myself – so wrapped up in the business that I didn't notice what was going on right under my nose!'

'What was going on?' I ask warily.

Is this to do with the newspaper article? Have the police been round asking questions? Have Mum and Paddy worked out that I am not seeing my friends every afternoon, but wandering around the moors in the dark with a boy I barely know and a couple of stolen ponies?

I really hope not.

It's not even as though our rescue has changed anything – Seddon has just bought more ponies who will suffer in exactly the same way as Spirit and Caramel. There is no way to stop him, and the knowledge makes me feel crushed, hopeless.

Mum looks tired, with shadows under her eyes, smudged eyeliner and a hopeless, defeated tilt to her shoulders. Fear curls in my belly.

'Mum? What is it?'

She picks up a letter typed on the school's headed paper, her hand shaking. 'Oh, Coco . . . I was so proud of her, so sure she'd turned the corner. And now this!'

The penny drops.

❀❀❀❀❀❀❀❀❀❀❀❀❀❀❀❀❀❀❀❀❀❀❀❀

'Honey,' I say flatly, and Paddy nods.

'We've been asked to come into school to discuss her continued absences and erratic grades,' Mum says. 'But her report was excellent – how can things have gone downhill so fast? It doesn't make sense!'

'Let me ring the school and find out,' Paddy suggests.

'Not yet – we have to give Honey a chance to explain,' Mum argues. 'Perhaps it's a mix-up . . . there could be a perfectly reasonable explanation for it all.'

'Charlotte, if we just speak to Mr Keating . . .'

'No,' Mum pleads. 'We'll talk to Honey first. If something's been going on, I want to hear it from her. I'm her mother, she'll tell me the truth!'

I doubt that somehow, but I stay silent and put the kettle on. Instead of making a flask of hot chocolate I brew a pot of tea and raid the cupboard for Jammie Dodgers.

Family trouble, I text Lawrie quickly. Mum upset. Might be a bit late getting to the meeting place.

Will go without you, he texts back. Family comes first. Take care xx

I stare at the message, wide-eyed. Two kisses? Does

❁❁❁❁❁❁❁❁❁❁❁❁❁❁❁❁❁❁❁❁❁❁❁

that mean anything, and if so, what? I would never have imagined that Lawrie was the kind of boy to add text kisses – after all, he can barely dredge up a smile for me most days.

By the time I've poured the tea and arranged the biscuits on a plate, Skye, Summer, Cherry and Honey come clattering in. Their chat fades to silence fast as they see Mum's face, tight-lipped.

'So . . . Honey?' she grates out, handing over the letter. 'Tell me this isn't true!'

Skye, Summer and Cherry huddle beside me, out of the line of fire, and Fred the dog nudges my hand with his nose. I stroke his ears and he leans against me, whining softly.

'It's a mistake, obviously,' Honey says, scanning the letter dismissively. 'Ridiculous. You've seen my report!'

'They can't both be right,' Mum says. 'What's going on, Honey?'

'Nothing! The computers at school must have been playing up, that's all – loads of things have been going wrong these last few days. Or maybe some stupid

✿✿✿✿✿✿✿✿✿✿✿✿✿✿✿✿✿✿✿✿✿✿✿✿✿

secretary has picked up last year's file? I am doing fine this term, you know I am!'

'We thought you were,' Paddy sighs. 'Now we're not too sure.'

Honey flings him an angry glance. 'Look, it's fine, all right?' she says. 'I was on the bus to school this morning – ask the others. And I was on the bus home; you can't argue with that. I haven't missed a day all term. Right, Summer? Skye? Cherry? We may not be in the same year but you must see me in the corridors sometimes . . .'

Cherry shrugs, and her eyes slide away from Honey's, evasive. She does not want to answer, and nobody can blame her – Honey has made her life a misery from day one.

Beside me, I can feel Summer shrink into herself, hiding behind her hair, arms wrapped around her body as if for protection. She was always the sister who stuck up for Honey, even when the rest of us despaired of her, but I'm not sure she will defend her now.

'I don't know,' she says in a whisper. 'I'm not at school all of the time any more, Honey, I have the day clinic thing twice a week. I . . . I can't say . . .'

❁❁❁❁❁❁❁❁❁❁❁❁❁❁❁❁❁❁❁❁❁❁❁❁

'I've seen you,' Skye chips in, taking the pressure off her twin. 'Once or twice. Maybe. Not for quite a while, though . . .'

'Oh, for goodness' sake!' Honey growls.

My sisters have never looked more uncomfortable. Nobody wants to break the 'sisters-don't-tell' rule, but all of us know it's time to stop covering up for Honey. I am glad I'm not at the high school, that nobody asks me. I would not want to tell how I see Honey come and go at all hours of the day and night, getting lifts from boys whose cars blare loud music and laughter. I would have to mention how she has been hanging out at the fair with hard-faced girls and tattooed boys, working on an art project that may or may not exist.

It's not even as if any of this seems to make my big sister happy.

'I don't know why they're saying all this,' she argues, shooting the twins a furious look. 'I'm in school every day, I told you. The letter's a mistake.'

'Well,' Paddy says, 'that's a relief. But we'll ring the school anyway, or call in to see Mr Keating tomorrow morning, let him know we got the letter. We can't ignore it, Honey. If it's some kind of computer error, they'll tell us – no harm done.'

'It's for the best,' Mum agrees. 'Set the record straight, sort it out.'

I watch Honey's face crumble, the confident mask replaced with anger, panic. Suddenly her excuses seem flimsy, desperate.

'I knew you wouldn't believe me!' she yells. 'You never do, any of you! Don't try and pretend that you care what I get up to – you really, really don't. All you care about are your horrible chocolates and that stupid order. Don't kid yourself – you're not going to make your fortunes. Those truffles will probably *poison* someone and then you'll be sorry! Sheesh, this whole family sucks!'

She storms out of the kitchen, slamming the door behind her.

'I don't know what to do,' Mum whispers. 'How did I miss this? How did I get it so wrong? Honey needs more help and support than I can give her – she's just so angry, so lost. No matter what I try to do, nothing ever changes.'

'We'll see Mr Keating in the morning, get to the bottom

of it,' Paddy promises. 'We can't let her throw her life away like this.'

Honey's timing could not be worse – my family is stressed and struggling as it is; we really do not need more of Honey's dramas. Later, subdued and slightly shaken, we are eating a makeshift supper of cheese and vegetable pie heated up from the freezer when she flounces back into the kitchen.

'I've been speaking to Anthony,' she announces smugly, holding out her mobile. 'He's had exactly the same letter, and everyone knows he is the biggest swot in Somerset. He's probably never missed a school day in his life. So he reckons it is *definitely* a computer glitch because the school has just emailed him to apologize. So can you check your emails and see if we've had one too?'

'We're eating,' Paddy says patiently. 'I'll check in a minute.'

'This is my reputation at stake here,' Honey says. 'It's important!'

Mum stands up, tight-lipped, and fetches her laptop. She opens it, checks her mail, and there, sure enough, is an email from Exmoor High. '*A faulty software installation*

❀❀❀❀❀❀❀❀❀❀❀❀❀❀❀❀❀❀❀❀❀

on the school IT system has resulted in some confusion, with warning letters being sent to students who are in fact performing very well at present,' she reads. 'How odd . . . I've never heard of anything like that before.'

'It happens all the time, apparently,' Honey says. 'So. A problem with the software system. OK? Don't all say sorry at once.'

'Well . . . I am sorry if we jumped to the wrong conclusion,' Mum says.

'Thank you,' Honey snaps. 'Now, I have a ton of homework, so I'd better get on with it.'

We watch her go.

'*If* we jumped to the wrong conclusion,' Mum repeats. 'But I don't think we did somehow. Take a look at this . . .'

She hands the laptop over to Paddy, who reads it carefully. 'It's from the school's email address all right. And the header looks official too . . .'

'Look closely,' Mum says.

We look at the address: *Exmoor High School, Graystone Lane* . . .

'What am I looking for?' Paddy frowns.

'They've spelt "Greystone" wrong,' Mum says. 'And I

❀❀❀❀❀❀❀❀❀❀❀❀❀❀❀❀❀❀❀❀❀❀❀

really don't think the school would make that mistake, do you?'

Paddy raises an eyebrow. 'Ah,' he says. 'Not so good. The punctuation is a bit dodgy too. It's from the school's email, but . . .'

'Something odd is going on here,' Mum says, her mouth settling into a thin line. 'Let's see what Mr Keating has to say about it in the morning.'

23

On Friday afternoon, after school, I am in the music room auditioning for Miss Noble; next door in the hall, the orchestra kids are warming up in a screech of trumpet blasts and cello twangs and bursts of unruly saxophone. Soon, with luck, I will be joining them.

I am playing a violin piece I have composed myself, and Miss Noble is looking quite amazed and very impressed. I think. I hit a few dud notes because playing violin in a classroom is very different from playing violin in an oak tree, but I think this just adds to the atmosphere. After all, I am twelve years old and mostly self-taught. Miss Noble will not be expecting perfection.

I don't think I will miss riding lessons at all, not once I am playing violin solos in the orchestra.

❀❀❀❀❀❀❀❀❀❀❀❀❀❀❀❀❀❀❀❀❀❀❀❀❀❀

The teacher holds her hand up, smiling. 'Thank you, Coco,' she says. 'A very . . . unusual style of playing. Full of character.'

I grin.

'Sadly, I won't be able to offer you a place in the orchestra on this occasion,' she tells me, and my face falls. 'You have a certain raw talent, but I'm afraid there's a little way to go before you reach orchestra standard. You would need to be able to read music too. Some lessons might be a good idea.'

'It's a no?' I double-check, feeling as crestfallen as if I've just been voted off *The X Factor*. 'Are you sure? If I could just play it again, with my gloves on, because that's how I usually do it . . .'

'Not this time, Coco,' Miss Noble says kindly. 'Take some lessons and try out again at the high school.'

I put my violin away in its case, pull on my panda hat and grab my schoolbag. The world is full of disappointments. Music teachers who do not recognize genius when they see it, landowners who treat their ponies like dirt, sisters who break the rules, boys who sulk and growl and sign off their texts with kisses just to confuse you. Lawrie

Marshall actually came up to me today in the lunch queue and asked how things were at home, and I just gulped and said everything was fine because I really did not want any kind of fuss with Sarah and the others around. They noticed anyhow and teased me all day about Lawrie fancying me, which did not help my stress levels, seriously.

There's an icy bite in the air as I trudge out towards the school gate. My heart is heavier than my schoolbag until I spot three familiar figures sitting on the wall.

'Coco!' Cherry calls, jumping down and running across the playground. 'Over here! We've come to kidnap you!'

'We're taking you for tea,' Skye adds, hooking an arm through mine. 'We went to the riding stables and some boy with smouldering eyes told us you'd given up on lessons, and that you'd be here, pursuing your musical career . . .'

'Lawrie Marshall,' Cherry says, with a knowing look. 'He is *so* not the way you described him.'

'He looks quite cool,' Summer tells me.

'Hot, you mean,' Skye corrects her twin. 'Anyway, here we are. Have you got your stuff? Shall we go?'

I allow myself to be led out of school and down towards

❀❀❀❀❀❀❀❀❀❀❀❀❀❀❀❀❀❀❀❀❀❀❀

the seafront cafe, my sisters talking all the time. It feels good to be with them and takes some of the sting out of being turned down for the orchestra. I remind myself that many great artists and musicians were not appreciated properly in their lifetimes.

'So why have you kidnapped me?' I ask, as we tumble into the warm, brightly lit cafe. 'Not that I am complaining, obviously . . .'

'Ah. World War Three is raging at home,' Skye explains as we order three big hot chocolates with whipped cream and chocolate flakes and a modest skinny latte for Summer. 'You do *not* want to be there right now. Honey's in *so* much trouble – Mum is furious and Paddy is banging the table with his fist and they are all waiting for Dad to call from Australia . . .'

We slide into a window seat, the sea in the distance grey and ominous in the dusk, and for once my sisters' faces are serious.

'So . . . what happened?' I ask.

'She's been expelled from school,' Summer whispers. 'Excluded, thrown out, asked to leave . . . and Anthony too!'

❀❀❀❀❀❀❀❀❀❀❀❀❀❀❀❀❀❀❀❀❀❀❀❀

I blink. 'But . . . why? Skipping lessons?'

'Worse than that,' Skye tells me. 'Mum and Paddy went in to see Mr Keating this morning, and everything came out. Honey's been truanting for months, going into Minehead on the school bus and then disappearing off to town. Turns out she'd met this boy who works at the fairground, and she was hanging out with him and his friends . . .'

That pulls me up short.

'I saw her,' I whisper. 'After the firework display in town – she was with these scary-looking girls, talking to a boy with tattoos. She told me she was working on an art project. I believed her. I am so stupid . . .'

'We've all been stupid,' Skye says. 'Trying to cover up for her, hoping she'd wise up and sort herself out. It's been going on way too long.'

'She's been fobbing the teachers off with forged letters saying she was ill,' Cherry tells me. 'Really ill – the letters talked about blood tests and scans and stays in hospital. She didn't say what was wrong, exactly, but she implied it was serious. The teachers were really upset, and nobody wanted to say anything.'

'Think they reckoned our family had enough troubles right now,' Summer says quietly. 'With me having . . . an eating disorder and everything. That's why they've been asking how she was, passing on worksheets and homework. Anthony was the main go-between, passing on letters and collecting work. I guess that means he's been doing most of it for her too.'

I bite my lip. 'But . . . how come Honey's school report didn't say anything?' I ask. 'It said she had perfect attendance, and that her grades were fine. And . . . what's Anthony got to do with all this, anyway?'

Cherry sips her hot chocolate. 'Mum and Paddy were there most of the day,' she says. 'It was a major investigation – Anthony's parents had to come in too, and everyone was trying to find out what was happening.'

'Honey's had Anthony dangling on a string for ages now,' Summer goes on. 'She's been going down to see him once or twice a week, in between seeing her fairground friends. Anthony has a crush on her; he'd do pretty much anything to please her.'

'And he's really brainy,' Cherry reminds me. 'Some kind of computer genius.'

✿✿✿✿✿✿✿✿✿✿✿✿✿✿✿✿✿✿✿✿✿✿✿

'So . . . ?'

Skye dunks her chocolate flake and bites into the end. 'You won't believe it,' she says. 'He's been hacking into the school computer system. He altered Honey's report and made it look like she'd got good grades and perfect attendance, and he tweaked some of her coursework marks too . . . scary!'

I almost choke on my hot chocolate, ending up with a dollop of whipped cream on my nose. It's not a good look.

'No way,' I breathe. 'That's . . . major! No wonder they've kicked her out, and Anthony. She must have known she couldn't get away with it!'

'I don't think she cared either way,' Skye shrugs. 'And Anthony's clever, he had it all planned out. He was sending letters to the school, as well, supposedly from the hospital, and from Mum and Paddy. Nightmare.'

'Last night's email blew it all,' Cherry explains. 'If Anthony had got the school address right, they might never have been found out.'

My head is spinning. Expelled from school? I don't think even Honey can wriggle out of this one. Finally, after years of pushing the boundaries, breaking the rules and behaving badly, my big sister has reached the end of the line. It's terrifying but kind of a relief at the same time.

'I should have lied,' Summer says into the silence. 'Last night. Said I saw Honey around at school, so Mum believed her excuses . . .'

'No,' Skye cuts in. 'You shouldn't, Summer. And nor should I. We didn't drop her in it, we were just honest. It's time we dumped that old "sisters-don't-tell" rule because Honey needs help, you know that – we've all known it for a while. She wasn't always this way . . .'

I frown, trying to remember the way things were before Dad left. It all seems hazy and long ago, a perfect world where the sun always shone and nothing ever went wrong, but I'm pretty sure it wasn't like that really. I do remember Honey, bright and beautiful and kind and confident, always laughing, always Dad's favourite.

Then he left us, and Honey turned from golden girl to rebel just about overnight. She yelled and shouted and blamed Mum for letting him go, but Mum couldn't have stopped him, of course – none of us could.

'What happens now?' I ask.

✿✿✿✿✿✿✿✿✿✿✿✿✿✿✿✿✿✿✿✿✿✿✿

'Paddy took us home, told us everything,' Skye shrugs. 'Mum's gutted. She called Dad in Sydney but he's in a meeting, so they're waiting for him to ring back, and Honey just looks sort of shell-shocked. You could cut the atmosphere with a knife. Paddy said it might be an idea to go and stay with friends tonight, stay out of the firing line. So Mum rang Tia's mum and she says we can all come over for an epic sleepover, me and Summer and Cherry and you. And Millie from school, and Cherry's friend Haruna.'

'We grabbed our PJs and sleeping bags, and your stuff too,' Cherry adds. 'Paddy dropped us at the riding stable to collect you, and when you weren't there we asked that stable boy and walked up to the school.'

I blink. 'So I have to go to Tia's?'

'Well, that's what Mum arranged,' Summer says. 'We should all stick together because I really don't recommend going back to Tanglewood right now.'

I try to picture the sleepover, a crush of teenage girls wrapped in duvets and sleeping bags, eating pizza and popcorn and dissecting every last detail of Honey's fall from grace. I don't think I could stomach it.

215

'Couldn't I go to Sarah's house instead?' I ask. 'I don't think I can face a big gang of your mates right now . . . it's quite a lot to take in.'

Skye frowns. 'Well, I suppose it'd be OK,' she says. 'As long as we know where you are. If you can just check with Sarah . . .'

I tap out a quick message on my mobile and a few moments later a reply bleeps through. No problem. See you soon

'It's fine,' I say. 'I can stay as long as I want.'

'Great.' Summer looks at her watch. 'I'll text Mum and let her know. We should go, y'know, we don't want to miss the six o'clock bus. The girls will be waiting.'

'We'll walk you along to Sarah's,' Skye says, ushering me out into the street. 'Make sure you get there OK.'

I know better than to argue – my sisters are in protective mode and it's not hard to work out why, what with everything that's happening at home. Skye and Summer would freak if they knew what I'd been up to these past few weeks – they still think I am six years old, some cute little kid in patched dungarees with a pet spider in a matchbox.

They deliver me to Sarah's gate, watch me walk along

216

the path and ring the bell, then sprint along to the bus stop as the Kitnor bus heaves into view, waving as they pile on board.

'See you tomorrow!' Skye yells. 'Have fun!'

The door opens and Sarah peers out. 'Oh,' she says. 'Hi, Coco. Didn't expect to see you tonight.'

'Flying visit,' I tell her. 'I've just come from orchestra practice, and I wanted to check whether we had maths homework this weekend or not.'

'We do,' Sarah says, frowning. 'Fractions and decimals for that test on Monday.'

'OK,' I say brightly. 'Great. See you then!'

I check that the bus has vanished, then wave and walk back down the path. Sarah watches me, puzzled, as I walk towards the lone figure on the corner, a boy leaning moodily against the wall, eating chips, checking his mobile, his bike silhouetted in the lamplight.

24

We finish up the chips and ride out of town, along the quiet lanes towards the hazel copse, me sitting on the bike seat with my arms round Lawrie's waist while he stands up, pedalling hard. I am still in school uniform, my schoolbag slung across my body, my violin case tied on to the back of the bike with bungees. The wind lifts my hair but it doesn't quite blow away my troubles – not today.

'What's up?' Lawrie asks finally, as we ditch the bike and hike up through the heather towards the ruined cottage. 'Why the mystery text? Friday's normally my day because of working at the stables.'

'And Saturday and Sunday are supposed to be mine, but you came up anyhow,' I remind him. 'I'm just fed up. I failed my audition for the school orchestra.'

'Well, you can't be good at everything,' he shrugs.

I want to ask why not, or point out that I am not asking to be good at everything, just one thing, for now at least, but it seems pointless.

'You can play for me, anyway,' Lawrie is saying. 'I don't know much about music but I quite like the sound of the violin. Sort of sad, but I bet I'd like it. Will you?'

'I might,' I tell him. 'Sometime. Maybe.'

'Is something else wrong?'

I sigh. 'My family are in crisis – again. Don't want to go home, don't want to talk about it . . .'

'Fair enough,' he shrugs.

The evening is bitterly cold and the dark velvet sky is sprinkled with a million stars. It's beautiful but freezing, the kind of night when your breath hovers in little clouds just beyond your lips. We trudge on in silence, but I can't keep quiet. The day's disasters are playing over and over in my head like a newsreel.

'My big sister's been expelled,' I blurt suddenly. 'She is fifteen years old, seeing a boy from the fairground, truanting from school. She got her friend to hack into the school computer system to fake school reports and told

❀❀❀❀❀❀❀❀❀❀❀❀❀❀❀❀❀❀❀❀❀❀❀

the teachers she had a serious illness. They're waiting for my dad to ring from Australia to decide what to do, but whatever it is won't be good. Honey has been pushing her luck for way too long.'

I pause for breath. For someone who doesn't want to talk about it, I am doing OK. I tell Lawrie about Honey's part in the stable fire this summer, her attempt to run away; how only a few weeks ago at the start of the autumn term, she was reported missing and turned up next day, completely oblivious to the panic she'd caused. The police warned her then they would call social services if she got into trouble again.

This is a different kind of trouble, but just as serious; is that why Paddy wanted us out of the house tonight? Are social services at Tanglewood right now, making notes, shaking their heads, planning my sister's future? I feel sick just thinking about it.

'OK. Not good,' Lawrie is saying. 'No wonder you don't want to go home – it sounds a bit full-on.'

'It is,' I say into the darkness, and suddenly an avalanche of hurt spills out, defensive, despairing.

'Everyone thinks we're so perfect, but we're really not.

❀❀❀❀❀❀❀❀❀❀❀❀❀❀❀❀❀❀❀❀❀❀❀❀❀

We live in a big house, but it doesn't belong to us – it's Grandma Kate's, and since Dad left we've had to run it as a B&B to make ends meet. We need the chocolate business to take off and we have this big order just now, but Paddy's had to halt production to sort this mess out. Oh yeah, and one of my sisters is anorexic and one is trying to smash what's left of our family into little bits . . .'

'I'm sorry, Coco,' Lawrie says.

I tilt my chin up proudly as we approach the ruined cottage. 'I don't usually go around telling other people my troubles. Don't want anyone feeling sorry for me.'

Lawrie nods. 'I understand. I won't tell anyone.'

'You'd better not.'

A thin whinnying sound drifts down through the darkness, and I stop short, frowning.

'The ponies,' Lawrie says, running forward through the heather. 'Quick . . . something's wrong!'

We push through the gate to Jasmine Cottage to find Spirit trotting jerkily through the overgrown garden, kicking at her swollen stomach, pushing herself against the hedge, crying out while Caramel paces patiently alongside her.

❀❀❀❀❀❀❀❀❀❀❀❀❀❀❀❀❀❀❀❀❀❀❀❀❀

'She's foaling,' Lawrie says, his face grave. 'I knew she was close, but I thought we had a little more time . . .'

Guilt and panic curdle inside me, cold and sour. I checked the Internet for information on delivering a foal, but with all the chaos at Tanglewood lately, I failed to follow it up. I made time to bake cupcakes and design posters, but not to find out how best to help a pony who needed me.

I can't remember a thing from the online article. What kind of a would-be vet am I? 'What do we do?' I ask.

'Get lanterns and hay and hope for the best,' Lawrie says.

He takes Spirit's head collar and presses his face against hers, whispering softly, quietening, calming her, walking her up and down while I light the lanterns and spread hay across the floor of the ruined kitchen. After a while, he leads Spirit in.

'Her waters have broken,' he tells me. 'It shouldn't take too long now – if things are straightforward she won't need us at all. Let's just hope that they are . . .'

Caramel crowds into the cottage kitchen, uneasy, curious, and Spirit stumbles to her knees on the hay, nostrils flaring. Lawrie soothes her and she slumps on to her side, tail swishing, eyes wide.

'There must be something I can do?' I ask. On TV, when babies are being born in unexpected places, people boil kettles and tear up clean sheets and gather towels while they wait for the ambulance to arrive. I am not sure it is the same for ponies, but even if it were, there is no way here to get hot water or clean linen, and no ambulance will be arriving any time soon.

'Well,' Lawrie says, 'how about you play that violin for us?'

'What, now?'

Lawrie nods, and although the whole idea of it is obviously crazy, I reach for my violin case, lifting out the glossy, curvy violin. Every time I play, my heart lifts up with music and takes me far away, to a place where anything is possible. Even when Mum banned me from playing in the house, even when my sisters made jokes about screeching ghosts and cats being strangled, nothing could spoil it for me . . . until today's failed audition. Gloom floods me all over again, but I push it away, determined. If anything can calm the crackle of tension and fear in the air, the violin can.

Spirit groans softly in the lamplight, dark eyes fringed with long lashes fixed on me as I start to play. Music swirls around the shadowy corners, filling up the darkness with a haunting lament that slowly builds into something brighter, braver. I play for ages, until Spirit's breathing steadies, until Lawrie grins in the lamplight.

'I think she's almost there,' he says. 'Look!'

I put my bow down, kneeling beside Lawrie as the foal is born, long legs first, wrapped in a sticky membrane. Time seems to slow. As I hold my breath, the head appears, and then finally the foal slides out into the hay and I am wiping the sticky membrane from its face as if I have done it a million times before. Lawrie is grinning and Spirit is resting now, nudging the foal gently.

'He's perfect,' I say, and my eyes brim with happy tears because in spite of everything that is messed up and wrong with my world, the newborn foal really is perfect, a kind of miracle.

'We could call him Star,' Lawrie suggests. 'It's such a clear sky tonight you can see whole constellations . . .'

'Perfect,' I say again.

My memory dredges up what I read on the Internet,

and I know that we have to let Spirit and her foal rest now before she breaks the cord. The website said something about iodine to disinfect, but we don't have any and I try not to worry; there wouldn't have been any in the wild, after all.

'It'll be a couple of hours before she delivers the placenta,' Lawrie says. 'I'll stay, obviously.'

'Me too,' I whisper. 'I can't go back to the house tonight; I told you.'

Then Lawrie makes a tiny fire in the grate so we don't all die of frostbite, and Spirit struggles to her feet and the cord breaks, and there doesn't seem to be any need for iodine.

'The violin was good,' he says. 'Who needs the school orchestra? You are clearly more of a ruined-cottage violinist, gloves and icicles and jasmine in the hair, at one with nature.'

I laugh. 'You're a music expert now? Well, whatever, I'll take the compliment. My fan club consists of you and two ponies.'

Lawrie grins. 'Three, actually. Star is your biggest fan. And we all have very good taste.'

I stroke the foal so gently that it feels like I am holding

my breath. Spirit looks on, calm and trusting. She's wrong to trust me, though. If anything had gone wrong tonight, the ponies would have been in danger – because of me.

I thought I had things all mapped out with no margin for error – but my plans are unravelling by the minute. Life is not a box of chocolates, a pick 'n' mix where I can choose just what I want; it turns out that someone has tricked me, switched the whole box for something less appealing. Lately, more and more, I find myself biting into something tough, tasteless, stale; something that leaves a bad taste in my mouth.

It turns out I am hopeless at the violin, and how am I supposed to stop bullies like Seddon and save the world when my own family is falling to bits right before my eyes? I am keeping so many secrets, telling so many lies to so many people that I can barely sleep at night. Not even Cherry, Sarah, Amy and Jayde know the whole story – they just know snippets of what's happening, my own edited version.

My big sister isn't the only one breaking the rules, the law.

Caramel comes close, nuzzling my hair, and I feel the

❀❀❀❀❀❀❀❀❀❀❀❀❀❀❀❀❀❀❀❀❀❀❀❀

gentle pressure of a hand on my shoulder. 'Hey,' Lawrie says. 'Don't go all slushy on me now . . .'

I wipe a sleeve across my eyes, fierce, furious. 'I'm not,' I lie. 'I just . . . got something in my eye. A speck of dust or something . . . OK?'

Lawrie nods, and I reflect that there is something to be said for having a mate like him, someone who just gets on with stuff and doesn't try to dig out your deepest, darkest secrets. And it is difficult to be sad for too long when a scruffy Exmoor pony is breathing down your neck and chewing the hood of your duffel coat, seriously.

I huddle next to the fire beside Lawrie, who hands me apples and chocolate, and we watch as Star battles to his feet, long legs buckling and sliding as he nudges against Spirit and begins to feed. My fingers begin to thaw a little as I hold them out to the flames.

'What will happen about your sister?' Lawrie asks quietly. 'What will your family do?'

'I don't know,' I admit. 'Mum and Paddy have given her so many chances . . . but the truth is, she doesn't want to be here, doesn't want to be a part of our family. That hurts – for all of us. She used to be Dad's favourite;

she thinks that if he were still around things would be different. Thing is, Dad's moved on – he never bothered seeing us when he was in London, and now he lives on the other side of the world.'

'We're not so different, you and me,' Lawrie muses. 'Our dads both let us down. What's your stepdad like?'

'Great,' I say easily. 'Paddy's good fun and he makes Mum happy – that's the biggest thing. He's working really hard to make us into a family, and I think he does care about Honey – if she'd just give him a chance!'

'Sounds like one of the good guys,' Lawrie says. 'You're lucky. Not everyone is like that.'

I shrug. 'Well, most people are OK, I guess . . .'

'Huh,' he says. 'I used to think that too, once. After Dad left, Mum wanted a new start, to put some distance between us and him. She got a job as a housekeeper for some holiday cottages; the work was easy and there was a rent-free flat thrown in. Then it all went pear-shaped, and now we're stuck here, trapped.'

'Trapped?' I echo. 'How come?'

Lawrie shrugs. The shutters come down again as if he has changed his mind, said too much.

❀❀❀❀❀❀❀❀❀❀❀❀❀❀❀❀❀❀❀❀❀❀❀

'I'll tell you sometime,' he says, getting up to fetch more firewood. 'Maybe. Don't worry about it. What does it matter how messed up our lives are right now? It won't be forever. One day soon you'll be a violin-playing vet, travelling from place to place on horseback, handing out panda cupcakes to the poor and needy . . . and I'll run my own stables back home in Cumbria. We'll look back at all this and laugh.'

'You think?' I ask.

'No, probably not,' he says. 'Maybe we'll end our days in prison. Coco and Marshall, the notorious under-age Exmoor horse rustlers . . .' He pulls his woolly scarf up over his nose, gangster style, raising his hands in surrender, and the two of us dissolve into laughter.

A couple of hours later, the birthing is safely over and Lawrie has cleared everything away and brought in fresh hay for Spirit and Star and Caramel. We sit for hours, huddled in blankets beside the crackling fire, watching the three ponies and talking about an imaginary future where no animals are ever ill-treated.

'Panda hats will be considered the height of fashion,' Lawrie declares. 'And all music lessons will be conducted a minimum of ten feet off the ground, in the branches of an oak tree.'

'All animals will be equal,' I add. 'Cruelty will be abolished and annoying Year Six boys with cake addictions and bullying tendencies will be hoisted up the school flagpole.'

'Certificates of excellence will be awarded for science students who succeed in singeing their own hair with a Bunsen burner. I don't know why we don't go into politics. We'd soon get this country straightened out – we'd be unstoppable!'

My laughter fades and I remember that in real life we don't have quite so much to laugh about, but I have never been the kind of person to accept defeat.

I bite my lip. 'Listen, Lawrie,' I say. 'I know it's risky, but . . . we have to rescue Seddon's new ponies. We don't have a choice, you know that, don't you?'

'Coco, just hold on –'

'We can't leave them there!' I argue. 'Seddon's a thug, you know that – he won't treat them well. We don't have to bring them up here – that would endanger Caramel and Spirit and Star. But if we get them out and take

❀❀❀❀❀❀❀❀❀❀❀❀❀❀❀❀❀❀❀❀❀❀❀❀

them somewhere safe – like the riding school perhaps – well, that would be a message to the police that we're not stealing them for profit. We could send a note to the police and to the *Gazette*, maybe, about how Seddon treats his animals . . .'

Lawrie frowns. 'It could work. We could tip off the police and the papers, then Jean and Roy wouldn't get into trouble. Maybe someone will actually check up on Seddon and find out what he's like. It wouldn't be stealing . . . more moving the ponies around. I think you're on to something, Coco!'

'I know I am,' I tell him. 'So . . . tomorrow night? I'll draft some letters for the police and the newspaper.'

'Meet in the woods by Blue Downs House then?' Lawrie suggests. 'At midnight?'

'I'll be there. And . . . I'll never forget this night, Lawrie. Spirit and Star . . . and, well, everything.'

'Nor me.'

I yawn and stretch, suddenly aware of how late it must be. Lawrie puts together a nest of cushions and blankets and I curl inside it, bone-weary, while he banks up the fire with fresh logs.

❀❀❀❀❀❀❀❀❀❀❀❀❀❀❀❀❀❀❀❀❀❀❀❀

I wake achey and cold, with the heavy arm of the school's moodiest boy flung over me beneath the blankets that cocoon us both, his breath warm on my neck, his hand holding mine.

Departures

25

The fallout from Honey's expulsion from school is still settling when I return home on Saturday morning. The chocolate factory is deserted, the kitchen looks like a bomb has hit it and Mum and Paddy look shattered, as if they haven't slept at all. Well, maybe they haven't.

Honey is stretched out on one of the blue velvet sofas, watching our *Bambi* DVD and eating crumpets. She looks unbothered, as if today is just any old Saturday and not the day after she got kicked out of Exmoor High. I remember the time I first watched *Bambi*, years ago when I was little, with Honey, Summer and Skye. I was mad about animals even then and I loved it – right up until the moment that Bambi's mum got shot. I cried so hard then that Mum had to switch it off, and my sisters grumbled and told me I was a baby, and not to be stupid because it was just a movie.

There's a lump in my throat as I flop down beside Honey now.

'You OK?' I ask. 'Are you grounded again?'

'Don't think so,' she shrugs. 'What's the point? They know I'll find a way round it. Besides, I don't care any more. I'm out of here!'

My mind buzzes with past threats of boarding school. 'What d'you mean?'

'Ask Mum,' Honey says. 'She and Paddy have got what they wanted – to be rid of me.'

'That's not true!' I argue. 'You're twisting things round!'

She shrugs. 'Whatever. It doesn't matter because I got what I wanted too. Sorry to ditch you, little sis, but I finally get to escape this dump. Apparently boarding school is too expensive – trust Paddy, stingy with the cash right to the last – but hey, this time it works in my favour. I'm going out to Australia to live with Dad. This time next week I'll be on a flight to Sydney!'

I feel cold all over. My big sister is a chancer, a drama

❀❀❀❀❀❀❀❀❀❀❀❀❀❀❀❀❀❀❀❀❀❀❀

queen, a rule-breaker. She's lazy, rebellious and sometimes downright bitchy, but I love her to pieces and I cannot imagine life without her.

'You can't!' I whisper. 'What about us?'

'What about you?' Honey asks. 'You've made your choice, Coco. You just can't see how Paddy has ruined this family, can you? If it wasn't for him, Dad and Mum might have been back together by now.'

'Honey, you know that's not true!'

'Well, it was possible, wasn't it?' she snaps. 'Until Mum married that loser! Now she puts him first the whole time. Admit it, we have hardly seen them this last week or two!'

'That's because of the department store order,' I argue. 'You're not being fair. Mum has done everything in her power to help you and Paddy is trying his very best too!'

Honey shrugs. 'His best isn't good enough,' she says. 'Not for me. Paddy doesn't belong here – he's not my dad, and he never will be!'

She picks up a fluffy cushion and hugs it to her, her lower lip quivering. I think Honey is a whole lot more bothered by all this than she is letting on. 'I can't get

❀❀❀❀❀❀❀❀❀❀❀❀❀❀❀❀❀❀❀❀❀❀❀❀❀❀

along with Cherry either – and the rest of you are so totally taken in by her,' she goes on. 'She's pushed me out – with Mum, with Shay, even with you . . .'

'No way!' I protest. 'Nobody could ever do that! Honey, please don't go away. If you could only try harder at school, stay away from the fairground crowd and just calm down . . . it's not too late!'

Honey shakes her head. 'I think it is. I've tried too, Coco – really I have. I just can't seem to get anything right, and the whole school thing has gone way too far. They wouldn't have me back even if I wanted them to, and trust me, I don't. I made one massive mistake trusting Anthony. It was his idea, about hacking into the school system and changing my report – I should have known we'd never get away with it. And now he's not even speaking to me – he says it's all my fault!'

I remember seeing Anthony at one of our beach parties in the summer, a misfit loner whose puppy-dog eyes trailed after Honey wherever she went. He had a major crush on her, but of course, Anthony has never even been on my sister's radar. It's all too easy to imagine him thinking up plots and plans to hike up her school grades, to please

✿✿✿✿✿✿✿✿✿✿✿✿✿✿✿✿✿✿✿✿✿✿✿

her, hoping she might see him differently. Instead it all backfired, and Anthony's perfect school career is over in one dramatic fall from grace. I guess that would cure a crush, all right.

'The truth is I don't fit in here any more,' Honey is saying. 'I am a walking disaster area. My friends are the kind of kids who think it's cool to break the rules. As for boys, the ones I like have "trouble" stamped all over them. And when things go wrong, not one of them is anywhere to be seen.'

'So change your friends, pick nicer boyfriends,' I say. 'You can still turn things around. Start over!'

'I'm going to,' Honey says. 'In Australia. I'll miss you, Coco-pops, of course I will, but we can stay in touch on Skype and SpiderWeb. I have tried about a million fresh starts here, you know that – I need something different. Dad's stepped up to the mark, finally – he's going to find a good school, hire tutors, make sure I pass some exams. He does care, Coco!'

'Of course he does,' I say, although I have to admit there has never been much evidence of it before. I can't say that to Honey, though.

❀❀❀❀❀❀❀❀❀❀❀❀❀❀❀❀❀❀❀❀❀❀❀❀❀

'I still miss Dad,' she tells me. 'Every day. And the rest of you seem to have forgotten him, and it makes me feel like such a freak for even caring . . .'

'We all miss him,' I tell her, and because there really isn't any more to say I put my arms round my big sister and hold her tight. She hugs me back, her face pressed against my shoulder, her beautiful hair soft beneath my fingers.

I look up and see that the DVD has reached the part where Bambi's mother gets shot, but this time it's Honey who's crying.

I sit at one end of the blue sofa, writing letters to the newspaper and to the police about Seddon and the way he treats his ponies, while Honey huddles at the other end, curled up under the blanket made of crochet squares she has had since she was tiny.

My sisters come home at midday and Mum and Paddy call a family meeting in the kitchen. Everyone is there except Honey, who has fallen asleep in the living room, the tail end of *Bambi* playing softly in the background.

'Is it true that you're sending her away?' I blurt out, as soon as Mum sits down. 'You can't, Mum, it's cruel!'

Skye kicks me hard under the table. 'Shut UP, Coco!' she whispers. 'That's not helping!'

Mum's eyes fill with tears, and I am instantly ashamed. 'It's not what I want,' she explains in a wobbly voice. 'It's what your sister wants . . . what she's wanted all along. She has used up all her chances here. She needs discipline, rules, support – we've tried to give her those things, Coco, you know that. It hasn't worked. Everyone is in agreement here, Mr Keating, the school counsellor, Honey's social worker . . .'

I gulp. 'She has a social worker?'

'Social services are trying to help us,' Paddy says. 'They've been aware of the problems since the summer, when Honey ran away. Once the police were involved, they were involved – but they want to help, Coco, we all do. We just want what's best for Honey.'

'And what's that?' Skye asks.

'A fresh start,' Paddy says. 'A chance to get away from the kids she's been seeing – well, most of them aren't kids, of course, and that's part of the problem. It's almost like a cry for help, and let's face it, the gentle approach hasn't worked. We need to do something different.'

✿✿✿✿✿✿✿✿✿✿✿✿✿✿✿✿✿✿✿✿✿✿✿✿

'Boarding school was one option,' Mum says. 'We looked into it, and there were a couple of places that gave great support to troubled teens like Honey – but right now, we can't afford the fees. If we knew that this big chocolate order was going to be a success it might be different, but we can't predict what will happen.'

'So Honey's dad has stepped in,' Paddy says. 'He's found a day school in Sydney that promises good grades and one-to-one tuition and counselling for girls like Honey.'

'What does that mean?' Summer asks. 'Who are these "girls like Honey"? Is it some kind of Australian boot camp?'

'Not at all,' Mum promises. 'It's very strict but very fair, a private school with a good reputation academically. It has an exceptional ethos, though – one that could really help Honey. It's all about encouraging self-esteem and healing hurts, turning negatives into positives. We've spoken with the head teacher, and she seems confident they can turn your sister around.'

'But . . . why does it have to be on the other side of the world?' I plead.

❀❀❀❀❀❀❀❀❀❀❀❀❀❀❀❀❀❀❀❀❀❀❀

Mum sighs. 'Because we don't know of any schools here that offer this kind of help,' she says honestly. 'And if we did, we probably wouldn't be able to afford them. Luckily, this particular school is near to Greg, and the fees are affordable, just about, if both we and Greg chip in.'

'You're sending her away,' I whisper.

Mum's eyes fill with tears. 'Coco, it's just until the summer . . . we can review things then, see what Honey wants. And, Coco, she wants this – a fresh start, away from bad influences, in a school that promises to get her back on the right track. She wants to be with Greg, you know that. I don't want this any more than you do, but we have to do something, Coco – your sister is right on the edge.'

I think of Dad, who is so busy with his high-flying business in Sydney that he barely has time to speak to us on Skype at Christmas; he has been known to forget our birthdays, our ages, our interests. OK, he is thousands of miles away in Australia, I know, but even when he lived in London he was kind of hopeless. I sometimes wonder if he'd forget he had kids at all unless Mum was there to remind him.

❀❀❀❀❀❀❀❀❀❀❀❀❀❀❀❀❀❀❀❀❀❀❀❀

I really hope the day school is good because if things are left to Dad, Honey won't be on the edge for much longer – she'll tumble right over it and go into freefall.

26

Lawrie whistles as I swerve my bike to a halt by the woodland at Blue Downs House just before midnight, stepping through the trees to greet me. 'Hey,' he says, looking at me so intently I can't quite meet his gaze. 'Everything OK at home?'

'Not really,' I tell him. 'Everything's about as bad as it possibly can be. I'll tell you later.'

'Where do your parents think you are right now?'

'Sarah's,' I say. 'Trust me, they have so much on their plate right now they won't even think of checking up.'

'Sure you want to do this?'

'Try and stop me,' I huff. 'I'm determined to get one thing right this week if it kills me . . .'

We walk slowly through the woods and past the

paddock, up to the edge of the stable yard. We watch the farmhouse until the last lights are extinguished, then unhook the gate and creep softly round the perimeter of the yard.

The ponies are stabled separately, side by side at the end of the block. One is a chestnut, the other a roan, and both are stocky, steady, calm. I falter for a moment; maybe Seddon will treat these two properly? Then I remember the way he treated Caramel, the state Spirit was in, and I know we have no choice but to carry on. The new ponies may be OK right now, but it's just a matter of time before Seddon crushes their spirit too. Getting these two out will blow the whistle on what he is doing, trigger an investigation and maybe stop him from ever working with animals again.

As we lead them out across the yard a plaintive, whining bark rasps out across the silence. Lawrie swears under his breath. 'Sheesh . . . I forgot about the blinkin' dog!'

He hands me the reins of the chestnut pony and moves towards the skinny mongrel quickly, palm outstretched, whispering softly. The guard dog quietens almost at once, but

❀❀❀❀❀❀❀❀❀❀❀❀❀❀❀❀❀❀❀❀❀❀❀

not before I see the curve of its ribs in the moonlight, the hollow of its belly. The dog is thinner than ever, shivering, cowering, tied to an outdoor kennel with a short rope that keeps her bowl of water tantalizingly out of reach.

'Think anyone heard?' Lawrie asks, petting the dog's head, glancing up towards the house. 'I hope not . . .'

Guilt churns inside me. As far as animal cruelty goes, this dog says it all – she's thin, scared, trembling, yet her tail still wags, hopeful, trusting. I can't believe we left her behind a fortnight ago; there is no way I can ignore her now.

'We're taking her,' I whisper. 'We have to, Lawrie!'

He looks at me in the moonlight, his blue eyes unreadable. Two weeks ago he would have curled his lip, said something harsh and cutting about sticking to the plan, but we've both changed a lot in that time. We have rescued two ponies and helped to bring a third into the world, and this morning I woke in front of a long-dead fire with Lawrie's hand in mine. My cheeks burn at the memory.

Lawrie nods calmly and drops to his knees to untie the rope, whispering softly to the dog as he struggles with the knot.

❁❁❁❁❁❁❁❁❁❁❁❁❁❁❁❁❁❁❁❁❁❁❁❁❁❁

I am watching from the shadows when suddenly a flashlight flares and a shot rings out, splitting the night in two.

'I'm OK,' Lawrie whispers. 'Are you? Get back, quick, so he can't see you!'

My heart thumps so hard it feels like it might burst right out of me, and I can barely breathe. I edge back into the darkness, leading the ponies out of sight, round the corner, behind an outbuilding.

A tall figure is raking the flashlight across the stable yard, and I make out James Seddon, shotgun in hand, his face a tight, cold mask of fury.

'What the hell are you doing, Lawrie?' he roars. 'Leave the dog be and get in the house! I thought you were one of those blasted burglars!'

Lawrie's eyes flicker to me once more, and I creep another step backwards, my heart pounding. The ponies clatter back with me, snuffling, shaking their heads, their breath hanging in the night air like smoke.

I don't understand what's going on, how Seddon knows Lawrie's name, why he's ordering him to get in the house; my head is too scrambled to even try to make sense of it. All I know is that James Seddon is striding towards us in the darkness, his shotgun swinging. I have never been so terrified in my life.

I watch Lawrie's fingers fumble as the dog whimpers and cowers.

'What's going on?' Seddon growls. 'I've told you before to leave that dog alone! She's not a pet, she's a guard dog, and not even a very good one – useless mutt didn't raise the alarm when those thugs took my ponies . . .'

Lawrie abandons the rope and tugs at the dog's collar. It unbuckles suddenly and the skinny mongrel lurches away from Seddon's grip, yelping with fear, running past me in the darkness. Startled, the ponies snort and huff and sidestep, clattering away from the outbuilding, and abruptly Seddon's flashlight swoops over us all, trapping us in the dazzling light.

He laughs, and the sick, harsh sound of it turns my bones to water.

'What's this?' he enquires. 'Don't tell me, a little rescue party! It's starting to make sense now. You took the others too, didn't you? To spite me . . .'

'She wasn't involved,' Lawrie mutters, nodding at me.

'Not the first time. And this was my idea too, so just let her go . . .'

'Don't worry, I know very well whose idea this was,' Seddon growls. 'You're a useless, pathetic excuse for a boy. I've tried to teach you how to have a backbone, how to be a man, but I can see that mere discipline won't do it. You need to be broken, just like the horses – you come from bad stock, you see. You're a loser, a waster, just like your dad.'

Lawrie tries to run but Seddon grabs him, hauling him back, throwing him roughly on to the ground. I think I am going to be sick; nausea seeps through me in waves, making me dizzy.

'Shhh, shhh,' I croon to the ponies, trying to calm their panic. 'Steady, now . . .'

A light goes on up at the house and a woman and child appear in the courtyard. The woman is pretty, with expensive clothes and carefully styled hair; the child is in pyjamas, sleepy and rumpled, but I recognize her instantly as the frightened girl I saw a fortnight ago.

'James?' the woman falters, pulling a mobile from her pocket. 'What's going on? Who is that? Shall I call the police?'

❀❀❀❀❀❀❀❀❀❀❀❀❀❀❀❀❀❀❀❀❀❀❀❀❀

'It's Lawrie!' the child shrieks.

Lawrie pulls free, struggling to his feet, but Seddon is too fast for him; furious, he throws Lawrie against the outbuilding wall and he slumps down, gasping, clutching his arm.

'Leave him *alone!*' the woman yells, running across the yard, the child at her heels.

Seddon turns, shouting that the three of them are worthless, ungrateful trash, and before I can understand what's happening he lashes out, slapping the woman so hard that a river of blood slides down from her pink-glossed lips.

Fury floods my body and logic deserts me. I run forward with the horses, yelling. Terrified, they drag free of my grip, bucking and rearing. The skinny dog appears from the shadows, barking madly, baring her teeth at Seddon, and in the chaos the chestnut pony rears again, catching Seddon on the temple so that he reels back awkwardly, falling to the ground.

We are running then, the child's small, cold hand in mine, the woman holding Lawrie as he clutches his damaged arm. 'The car,' she gasps. 'Head for the car – I have the keys!'

❀❀❀❀❀❀❀❀❀❀❀❀❀❀❀❀❀❀❀❀❀❀❀❀

We race across the stable yard towards the looming shape of a four-wheel drive parked on the driveway leading down to the road. The doors flash red in the darkness, unlocking, and we bundle inside, the skinny dog too.

'Quick, Mum, he's coming!' Lawrie says, and the engine roars and there's a screech of gravel and we're driving into the darkness, away from there.

27

'Is . . . is everyone OK?' Lawrie's mum asks, her voice shaking.

Somehow, everybody is. Lawrie's mum drives slowly through the darkened lanes. I can tell it's an effort for her to keep the car steady.

'We're going the wrong way,' Lawrie says after a minute. 'We have to go to Minehead, Mum, to the police . . . we have no choice this time!'

'I can't,' she whispers, and I can hear the fear in her voice. 'We can't . . .'

My head is starting to unscramble the jigsaw pieces; a moody, secretive boy who hates bullies, the little sister, a sense of amazement that stepdads could actually be cool. This is why Lawrie was feeding Caramel the first night

I went to Blue Downs House, how he knew about Spirit – and why he hates Seddon so much.

He lives with him.

'Drive to my place,' I say, taking charge. 'You're heading that way, and it's not far. You'll be safe there, I promise.'

Eventually the car limps to a halt on the gravel at Tanglewood, and I jump out and lean on the doorbell long enough to make lights spring on all over the house. By the time I have settled Lawrie, his mum and his sister in the warm kitchen and coaxed the frightened mongrel inside too, Mum and Paddy appear in the doorway in PJs and dressing gowns. My sisters crowd behind them on the staircase, wide-eyed.

'What on earth . . . Coco?' Paddy demands, but Mum just surveys the scene and puts the kettle on, fetching warm water and a clean flannel to bathe the woman's face.

'I'm Charlotte, and this is Paddy,' Mum says, matter-of-factly. 'Your name is . . . ?'

'Sandra Marshall,' the woman says, wincing as the warm water touches her broken skin. 'Sandy. These are my children, Lawrie and Jasmine . . .'

❀❀❀❀❀❀❀❀❀❀❀❀❀❀❀❀❀❀❀❀❀❀❀

'Lawrie's my friend from school,' I add. 'We were trying to rescue some ponies and it all got out of hand . . .'

'Way to go, little sis,' Honey says. 'Stepping into my shoes as the rebel-rouser already? I haven't even gone yet!'

'Honey, shhh, this is serious,' Mum says. 'What exactly happened here?'

'I don't know,' I tell her. 'But I think Lawrie's arm might be broken and the horses have gone and –'

'He hit my mum,' Jasmine says in a tiny voice. 'And he shot his gun!'

'Who did?' Mum echoes. 'Sandy, who did this to you?'

The whole story comes out then, the bits I know already and the bits I could only guess at; about the shotgun, the slap, the stolen horses, about a whole year of intimidation and bullying for Lawrie and his family.

They came to Somerset a year ago when Sandy found work with James Seddon's holiday-let business. Soon Seddon was dating her and moved the whole family in with him. He made them feel special with gifts and days out and endless promises . . . but before long he began to control everything they did. When Seddon began to show a darker side, a cruel, bullying streak, Lawrie had to stand by and watch as fear pulled his family apart.

'Where do the ponies come into all this?' Mum asks. 'This rescue you mentioned, Coco?'

'Seddon was the one who bought Caramel,' I explain. 'I went to see if she was all right and she really, really wasn't. Seddon drove her to exhaustion, made Jasmine watch until she fell down in the mud, crying. So I took Caramel away . . . me and Lawrie. We had to. There was another pony too, a mare in foal. We hid them on the moors, and when Lawrie told me Seddon had bought more ponies we tried to take them too, but the dog barked and Seddon came after us with a shotgun and it all went wrong . . .'

My sisters have moved into the kitchen, perched on the countertops or leaning against the Aga. Paddy has slipped out of the room. Jasmine has fallen asleep in Sandy's arms, Lawrie is curled up with the skinny mongrel.

Mum touches Sandy's hand. 'You have to call the police,' she says gently. 'You know that, don't you?'

'I can't,' she whispers. 'I really can't . . .'

✿✿✿✿✿✿✿✿✿✿✿✿✿✿✿✿✿✿✿✿✿✿✿✿✿

'You don't have to,' Paddy says, as he comes through the kitchen door. 'They're already on their way.'

The night goes crazy. Paramedics arrive and decide that Lawrie's arm isn't broken, that Sandy's cuts will heal and hopefully not scar; the police take a statement from Lawrie's mum, ask if she wishes to press charges, and dispatch officers to bring Seddon down to the station. It's daybreak by the time all that is done. My sisters have gone back to bed, and Lawrie and Jasmine are asleep in one of the guest rooms.

'You and I need a little talk,' Mum says, catching my arm as I try to slope upstairs. 'I'm glad you brought Lawrie and Sandy and Jasmine here, but . . . what on earth have you been thinking, Coco? Stealing ponies, wandering around on the moors in the dark? That was dangerous . . . I mean, really dangerous!'

Her eyes fill with tears and instantly I am flooded with guilt. Mum is right, of course – I may have acted with the best intentions, but still, I have broken the law and lied and taken so many risks that it has become second nature. Suddenly, it doesn't look daring or brave so much as downright foolhardy.

'Sorry, Mum,' I whisper. 'I just . . . didn't know what else to do!'

Mum wipes her eyes. 'You could have talked to me,' she says. 'I'd have listened, Coco, you know that, don't you? Together, we could have worked something out. But I really don't think I could bear to have another daughter in trouble. The family seems to be unravelling before my very eyes . . .'

'No, Mum!' I protest. 'That's not true! We're the best family in the world! We may not be perfect, but we're still pretty amazing, and that's thanks to you and Paddy. I'm fine, I promise, really I am! I'm so, so sorry!'

But Mum is crying again, and all I can do is put my arms round her and hold her close and promise I will talk to her if there's anything, anything at all, I am worried about in future. And I mean it. Forget boys and make-up and cramps and mood swings, this is what growing up is all about – learning from your mistakes, daring to admit that you don't know everything, and that sometimes, just maybe, you get things wrong.

It's hard. There's an ache inside my chest and I want to cry and argue and yell, but I won't, I can't. I am going

✿✿✿✿✿✿✿✿✿✿✿✿✿✿✿✿✿✿✿✿✿✿✿✿

to learn, listen, change. I am going to make Mum proud. I hold her tight and promise that everything will be OK.

In the end, Lawrie and his family stay with us for two weeks. Sandy helps out in the chocolate workshop, and it turns out she is a whizz at organizing and getting things to run smoothly. Pretty soon, the order is back on track.

As well as the police, the RSPCA are investigating Seddon, and the *Exmoor Gazette* runs a story on it all. Seddon has been shamed into handing the two newest ponies back to their original owner, while Jean and Roy at the stables take on Spirit and Star. Sheba the dog has gained weight and her fur looks glossy and healthy. She curls up in Fred's basket at night and runs rings round the garden with him during the day.

Lawrie and I are Year Eight heroes for all of five minutes, then targets for endless teasing about whether we are/aren't an item. For the record, we are not, but Lawrie has chilled out now his mum is away from Seddon; the moody, chippy veneer has dropped away to reveal a quiet, gentle boy who opens up a little more each day.

He surprises me sometimes. When I show Jasmine how

❀❀❀❀❀❀❀❀❀❀❀❀❀❀❀❀❀❀❀❀❀❀❀

to make my secret Coco Caramel cupcakes he joins in, whizzing up flour and eggs and butter and sugar; he sits beside me in the old oak tree, listening to my violin practice, looking at the stars, talking about the past, the future, a hundred different versions of each.

Eventually, of course, the future becomes the present.

The chocolate order is finished, the last consignment driven away. Sandy makes plans to go back to Kendal, staying with her parents until she can find a job and a flat. Jasmine and Lawrie will go back to their old schools, putting the past behind them.

I am pleased for the Marshalls, really I am, but the news leaves me feeling strangely deflated. On the day they leave, I sit in the old oak, legs swinging, gloomy. I have baked panda-face cupcakes for Jasmine, packed a bag with dog chews for Sheba, painted a good-luck card for all of them. Still, it feels like I am crying inside.

Lawrie comes out of the house and down through the garden, hauling himself up into the branches beside me.

'I don't want you to go,' I confess. 'I will miss you, Lawrie Marshall.'

'I'll miss you,' he counters. 'It's for the best, though.

The further Mum is from Seddon the better. Maybe things will be OK for your family too, now?'

'Sure they will. Your mum had the chocolate workshop running like clockwork. I can't believe we made that deadline after all!'

'With time to spare,' he tells me. 'Mum loved it. It's been like watching her wake up, start to believe in herself again – thanks to Charlotte and Paddy. And you, obviously.'

'What did I do?'

He shrugs. 'Without you, I'd never have dared stand up to Seddon. He'd knocked the fight out of us – all I could do was look out for Mum and Jas, make sure the animals were fed. Then you turned up with your mad plans and suddenly everything was different, we were in the middle of this big adventure. You gave me hope. OK, at first I thought you were a little bit crazy . . .'

'I am a little bit crazy,' I agree.

He grins. 'I know. I got to like it, after a while. It's been so long since I had a proper friend, and I think . . . I know . . . well, you're probably my best friend. Maybe more than a friend . . .'

I don't see it coming.

I have noticed the way he looks at me sometimes, his blue eyes sad and searching, noticed a crackle of energy between us sometimes when we touch by accident. I've laughed off my friends' suggestions that he fancies me, but I'd be lying if I said I hadn't wondered if he did. I'd be lying too, if I said I hadn't thought about Lawrie a little bit, dreamed even.

Still, I panic when he leans towards me, his fingers stroking my cheek, his lips brushing mine. I almost jump out of my skin, and that is not a good plan when you are six feet above the ground, sitting in an old oak tree.

I am pretty sure it's not the reaction Lawrie was hoping for.

I put my hand out, touch his cheek, his lips. His skin is cold beneath my fingers, but his lips are soft and warm.

'Hey,' I whisper. 'Lawrie, you're my best friend too, but . . . well, I don't think I'm ready for anything more right now. Is that OK?'

'I guess,' he says. 'I'll wait. I'll come back one day, I promise, and we'll both be older then and things will be different. Yeah?'

❀❀❀❀❀❀❀❀❀❀❀❀❀❀❀❀❀❀❀❀❀❀❀❀

'I hope so,' I tell him. 'We can write, can't we? And email, maybe.'

'Definitely. Listen, Coco, I hate goodbyes,' he says. 'Besides, I know we'll meet again. But if we don't, for whatever reason, there's one thing you have to know. I will never forget you, Coco Tanberry. Never.'

He slides down from the oak tree and walks away, and by the time the taxi arrives to take them to the station I am playing the violin, thinking of a boy with sad eyes, warm lips, unruly hair that falls across his face.

I guess I hate goodbyes as well.

A week ago we took Honey to Heathrow to catch her flight to Sydney. Honey looked small, lost, alone as she walked out through the security gates, and I panicked suddenly that we might lose her forever. Living with a stormcloud like Honey has never been easy, but I don't think I will ever get used to her not being around. In some ways, this has been the worst week of my life.

In other ways, it has been the best.

As I play, a pony comes towards me through the long grass, a rough-coated bay with a wild, dark mane and tail, her eyes soft and shining. Caramel watches me solemnly for a while, ears pricked as I play. It turns out that she really was Jasmine's birthday pony, but of course there will be no room for her at Jas and Lawrie's gran's house. Fitting three people and a skinny mongrel in is one thing; finding space for an Exmoor pony is something else entirely.

'You sent me cupcakes and jasmine flowers,' the little girl explained to me last week. 'Before you even met me. That was kind. And you saved Caramel and kept her safe, so . . . will you look after her for me now? Please?'

I promised that I would.

Just a few weeks ago I thought that if I had Caramel, all my troubles would be over; she's mine now, pretty much, but I have a feeling my troubles are just beginning. I said this to Honey at the airport last week, and she laughed and told me that I'd be fine, that I was just growing up. Well, maybe.

I slide down to the ground, put my violin away and take Caramel's halter, leading her up to the stable she shares with Humbug the sheep. I saddle her carefully, adjust her reins and swing up on to her back, and together we walk out through the field gate heading down, slowly, towards the beach.

❁❁❁❁❁❁❁❁❁❁❁❁❁❁❁❁❁❁❁❁❁❁❁❁

Caramel tosses her head in the wind and skitters a little as her hooves sink into the sand. We turn to face the vast shimmering expanse of ocean, now streaked with red and gold as the sun drops steadily lower in the sky, and I think of another afternoon, riding Caramel across the moors with Lawrie's arms round me. Then I shake the memory free and press my heels in gently and we bound forward into a canter, out along the beach, heads down, happy, glad to be alive.

The scrumptious series by

Cathy Cassidy

The Chocolate Box GIRLS

Cherry:
Dark almond eyes, skin the colour of
milky coffee, wild imagination, fiesty, fun . . .

Skye:
Wavy blonde hair, blue eyes, smiley, individual, kind . . .

Summer:
Slim, graceful, pretty, loves to dance, determined, a girl with big dreams . . .

Coco:
Blue eyes, fair hair, freckles, a tomboy who loves
animals and wants to change the world . . .

Honey:
Willowy, blonde, beautiful, arty and out of control, a rebel . . .

*Each sister has a different story to tell,
which will be your favourite?*

Cherry Costello is ...

shy, quiet, always on the outside . . .
sometimes finds it hard to separate
truth from fiction

14 years old

Born: Glasgow

Mum: Kiko

Dad: Paddy

Looks: small; slim; coffee-coloured skin;
straight, dark hair with a fringe, often
worn in little bunches

Style: bright skinny jeans, T-shirts,
anything with a Japanese theme

Loves: dreaming, stories, cherry blossom,
Irn-Bru, gypsy caravans

Prize possessions: kimono, parasol,
Japanese fan, photo of her mum
from long ago

Dreams: of being part of a family

www.cathycassidy.com

Skye Tanberry is ...

friendly, eccentric, individual, imaginative

13 years old - Summer's identical twin

Born: Kitnor

Mum: Charlotte

Dad: Greg

Looks: shoulder-length blonde hair,
blue eyes, big grin

Style: floppy hats and vintage dresses,
scarves and shoes

Loves: history, horoscopes,
dreaming, drawing

Prize possessions: her collection
of vintage dresses and the fossil
she once found on the beach

Dreams: of travelling back in
time to see what the past
was really like . . .

www.cathycassidy.com

Summer Tanberry *is ...*

quiet, confident, pretty, popular, and very serious about dance

13 years old - Skye's identical twin

Born: Kitnor

Mum: Charlotte

Dad: Greg

Looks: long blonde hair, always tied back in braids or a neat ballerina bun; blue eyes; moves gracefully

Style: anything pink . . . neat, pretty, fashionable clothes and dance-wear

Loves: dancing, especially ballet

Prize possessions: pointe shoes and tutu

Dreams: of going to the Royal Ballet School, becoming a professional dancer and one day running her own ballet school

www.cathycassidy.com

Coco Tanberry *is ...*

cheeky, energetic, friendly,
adventurous, crazy about animals

12 years old

Born: Kitnor

Mum: Charlotte

Dad: Greg

Looks: chin-length wavy blonde hair,
always tangled; blue eyes; freckles;
big grin

Style: tomboy: jeans, T-shirt, always
messy and dishevelled

Loves: animals, climbing trees,
swimming in the sea

Prize possessions: Fred the dog
and the ducks

Dreams: of having a llama,
a donkey and a parrot

www.cathycassidy.com

Honey Tanberry is ...

a drama queen: moody, selfish, often
sad . . . but also bright, charming,
organized and sweet

15 years old

Born: London

Mum: Charlotte

Dad: Greg

Looks: long, ringletty blonde hair
that reaches to her waist; blue eyes;
creamy skin; tall; slim

Style: cool: little print dresses, strappy
sandals, shades, shorts and T-shirts

Loves: drawing, painting, fashion,
music . . . and Shay Fletcher

Prize possessions: hair, diary,
sketchbook, turret bedroom

Dreams: of being a model, actress
or fashion designer

www.cathycassidy.com

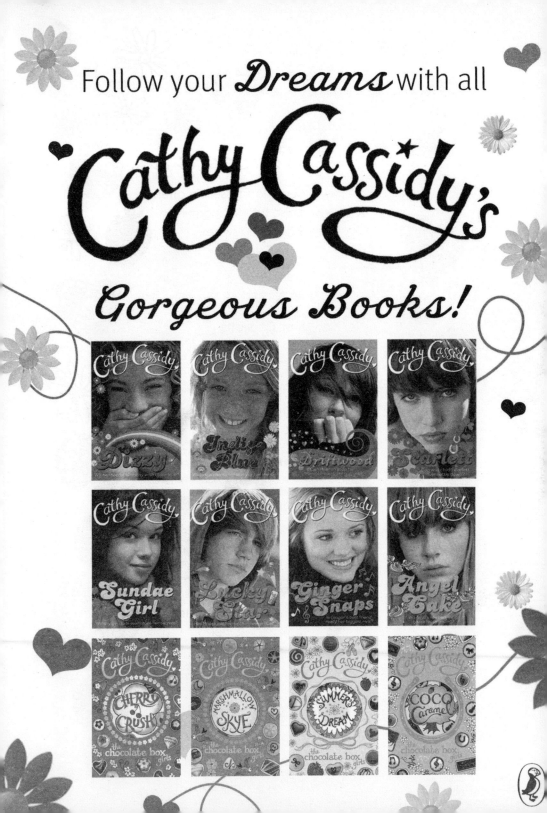

Which Chocolate Box Girl Are You?

Your perfect day would be spent . . .

a) visiting a busy vintage market
b) with your favourite canine companion on a long walk in the countryside
c) curled up on the sofa watching black-and-white movies with your boyfriend
d) window-shopping with your BFF
e) sipping frappuccinos in a hip city cafe

Your ideal boy is . . .

a) arty and sensitive
b) boy? No thanks!
c) a good listener . . . and a little bit quirky
d) polite and clever
e) good looking and popular – what other kind of boy is there?

Who's the first person you would tell about your new crush?

a) your sister – she knows everything about you
b) your pet cat . . . animals are great listeners
c) your BFF
d) your mum – she always has the best advice
e) no one. It's best not to trust anyone with a secret

Your favourite subject is . . .

a) history
b) science
c) creative writing
d) French
e) drama

Your school books are . . .

a) covered in paisley-print fabric
b) a bit muddy
c) filled with doodles
d) neat, tidy and full of good grades
e) rarely handed in on time

When you grow up you want to be . . .

a) an interior designer
b) a vet
c) a writer
d) a prima ballerina
e) famous

People always compliment your . . .

a) individuality. If anyone can pull it off you can!
b) caring nature – every creature deserves a bit of love
c) wild imagination . . . although it can get you into trouble sometimes
d) determination. Practice makes perfect
e) strong personality. You never let anyone stand in your way

Mostly As . . . *Skye*
Cool and eclectic, friends love your relaxed boho style and passion
for all things quirky.

Mostly Bs . . . *Coco*
A real mother earth, but with your feet firmly on the ground, you're
happiest in the great outdoors – accompanied by a whole menagerie
of animal companions.

Mostly Cs . . . *Cherry*
'Daydreamer' is your middle name . . . Forever thinking up crazy stories and
buzzing with new ideas, you always have an exciting tale to tell – you're
allowed a bit of artistic licence, right?

Mostly Ds . . . *Summer*
Passionate and fun, you're determined to make your dreams come
true . . . and your family and friends are behind you every step of the way.

Mostly Es . . . *Honey*
Popular, intimidating, lonely . . . everyone has a different idea about the
'real you'. Try opening up a bit more and you'll realize that friends are there
to help you along the way.

Catch all the latest
news and gossip from

Cathy Cassidy

at

www.cathycassidy.com

* Sneaky peeks at new titles
* Details of signings and events near you
* Audio extracts and interviews with Cathy
* Post your messages and pictures

Don't Miss a Word!

Sign up to receive a FREE email newsletter
from Cathy in your inbox every month!
Go to *www.cathycassidy.com*

Summer Fruit Skewers

For a refreshing healthy snack on those hot summer days, try making your own garden of fruit skewers.

You will need:

Your fave fruits (the best ones include kiwis, strawberries, grapes, oranges, and watermelon and pineapple slices)

10 or more wooden skewers

Heart, flower or butterfly cookie cutters

A shoe box (this will be your garden display)

What to do:

Using a chopping board carefully cut your chosen fruit into round shapes.

♥

One at a time, lay your slices of fruit on the board and cut into flower, butterfly and heart shapes using the cookie cutters.

♥

Carefully insert the skewers into the fruit to create a beautiful flower display.

Making a Flower:

 Cut a slice of pineapple into a flower shape and add to the skewer so it's horizontal. Then add a small strawberry to the very top to make the centre of the flower. Add a couple of grapes to the 'stem' of the flower to look like leaves. Try other methods and designs too!

Assemble Your Flower Garden:

Decorate your shoe box to make it look like a garden, using green paint, tissue paper, flower stickers, etc.

Cut small holes into the top of the shoe box.

Insert your flower skewers into the holes to create a flower border!

Top Tip!
For an extra-refreshing taste, serve with a yoghurt or cream-cheese dip!

www.cathycassidy.com

Coco's Lemonade

You need:

1 cup sugar
4–6 fresh lemons

Method:

Place one cup of sugar in a heatproof mixing jug and add one cup of boiling water, stirring gently until the sugar dissolves.

Use a lemon squeezer to squeeze the juice of 4–6 fresh lemons, enough to make a cupful.

Mix sugar-water and lemon juice together in a tall jug/pitcher and add 3–4 cups of water to taste.

Refrigerate for 30 mins and serve with lots of ice and slices of lemon.

For pink lemonade, slice up a bowlful of fresh strawberries and stir into the finished lemonade instead of lemon slices.

Find more yummy recipes at
www.cathycassidy.com

Yummy Ice-cream Sundaes

Banana Split

You need:
1 banana
vanilla ice cream
chopped nuts
chocolate sauce

Method:
Slice the banana in half lengthways, place in a dish and arrange three scoops of vanilla ice cream between the halves.

Decorate with a sprinkle of chopped nuts and a squoosh of chocolate sauce!

Chocolate Heaven

You need:
3 chocolate chip cookies, crumbled
4 squares chocolate, grated
vanilla ice cream
chocolate ice cream
chocolate sauce
aerosol cream

Method:
In a tall glass, layer a scoop of vanilla ice cream, a sprinkle of crumbled cookie, a scoop of chocolate ice cream and a layer of grated chocolate, and another scoop of vanilla ice cream and a layer of crumbled cookie. Top with a layer of squishy aerosol cream and decorate with grated chocolate and sauce . . . bliss!

Strawberry Sundae

You need:
fresh strawberries
plain frozen yoghurt
strawberry yoghurt
strawberry sauce

Method:
Cut most of the fresh strawberries into quarters then layer in a tall glass with the plain frozen yoghurt, strawberry yoghurt and an occasional squirt of strawberry sauce.

Repeat the layers until you reach the top of the glass. Finish off with the leftover strawberries and an extra squoosh of strawberry sauce!

How to make your very own friendship bracelets

Friendship bracelets are great fun to make, and even better to make with and for your best friend! There are lots of colours and patterns you can use to create a unique and special bracelet for your friend.

Method 1: The easiest way to make a friendship bracelet is by plaiting.

1. Choose 3 colours of thread that you like.
2. Take 2 strands of each colour.
3. Tie a knot in the end of the 6 strands and separate the different colours from each other.
4. Get your friend to hold the knotted end of the bracelet and start plaiting the 3 colours together.
5. Once the bracelet is long enough to go around your wrist, tie a knot in the other end.
6. Snip off any straggly ends and you're done!

Method 2: This is more difficult but you'll end up with a cool pattern.

1. Take 6 strands of thread – choose any colours you like.
2. Each strand represents a letter in the word **FRIEND**.
3. Tie a knot in the end of the 6 strands.

4. Arrange them in the order you like and ask your friend to hold the end.

5. Take the first string on the left **F** and wrap it over and around the next string **R** to make a knot. Pull up on **F** to tighten.

6. Make a second knot the same way with string **F** over and around string **R**. Pull up on **F** to tighten.

7. Drop string **R** and pick up string **I**. Make two knots with string **F** and around string **I**.

8. Repeat on strings **E**, **N** and the last string **D** making two knots on each with string **F**, now on the right. This makes a complete row.

9. Continue the next row by taking the first string on the left, now string **R**, and making two knots over and around the other strings.

10. With each row the string on the left is worked over the string on the right.

11. Once the bracelet is long enough to go around your wrist, tie a knot in the other end.

12. Snip off any straggly ends and you're done.

www.cathycassidy.com

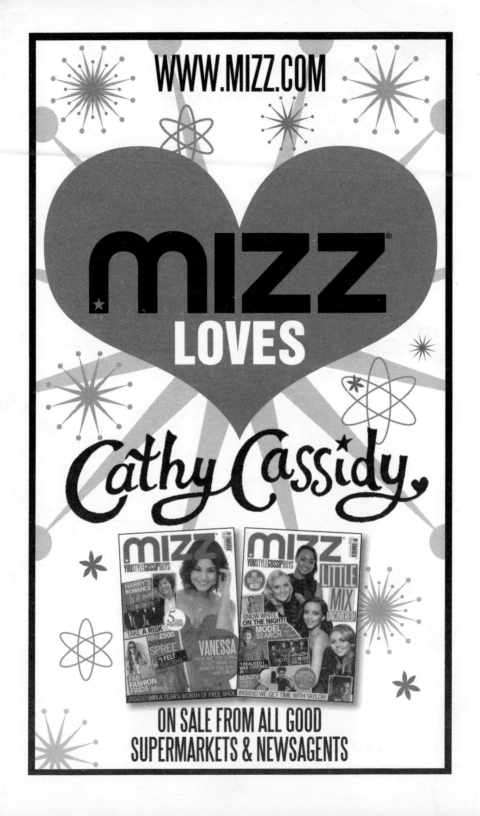

Best Friends are there for you in the good times and the bad. They can keep a secret and understand the healing power of chocolate.

Best Friends make you laugh and make you happy. They are there when things go wrong, and never expect any thanks.

Best Friends are forever,

Best Friends Rock!

Cathy Cassidy's
MY BEST FRIEND
Rocks!

Enter at:
www.cathycassidy.com

mizz
AWARD

Is your *Best Friend* one in a million?

Go to *www.cathycassidy.com* to find out how you can show your best friend how much you care

What Cathy Cassidy's

fans think ...

'I LOVE your books . . . I can't put them down' **Leyla**

'I can't wait until *Coco Caramel*!
You're my favourite author EVER!!' **Ellen**

'I can't wait till your other books come out,
The Chocolate Box Girls are the best!' **Ruby**

'Me and my best friend have read all of your books!' **Isabelle**

'I'm obsessed with reading your books –they are
just THE BEST! You rock Cathy!' **Momin**

More praise for Cathy!

'I was addicted to *Marshmallow Skye* . . . beautiful,
perfect and super moreish' *thebookaddictedgirl.blogspot.com*

'Writing as engaging as this is not easy to pull off' *Mail on Sunday*

'A great choice for older Jacqueline Wilson fans' *Irish Independent*

'Wittily written . . . from the heart' *Radio Times*

Write your own review at www.cathycassidy.com

DEMELZA

Demelza is the daughter of a Cornish miner and has been brought up in poverty and squalor. Now she has married Ross Poldark (chief figure of an earlier novel by Winston Graham), and, although Ross has great sympathy for the poor, he is one of the gentry and she finds she has much to learn of the ways of society and also of the ways of men—and of her husband. But their love is strong enough to survive the stormy early years of marriage, and they find great joy in the birth of their first child. The bitter struggles of the mining communities in the 18th Century form an authentic and fascinating background to this absorbing love story.

Winston Graham

DEMELZA

A Novel of Cornwall

1788-1790

THE BODLEY HEAD

LONDON

With the exception of actual historical personages
identified as such, the characters are entirely the
product of the author's imagination and have no
relation to any person or event in real life.

All rights reserved
ISBN 0 370 00540 6
Printed in Great Britain for
The Bodley Head Ltd
30 Bedford Square, London WCIB 3RP
by Redwood Burn Limited, Trowbridge
First published 1946
This edition 1960
Eighth impression 1985

DEMELZA
Book One

BOOK ONE

CHAPTER I   There could have been prophecy in the storm that blew up at the time of Julia's birth.

May month was not a time for heavy gales, but the climate of Cornwall is capricious as any child ever born. It had been a kindly enough spring, as kindly as the summer and winter that had gone before it; mild, soft, comfortable weather; and the land was already heavy with green things. Then May broke rainy and gusty, and the blossom suffered here and there and the hay leaned about looking for support.

On the night of the fifteenth Demelza felt her first pains. Even then for a while she gripped the bedpost and thought the matter all round before she said anything. All along she had viewed the coming ordeal with a calm and philosophical mind and had never troubled Ross with false alarms. She did not want to begin so late. Last evening she had been out in her beloved garden, digging round the young plants; then as it was going dark she had found a disgruntled hedgehog and had played with him, trying to persuade him to take some bread and milk, and had only come in reluctantly as the sky clouded and it went cold.

This now—this thing in the middle of the night—might yet be only the result of getting overtired.

But when it began to feel as if someone was kneeling on her backbone and trying to break it, she knew it was not.

She touched Ross's arm and he woke instantly.

"Well?"

"I think," she said, "I think you will have to fetch Prudie."

He sat up. "Why? What is it?"

"I have a pain."

"Where? Do you mean . . ."

"I have a pain," she said primly. "I think twould be as well to fetch Prudie."

He climbed quickly out of bed, and she listened to the scratch of flint and steel. After a moment the tinder caught and he lit a candle. The room flickered into view: heavy teak beams, the curtain over the door moving gently in the breeze, the low window seat hung with pink gro-gram, her shoes as she had kicked them off, one wooden sole upmost, Joshua's spyglass, Ross's pipe, Ross's book and a fly crawling.

He looked at her and at once knew the truth. She smiled a pallid apology. He went across to the table by the door and poured her a glass of brandy.

"Drink this. I will send Jud for Dr. Choake." He began to pull on his clothes, anyhow.

"No, no, Ross; do not send yet. It is the middle of the night. He will be asleep."

Whether Thomas Choake should be called in to her had been a dis-sension between them for some weeks. Demelza could not forget that twelve months ago she had been a maidservant and that Choake, though only a physician, owned a small estate which, even if it had been bought with his wife's money, put him on a level from which the likes of her would be seen as unimportant chattels. That was until Ross married her. Since then she had grown to her position. She could put on a show of refinement and good manners, and not at all a bad show at that; but a doctor was different. A doctor caught one at a disadvantage. If the pain was bad she would almost certainly swear in the old way she had learned from her father, not a few genteel "damn mes" and "by Gods," as any-one might excuse from a lady in trouble. To have a baby and be forced to act genteel at the same time was more than Demelza could look for-ward to.

Besides, she didn't want a man about. It wasn't decent. Her cousin-in-law, Elizabeth, had had him, but Elizabeth was an aristocrat born and bred, and they looked at things different. *She* would far rather have had old Aunt Betsy Triggs from Mellin, who sold pilchards and was a rare strong hand when it came to babies.

But Ross was the more determined and he had had his way. She was not unprepared for his curt, "Then he shall be woke," as he left the room.

"*Ross!*" She called him back. For the moment the pain had gone.

"Yes?" His strong, scarred, introspective face was half lit by the candle; the upgrowing dark hair was ruffled and hardly showed its hint of cop-per; his shirt was open at the throat. This man . . . aristocrat of them all, she thought . . . this man, so reserved and reserving, with whom she had shared rare intimacy . . .

"Would you?" she said. "Before you go . . ."

He came back to the bed. The emergency had come on him so quickly

8

in sleep that he had had no time yet to feel anything but alarm that her time was here and relief that it might soon be over. As he kissed her he saw the moisture on her face and a worm of fear and compassion moved in him. He took her face in his hands, pushed back the black hair and stared a moment into the dark eyes of his young wife. They were not dancing and mischievous as they so often were, but there was no fear in them.

"I'll be back. In a moment I'll be back."

She made a gesture of dissent. "Don't come back, Ross. Go and tell Prudie, that's all. I'd rather—you didn't see me like this."

"And what of Verity? You specially wanted Verity here."

"Tell her in the morning. Tisn't fair to bring her out in the night air. Send for her in the morning."

He kissed her again.

"Tell me that you love me, Ross," she said.

He looked at her in surprise.

"You know I do!"

"And say you don't love Elizabeth."

"And I don't love Elizabeth." What else was he to say when he did not know the truth himself? He was not a man who spoke his inmost feelings easily, but now he saw himself powerless to help her, and only words of his and not actions would give her aid. "Nothing else matters but you," he said. "Remember that. All my relatives and friends—and Elizabeth, and this house and the mine . . . I'd throw them in the dust and you know it—and you know it. If you don't know it, then all these months I've failed and no words I can give you now will make it otherwise. I love you, Demelza, and we've had such happiness. And we're going to have it again. Take hold of that, my sweet. Hold it and keep it, for no one else can."

"I'll hold it, Ross," she said, content because the words had come.

He kissed her again and turned and lit more candles; took up one and went quickly out of the room, the hot grease running over his hand. The wind had dropped since yesterday; there was only a breeze. He did not know the time, but it felt about two.

He pushed open the door on the other side of the landing and went across to the bedroom where Jud and Prudie slept. The ill-fitting bedroom door opened with a long squeak which merged into Prudie's slow rasping snore. He grunted in disgust, for the hot close sweaty smell offended his nose. The night air might be dangerous, but they could surely open the window during the day and let this stink out.

He went across and parted the curtains and shook Jud by the shoulder. Jud's two great teeth showed like gravestones. He shook again, violently. Jud's nightcap came off and a spot of the candle grease fell on

9

his bald patch. Jud woke. He began to curse; then he saw who it was and sat up rubbing his head.

"What's amiss?"

"Demelza is ill." How call her anything but Demelza to a man who had been here when she came as a tattered waif of thirteen? "I want you to go for Dr. Choake at once. And wake Prudie. She will be wanted too."

"What's amiss with her?"

"Her pains have begun."

"Oh, that. I thought ee said she were ill." Jud frowned at the piece of cooling tallow he had found on his head. "Prudie and me could manage that. Prudie d'know all that sort of panjandle. Tedn a 'ard thing to learn. Why, there's always such a dido about en I never can conceit. Tedn easy, mind, but once you've gotten the knack——"

"Get up."

Jud came out of bed, knowing the tone, and they woke Prudie. Her great shiny face peered through its tangle of greasy black hair as she wiped her nose on a corner of her night rail.

"Aw, my dear, I'll see to the mite. Poor maid." She began to fasten a pair of filthy stays over her shift. "I d'know how twas with my mother. She told me how twas when I was on the brew. Shifted I 'ad. Moved I 'ad. Twas a cruel chronic thing, they said. A weak, ailing little mouse, an' nobody believed I'd see the christening pot. . . ."

"Go to her as soon as you can," Ross said. "I'll get Darkie from the stables. You won't want her saddled."

"Mebbe I can ride bare-ridged that far," Jud said grudgingly. "Though if onct you d'make a slip in the dark, like as not you're pitched off on yer 'ead, and then snap goes yer neck and where are you?"

Ross ran down the stairs. On his way out he looked in at the new clock they had bought for the parlour. It wanted ten minutes to three. Dawn would not be long. Things were so much worse by candlelight.

In the stable he delayed to saddle Darkie, telling his fumbling fingers that every woman went through this: it became a commonplace of their existence, pregnancies following each other like the summer seasons. But he would see Jud safely off; if the fool slipped he might be hours. He would have gone himself if he could have trusted the Paynters alone with Demelza.

At the front of the house Jud was fastening his breeches under the lilac tree.

"Don't know as I shall rightly see me way," he said. "Dark as a blathering sack, tis. By rights I should 'ave a lantern on a pole. A long pole as I could 'old out——"

"Get up or you'll have the pole across your head."

Jud mounted. "What's to say as he won't come?"

"Bring him," said Ross, and gave Darkie a slap across the haunches.

When Jud turned in at the gates of Fernmore, the house of Thomas Choake, he observed disdainfully that the building was little more than a farmhouse, though they put on airs as if it was Blenheim. He got down and rat-tatted at the door. The house was surrounded by big pine trees, and the rooks and jackdaws were already awake, flying round in circles and being noisy. Jud raised his head and sniffed. All yesterday they'd been unsettled at Nampara.

At the seventh knock a window screeched above the door, and a nightcap appeared like a cuckoo out of a clock.

"Well, man, well, man! What is it? What's the damnation noise?"

Jud knew by the voice and eyebrows that he had flushed the right bird.

"Cap'n Poldark sent me for to fetch ee," he said, mumbling. "Dem—um—Mistress Poldark's took bad and they d'need you."

"What Mistress Poldark, man? What Mistress Poldark?"

"Mistress Demelza Poldark. Over to Nampara. 'Er that be going to have 'er first."

"Well, what's wrong? Didn't they say what was to do?"

"Ais. Tes her time."

"Nonsense, fellow. I saw her last week and I told Captain Poldark that there would be nothing until June. Go tell them I stand by that opinion."

The window slammed.

Jud Paynter was a man much interested in the malign indifference of man and providence to his own needs, and interested in not much else; but sometimes an accident roused him for other ends. This was one of the accidents. From feeling disgruntled at the simpering softness of Demelza and the misplaced harshness of Ross in turning him out on a bitter May morning without so much as a tot of rum, he came to reflect that Ross was his master and Demelza one of his own kind.

Three minutes later Dr. Choake put out his head again.

"What is it, man? You'll have the door down!"

"I was telled to fetch you."

"You insolent fellow! I'll have you thrashed for this!"

"Where's yer 'orse? I'll 'ave him out while you put yer drawers on."

The surgeon withdrew. Polly Choake's lisping voice could be heard in the background, and once her fluffy head passed the window. They were in consultation. Then Choake called down coldly:

"You must wait, fellow. We shall be with you in ten minutes."

Jud was sufficiently alive to the surgeon's peculiarities to know that by this Choake meant only himself.

Twenty-one minutes later, in icy silence, they set off. The rooks were still flying in circles and cawing, and at Sawle Church there was a great noise. Day was breaking. Streaks of watered green showed in the north-east, and the sky where the sun would rise was a bold pale orange behind the black ribs of the night. A wild sunrise and a strangely quiet one. After the winds of the last days the calm was profound. As they passed Grambler Mine they overtook a party of bal-maidens singing as they walked to work, their shrill fresh voices as sweet and young as the morning. Jud noticed that Will Nanfan's sheep were all gathered together in the most sheltered corner of the field.

Reflection on the quiet ride salved some of Dr. Choake's annoyance, for when they reached Nampara he did not complain, but greeted Ross stiffly and lumbered upstairs. There he found that the alarm was not a false one. He sat with Demelza for half an hour telling her to be brave and that there was nothing to be frightened of. Then, because she seemed constrained and was sweating a lot, he suspected a touch of fever and bled her to be on the safe side. This made her feel very ill, a result which pleased him for it proved, he said, that a toxic condition had existed and his treatment had brought on a normal and desirable inter-mission of the fever. If she took an infusion of bark once an hour it would prevent a renewal. Then he went home to breakfast.

Ross had been swilling himself under the pump trying to wash away the megrims of the night, and when he came through the house and saw a thickset figure riding up the valley he called sharply to Jinny Carter, who came every day to work in the house and had just arrived.

"Is that Dr. Choake?"

Jinny bent over her own child, which she brought on her back and kept in a basket in the kitchen. "Yes, sur. He d'say the baby won't be afore dinner at the early side, and he say he'll be back by nine or ten."

Ross turned away to hide his annoyance. Jinny looked at him with devoted eyes.

"Who helped you with your babies, Jinny?" he asked.

"Mother, sur."

"Will you go and get her, Jinny? I think I would trust your mother before that old fool."

She blushed with pleasure. "Yes, sur. I'll go right off. She'll be that glad to come." She started as if to go and then looked at her own baby.

"I'll see she comes to no harm," Ross said.

She glanced at him a moment in pleased embarrassment and then snatched up her white bonnet and left the kitchen.

Ross walked into the low hall, stood at the foot of the stairs, disliked the silence, went into the parlour and poured himself a glass of brandy, watched Jinny's brisk figure dwindling towards Mellin, returned to the kitchen. Little Kate had not moved, but lay on her back kicking and crowing and laughing at him. This mite was nine months old and had never seen its father, who was serving a two-year sentence in Bodmin Gaol for poaching. Unlike the two eldest, who took after their father, little Kate was a true Martin: sandy hair, blue eyes, tiny freckles already mottling the bridge of her button nose.

The fire had not been lighted this morning, and there was no sign of breakfast. Ross raked the ashes but they were dead; he picked up some kindling wood and set about lighting it, wondering irritably where Jud had gone. There must be hot water, he knew, and towels and basins; nothing was being prepared down here. Damn Choake for his impertinence, not even waiting to see him before he left.

Relations between the two men had been cool for some time. Ross disliked his inane wife, who had gossiped and whispered about Demelza; and when Ross disliked someone he found it hard to hide the fact. Now he fumed that he should be at the mercy of this obstinate stiff-necked unprogressive old fool who was the only physician within miles.

As the fire began to take Jud came in, and wind came with him and rushed round the kitchen.

"Thur's something blawing up," he said, eyeing Ross out of bloodshot eyes. "Seen the long black swell, 'ave ee?"

Ross nodded impatiently. There had been a heavy ground sea since afternoon yesterday.

"Well, tes breaking all ways. Scarcely ever did I see the like. It might be as someone was lashin' of un with a whip. The swell's nigh gone and the sea's all licky-white like Joe Trigg's beard."

"Keep your eye on Kate, Jud," Ross said. "Make some breakfast in the meantime. I am going upstairs."

At the back of his mind Ross was aware of the sound of wind rushing about in the distance. Once when he glanced out of the bedroom window his eyes confirmed that the swell had in fact quite broken up and the sea was stippled with white-lipped waves which crossed and recrossed each other in confusion, running heedlessly, colliding and breaking up into wisps of futile spray. The wind was as yet only gusty on the land, but here and there eddies rushed over the water, little winds, vicious and lost.

While he was there Demelza made a big effort to be normal, but he saw that she wished him gone. He could not help her.

Disconsolate, he went down again and was in time to greet Mrs. Zacky Martin, Jinny's mother. Flat-faced, competent, bespectacled and sneezing, she came into the kitchen with a brood of five small children dragging at her heels, talking to them, chiding them, explaining to

Ross that she had no one to trust them with—Jinny's two eldest and her three youngest—greeting Jud and asking after Prudie, commenting on the smell of frying pork, inquiring about the patient, saying she had a touch of ague herself but had taken a posset before leaving, rolling up her sleeves, telling Jinny to put the colewort and the motherwort on to brew, they being better than any doctor's nostrums for easing of the maid, and disappearing up the stairs before anyone else could speak.

There seemed to be a child on every chair in the kitchen. They sat like timid ninepins at a fair, waiting to be knocked off. Jud scratched his head and spat in the fire and swore.

Ross went back to the parlour. On the table was a bundle of crochet work that Demelza had been doing last night. A fashion paper which Verity had lent her lay beside it—something new and novel come to them from London; there had never been anything like it before. The room was a little dusty and unkempt.

It was fifteen minutes after six.

No birds singing this morning. A moment ago a ray of sunlight had fallen across the grass, but had been quickly put out. He stared at the elm trees, which were waving backwards and forwards as if with an earth tremor. The apple trees, more sheltered, were bending and turning up their leaves. The sky was heavy with racing clouds.

He picked up a book. His eyes scanned the page but took nothing in. The wind was beginning to roar down the valley. Mrs. Zacky came in.

"Well?"

"She'm doing brave, Cap'n Ross. Prudie and me'll manage, don't ee worry an inch. Twill all be over long before ole Dr. Tommie d'come back."

Ross put down the book. "Are you sure?"

"Well, I've had eleven o' my own and there's three of Jinny's. And I helped wi' two of Betty Nanfan's twins and four of Sue Vigus's, the first three out of wedlock." Mrs. Zacky hadn't fingers enough to count. "This won't be easy, not like Jinny's was, but we'll do a proper job, never you fear. Now I'll go get the brandy an' give the maid a tot o' that t'ease her up."

The house suddenly shuddered under a gust of wind. Ross stood staring out at the wild day, anger with Choake rising in him and seeking outlet like a part of the storm. Common sense told him that Demelza would be all right, but that she should be denied the best attention was intolerable. It was Demelza who suffered there, with only two clumsy old women to help her.

He went out to the stables, hardly aware of the storm that was rising about them.

At the stable door he glanced over Hendrawna and saw that clouds of spray had begun to lift off the sea and drift away like sand before a sandstorm. Here and there the cliffs were smoking.

He had just got the stable door open when the wind took it out of his hand, slammed it shut and pushed him against the wall. He looked up and saw that it would not be possible to ride a horse in the gale.

He set off to walk. It was only a matter of two miles.

A hail of leaves and grass and dirt and small twigs met him as he turned the corner of the house. Behind him the wind was tearing off mouthfuls of sea and flinging them to join the clouds. At another time he would have been upset at the damage to his crops, but now that seemed a small matter. It was not so much a gale as a sudden storm, as if the forces of a gathering anger had been bottled up for a month and must be spent in an hour. The branch of an elm came down across the stream. He stumbled past it, wondering if he could make the brow of the hill.

In the ruined buildings of Wheal Maiden he sat and gasped and groped for breath and rubbed his bruised hand, and the wind blew bits of masonry from the gaunt old granite walls and screamed like a harlot through every slit and hole.

Once through the pine trees, he met the full force of the storm coming in across Grambler Plain, bringing with it a bombardment of rain and dirt and gravel. Here it seemed that all the loose soil was being ploughed up and all the fresh young leaves and all the other small substances of the earth were being blown right away. The clouds were low over his head, brown and racing, all the rain emptied out of them and flying like torn rags before the frown of God.

Down in Fernmore, Dr. Choake was beginning his breakfast.

He had finished the grilled kidneys and the roast ham and was wondering whether to take a little of the smoked cod before it was carried away to be kept warm for his wife, who would breakfast in bed later. The early ride had made him very hungry, and he had set up a great commotion because breakfast was not waiting when he returned. Choake believed servants should not be allowed to get fat and lazy.

The loud knocking on the front door was hardly to be heard above the thunder of the wind.

"If that is anyone for me, Nancy," he said testily, lowering his eyebrows, "I am from home."

"Yes, sir."

He decided after a sniff to take some of the cod, and was irritated that it was necessary to help himself. This done, he settled his stomach against the table and had swallowed the first knifeful when there was an apologetic cough behind him.

"Begging your pardon, sir. Captain Poldark——"

"Tell him——" Dr. Choake looked up and saw in the mirror a tall dripping figure behind his harassed maid.

Ross came into the room. He had lost his hat and torn the lace on the sleeve of his coat; water followed him in a trail across Dr. Choake's best Turkey carpet.

But there was something in his eyes which prevented Choake from noticing this. The Poldarks had been Cornish gentlemen for two hundred years, and Choake, for all his airs, came from dubious stock.

He got up.

"I disturb your breakfast," said Ross.

"We—er—hm . . . Is something wrong?"

"You'll remember," said Ross, "that I engaged you to be with my wife in her lying-in."

"Well! She is going on well. I made a thorough examination. The child will be born this afternoon."

"I engaged you as a surgeon to be in the house, not as a travelling pedlar."

Choake went white round the lips. He turned on the gaping Nancy.

"Get Captain Poldark some port."

Nancy fled.

"What's your complaint?" Choake made an effort to outstare his visitor; the fellow had no money and was still a mere youngster. "We have attended your father, your uncle, your cousin and his wife, your cousin Verity. They have never found reason to call my treatment in question."

"What they do is their own affair. Where is your cloak?"

"Man, I can't ride out in this gale of wind. Look at yourself! It would be impossible to sit a horse."

"You should have thought of that when you left Nampara."

The door opened and Polly Choake came in with her hair in pins and wearing a flowing cerise morning gown. She gave a squeal when she saw Ross.

"Oh, Captain Poldark. I'd no idea. Weally, to see one like this! But the wind upstairs, faith, it upthets one to hear it! I fear for the woof, Tom, that I do, an' if it came in on my head I should be a pwetty thight!"

"You're not a pretty sight peeping round the door," snapped her husband irritably. "Come in or go out as you please, but have the goodness to decide."

Polly pouted and came in, and looked at Ross sidelong and patted her hair. The door slammed behind her.

"I never get used to your old Cornish winds, and thith ith a fair demon. Jenkin says there is five thlates off of the butterwy, and I doubt there'll not be more. How ith your wife, Captain Poldark?"

Choake slipped off his skullcap and put on his wig.

"That will not stand in the wind," said Ross.

"You're not going out, Tom? But you could not wide and scarthely walk. An' think of the danger of falling twees!"

"Captain Poldark is nervous for his wife," Choake said whitely.

"But thurely ith it that urgent tho thoon again? I wemember my mother said I was eight and forty hours a-coming."

"Then your husband will be eight and forty hours a-waiting," said Ross. "It is a whim I have, Mrs. Choake."

Pettishly the surgeon flung off his purple-spotted morning gown and pulled on his tail coat. Then he stumped out to get his bag and his riding cloak, nearly upsetting Nancy, who was coming in with the port.

The wind was a little abeam of them on the return. Choake lost his wig and his hat, but Ross caught the wig and stuffed it under his coat. By the time they climbed the rise near Wheal Maiden they were both gasping and drenched. As they reached the trees they saw a slight figure in a grey cloak ahead of them.

"Verity," said Ross as they overtook her leaning against a tree. "You have no business out to-day."

She gave him her wide-mouthed generous smile. "You should know it can't be kept a secret. Mrs. Zacky's Betty saw Jud and Dr. Choake on her way to the mine, and she told Bartle's wife." Verity leaned her wet face against the tree. "Our cow shed is down and we have the two cows in the brewhouse. The headgear of Digory's mine has collapsed, but I think no one is hurt. How is she, Ross?"

"Well enough, I trust." Ross linked his arm in Verity's and they began to walk after the stumbling, cloak-blown figure of the physician. He had often thought that if a man were allowed a second wife he would have asked his cousin, for her kindness and generosity and for the soothing effect she always had on him. Already he was beginning to feel shamefaced at his own anger. Tom Choake had his good points and naturally knew his job better than Mrs. Zacky Martin.

They caught up with Choake as he was climbing over the fallen elm branch. Two of the apple trees were down, and Ross wondered what Demelza would say when she saw the remnants of her spring flowers. When she did . . .

He quickened his pace. Some of his irritation returned at the thought of all the women milling about in the house and his beloved Demelza helpless and in pain. And Choake going off without a word.

As they entered they saw Jinny pattering up the stairs with a basin of steaming water, slopping some of it into the hall in her haste. She never even looked at them.

Dr. Choake was so distressed that he went into the parlour and sat on the first chair and tried to get his breath. He glared at Ross and said:

"I'll thank you for my wig."

Ross poured out three glasses of brandy. He took the first to Verity, who had collapsed in a chair, her fluffy dark hair contrasting with the wet streaks where the hood had not covered it. She smiled at Ross and said:

"I will go upstairs when Dr. Choake is ready. Then if all goes well I will get you something to eat."

Choake gulped down his brandy and passed his glass for more. Ross, knowing that liquor made him a better doctor, gave it him.

"We will breakfast together," Choake said, more cheerful at the thought of food. "We will just go up and set everyone's mind at rest; then we will breakfast. What have you for breakfast?"

Verity got up. Her cloak fell away and showed the plain grey dimity frock, the bottom eight inches embroidered with mud and rain. But it was at her face that Ross looked. She wore a full, uplifted, startled expression, as if she had seen a vision.

"What is it?"

"Ross, I thought I heard . . ."

They all listened.

"Oh," said Ross harshly, "there are children in the kitchen. There are children in the still-room and children for all I know in the clothes closet. Every age and size."

Verity said: "Ssh!"

Choake fumbled for his bag. All his movements were clumsy and he made a great deal of noise.

"That is not a grown child!" Verity said suddenly. "That is not a grown child!"

They listened again.

"We must go to our patient," said Choake, suddenly ill at ease and faintly sly. "We shall be ready for breakfast when we come down."

He opened the door. The others followed him, but at the foot of the stairs they all stopped.

Prudie was on the top step. She was still wearing her night shift, with a coat over it, and her great figure bulged like an overfull sack. She bent to look at them, her long pink face bulbous and shining.

"We've done it!" she shouted in her organ voice. "Tes a gurl. We've gotten a gurl for ee. 'Andsomest little mite ever I saw. We've knocked her face about a small bit, but her's as lusty as a little nebby colt. Hear 'er screeching!"

After a moment's silence Choake cleared his throat portentously and put his foot on the bottom step. But Ross pushed him aside and went up the stairs first.

CHAPTER II   Had Julia known the difference she would have thought it a strange countryside into which she had been born.

For hours a blight had stalked across it. So much salt was in the terrible wind that nothing escaped. The young green leaves of the trees turned black and withered, and when a breeze moved them they rattled like dry biscuits. Even the dandelions and the nettles went black. The hay was damaged and the potato crop, and the young peas and beans shrivelled and died. The rosebuds never opened, and the stream was choked with the debris of a murdered spring.

But inside Nampara, in the little world made up of four walls and bright curtains and whispering voices, life was triumphant.

Having taken a good look at her baby, Demelza decided that the infant was complete and wonderful to behold, once her poor bruised little face righted itself. No one seemed to know how long this would take—Ross thought privately that there might be lasting marks—but Demelza, of a more sanguine temperament, looked at the bruises and then looked out at the ravaged landscape and decided that nature in her own good time would work wonders on both. They should postpone the christening until the end of July.

She had ideas about the christening. Elizabeth had had a party for Geoffrey Charles's christening. Demelza had not been there, for that was four years ago come November, when she was less than nothing in the eyes of the Poldark family; but she had never forgotten Prudie's tales of the fine people invited, the great bunches of flowers brought from Truro, the feast spread, the wine and the speeches. Now that she had made her own debut, however modestly, into such society, there was no reason why they should not give a party for *their* child, as good or even better.

She decided to have two parties if Ross could be talked into it.

She put this to him four weeks after Julia was born, as they were taking tea together on the lawn before the front door of Nampara, while Julia slept soundly in the shade of the lilac tree.

Ross looked at her with his quizzing, teasing glance.

"Two parties? We've not had twins."

Demelza's dark eyes met his for a moment, then stared into the dregs of her cup.

"No, but there's your people and there's my people, Ross. The gentlefolk and the other folk. It wouldn't do to mix 'em, no more than you can't mix cream and—and onions. But they're both nice enough by themselves."

"I'm partial to onions," Ross said, "but cream cloys. Let us have a party for the country people: the Zacky Martins, the Nanfans, the Daniels. They're worth far more than the overfed squires and their genteel ladies."

Demelza threw a piece of bread to the ungainly dog squatting near.

"Garrick's no better looking for his fight wi' Mr. Treneglos's bull," she said. "I'm certain sure he's got some teeth left, but he d'swallow his food like a sea gull and expect his stomach to do the chewing."

Garrick wagged his two-inch stump at this notice.

"Here," said Demelza, "let me see."

"We could gather a very nice picking of the country folk," said Ross. "Verity would come too. She is just as fond of them as we are—or would be if she were let. You could even ask your father if it pleased you. No doubt he's forgiven me for throwing him in the stream."

"I thought twould be nice to ask father and brothers as well," Demelza said, "on the second day. I thought we could have that on the twenty-third of July, Sawle Feast, so that the miners would have the day off anyhow."

Ross smiled to himself. It was pleasant sitting here in the sun, and he did not mind her wheedling. Indeed he took an objective interest in what would be her next move.

"Yes, he's teeth enough to make a show," she said. "It is plain laziness, naught else. Would all your fine friends be too fine to be asked to dinner with a miner's daughter?"

"If you open his mouth much wider," said Ross, "you'll fall in."

"No, I shan't; I'm too fat; I'm getting a rare fudgy face; my new stays will scarcely lace. John Treneglos, I reckon, wouldn't say no to an invitation. And even maybe his slant-eyed wife would come if you was here for bait. And George Warleggan—you d'say his grandfather was a smith, so he's no call to be proud even if he is so rich. And Francis . . . I like Cousin Francis. And Aunt Agatha wi' her white whiskers and her bettermost wig. And Elizabeth and little Geoffrey Charles. We should be a rare boiling. And then," said Demelza slyly, "maybe you could ask some of your friends you go visiting at George Warleggan's."

A cool breeze stirred between them. It lifted a frill of Demelza's dress, flapped it idly and let it fall.

"Gamblers all," said Ross. "You would not want gamblers at a christening. And twice meeting at a card table is not a close acquaintance."

She loosed Garrick's slavering jaws and moved her hands to wipe them down the side of her dress. Then she remembered and bent to rub them on the grass. Garrick licked her cheek and a dark curl fell over one eye. The trouble with arguing with women, Ross thought, was that one was diverted from the point by their beauty. Demelza was not less lovely for being temporarily more matronly. He remembered how his first love Elizabeth had looked after Geoffrey Charles was born, like an exquisite camellia, delicate and spotless and slightly flushed.

"You can have your two christenings if you want them," he said.

For a moment, absurdly, Demelza looked a little troubled. Used to her sudden changes of mood, he watched her quizzically, and then she said in a small voice:

"Oh, Ross. You're that good to me."

He laughed. "Don't weep for it."

"No, but you are; you are." She got up and kissed him. "Sometimes," she said slowly, "I think I'm a grand lady, and then I remember I'm really only . . ."

"You're Demelza," he said, kissing her in return. "God broke the mould."

"No, he didn't. There's another one in the cot." She looked at him keenly. "Did you really mean all those pretty things you said before Julia was born? Did you, Ross?"

"I've forgotten what I said."

She broke away from him and went skipping across the lawn in her smart dress. Presently she was back. "Ross, let's go and bathe."

"What nonsense. And you but a week out of bed."

"Then let me put my feet in the water. We can go to the beach and walk in the surf. It is quiet to-day."

He gave her a pat. "Julia would suffer for your cold feet."

". . . I hadn't thought of that." She subsided in her chair.

"But," he said, "there is dry sand enough to walk on."

She was up in a moment. "I will go'n tell Jinny to keep an eye on Julia."

When she came back they walked to the edge of the garden where the soil was already half sand. They crossed a patch of wasteland, threading between thistles and tree mallows, and he lifted her over the crumbling stone wall. They ploughed through soft sand and were on Hendrawna Beach.

It was a soft summery day with white regiments of cloud mustered on the horizon. The sea was quiet, and the small wavelets turning their heads near the edge left behind them on the green surface a delicate arabesque of white.

They walked arm in arm, and he thought how quickly they had refound their old companionship.

Out in the sea were two or three herring boats from Padstow and one

21

from Sawle. They thought it Pally Rogers's boat and waved, but he took no notice, being more concerned with fish than friendship.

She said: "I think it would be a good thing if Verity came to both our parties. She needs the change and new notions to interest her."

"I hope you don't intend to have the child held over the font two days together."

"No, no, that would be the first day. The high folk would see that. The low folk will not mind if they are given plenty t'eat. An' they can finish up what's left from the day before."

"Why do we not also have a children's party," said Ross, "to finish up on the third day what has been left on the second?"

She looked at him and broke out laughing. "You mock me, Ross. Always you d'mock me."

"It's an inverted form of reverence. Didn't you know that?"

"But quite serious, do you not think it would be a good genteel notion to have such a gathering?"

"Quite serious," he said, "I'm disposed to gratify your whims. Isn't that enough?"

"Then I wish you would gratify me in another. I'm that worried over Verity."

"What is wrong with her?"

"Ross, she was not meant to be an old maid. She has so much in her warm-like and fond. *You* know that. Well, it isn't the life for her, tending Trenwith, looking to the farm and the house and caring for Elizabeth and Francis and Elizabeth's baby and old Aunt Agatha, and caring for the servants and ordering the supplies and teaching the old choir at Sawle Church and busying about helping the mine folk. That isn't what she did ought to be doing."

"It is precisely what she enjoys doing."

"Yes, if it was on her own, like, yes. If she was wed and with a home of her own it would make all the difference. Last September month when she was here wi' us at Nampara she looked betterer in no time, but now she's yellow as a saddle and that thin. How old is she, Ross?"

"Twenty-nine."

"Well, it is high time something was done."

Ross paused and threw a stone at two quarrelling sea gulls. Not far ahead, on the cliff top, were the buildings of Wheal Leisure, open now as a result of years of contriving on his part, open and employing fifty-six men and showing a profit.

"You have walked far enough," he said. "Back now."

Obediently she turned. The tide was coming in, eating quietly away at the sand. Every so often a wave would make a larger encroachment and then retreat, leaving a thin fringe of soapy scum to mark its limits.

He said amusedly: "Nine months ago you would not have Verity at any price. You thought her an ogre. When I wanted you to meet, you went as stiff as a pit prop. But since you met you have never ceased to pester me to find her a husband. Short of going to one of the old witches of Summercourt Fair and buying her a love potion, I know of no way of satisfying you!"

"There's still Captain Blamey," said Demelza.

He made a gesture of irritation.

"That too I've heard. And am growing a little tired of. Leave well alone, my dear."

"I shall never be wise, Ross," she said after a moment. "I don't even think I wish to be wise."

"I don't want you to be," he said, as he lifted her over the wall.

The following day Verity came. She had caught a bad chill from her wetting of a month ago, but now was well again. She cooed over the baby, said she was like them both and like neither of them, heard of Demelza's schemes for the christening and endorsed them without hesitation, tried valiantly to answer one or two questions Demelza had been afraid to ask Dr. Choake, and brought out a fine lace christening gown she had made for the child.

Demelza kissed her and thanked her, and then sat looking at her with such dark serious eyes that Verity broke into one of her rare laughs and asked what was to do.

"Oh, nothing. Will you take some tea?"

"If it is time."

Demelza pulled at the tassel by the fireplace. "I do naught but drink all day long since Julia came. And I reckon tea's better than gin."

The red-haired, fair-skinned Jinny came in.

"Oh, Jinny," Demelza said awkwardly. "Would you make us a dish of tea. Nice an' strong. An' make the water to boil before you put it on the leaves."

"Yes, ma'am."

"I can't believe that's me," said Demelza when she had gone.

Verity smiled. "Now tell me what's troubling you."

"You are, Verity."

"I? Dear, dear. Say at once how I have offended."

"Not offended. But if . . . Oh, it is me that will give the offence. . . ."

"Until I know the subject I can't advise you on that."

"Verity," Demelza said. "Ross told me once, after I'd been plaguing him for hours, told me about that you'd once been fond of somebody."

Verity did not move but the smile on her face became less soft, its curves slightly changed.

"I'm sorry that should trouble you," she said after a moment.

Demelza was now too far on to mind her words.

"What's testing me is whether it was right that you should've been kept apart, like."

A faint colour was moving in Verity's sallow cheeks. She's gone old-maidish and drawn-in, Demelza thought, just like when I first saw her; such a difference, like two people living in the same body.

"My dear, I don't think we can measure the behaviour of others by our own judgments. This is what the world is always at. My . . . father and brother have strong and considered principles and they acted on them. Whether it was right or wrong to do so is hardly for us to say. But what is done cannot be undone, and anyway, it is long since buried and almost forgot."

"Did you never hear of him again?"

Verity got up.

"No."

Demelza went and stood beside her.

"I *hate* it. I *hate* it," she said.

Verity patted her arm, as if Demelza had been the injured one.

"Will you not tell me about it?" said Demelza.

"No," said Verity.

"Sometimes telling helps—makes it easier, and that."

"Not now," said Verity. "Speaking of it now would be . . . digging an old grave."

She gave a little shiver of emotion (or distaste) as Jinny brought in the tea.

That evening Demelza found Jud in the kitchen alone. No one could have told from their behaviour whether these two liked each other or held to an armed neutrality. Jud had never been won over by Demelza quite as his wife had been. For long he had felt a grudge that this foundling who had once run at his bidding should now be in a position to order him; but then Jud was sure Fate was cruel to him in many ways. Given the choice, he would have preferred Demelza to some coxy-faced madam used to luxury and being waited on all ends.

"Jud," said Demelza, taking down the baking board and the flour and the yeast. "Jud, do you recollect a Captain Blamey who used to come here to see Miss Verity?"

"Do I just," said Jud.

"I must ha' been here then," said the girl, "but I don't recall nothing—anything about it."

"You was a little small tiddler o' thirteen," Jud said gloomily, "an' kep' in the kitchen where ye belonged to be. That's what."

"I don't suspect you remember much about it now," said the girl.

"No, I don't know, not I, when I was thur through un all, what next."

She began to knead the dough.

"What happened, Jud?"

He took up a piece of wood and began to whittle it with his knife, blowing a little between his two teeth. His shiny head with its fringe of hair gave him the look of a dissident monk.

"He'd killed his first wife by accident, like, hadn't he?" she asked.

"I see ee d'knaw all about un."

"No, not all. Some, not all, Jud. What happened here?"

"Oh, this Captain Blamey fellow, he was tinkering after Miss Verity for a rare time. Cap'n Ross put'n to meet here when they'd been foiled to meet else, an' one day Mister Francis and is fathur—'im they berred Septemby last—come over and found un in the parlour. Mister Francis called 'im to meet'n outside, and out they stamped wi' them duelling pistols that's hung by the window. Me they broft in to see fair play, as you'd only expect, as you'd be right to expect; and afore the day was five minutes olderer Mister Francis'd shot Captain Blamey and Blamey'd shot Francis. As tidy a bit of work as never you saw."

"Were they hurt?"

"Not as you'd say 'urted. Blamey'd taken a snick in the hand, and the other ball fetched in Francis's neck. Twas straight and fair doin', and Cap'n Blamey up on his 'orse and rid away."

"Have you ever heard tell of him since then, Jud?"

"Not a whisper."

"Don't he live at Falmouth?"

"When he's not to sea."

"Jud," she said, "I want for you to do something for me."

"Eh?"

"The next time Captain Ross rides to see Jim Carter I want you to do something."

Jud looked at her with his bloodshot bulldog eyes, old and wary.

"How so?"

"I want for you to ride to Falmouth and ask after Captain Blamey and see if he's there still and see what he's doing."

There was silence while Jud got up and spat emphatically in the fire. When it had finished sizzling he said:

"Go on with yer mooling, Mrs. Tedn for we to be setting the world in step. Tedn sense, tedn natural, tedn right, tedn *safe*. I'd as lief bait a bull."

25

He picked up his stick and his knife and walked out.

Demelza gazed after him. She was disappointed but not surprised. And as she looked at the dough, turning it slowly with floured fingers, there was a dark glint in the depths of her glance which suggested she was not discouraged.

CHAPTER III   The day of the christening broke fine, and inside Sawle Church the ceremony passed off well before thirty guests, Julia squinting self-consciously when her second cousin, the Rev. William-Alfred Johns, dripped water on her forehead. Afterwards everyone began to trek back to Nampara, some on horseback, others walking in twos and threes, chatting and enjoying the sun; a colourful procession straggling across the scarred countryside and gazed at with curiosity and some awe by the tinners and cottagers as they passed. They were indeed visitors from another world.

The parlour, large and accommodating as it was, was none too spacious for feeding a company of thirty, some of them with big hoop skirts and none of them used to being overcrowded.

Elizabeth and Francis had both come, and with them Geoffrey Charles, three and a half years old. Aunt Agatha, who had not been outside Trenwith grounds for ten years and not on a horse for twenty-six, had come over looking disgusted on a very old and docile mare. She'd never ridden sidesaddle before in forty-seven years of hunting and she thought it an indignity to begin. Ross got her settled in a comfortable chair and brought her a charcoal foot warmer; then he put some rum in her tea, and she soon brightened up and started looking for omens.

George Warleggan had come, chiefly because Elizabeth had persuaded him. Mrs. Teague and three of her unmarried daughters were here to see what was to be seen, and Patience Teague, the fourth, because she hoped to meet George Warleggan. John Treneglos and Ruth and old Horace Treneglos were here, variously out of interest in Demelza, spite, and neighbourliness.

They had also asked Joan Pascoe, daughter of the banker, and with her was a young man called Dwight Enys, who spoke little but looked earnest and likeable.

Ross watched his young wife doing the honours. He could not but compare Demelza with Elizabeth, who was now twenty-four and certainly no less lovely than she had ever been. At Christmas she had been a little piqued by the young Demelza's success, and to-day she had taken pains to see if she could rebuild her ascendancy over Ross, a matter that was becoming more important to her than it had once been. She was wearing a brocaded dress of crimson velvet, with broad ribbons round the waist and tiers of lace on the sleeves. To anyone with a sense of colour the rich crimson made her fairness mesmeric.

Hers was the loveliness of gracious, aristocratic womanhood, used to leisure and bred to refinement. She came from uncounted generations of small landed gentlefolk. There had been a Chynoweth before Edward the Confessor, and, as well as the grace and breeding, she seemed to have in her a susceptibility to fatigue, as if the fine pure blood was flowing a little thin. Against her Demelza was the upstart: bred in drunkenness and filth, a waif in a parlour, an urchin climbing on the shoulders of chance to peer into the drawing-rooms of her betters: lusty, crude, unsubtle, all her actions and feelings a stage nearer nature. But each of them had something the other lacked.

The Rev. Clarence Odgers, curate of Sawle-with-Grambler, was present in his horsehair wig; Mrs. Odgers, a tiny anxious woman who had somehow found room for ten children and spread not an inch in the doing, was at talk humbly over the boiled pike on parish problems with William-Alfred's wife, Dorothy Johns. A group of the younger people at the far end of the table were laughing together at Francis's account of how John Treneglos for a bet had last week ridden his horse up the steps of Werry House and had fallen off into Lady Bodrugan's lap, all among the dogs.

"It is a lie," said John Treneglos robustly above the laughter, and glancing at Demelza to see if she had some attention for the story. "A brave and wicked lie. True I came unseated for a moment and Connie Bodrugan was there to offer me accommodation, but I was back on the nag in half a minute and was off down the steps before she'd time to finish her swearing."

"And a round cursing you'd get, if I know her ladyship," said George Warleggan, fingering his beautiful stock, which failed to hide the shortness of his neck. "I'd not be astonished if you heard some new ones."

"Really, my dear," said Patience Teague, pretending to be shocked, and looking up at George slantwise through her lashes. "Isn't Lady Bodrugan rather an indelicate subject for such a pretty party?"

There was laughter again, and Ruth Treneglos, from farther along the table, eyed her elder sister keenly. Patience was coming out, breaking away as *she* had done from the dreary autocracy of their mother. Faith and Hope, the two eldest, were hopeless old maids now, echoing Mrs. Teague like a Greek chorus; Joan, the middle sister, was going the same way.

"Don't some of our young people dress extravagant these days," said

Dorothy Johns in an undertone, breaking off her more substantial conversation to look at Ruth. "I'm sure young Mrs. Treneglos must cost her husband a handsome penny in silks. Fortunate that he is able to gratify her taste."

"Yes, ma'am, I entirely agree, ma'am," Mrs. Odgers breathed anxiously, fingering her borrowed necklace. Mrs. Odgers spent all her time agreeing with someone. It was her mission in life. "And not as if she had been accustomed to such luxury at home, like. It seems no time at all since my husband christened her. My first came just after."

"She's grown quite fat since I saw her last," whispered Mrs. Teague to Faith Teague, while Prudie clattered the gooseberry pies behind her. "And I don't like her dress, do you? Unbecoming for one so recently—um—a matron. Worn with an eye for the men. You can see it."

"One can understand, of course," said Faith Teague to Hope Teague, passing the ball obediently a step downtable, "how she appeals to a certain type. She has that sort of full bloom that soon fades. Though I must say I'm quite surprised at Captain Poldark. But no doubt they were thrown together. . . ."

"What did Faith say?" said Joan Teague to Hope Teague, waiting her turn.

"Well, she's a fine little monkey," said Aunt Agatha, who was near the head, to Demelza. "Let me hold her, bud. Ye're not afraid I'll drop her, are you? I've held and dandled many that's dead and gone afore ever you was thought of. Chibby, chibby, chibby! There now, she's smiling at me. Unless it's wind. Reg'lar little Poldark she is. The very daps of her father."

"Mind," said Demelza, "she may dribble on your fine gown."

"It will be a good omen if she do. Here, I have something for you, bud. Hold the brat a moment. Ah! I've got the screws to-day, and the damned jolting that old nag gave me didn't help. . . . There. That's for the child."

"What is it?" Demelza asked after a moment.

"Dried rowanberries. Hang 'em on the cradle. Keep the fairies away. . . ."

"He hasn't had the smallpox yet," said Elizabeth to Dwight Enys, rubbing her hand gently over the curls of her small son, who was sitting so quietly on his chair beside her. "I have often wondered whether there is anything in this inoculation, whether it is injurious to a young child."

"No; not if it is carefully done," said Enys, who had been put beside Elizabeth and was taking in little except her beauty. "But don't employ a farmer to give the cowpox. Some reliable apothecary."

"Oh, we are fortunate to have a good one in the district. He's not here to-day," Elizabeth said.

The meal came to an end at last, and since the day was so fine people strolled into the garden. As the company spread out Demelza edged her way towards Joan Pascoe.

"Did you say you came from Falmouth, did I hear you say that, Miss Pascoe?"

"Well, I was brought up there, Mrs. Poldark. But I live in Truro now."

Demelza moved her eyes to see if anyone was within hearing.

"Do you chance to know a Captain Andrew Blamey, Miss Pascoe?"

Joan Pascoe cooed to the baby.

"I know *of* him, Mrs. Poldark. I have seen him once or twice."

"Is he still in Falmouth, I wonder?"

"I believe he puts in there from time to time. He's a seafaring man, you know."

"I've often thought I'd dearly like to go to Falmouth on a visit," Demelza said dreamily. "It's a handsome place they say. I wonder when is a good time to see all the ships in the harbour."

"Oh, after a gale, that is the best, when the vessels have run in for shelter. There is room enough for all to ride out the greatest storm."

"Yes, but I s'pose the packet service runs regular, in and out, just like clockwork. The Lisbon packet they say goes every Tuesday."

"Oh, no, I think you're misinformed, ma'am. The Lisbon packet leaves from St. Just's Pool every Friday evening in the winter and every Saturday morning in the summer months. The week's end is the best time to see the regular services."

"Chibby, chibby, chibby," said Demelza to Julia, copying Aunt Agatha and watching the effect. "Thank you, Miss Pascoe, for the information."

"My dear," said Ruth Treneglos to her sister Patience, "who is this coming down the valley? Can it be a funeral procession? Old Agatha will certainly smell a bad omen here."

One or two of the others now noticed that fresh visitors were on the way. Headed by a middle-aged man in a shiny black coat, the newcomers threaded their way through the trees on the other side of the stream.

"My blessed parliament!" said Prudie, from the second parlour window. "It's the maid's father. 'E's come on the wrong day. Didn ee tell him Wednesday, you black worm?"

Jud looked startled and swallowed a big piece of currant tart. He coughed in annoyance. "Wednesday? O' course I says Wednesday. What for should I tell Tuesday when I was told to tell Wednesday? Tedn my doing. Tedn me you can blame. Shake yer broom 'andle in yer own face!"

With a sick sensation in the pit of her stomach Demelza too had recognized the new arrivals. Her brain and her tongue froze. She could see disaster and could do nothing to meet it. Even Ross was not beside her at this moment but was tending to Great-aunt Agatha's comfort, opening the french windows for her to sit and view the scene.

But Ross had not missed the procession.

They had come in force: Tom Carne himself, big and profoundly solid in his new-found respectability; Aunt Chegwidden Carne, his second wife, bonneted and small-mouthed like a little black hen, and behind them four tall gangling youths, a selection from among Demelza's brothers.

A silence had fallen on the company. Only the stream bubbled and a bullfinch chirped. The cavalcade reached the plank bridge and came across it with a clomp of hobnailed boots.

Verity guessed the identity of the new arrivals and she left old Mr. Treneglos and moved to Demelza's side. She did not know how she could help Demelza unless it was merely by being there, but in so far as she could give a lead to Francis and Elizabeth that she meant to do.

Ross came quickly out of the house, and without appearing to hurry reached the bridge as Tom Carne came over.

"How d'you do, Mr. Carne," he said, holding out his hand. "I am grateful you were able to come."

Carne eyed him for a second. It was more than four years since they had met, and then they had smashed up a room before one of them ended in the stream. Two years of reformation had changed the older man; his eyes were clearer and his clothing good and respectable. But he still had the same intolerant stare. Ross too had changed in the interval, grown away from his disappointment; the content and happiness he had found with Demelza had softened his intolerance, had cloaked his restless spirit in a new restraint.

Carne, finding no sarcasm, let his hand be taken. Aunt Chegwidden Carne, not in the least overawed, came next, shook his hand, moved on to greet Demelza. As Carne made no attempt to introduce the four gangling youths, Ross bowed gravely to them and they, taking their cue from the eldest, touched their forelocks in response. He found a strange comfort in the fact that none of them was the least like Demelza.

"We been waiting at the church, maid," Carne said grimly to his daughter. "Ye said four o'clock and we was there by then. Ye'd no manner of right to do it afore. We was besting whether to go 'ome again."

"I said *to-morrow* at four," Demelza answered him sharply.

"Aye. So yer man said. But twas our right to be 'ere the day of the baptizing, an' he said the baptizing was for to-day. Yer own flesh an' blood 'as more call to be beside you at a baptizing than all these 'ere dandical folk."

A terrific bitterness welled up in Demelza's heart. This man, who had beaten all affection out of her in the old days, to whom she had sent a forgiving invitation, had deliberately come on another day and was going to shatter her party. All her efforts were in vain, and Ross would be the laughing stock of the district. Already, without looking, she could see the laughter on the faces of Ruth Treneglos and Mrs. Teague. She could have torn tufts from his thick black beard (showing streaks of grey now beneath the nose and under the curve of the bottom lip); she could have clawed at his sober, too-respectable jacket or plastered his thick red-veined nose with earth from her flower beds. With a fixed smile hiding the desolation of her heart she greeted her stepmother and her four brothers: Luke, Samuel, William and Bobby: names and faces she had loved in that far-off nightmare life that no longer belonged to her.

And they, at any rate, were overawed, not least by their sister, whom they remembered a managing drudge and found a well-dressed young woman with a new way of looking and speaking. They grouped round her at a respectful distance, answering gruffly her metallic little questions, while Ross, with all that grace and dignity of which he was capable when he chose, was escorting Tom Carne and Aunt Chegwidden round the garden, inexorably introducing them to the others. There was a steely politeness in his manner which bolted down the reactions of those who were not used to exchanging compliments with the vulgar classes.

As they went Tom Carne's eyes grew no more respectful at the show of fashion but harder and more wrathful at the levity these people seemed to consider suitable for a solemn day; and Aunt Chegwidden's mouth pinched itself in like a darned buttonhole as she took in Elizabeth's flamboyant crimson, Ruth Treneglos's tight low-cut bodice and Mrs. Teague's rows of pearls and richly frizzled wig.

At last it was over and talk broke out again, though on a subdued note. A tiny wind was getting up, moving among the guests and lifting a ribbon here and a tail coat there.

Ross motioned to Jinny to carry round port and brandy. The more everyone drank the more they would talk, and the more they talked the less of a fiasco it would all be.

Carne waved away the tray.

"I have no truck wi' such things," he said. "Woe unto them that rise up early in the morning that they follow strong drink, that continue until night till wine do inflame them! I've finished wi' wickedness and bottledom and set my feet 'pon a rock of righteousness and salvation. Let me see the child, dattur."

Stiffly, grimly, Demelza held Julia out for inspection.

"My first was bigger than this," said Mrs. Chegwidden Carne, breathing hard over the baby. "Warn't he, Tom? Twelve month old he'll be August month. A 'andsome little fellow he be, though tis my own."

"What's amiss wi' er forehead?" Carne asked. "Have ee dropped 'ur?"

"It was in the birth," Demelza said angrily.

Julia began to cry.

Carne rasped his chin. "I trust ye picked her godparents safe and sure. Twas my notion to be one myself."

Near the stream the Teague girls tittered among themselves, but Mrs. Teague was on her dignity, drawing down her eyelids in their side-slant shutter fashion.

"A calculated insult," she said, "to bring in a man and a woman of that type and to *introduce* them. It is an affont set upon us by Ross and his kitchen slut. It was against my judgment that I ever came!"

But her youngest daughter knew better. This was no part of any plan but was a mischance she might put to good use. She took a glass from Jinny's tray and sidled behind her sister's back up to George Warleggan.

"Do you not think," she whispered, "that we are remiss in straying so far from our host and hostess? I have been to few christenings so I do not know the etiquette, but common manners would suggest . . ."

George glanced a moment into the slightly oriental green eyes. He had always held the Teagues in private contempt, an exaggerated form of the mixed respect and patronage he felt for the Poldarks and the Chynoweths and all those gentlefolk whose talent for commerce was in inverse rate to the length of their pedigrees. They might affect to despise him but he knew that some of them in their hearts already feared him. The Teagues were almost beneath his notice, maleless, twittering, living on three per cents and a few acres of land. But since her marriage Ruth had developed so rapidly that he knew he must reassess her. She, like Ross among the Poldarks, was of harder metal.

"Such modesty is to be expected in one so charming, ma'am," he said, "but I know no more of christenings than you. Do you not think it safest to consult one's own interests and follow where they lead?"

A burst of laughter behind them greeted the end of an anecdote Francis had been telling John Treneglos and Patience Teague.

Ruth said in an exaggerated whisper: "I think you should behave more seemly, Francis, if we are not to have a reprimand. The old man is looking our way."

Francis said: "We are safe yet. The wild boar always raises its hackles before it comes to the charge." There was another laugh. "You, girl," he said to Jinny as she passed near, "is that more of the canary you have? I will take another glass. You're a nice little thing; where did Captain Poldark find *you?*"

The stress was almost unconscious, but Ruth's laugh left no doubt of the way she took it. Jinny flushed up to the roots of her hair.

"I'm Jinny Carter, sur. Jinny Martin that was."

"Yes, yes." Francis's expression changed slightly. "I remember now. You worked at Grambler for a time. How is your husband?"

Jinny's face cleared. "Nicely, sur, thank you, so far as—so far as . . ."

"So far as you know. I trust the time will pass quickly for you both."

"Thank you, sur." Jinny curtsied, still red, and moved on.

"You are taking small interest in your goddaughter, Francis," Ruth said, anxious to turn him away from his squireish mood. "The infant is getting well quizzed in your absence. I'm sure she would appreciate a sup of canary."

"They say all the vulgars are brought up on gin," said Patience Teague. "And look no worse for it. I was reading but the other day how many, I forget how many, million gallons of gin was drunk last year."

"Not all by babies, Sister," said Treneglos.

"Well, no doubt they will sometimes take ale for a change," said Patience.

This had all been watched though not heard by Tom Carne. He turned his sharp obstinate eyes upon Mrs. Carne.

"Thur's ungodliness 'ere, Wife," he said through his beard. "Tis no proper place for a cheeil. Tis no fitty company to attend on a baptizing. I suspicioned no less. Women wi' their wanton clothes and young princocks strutting between 'em, drinkin' and jesting. Tis worse'n ye d'see in Truro."

His wife hunched up her shoulders. Her conviction was of longer standing and was by nature less belligerent. "We must pray for 'em, Tom. Pray for 'em all, and your own darter among 'em. Maybe there'll come a day when they'll see the light."

Julia would not be quieted so Demelza seized the excuse to take her indoors. She was in a despairing mood.

She knew that however the day might turn now it was a black failure to her. Full-flavoured meat for the gossips. Well, let it come. There was nothing more she could do. She had tried to be one of them and failed. She would never try again. Let them all go home, ride off at once, so that she might have done with everything. Only that she might be left alone.

A few moments after she had gone Ruth succeeded in edging her friends within earshot of Tom Carne.

"For my part," she said, "I have no care for liquor unless it be brandy or port; I like a good heavy drink, soft to the taste and no bite until it is well down. Don't you agree, Francis?"

"You remind me of Aunt Agatha," he said. "The conceits of a woman of discretion."

There was another laugh, against Ruth this time.

They were passing by Tom Carne and he stepped forward, playing exactly into Ruth's hands.

"One of ye be the cheeil's godfather?"

Francis bowed slightly. Viewed from behind there seemed a hint of satire in the way the rising wind twisted his coattails.

"I am."

Tom Carne stared at him.

"By what right?"

"Eh?"

"By what right do ye stand for the cheeil at the seat of righteousness?"

Francis had won heavily at the faro tables last night and he felt indulgent.

"Because I was so invited."

"Invited?" said Carne. "Aye, mebbe you were invited. But are ee saved?"

"Saved?"

"Aye, saved."

"Saved from what?"

"From the Devil and damnation."

"I haven't had any communication on the point."

John Treneglos guffawed.

"Well, that's where ye're at fault, mister," said Carne. "Them as has paid no heed to God's call has no doubt hearkened to the Devil's. Tes one or the other for all of we. There's no betwixt an' between. Tes Heaven an' all the angels or hell-fire an' the brimstone pit!"

"We have a preacher among us," said George Warleggan.

Mrs. Carne pulled at her husband's sleeve. Although she professed to despise the gentry she had not Carne's genuine contempt for them. She knew that outside the small circle of their own meetinghouse people like this ruled the material world. "Come away, Tom," she said. "Leave 'em be. They're in the valley o' the shadow, and nought will move 'em."

Ross, who had gone with Demelza into the house to try to encourage her to face it out, came again to the front door. The wind was gusty. He saw the argument and at once moved towards it.

Carne had thrown off his wife's arm.

"Four years ago," he was proclaiming in a voice which carried all over the garden, "I was a sinner against God and served the Devil in fornication an' drunkenness. Nay, there was the smell of sulphur 'pon me an' I was nigh to Hell. But the Lord showed me a great light and turned me to salvation, an' joy an' glory. But them as has not laid hold o' the blessing and is living in wickedness an' unrighteousness has no call or sanction to stand before the Lord to answer for a puking cheeil."

"I hope you find yourself rebuked, Francis," said Ruth.

Francis refused to be provoked.

"For my part," he said, eyeing Carne, "I am a little perplexed at this sharp division of the sheep and the goats, though I know it is often done by people of your complexion. What is the hallmark of the change? Are we of different flesh, you and I, that death should bring you a golden crown and me a seat in Hell's cockpit? Who's to say that you are a better keeper of the brat's religion than I? I ask you that in genuine inquiry. You say you are saved. *You* say it. But what's to prove it? What is to hinder me from saying that *I* am Grand Vizier and Keeper of the Seven Seals? What is to prevent me from running round and announcing *I* am saved, mine is the Kingdom and yours the damnation: *I'm* going to Heaven, *you* go to Hell!"

John Treneglos broke into a huge gust of laughter. Carne's fleshy dogmatic face was purpled up and spotty with anger.

"Leave un be," said Mrs. Carne sharply, dragging at him again. "'Tis the Devil himself temptin' of ee to vain argument."

The christening guests, as if under the pull of a magnet, had all drawn in towards this noisy focal point.

Ross came up behind the group.

"The wind is rising," he said. "The ladies would be better indoors. Perhaps you would help Aunt Agatha, Francis?" He made a gesture towards the old lady who, with an ancient instinct for trouble, had left her window seat and was tottering unaided across the lawn.

"Nay," said Carne. "I'll not be under the same roof wi' such evil thoughts." He stared sharply at Ruth. "Cover yer breast, woman, tis shameful an' sinful. Women ha' been whipped in the streets for less."

There was an awful pause.

"Damn your insolence!" Ruth snapped back, flushing. "If—if there's whipping to be done it's you that'll get it. John! Did you hear what he said!"

Her husband, whose mind was not agile and, being set to see the funny side, had at first seen no further, now swallowed a guffaw.

"You impudent splatty old pig!" he said. "D'you know who you're speaking to? Make an apology to Mrs. Treneglos at once, or, damme, I'll have your coat off your back!"

Carne spat on the grass. "If the truth do offend then it edn the truth that's at fault. Woman's place is to be clothed modest an' decent, not putting out lures for men, shameless an' brazen. If she was my wife, by Jakes——"

Ross stepped sharply between them and caught Treneglos's arm. For a moment he stared into the flushed angry face of his neighbour.

"My dear John. A common brawl! With all these ladies present!"

"Look to your own business, Ross! The fellow is insufferable——"

"Leave him come," said Carne. "Tes two year since I was in the ring, but I've a mind to show 'im a trick or two. If the Lord——"

"Come away, Tom," said Mrs. Carne. "Come away, Tom."

"But it is my business, John," said Ross, still staring at Treneglos. "You are both my guests, never forget. And I couldn't permit you to strike my father-in-law."

There was a moment's stunned silence, as if, although they knew the truth, the mere statement of it had shocked and quieted them all.

John tried to wrench his arm out of Ross's grip. He didn't succeed. His face got still pinker.

"Naturally," said Ruth, "Ross would wish to support one who has connived at all his schemes all along."

"Naturally," said Ross, releasing the arm, "I would wish to be on agreeable terms with my neighbours, but not at the price of allowing a brawl before my front door. The ladies don't like torn shirts and bloody noses." He looked at Ruth and at the little pink spots showing through her make-up. "At least, some of 'em do not."

Ruth said: "It is quite strange, Ross, how you look upon things since you married. I don't think you were lacking in all courtesy before. I hesitate to think what influence can have been at work to turn you out so boorish."

"I want an apology," Treneglos shouted. "My wife was grossly insulted by that man, father-in-law or no. Damme, if he was of my own status, I'd call him out for what he said! Would you swallow such impudence, Ross? Lord save us, you'd be the last! Rot an' perish me if I'll be content——"

"The truth's the truth!" Carne snapped. "An' blasphemy don't aid un to be anything other——"

"Hold your tongue, man." Ross turned on him. "If we want your opinions we'll invite 'em at a proper time." While Carne was speechless, he turned back to Treneglos. "Modes and manners vary with the breed, John; those with the same code can speak the same language. Will you allow me as host to apologize for such offence as this may have given you or your wife?"

Hesitating, a little mollified, John flexed his arm and grunted and glanced at the girl at his side. "Well, Ross, you spit it out well enough. I have no wish to go against that. If Ruth feels——"

Outmanoeuvred, Ruth said: "I confess I should have taken it better at an earlier stage. Naturally if Ross wishes to protect his new relative . . . Some allowance must be made for those who know no better by those who do."

A sudden wail from near by caused them all to turn. Aunt Agatha, neglected in the quarrel, had made fair speed across the grass, but just when she was nearing her quarry a mischievous gust had caught her. They saw a barely recognizable old lady crowned with a scum of grey hair, while a purple bonnet and a wig bowled along towards the stream. Francis and one or two of the others at once went in pursuit. Following them, floating down the wind, came a stream of curses from a Carolinian world none of the others had known. Even the Dowager Lady Bodrugan could not have done better.

An hour later Ross went upstairs to find Demelza lying in a sort of dry-eyed grief on the bed. All the guests had amiably gone, by foot or on horseback, clinging to hats; skirts and coattails flying in the wind.

Demelza had helped to see them off, smiling with fixed politeness until the last had turned his back. Then she had muttered an excuse and fled.

Ross said: "Prudie is looking for you. We didn't know where you were. She wants to know what is to be done with some of the foodstuffs."

She did not answer.

"Demelza."

"Oh, Ross," she said, "I am in a sore state."

He sat on the edge of the bed. "Never worry about it, my dear."

"It will be the talk of the district. Ruth Treneglos an' all the other Teagues will see to that."

"What is there to fret about? Tittle tattle. If they have nothing better to do than prate . . ."

"I am that grieved. I thought I would show 'em that I was a fit wife for you, that I could wear fine clothes and behave genteel an' not disgrace you. An' instead they will all ride home snickering behind their hands. 'Have you not heard about Cap'n Poldark's wife, the kitchen wench . . .' Oh, I could die!"

"Which would displease us all much more than a brush with John Treneglos." He put his hand on her ankle. "This is but the first fence, child. We have had a check. Well, we can try again. Only a faint heart would give up the race so soon."

"So you think I am a faint heart." Demelza withdrew her foot, feeling irrationally irritated with him. She knew that, of all the people this

37

afternoon, Ross had come out best. She faintly resented it because she felt that no one who cared could have been so unruffled; and because of this she faintly resented his manner now, seeing in it more patronage than sympathy, disliking for the first time his use of the word "child," as if it spoke more of condescension than love.

And at the back of everything was Elizabeth. Elizabeth had scored to-day. She had looked so beautiful, so poised and graceful, standing in the background, taking no part in the squabble. She had been content to be there. Her existence was enough, just her as a contrast, as an example of all Ross's wife was not. All the time he was sitting here, patting her foot and idly consoling her, he would be thinking of Elizabeth.

"The old man's Methodism," said Ross, "was grafted on a well-established tree. Moderation is not in him. I wonder what Wesley would say."

"Jud was at fault for ever telling 'em there was to be two parties," Demelza cried. "I could kill 'im for that!"

"My dear, in a week it will all be forgot and no one the worse. And to-morrow we have the Martins and the Daniels and Joe and Betsy Triggs and Will Nanfan and all the others. They will need no prompting to enjoy themselves and will jig on the lawns; and do not forget the travelling players are coming to give a play."

Demelza turned over on her face.

"I cannot go on, Ross," she said, her voice remote and muffled. "Send 'em all back word. I have done my most, and that is not enough. Maybe it's my own fault for takin' pride in pretending to be what I never can be. Well, it's over now. I cannot face any more. I ha'n't the heart."

CHAPTER IV   Three days before the christening there had been a stormy meeting of the Wheal Leisure venturers at which Ross and Dr. Choake had again got at loggerheads, Ross being all for development—Choake called it gambling—and Choake for consolidation—Ross called it obstruction—and the argument had ended by Ross's offering to purchase Choake's share of the mine for three times what he had put in. With great dignity Choake had accepted, so the morning after the christening Ross rode in to Truro to see his banker about raising the money.

Harris Pascoe, a little ageless man with steel spectacles and a stammer, confirmed the view that the mortgage on Nampara could be raised to cover it, but thought the purchase fantastically unbusinesslike at the price. Copper was at seventy-one now, and no one knew where it would end. There was a good deal of bitterness felt for the smelting companies, but what could you expect when often the metal had to lie idle for months before a buyer could be found? Ross liked Harris Pascoe and saw no point in arguing his own side of the case.

On his way out of the house he passed a young man whose face was known to him. He raised his hat and would have passed on, but the man stopped.

"How d'you do, Captain Poldark. It was kind of you to have me yesterday. I'm a stranger in these parts and appreciated your welcome."

Dwight Enys, whom Joan Pascoe had brought to the party. He had a good head and face; a look of courage strengthened the boyish turn of his cheek and jaw. Ross had never quite passed through this stage. He had gone to America a lanky youth and come back a war veteran.

"Your name suggests a local connection."

"I have second cousins here, sir, but one does not always wish to presume on relationship. My father came from Penzance, and I have been in London studying medicine."

"Is it your intention to go in for the profession?"

"I graduated as a physician early this year. But living in London is expensive. I thought to settle in this neighbourhood for a time to go on with my studies and to keep myself by taking a few patients."

"If your interest is in undernourishment or miners' complaints you will have subjects for your study."

Enys looked surprised. "Has someone told you?"

"No one has told me anything."

"It is the lungs really. It seemed to me that if one was to practise at the same time the proper place was among a mining community where consumption of the lungs is widespread."

The young man was losing his shyness.

"In the matter of fever too. There is so very much to be learned and experimented on. . . . But no doubt I bore you, sir. I am inclined to run on. . . ."

Ross said: "The surgeons I know are much more prone to talk of their successes in the hunting field. We must speak of it again."

After going a few paces he stopped and called Enys back.

"Where do you intend to live?"

"I am staying with the Pascoes for a month. I shall try to take a small house somewhere between here and Chacewater. There is no other medical man in that vicinity."

Ross said: "You know, perhaps, that I am interested in a mine which you may have seen from my house yesterday?"

"I did notice something. But no, I hadn't heard. . . ."

"The post of mine surgeon is at present vacant. I think I could get it for you if you were interested. It is very small of course; about eighty men at present, but it would bring you in some fourteen shillings a week and you would gain the experience."

Dwight Enys's face flushed with pleasure and embarrassment.

"I hope you did not think . . ."

"If I thought that I should not have suggested it."

"It would be a great help to me. That kind of work is what I wish. But . . . the distance would be considerable."

"I take it you have not settled on a house. There is scope in our neighbourhood."

"Is there not a surgeon of some repute?"

"Choake? Oh, there's room enough. He has private means and doesn't overwork. But think of it and let me know what you decide."

"Thank you, sir. You're very kind."

And if he's any good, Ross thought as he turned out into the street, I'll see if he can do something for Jim when he comes out, for Choake could not have done less. Carter had been in prison over a year now, and since he had somehow survived in spite of his morbid lung there seemed a hope that he would live through the next ten months and be restored to Jinny and his family. Ross had seen him in January and found him thin and weak; but, for prison life, conditions in Bodmin were supportable. Jinny and her father, Zacky Martin, had seen him twice, walking in one day and back the next; but twenty-six miles each way was too much for a girl who was still nursing her baby. He thought he would take her in himself sometime.

The quarrel with Choake would leave him irritatingly short of money just when he had begun to see his way clear to spend more on the luxuries of life. The necessities too, for he badly needed another horse. And the birth of Julia had involved him in fresh expense which he could not avoid and did not want to avoid.

He was annoyed with himself for having been so reckless.

He turned in at the Red Lion Inn, which was crowded, and chose a seat in the recess by the door. But his entry had not been unnoticed and after the potboy had been with his order a discreet footstep sounded near by.

"Captain Poldark? Good day to you. We do not often see you in town."

Ross looked up, a not very welcoming expression in his eyes. It was a man called Blewett, manager and part shareholder in Wheal Maid, one of the copper mines of the Idless Valley.

"No, I have no time to spare except for business visits."

"May I sit with you? The wool merchants in the parlour have no interest for me. Thank you. I see the price of copper has fallen again."

"So I have just learned."

"It must stop soon or we shall all be in bankruptcy."

"No one deplores that more than I," said Ross, reluctantly finding common cause with this man whom he disliked only for breaking into his private thoughts.

"One hopes for almost anything to stop the downward trend," Blewett said, setting down his glass and moving restlessly. "We have lost eight hundred pounds in trading this year. It is a big sum for people like ourselves."

Ross glanced up again. He saw that Blewett was really worried; there were dark pouches under his eyes, and his mouth sagged. Before him—and not far away—was the debtors' prison and starvation for his family. It was that which had made him risk the rebuff of a man who had a reputation for being unapproachable. Perhaps he had just come from a meeting with his fellow venturers and felt he must talk or suffocate.

"I don't think conditions can remain long as they are," Ross said. "There is an increasing use of copper in engines of all kinds. As the towns use more the price will recover."

"On a long view you may be right, but unhappily we are all committed to a short-term payment of loan interest. We have to sell the ore attle cheap to exist at all. If the copper and smelting companies were honestly run we might eke out this bad period. But what chance have we to-day?"

"I don't think it can be to the interest of the smelters to keep the prices down," Ross said.

"Not the market price, no, sir, but the price they pay us. It's all a ring, Captain Poldark, and we know it," Blewett said. "What chance have we of getting fair returns where the companies do not bid one against another!"

Ross nodded and stared at the people moving in and out of the inn. A blind man was feeling his way towards the bar.

"There are two ways to combat the evil."

Blewett grasped at the implication of hope. "What do you suggest?"

"I'd suggest what is not possible. The copper companies never hurt themselves by competitive bidding. Well, if the mines were in similar unity they could withhold supplies until the copper companies were prepared to pay more. After all, they cannot live without us; we are the producers."

"Yes, yes. I see what you mean. Go on."

At that moment a man passed the low window of the inn and turned in at the door. Ross's thoughts were on what he had been saying, and for some moments the familiar stocky figure and slightly wide-legged walk made no mark in his mind. Then he was jerked into attention.

The last time he had seen the man was years ago riding up the valley out of Nampara after his fight with Francis, whilst Verity stood and watched him go.

Ross lowered his head and stared at the table.

Between his eyes and the table top—as if he had been staring at the sun—was the visual image of what he had just seen. Fine blue coat, neat black cravat, lace at sleeves; stocky and rather impressive—the face was different, though; the lines deeper about the mouth, the mouth itself was tighter as if for ever held in, and the eyes full of self-assertion.

He did not look either way but went straight through into one of the parlours. A fortunate escape.

"What we need, Captain Poldark, is a leader," said Blewett eagerly. "A man of position who is upright and confident and can act for us all. A man, if I may say so, such as yourself."

"Eh?" said Ross.

"I trust you will pardon the suggestion. But in the mining world it is everyone for himself and Devil take your neighbour. We need a leader who can bind men together and help them to fight as a body. Competition is very well when the industry is booming, but we cannot afford it at times like these. The copper companies are rapacious—there is no other word. Look at the waste allowance they demand. If we could get a leader, Captain Poldark . . ."

Ross listened with fitful attention.

"What is your other suggestion?" Blewett asked.

"My suggestion?"

"You said there were two ways of combating the evil of our present conditions. . . ."

"The other solution would be for the mines to form a copper company of their own—one which would purchase the ore, build a smelting works close at hand and refine and sell their own products."

Blewett tapped his fingers nervously on the table.

"You mean—to—to . . ."

"To create a company which would bid independently and keep its profits for the men who run the mines. At present what profits there are go to South Wales or into the hands of merchants like the Warleggans, who have a finger in every pie."

Blewett shook his head. "It would take a large amount of capital. I wish it had been possible——"

"Not more capital than there was, than perhaps there is; but far more unity of purpose."

"It would be a splendid thing to do," said Blewett. "Captain Poldark, you have, if I may say so, the character to lead and to create unity. The companies would fight to squeeze the newcomer out, but it—it

42

would be a hope and an encouragement for many who see nothing but ruin staring them in the face."

Desperation had given Harry Blewett a touch of eloquence. Ross listened half in scepticism, half seriously. His own suggestions had become more clearly defined as he made them. But he certainly did not see himself in the role of leader of the Cornish mining interests. Knowing his men, their independence, their obstinate resistance to all new ideas, he could see what a tremendous effort would be needed to get anything started at all.

They sipped brandy over it for some time, Blewett seeming to find some comfort in the idle talk. His fears were the less for having been aired. Ross listened with an ear and an eye for Andrew Blamey.

It was nearly time to leave, Demelza, sorely stricken, having been persuaded overnight to go on with her second party. Blewett brought another man to the table, William Aukett, manager of a mine in the Ponsanooth Valley. Eagerly Blewett explained the idea to him. Aukett, a canny man with a cast in one eye, said there was no question but that it might save the industry—but where was the capital coming from except through the banks, which were tied up with the copper companies?

Ross, driven a little to defend his own idea, said well, there were influential people outside the copper companies. But of course this was no seeking venture that could be floated for five or six hundred. Thirty thousand pounds might be nearer the figure before it was ended—with huge profits or a complete loss as the outcome. One had to see it on the right scale before one could begin to see it at all.

These comments, far from depressing Blewett, seemed to increase his eagerness; but just as he had taken out a sheet of soiled paper and was going to call for pen and ink a crash shook the pewter on the walls of the room and stilled the murmur of voices throughout the inn.

Out of the silence came the sound of someone scrambling on the floor in the next parlour. There was a scurry of feet and the flash of a red waistcoat as the innkeeper went quickly into the room.

"This is no place for brawling, sir. There's always trouble when you come in. I'll have no more of it. I'll . . . I'll . . ."

The voice gave out. Another's took its place, Andrew Blamey's, in anger.

He came out, ploughing his way through those who had crowded to the door. He was not drunk. Ross wondered if drink ever had been his real trouble. Blamey knew a stronger master: his own temper.

Francis and Charles and his own early judgment had been right after all. To give the generous softhearted Verity to such a man . . .

Demelza must be told of this. It would put a stop to her pestering.

"I know him," Aukett said. "He's master of the *Caroline*, a brig on

Falmouth–Lisbon packet service. He drives his men; they say too he murdered his wife and children, though in that case how it comes that he is at large I do not know."

"He quarrelled with his wife and knocked her down when she was with child," Ross said. "She died. His two children were not concerned in it, so far as I am informed."

They stared at him a moment.

"It's said he has quarrelled with everyone in Falmouth," Aukett observed. "For my part I avoid the man. I think he has a tormented look."

Ross went to get his mare, which he had left to-day at the Fighting Cocks Inn. He saw nothing more of Blamey, but his way took him past the Warleggans' town house and he was held up for a moment by the sight of the Warleggan carriage drawing up outside their door. It was a magnificent vehicle made of rich polished wood with green and white wheels and drawn by four fine grey horses. There was a postillion, a driver and a footman, all in green and white livery, smarter than any owned by a Boscawen or a de Dunstanville.

The footman leapt down to open the door. Out of the carriage stepped George's mother, fat and middle-aged, wreathed in lace and silks but personally overshadowed by all the finery. The door of the big house came open and more footmen stood there to welcome her in. Passers-by stopped to stare. The house swallowed her. The magnificent carriage drove on.

Ross was not a man who would have gone in for display had he been able to afford it; but the contrast struck him to-day with special irony. It was not so much that the Warleggans could afford a carriage with four horses while he could not buy a second horse for the necessary business of life, but that these merchant bankers and ironmasters, sprung from illiteracy in two generations, could maintain their full prosperity in the middle of a slump, while worthy men like Blewett and Aukett—and hundreds of others—faced ruin.

CHAPTER V   The second christening party went off without a hitch. The miners and small holders and their wives had no mental reserves about enjoying themselves. It was Sawle Feast anyway, and if they had not been invited here most of them would have spent the afternoon in Sawle dancing or playing games or sitting in one of the kiddleys getting drunk.

The first half-hour at Nampara was a little constrained while the guests still remembered they were in superior company; but very soon the shyness wore off.

This was a summer feast in the old style, with no newfangled dainties to embarrass anyone. Demelza and Verity and Prudie had been working on it from early morning. Huge beef pies had been made: repeated layers of pastry and beef laid on top of each other in great dishes with cream poured over. Four green geese and twelve fine capons had been roasted; cakes made as big as millstones. There was bee wine and home-brewed ale and cider and port. Ross had reckoned on five quarts of cider for each man and three for each woman, and he thought that this would just be enough.

After the meal everyone went out on the lawn, where there were races for the women, a Maypole for the children and various games, drop the handkerchief, hunt the slipper, blind man's buff, and a wrestling competition for the men. After some bouts, the final match was between the two Daniel brothers, Mark and Paul, and Mark won, as was expected of him. Demelza presented him with a bright red kerchief. Then, having worked off some of their dinner, they were all invited in again to drink tea and eat heavy cake and saffron cake and gingerbreads.

The event of the evening was the visit of the travelling players. In Redruth the week before Ross had seen a tattered handbill nailed on a door, announcing that the Aaron Otway Players would visit the town that week to give a fine repertory of musical and sensational plays both ancient and modern.

He had found the leader of the company in the larger of the two shabby caravans in which they travelled and had engaged him to do a play in the library at Nampara on the following Wednesday. The lumber in the library had been moved to one end, the half-derelict room brushed out and planks put across boxes for the audience to sit on. The stage was defined by a few pieces of curtain cord tied together and stretched across the end of the room.

They performed *Elfrida or The Lost Wife*, a tragedy, by Johnson Hill, and afterwards a comic play called *The Slaughter House*. Jud Paynter stood at one side and came forward to snuff the candles when they grew too smoky.

To the country people it had all the thrill and glamour of Drury Lane. There were seven in the company; a mixed bag of semigipsies, ham actors and travelling singers. Aaron Otway, the leader, a fat sharp-nosed man with a glass eye, had all the showmanship of a huckster, and spoke the prologue and the *entr'acte* through his nose with tremendous gusto; he also acted the crippled father and the murderer, for which last part he wore a black cape, an eyeshade and a heavy black periwig. His time, like his cup later in the evening, was well filled. The heroine's part was played by a blonde woman of forty-five with a goitrous neck and large bejewelled hands; but the best actress of the company was a dark pretty slant-eyed girl of about nineteen, who acted the daughter with an unconvincing demureness and a woman of the streets with notable success.

Ross thought that with proper training she would go far. The chances were that neither opportunity nor training would come her way and that she would end up as a drab lurking at street corners or hang from a gibbet for stealing a gentleman's watch.

But other notions flickered through the head of a man sitting near. The gaunt Mark Daniel, tall and long-backed and powerful, was thirty, and never in his life had he seen anything to compare with this girl. She was so slender, so sleek, so glistening, so dainty, the way she stood on her toes, the way she bent her neck, her soft sibilant singing, the ochreous candle-reflecting glint of her dark eyes. To him there was nothing facile in her demureness. The smoky light showed up the soft young curve of her cheeks, the cheap gaudy costumes were exotic and unreal. She looked different from all other women, as if she came from a purer finer breed. He sat there unspeaking through the play and the singing which followed, his black Celtic eyes never leaving her when she was to be seen and staring vacantly at the back cloth when she had gone behind it.

After the play was over and drinks had gone all round, Will Nanfan got out his fiddle, Nick Vigus his flute and Pally Rogers his serpent. The benches were pushed back to the walls and dancing begun. These were not graceful restrained minuets but the full-blooded dances of the English countryside. They danced "Cuckolds All Awry," "All in a Garden Green" and "An Old Man's a Bedful of Bones." Then someone proposed "The Cushion Dance." A young man began by dancing round the room with a cushion, until after a while he stopped and sang "This dance I will no farther go," to which the three musicians replied in chorus, "I pray ee, good sir, why say so?" Then the dancer sang, "Because Betty Prowse will not come to," and the musicians shouted back, "She must come to whether she will or no." Then the man laid his cushion before the girl, she knelt on his cushion and he kissed her. After that they had to circle the room hand in hand singing, "Prinkum, prankum, is a fine dance, an' shall us go dance it over again." Then it was the girl's turn.

All went well and fun was fast until the old people were drawn in. Then Zacky Martin, intent on mischief, called out Aunt Betsy Triggs. Aunt Betsy, known for a comic when she got going, danced round with Zacky with a great flutter of skirts as if she was sixteen, not sixty-five. When it came to her turn to go alone she made a war dance of it, and at length she stopped at the end of the room. There was a great roar of laughter, for only one man was sitting there.

"This dance I will no farther go," she screeched.

"I pray ee, good ma'am, why say so?" shouted everybody in reply.

"Because Jud Paynter will not come to!" said Aunt Betsy.

Another roar and then everybody chorused:

"He *must* come to, whether he will or no!"

There was a sudden scuffle and shouts of laughter as several men pounced on Jud just as he was going to sneak away. Protesting and struggling he was brought to the cushion; he would not kneel so they sat him on it. Then Aunt Betsy flung her arms round his neck and kissed him lavishly—so lavishly that he overbalanced and they both went rolling on the floor together, boots and skirts flying. After more uproar they got to their feet and circled the room together, Jud sheepishly joining in the rest, his bloodshot bulldog eyes half peevish, half wily. It was now his choice. Even with Prudie watching it was still his choice, and she could do nothing, it being only a game.

When he was left alone he plodded slowly round, trying to remember what he had to sing. At last he stopped.

"Here I stays!" he said.

There was more laughter, so much that people could hardly answer him.

"I pr-pray ee, good sir, why say so?"

"Cos I wants Char Nanfan, that's why, see?" Jud glared round as if expecting opposition, showing his two great teeth.

Will Nanfan's second wife was one of the comeliest women in the room, with her great fair plaits bound about her head. Everyone looked to see how she would take it, but she pulled a face and laughed and meekly went forward and knelt on the cushion. Jud viewed the prospect with pleasure for a moment, then wiped his mouth slowly along the back of his sleeve.

He kissed her with great relish, while all the young men in the room gave out a groan.

Jud lingered on, but there suddenly came a great shout from Prudie, who could bear it no longer.

"Leave go, yer great ox! No call to make a meal of 'er!"

Jud hastily straightened up amid more shouts of laughter, and it was noticed that when he fell out of the ring he went back to his corner, which was a long way from his wife.

After a bit the game finished and the dancing began again. From all this Mark Daniel had held aloof. He had always looked down on such prancing as effeminate (his was a silent, gaunt uncompromising maleness, unimpressionable and self-sufficient), but now he noticed that two or three of the actors, having finished their supper, were joining in.

He could hold back no longer and risked an eight-handed reel, which needed no delicacy of step. Then, rubbing his chin and wishing he had shaved more carefully, he joined in a country dance. At the other end of the long line of people he saw the girl. Keren Smith they said her name was. He could not keep his eyes off her, and danced almost as if he did not see the people opposite him.

And in some way the girl knew of his gaze. She never once looked at him, but there was something in her expression which told him she knew, a little self-conscious pursing of her young red lips, the way once or twice she pushed back her hair and tossed her head. Then he saw that for a second or two they would have to dance together. He stumbled and felt the sweat start. The moment was near, the next couple were dancing back to their places: he was off down the line, and she coming to meet him. They met, he grasped her hands, they danced round, her hair flying, she looked up once straight into his eyes; the look was blinding, dazzling; then they separated, he back to his place, she to hers. Her hands had been cool, but the palms of his were tingling as if they had met ice, met fire, been shocked by the touch.

The dance was over. He walked solidly back to his corner. Other people about him were talking and laughing and did not notice any change. He sat down, wiped the sweat off his forehead and calloused hands, which were twice the size of hers and could have crushed them to pulp. He watched her covertly, hoping for another glance but not getting it. But women, he knew, could look without looking.

He joined in nearly all the rest hoping that he might come near her again, but it did not happen. Nanfan's son, Joe Nanfan, who ought to have known better, had somehow got talking to her, and he and a wizened little man from the troop took her attention.

Then the party began to break up. Before any grownups left, Zacky Martin, "scholar" of the neighbourhood and father of Jinny, got up and said a little piece, about what a brave time they had had, one and all, and how they'd all eaten enough to last 'em a week and drunk enough to last 'em a fortnight and danced enough to last 'em a month. And how twas only fitty here and now to say thank you kindly for a handsome day and all the generosity, to Captain Poldark and Mistress Poldark, and Miss Verity Poldark, and to wish long life and prosperity to them and theirs, not forgetting Miss Julia, and might she grow up a pride to her father and mother as he was sure she would, and that was all he had to say except thank you kindly again and good night.

Ross had them all served with a stiff glass of brandy and treacle.

When they had drunk it he said, "Your good wishes are of great value to me. I want Julia to grow up in this countryside as a daughter of mine and as a friend of yours. I want the land to be a part of her inheritance and friendship her earning from it. I give you our good wishes for the health and happiness of all *your* children, and may we all see a prosperous county and better times together."

There was a rapturous cheer at this.

The Martins stayed behind—Mrs. Zacky to help her daughter with the clearing up—so the Daniels went home alone.

Leading the way Grannie Daniel and Mrs. Paul supported Mark's elder brother between them; then just behind, like frigates behind ships of the line, came Paul's three young children. A little to the left, heads close together in whispered talk, were Mark's two sisters, Mary and Ena; at the rear Old Man Daniel hobbled and grunted, and the long silent figure of Mark made up the convoy.

It was a pleasant July night with the western sky still luminous, as from the reflection of a lighted window. Now and then a cockchafer would drone past their ears and a bat lift fluttering wings in the dusk.

Once they had left the stream behind, the only babble was that of Grannie Daniel, a hearty fierce old woman in the late seventies.

The convoy, shadowy uneven figures in the shadowy half dark, breasted the rise of the hill, bobbed and stumbled on the sky line for a few seconds and then plunged down towards the cluster of cottages at Mellin. The valley swallowed them up and left only the quiet stars and the night glow of summer over the sea.

In his bed Mark Daniel lay very quiet listening. Their cottage, set between the Martins and the Viguses, had only two bedrooms. The smaller of these was used by Old Man Daniel and his mother and the eldest of Paul's three children. The other one Paul and his wife Beth and their two younger children took, while Mary and Ena slept in a lean-to at the back of the cottage. Mark slept on a straw mattress in the kitchen.

Everyone was a long time settling off, but at last when the house was quiet he stood up and drew on his breeches and coat again. He did not put on his boots until he was safe outside.

The silence of the night was full of tiny noises after the enclosed silence of the cottage. He set off in the direction of Nampara.

He did not know what he was going to do, but he could not lie and sleep with this thing inside him.

This time there was no silhouette on the sky line, but for a moment the trunk of a tree thickened and then a shadow moved beside the ruined engine house of Wheal Grace.

Nampara was not yet in darkness. Candles gleamed behind the curtains of Captain Poldark's bedroom and there was a light flickering about downstairs. But it was not for these that he looked. Some way up the valley beside the stream were the two caravans which housed the strolling players. He went towards them.

He saw as he drew nearer that there were lights here too, though they had been screened by the hawthorn and wild nut trees. For a man of his size he moved quietly, and he came close to the larger caravan without raising an alarm.

No one was asleep here or thought of it. Candles burned and the players were sitting about a long table. There was much talk and laughter and the chink of money. Mark crept near, keeping open a wary eye for a possible dog.

The windows of the caravan were some distance from the ground, but with his great height he could see in. They were all here: the fat man with the glass eye, the blowsy leading woman, a thin fair man who had played the hero, the shrivelled little comedian . . . and the girl. They were playing some card game, with thick greasy cards. The girl was just dealing, and as she laid a card each time opposite the thin fair man she said something that made them all laugh. She was wearing a kind of Chinese smock and her black hair was ruffled as if she had been running her hands through it; she sat now holding her cards, one bare elbow on the table and a frown of impatience growing.

But there is a stage when even the slightly imperfect is an added lure; somehow Mark was grateful for this falling short from divinity: he stood there looking in, one great hand holding back a prickly hawthorn bough, the uncertain light from the window setting shadows and mock expressions on his face.

There was a sudden roar of laughter, and in a moment the comedian was gathering in all the pennies on the board. The girl was angry, for she flung away her cards and stood up. The fair man leered at her and asked a question. She shrugged and tossed her head; then her mood changed, and with incredible swift grace she slid, pliant as a sapling, round the table to bend and kiss the comedian's bald head, at the same time drawing two pennies away from under his lifted fingers.

Too late, he saw through it and snatched at her hand, but she danced away, showing her fine teeth in glee, and took shelter behind the fair man, who fended off the angry comedian. Almost before Mark could realize it, she was out of the caravan, banging the door and giggling with triumph. Too occupied to notice him in the dark, she ran towards her own caravan fifty yards up the valley.

Mark sank back into the shadows as the comedian came to the door and shouted and swore after her. But he did not follow, for the blowsy woman squeezed past.

"Leave her go," she said. "You ought to know she's still a child, Tupper. She can't bear to lose at a game of cards."

"Child or not, she stole the price of a glass of gin! I've seen folk ducked and whipped for less! Who do she think she is; Queen o' Sheba, with her airs? Dang and rot all women! I'll have her in the morning. D'you 'ear, Kerenhappuch! I'll 'ave you in the morning, you sneavy little dumdolly!"

The answer was the slamming of a door. The leader of the troop elbowed his way past the woman.

"Stop this noise! Don't forget we're still on Poldark land, friends, an' though he's treated us good, you wouldn't get soft smoothing if you found yourself on the wrong side of him! Leave the little neap alone, Tupper."

The others, grumbling and talking, went in, the woman walking across to the other caravan.

Mark stayed where he was, crouching in the bushes. There was nothing more he could do or see, but he would wait until all was quiet. He would not sleep if he went home, and he was due at Grambler Mine at six.

There was a light now in the other caravan. He straightened up and moved in a semicircle towards it. As he did so the door of the caravan opened and someone came out. There was the clatter of a bucket, and he saw a figure coming towards him. He ducked down into the bushes.

It was Keren.

She passed close to him and went on her way whistling some song softly between her teeth. The clank, clank of the wooden bucket went with her, blatant among the softer noises of the copse.

He followed. She was making for the stream.

He came up with her as she knelt to scoop up a bucketful. They were some distance from the caravan, and he watched a moment and heard her swear impatiently, for the stream was shallow and she never had the bucket more than a third full.

He stepped out of the bushes.

"You rightly d'need a pot or a pan to——"

She turned and half screamed.

"Leave me alone you . . ." Then she saw it was not the comedian and screamed louder.

"I mean no 'arm," said Mark, his voice quiet and sounding firm. "Hush, or you'll rouse the valley."

She stopped as quickly as she had begun and stared up at him.

"Oh . . . it's you. . . ."

Half pleased to be known, half doubtful, he looked down at the delicate oval of her face.

"Yes." It was lighter here away from the overhanging trees. He could see the moist gleam of her bottom lip.

"What d'you want?"

"I thought to aid you," he said.

He picked up the bucket and went out into the middle of the stream where there was a narrow channel. Here he was able to fill the bucket and brought it to her side.

"What're you doin' sneakin' around here so late at night?" she asked sharply.

He said: "I reckon I liked that, what you did to-night. I . . . liked that play."

"Do you live . . . at the house?"

"No. Over there."

"Where?"

"Down in Mellin Hollow."

"What d'you do?"

"Me? I'm a miner."

She moved her shoulders distastefully. "That's not a pretty job, is it?"

"I . . . liked the play acting," he said.

She looked at him obliquely, taking in the size of him, the set of his shoulders. She could see no expression on the shadowy face turned to her.

"Was it you that won the wrestling?"

He nodded, not showing his pleasure. "But you wasn't——"

"Oh, I wasn't there. But I heard."

"That play," he began.

"Oh, that." She pouted her lips, turning her profile against the lighter sky. "Did you like me in it?"

". . . Yes."

"I thought you did," she said calmly. "I'm pretty, aren't I?"

". . . Yes," he answered, forcing out the word.

"You'd best be going now," she advised.

He hesitated, fumbling with his hands. "Won't you stay and talk for a while?"

She laughed softly. "What for? I got better ways of passing my time. Besides, I'm surprised at you. It's very late."

"Yes," he said, "I know."

"You'd best be off before they come lookin' for me."

"Shall you be at Grambler to-morrow night?"

"Oh, yes. I expect."

"I'll be there," he said.

She turned and picked up the bucket.

"I'll carry that," he said.

"What? Back to the camp? No, indeed."

"I'll look for ee to-morrow," he said.

"I'll look for you too," she answered back over her shoulder, carelessly.

"You will?"

"Yes . . . maybe." The words floated to him, for she had gone, the clank of the bucket dulled and sibilant now as it receded.

He stood a moment. "All right, then!" he called.

He turned and walked home under the quiet stars, his long powerful stride longer than ever and his slow steady careful mind moving in uncharted seas.

CHAPTER VI   Demelza a few mornings later was eating a silent breakfast and scheming. Ross should have known by now that silence at a mealtime was an ominous symptom. For a few days after the christening catastrophe she had been subdued, but that had been gone some time now. Although she had fully intended to brood her nature had defeated her.

"When was it you was thinking to ride in an' see Jim?" she asked.

"Jim?" he said, coming down from thoughts of copper companies and their misdeeds.

"Jim Carter. You said you was minded to take Jinny in with you next time."

"So I am. I thought next week. That's if you can spare her and have no objections."

Demelza glanced at him.

"It is all one to me," she said awkwardly. "Shall you be one night away?"

"The gossips have minds like a jericho, and there are some who will whisper over my riding off in the company of a serving maid. Er . . ." He paused.

"Of *another* serving maid?"

"Well, if you put it so. Jinny is not uncomely and they will have no regard for my good name."

Demelza put up two fingers to push away a curl.

"What's your own mind, Ross?"

He smiled slightly. "They may whisper till their tongues swell, and have done before to-day."

"Then go," she said. "I'm not afeared of Jinny Carter, or the old women."

Once the day had been fixed, the next thing was to get a message

53

over to Verity. On the Monday morning, Ross being busy at the mine, she walked the three miles to Trenwith House.

She had only been to the house of her superior cousins-by-marriage once before; and when she came in sight of its mullioned windows and mellow Elizabethan stone she modestly made a circuit to come upon it again from the rear.

She found Verity in the still-room.

Demelza said: "No, thank ee. We're brave an' well. I came to ask you for the loan of a horse, Verity dear. It is rather a secret, I didn't wish for Ross to know; he's going, next Thursday he's going to Bodmin to see Jim Carter that's in prison an' takin' Jinny Carter with him, so that there's no horse for me to go to Truro, as I wanted to go while Ross is away."

Their eyes met. Demelza, though slightly breathless, looked empty of guile.

"I'll lend you Random if you wish. Is this to be a secret from me also?"

"No, indeed," Demelza said. "For I couldn't borrow a horse if it was a secret from you, could I?"

Verity smiled. "Very well, my dear, I'll not press you. But you cannot go to Truro alone. We have a pony we can loan you for Jud."

"There's no tellin' what time Ross'll be gone on Thursday, so we'll walk over for the horses if it is all the same to you, Verity. Maybe you'll leave us come in this way, then Francis and—and Elizabeth wouldn't know."

"It is all very mysterious, I assure you. I trust I'm not conniving at some misadventure."

"No, no, indeed. It is just . . . something I have had a mind to do for a long time."

"Very well, my dear."

Verity smoothed down the front of her blue dimity frock. She looked plain and prim this morning. One of her old-maidish days. Demelza's heart almost failed her at the enormity of her intention.

Ross looked about him with an appreciative eye as he rode up the valley early on Thursday morning with Jinny Carter silent beside him on old near-blind Ramoth. This land of shallow soil soon exhausted itself, and one had to give the ground ample time to recover from a cereal crop; but the fields he had chosen for this year were bearing well. They were all colours from pea green to a biscuit brown. A good harvest would be some compensation for the storm damage in the spring.

As he disappeared over the hill Demelza turned and went indoors. All the day was before her now, all to-day and part of to-morrow if necessary; but Julia put a shorter time limit on her actions. If she was fed at seven she would do well enough with some sugar and water at noon, which Prudie could give her, and then she would last out till five.

Ten hours. There was much to do in the time. "Jud!"

"Ais?"

"Are you ready?"

"Well, pick me liver, I only seen Mr. Ross out of the 'ouse two minutes."

"We've precious little time to waste. If I ain't—if I'm not back before five little Julia'll be cryin' out, and me perhaps miles away."

"A danged misthought notion from last to first," said Jud, putting his bald fringed head round the door. "There's them as'd say I'd no leave to lend meself to such fancy skims. Tedn sensible. Tedn right. Tedn '*uman*. . . ."

"Tedn for you to argue all morning," said Prudie, appearing behind him. "Ef she say go, go and begone. Ef there's a dido with Mr. Ross that's for she to suffer."

"I aren't so sartin," said Jud. "I don't know, not I. There's no saying wi' womenfolk 'ow they'll jump when the screw's on 'em. Cuzzle as a cartload o' monkeys. Well, I'm warning ye. If I take the fault for this, may I be 'anged for a fool." He went off grumbling to get his best coat.

They left soon after seven and picked up the horse and pony at Trenwith House. Demelza had dressed herself carefully to-day in her new close-fitting blue riding habit cut after a masculine style, with a pale blue bodice to give it a touch of something different and a three-cornered small brimmed hat. She kissed Verity and thanked her very affectionately, as if she thought the warmth of her hug would make up for all the deceit.

Jud's presence was useful, for he knew the way to Falmouth across country by narrow lane and mule track, and they touched no town or village where they might be recognized.

Nothing in these hamlets passed unnoticed or unremarked. Every tinner and farm worker stopped in his work, hand on hips, to look over the ill-assorted couple, Jud ugly and whistling on his little shaggy pony, she young and handsome on her tall grey horse. Every cottage had its peering face.

They had no watch between them, but two or three hours before midday they caught a gleam of blue and silver water, and she knew she must be near.

They lost the river among the trees and began sharply to pick their way down a dusty hill with cart ruts, and found themselves among cottages. Beyond the cottages was a great landlocked harbour and the masts of ships. Now her heart began to beat. The hazard of the day began. All her private imaginings in the quiet of the night were to come up against the hard and difficult truth. Her own view of Verity's lover, a soft-spoken, handsome middle-aged sailor, and the picture that Ross had raised by his description of the scene in Truro; these had to be reconciled and confronted with the truth before anything else was begun.

After a few minutes they reached a cobbled square, and the water glittered like a silver plate between some houses of larger size. There were plenty of people in the streets who seemed in no hurry to move aside for a couple of riders. Jud pushed his way through shouting and swearing.

At the other side they looked upon a quay pyramided with merchandise which was being unloaded from a longboat. Demelza stared about her, faintly mesmerized. A group of blue-coated sailors with pigtails stared up at the girl on the horse. A big Negress went by; and two dogs were quarrelling over a crust. Someone leaned out from an upper window and threw more refuse in the road.

"Wot now?" said Jud, taking off his hat and scratching his head.

"Ask someone," she said. "That's the proper way."

"Thur's no one t'ask," said Jud, staring round at the crowded square. Three important-looking sailors with gold braid on their uniforms were past before Demelza could decide. Jud sucked his two great teeth. She edged her horse past some urchins playing in the gutter and closed up to four men who were talking together on the steps of one of the large houses. Prosperous merchants, fat-stomached and bewigged.

She knew that Jud should have done the asking but could not trust his manners. At that moment Random chose to side-step, and the clatter of his hooves on the cobbles took their attention.

"I beg your pardon for the interference," Demelza said in her best voice, "but could you please to direct me to the house of Captain Andrew Blamey."

They all pulled off their hats. Nothing quite like that had ever happened to Demelza before. They took her for a lady and it made her blush.

One said: "Pardon me, ma'am, I didn't catch the name."

"Captain Andrew Blamey of the Lisbon packets."

She caught an exchanged glance.

"He lives at the end of the town, ma'am. Down this street, ma'am. Perhaps one third of a mile. But the packet agent would direct you, if you called on him. He could also inform you if Captain Blamey is home or at sea."

"He's home," said another. "The *Caroline's* due to sail on Saturday forenoon."

"I'm greatly obliged to ye," said Demelza. "Down this street, you said? Thank you. Good day."

They bowed again; she touched her horse and went off. Jud, who had been listening with his mouth open, followed slowly, muttering about fine feathers.

They trekked up a long narrow lane, mainly squalid huts and court-yards with here and there a house or a tiny shop, the land climbing steeply away among trees and scrub to the right. The harbour held two or three dozen ships in an almost closed hand: she had seen nothing like it in her life, accustomed as she was to the sight of an occasional brig or cutter beating away from the land on the dangerous north coast.

They were directed to one of the better houses with a room built out over the front door to form a pillared porch. This was more imposing than she had expected.

She got down stiffly and told Jud to hold her horse. Her habit was thick with dust, but she knew of no place to go and tidy herself.

"I'll not be long," she said. "Don't go away an' don't get drunk or I'll ride home wi'out you."

"Drunk," said Jud, wiping his head. "No one 'as the call to leave that at my door. Many's the week as passes an' never a drop of liquor. Many's the time I ain't gotten the spittle for a fair good spit. That dry. An' you says drunk. *You* says drunk. Why, I mind the time when you was tiddley on account of findin' a bottle o' grog, an' twas——"

"Stay here," said Demelza, turning her back. "I'll not be gone long."

She pulled at the bell. Jud was a spectre of old times. Forget him. Face this. What would Ross say if he could see her now? And Verity. Base treason. She wished she had never come. She wished . . .

The door opened and Jud's grumblings died away.

"I wish to see Captain Blamey, please."

"He bain't in, ma'am. He did say he'd be back afore noon. Would ye wait?"

"Yes," said Demelza, swallowing and going in.

She was shown conversationally into a pleasant square room on the first floor. It was panelled with cream-painted wood and there was a model ship among the littered papers on the desk.

"What name sh'll I tell him?" asked the old woman, coming to the end of her chatter.

At the last moment Demelza withheld the vital word. "I'd better prefer to tell him that myself. Just say a—er—someone . . ."

"Very well, ma'am."

The door closed. Demelza's heart was thumping in her breast. She listened to the woman's self-important footsteps receding down the stairs.

The documents on the desk took her curiosity, but she was afraid to go over and peer at them and her reading was still so slow.

A miniature by the window. Not Verity. His first wife whom he had knocked down to die? Little framed silhouettes of two children. She had forgotten his children. A painting of another ship, it looked like a man-of-war. From here she found she could see the lane outside.

She edged nearer the window. Jud's shiny head. A woman selling oranges. He was swearing at her. Now she was swearing back. Jud seemed scandalized that anyone could match his own bad words. "Captain Blamey," she would say, "I have come to see ee—to see you about my cousin." No, first she'd best make sure he was not married again to someone else. "Captain Blamey," she would begin. "Are you married again?" Well, she couldn't say that. What did she hope to do? "Leave it alone," Ross had warned. "It's dangerous to tamper with other people's lives." That was what she was doing, against all orders, all advice.

There was a map on the desk. Lines were traced across it in red ink. She was about to go and look when another noise in the street drew her notice again.

Under a tree a hundred yards back were a group of seamen. A rough lot, bearded and pigtailed and ragged, but in the middle of them was a man in a cocked hat talking to them in some annoyance. They pressed around him, angry and gesticulating, and for a moment he seemed to disappear among them. Then his hat showed again. The men stepped back to let him through, but several still shouted and shook their fists. The group closed up behind and they stood together staring after him. One picked up a stone but another grasped his arm and stopped him from throwing it. The man in the cocked hat walked on without glancing behind.

As he came nearer the house Demelza felt as if the lining of her stomach was giving way. She knew by instinct that this was the person she had plotted and schemed and ridden twenty miles to see.

But for all Ross's warnings she had not imagined he would be like this. Did he never do anything but quarrel with people, and was this the man for loss of whom Verity was sere and yellow before her time? In a flash Demelza saw the other side of the picture, which up till now had evaded her, that Francis and Old Charles and Ross might be right and Verity's instinct at fault, not theirs.

In panic she looked at the door to gauge her chance of escape; but the outer door slammed and she knew it was too late. There was no drawing back now.

She stood rigidly by the windows and listened to the voices below in the hall. Then she heard a tread on the stairs.

He came in, his face still set in hard lines from his quarrel with the seamen. Her first thought was that he was old. He had taken off his cocked hat and wore his own hair: it was grey at the temples and specked with grey on the crown. He must be over forty. His eyes were blue and fierce and the skin was drawn up around them from peering into the sun. They were the eyes of a man who might have been holding himself always ready for the first leap forward of a race.

He came across to the desk and put his hat on it, looked directly at his visitor.

"My name is Blamey, ma'am," he said in a hard clear voice. "Can I be of service to you?"

All Demelza's prepared openings were forgotten. She was overawed by his manner and his authority.

She moistened her lips and said: "My name is Poldark."

It was as if some key had turned in the inner mechanism of this hard man, locking away before it could escape any show of surprise or sentiment.

He bowed slightly. "I haven't the honour of your acquaintance."

"No, sir," said Demelza. "No. You d'know my husband, Captain Ross Poldark."

There was something ship-like about his face, jutting and aggressive and square, weathered but unbeaten.

"A few years ago I had occasion to meet him."

She could not shape the next sentence. With her hand she felt the chair behind her, and sat in it.

"I've rid twenty miles to see you."

"I am honoured."

"Ross don't know I've come," she said. "Nobody knows I've come."

His unflinching eyes for a moment left her face and travelled over her dusty dress.

"I can offer you some refreshment?"

"No. . . . No. . . . I must leave again in a few minutes." Perhaps that was a mistake, for tea or anything would have given her ease and time.

There was a strained pause. Under the window the quarrel with the orange woman broke out afresh.

"Was that your servant at the door?"

"Yes."

"I thought I recognized him. I should have known."

His voice left no doubt of his feelings.

She tried once again. "I—mebbe I shouldn't ought to have come, but I felt I must. I wanted to see you."

"Well?"

"It is about Verity."

Just for a moment his expression grew embarrassed; that name could no longer be mentioned. Then he abruptly glanced at the clock. "I can spare you three minutes."

Something in the glance quenched the last of Demelza's hopes. "I been wrong to come," she said. "I think there's nothing to say to you. I made a mistake, that's all."

"Well, what is it you made a mistake in? Since you are here you'd best say it."

"Nothing. Nothing will be any use saying to the likes of you."

He gave her a furious look. "I ask you, tell me."

She glanced at him again.

"It is about Verity. Ross married me last year. I knew nothing about Verity till then. An' she never told me a thing. I persuaded it out of Ross. About you, I mean. I love Verity. I'd give anything to see 'er happy. An' she isn't happy. She's never got over it. She's not the sort to get over it. Ross said it was dangerous to meddle. He said I must leave it alone. But I couldn't leave it alone till I'd seen you. I—I thought Verity was right an' they was wrong. I—I had to be sure they was right before I could let it drop."

Her voice seemed to go on and on, into an arid empty space. She said: "Are you married again?"

"No."

"I schemed to-day. Ross has gone Bodmin. I borrowed the horses and came over with Jud. I'd best be getting back, for I've a young baby at home."

She got up and slowly made for the door.

He caught her arm as she went past him.

"Is Verity ill?"

"No," Demelza said angrily. "Ailing but not ill. She looks ten years olderer than her age."

His eyes were suddenly fierce with pain.

"D'you not know the whole story? They cannot fail to have told you the whole story."

"Yes, about your first wife. But if I was Verity——"

"You're not Verity. How can you know what she feels?"

"I don't, but I——"

"She never once sent me any word. . . ."

"Nor you never sent her any word neither."

"Has she ever said anything?"

"No."

"Then it's pitiable. . . . This attempt on your part . . . this—this intrusion. . . ."

"I know," said Demelza, nearly crying. "I know now. I thought to help Verity, but I wisht now I'd never tried. You see, I don't understand. If folk in our way love one another it is more than enough to bring 'em together, drink or no. If the father's against it then that's some reason, but now the father's dead an' Verity's too proud to make any move. And you—and you . . . But I thought you were different. I thought——"

"You thought I was likely to sit moping my time away. No doubt the rest of your family has long since written me off as a failure and a drunkard, drooling in taprooms and lurching home of a night. No doubt Miss Verity has long since agreed with her weakling brother that it was better for all that Captain Blamey was sent about his business. What for——"

"How dare you say that of Verity!" Demelza cried out, standing up to him. "How dare you! An' to think I've rid myself sore to hear it! To think I've schemed and plotted and lied and borrowed the horses and one thing and the next. An' to say such of Verity when she's ill for pining of you! Judas God! Leave me get out of here!"

He barred her way. "Wait."

His epaulettes and gold braid no longer counted.

"Wait for what? For more insults? Let me past or I shall call Jud!"

He took her arm again. "It is no reflection on you, girl. I grant you did it all from the best of motives. I grant you your good will——"

She was trembling, but with great self-control did not try to wrench her arm free.

For a moment he did not go on, but peered at her closely as if trying to see all that she had not said. His own anger was suddenly in ashes. He said:

"We've all moved on since those days, grown, changed. It's—you see, it's all forgotten, behind us—but it has left us bitter. There were times when I ranted and railed—if you understood—if you'd known it all you'd see that. When you stir up old things best forgotten you're bound to stir up some of the mud that's settled round 'em."

"Leave go my arm," she said.

He made a brief awkward gesture and turned away. She went stiffly to the door and grasped the handle.

She glanced back. He was staring out towards the harbour. She hesitated a second longer and there came a knock at the door.

No one answered it. Demelza stepped aside as the handle turned. It was the woman who looked after him.

"Beg pardon. Did you want something, sir?"

"No," said Blamey.

"Your dinner's ready."

Blamey turned and glanced at Demelza.

"Will you stay and take a meal with me, ma'am?"

"No," said Demelza. "Thank you. I'd best be getting back."

"Then perhaps you will first show Mistress Poldark to the door."

The woman bobbed. "Yes, surely, sir."

Conversationally she led Demelza downstairs again. She warned her to mind the step for the light was none too good, the curtain being drawn to keep the carpet from fading as this window looked due south. She said the day was warm and there might be thunder, it being a bad sign that St. Anthony's Head was so clear. Still talking, she opened the front door and wished her visitor good day.

Outside in the street Jud was sitting blinking on a stone wall beside her pony. He was sucking an orange he had filched from the orange woman's cart.

"Finished already, Mrs.?" he said. "Reckoned 'e'd soon do for ee. Well, all's for the best, I reckon, as leaves well alone."

Demelza did not reply. Captain Blamey was still watching her from the upper room.

CHAPTER VII   Julia had wind and was thoroughly cross; Demelza had sore buttocks and was thoroughly disheartened. They made a mopish pair, while Jud took the two animals back to Trenwith and Prudie grumbled over the evening meal.

Julia, fed and changed, went into a fitful sleep but Demelza, feeding by herself for the first time in the parlour, swallowed her food anyhow and in lumps, hating the thought of her own defeat but knowing that the defeat was final. Ross had been right. Even Francis had been right. There would never have been hope for a happy marriage for Verity. And yet . . .

Oh, well . . .

There broke upon her deep reflections, levering a way like a swollen female Caliban into her absent mind, the amorphous figure of Prudie. It stood there beside the boiled beef talking at her, making growling and discordant claims on her attention, until at last she was forced to give it.

"Eh?" she said.

Prudie stared back at her, seeing that she had been wasting her breath.

"Got the mullygrubs, 'ave ee, an?"

"No, Prudie, but I'm feeling tired an' cross. And I'm that sore I can scarce sit down. I can't reckon how it is but everytime I touch a bone I go 'Oohh!' "

"There's naught t'wonder at in that, maid. . . . 'Osses, I always d'say, is not for ridin' whether saddled or bare-ridged, side-sat or ascrode. Have 'em hitched to a cart an' that's different. But then a ox do do as well, an' twice as peaceable. Only onct 'ave I bin on a 'oss an' that were when Jud brought me from Bedruthan nigh on sixteen year ago. Twere an irkish kind of a journey, up 'ill an' down dell, wi' no rest neither for flesh nor bone. That night I smeared axle grease all over me what's-it, an' none too soon for taking care, else the skin would've bursten, I bla'. I tell ee what I'll do for ee. When you've took yer clothes off I'll come rub ee over them parts wi' some balsam I got at Marasanvose Fair, an?"

"I'll be well enough," said Demelza. "Leave me be. I'll sleep on my face to-night."

"Well, that's as you d'please. I came to tell ee that Mark Daniel's outside by the kitchen door besting whether to come in and see you or no."

Demelza sat up and winced. "Mark Daniel? What does he want with me?"

"Nothin' by rights. He come first at noon. They're from home, I says, an'll not be back, she afore supper, I says, an' he afore cockshut to-morrow, I says. Oh, he says, an' goes off an' comes back and says what time did ye say Mistress Poldark would be back, he says, an' I says supper to-night, I says, an' off he d'go wi' his long legs stalking."

"Has he asked for me to-night?"

"Aye, and I told him you was suppin' an' not to be disturbed by the likes of he. Gracious knows, there's enough fuss one way and the next without all the bal-men in district callin' round to pass the time o' day."

"He must want more than that," Demelza said, and yawned. She straightened her frock and patted her hair. "You'd best show him in."

She felt lonely and important to-night. The last time Ross had ridden to Bodmin she had had Verity to stay.

Mark came in twisting his cap. In the parlour he looked enormous.

"Oh, Mark," she said, "did you want to see Ross? He's from home and is lying to-night at Bodmin. Was it important or shall you wait until to-morrow?"

He looked younger too in the evening light and without his cap, his head bent for fear of the ceiling beams.

"I wish twas easier to explain, Mistress Poldark. I did ought to have called in to Cap'n Ross yesterday, but twasn't quite decided then, an' I didn't fancy to tell my chickens afore they was bealed. An' now—an' now there's the need to hurry, because . . ."

Demelza rose, careful to avoid grimaces, and went to the window. It would not be dark yet for an hour, but the sun was winking out behind the western rim of the valley and shadows were deepening among the trees. She knew that Mark was a special friend of Ross's, second only to Zacky Martin in his confidences, and she was a little flustered at his call.

He was waiting for her to speak and watching her.

"Why don't you sit down, Mark, an' tell me what it is that's troubling you?"

Presently she looked round and saw that he was still standing.

"Well, what is it?" she said.

His long dark face twitched once. "Mistress Poldark, I have the thought to be married."

She gave a little relieved smile.

"Well, I'm glad, Mark. But why should that be worrying you?" As he did not speak she went on: "Who have you the mind for?"

"Keren Smith," he said.

"Keren Smith?"

"The maid that came wi' the travelling players, mistress. The dark one wi' the—wi' the long hair and the smooth skin."

Demelza's mind went back. "Oh," she said. "I know." She did not like to sound unpleased. "But what do she say to it? Are they still hereabouts?"

They were still hereabouts. Standing by the door, grim and quiet, Mark told his story. And much that he did not say could be guessed. Almost every night since their first meeting he had followed the players round, watching Keren, meeting her afterwards, trying to persuade her of his sincerity and his love. At first she had laughed at him, but something in his great size and the money he pressed on her at last won her interest. Almost as a joke she had accepted his advances and then suddenly found that what he had to offer was no light thing after all. She had never had a home and had never had a suitor like this.

Mark had seen Keren last night at Ladock. By Sunday of this week they would be at St. Dennis on the edge of the moor. She had promised to marry him, promised faithfully on one condition. He must find somewhere for them to live; she would not share his father's house, crowded already, for a single day. Let him only find somewhere just for her alone before Sunday and she would run away with him. But if the company once travelled beyond St. Dennis she would not, she said, have the heart to come back. From there they would begin the long trek to Bodmin and not even if Mark took a pit pony for her would she face the moors a second time. It was a flight from St. Dennis or nothing. And it was up to him.

"And what do you think to do, Mark?" Demelza asked.

The Cobbledicks had moved into the Clemmow's old cottage; so there was no place empty at all. What Mark had in mind was to build himself a cottage before Sunday. His friends were ready to help. They had picked a possible spot, a piece of rough wasteland looking over on to Treneglos property though still on Poldark land. But with Captain Ross away . . .

It was strange to think of the feelings of love stirring in this tough, short-spoken, gaunt man; stranger still to think of the wayward pretty May fly who had wakened them.

"What d'you want for me to do?" she asked.

He told her. He needed leave to build. He thought he might rent the land. But if he waited until to-morrow it meant missing a whole day.

"Isn't it too late already?" she asked. "You can't ever build a cottage by Sunday."

"I reckon we can just do un," he said. "There's clay to hand and, private like, thinkin' it might come, I been gathering stuff of nights. Ned Bottrell over to Sawle has got thatchin' straw. We can make do, if only tis a four walls and roof to 'er head."

Words were on Demelza's tongue to say that any woman who made such conditions ought to be left where she belonged; but she saw from Mark's look that it wouldn't do.

"What land is it you want, Mark?"

"Over the brow beyond Mellin. There's a piece of old scrub an' furse, an' some attle from an old mine ditch. By the bed o' the leat as dried up years ago."

"I know it. . . ." Her mind went over the issue. "Well, it is not really in my hand to give it to you. What you must do is think to yourself: I'm an old friend, wouldn't Captain Ross let me have this bit o' scrubland to build my cottage?"

Mark Daniel looked at her a moment, then slowly shook his head.

"Tis not for me to decide, Mistress Poldark. Friends in a manner of saying we been all our lives; grown up head by head. We've sailed together, running rum and gin, we've fished together on Hendrawna Beach, we've wrastled together when we was tackers. But when all's done he belong up here and I belong down there, and—and I'd no more think to take what was his wi'out a by-your-leave than he'd think to take mine."

All the garden was in shadow now. The bright sky seemed to have no link with the gathering dusk of the valley, the land had fallen away into this abyss of evening while the day still blazed overhead. A thrush had caught a snail and the only sound outside was the *tap-tap-tap* as he swung it against a stone.

"If tis not in your power to do it," said Mark. "Then I must see for a piece o' land elsewhere."

Demelza knew what chance he had of that. She found when she turned from staring at the sky that she could only see his eyes and the firm parenthesis of his cheekbones. She went across and picked up flint and steel. Presently her hands were lit up, her face, her hair, as the first candle sputtered and glowed.

"Take an acre measuring from the bed o' the dry stream, Mark," she said. "I can't say more'n that. How you shall hire it I've no notion, for I'm not learned in figures an' things. That's for you an' Ross to make out. But I promise you you shall not be moved."

The man at the door was silent while two more candles were lit from the first. She heard him stir and shuffle one foot.

"I can't thank you right, mistress," he said suddenly, "but if there's service to be done for you or yours leave me know."

She lifted her head, and smiled across at him.

"I know that, Mark," she said.

Then he was gone and she was left alone with the candles lifting their heads in the lightening room.

CHAPTER VIII   Some ground haze gathered with the dark, and that night the moon came up like a bald old redskin peering over a hill. In the hollow of Mellin and the barren declivity of Reath beyond, it looked down upon a string of black figures, active and as seeming aimless as ants in the sudden light of a lantern, moving backwards and forwards over the hummock of moorland beyond Joe Trigg's cottage and down towards a path of rubble-scarred ground sloping indeterminately east.

The building was on.

There were nine to help him at the start: Paul, his brother and Ena Daniel, Zacky Martin and his two eldest boys, Ned Bottrell, who was a cousin from Sawle, Jack Cobbledick and Will Nanfan.

First there was the site to be marked; and this must be level enough to support the four walls. They found a patch and cleared it of stones, about a hundred yards from Reath Ditch. Then they roughly marked it into a rectangle and began. The walls were to be made of clay, beaten hard and mixed with straw and small stones. When Ross killed a bullock at the time of the christening Zacky had helped him and had been given a bag of bullock hair off the hide. This was used now, being stirred in with the clay and the stones and the straw to make a binding mixture. Four great boulders were used for the corners of the house, and from one to another of these a rough trough was built of wood about two feet wide and two deep. Into this the clay and stones and all the rest were shovelled and stamped down and left to set while more was mixed.

At eleven the three youngsters, being on the early core, were sent home to sleep, and at midnight Cobbledick turned his long high-stepping stride towards bed. Zacky Martin and Will Nanfan stayed until three, Paul Daniel until five, when he had just time to get home and have a plate of barley bread and potatoes before going on to the mine. Ned Bottrell, who ran his own little tin stamp, left at eight. Mark went steadily on until Beth Daniel came over with a bowl of watery soup and a pilchard on a chunk of bread. Having worked without a break for nearly fourteen hours, he sat down to have his food and stared at the result. The foundations were in and the walls just begun. The area of the cottage was slightly larger than intended, but that would be all to the good; there would be time for partitioning off when She was in it. To get her in it: that was his obsession.

This morning early the little children had been round before they went off to the fields; then later three or four of their mothers, staying an hour to help and talk or looking in on their way to work. Everyone had taken his cause to heart and no one had any doubt that he would have his house before Sunday. They might have been critical of the marriage since no one wanted a stranger, but Mark Daniel being who he was and popular, people were willing to swallow their prejudices.

At seven that evening Zacky Martin, Will Nanfan and Paul Daniel, having had a few hours' sleep, arrived back, and later they were joined by Ned Bottrell and Jack Cobbledick. At ten another figure came out of the cloud-shadowed moonlight behind them, and Mark saw by his height that it was Ross. He stepped down the ladder and went to meet him.

As they neared each other likeness might have been remarked between these men. They were of an age, ran to bone rather than flesh, were dark and long-legged and indocile. But at close quarters difference was more noticeable than sameness. Daniel, darker-skinned but sallow with underground work, had a stiffness that the other lacked, was broader in the jaw and narrower at the temples, his hair straight and close-cropped and black without the copper. They might have been distant relatives branching far from a common line.

"Well, Mark," said Ross as he came up. "So this is your house?"

"Yes, Cap'n." Mark turned and stared at the four walls now nearly roof-high, at the gaping sockets where the windows should go. "So far as it is made."

"What have you for floor joists?"

"There's wreck timber enough, I reckon. And these pit props. The planchin' will have to wait till later."

"For an upper room?"

"Ais. I thought it could be builded in the thatch; twill save the wall-building, for I've no more straw to spare—nor time."

67

"You've time for nothing. What of the windows and door?"

"Father will loan us his door till I can make another. An' he's hammering up some shutters for us over home. Tis all he can do with his rheumatics. They'll pass for the time."

"I suppose," Ross said, "you're making no error, Mark. In choosing this girl, I mean. D'you think she will settle down here after roaming the countryside?"

"She's never had no home, not since she can mind anything. That is the more reason why she should want one now."

"When are you to be married?"

"Monday first thing ef all d'go well."

"But can you?"

"Yes, I reckon. A fortnight gone she promised she'd wed me and I asked parson to call the banns. Then she changed her mind. This Sunday will be the third time. I'll take her over to Parson Odgers Monday so soon as we're back."

Behind his words lay the shadow of a fortnight's struggle. The prize had one minute looked close within his hand and the next as remote as ever.

"Mistress Poldark'll 'ave told you," Mark went on.

"She told me."

"Did I do right in askin' her?"

"Of course. Take more of this bottom if you wish to reclaim it, Mark." Mark inclined his head. *"Thank ye, sir."*

"I'll have the deed drawn up to-morrow." Ross stared at the shapeless yellow mound. "It is possible I can find you a door."

They were not acting at St. Dennis but were resting before the long trek to Bodmin to-morrow. This week they had gradually left the civilized west of Cornwall behind and had moved off towards the northern wilderness. For Keren each day had been worse than the last; the weather was too hot or too wet, the barns they played in impossible to manage, leaky and rat-infested or too small to move in. They had made barely enough to keep hunger away, and Aaron Otway, who had been consoling himself as he always did when times were bad, was sometimes almost too drunk to stand.

As if to set her decision on firm lines last night at St. Michael was the worst fiasco of all. The persistent rain had kept away all but seven adults and two children, and the players had had to act on wet and smelly straw, with constant drippings on their heads. Tupper had found a fever and had lost the ability (or desire) to make people laugh, and the audience just sat and gaped through it all.

They were to have spent the end of Sunday cleaning up the two caravans ready for a triumphal entry into Bodmin, Otway's idea for attracting an audience on Monday night; but he had been drunk all day and the others were too out-of-sorts or listless to make any move, once they had found a field and turned their animals out to grass. If a wheel fell off to-morrow or an axle broke for lack of grease, well let it.

She had her things packed in a basket, and at what she thought to be midnight she carefully slipped out of her bunk and made for the door. Outside it was fine, and with a shawl about her head she crouched by the wheel of the wagon waiting for Mark.

It was slow waiting, and she was not a patient girl, but to-night she was so set on leaving her present company that she stayed on and on, cursing the summer chill of night and wishing he'd make haste. Minutes passed that seemed like days, and hours that might have been months. Crouching there with her head against the hub of the wheel, she fell asleep.

When she woke she was stiff and chilled through, and behind the church on the hill was a lightening of the sky, the dawn.

She came to her feet. So he'd let her down! All this time he'd been playing with her, making promises he had no intention to keep. Tears of fury and disappointment started into her eyes. Careless of noise she turned to go in, and as she touched the handle she saw a tall figure hurrying across the field.

He came at a shambling half run. She did not move at all until he came up with her and stood seeking his breath and leaning against the caravan.

"Keren . . ."

"Where've you been?" she said wildly. "All night! All this night I've been waiting! Where've you been?"

He looked up at the window of the caravan. "You got your clo'es? Come."

His tone was so strange, short of its usual respect, that she began to move with him across the field without arguing. He walked straight enough now but stiffly, as if he could not bend. They reached the lane.

At the church she said angrily: "Where've you been, Mark? I'm chilled to the marrow! Waiting all the night through."

He turned to her. "Eh?"

She said it again. "What's amiss with you? What's kept you?"

"I was late startin', Keren. Late. Twas no easy job building a house. . . . At the last . . . there was last things to do. . . . Didn't start till ten. Thought I should make up by running all the way. . . . But I mistook the road, Keren. I ran wrong . . . kept on the main coach road instead o' turning for St. Dennis. . . . I went miles. . . . That's why

I came on ee from be'ind. . . . Lord save us, I never thought to find ye in time!"

He spoke so slow that at last she realized he was dead-tired, almost out on his feet. Surprise and disappointment made her snap at him, for she had always been pleased at his strength. This was a letdown; surely this great moment of his life should have been enough to liven him up all over again.

They walked on quietly until full day, when a fresh breeze blowing in from the sea seemed to give him a new lease, and from then on he steadily came round. She had put aside some dough cakes from last night's supper, and these they shared at the side of the road. Before they made St. Michael he was the stronger of the two.

They stopped at a tollhouse and bargained for some breakfast and rested. The sight of Mark's clinking purse put Keren in a good humour again, and they set off brightly enough on the next lap with her arm linked in his. Only another eight or nine miles to go and they would be there well before noon. She was quite excited now, for novelty always appealed to her; and though she had never in her darkest dreams thought of marrying a miner there was something romantic in the idea of running away and in going to church and making solemn vows and going back with him to a house specially built for her, for them. It was like one of the plays she acted in.

After a time came the discomfort of sore heels, and she went lame. They rested again and she bathed her feet in a stream. They went on, but not very far, and at length he picked her up and began to carry her.

She enjoyed this for a time, it was so much easier than walking and she liked to have his great arms about her and to feel his lungs breathing in the air. People stared, but she did not mind this until they came to a hamlet and walked down the winding muddy lane between the cottages, followed by a trickle of half-naked jeering urchins. She was indignant and wanted him to lay about him, but he walked stolidly on without a glimmer of a change of expression.

After that he carried her in the open country and set her down when a cluster of cottages came in sight. So they made progress but it was slow, and the sun, peering through a rift of cloud, was high as they reached the gates of Mingoose.

A mile and a half to Mellin; then two miles to Sawle Church. If they were not there before noon the wedding would have to wait until to-morrow.

He hastened his steps and at last set her down on the Marasanvose track, with Mellin just over the next rise. They had no time to go and see his cottage. She washed her face in a little pool and he did the same. Then she combed her hair with a property comb she had "borrowed," and they limped down into Mellin.

Little Maggie Martin saw them first and went screaming in to her mother that they were here at last. When they reached the first cottage everyone had turned out to meet them. Most of the able-bodied were asleep or at work; but the very old and the very young and one or two of the women did their best to make it a hearty welcome. There was no time to waste in talk, and Mark Daniel and his bride-to-be set off at once for Sawle. But now they were the head of a comet with a tenuous tail, made up of Grannie Daniel and Aunt Betsy Triggs and Mrs. Zacky and Sue Vigus and a sputter of excited toddlers.

They hurried, Mark with his great strides nearly outdistancing Keren in the last stages; but it was twenty minutes to noon when they reached Sawle Church. Then they could not find Mr. Odgers. Mrs. Odgers, confronted by a dark, gaunt, hollow-eyed unshaven man with a desperate and ungenteel manner, confessed timidly that Mr. Odgers had given them up and she had last seen him going out into the garden. It was Aunt Betsy who flushed him from behind a black-currant bush, and by then it was ten minutes to twelve. He began to raise objections as to legality and haste, until Mrs. Zacky, flat-faced and spectacled and persuasive, took him by one thin arm and led him respectfully into church.

So the spiritual bond was sealed, with the clock in the vestry striking twelve as Mark put a brass ring on Keren's long slender hand.

After the usual formalities (Mark Daniel, his mark; Kerenhappuch Smith, proudly written) they had to call in at Ned Bottrell's cottage near the church and have their health drunk in cider and ale; and it was some time before they could begin the walk back to Mellin. Then the walk became a triumphal procession, for it was the end of the morning core. Something in "bachelor" Mark's dogged courtship and his house-building had caught the imagination of the miners and bal-girls, and a whole group of them joined on and escorted the newlyweds back to Mellin.

Keren was not quite sure how to take all this, how far she should unbend towards these people she was coming to live among. She took a dislike to old Grannie Daniel, and she thought Beth Daniel, Paul's wife, a plain drudge who couldn't open her mouth because of jealousy. But some of the men seemed nice enough and ready to be friendly in a rough but respectful way. She looked up at them out of the corners of her eyes and let them see that they were more acceptable than their womenfolk.

As a special treat they had a big dish of tea and rabbit pasties with leeks and baked barley crusts, and it all passed off pretty well. There were bursts of conversation and as sudden silences, when everyone seemed to be watching everyone else; but this was the first time any of them except Mark had met her and it was bound to be strange.

By the time it was all over the day was done. At Mark's request there was to be no joking or following them to the new house. He'd earned his quiet now.

The evening sun was warm on their backs as they climbed the rise out of Mellin, and it had lit up all the west with a gold light. The contrast of colour was vivid where the bright sky met the cobalt sea.

They went down towards their cottage. Presently she stopped.

"Is that it?"

"Yes."

He waited.

"Oh," she said, and went on.

They came near to the door. He thought how commonplace and rough it was, seeing the house he had built behind the figure of the girl he had married. Everything was so crude, made with loving hands maybe; but crude and rough. Loving hands were not enough, you had to have skill and time.

They went in, and he saw that someone had lit a big fire in the open chimney he had made. It burned and crackled and roared and made the rough room cheerful and warm.

"That's Beth's doing," he said gratefully.

"What is?"

"The fire. She slipped out; I wondered why. She's a rare good one."

"She doesn't like me," said Keren, rustling the clean straw underfoot.

"Yes, she do, Keren. Tedn that but only that she's Methody and don't hold wi' playgoing an' such like."

"Oh, she doesn't," said Keren ominously. "What does she know about it, I'd like to know."

Mark stared round.

"It's . . . awful rough for you, Keren. But it has all been builded in four days and twill take weeks to make it just so as we shall want it."

He looked at her expectantly.

"Oh, it's nice," said Keren. "I think it's a nice house. Fifty times better than those old cottages over the hill."

His dark face lighted up. "We'll make it betterer as we go along. There's—there's much to be done. Twas only giving you a roof that I was about."

He put his arm round her tentatively, and when she put up her face he kissed her. It was like kissing a butterfly, soft and frail and elusive.

She turned her head. "What's in there?"

"That's where we'll sleep," he said. "I'd intended for a room upstairs, but tedn near finished yet. So I made this for the time."

She went into the next room and her feet again felt straw underfoot. It was like living in a cattle shed. Oh, well, as he said, it could be changed.

He went across and pushed open the shutter to let the light in. There was a big wooden shelf across one corner of the room, raised about a foot from the floor. On it was a sack mattress stuffed with straw and two thin blankets.

"You should have built the house facing west," she said, "then we'd have had the evening sun."

"I didn't think o' that," he said, crestfallen.

It was hers. Hers alone to do with as she chose, that was something.

"D'you mean you made all this house since I saw you last?" she said.

"Yes."

"Lord sakes," she said, "I can scarcely credit it."

This delighted him and he kissed her again. Presently she wriggled out of his arms.

"Go leave me now, Mark. Go sit by the fire an' I'll join you presently. I'll give you a surprise."

He went out, bending his great height in the door.

She stood for a time staring out of the window, at the barren prospect of the gully with the dried-up stream and the mining rubble all around. Up the other side of the valley the ground was better; there was the turret of a house and trees. Why hadn't he built up there?

She went across and put her fingers on the bed. Well, the straw was dry. It wasn't so very long since she'd slept on wet straw. And it could be made so much better still. After the first disappointment her spirits rose. No more wrangling with Tupper or smelling Otway's drunken breath. No more hunger or dismal treks across moors and bogs. No more playing to empty pigsties and half-wit yokels. This was home.

She moved to the window again and closed one of the shutters. A group of sea gulls flying high looked gold and pink in the sunlight against the cloudy eastern sky. The light was failing in this shallow rift in the moor, especially in the house—always it would be dark early in this house with all the windows facing the wrong way.

She knew he would be waiting for her. She did not shirk her part of the bargain but looked towards it with a faint sensuous lassitude. She slowly undressed, and when she had taken everything off she shivered a little and closed the other shutter. In the semidarkness of the new room she passed her hands caressingly down her smooth flanks, stretched and yawned, then put on her black and pink faded smock and fluffed out her hair. This would do. He'd be overcome as it was. This would do.

Bare feet rustling in the straw, she passed through to the kitchen and thought for a moment he had gone out. Then she saw him sitting in the shadows on the floor, his head against the wooden bench. He was asleep.

She was angry in a moment.

"Mark!" she said.

He did not reply. She went over and knelt beside him and stared into his dark face. He had shaved at Mellin, but already his strong beard was beginning to sprout again. His face was hollow and shadowed with fatigue, his mouth half open. She thought how ugly he was.

"Mark!" she said again, loudly.

His breathing went on.

"Mark!" She grasped the collar of his jacket and roughly shook him. His head tapped against the bench and his breathing halted, but he showed no signs of waking.

She got up and stared down at him. Anger began to give way to contempt. He was as bad as Tupper, lying there so limp and so foolish. What had she married, a man who fell dead-asleep on his wedding night, who hadn't the spark to be excited, who went to *sleep*? It was an insult to *her*. A great insult.

Well, it was as he chose. She was not all that particular. If he wanted to snore away there like a great black dog, well . . . It was his loss, not hers. She'd not defaulted. Let him be. She gave a short laugh, and then began to giggle as she saw the funny side of it. She giggled and giggled as she moved slowly away from him towards the other room. But her laughter was softer now so that she should not wake him.

CHAPTER IX   On his daylight visit to the cottage at Reath, Ross had also noted the turret among the trees on the farther slope. It was one of the gatehouses of Mingoose and was now in a bad state, but there were a number of usable rooms still and Ross had an idea.

He took it to Mr. Horace Treneglos, who tramped across regularly to inspect their mine now that it was showing a return.

"Who is this Dwight Enys, what?" Mr. Treneglos shouted. "Think you he's worth encouraging? Think you he's experienced at his profession?"

"Enys is eager, sharp and keen. It is good to encourage youth, and Choake has no intention of serving us since I quarrelled with him."

"I wisht we'd found a quieter place for our lode," said Mr. Treneglos, clutching at his hat. "It is always so demmed windy up here. For my part, as you know, I've no great fancy for these physical people, young or old. But I'm out to please you, and if the Gatehouse would satisfy

74

the stripling he may have it at some nominal rent for the repairing."

A fortnight later there was a ticketing at Truro, to which Wheal Leisure Mine was sending two parcels of ore; so Ross rode in early and called on the Pascoes before the auction began. Dwight Enys was away, but he wrote him a note and left.

Samples of the ore to be marketed had already been examined and tested and whispered over by agents of the copper companies; and at these ticketings it was left only for the various companies to put in a bid for the ore. Not for them the vulgar excitement of a common auction, where one buyer ran another up higher than he wanted to go. Instead each company put in a bid in writing, the chairman opened these offering tickets and the consignments of copper went to the company which had put in the highest bid.

To-day the bidding was even poorer than of late, and some parcels of ore went for less than half their real value. It was the custom of the companies when they did not want a particular parcel to put in a very low bid nevertheless, and if, as not infrequently happened, every other company did the same, one of these low bids made the sale. This meant a heavy loss for the mine concerned, and in the present state of trade no mine could afford it.

A great dinner at the inn always followed the ticketing, given by the mines, at which buyers and sellers—the lions and the lambs, as a wry humorist called them—sat down together; but to-day there was a noticeable lack of good spirits among the feasters. Ross had been surprised to see Francis at the sale—usually the manager of Grambler came—and he knew it to be a sign that his cousin was making a last bid to keep Grambler Mine on its great unwieldy feet.

To-day for all his poise he looked harassed and inept, and as if threatened by spectres which existed in half-ignored corners of his mind.

On his left Ross had Richard Tonkin, the manager and one of the shareholders in United Mines, the largest tin- and copper-producing combine in the county; and halfway through the meal Tonkin whispered in Ross's ear:

"I trust you have made some progress with your scheme."

Ross looked at him.

"You mean the extension at Wheal Leisure?"

Tonkin smiled. "No, sir. The project for forming a copper smelting company to promote the interests of the mines."

Ross's look became a stare. "I have no such project in hand, Mr. Tonkin."

The other man was a little incredulous. "I hope you are joking. Mr. Blewett told me . . . and Mr. Aukett . . . that there was some prospect of such a scheme. I should have been very happy to lend my aid."

"Mr. Blewett and Mr. Aukett," said Ross, "made much of a chance discussion. I have not given it another thought."

"That comes as a very great disappointment to me. I was in hope—others too were in hope—that something would arise from it. There can surely be little doubt that we have need of such a company."

The dinner broke up with men going off in twos and threes to find their horses and ride home before dusk, some staying at the table to sup a last glass of port or nod tipsily over a snuffbox, others talking in groups on the way downstairs or at the door of the inn.

Ross stayed behind to talk with Francis. Though there was now no ill will between them they saw little of each other. Ross had heard that Grambler Mine had been reprieved for the time being, but he kept the conversation to family topics, being afraid of treading on Francis's sensitive corns.

Chatting amiably, they went downstairs, when the innkeeper touched Ross on the arm.

"Beg your pardon, sir, but would you oblige a man by steppin' this way, just for a small matter of a moment or two? An' you too, sir, if tis agreeable an' convenient."

Ross stared at him and went down two steps into his private parlour. It was a gloomy little room, for the window looked out upon a high wall, but occupying this room in varying positions of comfort were fourteen men.

Francis, following him in, stumbled over the house cat, swore and raised his foot to kick away the obstruction, then saw what it was and picked the animal up by its scruff, coming into the room close behind Ross and elbowing him farther in.

"God's my life," he said, looking round.

It was not until Ross recognized Tonkin and Blewett and Aukett among the men that he smelt what was in the wind.

"Sit down, Captain Poldark," said Harry Blewett, vacating a chair by the window. "Glad we was able to catch you before you took your leave."

"Thanks," said Ross, "I'll stand."

"Damme," said Francis, "it looks like a pesky Bible meeting. Here, beast, you shall be chairman, and mind you call us to order." He leaned forward and dropped the cat on the empty seat.

"Captain Poldark," Tonkin said, "it was fortunate that you were late in coming down, for we have had the chance of talking together here in private; those of us you see around you; and no doubt you have an idea what our subject has been."

"I have an idea," said Ross.

"Sink me if I can say the same," remarked Francis.

"We would like your word, sir," a big man called Johnson leaned across and said to Francis, "that anything that passes here is in the strictest confidence."

"Very well."

"We may take it that you find no satisfaction in the business done to-day?" Richard Tonkin asked.

Grambler had been one of the worst sufferers. "You may take that," said Francis, "and pin it where you will."

"No, well, there's many of us here feels quite the same. And we've met here and now to say what's to be done by it."

Francis said: "Then we're here to set the world to rights. It will be a long session."

"Not so long as might be," Tonkin said quietly. "For we have a plan in mind, Mr. Poldark, which is to form a copper company of our own, one which will exist outside the ring, will give fair prices for the ore, will smelt the copper in this county, and will market the refined product direct. All of us here, more than a dozen, are willing to join together, and between us we stand for a fair share of the mines in this area; and between us, even in these hard times, we can lay our hands on a measure of cash. But this is a small beginning, Mr. Poldark, to what will surely come to us when the project gets about—if it can be done privately and in the right way. And there's some of the richest mines not here to-day. In good times unfair prices can be borne because there is a margin for all; but in bad times like the present there's only one way out short of bankruptcy for half of us here!"

There was a deep murmur of assent from the men in the room. Ross saw that most of the principal sellers of to-day were present. He realized that something was in motion now that could not be stopped. Tonkin was the eloquent one: he put into words what the others felt.

"Well, it all rings very agreeable, I believe you," said Francis. "But you'll be biting off no small mouthful of trouble, one way with another. The copper companies want no cutthroat competition and the banks will be behind 'em. Certain people——"

"Well, trouble's better'n starvation," Blewett said.

"Aye, we're not afraid of trouble!"

Francis raised his eyebrows slightly. "I would not disagree with you, gentlemen."

"Mind you," said Tonkin, "all this is but a beginning. I know—we all know—there's things to be faced. What's right and just isn't always easy to come by. But while we were all here together was a convenient time to see the wheels set in motion. And before we begin, we wish to know who's for us in the venture. For who is not for us——"

"Is against you?" Francis shook his head. "Far from it. For who is not instantly for you may have obligations of his own to consider. It does not follow that he may not wish you well." Francis turned an eye on Ross. "What is my cousin's view of the matter?"

Tonkin said: "It was your cousin who first suggested it."

Francis looked surprised. "Well, Ross, I had no idea. Nor should I ever have guessed, for as your own mine . . ."

Ross said nothing and his face showed nothing.

"There are disadvantages, we know," said Tonkin, "but if it becomes a working reality we shall do away with many of the present anomalies. Look, sir, we cannot go on as we are to-day. Unless there is some change, in a year we shall all be gone. I say for my part, let us undertake this venture with all speed and courage. I would rather fail fighting than lying down and waiting for the end!"

"Well," said Francis, and adjusted the lace on his cuff, "I don't doubt you'll give the copper companies a run for their money. And I wish you all good fortune, for God knows we have had none of late. For my part I would prefer to consider the proposal further before making a move. But I wish you well, gentlemen, I wish you well. By the way, who is to take the initiative in your venture. There must be a leader, must there not? Is it to be you, Mr. Tonkin?"

Tonkin shook his head. "No, sir. I couldn't do it. I'm not at all the right man. But we are all agreed who is the right man if he will undertake it, are we not, gentlemen?"

CHAPTER X Demelza had been expecting Ross since five. At six she prepared supper, making it lighter than usual, for she knew he came back from these ticketings satiated with food and drink and grumbling at the waste of time.

Towards seven she had her supper and thought she would walk up the valley to see if she could meet Ross. Julia was fed; her garden was not crying for attention; she had practised on the spinet just before dinner; her mind was at ease. Very nice. She would walk.

The joys of leisure, rarely indulged, had not yet lost a grain of their newness. This of all things was what made her happiest in the life of a lady. In her childhood she had always worked until there was nothing but a sleep of exhaustion left, and slept until a boot or a shout roused her. As a servant at Nampara she had had her quieter times, but the best of these had been stolen, furtive; nervous alertness woven in with her pleasure. Now if she chose, if she felt like it, she could idle with all the world to see. The very energy of her ordinary ways made these times all the sweeter. She was a lady, wife of Ross

78

Poldark, whose ancestry in these parts went back hundreds of years. The children of her body, Julia first, would be called Poldark, with a good home, money enough, a root, upbringing, a legacy of culture. Sometimes her heart swelled at the thought.

She walked up the valley listening to the first crickets making themselves heard in the undergrowth, and stopping now and then to watch the young birds squabbling in the branches of the elms or an occasional frog hop and slither by the edge of the stream. At the top, by the ruins of Wheal Maiden, she sat down on a block of stone and hummed a little tune and screwed up her eyes for the sight of a familiar figure. Beyond the smoke of Grambler you could see the tower of Sawle Church. From here it looked to be leaning towards the south-west, as a man will in a gale. All the trees leaned the other way.

"Mistress Poldark," said a voice behind her.

She leapt up.

Andrew Blamey had called.

"I hope you'll accept my excuses, ma'am. I hadn't any thought of scaring you."

He was standing beside her, thinking that the shock had brought her near to fainting. But it would have taken far more than that to send Demelza over. He kept a hand at her elbow until she was again sitting on the wall. Out of the corner of her eye she thought there was no arrogance in his expression.

She had sworn aloud at the shock, forgetting her manners and annoyed with herself the moment after.

"It is a bad beginning," he said, "to have come here with an apology to make and to need another at the outset."

"I had not thought to see you in these parts."

"Nor I to see myself, ma'am. Ever again."

"Then what brings you here, Captain Blamey?"

"Your visit to me. For after it I have had no peace of mind."

He kept moistening his lips and frowning a little, as if with turns of pain.

She said: "How did you—— Have you walked from Falmouth?"

"I came on foot from Grambler, hoping to be less conspicuous if you should have company. I was in Truro this forenoon and saw both your husband and—and Francis Poldark. Knowing they would be away, the need was too strong."

"I am expecting Ross back any moment."

"Then I'd best say what can be said while there is time. No doubt you took a very bad opinion of me from our first meeting, Mrs. Poldark."

Demelza stared at her feet. "I was a small matter put out."

"Your visit was sprung on me. It was something I had put away. . . . Its—its sudden outcropping brought with it all the bitterness." He put his hat down on the wall. "I am, I grant, a man of strong temper. To control it has been the work of a lifetime. Sometimes still there are moments when the struggle returns. But God forbid that I should quarrel with those who wish me well."

"Not even your own sailors?" said Demelza, faintly malicious for once. He was silent.

"Please go on," she said.

"The sailors quarrel with all their captains just now. For years they have eked out their poor wages by smuggling goods into the ports on each voyage. But it has come to such a pass that we are held to blame. Captain Clarke in the *Swan of Flushing* was detained in Jamaica under prosecution, and others will fare the same. So we have reached an agreement on the belongings that each sailor shall carry. It's not surprising they dislike it, but this is no personal quarrel between my crew and myself: it is a commotion throughout the packet service."

"I beg pardon," she said.

"I met you that day already angry from a disturbance. When you spoke it seemed at first an interference. Only later I came to count the exertion you had been to. Then I wished it was possible to have you back to thank you for what you had done and said."

"Oh, it was nothin'. It was not *that* I wanted, if you understand——"

"Since then," he said, "there has been no peace of mind. To Lisbon and back I carried what you said of Verity. You were allowed time to say little enough, maybe. But . . . Verity had never got over it. You said that, didn't you? And that she was ten years older than her age. How often I've thought of what it means. Ailing but not ill, you said. Because of me. Ailing but not ill. Ten years older than her age. You know, I never knew what Verity's age was. All the time I had her love. We didn't think of such things. I am forty-one, ma'am. She didn't look old when I knew her. Is that what her brother and father have saved her for? There's no more rest until I've seen her. That much you've done, Mistress Poldark, whatever the outcome. The move is with you again. That's what I came to say."

His eyes had been on her the whole time he was speaking, and she had not felt able to break from his gaze. At last her glance moved to the plain of Grambler; she got up.

"He's coming, Captain Blamey. You'd best not be seen here."

Blamey stared down with puckered eyes. "Is *he* against me now? He wasn't at the time."

"Not *against* you. He was against me stirring up what he thought should be left alone. He'd be angry with me if he knew."

He looked at her. "Verity has a good friend in you, ma'am. You take risks for your friends."

"I have a good friend in Verity," she said. "But don't stand there or he'll see you. Let us move behind the wall."

"What is the best way back?"

"Those fir trees. Wait there until we have gone down."

"When can I see you again? What arrangements can be made?"

She wracked her brain for a quick decision. "I can't say now. It depends—on Verity. . . . If——"

"Shall you tell her?" he said eagerly.

"I don't think so. Not at the start. I—hadn't thought more because I'd give up hope of ever anything being done—since I came to Falmouth. It will depend how I can arrange . . ."

"Write me," he said. "Care of the packet offices. I'll come."

She bit her lip, for she could hardly form her letters. "All right," she promised. "I'll leave you know. What if you're away?"

"I sail on Saturday, there's no choice for that. Set a time for the third week of next month if possible. It will be safer that way. If——"

"Look," said Demelza urgently. "Twill be in Truro; that's safest. I'll send you word, just a place and a time. I can't do more'n that. It will be up to you then."

"Bless you, ma'am," he said, and bent and kissed her hand. "I'll not fail you."

She watched him leave the shelter of the mine building and run quickly to the trees. At her first meeting in Falmouth she could not imagine what Verity had seen in him to take his loss so to heart. After this she was more able to understand.

The sun had set before Ross reached her. Over the land the smoke from Grambler was rising and blowing across the cottages and drifting towards Sawle. Here in the ruins the crickets were very busy, sawing away among the grass and the stones.

He jumped off Darkie when he saw her and his preoccupied face broke into a smile.

"Well, my love, this is an honour. I hope you've not been waiting long."

"Four hours behindhand," she said. "I should be grown to the stone if I had come here at five."

"But as you didn't your attachment is so much the less." He laughed and then looked at her. "What's wrong?"

She put her hand up and fondled the mare's soft nose.

"Nothing. Except that I been picturing you thrown off by poor Darkie here, or set upon by rogues and robbers."

"But your eyes are shining. In the distance I thought they were glow beetles."

She patted his arm but kept her glance on Darkie. "Don't tease, Ross, I was glad to see you back, that's all."

"Flattered but unconvinced," he commented. "Something has excited you. Kiss me."

She kissed him.

"Now I know it is not rum," he added.

"Oh! Judas!" She wiped her mouth distastefully. "What insult next! If that is all you kiss me for, to pry and spy into my liquors . . ."

"It's a sure way."

"Then next time you suspect him I hope you'll try it on Jud. 'Aye, Mester Ross,' he'll say. 'Gladly,' with a belch, he'll say. An' round your neck his arms'll go like a linseed poultice. Or Prudie, why don't you try your chance on Prudie? She has no beard and a comfortable soft sort of reception. She didn't have a chance at our party, and no doubt you'll not mind her fondness for onions. . . ."

He picked her up and set her sideways on the saddle of his horse, where she had to clutch his arm for fear of falling backwards. In the process her dark eyes looked into his grey ones.

"I think tis you that's excited," Demelza said, seizing the attack before he could. "You've been in mischief this day, I'll lay a curse. Have you thrown Dr. Choake in a pool or robbed George Warleggan at his bank?"

He turned and began to lead his horse down the valley, one hand firmly and pleasurably on Demelza's knee.

"I have some news," he said, "but it is dusty stuff and will not move you. Tell me first how you've spent the day."

"Tell me your news."

"You first."

"Oh . . . In the forenoon I went to call on Keren Daniel and renew our acquaintance. . . ."

"Did she please you?"

"Well . . . She has a small pretty waist. And small pretty ears. . . ."

"And a small pretty mind?"

"It is hard to say. She thinks well of herself. She wants to get on. I believe she d'think that if only she'd seen you first I'd never've stood a chance."

Ross laughed.

"An' would I?" said Demelza, curious.

He said: "Insults I have grown accustomed to bear. But, imbecility is something I cannot cope with."

"What long words you d'use, grandpa," Demelza said, impressed. They went on down the valley. A few birds were still chattering in the coloured close of the evening. On Hendrawna Beach the sea had gone a pale opal green against the warm brown of cliff and sand.

"And your news?" she said presently.

"There is a scheme afoot to rival the copper companies by forming a company of our own. I am to lead it."

She glanced at him. "What does that mean, Ross?"

He explained, and they crossed the stream and reached the house. Jud came ambling out to take Darkie, and they went into the parlour, where supper was still laid for him. She was about to light the candles but he stopped her. So she sat on the rug and leaned her back against his knees, and he stroked her face and hair and went on talking while the light faded right away.

"Francis was not willing to enter with us at the start," he said. "And I don't blame him, for the very continuance of Grambler hangs on Warleggan good will. That will be the trouble for many. They are so deeply involved with mortgages and things that they dare not risk offending those who hold them. But a compromise was suggested and our enterprise is to be a secret one."

"Secret?" said Demelza.

"If the company is formed it shall be formed by a few people who will act for those who do not wish their names known. I think it will work."

"Shall you be secret, then?"

His long fingers moved down the line of her chin.

"No. I have nothing at stake. They can't touch me."

"But doesn't Wheal Leisure owe some money to the bank?"

"To Pascoe's Bank, yes. But they are not connected with the copper companies, so that is safe enough."

"Why should you have to take all the risks and let other men shelter behind you?"

"No, no. There are others that will help openly; a man called Richard Tonkin. One called Johnson. Many of them."

She moved a moment restlessly. "And how far will it touch us?"

"I—may be more from home. It's hard to say."

She stirred again. "I'm not at all sure I like it, Ross."

"Nor I, that part of it. But there was no other they would choose for leader. I tried. . . ."

"We should be pleased at that."

"It's a compliment to be chosen. Though no doubt before this is done I shall curse my weakness in taking it. There is the need of this enterprise, Demelza. I didn't want the advancing of it, but I found I couldn't refuse."

"Then you must do what you think best to do," she said quietly.

There was silence for some time. Her face was quiescent between his hands. The electricity had gone out of her now, that tautness of mind, the elfish vitality of spirit which he could always sense when she had something special on or was in one of her "moods." His news had deflated her, for she did not want him more gone from her than now. She longed to have more in common with him, not less.

He bent and put his face against her hair. Vibrantly alive, like herself, it curled about his face. It smelled faintly of the sea. He was struck by the mystery of personality, that this hair and the head and person of the young woman below it was his by right of marriage and by the vehemently free choice of the woman herself, that this dark curling hair and head meant more to him than any other because it made up in some mysterious way just that key which unlocked his attention and desire and love. Closely, personally attached in thought and sympathy, interacting upon each other at every turn, they were yet separate beings irrevocably personal and apart, and must remain so for all efforts to bridge the gulf. Any move beyond a point fell into the void. He did not know at this moment what she was thinking, what she was feeling. Only the outward symbols he had come to understand told him that she had been excited and nervously alert and now was not. Her mind instead was exploring this new thing he had told her, trying to foresee what even he could not foresee who knew and understood so much more.

"A letter came for you this afternoon," she said. "I don't know who twas from."

"Oh, from George Warleggan. I met him this morning. He said he had written to invite me to another of his parties and I should find the invitation at home."

She was silent. Somewhere in the depths of the house Jud and Prudie were arguing; you could hear the deep growl of Prudie's complaint and the lighter growl of Jud's answer, like two dogs snarling at each other, the mastiff bitch and the crossbred bulldog.

"This will make enmity between you an' George Warleggan, won't it?"

"Very likely."

"I don't know that that's good. He's very rich, isn't he?"

"Rich enough. But there are older and stronger interests in Cornwall, if they can be roused."

There was a clash of pans from the kitchen.

"Now tell me," Ross said, "what was exciting you when I met you at Wheal Maiden?"

Demelza got up. "Those two old crows'll wake Julia. I must go and separate them."

CHAPTER XI   Dwight Enys, very gratified, rode over on the following day. Together they went to see the Gatehouse in the clump of trees beyond Reath Cottage, and Keren Daniel stood at a window and watched them ride past and thought her own strange thoughts. Demelza had been nearer divining her mind than Keren ever imagined.

Ross was surprised to find that Enys too had an invitation to the Warleggan party; and when he arrived there on the day he soon located him standing rather defensively against the wall in the reception-room.

There was a sprinkling of ladies among the guests and Ross kept his eyes and ears open. All society whispered of some woman Francis was paying attention to, but so far he had never seen her. Uncle Cary Warleggan was here to-night. Cary was not quite on the same respectable level as brother Nicholas and nephew George, and though he was one of the trio which was stretching its financial fingers all over west Cornwall, he generally kept in the background. He was tall and thin and bloodless, with a long nose, which he spoke through, and a wide tight crease of a mouth. Also present was a miller called Sanson with fat hands and a sharp sly look half masked by a habitual blink.

Ross strolled about with Dwight for a while, through the reception-rooms and then out upon the lawns, which ran down to the river at the back of the house. He mentioned Jim Carter and his imprisonment in Bodmin, and Enys said he would gladly go and see the young man any time.

When they returned to the lighted house Ross saw a tall young woman with shining black hair standing beside Francis at the hazard table. His deferential attitude left no doubt.

"A twelve as I'm alive! You nick," said the lady, her voice slow and deep with a not-unattractive burr. "And a bad dream to you, Francis. Always you was lucky at this game."

She turned her head to glance round the room, and Ross felt as if he had touched hot metal.

Years ago when he had left the Assembly Rooms sick at heart and desperate and had gone to the Bear Inn and tried to drink his misery away, there had come to him a tall, gaunt young harlot, distinctive and unusual but down-and-out, importuning him with her wide bold eyes and drawling tongue. And he had gone with her to her derelict hut and tried to drown his love for Elizabeth in a tawdry counterfeit passion.

He had never known her name except that it was Margaret. He had never known anything about her. Not in any wild dream had he thought to find this.

All evidence of poverty gone. She was powdered and scented and so hung with bracelets and rings that at every move she rustled and clinked.

At that moment George Warleggan came into the room. Beautifully dressed and thick-necked and bland, he came over at once to the two gentlemen by the door. Margaret's eyes followed her host and they reached Ross. Seen from this side with the scar, he was unmistakable. Her eyes widened. Then she gave way to a hearty burst of laughter.

"What is it, my love?" Francis asked. "I see nothing comical in a four and a three when you need a ten for a chance."

"Mrs. Cartland," said George, "may I introduce Captain Poldark, Francis's cousin. Mrs. Margaret Cartland."

Ross said: "Your servant, ma'am."

Margaret gave him the hand in which she held the dice shaker. How well now he remembered the strong white teeth, the broad shoulders, the feline, lustful dark eyes. "Me lord," she said, boldly using her old name for him, "I've looked for this introduction for years. I've heard such *tales* about you!"

"My lady," he said, "believe only the most circumstantial—or those that are witty."

She said: "Could any of them fail to be, that concerned you?"

His eyes travelled over her face. "Or any not seem to be, ma'am, with you to recount them."

She laughed. "Nay, it is the stories that *can't* be told that I find most diverting."

He bowed. "The essence of a good joke is that only two should share it."

"I thought that was the essence of a good bed," said Francis, and everybody laughed.

Later Ross played whist, but towards the end of the evening he came upon the lady alone at the foot of the stairs.

She dropped him a rather sarcastic curtsy, with a rustle of silk and a clink of bracelets. "Captain Poldark, how fortunately met."

"How surprisingly met."

"Not so polite out of company, I see."

"Oh, I intend no impoliteness to an old friend."

"Friend? Wouldn't you put it higher than that?"

He saw that her eyes, which he had always thought quite black, were really a very deep blue.

"Higher or lower as you count the matter," he said. "I'm not one for splitting hairs."

"No, you was always a willing man. And now you're married, eh?"

He agreed that he was.

"How monstrous dull." There was sarcastic laughter in her voice which provoked him.

"Should you despise marriage who appear to have followed it?"

"Oh, Cartland," she said. "He's wed and dead."

"Did you put that on his stone?"

She laughed with feline good humour.

"It was the colic put him away, but not before his time, he was forty. Ah, well. May he rest quieter for knowing I've spent his money."

George Warleggan came down the stairs. "You find our new guest entertaining, Margaret?"

She yawned. "To tell the truth when I have eaten so well almost anything will entertain me."

"And I have not yet eaten," said Ross. "No doubt, ma'am, that explains our difference in sentiment."

George glanced sharply from one to the other but he made no comment.

It was midnight before Ross left, but Francis stayed on. He had lost heavily at faro and was still playing, the number having been reduced to four: Cary Warleggan, who had also lost, Sanson, who was banker and had won all evening, and George, who had come in late to the game. Margaret was there watching the play, her hand resting lightly on Francis's shoulder. She did not look up as Ross left.

Dwight Enys moved to his half-ruined Gatehouse and took up his duties as bal-surgeon to Wheal Leisure; and Keren Daniel settled with a smothered discontent into her life as a miner's wife; and Demelza, taken apparently with a sudden mood, practised her letters with fanatic zeal; and Ross was much away in the company of the talented and persuasive Richard Tonkin, interviewing, discussing, contriving, estimating—working to bring a pipe dream down to the shape of reality.

Life moved on and Julia grew and her mother began to feel her gums for signs of teeth; the price of copper dropped to sixty-seven pounds and two more mines closed; there were riots in Paris and starvation in the provinces; Geoffrey Charles Poldark had the measles at last; and the physicians attending the King found it hard to follow his mathematics on the subject of flies.

It came to the time for Demelza to write her letter, and she did so with great care and many false starts.

DEAR CAP BLAMY,

HAVE THE GOODNESS TO MET US AT MISTRESS TRELASKS SILK MERCER SHOP IN KENWEN STREET TWENTY OCTOBER IN THE FORENOON VERYTY WILL NOT NO SO I BEG OF YOU TO TAKE US BY CHENSE.

SIR, I AM, WITH DUE RESPECT,

YOUR FRIEND AND SERVANT,

DEMELZA POLDARK.

She was not sure about the last part, but she had taken it from a book on correspondence Verity had lent her, so it must be all right.

Lobb, the man who acted as postman, was due on the morrow, so after her fiftieth reading she sealed the letter and addressed it in her boldest writing to: CAPTEN BLAMY, PACKUT OFFICES, FALMOUTH.

There was still a week to go, with all the possible chances of mishap. She had Verity's promise on the excuse that she wanted advice on the buying of a cloak for the winter.

As she walked back down the valley with the *Mercury* tucked under one arm and with Garrick making rude munching sounds at her heels she saw Keren Daniel moving across the valley almost to cut across her path.

This was all land belonging to Ross. It was not an enclosed estate, Joshua having been content to set a few stone posts to mark the limits of his land; but Nampara Combe was generally acknowledged as being within a special sphere of privacy on which the thirty or forty cottagers did not intrude unless invited.

It was clear that Keren did not know this.

This morning she was hatless, with her crisp curling black hair blowing in the wind and wore a brilliant scarlet dress of some cheap flimsy material she had filched from the property box. The wind blew it about the curves of her figure, and it was caught provocatively round her waist with a tight green girdle. It was the sort of dress which would make the men look and the women whisper.

"Good morning," said Demelza.

"Good morning," said Keren, eyeing her covertly for unfavourable comparisons. "What a wind! I mislike wind greatly. D'you never have nothing but wind in these districts?"

"Seldom," said Demelza. "For my part, now, I like a suggestion of breeze. It stirs up the smells and keeps 'em circulated and makes everyone more interesting. A place without wind'd be like bread without yeast, nothing to keep it light. Have you been shopping?"

Keren looked at her keenly a moment to make sure what was intended. Failing, she glanced at her basket and said:

"To Sawle. It is a miserable small place, isn't it? I suppose you do all your shopping in Truro."

"Oh, I like to buy from Aunt Mary Rogers whenever it is feasible. She's a brave kind soul for all her fat. I could tell you things about Aunt Mary Rogers . . ."

Keren looked uninterested.

"And then there's pilchards," said Demelza. "Sawle pilchards are the best in England. Mind you, it has been a rare bad season for 'em, but last year was wonderful. It set 'em up for the winter. What they'll do this year is beyond imagining."

"Mistress Poldark," Keren said, "don't *you* think Mark is worth something better than being a common ordinary miner? Don't you?"

Surprised, Demelza stared at the sudden question. She said: "Yes. Maybe. I hadn't thought to look at it that way."

"Nobody does. But look at him: he's strong as an ox; he's sharp enough; he's keen; he's a worker. But Grambler Mine is a dead end like. What can he do but work an' work, day in day out for a starvation wage till he's too old an' crippled like his father. An' then what's to become of us?"

"I didn't know twas so near starvation," Demelza said. "I thought he made a fair wage. He's on tribute, isn't he?"

"It keeps us. No more."

Demelza saw a horseman come over the hill.

"My father was a miner," she said. "Tributer like Mark. Still is. He made a fair wage. Up an' down of course, an' nothing startling at the best. But we should have managed if he hadn't swilled it all away at the gin shops. Mark don't drink, do he?"

Keren moved a stone about with her foot.

"I wondered if it was ever possible Captain Poldark ever had a vacancy in his mine, you see; a vacancy for something better. I only wondered. I thought it might be. Those on tribute there are doing well, they say; and I thought maybe there might be something better sometime."

"I've nought to do with it," Demelza said. "But I'll mention it." It was not Ross on the horse.

"Mind," said Keren, tossing her hair back, "we're nice and comfortable and all that. It isn't that one *needs* to ask favours, so to say. But Mark is so behindhand in that. I said to him one day, 'Why don't you go ask Captain Ross; you're a friend of his; he couldn't bite you; maybe he's never thought of you in that way; nothing venture, nothing have.' But he just shook his head and wouldn't answer. I always get angry when he won't answer."

"Yes," said Demelza.

The horseman was coming through the trees now, and Keren heard him and looked over her shoulder. Her face was slightly flushed and slightly resentful, as if someone had been asking a favour of *her*. It was Dwight Enys.

"Oh, Mrs. Poldark. I have just been to Truro and thought to call in on the way back. Is Captain Poldark at home?"

"No, he's in to Redruth, I b'lieve."

Dwight dismounted, handsome and young. Keren glanced quickly from one to the other.

"I have a letter here, that's all. Mr. Harris Pascoe asked me to deliver it. May I presume to leave it with you?"

"Thank you." Demelza took the letter. "This is Mistress Keren Daniel, Mark Daniel's wife. This is Dr. Enys."

Dwight bowed. "Your servant, ma'am." He was not sure from the girl's dress to what class she belonged, and he had forgotten who Mark Daniel was.

Under his gaze Keren's expression changed like a flower when the sun comes out. While she spoke she kept her eyes down, her long black lashes on the dusky peach bloom of her cheeks. She knew the young man, having seen him two or three times from her window after that first glimpse of him with Ross. She knew that he had come to live in that turreted house half hidden in a clump of trees just up the other side of the valley from her own cottage. She knew that he had never seen her before. She knew the value of first impressions.

They walked down together towards Nampara House, Keren determined that she should not leave the other two until she was forced. At the house Demelza invited them in for a glass of wine, but to Keren's great disappointment he refused. Keren, quickly deciding that a few minutes of Dr. Enys's company was worth more than the interest of seeing the inside of Nampara House, refused also; and they left together, Dwight leading his horse and walking beside Keren.

The twentieth of October was a windy day with dust and dead leaves blowing and the promise of rain. Demelza was on edge, as if she had a long-distance coach to catch; and Verity was amused by her wish to get into Truro by eleven at the latest. Demelza said that it wasn't nervousness for herself but that Julia had been restless in the night and she suspected she was a bit feverish.

At that Verity suggested they might postpone the visit: they could very easily ride in another day when it was more convenient. It would have suited her, for the date had come round for the quarterly meeting of the Grambler shareholders. But Demelza now seemed more than ever keen to go. . . .

This time they had Bartle for company, for Jud was growing ever more wayward.

Halfway there it began to rain, a thin damp drizzle moving across the country like a mesh of fine silk, slower than the low bags of cloud which spun it. About three miles from Truro they saw a crowd of people stretching across the road. It was so unusual to see many people about in the middle of the day that they reined in.

"I think tis a pile o' miners, ma'am," said Bartle. "Mebbe tis a feast day we've forgot."

Verity went forward a little doubtfully. These people did not look as if they were celebrating.

A man was standing on a cart talking to a compact group gathered around him. He was some distance away, but it was clear that he was giving expression to a grievance. Other groups of people sat on the ground or talked among themselves. There were as many women as men among them, all poorly dressed and some with young children. They looked angry and cold and desperate. A good many were actually in the lane, which here ran between clearly defined hedges, and hostile looks met the two well-dressed women on horseback with their well-fed groom.

Verity put a bold front on it and led the way slowly through: and silently they were watched and sullenly

Presently the last were left behind.

"*Phhh!*" said Demelza. "Who were they, Bartle?"

"Miners from Idless an' Chacewater, I bla'. These are poor times, ma'am."

Demelza edged her horse up to Verity's. "Were you scairt?"

"A little. I thought they might upset us."

Demelza was silent for some moments. "I mind once when we were short of corn in Illugan. We had potatoes an' water for a week—and mortal few potatoes."

For the moment her attention had been diverted from the plot on hand, but as they reached Truro she forgot the miners and only thought of Andrew Blamey and what she had engineered.

CHAPTER XII   Truro wore its usual Thursday-morning appearance, a little untidier than most days because of the cattle market of the afternoon before. They left Bartle in the centre of the town and made their way on foot, picking a fastidious path over the cobbles and through the mud and refuse.

There was no sign of a stocky figure in a blue-laced coat, and they went into the little dress shop. Demelza was unusually fussy this morning; but at length Verity persuaded her to pick a dark bottle-green cloth which would not clash with any of the clothes she already had and which greatly suited the colour of her skin.

When it was all over Demelza asked the time. The seamstress went to see, and it was just noon. Well . . . she'd done her part. She could do no more. No doubt the date was wrong and he was still at sea.

The little bell in the shop pinged noisily and her heart leapt, but it was only a Negro page boy to ask whether the Hon. Maria Agar's bonnet was finished.

Demelza lingered over some silk ribbons, but Verity was anxious to get her own shopping done. They had arranged to take a meal at Joan Pascoe's, an ordeal Demelza was not looking forward to, and there would be little time for shopping after that.

There were more people in the narrow street when they left the shop. A cart drawn by oxen was delivering ale at a near-by gin shop. Ten or twelve urchins, undersized, barefoot and scabby, and wearing men's discarded coats cut down and tied with string, were rioting among a pile of garbage. At the end of the street by the West Bridge a sober merchant had come to grief in the slippery mud and was being helped to his feet by two beggars. A dozen shopping women were out, most of them in clogs and with loops to their wrists to keep their skirts out of the dirt.

"Miss Verity," said a voice behind them.

Oh, God, thought Demelza, it has come at last.

Verity turned. Riding and shopping brought a delicate flush to her cheeks which they normally lacked. But as she looked into Andrew Blamey's eyes the colour drained away: from her forehead, her lips, her neck, and only her eyes showed their blue greyness in a dead-white face.

Demelza took her arm.

"Miss Verity, ma'am." Blamey glanced for a second at Demelza. His own eyes were a deeper blue, as if the ice had melted. "For years I dared to hope, but no chance came my way. Lately I had begun to lose the belief that someday . . ."

"Captain Blamey," said Verity in a voice that was miles away, "may I introduce you to my cousin, Mistress Demelza Poldark, Ross's wife."

"I'm honoured, ma'am."

"And I, sir."

"You are shopping?" Blamey said. "Have you engagements for an hour? It would give me more pleasure than I can express . . ."

Demelza saw the life slowly creeping back into Verity's face. And with it came all the reservations of the later years.

"I don't think," she said, "that any good can come of our meeting, Captain Blamey. There is no ill thought for you in my heart . . . But after all this time we are better to renew nothing, to assume nothing, to— to seek nothing. . . ."

"That," said Andrew, "is what I passionately challenge. This meeting is most happy. It brings me the hope of—at least a friendship where hope had—gone out. If you will——"

Verity shook her head. "It's over, Andrew. We faced that years ago.

Forgive me, but there is much we have to do this morning. We will wish you good day."

She moved to go on, but Demelza did not stir. "Pray don't consider me, Cousin. I can do the shopping on my own, truly I can. If—if your friend want a word with you, it is only polite to grant it."

"No, you must come too, mistress," said the seaman, "or it would be talked of. Verity, I have a private room as it happens at an inn. We could go there, take coffee or a cordial. For old times' sake. . . ."

Verity wrenched her arm away from Demelza. "No," she said hysterically. "No! I say no."

She turned and began to walk quickly down the street towards the West Bridge. Demelza glanced frantically at Blamey, then followed. She was furious with Verity, but as she caught up with her and again took her arm, slowing her footsteps, she realized that Andrew Blamey had been prepared for this meeting while Verity had not. Verity's feelings were just the same as Blamey's had been that morning she went to Falmouth, a shying away from an old wound, a sharp-reared hostility to prevent more hurt. She blamed herself for not warning Verity. But how could she have done that when Verity——

Coming to her ears were all sorts of noises and shouts, and in her present upset and confused state she came to link them with Blamey.

"You've left him far behind," she said. "There's no hurry now. Oh, Verity, it would ha' been fine if you'd given him a hearing. Really it would."

Verity kept her face averted. She felt stifled with tears, they were in her throat, everywhere but her eyes, which were quite dry. She had almost reached the West Bridge and tried to push her way towards it, but found herself blocked by a great number of people who seemed to be talking and staring up the way she had come. Demelza too was holding her back.

It was the miners, Demelza saw now. By the West Bridge there was a centre block of ancient houses with narrow streets like a collar about them, and in this roundabout the miners who had come down River Street were milling, jostling each other, packed tight together, shouting and shaking their weapons. They had lost direction, being set for the Coinagehall, but this junction of streets and alleys had confused them. Half a dozen of their number and several ordinary people had been pushed into the stream by the pressure from behind, and others were fighting in the mud to avoid following; the old stone bridge was packed with people struggling to get across it. Demelza and Verity were on the very edge of the maelstrom, twigs circling the outer currents and likely at any time to be drawn in. Then Demelza glanced behind her and saw people, miners, grey and dusty and angry, coming in a mass down Kenwyn Street.

They were caught between two floods.

"Verity, look!"

"In here," said a voice, and her arm was grasped. Andrew Blamey pulled them across the street to the porch of a house. It was tiny, it would just hold the three of them, but they might be safe.

Verity, half resisting, went with them. Andrew put Demelza behind him and Verity by his side, protecting her with his arm across the door.

The first wave of the flood went past them, shouting and shaking fists. It went past them at speed. Then came the impact of the crowd at the bridge; the speed slackened as rushing water will slacken and fill up a narrow channel once there is no further escape. The miners became eight, ten, fifteen, twenty abreast in the narrow street and some of the women began to scream. They filled the whole of Kenwyn Street, a grey and haggard horde as far as you could see. Men were being pressed against the walls of the houses as if they would burst them open; glass cracked in the windows. Blamey used all his strength to ease the pressure in the doorway.

No one could tell what was happening, but the earliest comers must have found their direction, and this began to ease the congestion beyond the bridge. The flood began to move turgidly away across the neck of the bridge. Pressure eased, the crowd ebbed, at first slowly, then more quickly towards the centre of the town.

Soon they were stumbling past in ragged columns and the three in the porch were safe.

Andrew lowered his arm. "Verity, I beg of you to reconsider . . ." He caught sight of her face. "Oh, my dear, please. . . ."

She pushed past him and plunged into the crowd.

The movement was so swift and reckless that neither of the others was quick enough to follow.

Then Blamey went shouting, "Verity! Verity!" over the heads of the people who separated them, and Demelza followed.

But even that second was enough to set people between them, and he with his greater strength, fighting ahead to catch Verity, soon widened the gap until Demelza lost sight of him.

Demelza was above average height, but they were all tall men ahead of her and she pushed and turned and craned her head to no purpose. Then as they neared the bottleneck of the bridge she had no room or strength to look for the others; she could only fight for herself to avoid being diverted and pushed into the river. Men and women were squeezed upon her from all sides, elbows and staves poking and pressing and jerking; the great crowd animal seized her breath and gave her nothing in return. For moments they were stationary, shouting and sweating and cursing; then, suddenly silent, they would surge one way or another. Several times she lost her foothold altogether and went along without using her legs, at others she stumbled and had to clutch at her neighbours to save herself from going under. Quite near her a woman fell and was trampled on by the crowd. Then another fainted, but she was picked up and dragged along by a man beside her. Beyond her sight there were splashings and screamings and the clash of staves.

Even past the bridge the very narrow street gave no good outlet.

Near its objective, the crowd was getting angrier, and its anger took more of the air, consuming it in great waves of heat and violence. Lights and spots danced before Demelza's eyes, and she fought with the others for room to live. At last they were out of the worst press and bearing down Coinagehall Street. The crowd was making for the big corn warehouses which stood beside the creek.

Captain Blamey was away to her right—she saw him suddenly—and as she began to recover she tried to fight towards him.

The press grew again, bore her forward and slowly brought her to a standstill, surrounded by angry sweating miners and their women. Her good clothes were too conspicuous.

Before the big doors of the first warehouse citizens and burghers of the town were gathered to defend the rights of property. A fat, soberly clad man, the Citizen Magistrate, was standing on a wall, and he began to shout soundlessly into the great growling noise of the mob. Beside him was the corn factor who owned the warehouse, a fat man with a habit of blinking, and two or three constables of the town. There were no soldiers about; the justices had been taken by surprise.

As Demelza pushed her way towards the corner, where Blamey was, she saw Verity. He had found her. They were standing together against a stable door, unable to move farther for the crowd of people about them.

The magistrate had turned from reason to threat. While all that could be done would be done, that did not mean that those who broke the law would not be punished according to the law. He'd remind them of the trouble at Redruth last month when one of the rioters had been sentenced to death and many thrown into prison.

There were cries of "Shame!" and "Cruel an' wicked!"

"But we want no more'n what's right. We want corn to live by like the beasts o' the field. Well, then, sell us corn at a fair an' proper price an' we'll go home wi' it peaceable. Name us a price, mister, a fair an' proper price for starving men."

The magistrate turned and spoke to the corn factor beside him.

Demelza pushed her way between two miners, who glared at her angrily for the disturbance. She had thought to cry out to catch Verity's notice, but changed her mind.

The justice said: "Mr. Sanson will sell you the corn at fifteen shillings a bushel as a concession to your poor and needy families. Come, it is a generous offer."

There was a growl of anger and dissent, but before he replied the little miner bent to consult with those around him.

At last Demelza got within speaking distance of her friends, but they were separated from her by a handcart and a group of women sitting on the handcart, and she did not see how she could get nearer. Neither Andrew nor Verity saw her, for their gaze was towards the parley at the doors of the warehouse, although it might never have been happening for all they took in.

"Eight shillings. We'll pay ye eight shillings a bushel. Tis the very top we can afford, an' that'll mean hardship an' short commons for all."

The corn merchant made an expressive gesture with his hands before even the magistrate turned to him. There was a roar of hostility from the crowd, and then suddenly in the silence which followed Demelza heard Andrew's voice speaking low and quick.

". . . to live, my dear. Have I expiated nothing, learned nothing in these empty years? If there's blood between us, then it's old and long dry. Francis is changed, that I can see, though I've not spoken to him. But you have not changed, in heart you have not. . . ."

There was another roar.

"Eight shillings or nothing," shouted a miner. "Speak now, mister, if it's to be peace, for we can 'old back no longer."

Verity put up a gloved hand to her eyes.

"Oh, Andrew, what can I say? Are we to have all this again . . . the meeting, the parting, the heartache?"

"No, my dear, I *swear*. Never the parting. . . ."

Then it was all lost in the roar that greeted Sanson's obstinate refusal. The little miner went from his perch as if a hand had plucked him, and there was a great surge forward. The men on the steps of the granary put up a show of resistance, but they were leaves before a wind. In a few minutes tinners were hacking with their staves at the padlock on the door of the warehouse, and then quickly the doors were open and they surged in.

Demelza clung to the handcart to stop herself being carried towards the warehouse, but then men seized the handcart to load it up with grain, and she had to give way and press herself against the stable door.

"Demelza!" Verity had seen her. "Andrew, help her. They will knock her down."

Verity clung to Demelza's arm as if Demelza were the one who had forsaken it. The tears had dried on her face, leaving it streaky and uncomely. Her black fine hair was awry and her skirt torn. She looked unhappy—and painfully alive.

Those inside the warehouse were passing out sacks of grain to those who were waiting for them, and mules, which had been held in the background, were already coming down the street to be laden with the booty. The warehouse, drawing all towards it as a gutter will draw water, was thinning out the people near Demelza and Verity.

"This way," said Blamey, "there is a good chance now. Better than later, for maybe they will start drinking when the corn's away."

He led them back to Coinagehall Street, which was clear of the tinners. But the townsfolk were out in their numbers, talking nervously together and discussing how best to prevent the looting from becoming widespread. The miners had come into town on a fair grievance, but appetite feeds an appetite and they might stay.

"Where are your horses?" asked Blamey.

"We were to have eaten with the Pascoes."

"I'd advise you to defer it to a later day."

"Why?" said Demelza. "Could you not dine there too?"

Blamey glanced at her as they walked round Middle Row.

"No, ma'am, I could not, and though no doubt their bank building is strong and you would be safe inside it, you would later face the problem of leaving it to ride home, and the streets may not be safe by then. If you dine with the Pascoes, then be prepared to stay the night."

"Oh, I could not do that!" said Demelza. "Julia would need me, an' Prudie is so wooden."

"Andrew," said Verity, her steps slowing, "won't you leave us here. If Bartle sees you the news of this meeting may reach Francis, and it may seem to him like a deliberate, a—a . . ."

"Let it," said the seaman. "There may be other rioters about. I have no intention of leaving you until you are safe out of this area."

Bartle was in the stables, and while the horses were being saddled they sent a messenger to the Pascoes. Then they were up and away.

There were no rioters in Pydar Street, but people had come out of their houses and were gazing apprehensively down the hill. Some carried sticks themselves.

At the top of the hill the way was too narrow to ride three abreast in comfort, so Demelza, taking things into her own hands, first told Bartle to go a little ahead to see if there were any pickets or rioters and then spurred her own horse forward to join him.

Thus they rode home in silence, two by two, under the lowering sky. Demelza tried to find a little conversation with Bartle, while at the same time straining her ears for sound of talk behind. She did not catch it, but a little took place, a few low words now and then, the first signs of green in a desert after rain.

CHAPTER XIII   Jud had been fairly behaved for so long that Prudie overlooked the signs of a change. The settled domestic life of Nampara—so unlike old Joshua's regime—had had a pacifying effect on her own impulses and she had come to think that the same was true of him. Ross left early in the morning—he was away three and four days a week now—and when Demelza was out of sight Prudie settled herself in the kitchen to brew a dish of tea and talk over the week's scandal with Jinny Carter, overlooking the fact that an hour ago she had caught Jud taking a sup of gin while he milked the cows.

Jinny, in an odd way, had come to fulfil for Prudie much the same function that Demelza had done; in short, she now did most of the rough work of the house and left Prudie to potter and to brew her tea and gossip and complain of her feet. When Demelza was about it wasn't quite as easy as that, but when she went out things settled into a very comfortable groove.

To-day for once Jinny had been talking of Jim, of how thin and ill he had looked, of how she nightly prayed that the next eight months would slip away so that he might be free to come home. Prudie was glad to hear that she had no thought of leaving her work at Nampara. There was to be no more going down the mine for Jim, Jinny said. She had made him promise he would come back and work on the farm. He had never been so well as when he worked here and they never so happy. It wasn't mining wages, but what did that matter? If she worked they could make do.

Prudie said oh, there was no tellin', things was upsy down and it might be that them as worked on a farm would soon be earning more than them as went below, if half she'd heard tell of copper and tin was true. Look at Cap'n Ross, galloping about the countryside as if Old Scratch was at his coattails, and what was the use? What was the good of trying to puff life into a cold corpse? Better if he saved his smith's fees and looked to his own taties.

During this Jinny was in and out the kitchen three or four times, and on her last return wore an anxious look on her thin young face.

"There's someone in the cellar, Prudie. Truly. Just now as I were passing the door . . ."

"Nay," said the other woman, wiggling her toes. "You're mistook.

Twas a rat maybe. Or wur it little Julia a-stirring in 'er cot, an? Go see, will ee, and save my poor feet."

"Couldn' be that," said Jinny. "It were a man's voice—grumble, grumble, grumble, like an old cart wheel—coming up from the cellar steps."

Prudie was about to contradict her again, but then with a thoughtful look she pulled on her slippers and rose like the side of a mountain creakily out of her chair. She flapped out into the hall and peered through the cellar door, which opened in the angle made by the stairs.

For a few seconds the murmur was too indistinct to catch any words, but after a while she heard:

"There was an old couple an' they was—was poor.
Tw—tw—tweedle, go tweedle, go twee."

"Tes Jud," she said grimly to the anxious Jinny. "Drownin' his guts in Cap'n Ross's best gin. 'Ere, stay a breath, I'll root en out."

She flapped back to the kitchen. "Where's that there broom 'andle?"

"In the stable," said Jinny. "I seen it there this morning."

Prudie went out to get it, Jinny with her; but when they came back the song in the cellar had stopped. They lighted a candle from the kitchen fire and Prudie went down the stairs. There were several broken bottles about but no signs of Jud.

Prudie came up. "The knock-kneed 'ound's wriggled out while we was away."

"Hold a minute," said Jinny.

They listened.

Someone was singing gently in the parlour.

Jud was in Ross's best chair, with his boots on the mantelpiece. On his head, hiding the fringe and the tonsure, was one of Ross's hats, a black riding hat turned up at the brim. In one hand was a bottle of gin and in the other a riding crop, with which he gently stirred the cradle in which Julia slept.

"Jud!" said Prudie. "Get out o' that chair!"

Jud turned his head.

"Ah," he said, in a ridiculous voice. "C-come in, good women all, good women all, g-good women. Your servant, ma'am. Damme, tis handsome of ee to make this visit. Tedn what I'd of expected in a couple o' bitches. But there, one 'as to take the rough wi' the rough; an' a fine couple of bitches ye be. Pedigree stock, sir. Never have I seen the likes. Judgin' only by the quarters, tis more'n a fair guess to say there's good blood in ee, an' no missment." He gave the cradle a prod with his riding crop to keep it rocking.

Prudie grasped her broom.

" 'Ere, dear," she said to Jinny, "you go finish yer work. I'll deal with this."

"Can you manage him?" Jinny asked anxiously.

"Manage 'im. I'll *mince* 'im. Only tis a question of the cradle. We don't want the little mite upset."

When Jinny had gone, Jud said: "What, no more'n one lef'? What a cunning crack ye are, Mishtress Paynter, gettin' quit o' she so's there'll be less to share the gin." His little eyes were bloodshot with drink and bleary with cunning. "Come us in, my dear, an' lift your legs up. I'm the owner 'ere; Jud Paynter, eskewer, of Nampara, mashter of hounds, mashter of cemeteries, Justice of the Peace. 'Ave a sup!"

"Pah!" said Prudie. "Ye'll laugh on the other side of yer head if Cap'n Ross catches ee wi' yer breeches glued to 'is bettermost chair. Ah . . . ye dirty glut!"

He had upended his bottle of gin and was drinking it in great gulps, so that bubbles leapt up the side of the bottle.

"Nay, don't ee get scratchy, for I've two more by the chair. Ye've overfanged notions o' the importance of Ross an' his kitchen girl in the scum of things. 'Ere, 'ave a spur."

Jud leaned over and put a half-empty bottle on the table behind him. Prudie stared at it.

"Look!" she said. "Out o' that chair or I'll cleave open yer 'ead with this broom. An' leave the cheeil alone!" The last words came in a screech, for he had given the cradle another poke.

Jud turned and looked at her assessingly; through the blear of his gaze he tried to see how far his head was in danger. But Ross's hat gave him confidence.

"Gis along, you. 'Ere, there's brandy in the cupboard. Fetch it down an' I'll mix ye a Sampson."

This had once been Prudie's favourite drink: brandy and cider and sugar. She stared at Jud as if he were the Devil tempting her to sell her soul.

She said: "If I d'want drink I'll get it and not akse you, nor no other else." She went to the cupboard and genteelly mixed herself a Sampson. With greedy glassy eyes Jud watched her.

"Now," said Prudie fiercely, "out o' that chair!"

Jud wiped a hand across his face. "Dear life, it d'make me weep to see ee. Drink un up first. An' mix me one too. Mix me a Sampson wi' his hair on. There, there, be a good wife now."

A "Sampson with his hair on" was the same drink but with double the brandy. Prudie took no notice and drank her own. Then, gloomily, she mixed herself another.

"Tend on yerself," she said. "I never was yer wife, and well you d'know it. Never in church proper like a good maid should. Never no passon to breathe 'is blessing. Never no music. Never no wedden feast. Just *took*, I was. I wonder you d'sleep of nights."

"Well, a fine load ye was," said Jud. "An' more's been added. Half enough to fill a tin ship now. And you didn want no wedden. Gis along, you old suss. Twas all I could do to get ee 'ere decent. Ave a drink."

Prudie reached for the half-empty bottle.

"Me old mother wouldn have liked it," she said. "Tes fair to say she was happier dead. The only one she reared, I was. One out of twelve. Tes hard to think on after all these year."

"One in twelve's a fair portion," said Jud, giving the cot another push. "The world's too full as tis, and some should be drownded. Ef I 'ad me way, which mebbe I never shall an' more's the pity, for there's precious few has got the head on 'em that Jud Paynter have got, though there's jealous folk as pretend to think other, and one o' these days they'll 'ave the shock of their lives, for Jud Paynter'll up and tell 'em down-souse that tes jealous thoughts an' no more d'keep away a recognition which, if he 'ad un, would be no more than any man's due who's got the head on 'im, where was I?"

"Killin' off me little brothers and sisters," said Prudie.

"Ais," said Jud. "One in twelve. That's what I d'say, one in twelve. Not swarming like the Martins an' the Viguses and the Daniels. Not swarming like this house'll be before long. Put 'em in the tub I would, like they was chets."

Prudie's great nose was beginning to light up.

"I'll have no sich talk in my kitchen," she declared.

"We bain't in your kitchen now, so hold yer tongue, you fat cow."

"Cow yerself, and more," said Prudie. "Dirty old gale. Dirty old ox. Dirty old wort. Pass me that bottle. This one's dry."

In the kitchen Jinny waited for the crash and commotion of Jud's punishment. It did not come. She went on with her work. Since her youngest, Kate, had begun to get her fingers in things she had given up bringing her to work and had left her in the care of her mother, to grow up along with the other two and with the younger ones of Mrs. Zacky's brood. So she was all alone in the kitchen.

Presently she finished her work and looked about for something else. The windows could do with a wash. She took out a bucket to get water from the pump and saw her eldest, Bengy Ross, coming trotting over the fields from Mellin.

She knew at once what it was. Zacky had promised to let his daughter know.

She went to meet the child, wiping her hands on her apron.

Bengy was now three and a half, a big boy for his age, showing no hurt for his ordeal except the thin white scar on his cheek. She met him at the edge of the garden by the first apple trees.

"Well, dear?" she said. "What did Gramfer say?"

Bengy looked at her brightly. "Gramfer d'say mine be to close next month, Mam."

Jinny stopped wiping her hands. "What . . . all of it?"

"Ais. Gramfer say tis all to close down next month. Mam, can I 'ave an apple?"

This was worse than she had expected. She had thought that they might let half of it go and keep the richer lode. She had hoped no worse. If all Grambler was to close it meant the end of everything. A few lucky ones might have savings to last the winter. The rest would find other work or starve. There was no other work about unless a few got on at Wheal Leisure. Some might try the lead mines of Wales or the coal mines of the Midlands, leaving their families here to see for themselves. It would be a breakup of lives, of homes.

Now there would be no choice for Jim when he came out. He would be lucky even to be taken on at the farm. She had lived all her life in the shadow of Grambler. It was no light-seeking venture, easy begun and easy done. There had been ups and downs, she knew, but never a closure. She did not know how many years it had been going, but long before her mother was born. There had been no village of Grambler there before the mine: the mine *was* the village. It was the centre point of the district, the industry, a household name, an institution.

She went in and picked out a ripe apple from among the "resters" in the still-room, gave it to Bengy.

She must tell Jud and Prudie—at least tell Prudie, if Jud was not yet in his senses.

Bengy trailing at her heels, she went into the parlour.

Ross heard the news as he was riding home from his meeting with Richard Tonkin, Ray Penvenen and Sir John Trevaunance. An elderly miner, Fred Pendarves, shouted it to him as he was passing the gibbet at the Bargus crossroads. Ross rode on thinking there would be no mines left to profit by their scheme if things went on like this much longer. He had come away from Place House, Trevaunance, in an encouraged mood, for Sir John had promised them his influence and his money, provided they built the copper smelting works on his land; but the news of Grambler's closure set this optimism back.

He rode slowly down Nampara Combe and reached his house, but he did not at once take Darkie to her stable. He had the half thought of going to see Francis.

In the hall he paused and listened to the raised voices in the parlour. Was Demelza entertaining company? He was not in the mood for company.

But that was Jud's voice. And Jinny Carter's raised too. Jinny *shouting!* He went to the door, which was an inch open.

"It is a lie!" Jinny was in tears. "A wicked filthy lie, Jud Paynter, and you did ought to be whipped, sittin' there in your master's chair drinking his brandy and uttering such falseness. You did ought to be scourged wi' scorpions like they say in the Bible. You horrible nasty beast you——"

"Hearear," said Prudie. "Thash ri', dearie. Give un a clunk on the head. 'Ave my stick."

"You bide in yer own sty," said Jud. "Cabby ole mare. I'm not saying nothin' but what's said by others. Look for yerself. Look at the lad's scar, there on 'is face. Poor lil brat, tedn his fault. But is it wonder folk d'say twas put there as a mark by Beelzebub himself to mark 'is true father for all to see. Folks d'say—and who can blame 'em—who ever see two scars more alike? Like father like son, they d'say: Ross and Bengy Ross. An' then, they d'say: Look he was riding off again wi' she last month but one all the way to Bodmin, and lay there *the night*. Tedn my talking, but tedn surprising there's talk. An' all the weepin' an' shoutin' in Gristledom won't stay it."

"I'll hear no more," cried Jinny. "I comed in here to tell you about Grambler, an' you turn on me like a horrible drunk old dog! An' you, Prudie, I should never have believed it if I hadn't seen it with my own eyes!"

"Ushush! Don't take on so, maid. I'm jush sitting here quiet-like to see Jud gets up to no mishchief. After all's done an' said——"

"An' as for that poor lil brat thur," said Jud, "tedn reasonable to blame he. Tedn smart. Tedn proper. Tedn just. Tedn fitty——"

"I wish Jim was here! Bengy, come away from the beast. . . ."

She burst out of the parlour with a wild look and her face streaked with tears. She clutched her eldest child by one hand. Ross had drawn back but she saw him. She instantly went very white, the red patches on her face showing up like blotches. Her eyes met his in fright and hostility. Then she ran into the kitchen.

Demelza reached home soon after, having walked across the cliff way from Trenwith. She found Julia still asleep through all the noise and Prudie with her head in her apron weeping loudly beside the cradle. The parlour reeked, and there were two broken bottles on the floor. Chairs were overturned and Demelza began to suspect the truth.

But she could get no sense out of Prudie, who only wailed the louder when she was touched and said they'd both seen the last of Jud.

Demelza fled into the kitchen. No sign of Jinny.

Noises in the yard.

Ross stood by the pump working it with one hand while in the other he held a horsewhip. Jud was under the pump.

Every time he tried to get away from the water he took a crack from the horsewhip, so he had given it up and was now drowning patiently.

"Ross, Ross! What is it! What has he done, Ross?"

He looked at her.

"Next time you take the day for shopping," he said, "we will see that better arrangements are come to for the care of our child."

The seeming injustice of this took her breath away.

"Ross!" she said. "I don't understand. What has happened? Julia seems all right."

Ross cracked his whip. "Get under there! Learn to swim! Learn to swim! Let's see if we can wash some of the nasty humours out of you."

"Humours" might have been "rumours," but Demelza did not know that. She turned suddenly and ran back into the house.

Verity got right home without hearing anything of the decision. They had parted from Captain Blamey at the St. Ann's Fork, and then Demelza had dismounted at the gates of Trenwith and Verity and Bartle went up the drive alone.

Elizabeth was the only one who looked up at Verity's coming in, for Aunt Agatha did not hear it and Francis did not heed it.

Elizabeth smiled painfully. "Did the Pascoes let you leave so soon?"

"We didn't go," said Verity, pulling off her gloves. "There were miners rioting in the town and—and we thought it wise to leave before the disorder grew worse."

"Ha!" said Francis from the window. "Rioting indeed. There'll be rioting in other parts soon."

"For that reason, I had not the time to get you the brooch, Elizabeth. I am so sorry, but perhaps I shall be able to go in next week——"

"All these years," said Aunt Agatha. "Damn me, twas old afore I was born. I mind well old Grannie Trenwith telling me that her grandpa-by-marriage, John Trenwith, cut the first goffin the year afore he died."

"What year was that?" Francis said moodily.

"But if you was to ask me how long ago that was, I shouldn't know. I'd say ye'd best look in the Bible. But it was when Elizabeth was an old queen."

Quite slowly the import of the whole scene came to Verity. The meeting of this morning had gone from her mind. She had ridden away from

Trenwith obsessed by the decisions that were to be taken in her absence. She had ridden back and not given it a thought.

"You don't mean——"

"Then the first underground shaft was put in by the other John seventy or eighty year later. That was the one Grannie Trenwith married. All those years an' never closed. It isn't long since we drew thousands a year out of it. It don't seem right to let it all go."

With a sudden subtlety unnatural in her, Verity played up to their assumption.

"From what I heard," she said, "I wasn't quite sure . . . Does it mean the whole mine? Everything?"

"How could it be otherwise?" Francis turned from the window. "We can't keep one part drained without the other."

"Why, when I was growing up," said Aunt Agatha, "there was money to play with. Papa died when I was eight, and I mind how Mama spent money on the memorial in Sawle Church. 'Spare no expense,' I heard her say. I can hear her now. 'Spare no cost. He died as surely of his wounds as if he'd fallen in battle. He shall have a worthy stone.' Ah, Verity, so you're back, eh? You're flushed. Why're you so flushed? Tis nothing to warm the blood, this news. It be the downfall of the Poldarks, I can tell ye."

"What will this mean, Francis?" Verity asked. "How will it affect us? Shall we be able to go on as before?"

"As shareholders, it will affect us not at all except to destroy the hope of a recovery and to stop us throwing good money after bad. We have drawn no dividend for five years. For mineral rights we have been taking upwards of eight hundred pounds a year, which will now cease. That's the difference."

Verity said: "We can hardly then continue——"

"It will depend on our other commitments," Francis said irritably. "We have the farm to work. We own all Grambler village and half Sawle, for what the rents will be worth after this. But if our creditors will be indulgent, there will be a minimum incoming which will make life supportable even if hardly worth supporting."

Elizabeth got up, sliding Geoffrey Charles quietly to the floor.

"We shall manage," she said quietly. "There are others worse than we. There are ways we can save. This cannot last for ever. It is just a question of keeping our heads above water for the time."

Francis glanced at her in slight surprise. Perhaps he had half expected her to take a different line, complaining and blaming him. But she always turned up trumps in a crisis.

"Now," said Geoffrey Charles, glancing angrily at his father, "can I make a noise now, Mama? Can I make a noise now?"

"Not just yet, dear," said Elizabeth.

Verity muttered an excuse and left them.

Slowly she climbed the broad spacious stairs and glanced with new eyes about her as she did so. She walked down the square low passage with its fine Tudor Gothic windows looking out on the small green central square, with its climbing roses, its fountain that never played and its solidly paved path. Everything about the house was solid, well shaped, built to please and built to last. She prayed it would never have to go.

In her own room she avoided looking at herself in the mirror lest she should see there what had been noticeable to Aunt Agatha's sharp old eyes.

This window looked out on the yew hedge and the herb garden. In the bitterness of four years ago she had looked this way. She had found some comfort here in all the big crises of her life.

She did not know if this was a big crisis or not. Perhaps, looking back, it would not seem so. Grambler was closing, that alone meant a wholesale change in the life of the district. Grambler was closing.

But why not be honest? That was not her crisis. It touched her money, but living the sort of life she did, money had always been remote from her. It touched her people then. Yes, acutely; it concerned all the people she knew and liked, not only in this house but in the district. It would affect the choir she taught and make ten times harder her work to help the poor. This morning, this morning, they had been her people. What, then, had changed?

Why wasn't she more upset for them? Why was she not as miserable as she ought to be? Why not? Why not?

The answer was plain if she had the courage to own it.

She pressed her hot face against the glass of the window and listened to the beating of her heart.

CHAPTER XIV   Jud and Prudie had to leave. On that Ross was adamant. In many ways an easygoing man, he would have tolerated much for the sake of loyalty. Jud's drunkenness he had long been used to, but Jud's disloyal slander could not be swallowed at any price. Besides, there was the child to be thought of. They could never be trusted with her again.

He had them before him next morning and gave them a week to get out. Prudie looked tearful, Jud sullen. Jud thought he had talked Ross round before and in a week could talk him round again. In this he was mistaken. It was only when he discovered it that he became really alarmed. Two days before they were due to go Demelza, taking pity on Prudie, suggested that she might be able to persuade Ross to keep *her*, if she would separate from Jud; but at the last Prudie was faithful and chose to go.

So in due time they left, burdened up with all sorts of lumber and belongings. They had found a tumble-down shack, half cottage, half shed, which was the first house in Grambler at this end of the straggling village. It was dismal and derelict, but the rent was practically nothing and it was next to a gin shop, which would be very convenient.

Their leaving was a tremendous upheaval, and when they had gone Nampara seemed a strange house; one was constantly listening for the flop of Prudie's slippers or the harsh tenor of Jud's grievances. They had been sloppy, idle incompetent servants but they had grown into the marrow of life, and everyone felt the loss. Demelza was glad they had not gone far, for her friendship with Prudie was of too long a standing to break in a few days.

In their place Ross took a married pair called John and Jane Gimlett, a plump couple in the early forties. Five or six years ago they had come to Grambler from north Cornwall to find work in the then still-prosperous west and he had set up as a journeyman shoemaker. But it had not gone well and they had both been working at a tin stamp for over a year. They seemed tremendously eager, willing, competent, clean, good-tempered and respectful—all things the opposite of Jud and Prudie. Only time would show how this would last.

Two days after the drunken fracas Ross had some further trouble with his small staff.

"Where's Jinny this morning?"

"She's left," answered Demelza moodily.

"Left?"

"Last night. I intended to have telled you but you were so late back. I can't make head or tail of it."

"What did she say?"

"She said she'd be happier looking after her three children. It was no good me saying all her mother's family would soon be out of work, for she just closed her lips tight and said she wanted to leave."

"Oh," said Ross, stirring his coffee.

"It is all to do with that trouble on Thursday afternoon," said Demelza. "Maybe if I knew what it was about I could do something. I mean, *she* wasn't drunk. Why should *she* leave?"

"I have a notion," said Ross.

"I don't see why I should be the only one left in the dark, Ross. If you know, then you did ought to tell me."

Ross said: "You remember when I took Jinny to Bodmin I said there'd be talk?"

"Yes."

"Well, there *is* talk, and Jud was repeating it when I got home. And there are all sorts of poisonous brews being added from the past. That is another reason why Jud must go—apart from Julia."

"Oh," said Demelza, "I see."

After a moment Ross said: "Perhaps Jinny does not know Jud is leaving. When——"

"Yes, she does. Prudie told her yesterday."

"Well, I will go and see Zacky, that's if you want her back."

"Of course I want her back. I like her."

"I have to see Zacky anyway. I have something to offer him."

"Well, that'll cheer up Mrs. Zacky. I've never seen her downcast before. What's it to be?"

"In our venture in copper buying we want an agent, a man unknown in the trade who will act for us and take the limelight. I think I can get Zacky the appointment. He's no ordinary miner, you know."

"What of Mark Daniel?"

"What about him?"

"You remember I said Keren had asked me if you'd anything good for him?"

"Ye-es. But this would not do, Demelza. We need a man who can read and write and can handle sums of money in a civilized fashion. And one who has a certain knowledge of the world. Zacky's is the minimum that could be acceptable. Besides, we need a man we can trust completely. We must have absolute secrecy. Anything less might be fatal. Of course I would trust Mark with my life . . . but he is not quite the free agent that he was. I feel that, however steady a man is, if he has an unstable wife to whom he is devoted, then there is a corrosion at work on his own foundations."

Demelza said: "I don't know what Keren would say if she heard that. Twould never occur to her that she might be a *drag* on Mark."

"Well, she'll not hear it, so set your mind at rest."

Keren at the moment was up a ladder. For two days it had rained, and the weather had found its way through Mark's thatching. It had come into the kitchen and then into the bedroom, and last night there had been drips of water falling on their feet.

Keren was furious. Of course Mark had spent the best part of his leisure up this ladder in the rain, but it was her view that in the two months of their married life he should have spent much more time making the house weatherproof. Instead, every wet day he had worked on the inside of the house and every fine day he had been in the garden.

He had done wonders there, had carried away many tons of stone and with them had built a wall surrounding the plot of land. The wall stretched right round now, a monument to one man's tireless energy, and inside the wall the land was being dug and raked and weeded and made ready for next season's crops. And in a corner by the house Mark had built a lean-to shed leading into a small walled compound where later he hoped to keep pigs.

Marriage was a disappointment. Mark's love-making, though sincere, was rough and unromantic and devoid of finesse, and Mark's conversation when he was not making love scarcely existed. Then there were the long hours he was away at the mine, and the weekly change of cores, so that one week he was up getting his breakfast at five, and another week he was coming home to sleep at six-thirty, waking her up but refusing to be wakened when she got up herself. Even this core when he went down at two in the afternoon left her with the whole evening alone. It had been the most exciting one in the early days, for he used to come home just before eleven and strip and wash himself and shave and then they'd get into bed together. But the novelty of that had worn off and usually she found an excuse to avoid his clumsy caresses. It was all so different from the part she had played in *The Miller's Bride*.

He had just gone now, hurrying away to be there in time, and she was left with nine hours to kill. He had had no time to move the ladder so she thought she would try to mend the thatch herself. She was of the opinion that adaptability was enough to solve all problems. She found where he had been working, and picked her way across the damp thatch. It was fine this morning, but there was the promise of more rain. She would like to see his face if he came home in a drenching downpour to-night and found the house quite dry within.

From where she sat now she had a clear view of Dr. Enys's turreted house, and she was sorry that the trees about it did not lose their leaves in winter. Three times since that meeting at Nampara she had caught glimpses of him, but they had not exchanged a word. She sometimes thought she would lose the use of her tongue, for few of the neighbours from Mellin came over, and when they did they were not encouraged by their reception. The only person Keren had made a friend of was little Charlie Baragwanath, who usually called in on his way back from work.

For some time now Keren had been having doubts of her own wisdom in leaving the travelling company for this buried-alive existence. She tried sometimes to remember the hardships and discouragements of that life, just to reassure herself; but distance was blurring the view. Even the money she had hoped to find here was not all it seemed. Mark had some money and was generous with it in a way; but the habits of a lifetime could not change in a week. He would give her money to spend as a lump sum, but he did not like to see money spent as a regular thing, to see it frittered. He had made it plain to Keren that his purse had a limit, and once his purse was empty only the severest pinching and saving would fill it again.

Not perhaps even that now that Grambler was going.

She leaned out to tuck in a piece of thatch and bind it, and as she did so her foothold grew uncertain. Quite gently she began to slide down the roof.

"Well," said Zacky, rubbing his bristle, "it is more'n kind of you. I'll not pretend but that I'd like to try it. Mother'll be fair delighted to think there will be money coming in without a break. But I couldn't take that much money, not to start. Give me what I been earning from my pitch, that's fair and proper."

"As an employee of the company," Ross said, "you'll take what you're given. I'll see you have good notice when you'll be wanted. It may mean a few absences from your pitch during the last week or so."

"That's no matter. The zest is out of it anyway. I don't know what half o' them will do this winter."

"And now," said Ross, "I should like a word with Jinny."

Zacky looked a trifle constrained. "She's inside with Mother. I don't know what's got her, but she seem set in her own way. We can't reason with her same as we belonged to when she was a maid. Jinny! Jinny! Come out for a breath. There's a gentleman to see you."

A long pause followed. Finally the door of the cottage opened and Jinny stood there but did not come out.

Ross went over to her. Zacky did not follow but scraped his chin with the ball of his thumb and watched them.

"Captain Poldark," Jinny said, dropping him a slight curtsy but not raising her eyes.

He did not beat about the bush. "I know why you have left us, Jinny, and sympathize with your feelings. But to give way to them is to conform to rules set down by the evil-minded. Through Jud Paynter and his drunkenness they were able to leave a nasty smear across my house and across your reputation. For that he has been got rid of. It would be a mistake for you to give life to the story by taking notice of it. I should like you to come as usual to-morrow."

She looked up and met his glance.

"Twill be better not, sur. If such stories be about, gracious knows where they'll end."

"They'll end where they began, in the gutters."

She was so terribly embarrassed that he was sorry for her. He left her there and returned to Zacky, who had been joined by his wife.

"Leave 'er be for a while, sur," said Mrs. Martin. "She'll come round. I'll not be long, Zacky. I just be going over to Reath Cottage. Bobbie's been in to say Keren Mark Daniel's met with a accident."

"What has she done?"

"Slided off the roof. Breaked her arm an' what not. I thought I'd just go'n see if I can be of 'elp. Not as I've a great taking for the maid, but it is only neighbourly to make sartin, as Mark's down the bal."

"Is she alone?" Ross asked. "I'll come with you if she needs any attention."

"No, sur; Bobbie says Dr. Enys is there."

He had been there twenty minutes. By great good fortune he had heard her shouting and had been the first on the scene.

After the first shock of the fall she had half fainted for some minutes, and when she came round she had nearly fainted again each time she moved her arm.

So she had sat there for an eternity, her head throbbing and her mouth dry with sickness. And then he had heard her cries and climbed across the ditch and come over to her.

After that, although there was pain and distress there was also comfort and happiness. He had carried her inside and put her on the bed, and his quick professional hands exploring her body were to her like the hands of a lover new-welcomed and at home.

He said: "You've fractured the bone. Your ankle will be well enough with rest. Now I must set your arm. It will hurt, but I'll be as quick as possible."

"Go on," she said, looking at him.

He had a roll of bandage in his pocket and found two splints among Mark's carpenterings. Then he gave her a drink of brandy and set her arm. She bit her teeth together and never made a sound. Tears came into her eyes, and when he had finished they rolled down her cheeks and she brushed them away.

"That was very brave of you," he said. "Take another drink of this."

She took it because it was in his flask, and began to feel better. Footsteps sent him to the door and he told Bobbie Martin to go for his mother. It had taken less than a month to teach him that if anyone in the district needed a good turn they sent for Mrs. Zacky, whose twelve children never impeded her instinct for mothering the neighbourhood.

Then he sat on the bed and bathed her other elbow and bathed her ankle and tied it up. This was sheer bliss to her and her eyes would have let him see it if he had not kept his own on the business in hand. All this done, he talked to her in a tone that had become steadily more dry and professional in the last ten minutes, suggesting that she should call her husband out of the mine.

But she was set against this, and when Mrs. Zacky's flat face and spectacles showed in the doorway she greeted her so sweetly that Mrs. Zacky thought the district had summed up Mark's wife too quick and too drastic.

Dwight Enys stayed a little longer, his handsome face sober but youthful, telling Mrs. Zacky what to do. Then he took Keren's hand and said he would call again in the morning.

Keren said in a soft contralto: "Thank you, Dr. Enys. I didn't know anyone could be so kind."

He flushed slightly. "Cruel to be kind. But you took it all well. The arm will give you pain to-night. Do, please, stay in bed. If you get up you may raise a temperature, and then it will be perhaps a long job."

"I'm *sure* I shall be all right," Keren said. "I'll do *anything* you say."

"Very well. Good day to you. Good day, Mrs. Martin."

CHAPTER XV   Grambler was to close on the twelfth of November, and the day came still and misty with a humid air and a threat of rain. Unhealthy weather, Dr. Choake said, which raised up all the putrid vapours. They had run the engine this long to finish the coal in stock.

There were three pumps to the mine. Two engines—both modernized but both left hopelessly out of date by Watt's invention of the separate condenser—and a great water wheel of thirty feet diameter, worked by the Mellingey Stream.

At noon a small party of men gathered in the big central engine house. Present were Francis Poldark, Captain Henshawe, the "grass" captain, Dunstan, Dr. Choake, the two chief enginemen, Brown and Trewinnard, the purser and a few other officials. They stood there and coughed and avoided each other's eyes, and Francis took out his watch.

Up and down went the great bob, to the rattle of the chains, the roar of the furnace and the suck and splash of water with its dull inrush through the leather valves. From the house the mine spread away like a great beast, unsightly, unordered; wooden sheds, stone huts, thatched air shafts, water wheels, washing floors, horse whims, mounds of refuse and stone and cinders, the accumulations, additions and wastages of years. And here and there, running away down little valleys like tributaries of the mine, were the cottages of Grambler village.

Francis looked at his watch.

"Well, gentlemen," he said, raising his voice, "the time has come for the closure of our mine. We have worked together many years, but the times have beaten us. Someday perhaps this mine will be restarted and we shall all meet here again. And if we have not that good fortune our sons may enjoy it in our stead. It is now twelve noon."

He reached up to the lever which controlled the steam in its passage from the giant boiler of the engine, and pulled it down. The great engine bob paused in its stroke, hesitated, lumbered to a stop. Meanwhile the engineman had moved round and opened a valve, and there was a sigh of escaping steam as it rose white in the still, misty air, hovered and seemed reluctant to disperse.

A silence fell on the company. It was not that the engine had never stopped before: it was halted monthly for the boilers to be cleaned; and there had been any number of breakdowns. But this silence was heavy with the knowledge of what it brought.

With an impulse foreign to himself Francis took up a piece of chalk and on the side of the boiler chalked the word RESURGAM.

Then they filed out of the house.

Over at the Sawle end of the mine the smaller engine "Kitty" was still chattering and thumping. Captain Henshawe raised his hand. The signal was seen, and Kitty thumped and muttered herself into silence.

Now all that was left was the water pump; but this used no fuel and needed little attention, so it was allowed to go on.

The last shift of the tut-workers had been told to come up at twelve, and as the group of men walked slowly towards the offices the miners were appearing in twos and threes at the mouth of the engine shaft, carrying up their picks and shovels and drills for the last time.

A mixed company, they formed a long slow caterpillar to file past the purser and take their last wages. Bearded or clean-shaven, young or middle-aged, mostly small and pallid, wiry and uncouth, sweat-stained and mineral-stained, grave-eyed and silent, they took their shillings and made their "marks" of receipt in the cost book.

Francis stood there behind the purser, exchanging a word with one or another of the men, until they were all paid. Then he shook hands with Captain Henshawe and walked home alone to Trenwith.

The engineers had gone back to their engines to go over them and decide what could be dismantled and sold for scrap; the purser was adding up his books, the manager and the grass captain began a wide tour of the buildings to take final account of what stock was left.

Henshawe changed into old clothes and a miner's hat and went down to make a last inspection.

With easy familiarity he climbed down the shaft to the forty-fathom level, and there stepped off into the tunnel in the direction of the richer of the two bearing lodes, the "sixty" level.

After walking about a quarter of a mile, he began to drop with the tunnel, picking his way past mounds of dead ground and climbing down ladders and across slippery slopes through mazes of timber used to shore up the roof and sides. He ploughed through water and at length heard the steady pick, pick and bang, bang, bang of men still at work.

There were about twenty tributers left. If they could mine a few more shillings' worth it would all add up on their accounts sheet with the company and would help in the struggle with poverty which would soon begin.

Zacky Martin was there, and Paul Daniel and Jacka Carter, Jim's young brother, and Pally Rogers. They were all stripped to the waist and sweating, for the temperature here was hotter than the hottest summer's day.

"Well, boys," said Henshawe, "I thought I'd come tell you that Big Bill and Kitty have stopped."

Pally Rogers looked up and wiped an arm across his great black beard. "We reckoned twas about time."

"I thought I'd tell you," Henshawe said, "just to leave you know."

Zacky said: "We should have a few days. There's been no weight of rain."

"I shouldn't bank on too much. She's always been a wet mine. And how will you get the stuff up?"

"By the east shaft. The Curnow brothers are keeping the horse whim going. We'll have to haul it as best we can to there."

Henshawe left them and went on as far as he could until he reached the flooded eighty-fathom level. Then he turned and went back, found his way through more water to the poorer west lode and made sure that nothing of value had been left. A few rusty tools, a clay pipe, a broken barrow.

It was two o'clock by the time he came up. The unnatural silence greeted him all round. Kitty still steamed a little in the quiet. A few men were pottering about the sheds, and about twenty women were out washing clothes in the hot water from the engine.

Henshawe walked into the changing-shed to put on his own clothes, and saw a half dozen men gathering at the shaft head. He thought of shouting, and then realized that it was the relieving men going down to take over work from their partners. He shrugged his shoulders and turned away. Tributers were a hardy breed.

By eight the following evening the water had risen a good deal but the lode was still untouched. Mark Daniel sent one of the others up to tell those who would come down and relieve them.

Up above it was a ghostly night, dark and gossamer-damp, marking the silence and emptiness of the mine buildings. Usually there were dozens in the changing-sheds, lights in the engine houses, the engineers to pass a word with, all the reassurance of companionship. Now there was no heat, no talk except the exchange of a muttered word among themselves, no light except from two lanterns.

They blew these out after lighting their candles and stolidly took to the ladders: Nick Vigus and Fred Martin and John and Joe Nanfan and Ed Bartle and sixteen others.

By four in the morning some of the lode was covered. They were working in water, and there were deep lakes in low-lying parts of the plot behind them. There was, however, a ledge round; and at a push they could still get away by the east shaft. Nick Vigus went up ahead to tell the newcomers the situation. There was a consultation, and Zacky Martin and the others decided to go down, for there was a chance of a few hours more.

At seven a fall of stone and rubble into one of the pools brought them to a halt. They spent another hour tugging away a few last buckets of ore up the side of the tunnel until they could attach it to a rope and get it pulled along the back of an exhausted lode to the east shaft. Then they climbed up a few feet and sat **and** watched the water lapping round the long black cavern which had been their working home for months past.

One by one they picked their way out, through the old workings and out of the mine.

Zacky Martin was the last to leave. He sat on the edge of the underground shaft and lit his pipe and stared down at the water, which rose so quietly that it hardly seemed to rise at all. He sat there nearly an hour, smoking and rubbing his chin and occasionally spitting, his eyes under their candle thoughtful and steady.

It might be weeks yet before there was a full house of water, but already the "sixty" was gone. And that was the best.

He came to his feet, sighed and began to pick his path in the wake of the others, past deserted windlasses, broken ladders, pieces of timber and piles of rubble. It was a honeycomb this upper part, a crazy twisting and turning with tunnels going off in every direction, most of them blind, where earlier miners had driven in search of fresh ore. There were underground shafts to trap the unwary and great hollow caves with dripping roofs.

Eventually he came out at the main shaft at the "thirty" level. Pick and shovel over one shoulder, he began to climb up it for the last time, taking it in slow steady stages from platform to platform, as became an old-timer. Now the quietude struck him again.

He reached the surface and found that the November day, hardly breaking when he went down, had fallen into a wet mist. It covered the countryside in a blanket, and only near things were clear.

Everybody had gone home. The Curnow brothers had stopped the water pump, and the ore they had raised these two days was dumped in heaps beside the east shaft. It would have to be accounted later, but nobody had the heart to begin it to-day. Even the fat familiar figure of the purser was not to be seen.

After resting a minute or two Zacky picked up his shovel and pick again and turned to go home. As he did so he saw Paul Daniel waiting by the engine house.

"I thought I'd make sartin you was out," Paul said, rather apologetic as Zacky reached him. "You was a long time after the rest of us."

"Yes," said Zacky. "Just had a last look round."

They walked off together towards Mellin.

And then the mine was quite deserted and alone in the mist. And the silence of its inactivity and the silence of the windless misty day was like a pall on the countryside. No rough boot jarred upon the old paved way between the office and the changing-shed. No voice called from the engine house or shouted a joke across the shaft. No women clustered to-day about the engine to get hot water for their clothes. No bal-maidens or spallers talked and chattered on the washing floors. All was in place but nothing stirred. Grambler existed but no longer lived. And in its vitals the water was very slowly filling up the holes and the bur-rowings of two hundred years.

The mine was still and the day was still and no man moved. Only somewhere up in the mist a sea gull was abroad, and crying, crying, crying.

BOOK TWO

CHAPTER I   On Friday April the third 1789 a ticketing took place in the upstairs dining-room of the Red Lion Inn. The low panelled room was already set out for the customary dinner that was to follow.

There were about thirty men, grouped in chairs round an oblong table raised on a wooden dais by the window. Eight of the men represented eight copper companies. The others were managers or pursers of the mines offering the ore. As was the custom the chair was taken by the manager of the mine which had the largest parcel to offer, and to-day this fell upon Richard Tonkin.

He sat at the middle of the table, with the ticket offers in heaps before him and flanked by a representative of the miners and the smelters. The faces of the men were grave and there was little of the good-humoured raillery of prosperous times. Copper—the refined product—was now fetching fifty-seven pounds a ton.

As the clock struck one, Tonkin got up and cleared his throat.

"The auction is open, gentlemen. There are no further offerings? Very good. I have first to dispose of a dole of ore from Wheal Busy."

With the two men beside him to supervise he opened the first lot of tickets and entered the bids in a ledger. One or two men shuffled their feet and the purser of Wheal Busy took out his notebook expectantly.

After a few moments Tonkin looked up.

"Wheal Busy ore is sold to the Carnmore Copper Company for six pounds seventeen shillings and sixpence a ton."

There was a moment's silence. One or two men looked around. Ross saw an agent frown and another whisper.

Tonkin went on. "Tresavean. Sixty tons."

He opened the second box. There was another consultation as the figures were written in the ledger.

Tonkin cleared his throat. "Tresavean ore is sold to the Carnmore Copper Company for six pounds seven shillings a ton."

Mr. Blight of the South Wales Copper Smelting Company got up. "What name did you say, Mr. Tonkin?"

"Tresavean."

"No. The name of the buyers."

"Carnmore Copper Company."

"Oh," said Blight, hesitated, sat down.

Tonkin picked up his list again, and for a few minutes the auction went on as before.

"Wheal Leisure," Tonkin said. "Parcel of red copper. Forty-five tons." The man on Tonkin's right leaned across to look at the bids.

"Wheal Leisure ore is sold to the Carnmore Copper Company for eight pounds two shillings a ton."

Several men looked at Ross. Ross looked at the end of his riding crop and smoothed down a piece of frayed leather. Outside in the yard they could hear an ostler swearing at a horse.

There was some talk at the table before Tonkin read out the next name. But he had his way and went on:

"United Mines. Three doles of ore. Fifty tons in each."

Entries in the ledger.

"United Mines," said Tonkin. "First parcel to Carnmore at seven pounds one shilling a ton. Second parcel to Carnmore at six pounds nineteen shillings and sixpence. Third parcel to the South Wales Smelting Company at five pounds nine shillings and ninepence."

Blight was on his feet again, his raddled little face sharp under its wig, like a terrier that has been shown the bait once too often.

"Sir, I dislike to intervene. But may I say that I do not know of the existence of any such smelting company as the Carnmore?"

"Oh," said Tonkin. "I am assured it exists."

"How long has it existed?" asked another man.

"That I could not say."

"What proof have you of its *bona fides*?"

"That," said Tonkin, "will very soon be put to the proof."

"Not until next month when payment is due," said Blight. "Then you may find yourselves with all these parcels of ore still on your hands."

"Aye! Or collected unpaid for."

Tonkin stood up again. "I think, gentlemen, we may ignore the last danger. Personally I do not see that as mining agents we can afford to offend a newcomer among our clients by—by casting doubts on his good faith. There have been newcomers in the field before. We have always taken them on their merits and have not been disappointed. It is not five years since we first welcomed the South Wales Copper Smelting Company among us, and that firm has become one of our largest buyers."

"At starvation prices," said someone *sotto voce*.

Blight was on his feet again. "We came into the field, I may remind Mr. Tonkin, vouched for by two other companies and with a guarantee from Warleggan's Bank. Who is standing guarantee here?"

There was no answer.

"Who is their agent?" demanded Blight. "You must have had contact with someone. If he is here, let him declare himself."

There was silence.

"Ah," said Blight, "as I thought. If——"

"I'm the agent," said someone behind him.

He turned and stared at a small, roughly dressed man in the corner by the window. He had blue-grey eyes, freckles across the bridge of a large intelligent nose, a humorous mouth and chin. He wore his own hair, which was reddish-gone-grey and cut short after the fashion of a working man.

Blight looked him up and down. He saw that he had to deal with a person in an inferior class.

"What is your name, my man?"

"Martin."

"And your business here?"

"Agent for the Carnmore Copper Company."

"I have never heard of it."

"Well, that's a surprise to me. Chairman up there's been talking of nothing else since one o'clock."

One of the copper agents beside Tonkin rose.

"What is your purpose, sir, in bidding for this great quantity of copper?"

"Same as yours, sir," said Zacky respectfully. "To smelt it and sell it in the open market."

"I take it you are the agent for a—a newly formed company."

"That's so."

"Who are your employers? Who finances you?"

"The Carnmore Copper Company."

"Yes, but that's a name," interrupted Blight. "Who are the men who make up and control this company? Then we shall know where we stand."

Zacky Martin fingered his cap. "I think tis for they to choose whether to give out their names or no. I'm but their agent—same as you—making bids on their behalf—same as you—buying copper for 'em to smelt—same as you."

Harry Blewett could sit by no longer. "De we yet know the names of the shareholders of the South Wales Smelting Company, Blight?"

Blight blinked at him a moment. "Are you behind this scheme, Blewett?"

"No, answer your own question first!" shouted another manager.

Blight turned on him. "You know well that we came in fully vouched for by friends. Tisn't our reputation that's in question, and——"

"Nor neither is it theirs! Let 'em default, and then you can talk!"

Tonkin rapped on the table. "Gentlemen, gentlemen. This is no way to behave. . . ."

Blight said: "When was the samples taken, Tonkin? Not when all the other agents went round. There must be collusion in this. There was no stranger among us when any of the sampling was done."

"I mistook the day," Zacky said. "I comed around the day after and was kindly allowed the oppor-tunity to sample them by myself. Twas no benefit to the mines."

"That's not fair doing, Mr. Tonkin. There's some sort of collusion in this——"

"Fair enough," said Aukett, squinting horribly in his excitement. "What's there amiss in it? No collusion such as might be set at the door of certain interests I could mention——"

"Who are you——"

"Now look ee here," said Zacky Martin, in a quiet voice that grad-ually made itself heard because everyone wanted to listen. "Look ee here, Mister Blight. And you other gentlemen too that seem a shade set about by me and my doings. I've no mind to be awkward or to put a stave in anyone's wheel, see? I want everything amiable and above-ground. Me and my friends is thinkin' of starting a little smelting works of our own, see, and we did think to buy up some o' the copper to-day just to lay in a little store handy-like."

"Smelting works? Where?"

"But we didn't think to lay the other companies by the ears—far from it. That's not our way. And if so be as we've bought more'n our share to-day—well, I reckon I'll take it on myself to sell back a parcel or two to any of you other companies that are disposed to buy. In a friendly fashion as the saying goes; no bones broke or harm meant. At the price I give to-day. No profit wanted. I'll be at the next ticketing and buy more then."

Ross saw Blight's expression change. One of the other brokers began to speak, but Blight interrupted him.

"So that's the game, eh? More than ever this stinks of arrangement. A pretty scheme, eh, to hoist the prices and put the legitimate dealers in a false box. No, my man, you and your friends—and I doubt not there's some here to-day—will have to think of another contrivance to catch us old hands. Keep your ore and take it to your new smelting works and *pay for it* at the end of the month, else you'll have all the mine managers whining to you before ten o'clock of the following day!"

Johnson got up, nearly cracking his big head on the beam above him. "There's no call for abuse, Blight. And if so be as the money does not forthcome, we'll not come whining to you!"

Richard Tonkin rapped the table again.

"Let us complete the auction."

This time he had his way, and quietness reigned until all the ore was sold. About two thirds of the total—all the best quality stuff—was bought by the Carnmore Company. It was a transaction which amounted to some five thousand pounds.

Then everyone sat down to dinner together.

It was the first real clash there had been between the two sides of the industry. Most of the grumbling had been done in private corners. After all the copper companies were the customers, and one did not in common sense seek out quarrels with such folk.

Zacky Martin sat some distance from Ross. They caught each other's eye once, but no gleam of recognition showed.

There was less talk than usual; men spoke together in lowered tones and with some constraint. But the wine had its effect, and the quarrel (and the deep rift of bitterness lying under the quarrel) was temporarily put away. To-day there was little said of affairs outside the county. Their own shadows loomed too large. The countryside was emerging from the worst winter in living memory—worst for conditions of life and one of the severest for weather. During January and February all Europe had lain under an icy hand, and even in Cornwall there had been weeks of frost and black east winds. Now that April was here and the worst over, men's minds turned to more hopeful things, not only to the summer ahead but to the chance of a kinder working life. Search where you would, there were no signs of a betterment, but at least the spring was here.

The agent of one of the older copper companies, a bluff rugged man called Voigt, told of the riots there had been in Bodmin last week.

"It were only a chance I was there," he said. "Just passing through in the coach. A mercy I'm alive, I assure you. They stopped the coach afore it reached the inn because they'd heard there was a corn factor within. Happily he'd not travelled; but we suffered who had. Out we was dragged with no ceremony and small comfort, and smash! went the coach, over on its side; glass and woodwork breaking, horses kicking in the road. Then some rascals put hammers to the wheels, and they were in pieces in no time. A good fortune for me I had not the opulence to be mistook for him they wanted; but a merchant from Helston was upended and rough-handled before they knew their mistake. I was relieved when they left us go."

"Was there much damage in the town?"

"Oh, yes, of a light nature. There was looting too and some who tried to stop 'em was ill-used. Even when the military came they showed fight and had to be drove off like in a pitched battle."

"There'll be hangings for that," said Blight. "Some example must be made."

"They took half a hundred of them into custody," said Voigt. "The gaol's filled to overflowing."

Ross's eyes met Zacky's for the second time that day. They were both thinking of Jim Carter, whose time of discharge was drawing near. The gaol had been full enough before.

Ross did not look at Zacky again. Neither did he speak to Richard Tonkin or Blewett or Aukett or Johnson after the dinner. Curious eyes would be watching.

He left the inn and walked round to see Harris Pascoe. The banker rose to greet Ross and diffidently inquired how the purpose of the day had gone.

Ross said: "You will have drafts of about four thousand eight hundred pounds to pay on the Carnmore account next month."

Pascoe pursed his lips. "You b-bought more than you expected?"

"We bought all we could while the price was low. Once they realize we are in earnest they will likely try to outbid us. But with that stock we shall be safe for some months."

"Was there any inquiry?"

Ross told him. Pascoe fumbled rather nervously with the snuff-stained cambric of his stock. He was in this scheme as their banker, but he had no stomach for conflict. He was in all his dealings a man of peace, using his own money for principled ends, but not caring to defeat the *un*-principled. He liked to look on money in an academic way: figures to be squared with other figures, balances to be brought to an equilibrium; it was the mathematics of his business which appealed to him most of all. Therefore while applauding the intention of this group of men, he was a little nervous lest they should become a worry and a disturbance to his peace of mind.

"Well," he said at length, "there you have the first responses of the agents and other small fry. I fancy that the men behind them will express their disapproval more subtly. The next ticketing will be the testing time. I doubt if you'll ever provoke an overt protest again."

"The essential thing is to keep them mystified," Ross said. "Some of the facts will leak out quick enough with Zacky Martin living on my land and the smelting works being built on Trevaunance property."

"It is surprising that the smelting works has been kept a secret so long."

"Well, all the components were shipped direct and housed around the disused pilchard cellars. Sir John put out the story that it was a new engine for his mine."

Pascoe drew towards him a sheet of paper and made two more brief entries on it with his scratchy quill. This was the first printed billhead of the Carnmore Copper Company, and on it in watery ink the banker had entered all the particulars of the company. He had begun with the chief shareholders.

Lord Devoran,
Sir John Michael Trevaunance, Bart.,
Alfred Barbary, Esq.,
Ray Penvenen, Esq.,
Ross Vennor Poldark, Esq.,
Peter St. Aubyn Tresize, Esq.,
Richard Paul Cowdray Tonkin,
Henry Blewett,
William Trencrom,
Thomas Johnson.

An imposing list. The company was floated with a capital of twenty thousand pounds, of which twelve thousand pounds was paid up and the rest on call. They were also going into business as merchants, to supply the mines with all the stuff of their trade. It would give them a small steady basis of business to rely on outside the main object of the company.

Pascoe knew that there were men who would be very interested to see this sheet of paper. It would be better locked up. He rose and went to his safe in the corner of the room.

"You'll take t-tea with us, Captain Poldark? My wife and daughter are expecting you."

Ross thanked him but said no. "Forgive me, but to get home in good time from one of these days is a treat I look forward to. It has been all riding this winter. My wife complains she has none of my company."

Pascoe smiled gently as he turned the key in the safe. "The complaint from a wife has a novelty you do well to consider. A p-pity your cousin Francis could not join the shareholders of the company."

"He is much too closely committed with the Warleggans. Privately we have his good will."

The banker sneezed. "Verity was in to stay the night early this week. She is looking in improved health, don't you think?"

"They have all stood up to the closing of Grambler better than I expected."

Pascoe walked with him to the door. "You have heard, I imagine, that there are r-rumours again attaching to Miss Verity's name."

Ross stopped. "I have heard nothing."

"Perhaps I should not have m-mentioned it, but I thought you should know. You and she have always been so close to one another."

"Well, what is the rumour?" Ross spoke with impatience. Pascoe did not know the cause of Ross's bitter hostility to the word.

"Oh, well, it is to do with that Blamey fellow. Word has c-come from several sources that they have been seen meeting again."

"Verity and Blamey? What are your sources?"

"If you prefer to disregard it, pray forget I spoke. I have no wish to pass on irresponsible gossip."

Ross said: "Thank you for the information that it is abroad. I'll take steps to smoke it out."

CHAPTER II   As he rode home his thoughts were not stable for a moment. Eighteen months ago he had known himself happy and with prevision had tried to hold the mood as long as it would stay. He was not now discontented, but he was too restless, too preoccupied. Each day led so relentlessly to the next, linked by cause and effect, anticipation and result, preparation and achievement. The chance suggestion made to Blewett nine months ago had led him into a web of new things.

Verity and Blamey? The arrogant man he had seen on the day after Julia's christening had lost everything he had ever had in common with the gentle self-restrained Verity. It could not be. Some evil-minded old crone had hatched it from her own brooding. There was as much truth in it as the slander he had heard on Jud's lips.

There had been no reconciliation between himself and the Paynters. Demelza visited Prudie sometimes, but that was all. Jud was working irregularly for Trencrom, who could always use a man with sailing experience and no scruples. In between times he went the round of the kiddleys and lectured men on their shortcomings.

As for the Gimletts, they had fulfilled all their earlier promise. With plump bounding good humour they trotted about the house and the farm, often working from pleasure when need was satisfied. Jinny had been back at Nampara since Christmas. In the end she had asked to return, common sense and lack of money prevailing over her shyness.

Ross had not seen Jim again, though all winter he had thought of riding to Bodmin and taking Dwight Enys with him. The copper company had taken all his attention. Many a time he had wished he could resign. He was short of the tact and patience to gain the interest of the men of substance, to support their interest when gained and to make all sorts of little adjustments to placate their self-esteem. For that Richard

Tonkin was invaluable. Without Richard Tonkin they would have been lost.

But without Ross too they would have been lost, although he did not realize it. He was the stiffening, the unyielding element and a large part of the driving power. Men accepted his integrity where with another they would have asked: "What has he to gain?"

Well, the company was on its feet now, alive and ready to begin the struggle. And the winter was over, and men and women had come through it (most of them); and the children had whimpered and survived (some of them). The law made it difficult for men to move out of their own district—lest they become a burden upon another parish—but a few had trekked to the waterfronts of Falmouth and Plymouth or to seek a pittance in the inland towns. The rapid-growing population of the mining districts had been checked in a single year.

And the King had gone mad and fought with his gaolers and been ill-treated by them and had torn up his curtains; and young Pitt, his patron locked away, had been preparing for retirement from public life, bowing to the whims of Fate and considering a career at the Bar; and the Prince of Wales, with Mrs. FitzHerbert to restrain his worst blatancies, had come back from Brighton to accept a regency, which young Pitt had the insolence to oppose.

And the King had recovered just in time to put his son's hopes out of joint; so all was back where it began, except that George's dislike for Whigs was only less than his dislike for his own family.

And Hastings had come to trial at last. And a clergyman called Cartwright had brought out an extraordinary thing for weaving, which was a power loom worked by a steam engine.

In America the Union was complete; a new nation was born, said the *Sherborne Mercury*, of four million people—one quarter black—which might someday be counted of importance. Prussia had spent the winter putting down the freedom of the press and signing an alliance with Poland to guard her back door if she attacked France. France had done nothing. A palsy had fallen on the splendid court while men died of hunger in the streets.

And Wheal Leisure had moderately prospered all through the winter, though the money Ross made had gone quickly enough, most into the Carnmore Company. A little went to buy a horse for Demelza, and a small nest egg of two hundred pounds he was keeping by for emergency.

As he neared Grambler he saw Verity coming towards him from the direction of the village.

"Why, Ross, imagine meeting you," she said. "I have been over to see Demelza. She complains that you neglect her. We have had a long talk, which would have lasted until sundown if Garrick had not upset the tea tray with his tail and wakened Julia from her afternoon nap. We have chattered away like two old fish jousters waiting for the nets to come in."

Ross glanced at his cousin with new eyes. There was something in her gaze, her manner was lively. He got down in alarm.

"What have you been hatching in my house this afternoon?"

The question was so well directed that Verity coloured.

"I went over to see if the Sherborne man had brought you an invitation as he had us. Curiosity, my dear. Women are never satisfied unless they know their neighbours' business."

"And has he?"

"Yes."

"An invitation to what?"

Verity tucked in a wisp of hair. "Well, cousin, it is waiting you at home. I hadn't thought to mention it but you surprised it out of me."

"Then let me surprise the rest, so that I may know all the news at once."

Verity met his eyes and smiled. "Have patience, my dear. It is Demelza's secret now."

Ross grunted. "I have not seen Francis or Elizabeth. Are they prospering?"

"Prospering is not the word, my dear. Francis is so heavy in debt that it looks as if we shall never struggle clear. But at least he has had the courage to withdraw from the Warleggan circle. Elizabeth—well, Elizabeth is very patient with him. I think she is glad to have him more at home; but I wish—perhaps her patience would be more fruitful if it had a little more understanding in it. One can be kind without being sympathetic. I—— Perhaps that is unjust." Verity looked suddenly distressed. "I don't take Francis's part because he is my brother. Really it is all his fault . . . or—or seems to be. . . . He threw away his money when he had it. If the money he squandered had been available there would have been more to finance the mine at the last. . . ."

Ross knew why Francis stayed away from the Warleggans and drank at home: Margaret Cartland, finding his money gone, had thrown him over.

"Demelza will blame me for keeping you, Ross. Be on your way, my dear; you must be tired."

He put his hand on her shoulder a moment and looked at her. Then he got on his horse. "Tired of hearing men talk of their mines and the price of copper. Your conversation has more variety, and you never give me the opportunity of tiring of it. Now you keep your secrets for Demelza and run away before I come home."

"Indeed not, Ross," Verity said, blushing again. "If I call when you are away it is because I think Demelza may be lonely; and if I go before you come it is because I think you want your hours at home with her. You offend me."

He laughed. "Bless you. I know I do not."

He rode on. Yes, there was a change. Twice he had been on the point of mentioning Blamey's name, twice he had baulked at the fence. Now he was glad. If there was anything there, let it be hidden from him. He had borne the responsibility of knowing once.

As he passed Grambler Mine he glanced over it. One or two windows of the office had been blown in and sprays of weeds grew here and there between the stones of the paved path. Wherever was metal was brown rust. The grass round the mine was an unusual vivid green, and in some corners heaps of blown sand had gathered. Some children had made a rough swing out of a piece of old rope and had hung it across a beam of the washing floors. A dozen sheep had wandered up to the engine house and were grazing peacefully in the afternoon silence.

He moved on and reached his own land and rode down into the valley; and from far off could hear Demelza playing the spinet. The sound came up to him in a sweet vibration, plaintive and distant. The trees were green-tipped and the catkins were out and a few primroses bloomed in the wet grass. The music was a thread of silver woven into the spring.

A fancy took him to surprise her, and he stopped Darkie and tethered her at the bridge. Then he walked to the house and came into the hall unnoticed. The parlour door was open.

She was there at the spinet in her white muslin frock, the peculiar expression on her face which she always took on when reading music, as if she were just going to bite an apple. All the winter she had been taking lessons from the old woman who had been nurse to the five Teague girls. Mrs. Kemp came once a week, and Demelza had shot ahead.

Ross slid into the room. She was playing the music from one of Arne's operas. He listened for some minutes, glad of the scene, glad of the music and the bordering quiet. This was what he came home for.

He stepped silently across the room and kissed the back of her neck.

She squeaked, and the spinet stopped on a discord.

"A slip o' the finger and *phit*, yer dead," said Ross in Jud's voice.

"Judas! you give me a fright, Ross. Always I'm getting frights of some sort. No wonder I'm a bag of nerves. This is a new device, creepin' in like a tomcat."

He took her by the ear. "Who has had Garrick in here where he does not belong, breaking our new Wedgwood? A dog—if he can be called that—no smaller than a cow. . . ."

"You have seen Verity, then? Did she tell you of our—of our . . ."

He looked into her eager, expectant face. "Of our what?"

"Our invitation."

"No. What is that?"

"Ha!" Pleased, she wriggled free from him and danced away to the window. "That's telling. I'll tell you to-morrow. Or maybe next day. Will that do?"

His keen eyes went round the room and instantly, irritatingly noticed the slip of paper folded under the spice jar on the table.

"Is this it?"

"No, Ross! You mustn't look! Leave it be!" She ran across and they both reached it together, struggled, laughed, her fingers having somehow got inside his. The parchment tore down the middle, and they separated, each holding a piece.

"Oh," said Demelza, "now we've spoiled it!"

He was reading. " 'On the occasion of the day of national Majesty the King and the mayor will hold——' "

"Stop! stop!" she said. "My part comes in between. Begin again."

" 'On the occasion of the day of national——' "

" 'Thanksgiving,' " she put in, " 'set aside to celebrate the recovery to health of His——' Now it's your turn."

" 'Majesty the King, namely April the twenty-third next, the Lord——' "

" 'Lieutenant of Cornwall, the High Sheriff, the Burgesses——' "

" 'And the Mayor of Truro will hold a Grand Assembly and Ball at the Assembly Rooms——' "

" 'Commencing at eight o'clock of that day, preceded by——' "

" 'Bonfires and general rejoicings.' " He looked at his paper again. " 'Captain Poldark are invited.' "

" 'And Mrs.,' " she cried, " 'to attend.' 'Captain and Mrs. Poldark are invited to attend.' "

"It says nothing about that on my invitation," he objected.

"There! there!" She came up to him and fitted the torn paper with his own piece. " 'And Mrs.' See, we shall both go this time."

"Do we each walk in with our own piece?" he asked. "They would not admit you just as 'Mrs.' It's altogether too vague."

"I do not wonder," she said, "that they put you to drive the copper companies; for you would drive anyone into bad thoughts."

"Well, anyway the invitation is useless now," he said, making a move to drop his half in the fire.

"No, Ross! No!" She caught at his hand and tried to stop him. After a moment or two his mood changed; he gave up the struggle and caught her to him and kissed her.

And as suddenly she was quiet, breathing quickly like an animal which knows it has been caught.

"Ross, you shouldn't do that," she said. "Not in the day."

"How much of our crockery did Garrick break?"

"Oh . . . but two saucers."

"And how many cups?"

"One, I think. . . . Ross, we shall go to this Assembly?"

"And who let him in here?"

"I think, I believe he just sort of sneaked in. You d'know what he is like. Will never have no for an answer. One minute he was outside and the next he was in." She wriggled in his grip but this time he had her fast. Her flushed cheek was close to his and he put his nose against it, liking the smell. "And what of Verity? What news had she?"

"Am I a dandelion?" she said, "to be snuffed over. Or a carrot to be hung before a—a . . ."

"A donkey's nose?" He laughed. Then she laughed, and their laughter infected each other.

They sat down on the settle and giggled together.

"I shall wear my apple green and mauve," she said presently; "the one I wore at Trenwith the Christmas before last. I don't think I am any fatter now."

Ross said: "I shall wear a secondhand wig with curls on the forehead, and scarlet stockings and a coat of green silk embroidered with field mice."

She giggled again. "Do you think we should be allowed in as Mrs. and Miss Poldark?"

"Or two ends of a donkey," he suggested. "We would throw lots who was to be the tail."

A few minutes later Jane Gimlett put her plump, tidy little head round the door; and they sat there together on the settle and laughed at her.

"Oh, I beg pardon," she said hastily. "I didn't know you was back, sur. I thought something was amiss."

Ross said: "We have an invitation to a ball and by mischance have torn it up. One piece is here and one piece is there. So we were considering what was the best to do."

"Oh, sur," said Jane, "I should stick the twin halves together with a mix of flour paste. Put 'em on a piece o' newsprint to hold 'em firm. No one would be able to make head nor tail of it as it is."

At that they looked at each other and laughed again—as if Jane Gimlett had told them a very funny joke.

That night before they went to sleep Ross said:

"Now that we are in our right minds again, tell me: Has Verity mentioned Captain Blamey to you of late?"

The question came as a shock to Demelza. She had a sharp struggle with her conscience.

"Why do you ask?"

"There is a rumour that she is meeting him."

"Oh?" said Demelza.

"Well?" he said, after a wait.

"I wouldn't like to say, Ross. I wouldn't like to say that she hadn't, and then again I wouldn't like to say that she had."

"In shorter words, you wouldn't like to say anything at all."

"Well, Ross, what's given in confidence it isn't fair to repeat even to you."

Ross thought this over.

"I wonder how she met him again. It was most unfortunate."

Demelza said nothing, but crossed her fingers in the dark.

"There can't be anything serious meant now," Ross said uneasily. "That moody bully. Verity would be mad to go on with it, whatever the chances were before. All that bitterness will begin again if Francis gets to know."

Demelza said nothing, but crossed her legs as well.

"When I heard it I discounted it," he went on. "I could not believe that Verity would be so foolish. You are very silent."

"I was thinkin'," said Demelza quietly, "that if the—if they still feel the same after all these years, it must never *really* have broke at all."

"Well," he said after a pause, "if you can't tell me what is happening you can't. I won't pretend I'm not disturbed, but I am only glad *I* didn't bring them together. I am more than sorry for Verity."

"Yes, Ross," she said. "I see just how you feel. I'm awful sleepy. Can I go to sleep now?"

CHAPTER III   It rained all night, but by eight the day was clearing and a fresh soft wind blew from the south-west. Mark Daniel had spent his whole morning in the garden, but at half an hour after noon he came in to eat his dinner and get ready for the mine. Keren had made a herb pie out of things she had been able to gather and had flavoured it with two rabbit legs she had bought from Mrs. Vigus.

For a time they ate without speaking. In Mark silence was usual, but in Keren it meant either a new grievance or sulks over an old. He glanced at her several times as they sat there.

To test her mood he tried to think of something to say.

"Things is coming up too fast to be safe; it is as if the spring is two months on. I hope there'll be no frost or bitter wind like last year."

Keren yawned. "Well, we ought to have something after that January and February. I've never known such months, not anywhere."

(She blamed him for the weather now, as if the Cornish climate were a part of the general fraud practised on her by marriage.)

"The thrushes in the May tree will be hatching out any time now," he said. "Reckon they're so early they'll be sitting a second time."

There was another silence.

"Peas an' beans'll be a month early too," said Mark. "We owe thanks to Captain Poldark for they, for giving us the seeds."

"It would have looked better for him to have found you better work instead." She had no good to say of the Poldarks.

"Why, I have a pitch at Wheal Leisure. More he couldn't do."

"And a poor pitch it is. Brings you in not half what the Grambler one used to."

"All the best pitches was taken, Keren. Some would say it was my own fault to have took it, for he offered me contract work. Paul was saying but yesterday forenoon we was lucky to have work at all."

"Oh, Paul . . ." said Keren contemptuously. "What's Zacky Martin doing, I should like to know? He's working for Captain Poldark, isn't he? I'll wager he's not working miner's hours for a few shillings a week. Why, the Martins've never been better set in their lives. Zacky's been away here and away there—pony provided and all. Why couldn't they give you a job like that?"

"Zacky's more eddicated than me," said Mark. " 'Is father rented a few acres an' sent him to school till he were nine. Everyone round here d'know that Zacky's a cut above we."

"Speak for yourself," Keren said, getting up. "Reading and writing's easy to learn. Anyone can learn it if they've the mind to. Zacky only seems clever because all you folks are slothful and ignorant."

"Aye, I speak for myself," Mark said quietly. "I well know you're different too, Keren. You're cleverer than Zacky or any. An' maybe it's sloth that folk don't learn more an' maybe it ain't. You'll acknowledge it is easier-like to get your letters as a tacker at school than when you're more growed, and one by one, all by yourself wi' no one to learn you. I went as a buddle boy when I were six. I'd no care for letters when I come home from that. Since then I been working wi'out a break except for feast days. Maybe I should ha' learned instead of wrestling, but that's the way of things. An' you can't say I'm idle about the house here and now."

Keren wrinkled her nose.

"Nobody said you was idle, Mark; but you get little enough for all your sweat. Why, even the Viguses are better off than us—and him without work at all."

"Nick Vigus is a slippery rogue, an' twas he got young Jim Carter into trouble. You wouldn't want for me to spend all my time poaching or mixing cheap poisons to sell as gin?"

"I'd want you to make some money," said the girl, but she spoke in a softer voice. She had gone to the open door and was staring across the valley.

Mark finished his meal. "You've eaten little or nothing," he said. "You'll keep no strength in you that way."

"My strength's all right," Keren said absently.

"Besides, it is wrong to waste food."

"Oh, eat it yourself," she said.

Mark hesitated, and then slowly scooped the piece of pie she had left back into the tin dish.

"Twill stand till to-morrow."

She glanced away impatiently to the north. Several figures were moving over the hill.

"It's time you were off."

She stood at the door watching him while he put on his heavy boots and pulled on his coarse drill coat. Then he came to the door and she went out to let him pass.

He looked at her, with the sun striking lights in her curly hair and her dark elfish eyes turned away.

"Don't ee take on about we, Keren," he said gently. "We'll come through all right, never fear. This bad time won't last for ever an' we'll soon be on our feet again."

He bent his great body and kissed her on the neck. Then he moved off a little stiffly in the direction of the mine.

She watched him go. We'll come through all right, she thought; through to what? This cottage and children and middle age? We'll soon be on our feet again. For what? For him to keep on going down the mine, making a bit more money or a bit less for ever and ever until he is too old and crippled like the old men over the hill. Then he'll be here about the house all day long, as they are; while I bring up the last of the children and do menial jobs for the Poldarks to eke out.

That was the best she could look for. She'd been a fool to think she could change him. He didn't *want* to change. Born and bred a miner, he had no horizon but digging for copper and tin. And although he was a great worker and a craftsman he hadn't the learning or the initiative to be able to rise even in the mine. She saw it all clear enough. He was a goat tethered to the peg of his own character and could only consume the riches of the earth which came within his range. And she had bound herself to stay in his circle for the rest of her life. . . .

Tears came to her eyes and she turned back into the cottage. Mark had done much to better the inside during the winter months, but she saw none of it. Instead she swept through into their bedroom and changed her plain dimity frock for the challenging one of flimsy scarlet with the green cord girdle. Then she began to comb her hair.

In ten minutes with her face sponged and powdered, her rich hair glossy and crisp, theatrical sandals on her bare feet, she was ready.

She slipped out of the house and ran quickly down the hill to the bed of the dried-up stream, climbed across it, and ran up the other side towards the wood. Very soon, her breath coming in swift gasps, she was standing before the door of the Gatehouse.

Dwight Enys himself opened it.

Against his better judgment something kindled in his eyes when he saw her standing there with her hands behind her back and the wind ruffling her hair.

"Keren. What brings you here at this time of the day?"

She glanced over her shoulder. "May I come in before all the old women see me and begin to whisper?"

He hesitated and then opened the door wider. "Bone is out."

"I know. I saw him go early."

"Keren. Your reputation will be worth nothing."

She walked ahead of him down the dark corridor and waited for him to open the door into his living-room.

"It gets more cosier every time I see it," she said.

The room was built long and narrow with three slender Gothic windows looking over the hill towards Mingoose. The manner was less medieval than in the other rooms, and he had chosen it as his parlour and furnished it with a good Turkey carpet and some comfortable old chairs and a bookcase or two. It was also the only room with a good fireplace; and a bright fire burned there now, for Enys had cooked his meal on it.

"What time will Bone be back?"

"Oh, not yet; he has gone to see his father, who has had an accident. But how did you see him go?"

"I just watched," she said.

He looked at her kneeling there. She had interrupted his reading. It was not the first time now nor even the fifth, though her arm was long since better. One side of him was displeased, indignant; the other, not. His eyes took in the gracious curve of her back, like a bow slightly bent, ready at any moment to quiver and straighten. He looked at the faint obverse curve of her throat, at the flamboyant colour of the dress. He liked her in that best. (He thought she knew it.) But to come here to-day, and deliberately.

"This must stop, Keren," he said. "This coming——"

The bow straightened and she looked up as she interrupted him. "How *can* I, Dwight? How *can* I? I so look forward to coming here. What does it matter if I am seen? What does it matter? There's no harm in it. There's nothing else I care about."

He was surprised by her vehemence and a little touched. He came over to the fire and stood with a hand on the mantelpiece looking down on her.

"Your husband will get to know. He could not like your coming here."

"Why not?" she said fiercely. "It is the only little change and—and company I get. A change from the sort of common folk who live around here. There's not one of 'em been further than a couple of miles from where they were born. They're so narrow and small. All they think to do is work and eat and sleep like—like animals on a farm. They just don't see farther than the top of St. Ann's Beacon. They aren't more than half alive."

He wondered what she expected in marrying a miner.

"I think," he said gently, "that if you look deeper you will find all sorts of good things in your neighbours—and in Mark too, if you're dissatisfied with him. Narrow, I grant you, but deep. They have no charity outside the range of their understanding, but within it they are loyal and kind and honest and God-fearing and brave. I have found that in the short time I have been here. Forgive me if I seem to preach, Keren, but in meeting them try to meet them on *their* ground for a change. Try to see life as they see it. . . ."

"And become one of them."

"Not at all. Use your imagination. In order to understand it's not necessary to *become*. You are criticizing their lack of imagination. Show that you are different, that you do not lack it. I think in the main they are a fine people and I get on well with them. Of course, I know I have the advantage of being a surgeon——"

"And a man." She didn't add, "And a very handsome one." "That's very well, Dwight, but you haven't married one of 'em. And they accept you because you're far enough above them. I'm betwixt and between. I'm one of them but I'm a stranger and always will be. If I couldn't read nor write and'd never seen the world they might forgive me in time, but they never will now. They'll be narrow and mean to the end of their days." She blew out a little sigh from between pursed lips. "I'm that unhappy."

He frowned at his books. "Well, I am not that much beset with company that——"

She got up eagerly. "I may come then? I may stay a little? You find it none too bad to talk to me? I promise I'll not bore you with my grief. Tell me what you are doing now, what you are studying, eh?"

He smiled. "There's nothing in that would interest you. I——"

"Anything would interest me, Dwight. Really it would. Can I stay a few hours to-day? Mark has just gone below. I'll promise not to talk. I'll not be in your way. I can cook you a meal and help you."

He smiled again, a little ruefully. He knew of old what this offer meant; an enthusiastic approach to his interests, a wide-open, wide-eyed receptiveness on her part, which changed by curious subtle feminine gradations until *his* interest became centred on *her*. It had happened before. It would happen again to-day. He did not care. In fact there was a part of him that looked forward to it.

Two hours had passed, and the expected had not quite happened.

When she came in he had been preparing for record a table of the lung cases treated since his arrival, the type of disease so far as he was able to place it, the treatment given and the results yielded. And for once her interest had held. She had written down the details as he read them out; and as a result he had done the work of three hours in half the time.

She wrote a big unformed hand clearly and well. She seemed to grasp quickly what he said, even when the terms bordered on the medical.

When it was done he said: "You've been a real help to-day, Keren. I'm grateful for that. It's good of you to have spent this time and patience on my dull records."

Again for the first time she did not bridle and respond to his praise. She was reading part of what she had written and her pretty petulant little face was serious and intent.

"This cold water," she said. "What does it mean, Dwight? Look here: for this man Kempthorne you order nothing but cold water and goat's milk. How will that aid him? It is hard on the fellow to be given nothing at all."

"Oh, I made him up some pills," Dwight said. "Just so that he would feel better, but they were only made of meal, baked hard."

"Well, why did you not treat him then? Had he done you a bad turn?"

Enys smiled and came over to her.

"Both lungs are affected at the top, but not too serious yet. I have put him on a strict regime if he will follow it: four miles' walking a day, drinking goat's milk with his meals when he can get it, sleeping in the open when it is fine. I have odd notions about things, Keren; but he is one of the best cases so far and is on the mend. I am sure he is better than if I had given him the leeches and antimony and the rest."

Her hair was brushing his cheek. She turned her head and looked up at him, her full red lips slightly parted to show the gleam of her teeth. "Oh, Dwight," she said.

He put his hand on hers on the table. His was a little unsteady.

"Why do you come here?" he said sharply, averting his eyes as if ashamed.

She turned towards him without moving her hand.

"Oh, Dwight, I'm sorry."

"You're not. You know you're not."

"No," she said. "I'm not. Nor never could be."

"Then why say it?"

"I'm only sorry if you dislike me."

Staring at her as if he had not heard, he said: "No . . . not that."

He put his hands on her shoulders and bent his head and kissed her. She leaned a little against him and he kissed her again.

He drew back.

She watched him walk over to the windows. It had been a boy's kiss, gentle and sincere. What a mixture he was, she thought. A graduate in the physical profession, learned, and full of new ideas; he could go round these homes, speak with authority, operate, mend broken arms, treat fevers, attend women in childbed. But in his very own life, where close things like love were touched, he was inexpert and shy.

The thought pleased her more than the kiss had done—the implications of the kiss more than either.

She hesitated, looking at his back, uncertain what to do now. Neither of them had spoken. Everything was new between them from this moment: there were no signposts to follow, no tracks or beaten ways.

Everything was new and everything was changed. But a wrong word or act might set it back again, farther back than ever before. This moment might lead to tremendous things. Or it might lead to the blind alley of a broken friendship. Every normal impulse urged her to go on, to snatch at this thing which might not come again for months, perhaps never at all. Normally Bone was close at hand, whistling or making a noise. She thought that now in the isolation, in the emotion, there was no brake.

But with a queer view into his mind she saw that if she did that, if everything happened on the leaping tide of the moment, he might come to regret it almost at once, might come to hate her or despise her as a common woman who had led him to this; whereas if he had time to think it over, to come to the desire slowly and on his own, then he

136

would be unable to put the act on her. It would sit squarely on his own shoulders and he might never even wish to throw it off.

Besides, that way, anything might happen.

She went slowly up to him and stood by him at the window. His face was tense as if he was by no means sure of himself.

She touched his hand. "You make me very proud," she whispered, remembering a line out of *Elfrida;* and turned and went out of the room and left the house.

CHAPTER IV   That week another invitation reached the Poldarks. George Warleggan had decided to hold a party on the day of the celebrations. His guests would sup at Warleggan House, then go on to the Assembly Rooms for the evening, returning to Warleggan House to sleep. He would be glad if Ross and his wife would be of that number.

Ross wanted to refuse. With a rupture certain between himself and George he had no wish to be beholden to him. But for Demelza it was the last step of ambition to see the Warleggans at home, and though she trembled and hesitated after the fiasco of the christening, she would have been desperately disappointed to miss it.

So Ross chose to give way and, once the acceptance had gone, he quietly looked forward to the day, as he always looked forward to taking Demelza out. When Mrs. Kemp came she was not allowed to go near the spinet but instead was pressed into teaching Demelza the steps of the more popular dances and giving her lessons in deportment.

Since Demelza's good humours were so pervasive as to give a lead to the whole house, the mood at Nampara became one of pleasurable anticipation. Julia, kicking in her cot, crowed and laughed and joined in the fun.

On the sixteenth of April, Ross had gone up to the mine and Demelza and Jinny and Jane were brewing mead. They were enjoying themselves. They had stirred six pounds of honey into a couple of gallons of warm water and added some dried elder flowers and ginger. This was on the fire to boil in a large pan, and Jane was skimming it with a spoon whenever a frothy scum formed on the surface.

Upon this domestic scene fell the shadow of Zacky Martin aslant in the afternoon sun. As soon as she saw him Demelza knew something was wrong. No, Captain Poldark was not here, he would be up at the mine. Zacky thanked her stolidly enough and moved off.

Jinny ran to the door as he went. "Father. What's amiss? Is it to do wi' Jim?"

"No, there's no call for you to worry," said Zacky. "It was just that I wanted for to see Cap'n Ross on a point or two."

"Well, I thought——" said Jinny, half reassured. "I thought as . . ."

"You'll need to get used to me in and about the house now, Jinny. I'm workin' for Cap'n Ross, you did ought to know that."

She watched him move away and then returned to the kitchen with a troubled face.

Zacky found Ross talking to Captain Henshawe among the mine buildings on Leisure Cliff. He gave Zacky an inquiring glance.

"Well, sir, it is about Jim. You mind what that man said at the ticketing about Bodmin Gaol being crowded with the rioters who'd be there till next sessions?"

Ross nodded.

"Well, this morning, getting about more, y'understand on business, as I do now, I heard tell that many of the old prisoners had been moved to other gaols to make room."

"Was the word reliable, d'you judge?"

" 'S, I reckon. Joe Trelask's brother has been moved; an' Peter Mawes said as how all our Jim's cell was to go to Launceston."

"Launceston." Ross whistled slightly.

"They say it's bad there?"

"It has a poor name." No point in alarming Zacky further. "But this moving of a man about due for release is monstrous. Who ordered it? I wonder if it is true."

"Peter Mawes was straight from Bodmin. I thought I should tell you. I thought ye'd wish to know."

"I'll think over it, Zacky. There may be some way of coming at the truth quickly."

"I thought you should wish to know." Zacky turned to go. "I'll be out in the morning, sur, to see ee over the wet and waste deduction."

Ross went back to Henshawe; but he could not bring his mind to what they had been discussing. He had always been perversely attached to Jim, and the thought that he might have been moved twenty miles farther from home to the worst prison in the west—possibly on the decision of some puffed-up jack-in-office—irritated and concerned him.

For the rest of the afternoon he was busy at the mine, but when he had finished he walked across to see Dwight Enys.

As he came to the Gatehouse he noticed the improvements Enys had made; but passing the window of Dwight's own living-room, the windows being open, he heard someone singing. To his surprise it was a girl's voice, not very loud but quite distinct.

He did not pause in his stride but as he walked round to the front door the words followed him:

"My love is all Madness and Folly,
    Alone I lye,
    Toss, tumble and cry,
What a happy creature is Polly!
Was e'er such a Wretch as I!
With rage I redden like Scarlet. . . ."

He knocked with the light stick he carried.

The singing ceased. He turned and stood with his back to the door watching a robin searching among the stones for moss for his nest.

Then the door opened. Dwight's face, already slightly flushed, coloured deeper when he saw who it was.

"Why, Captain Poldark, this is a surprise! Will you step inside, please."

"Thank you." Ross followed him into the living-room, from which three minutes before the song had come. There was no one there.

But perhaps because of his knowledge he seemed to detect a subtle arrangement of the room which spoke of a visitor just gone.

Ross stated his business, the news of Jim Carter, and that he proposed to take the coach to-morrow and discover the truth. He wondered if Enys would be interested to go with him.

Dwight at once accepted, his eagerness showing through his embarrassment, and they made an arrangement to meet early and ride into Truro.

Ross walked home wondering where he had heard the woman's voice before.

To keep Jinny from worrying she was not told; but Demelza was prepared to worry over her own man. She never liked Ross going into the confined atmosphere of a prison, which was poisonous at the best; and a journey as far as Launceston across the dangerous wastes of the Bodmin moors seemed set with every kind of hazard.

They left after an early breakfast and when they reached Truro, Ross did some shopping.

Mistress Trelask, just taking the sheets off her stock, was fluttered by the arrival of a tall serious-looking man who introduced himself and said he understood Mistress Trelask had been patronized by his wife and knew her measurements. This being so, he had a mind to buy a new evening gown for his wife to be made and delivered for the celebration ball.

Mistress Trelask, like a hen caught in a small shed, fluttered and flapped noisily, bringing down in hasty confusion new silk satins and brocades and tonquedelles and velours, before the sting in the end of her visitor's sentence made her qualify the sale by the grave doubt of her ability to make anything in the time, so much being already on hand.

Her visitor, who had shown interest in an expensive silver brocade silk, thereupon took up his hat and wished her good morning.

Mistress Trelask immediately flapped a great deal more, and called up her daughter; they chirped together and made little notes and played with pins, while the shopper tapped his boot. Then they said they would see what they could do.

"It is a condition of sale, you understand."

"Yes," said Miss Trelask, wiping away a tear, "I take it so, sir."

"Very well, then; let us have the business in hand. But you must aid me in it, for I have no knowledge of women's things and want the latest and best."

"We'll see you get everything after the most fashionable rate," said Mrs. Trelask. "When could Mrs. Poldark call for a fitting?"

"There will be no fitting unless it is on the day of the Assembly," Ross said. "I want this as a surprise. If it is not quite right my wife can call in in the afternoon."

At this there were more flutterings, but the floodgates of concession were already open and they presently agreed.

Later Ross made for a tiny shop with a creaking sign which read: S. Solomon. Goldsmith and Pewterer.

"I want to see something for a lady," he said. "Something to wear in her hair or round her neck. I have not the time to examine many pieces."

The tall old man bent his head to lead Ross into the dark room at the back and brought out a tray with a half dozen necklaces, three cameo brooches, a few pearl bracelets for the wrist, eight rings. There was nothing that attracted him. The largest of the pearl necklaces was priced at thirty pounds, which seemed more than its value.

"Pearls are so fashionable, sir. We cannot get them. All the smaller ones are used for decorating gowns and hats."

"Have you nothing else?"

"It does not pay me to have better things, sir. Perhaps I could get you something made?"

"I wanted it for next week."

The shopkeeper said: "I have one little thing I bought from a seaman. Could that interest you?"

He took out a gold filigree brooch set with a single good ruby and a circlet of small pearls. It was foreign, probably Venetian or Florentine. The man watched Ross's eyes as he picked it up.

"What is the price?"

"It is worth at least a hundred and twenty pounds, but I might wait long for a sale and I do not fancy to risk it by mail to Plymouth. I will take a hundred guineas."

"I'll not pretend to bargain," Ross said, "but ninety pounds was the amount I had set aside to spend."

The shopkeeper bowed slightly. "I do not bargain myself. Do you, pardon me, intend to pay cash?"

"By draft on Pascoe's Bank. I will pay to-day and call for the brooch this day week."

"Very good, sir. I will take ninety—ninety guineas."

Ross rejoined Dwight in time to take the coach, and they were in Bodmin early in the afternoon. There the coach stayed long enough for people to eat a meal and for Ross to discover that the rumour he had come to sound was no rumour at all. Jim had gone.

They missed their meal but caught the coach on its last stage. As it set out for the long lonely trek across the Bodmin moors among the barren hills and the woodless valleys Ross noticed that the driver and his companion each carried a musket on the box beside them.

But to-day the crossing was uneventful and they had leisure to admire the changing colours of the land under a play of blue sky and cloud. They reached Launceston soon after seven and took rooms at the White Hart.

The gaol was on the hill within the grounds of the old ruined Norman castle, and they made their way towards it through a narrow tangle of streets and across a rising path between laurels and bramble until they came to the outer wall of what once had been the castle keep. A padlocked iron gateway led through an arch, but no one answered their knocking or shouting. A thrush twittered on a stunted tree and far overhead in the evening a lark sang.

Dwight was admiring the view. On this high ground you could see the moors stretching away on all sides, north towards the sea, which gleamed like a bared knife in the setting sun, and east and south across the Tamar into Devon and the wild purples of Dartmoor. No wonder the Conqueror had chosen the place to build his castle to dominate all the approaches from the west. Robert, his half brother, had lived here and gazed out over all this foreign territory, which had now come to him and must be settled and pacified.

Dwight said: "There's a cowherd by that fallen fence. I'll ask him."

While Ross made the gate echo, Dwight went across and spoke to a dark-faced man in the canvas hat and smock of a farm labourer. He was soon back.

"At first I could make no sense of him. They speak quite different in these parts. He says everyone in the prison is ill of fever. It lies over there on the green, just to the right of our gate. He does not think we shall get in to-night."

Ross stared through the bars. "And the gaoler?"

"Lives distant. I have his address. Behind Southgate Street."

Ross frowned up at the wall. "This could be climbed, Dwight. The spikes are rusty and would pull out of the wall."

"Yes, but we could do no good if the gaol itself were locked."

"Well, there's no time to waste, for it will be dark in an hour."

They turned and went down the hill again.

It took them time to find where the gaoler lived and minutes hammering on the door of the cottage before it came open a few inches and a ragged, spotty, bearded man blinked out. His anger wavered a little when he saw the dress of his visitors.

"You are the gaoler of the prison?" Ross said.

"Iss."

"Have you a man in your custody named Carter, new moved from Bodmin?"

The gaoler blinked. "Mebbe."

"We wish to see Carter at once."

"It bain't time for visiting."

Ross put his foot quickly in the jamb of the door. "Get your keys or I'll have you dismissed for neglecting your duty."

"Nay," said the gaoler. "It be sundown now. There's the fever abroad. It bain't safe to go near——"

Ross had thrust open the door again with his shoulder. A strong smell of cheap spirits was in the air. Dwight followed into the room. An ancient woman, misshapen and tattered, crouched over the hearth.

"The keys," said Ross. "Come with us or we'll go ourselves."

The gaoler wiped his arm across his nose. "Where's your authority? Ye must have authority——"

Ross took him by the collar. "We have authority. Get the keys."

In about ten minutes a procession started through the cobbled alleys towards the summit of the hill, the ragged gaoler in the lead carrying four great keys on a ring. Faces watched them go.

As they climbed above the town the sunset flared and the sun dipped and was gone.

The cowherd had driven in his cows and the ruin looked shadowy and silent. They reached the iron gate and passed through it under the stone arch, the gaoler leading the way with slowing steps towards a moderate-sized square building in the centre of the green.

The man's lagging footsteps came to a stop. "It be overlate to enter in. Ye maun show me the authority. There's fever in plenty. Yesterday one of 'em died. I'm not sure which twas. My mate——"

"How long since you were here yourself?"

"Nay, but the day before. I would ha' been over to-day, but for me mother an' 'er bein' ill. I sent over the food. Ye maun show yer authority——"

There was a sudden burst of cries, growing in tone and number, animal not human, barks and moans and grunts, not words. The prisoners had heard them.

"There," said the gaoler, as Ross drew back. "Ye see. Twould be unfit fur self-respectin' gents to go nearer. There be fever——"

But Ross had moved back to look for a window and now saw one set high in the wall on his right. The building was two-storied, and the window was to provide some light and ventilation for the dungeons on the ground floor. It was not three feet long and less than eighteen inches high, being set with thick bars. The cries and shouts came from here but echoed hollow, and it was clear that the window was out of reach of the inmates.

"Open the door, man," Ross said. "Here, give me the keys!"

"Not that way!" said the gaoler. "It ain't been opened that way since they was put in. Come you up to the chapel above and I'll open the trap door where the food d'go down. Tes a danger for fever, even that, I tell ee. If ye've a mind——"

Dwight said: "It will be dark in ten minutes. We have no time to lose if we wish to see him to-day."

"See here," said Ross to the gaoler. "This gentleman is a surgeon and wishes to see Carter at once. Open this door or I'll crack your head and do it myself."

The gaoler cringed. "It be as much as me job's worth, damme—— 'Ere, I'll open of it. . . . Mind, I take no blame, fever or no. . . ."

The great door was unlocked and opened against their pressure, groaning on rusty hinges. Inside it was quite dark, and as they entered a terrible stench hit them. Ross was a man of his age and had travelled in rough places; Dwight was a doctor and had not neglected his duties; but this was new to them both. The gaoler went outside again and hawked and spat and hawked and spat. Ross caught him by the scruff and pulled him back.

"Is there a lantern here?"

"Iss, I reckon. Be'ind the door."

Trembling, he groped among the refuse and found the lantern. Then he scratched at his tinderbox to get a spark for the candle.

Inside the prison, after all the noise, silence had fallen. No doubt they thought more felons were to be added to their number.

As his eyes grew used to the dark, Ross saw they were in a passage. On one side the window let in the faint glimmer of the afterglow. On the other were the cells or cages. There were only three or four, and all of them small. As the tinder rag at last caught and the candle was lit, he saw that the largest of the cages was not more than three yards square. In each of them there were about a dozen convicts. All down the cages terrible faces peered between the bars.

"A pest spot," said Dwight, walking down with his handkerchief to his nose. "God, what an offence to human dignity! Are there sewers, man? Or any medical attention? Or even a chimney?"

"Look ee," said the gaoler by the door, "there's sickness an' fever. We'll all be down ourselves afore long. Let us go out an' come again to-morrow."

"In which cell is Carter?"

"Save us, I dunno. I dunno one from t'other, s'elp me. Ye'd best find him yourself."

Pushing the gaoler with his quavering lantern before him, Ross followed Dwight. In the last and smallest cage were a half dozen women. The cell was barely big enough for them to lie down. Filthy, emaciated, in rags, like strange devils they screeched and skirled—those of them who could stand—asking for money and bread.

Sick and horrified, Ross went back to the men.

"Quiet!" he shouted to the clamour that was growing again.

Slowly it died.

"Is Jim Carter among you?" he shouted. "Jim, are you there?"

No answer.

Then there was a rattle of chains and a voice said: "He is here. But in no fit state to speak for himself."

Ross went to the middle cage. "Where?"

"Here." The demons of the pit moved away from the bars, and the gaoler's lantern showed up two or three figures lying on the floor.

"Is he—dead?"

"No, but t'other one is. Carter is with the fever bad. And his arm . . ."

"Bring him to the bars."

They did so, and Ross gazed on a man he would not have recognized. The face, wasted and with a long straggling black beard, was covered with a blotchy red rash. Every now and then Jim stirred and muttered and spoke to himself in his delirium.

"It is the petechial type," Enys muttered. "It looks to be past its height. How long has he been ill?"

"I don't know," said the other convict. "We lose count of days, as you will understand. Perhaps a week."

"What is wrong with his arm?" Enys said sharply.

"We tried to check the fever by letting blood," said the convict. "Unhappily the arm has festered."

Dwight looked at the delirious man a long moment, then stared at the speaker.

"What are you in this place for?"

"Oh," said the other, "I do not think my case can interest you, though at a happier meeting I might entertain you for an idle hour. When one has not the benefit of a patrimony one is sometimes forced to eke out one's livelihood by means which your profession, sir, prefers to keep in its own ranks. Natural that——"

Ross had stood up. "Open this door."

"What?" said the gaoler. "What for?"

"I am taking this man away. He needs medical attention."

"Aye, but he be servin' a sentence, an' nothing——"

"Damn you!" Ross's mounting anger had bubbled over. "Open this door!"

The gaoler backed against the cage, looked round for a way of escape, found none, and his eyes again met those of the man confronting him. He turned quickly, fumbled with the great keys, unlocked the door in haste, stood back sweating.

"Bring him out," said Ross.

Dwight and the gaoler went in, their feet slipping over ordure on the damp earth floor. Happily Jim was not one of those chained to another prisoner. They picked him up and carried him out of the cage and out of the prison, Ross following. On the sweet grass outside they laid him down, and the gaoler went stumbling back to lock the doors.

Dwight mopped his forehead.

"What now?"

Ross stared down at the wreck of a human being stirring in the half-dark at their feet. He took great breaths of the beautiful fresh evening air, which was blowing like the bounty of God over from the sea.

"What chance is there for him, Dwight?"

Dwight spat and spat. "He should survive the fever. But that meddling fool in there . . . though he did it for the best. This arm is mortifying."

"We must get him somewhere, under cover. He can't survive the night out here."

"Well, they will not have him at the White Hart. As well ask them to house a leper."

The gaoler had locked up his prison again and was standing by the door watching them with an envenomed gaze. But he was coming no nearer.

"There must be a shed somewhere, Dwight. Or a room. All men are not inhuman."

"They tend to be where fever is concerned. It is self-preservation. Our only resort, I should say, is a stable somewhere. A little from the prison would be better, lest the gaoler makes an early report on our doings."

"There may be a hospital in the town."

"None that would take such a patient."

"I'll be all right, Jinny. They won't catch me," came in a husky voice from the figure at their feet.

Ross bent down. "Give me a hand. We must get him somewhere, and at once."

"Avoid his breath," said Dwight. "It will be deadly at this stage."

CHAPTER V   Jim was laughing while they undressed him. It was a peculiar cross-grained broken sound. Now and again he would begin to talk, but it was senseless stuff, now in conversation with a prisoner, now with Nick Vigus, now with Jinny.

They had found a store-barn—some relic, from its architecture, of the early history of the town—and had taken possession, turning out the chickens and the bullock cart and the two mules before informing the farmer who owned it. Then a mixture of bribery and threats had withstood his anger. They had bought two blankets from him and two cups and some milk and some brandy. They had lit a fire at the end of the barn—the farmer had come back to shout about this but, being terrified of the fever, had done nothing more.

So now Dwight made his examination by the light of two candles and the smoky glimmer of the fire. Ross had taken the last of Jim's clothes and flung them outside, and he came back to find Enys gingerly touching the boy's poisoned arm. He lifted one of the candles and looked at it himself. Then he straightened up. He had seen too many cases like it in the fighting in America.

"Well?" he said.

"Well, I must take that arm off if he is to stand a chance, Ross."

"Yes," said Ross. "And what chance is there then?"

"Somewhat less than an even one, I should say."

"There is not much to commend it. He loses his arm and the poison begins again."

"Not of necessity."

Ross went to the door and looked out into the darkness. "Oh, God," he said. "He is in too poor a shape, Dwight. Let him die in peace."

Dwight was silent a moment, watching the delirious man. He gave him brandy and Jim swallowed it.

"He would feel little, I believe. I am not happy to let him go without a chance."

146

"Have you done it before?"

"No, but it is a straightforward thing. Merely a matter of common anatomy and common precaution."

"What precautions can you take here? And what have you here to do it with?"

"Oh, I could get something. The precautions are to prevent loss of blood or further poisoning. Well, a tourniquet is simple and . . . we have a fire and plenty of water."

"And the fever?"

"Is on the wane. His pulse is slowing."

Ross came back and stared at the emaciated bearded figure.

"He had a year or two of happiness with Jinny. They had that together before one thing after another went wrong. He never had health in the best of times. He will be a cripple now, even if he survives. Yet I suppose we must give him the chance. I would like to wring someone's neck for this."

Dwight got up. "Notice how our own clothes stink. We should do better to burn them after this." He looked at Ross. "You can help me with the operation?"

"Oh, I can help you. I am not likely to faint at blood. My queasiness is at this waste of a young life. I could vomit over that; and would quick enough if the magistrates were here who sent him to gaol. . . . When has it to be?"

"As soon as we can assemble ourselves. I will go and find a barber surgeon in the town and borrow some things of him. I will also call at the White Hart and bring my own bag here."

Dwight picked up his hat and went out.

Ross sat down beside Carter and filled up the cup with brandy. He intended to get as much down the sick man as possible, and he would take some himself from the other cup. The nearer they all were to being drunk the better. Enys was right. Everything stank from that visit to the prison: the boots on his feet, his gloves, his stock, even his purse. Perhaps his nostrils were wrong. Celebrations for the King's recovery indeed! All those preparations of yesterday and last week seemed cut off from to-night by the gulf of Launceston Gaol.

" 'Ere, steady on," said Jim, and coughed loosely. "I can 'old me own, I can, and well enough."

Jim could hold his own. The tattered scarecrow lying on the blanket with fever in his veins and poison creeping up his arm, that bearded derelict of a young man could hold his own. No doubt, so far as he had conscious will, he would try for Jinny's sake as he had done in the past. As he had done in the past. This was the crucial test.

Great shadows stirred and moved on the wall behind them. In the flickering firelight, sitting among the straw and the chaff and the feathers, Ross bent and gave the boy another drink of brandy.

On the morning of the twenty-second Ross was still away and Demelza had spent a sleepless night. At least she thought it sleepless, although she had in fact spent the time in a succession of dozes and sudden wakenings, fancying she heard the beat of Darkie's hooves outside her bedroom window. Julia had been fretful too, as if aware of her mother's unease; though with her it was no more than a sore gum.

Demelza wished she could have a sore gum in place of her own gnawing anxiety. As soon as light came she was up, and chose to revert to her old custom of going out with the dawn. But to-day, instead of making up the valley for flowers, she walked along Hendrawna Beach with Garrick at her heels.

There was a good deal of driftwood left by the tide, and she paused here and there to turn something over with her foot to see if it was of special value. She still sometimes had to remember that what would have been well worth the salving a few years ago now was beneath her station to bother with.

As the light grew she saw that they were changing cores at Wheal Leisure, and a few minutes later several figures came on the beach, miners who had finished their eight hours and were doing a bit of beachcombing to see what could be carried home to breakfast. The sea had not been generous of late, and every tide the beach was picked clean by the searchers. Nothing was too small or too useless. Demelza knew that this winter even the snails in the fields and lanes had been gathered to make broth.

Two or three small wiry men passed her, touching their caps as they went; then she saw that the next was Mark Daniel; and he did not seem interested in the harvest of the tide.

Tall and stiff, with a mining pick over his shoulder, he ploughed his way across the soft sand. Their paths crossed, and he looked up as if he had not noticed her.

She said: "Well, Mark, how are you going along? Are you comfortable-like in your new house?"

He stopped and glanced at her and then looked stolidly out over the sea.

"Oh, aye, ma'am. Well-a-fine. Thank ye, ma'am, for the asking."

She had seen very little of him since the day he had come to beg the land. He was thinner, gaunter—that was not surprising, for so was almost everyone—but some new darkness moved at the back of his black eyes.

She said: "The tide has left us nothing this morning, I b'lieve."

"Eh? No, ma'am. There are them as say we could do with a profitable wreck. Not as I'd be wishing hurt to anyone. . . ."

"How is Keren, Mark? I have not seen her this month; but to tell truth there is so much distress in Grambler village that makes us seem well placed. I have been helping Miss Verity with her people there."

"Keren's brave 'nough, ma'am." A sombre gleam showed. "Is Cap'n Poldark back yet, if ye please?"

"No, he's been away some days, Mark."

"Oh. . . . It was to see he I was comin' this way. I thought as he was back. John told me . . ."

"Is it something special?"

"It can bide." He turned as if to go.

She said: "I'll tell him, Mark."

He said hesitatingly: "You was a help to me last August, and I ain't forgot, mistress. But this—this is something better only spoke of between men. . . ."

"I expect he'll be here before morning. We have an invitation in Truro for to-morrow. . . ."

They separated, and she walked slowly on along the beach. She ought to be getting back. Jinny would be at Nampara now, and Julia was still restless.

Some seaweed crunched behind her, and she turned to find that Mark had followed.

His black eyes met hers. "Mistress Poldark, there's bad things being spoke of Keren." He said it as if it were a challenge.

"Was that what you wanted to say?"

"There's tales bein' spread."

"What tales?"

"That she be going with another man."

"There are always tales in these parts, Mark. You know that the grannies have nothing else to do but whisper over their fires."

"Aye," said Mark. "But I'm not easy of mind."

No, thought Demelza, neither should I be, not with Karen. "How can Ross help you?"

"I thought to have 'is view on what was best. I thought he'd know betterer than me."

"But is—is there any man specially spoken of?"

"Aye," said Mark.

"Have you said anything to Keren? Have you mentioned it to her?"

"No. I ha'n't the heart. Mistress, I ha'n't the heart. We've only been wed eight months. I builded the cottage for she. I can't put myself to believe it."

"Then don't believe it," Demelza said. "If you've not the mind to ask her straight, leave it be and do no more. There's always evil tongues in this district, and like serpents they are. Maybe you know the things that used to be whispered about me. . . ."

"No," said Mark, looking up. "I never took no heed of such talk . . . not—not before . . ."

"Then why take heed of it now? Do you know, Mark, that there's whispers about that Captain Poldark is the father of Jinny Carter's first child, all on account of them having scars similar placed?"

"No," said Mark. He spat. "Beg pardon, ma'am, but tis a cabby lie. I know that; an' so do any other right-minded man. A wicked lie."

"Well, but if I chose to think there was truth in it I might be just as miserable as you, mightn't I, Mark?"

The big man looked at her, an uncertain but noticeable reassurance on his face. Then he looked down at his hands.

"I near strangled the man who told me. Maybe I was overhasty. I've scarce done a stroke at the mine these two days."

"I know how you must have felt."

Suddenly he sought justification and, finding it, found suspicion again.

"You see—you see, she's that pretty an' dainty, mistress. She's far above the likes of me. Maybe I did wrong in plaguing her to wed me; but—but I wanted her for wife. She's too good for a miner's wife, and when I know that, I d'feel anxious. I get hard and overhasty. I get suspecting. And then when there's whispers, and a man who belongs to call himself friend takes me aside and says—and says . . . It is easy to slip, Mistress Poldark, and feel there's truth in what may be lies." He considered the sea. "Dirty lies. If they bain't . . . I couldn't stand by. So 'elp me, I couldn't. Not and see 'er go to another. No. . . ." The muscles of his throat worked a moment. "Thank ye again, ma'am. I'm more in your debt. I'll forget and start anew. Maybe I'll come and see Cap'n Poldark when he is home; but maybe what you've said'll put things straight in my mind. Good day to ye."

"Good day," said Demelza, and stood watching his great figure striding east towards the sand hills and his home. She began to walk back the way she had come, towards Nampara. Who is Keren carrying on with? she thought, instinctively believing what she had sought to discredit. Who *is* there that she could carry on with? Keren, who affected to look down on all the cottage folk.

When Ross came back she would mention it to him, see what he said. It looked as if someone ought to warn not Mark but Keren. She would be very sorry for Keren—and the man—if Mark found them out. Keren should be told that her husband was suspicious. It might just frighten her off someone and perhaps save a tragedy. She would remember to tell Ross when he came home.

Then as she climbed the wall from the beach she saw Ross dismount at the door of Nampara and go into the house; and she ran quickly up the slope calling him. Mark Daniel and Keren were forgotten, and would stay forgotten for a long time.

CHAPTER VI   She found him in the parlour taking off his gloves.

"Ross!" she said. "I thought you was never coming home. I thought——"

He turned.

"Oh, Ross," she said. "What's to do?"

"Is Jinny here yet?"

"I don't know. I don't think she can be."

He sat down. "I saw Zacky early. Perhaps he was able to tell her before she left."

"What is it?" she asked.

He looked up at her. "Jim is dead."

She faltered and looked at him, then dropped her eyes. She came over and took his hand.

"Oh, my dear . . . I'm that sorry. Oh, poor Jinny. Ross, dear . . ."

"You should not come near me," he said. "I have been in infection."

For answer she pulled up a chair beside him, stared again at his face.

"What happened?" she said. "Did you see him?"

"Have you brandy?"

She got up and brought him some. She could tell he had drunk a good deal already.

"He had been taken to Launceston," he said. "We found him in gaol with the fever. The place should be burned down. It is worse than an ancient pest house. Well, he was ill and we took him out. . . ."

"You took him out?"

"We were stronger than the gaoler. We carried him to a barn and Dwight did what he could. But a quack doctor had let blood while he was in the gaol, and his arm had festered and gone poor. There was only one hope, which was to have it off before the poison spread."

"His—his arm?"

Ross finished the brandy at a gulp.

"The King and his ministers should have been there—Pitt and Addison and Fox; and Wilberforce, who weeps over the black slaves while forgetting the people at his own door, and the fat Prince with his corsets and his mistresses. . . . Or perhaps they would have been entertained by the spectacle, they and their powdered and painted women; Heaven knows, I have lost hope of understanding men. Well, Dwight did his best and spared no effort. Jim lived until the early morning; but the shock was too great. At the end I think he knew me. He smiled and seemed to want to speak but he had not the strength. So he went: and we saw him buried in Lawhitton Church and so came home."

There was silence. His vehemence and bitterness frightened her. Upstairs, as from a homely world, was the sound of Julia grizzling. Abruptly he rose and went to the window, stared out over his well-ordered estate.

"Was Dr. Enys with you in all this?" she asked.

"We were so tired yesterday that we lay last night in Truro. That is why we are here so early to-day. I—saw Zacky on the way home. He was riding on company business but turned back."

"It were better that you had not gone, Ross. I——"

"It is bad that I did not go a fortnight sooner. Then there would have been hope."

"What will the magistrates and the constables say? That you broke into the gaol and helped a prisoner to escape, Ross. Will there not be trouble over that?"

"Trouble, yes. The bees will hum if I do not plaster them with honey."

"Then . . ."

"Yes, let them hum, Demelza. I wish them good fortune. I should be almost induced to go among 'em as arranged at to-morrow's celebrations if I thought they might catch the fever from me."

She came urgently up to him. "Don't talk so, Ross. Do you not feel well? Do you feel you have caught it?"

After a moment he put his hand on her arm, looking at her and seeing her for the first time since he came home.

"No, love. I am well enough. I should be well, for Dwight took strange precautions which seemed to please him: washing our clothes and hanging them over a burning pitch barrel to get out the stink of the gaol. But do not expect me to dance and play with these people to-morrow when their handiwork is still fresh in my mind."

Demelza was silent. Between the thankfulness that Ross was home—perhaps safe but at least home—and the sorrow for Jim and Jinny, a desolation was beginning to appear, a knowledge that all her own plans were in ruin. She might have argued but she had neither the tongue nor the lack of loyalty to do so.

For it did seem to her just then a matter of loyalty. He must do as he chose and she, at whatever disappointment, must accept it.

He was not at all himself that day. She, who had known Jim little enough, wondered at the bitterness of his loss. For it was bitterness as well as sorrow. He had known Jim's loyalty to himself and had given a greater loyalty in return. Always it seemed to him he had striven to help the young man and always his efforts had come too late. Well, this was the last effort and the failure was final. At five he went to see Jinny. He hated the thought of meeting her but there was no one else to do it.

He was gone an hour. When he came back she had a meal ready for him, but at first he would not touch anything. Later, coaxingly, like tempting a child, she got him to taste first one thing and then another. It was a new experience for her. At seven Jane cleared the table and he sat back in his chair by the fire, stretching his legs, not appeased in mind but quieter in body and just beginning to relax.

And then the frock came.

Demelza frowned at the great box and carried it in to Ross, only just getting through the parlour door.

"Bartle has just brought this," she said. "Over from Trenwith. They sent into Truro to-day for provisions, and Mistress Trelask asked would they deliver this. What can it be?"

"Is Bartle still there? Give him sixpence, will you."

Ross stared at the box bleakly until Demelza came back. Then she too stared at it, between glances at him.

"I thought it was a mistake. I thought Bartle must have brought it wrong. Have you been buying something at Mistress Trelask's, Ross?"

"Yes," he said. "It seems like a year ago. On my way to Launceston I called in to order you a frock."

"Oh," said Demelza, her dark eyes widening.

"For the celebrations to-morrow. That was when I still thought we should go."

"Oh, Ross. You're that kind. Could I see it?"

"If you've the interest," he said. "It will do for sometime in the future."

She fell on the box and began to pull at the cord. She at last wriggled it free and lifted the lid. She pulled out some sheets of paper and loose cloth packing and stopped. She put in her fingers and began to lift out the gown. It shimmered silver and scarlet.

"Oh, Ross, I never thought . . ."

Then she put it back and sat on her heels and began to cry.

"It will do for some other time," he said again. "Come, you do not dislike it?"

She did not answer but put her hands to her face, and the tears trickled through her fingers.

He reached for the brandy bottle but found it empty.

"We could not enter with any enjoyment into the visit to-morrow, not now, with this fresh in our minds. *Could* you?"

She shook her head.

He watched her for some moments. His mind was fumed with brandy but he could not see her crying like this without discomfort.

"There is something else in there if you will look. At least, I asked that a cloak should be sent."

But she would not look. And then John showed Verity in.

Demelza got quickly up and went to the window. Without handkerchief, she stared hard at the garden and wiped her cheeks with her hands and with the lace cuffs of her frock.

"I am *de trop*," Verity said. "Well, it's no good to withdraw now. I knew I should not have come to-night. Oh, my dear, I am so sorry about Jim."

Demelza turned and kissed her but did not meet her eyes.

"We—we have been a little upset, Verity. It is tragical about Jim, is it not. . . ." She went from the room.

Verity looked at Ross. "Forgive me for being so intruding. I had intended coming over yesterday but have been busy getting Elizabeth off."

"Off?"

"With Francis. They are sleeping for two nights at the Warleggans. I stayed behind and thought you might allow me to ride in with you to-morrow."

"Oh," said Ross. "Yes, if we were going."

"But I thought it was settled long since. You mean . . ." Verity sat down. ". . . because of Jim."

Sombrely he reached out and kicked at the log on the fire. "Verity, I have a strong stomach, but the sight of a powdered head would turn it."

Verity's glance had several times strayed to the open box.

"This is what Bartle brought? It looks something like a frock."

In a few words Ross told her. Verity pulled at her gloves and thought what a strange man Ross was, at once a cynic and a sentimentalist, a strange blend of his father and his mother and a personal x equation belonging to neither. Abstemious enough by the standards of the day, he was now drinking himself into an ugly stupor over the death of this boy, who had not even been employed by him for a year or more before his imprisonment. An ordinary man in his station would have passed over the loss with a grunt of regret and not have ventured within two miles of a gaol to prevent it. And this gesture of the frock . . . No wonder Demelza wept.

They were all sentimentalists at heart, the Poldarks, Verity thought, and she realized suddenly for the first time that it was a dangerous trait, far more dangerous than any cynicism. She herself at this moment, happy among all the distress and discontent; life was full for her again, and she had no right to let it be on the strength of a *mésalliance* which might any time end in disaster, which was a deliberate closing of the eyes to one side of life, a forgetting of the past and a planning for an unrealizable future. Sometimes in the night she woke up cold at the thought. But in the day she went on and was happy.

Francis too. Half his ailments came from the same source. He expected too much of life, of himself, of Elizabeth. Especially of Elizabeth. When they failed him he resorted to gambling and to drink. He wouldn't come to terms. None of them would come to terms.

"Ross," she said at last, after the silence, "I do not think you are wise to stay away to-morrow."

"Why?"

"Well, you would disappoint Demelza desperately, for she has been building on this ever since the word came, and however much she may grieve for Jim and Jinny she will bitterly regret it if she does not go. And this frock you have rashly and beautifully bought will heap coals of fire on her disappointment. Then you would disappoint me, who would now have to ride in alone. But most important you should go for your own sake. You can't help poor Jim now. You have done your most, and can't reproach yourself for that. It will do real harm to sit and mope here. And your move in forcing the gaol will not be popular. Your presence among people to-morrow will emphasize that you are one of their class, and if they contemplate any move it will, I think, give them pause."

Ross got up and stood a moment leaning against the mantelpiece.

"Your arguments fill me with disgust, Verity."

"Everything at the moment, my dear, no doubt seems disgusting. I know the mood too well. But being in that mood, Ross, is like being out in the frost. If we do not keep on the move we shall perish."

He went over to the cupboard and looked for another bottle of brandy. There was none there.

He said suddenly, confusedly: "I cannot think straight to-night. Demelza said she did not wish it."

"Well, she would say that."

He hesitated. "I'll think it over, Verity, and send you word in the morning."

CHAPTER VII   When in the end, without consulting anyone further, Ross decided to go to the celebrations after all, and when, after an uneventful ride in, Demelza found herself shown up into one of the bedrooms of the Great House, the town house of the Warleggans, there were several worms of discomfort within her to spoil the first flush of excitement.

First there was compassion for Jinny, who last night had tried to hang herself from a beam in her own kitchen; second there was anxiety about Ross, who had not yet been entirely sober since his return and carried his drink like a gunpowder keg which any chance spark might set off; third there was unease over Julia, who had been left in the care of Mrs. Tabb at Trenwith.

But all these reservations, vital though they were, could not quite destroy the pleasure of the adventure.

Some inherent good taste told her that this house had nothing to equal the Elizabethan charm of Trenwith, but she was overwhelmed by its bright furnishings, its soft carpets, its glittering chandeliers, its many servants. She was overwhelmed by the large number of guests and the easy familiarity with which they greeted each other, their expensive clothes, their powdered hair and patched faces and their gold snuffboxes and glittering rings.

They were all here; George Warleggan had seen to that; it was like a preliminary regal reception before the public entertainment of the ball. Or all were here who would come. The Lord Lieutenant and his family had politely declined; so had the Bassetts, the Boscawens and the St. Aubyns, not yet ready to put themselves on a level with these wealthy upstarts. But their absence was unremarked except by the perceptive or the malicious. Demelza had a confused recollection of meeting Sir John This and the Hon. Someone Else, and had passed in a dazed fashion in the wake of a servant up the stairs to her bedroom. Now she was waiting for the arrival of a maid, who was coming to help her put on her new gown and to dress her hair. She was in a panic about it and her hands were cold; but this was the price of adventure. She knew herself far better able to cope with John Treneglos, who traced his ancestry back to a Norman count, than to face the prying eyes of a saucy servant girl who if she didn't know what Demelza had been would soon be ready to guess.

Demelza sat down at the dressing table and saw her flushed face in the mirror. Well, she was really here. Ross had not come up yet. Dwight Enys was here, young and handsome. Old Mr. Nicholas Warleggan, George's father, big and pompous and hard. There was a clergyman called Halse, thin and dried-up but vigorous-looking and moving among the aristocracy like one of them, not cringing for a bone like Mr. Odgers of Sawle-with-Grambler. Dr. Halse and old Mr. Warleggan, Demelza knew, had been among the magistrates who had sentenced Jim. She was afraid for what might happen.

A knock came at the door and she checked an impulse to start up as a maid entered. "This has come, ma'am. I was told to bring it up to you. Thank you, ma'am. A dressing maid'll be along in just a few minutes."

Demelza stared at the packet. On the outside was written: "Rs. Poldark, Esquire," and over that Ross had just scrawled in ink not yet dry: "For delivery to Mrs. Demelza Poldark."

She pulled at the wrapping, took out a small box, parted some cotton packing, gasped. After a moment, gingerly, as if afraid of burning herself, she put in a finger and thumb and drew out the brooch.

"Oh," she said.

She lifted it and held it to her breast so that she could see the effect in the mirror. The ruby glowed and winked at her. This gesture of Ross's was tremendous. It melted her. Her eyes, black and liquid with emotion, glowed back at herself above the ruby. This gift, if anything, would give her confidence. With a new dress and *this* no one surely could look down on her. Even the maids could hardly do so.

Another knock at the door and another maid entered. Demelza blinked and hastily crumpled up the packing in which the brooch had come. She was glad to see they had sent an elderly maid.

Well, she was in it. It wasn't decent, she was sure of that, but the maid didn't seem to think anything was amiss. Of course other women wore this sort of thing; it was all the fashion; but other women might be used to this sort of gown; she was not.

It was the same general shape as the afternoon gown Verity had bought her, only more so. The afternoon dress was cut away from her neck and the tops of her shoulders, but this one was so much lower. It was amazingly ruched at the sides, and there was a lot of beautiful lace hanging over her hands, where she didn't need it. How Ross had bought it she could not conceive. It had cost a pretty penny, that was clear. He spent money on her as if it was chaff. Dear, dear Ross! Unbelievably dear. If only poor Jim's death had not come between these presents and their wearing, how happy to-night would be!

The maid had just finished her hair, piling it up and up. Since Julia's birth she had not kept it clipped but had let it grow, and the sudden luxuriance of her surroundings as Ross's wife had seemed to give great richness to it so that its darkness fairly gleamed with colour. The maid had brought her powder box, but she instantly concurred in Demelza's refusal; such hair was not to be whitened. She did not however agree with Demelza's hesitant refusal of make-up, and she was now attending to my lady's face. Demelza's restiveness under her hands had the result of keeping her dresser's enthusiasm within bounds, and she came out of it with her dark eyebrows slightly lengthened, only a moderate amount of powder to harden the soft glow of her skin and an excusable amount of rouge on her lips.

"One patch or two, ma'am?" said the maid.

"Oh, none, thank ee. I have no liking for 'em."

"But ma'am would not be finished without one. May I suggest one just below the left eye?"

"Oh, well," said Demelza. "If you think so."

Five minutes later, the jewel on her breast, she said:

"Can you tell me which is Miss Verity Poldark's room?"

"The second down the passage, ma'am. On the right-hand side."

Sir Hugh Bodrugan tapped his snuffbox with hairy fingers.

"Damme, who's that filly just come in the room, Nick? The one wi' the dark hair and the pretty neck. With one of the Poldarks, ain't she?"

"I've never put eyes on her before. She's a pridey morsel to look at."

"Reminds me of my mare Sheba," said Sir Hugh. "Same look in her eyes. She'd take some bridling, I'll lay a curse. Damme, I'd not refuse the chance."

"Enys, you know the Poldarks. Who's that handsome creature Miss Verity has just led in?"

"Captain Poldark's wife, sir. They have been married about two years."

Sir Hugh brought his thick eyebrows together in an effort of remembrance. Thinking was not his favourite pastime.

"Aye, but was there not some story that he'd married below him; a farm wench or some such?"

"I could not say," Dwight answered woodenly. "I was not here at the time."

"Well, maybe that is she," said Nick.

"Lord's my life, I'll not believe it. Farm wenches just don't come that way. Or not on my estate. I only wish they did. I only wish they did. Nay, she's no vulgar: her flanks are too long. Here, Enys, you know the lady. Grant me the favour."

She had come down thinking she would find Ross, but in this crowd it would be all but impossible. A footman stood beside her, and she and Verity took a glass of port. Somebody called Miss Robartes monopolized Verity, and before she knew it they were separated. People began talking to her, and she answered them absently. As always port helped her, and she thought how wrong Ross had been to deny it her at the christening. It was specially needed to-night to give her confidence about her frock. Then she saw Dwight Enys bearing down on her and she greeted him with relief. With him was a beetle-browed, stocky elderly man with a hairy nose, and Dwight introduced him as Sir Hugh Bodrugan. Demelza looked at him with quickened interest and met a gaze that surprised her. She'd seen that look in a man's eyes twice before: once from John Treneglos at the Christmas party the year before last, once to-night from a stranger as she came down the stairs.

She breathed it in for a moment before curtsying.

"Your servant, ma'am."

"Sir."

"Cod, ma'am, Dr. Enys tells me you are Mrs. Poldark from Nampara. We've been neighbours two years and not met before. I hurry to repair the omission." Sir Hugh snapped his fingers to a footman. "Wine for this lady, man, her glass is empty."

Demelza sipped another glass. "I have heard of you often, sir," she answered.

"Indeed," Sir Hugh puffed out his cheeks. "And I trust that the report was not disfavourable, eh?"

"No, sir, not at all. I hear that you keep plump pheasants which are a trouble to the poor poachers when they come to steal 'em."

Sir Hugh laughed. "I have a heart too, and no one has ever stole that yet neither."

"Perhaps like the pheasants you keep it too well guarded."

She noticed Dwight looking at her in surprise.

"Nay, ma'am," said Sir Hugh, making eyes at her downright, "it is not guarded at all for them as knows how and when."

"Good God, Hughie," said his stepmother, coming on them suddenly. "I thought you'd gone without me, you wicked old devil. Seen about the carriage, have you? I can't tramp across in all this falallery." The Dowager Lady Bodrugan, who was twenty years younger than her stepson, hitched up her fine satin cloak in a disgusted fashion and stared Demelza up and down. "Who is this? I haven't the pleasure, miss."

"This is Captain Ross's wife. From Nampara. Damme, I was saying we've been lax in our manners not asking 'em over to an evening of whist. . . ."

"D'you hunt, mistress?" demanded Constance Bodrugan.

"No, ma'am." Demelza finished her port. "I have some sympathy for the foxes."

Lady Bodrugan stared. "Pah, a Methody or some such! I smelt it. Let's see, weren't you a miner's daughter?"

Inwardly Demelza trembled with sudden unruly anger. "Yes, ma'am. Father hung at Bargus for the crows to pick; an' Mother was a highwaywoman an' fell over a cliff."

Sir Hugh roared with laughter. "Serves you right, Connie, for your quizzing. Take no account of my stepmother, Mrs. Poldark. She barks like her hounds, but there's little vice in it."

"Damn you, Hugh! Keep your apologies for your own behaviour. Just because you feel——"

"Why, there!" John Treneglos pushed his clumsy way into the circle. For once he was dressed up, and his freckled sandy face was already flushed with drink. "Hugh and Connie, tagging at each other as usual. I might have known! And Mistress Demelza," he added with assumed surprise. "Well, now, here's a good meet. Tallyho! Mistress Demelza, I want you to promise me the first country dance."

"Well, that you can't have, John," said Sir Hugh. "For she's promised it to me. Haven't you, ma'am. Eh?" He winked.

Demelza sipped another glass which someone had put into her hand. It was the first time she had seen John Treneglos since his quarrel with her father, but he seemed to have ignored or forgotten that. Out of the corner of her eye she saw Ruth Treneglos edging her way through the crowd towards her husband.

"I thought that was the second, Sir Hugh," she said.

She saw "the look" come strongly into John Treneglos's eyes as he bowed. "Thank ee. I'll be waiting to claim the first."

"Here's Captain Poldark," said Dwight, almost with a note of relief in his voice.

Demelza turned and saw Ross and Francis and Elizabeth entering the room together. Dear life, she thought, what do these men think they are? There isn't one of 'em I'd glance at twice with Ross in the room. The strong bones of his face stood out hard and severe to-night, the scar hardly showing at all. He wasn't looking for her. Beside him Francis was slight. By the colour and shape of their eyes they might have been brothers.

They might have been brothers entering a hostile room and preparing to fight. Demelza wondered if others read their expression the same, for the noise and chatter in the room grew less.

Then George Warleggan came smiling suavely up and began to move among the guests, remarking that it wanted ten minutes to eight.

The night was fine, and Demelza persuaded Ross to walk to the Assembly Rooms. The distance was nothing, and if they picked their way they would get there clean. There were already a lot of people in the streets, many of them drunk, and Demelza had the wish to see how her own kind were enjoying the night.

Two great bonfires roared, one in the cockpit overlooking the town, the other in High Cross opposite the Assembly Rooms. It was rumoured that there were to be fireworks at Falmouth, but this sophistication was not for Truro. In places lanterns had been hung on poles in the narrow streets, and the quarter moon had not yet set, so there was a fair amount of light.

Demelza wanted too to rebuild her contact with Ross. The sudden admiration of those men had surprised and elated her, but they really didn't mean anything at all. She wanted to be with Ross, to keep his company, to encourage his enjoyment, to have his admiration. But she couldn't break down the wall that his anger and resentment had set up. It was not resentment against her, but it kept her outside. Even his concern for the success of the copper company—overriding this winter—had been forgotten. She had tried to thank him for his wonderful gift but he hadn't seemed to respond.

Just for a moment his eyes had changed, warmed when he saw her in the frock, but she had not been able to keep his interest, to keep him away from his thoughts.

They reached the steps of the Assembly Rooms and paused to look back. The bonfire was roaring and crackling in the centre of the little square. Round it the figures were moving and dancing, yellow and black in the flickering flame-light. Beyond and to the right the bow windows of the houses were dotted with faces, old people and children watching the fun. To the left the light wavered through the quiet trees and set white among the gravestones. Then a carriage and a sedan chair drew up at the door of the Rooms, and Ross and Demelza turned and went up the stairs.

CHAPTER VIII   A gathering at which the Lord Lieutenant of the County was present was a gathering of importance. For the Lord Lieutenant was the King's Man, and from him came all things great and small. Or, to be explicit, what came from him were appoointments to be Justice of the Peace, and to be a J.P. meant to be the possessor of undisputed local power. For good or ill the J.P.s ruled, unchecked by Privy Council or the public purse. So the Lord Lieutenant was a man to be sought after, flattered and fawned on.

To-night there was to be cardplaying, toasts, dancing and a wide range of refreshments. The room had been hung with red, white and blue streamers, and behind the dais, where the band played, a big painting of King George was set up.

Almost as soon as she got there Demelza saw Andrew Blamey. He had taken up a quiet place where he could see the door, and she knew he was watching for Verity. Her heart began to thump for an extra reason, for Verity was coming with Francis and that might mean trouble.

Being at the Warleggans had given her some idea what to expect, and the arrival of the people she had moved among there gave her time to take a grip. It was extraordinarily pleasing and reassuring too to see and be greeted by other people she had met before. Joan Pascoe spoke to her and introduced a young man called Paul Carruthers, who was an ensign in the Navy. Dr. and Mrs. Choake were there, but they kept their distance. Patience Teague unexpectedly attached herself; Demelza was very flattered until she began to suspect it was because she was in the party of George Warleggan. Then a fat pale man called Sanson (whom she remembered at the food riots) pushed his way in, blinking all the time, and took Ross in conversation. It was something about some gaming loss he had had. Before she knew it they were separated.

She was surrounded with people she did not know or knew slightly. Sir Hugh was here again and John Treneglos and a man called St. John Peter, better-looking than the others and young. Several of them were talking to her and she was answering them absent-mindedly, keeping her attention for the other things. Which was the Lord Lieutenant, how did they ever get so many candles burning so even, could she get back to Ross, had Andrew Blamey moved from his corner, what sort of flowers were they in the tall vases, was her frock holding up, would she ever be able to dance with her hair so high? Several times the people about her laughed, and she wondered anxiously if one of the others had said something witty or she had somehow made a fool of herself.

She needed a drink, that was certain. The three ports at the Warleggans had made her feel well and confident, but the confidence was wearing off. More courage was needed out of a glass.

Suddenly there was a whirring noise from the band and all the noise ceased as if you had rubbed it off a slate and people stood up stiff and she realized they were playing "God Save the King." Very soon everyone joined in, and they sang it to the roof. When it was over the noise broke and rippled over the floor again. Then someone had found her a seat between Patience Teague and Joan Pascoe, and she was trying to fan herself with the fan Verity had loaned her.

Dwight Enys arrived with another young man, and she thought she saw the colour of Verity's dress.

Someone at the far end of the hall was speaking, but she could not see without standing up and she only heard words here and there, about "our Gracious Majesty" and "Divine Providence," and "all his people" and "thankful hearts." Then the voice stopped and there was a ripple of applause. Faintly could be heard the scrape of bass viols tuning up. Several men came about her. They wanted her to dance the first minuet. Where was Ross? She looked up at the faces and inclined her head slightly at St. John Peter. Then a man called Whitworth, good-looking but dressed in an absurdity of fashion, pressed her for the second. She accepted but refused any for the third. Ross would come back.

The band struck up and no one went on the centre of the floor at all except two quite old people, very grand, who led off all by themselves. Then after a minute or two the band paused and everyone applauded again and began forming up.

She went out with St. John Peter, who noticed that his partner's expression had changed, from that rather absent, ready-for-flight look which her talk proved so takingly deceptive, to a faint frown of serious thought. He wondered at her lack of response to his sallies. He didn't realize that she needed all her care to remember what Mrs. Kemp had taught her.

Presently she found she could do well enough, and as the dance came to an end and they waited for the repeat she knew she had nothing to fear.

Near by Joan Pascoe said: "We never see you now, Dwight. Do you never ride in to Truro?"

"I am very occupied," said Dwight, flushing at the hint of reproach in her voice. "The work of the mine takes much of my time, and there are so many interesting cases in the district."

"Well, you can always pass a night or take a meal with us when you come in for your drugs. Mama and Papa will be pleased to see you."

"Thank you," he said a little stiffly. "Thank you, Joan. I'll surely keep it in mind."

They separated and bowed and the figure re-formed.

". . . George is very popular to-night," St. John Peter said, inclining his head towards the painting at the end of the hall. "I remember well how he was abused over the American war."

"How old is he?" Demelza asked.

"Who?"

"The King."

"Oh, about fifty, I should say."

"I wonder what a mad king thinks he is," she said. "Twould be queer if he mistook himself for the King of England."

St. John Peter laughed. "You know we are cousins, ma'am?"

"Who? You and the King?"

"No. You and I. Ross's grandmother and my grandfather were brother and sister."

"But Ross's grandmother wasn't my grandmother."

"No. Cousins-in-law. That makes it more refreshing, don't you think?"

"Quite refreshing," said Demelza absently. "Faith, I am most refreshed."

Peter laughed again as they moved apart.

". . . You should not have come to-night, Andrew," Verity said. "People have seen us already. In a day or two the whole district will know."

"It is what I wished. No good can come of secrecy, my love. Let's face it out together."

"But I'm afraid for Francis. If he sees you to-night he may cause trouble. He is in the wrong mood."

"Have we to wait for ever to get him in the right one? He can't stop us. He may even not object strongly now. He has grown up, is not the young hothead. We can't go on with these secret meetings. There's nothing underhand in our love. Why should there be? Why should it be warped and distorted by my old sin, which I've paid for again and again? I intend to see him to-night."

"No, not to-night, Andrew. Not to-night. I have a feeling . . . A foreboding."

The flute, the hautboy and the strings were playing an old Italian minuetto, graceful and refined. The strains of the music, thin and unforced though they were, reached every corner of the dance-room and penetrated through to where the refreshments were being served, to the rest-room, to the card-room. . . .

. . . Sanson had said when they met at the door: "I have been looking to the opportunity to play you again, Captain Poldark. The good cardplayer is very rare and it is a pleasure to sit with such an expert one."

"Thank you, I've no taste for gaming to-night," Ross had said.

"I find that most disappointing, Captain Poldark. Last time you were very successful at my expense, and I had looked forward to the opportunity of levelling our scores. Most disappointing." He said this in a deliberate voice.

"I'm here to escort my wife. That being so, it wouldn't fill my purpose to spend the evening in the card-room."

"Which is your wife? I would like the pleasure."

Ross looked about, but Demelza had been surrounded.

"Over there."

"She seems well attended, if I may say so. Might I suggest a short game, just while the evening is warming up?"

Ross caught sight of Mrs. Teague in an astonishing dress of light green and gold gauze, with green foil leaves and gold spangles. With her was Elizabeth's mother, Mrs. Chynoweth, whom he detested. At that moment George Warleggan arrived with Francis and Elizabeth.

"Ah, Sanson," he said, "there'll be no pleasure dancing in this crush. Have you got a table?"

"I have seats saved. But they will be gone if we don't hurry. I was prevailing on Captain Poldark to join us."

"Come along," said George. "With Francis we can make a foursome."

"Captain Poldark has not the taste for it to-night," Sanson said. "I am sixty guineas out, and had hoped to recoup myself——"

"Or go sixty guineas outer?" suggested George. "Come, Ross, you can't refuse the dear fellow his fair revenge. Francis is eager to start. Don't spoil the game."

There were too many people here, people of the kind who had sent Jim to prison. Painted and powdered up, dressed to the eyes, high-heeled, fan-flicking, snuffbox-clicking, people with titles, people wanting titles, place holders, place seekers, squires, squireens, clergymen with two or three rich livings, brewers, millers, iron, tin and copper merchants, ship owners, bankers. People of his own class. People he despised.

He turned. "What do you want? What do you wish to play?"

". . . Where is Francis?" Mrs. Chynoweth asked peevishly a few minutes later. "The dancing has begun and you are not dancing, Elizabeth. It's not good enough, really it is not! He might be here at least to commence with his wife, if nothing more. It will make more talk. Go and see where he is, Jonathan."

"Yes, my pet."

"Do sit down, Father," Elizabeth said. "Francis is in the gaming-room with Ross and George; I saw them enter. He will not come back for you. Leave him for a little."

"It's not good enough. Really it's not good enough. And if Francis was not coming, why did you refuse that Dr. Enys and those other gentlemen? You are too young to spend your evening sitting by the wall. The first gathering you have permitted yourself in so many years, and then to squander the time." Mrs. Chynoweth fanned herself vigorously to show her frustrations. The last years had changed her cruelly. At Elizabeth's wedding she had been a beautiful woman, but her illness and the doctors' treatment had distorted the eye of which she had lost the sight, and her face was swollen and drawn. She was a deeply disappointed woman too, for Elizabeth's marriage, of which she had hoped so much, had gone just the same way as her own—or even worse, for Jonathan had never dared to get his name linked with another woman; he had only lost money irritatingly and steadily for twenty-six years.

"Elizabeth," said George Warleggan, coming on them suddenly, "grant me the favour of the second dance."

She looked up and smiled at him. "I promised you the first, but you were busy with your gaming."

"No, I was seeing the others settled. I had no thought but to be in time. Mrs. Chynoweth"—he hunched his big shoulders and bowed—"how charming you look to-night. You only do wrong to sit beside Elizabeth, whose beauty has no match. I swear her seat will be occupied the moment I take her away."

Mrs. Chynoweth bridled like a girl at her first compliment, and when people began forming up and Elizabeth had left them she sighed.

"A shame, a wicked shame, Jonathan!"

"What, my pet?"

"That Elizabeth should have thrown herself away on one of the Poldarks. We were too hasty. What a supremely good match she would have made with George."

"A bit of an upstart, what?" said Jonathan, stroking his silky beard. "No class about him, you know."

"Blood is overrated," said his wife impatiently. She was tempted to say she had made the mistake of marrying it. "It takes but a generation to make class, Jonathan. Times have changed. Wealth is what counts."

The dance began.

Demelza was recovering her confidence, but her throat was parched.

"A clergyman?" she said in a puzzled voice, looking at her partner's double-breasted cutaway coat, canary embroidered waistcoat, brown silk breeches and striped stockings. "No, I would not have guessed it."

The newly ordained vicar of St. Trudy and St. Wren squeezed her hand.

"Why not, eh, why not?"

"The one I know at Grambler wears a patched suit an' a straw wig."

"Oh, pooh, no doubt some poor little clerk doing duty for his master."

"What are you?" she asked. "A bishop?"

Whitworth bowed low. "No, mem, not yet. But with your encouragement, mem, I soon would be."

"I didn't know clergymen danced," she said.

"It is an accomplishment some of us have, mem."

"Like bears?" she suggested, looking at him.

Whitworth broke into a low laugh. "Yes, mem, and we can hug too."

"Oh, I'm that frightened." She bowed to him with a little pretended shiver.

The young man's eyes kindled. He could hardly wait until they came together again to continue.

. . . George and Elizabeth had been dancing in well-mannered silence. Then George said:

"Elizabeth, you ravish me in that gown. I sigh to be a poet or a painter. There's such purity of colour, such beauty of line. . . ."

She smiled up at him more warmly than she had ever done before.

She had been thinking of Geoffrey Charles at home at Trenwith without her protective care; but George's words recalled her.

"Really, George, you're too kind. But I should take your compliments more seriously if you were less free of them."

"Free? My dear, I am never free with my compliments. With whom have I ever been free except with you, whom I admire and reverence?"

"Sincere, then," she said. "Is it sincere to praise my poor mother?"

He glanced at the couple by the wall. No one had come to occupy Elizabeth's seat.

"No, I confess it is not. But I have the respect for her that I would naturally have for your mother, and I sympathize with her in her misfortune. She has been a beauty, remember, or a near beauty, used to the praises of men. How must she feel now, never to know a second glance except perhaps in compassion?"

Elizabeth looked quickly up at her partner. It was the most sensitive thing she had ever heard him say.

"You're *very* kind, George," she said quietly. "You always are. I'm afraid you have little reward for your—for your attendance on me. I'm a dull creature these days."

"My reward is in your friendship and confidence. As for your being a dull creature, how can what is treasured be dull? You are lonely, agreed. You spend too much of your time at Trenwith. Your child is grown now; you should come more often to Truro. Bring Francis if you——"

"Bring Francis to the gaming tables again? It is the only reward for the end of Grambler, that he sees less of the green cloths and more of his family."

George was silent a moment. He had gone wrong there.

"Is Francis good company now that he stays at home?"

Elizabeth bit her lip. "I have my house and my child. Geoffrey Charles is not yet five. He's delicate and still needs watching."

"Well, promise at least that this is not an isolated occasion. Come again to stay with me in town or at Cardew. I in turn will promise not to encourage Francis at the cards. In fact I'll undertake never to play with him if that would please you."

"He is playing now, George."

"I know, my dear. It was unfortunate but there was no stopping him."

CHAPTER IX   In the card-room there was the prospect of mischief.

Four tables were occupied, one of faro, one of basset and two of whist. Francis always played faro if he could, but the first person he saw on entering was Margaret Cartland sitting at the faro table with her new friend, a man called Vosper. She turned and waved with ironical good humour, but Francis bowed and at once moved to an empty whist table, ignoring the four seats Sanson had kept for them. Ross, not caring either way or about anything, followed him. They sat down opposite each other, and Sanson took one of the other chairs. George Warleggan, however, was talking with a man in black by the door, and presently he came across and said that as several gentlemen were here before him, he was standing down in favour of one of them. Of course, they all knew Dr. Halse.

At the Warleggans, Ross had avoided the man. Since he was there as a guest he did not seek trouble, but with the horror of Launceston fresh in his mind the sight of this cleric-cum-scholar-cum-magistrate, who more than anyone on the bench at the time had been responsible for Jim's sentence, was a goad in a raw place.

When Dr. Halse saw who was at the table he hesitated a moment, then came forward and took his seat opposite the miller. Ross did not speak.

"Well," said Francis impatiently, "now we are set, what are the stakes?"

"A guinea," suggested Sanson. "Otherwise the exchange of money is slow. Do you agree, sir?"

"It is more than my customary stake," said Dr. Halse, sniffing at his handkerchief. "So heavy a hazard makes the game overserious. We do not do well to put this burden on our pleasures."

"Perhaps you would prefer to wait for another table," said Ross.

It was the wrong tone for the hardy doctor. "No," he said through his nose; "I do not think I shall. I was here first and intend to remain."

"Oh, don't let us begin with an argument," said Francis. "Let it be half a guinea and have done."

Polly Choake peered into the gaming-room and withdrew.

"What ith the matter with the Poldark couthins?" she whispered to Mrs. Teague. "They came to the Athembly like they wath two tigers thtalking after pwey. Never tho much as glanthing left or right, in they go and settle to cards afore ever the Lord Lieutenant has made hith thpeech. And there they thit glowering away and playing as if the Devil wath in 'em both."

Mrs. Teague's creased eyelids came down knowingly at the sides. "But didn't you hear about Francis, dear? That woman has thrown him over. After the way he's frittered money on her too. And as for Ross, well, what else could you expect; no doubt he's bitterly regretting having married that cheap hussy who's showing herself up so bad to-night. I shouldn't be a bit surprised if he took to drink serious."

Polly Choake glanced across the room. She had not noticed that Demelza was showing herself up, but she welcomed the opinion and instantly concurred in it.

"I think it wicked the way thome mawwied women behave theirselves. Thwowing theirselves about the woom. An' of course the men encourage it. I'm thankful the doctor ith above thuch behaviour."

". . . Who is that young person dancing with your son, Lady Whitworth?" asked the Hon. Mrs. Maria Agar, lowering her lorgnette.

"I am not sure. I have not yet had the favour of an introduction."

"She is quite beautiful, don't you think? A small matter—how shall I put it—different. I wonder if she is from London?"

"It is very possible. William has many friends there."

"I have noticed she dances rather different too; more—how shall I put it—more lilt in the body. I wonder if that is the new style."

"No doubt. They say that at Bath one has to be continually taking lessons to be up with the new steps."

"I wonder who she is with, which party she came with."

"I have no idea," said Lady Whitworth, knowing well enough it was the Warleggans but holding her fire until she was on firmer ground.

The second dance came to an end. Demelza looked about for Ross but saw only other men. So many men seemed to want the third dance that she thought there must be a great shortage of women. Inclination getting the better of good manners, she said she was a little thirsty, and almost at once an embarrassing number of drinks were brought. A trifle primly she chose port and promised the third dance to one William Hick. Not till the band struck up did she realize it was the first country dance, and John Treneglos, sandy and rough, came over to claim it. There was a sharp exchange between him and William Hick, and Treneglos looked as if he was going to throw Hick off the floor.

"Dear, dear," said Demelza, as she was led away by John, "how you do growl at the smallest thing. I never knew there was so many fierce men about."

"Young princock," said Treneglos. "Young upstart."

"Who, me?" she asked.

"No, bud. Of course not you, bud. Young Hick, I mean. These town dandies think they can bluster their way in anywhere. He's found he is mistook. And will find it more if he prances in my stable again."

"Dear life. I don't like the ring of that. Must we all be put in stables even at a ball? Why not kennels, an' then you can call women what you really think them."

Treneglos lost his ill humour and guffawed aloud with laughter, so that many people looked. Ruth Treneglos, dancing near with Dr. Choake, shot them a venomous glance.

"No, chit, I'd make exceptions even to that rule, though I'll confess there's many it would be convenient for."

"An' where d'you put the buds and the chits?" she asked. "D'you grow them in your garden or pin 'em on sheets of paper like butterflies?"

"I cherish 'em and nourish 'em. To my bosom, dear girl. To my bosom."

She sighed. The port was just going down. "How uncomfortable for the chits."

"None of them have complained so. You know the old saying: 'Them as tries never flies.'" He laughed again.

"I thought," she said, "it was: 'Them as never tries never cries.'"

"It may be over Illugan way, but at Mingoose we're bolder."

"I don't live at either. I live at Nampara, where we have our own modes and customs."

"And what are they, pray?"

"Oh," she said, "they can only be learned by experience."

"Ha," he said. "Well, I crave that experience. Will you learn me?"

She raised her eyebrows at him. "I wouldn't really dare. I'm told you're so good at games."

Verity and Blamey had sat out this dance together in the refreshment-room.

Andrew said: "There's nothing in our way. A few people will not forget, they hold to the old memories. But that is unimportant beside the many who have forgotten or never knew. There's no cause ever again for bitterness between us. You have only to take this step. I have a good lodging—half a house—in the centre of Falmouth, very convenient and comfortable. We can settle there until a better is found. Five years ago perhaps not, but now I can afford the luxuries you need and desire——"

"I need no luxuries, Andrew. I would have married you before and gladly and worked and lived in any small cottage. It never has been that. I should be happy and proud to share your life. I—I had always thought I could make a home for you . . . in a way that you did not have before. I still want to. . . ."

"My dear, that's what I wished to hear."

"Yes, but hear me out. It is not luxuries—or popularity if that is short. It is a quiet mind. Our attachment broke last time on my family's opposition. My father and Francis. Perhaps you can excuse them; perhaps not. Well, Father is dead. It isn't pleasant to feel I should be going against his strongest opinions—that I should be disobeying his most express wishes. But I would—I feel I could reconcile that. I feel that . . . he'll understand now and forgive me. Not so Francis."

"That's why I want to see him."

"Well not to-night, Andrew. My dear, I know how you feel. But try to be patient. Francis is two years younger than I am. I—I remember him since he could just walk. Mother died when I was fourteen and he twelve. In a way I have been more than an ordinary sister to him. He has been spoilt all his life. His moods anger me often, but I love him— even for his faults. He's so headstrong and rash and impulsive and— and lovable with it. I know so well his wry sense of humour when he can almost always laugh at himself, his generosity when he can give away money that he greatly needs, his courage when it's most required. He's so much like my mother in all those things. I've noticed it and watched it all these years. That's why, if you can understand, I want to get his willing consent to our marriage. I don't want to quarrel with him and leave a bitter break between us. Especially now, when he is hard hit from other things. Trust me a little longer. I want to pick just the right time to speak to him, when we're alone and will not be interrupted. I think I can do it then."

The seaman had been watching the expressions come and go in her eyes. He stirred restlessly.

"I'll trust you; of course I'll trust you. That goes without question. But . . . things can't be put off indefinite. Events have to move on. Once they're put in train there's no stopping them. We've met several times now, and our meeting has not gone unremarked. Perhaps it was unwise of me to stop it. Do you know that one of my brother captains in Falmouth knew I was meeting a woman in Truro? That's how far it has gone, and that was one reason why I came here to-night. It is not fair to expose you to sly glances and whispering tongues. If you do not tell Francis someone else will."

"I wish you would go, Andrew," she muttered. "I have a feeling that things would go wrong if you met here."

. . . In the card-room Ross and Francis had won five guineas of their opponents' money.

"You did not return my trump lead, Doctor," said Sanson, taking snuff. "Had you done so we should have saved the game and the rubber for a breathing spell."

"I had only two trumps," said Halse, austere. "And no suit to establish if they were cleared."

"But I had five," said Sanson, "and a good suit of spades. It is an elementary principle to return one's partner's lead, sir."

"Thank you," said Halse; "I am acquainted with the elementary principles."

"No one can question," Ross said to Sanson, "that your partner has all his principles at his finger tips. It is a general misfortune that he does not make use of them."

Dr. Halse took out his purse. "The same might well be said of your manners, Poldark. Ignorance, which is the only excuse, can hardly be your plea. Several times you have been gratuitously offensive. One can only speculate on the bad humours which come of an ill-spent life."

"Offensive?" Ross said. "And to a Justice of the Peace, who compounds all the virtues of magistracy, except perhaps peace and justice, in his person. No, you do me wrong."

The doctor had gone very pinched about the nostrils. He counted out five gold coins and stood up. "I may tell you, Poldark, that this insulting attitude will do your case no good. No doubt the common people you mix with have blunted your faculties as to what may and may not be said in refined society. In such circumstances one is inclined to pity rather than to condemn."

"I agree," Ross said, "that it alters one's perspective. You should try such mixing, man, you should try. It would enlarge your outlook. I find the experience even enlarges one's sense of smell."

Other people were listening now. Francis grunted as he pocketed the money. "You're drastic to-night, Ross. Sit down, Halse. What's the point in life except to gamble. Come about, and cut for another rubber."

"I have no intention of cutting at this table again," said the clergyman.

Ross was watching him. "Have you ever been in a gaol, Dr. Halse? It is surprising the variety and fullness of stench that thirty or forty of God's creatures—I suppose they are God's creatures, though I defer to an expert view—can give off if confined for weeks in a small stone building without drains, water or attention. It becomes not so much a smell as a food. For the soul, you understand."

"The matter of your behaviour at Launceston has not gone unremarked," Dr. Halse said fiercely, like a dry, brittle, angry dog. "Nor will it escape our full attention very shortly. There will be a meeting of the justices concerned, of whom I may say I am one, to decide——"

"Give them this message," said Ross, "that I have shown greater forbearance sitting at table with one of their number and not breaking his head than they if they opened all the crawling fever gaols in Cornwall and let the prisoners free."

"You may be sure they shall have a full account of your grossness and vulgarity," the doctor snapped. All the room was attending. "And you may understand that if it were not for my cloth I would call you out for what you have said to me."

Ross got slowly to his feet, uncoiling himself from the low table.

"Tell your fellows when you see them that it would give me pleasure to meet any of them who can spare the time from their high offices and have not the impedimenta of holy living to maintain. Especially those responsible for the upkeep of Launceston Gaol. But let the invitation be catholic, for I feel catholic towards them."

"You offensive young drunkard!" The clergyman turned sharply on his heel and left the card-room.

A moment's silence fell on the people he had left. Then Margaret Cartland broke into a peal of her infectious laughter.

"Well done, His Lordship! Let the church keep to its own offices and leave the rest to us. Never have I heard a prettier squabble over a mere game of trumps. What did he do, let you down with a revoke?"

Ross took a seat opposite her at the faro table. His glance at her was so disquieting that even she was checked.

Ross said: "Get on with the game, Banker."

Margaret's bold impertinent eyes travelled round the room.

"Come, Mr. Francis, follow your cousin's lead! Lay a stake on the spade queen; she is poorly backed and we should be patriotic to-night."

"Thank you." Francis met her gaze. "I have learned never to stake on women. It is close in here; I will take a breath of air."

There had been another minuet; and in the refreshment-room Verity at last persuaded Andrew to leave. She had done so on the undertaking that she should talk to Francis within the week. A little incautiously, perhaps feeling the need to prove her sincerity to him, she walked with him round the edge of the floor, carefully avoiding the card-room, until they reached the main doors of the hall. A footman opened them and they went out. Coming up the stairs from the street below was Francis.

CHAPTER X   Demelza was beginning to feel like a lion tamer who has been putting his pets through their paces and finds them getting out of hand. She didn't know whether to brazen it out or run for safety. The smaller lions she could manage very well: men like Whitworth, William Hick and St. John Peter. But the big beasts, like John Treneglos, and the old lions, like Sir Hugh Bodrugan, were a different matter. Relays of port had added courage to natural wit; but there was a limit to her resource and she was thankful it was all happening in a public room, where they couldn't snarl over her more openly. If she had been the perspiring sort she would have perspired a lot.

Recently Ensign Carruthers, whom Joan Pascoe had introduced, had come to swell the numbers. A young man called Robert Bodrugan had also put in an appearance but had quickly been sent off by his hairy uncle. The ball of conversation kept flying at her and she would toss it back at someone indiscriminately. They laughed at almost everything she said, as if she were a wit. In a way it was all very enjoyable, but she would have liked it in smaller measure to begin. And every now and then she stretched her neck to peer over someone's shoulder in search of Ross.

It was in doing this that she caught sight of Verity re-entering the ballroom from the outer door. She knew instantly by her eyes that something was seriously wrong.

After a moment Verity slowed her steps and was lost to view by the dancers forming up for a gavotte. Demelza rose to her feet also.

"No, no," she said to several men and moved to pass through them. They parted deferentially and she found herself free. She looked about.

"Come, miss," said Sir Hugh at her shoulder, but she moved on without answering him. Verity had turned, was walking quickly away from her towards the ladies withdrawing-room. Demelza followed, walking round the floor by herself with her unusual long-legged stride and with a confidence she would not have known an hour ago.

Near her quarry, she found her way barred by Patience Teague and her sister Ruth Treneglos and two other ladies.

"Mistress Demelza," said Patience, "permit me to introduce two of my friends who are anxious to meet you. Lady Whitworth and the Hon. Mrs. Maria Agar. This is Mistress Poldark."

"How d'you do," said Demelza, sparing a moment to eye Ruth warily, and curtsying to the ladies in the way Mrs. Kemp had taught her. She instantly disliked the tall Lady Whitworth and liked the short Mrs. Agar.

"My dear child," said Lady Whitworth, "we have been admiring your dress ever since the Assembly began. Quite remarkable. We thought it had come from London until Mrs. Treneglos assured us to the contrary."

"Tisn't the dress," said Mrs. Agar. "'Tis the way it's worn."

"Oh, thank you, ma'am," Demelza said warmly. "Thank you ma'am. I'm that gratified to have your praise. You're all too kind. Much too kind. And now, if you'll forgive me I am this moment hurryin' to find my cousin. If you'll——"

"By the way, dear, how is your father?" Ruth asked, and tittered. "We have not seen him since the chistening."

"No, ma'am," Demelza said. "I'm very sorry, ma'am, but father is overparticular who he meets."

She bowed to the ladies and swept past them. Then she entered the withdrawing-room.

There were two maids in the little stuffy room, and three ladies and piles of cloaks and wraps. Verity was standing before a mirror, not looking into it but looking down at the table in front of her, doing something with her hands.

Demelza went straight across to her. Verity was pulling her lace handkerchief to shreds. "Verity. What is it? What is it?"

Verity shook her head and could not speak. Demelza glanced round. The other women had not noticed anything. She began to talk, about anything that came into her head, watching Verity's lips tremble and straighten and tremble again. One lady went out. Then the other. Demelza pushed a chair up behind Verity and forced her to sit down.

"Now," she whispered, "tell me. What is it? Did they meet? I was afeared they might."

Verity shook her head again. Her hair, as hard to confine as dark thistledown, was coming undone in her distress. As three more women came chattering in Demelza stood up quickly behind Verity's chair and said:

"Let me tidy your hair. It is all this dancin' has loosed the pins. Sit quite still an' I'll have it right in a jiffy. How warm it is in there! My hand is quite exhausted wi' working my fan."

She went on talking, taking out pins and putting them in again, and once or twice when Verity's head began to tremble she put her fingers, cool and firm for all the port, on Verity's forehead, resting them there until the spasm passed.

"I can't go through it all again," Verity said suddenly in an undertone. "Not all that again. I knew it might come, but now I can't face it. I—I can't face it."

"Why should you?" Demelza said. "Tell me what happened."

"They—they met as he was going. At the top of the stairs. I knew it would be wrong to-night. I have been waiting an opportunity, but Francis has been cross-grained for weeks. They had another terrible quarrel. Andrew tried to be conciliatory, but there was no arguing with him. He struck Andrew. I thought Andrew was going to kill him. Instead of that he just looked at Francis—I felt somehow that his contempt was for me as well . . ."

"Oh, nonsense. . . ."

"Yes," said Verity. "I did. Because I wanted the best of both worlds. Because I had wanted to keep Francis's affection as well as Andrew's and had been afraid to tell Francis. If I'd told him before, this would never have happened—not like this. I've been afraid to come out into the open. I've been—timid. I think it's the one weakness Andrew cannot countenance——"

"You're wrong, Verity. Nothing matters if you feel for each other like you do. . . ."

"—So he went. Without a glance or a word for me. That was worse than last time. I know now I shan't ever see him again. . . ."

In the card-room Ross had lost thirty guineas in as many minutes and Francis nearly as much in half the time. Francis had come back to the room after his airing with a face grey with anger.

He had sat down at the faro table without speaking and no one had addressed him; but the expressions of the two cousins were casting a blight over the game. Even the banker, a man named Page, seemed ill at ease; and presently Margaret Cartland yawned and got up, slipping a few pieces of gold back into her purse.

"Come, Luke, we've been in the saddle too long. Let's take a little stroll round the ballroom before the reels begin."

Her new lover rose obediently; he glanced uneasily at Francis but Francis ignored them as they went out.

At the door, her hand possessively on Vosper's arm, she surveyed the scene of the dance. It came to an end as she watched, the formal arrangements broke up into knots which themselves gradually dispersed as people moved off towards the refreshment-room or to corners under the ferns.

"These dainty dances bore me excessively," she said. "All that posturing with no result."

"You prefer your posturings to have some result," said Vosper. "I'm glad to learn it."

"Oh, tut, naughty," she said. "Remember where we are. Oh, damn, I believe it is the interval."

"Well, no matter; I can use my elbows as well as the next, sweet."

Margaret continued to survey the floor. There was one knot which refused to break up. It was largely men, but she saw a woman or women somewhere in the middle. Presently the knot, like a swarm of bees, began to move towards a few vacant chairs, occupied them; and then a section of the drones moved off in search of food and drink. Now she was able to see that there were two women concerned, a pleasant-faced, sad-looking person of about thirty and a striking girl with a mass of dark hair and very clear-cut shoulders above a shimmering frock with crimson ornaments.

"Sit in the card-room, my sweet," said Vosper. "I'll bring you something there."

"No, let 'em fight. Tell me, who's that young woman over there? The one in silver with her chin tilted. Is she from this district?"

Vosper raised his quizzing-glass. "No idea. She has a pretty figure. Hm, quite the belle. Well, I'll go get you some jellies and heart cakes."

When he had gone Margaret stopped a man she knew and found out who the two women were. A little surprised smile played round her lips at the news. Ross's wife. He playing faro with a bitter and angry face while she flirted with a half dozen men and paid him no attention. Margaret turned and looked at Ross as he staked money on a card. This side you could not see the scar.

She wasn't sorry this marriage was a failure. She wondered if he had any money. He had all the aristocrat's contempt for small amounts, she knew that; but it was the income that counted, not the small change. She remembered him five years ago in that hut by the river and wondered if she had any chance of offering him consolation again.

Luke Vosper came back but she refused to go in, preferring to stand at the door and watch the scene. Some ten minutes later the banker drew out the last two cards of a deal and this time Ross saw he had won. As he gathered in his winnings he found Margaret Cartland stooping beside him.

"Me lord, have you forgot you have a wife, eh?"

Ross looked up at her.

Her big eyes were wide. "No joke, I assure you. She's quite the sensation. If you don't believe me, come and see."

"What do you mean?"

"No more than I say. Take it or leave it."

Ross got to his feet and went to the door. If he had thought of Demelza at all during this last hour he had thought of her in Verity's safekeeping. (It never occurred to him to think of Verity in Demelza's.)

The first dance after the interval was to begin shortly. The band was back on its platform tuning up. After the quiet of the card-room the talk and laughter met him. He looked about, aware that both Margaret and Vosper were watching him.

"Over there, me lord," said Margaret. "Over there with all those men. At least, I was told it was your wife, but perhaps I was misinformed. Eh?"

It was to be another gavotte, less stately and sedate than the minuet and popular enough to get most people on the floor. Competition for Demelza was still strong. During the interval and fortified by some French claret for a change, she had put forward all her talents in conversation to take notice from Verity, who was sitting mute beside her.

It was really her own fault that at this stage the snarling grew worse; for, what with thinking of Verity and her anxiety for Ross, she had been careless what she said, and no less than three men thought she had promised the dance. John Treneglos had been dragged away for a time by his furious wife; but Sir Hugh Bodrugan was one of the three, trying by weight and seniority, she thought, to carry her off from Whitworth, who was relying on his cloth to support him in the face of Sir Hugh's scowls; the third was Ensign Carruthers, who was sweating a lot but was sticking to the Navy's tradition and not striking his flag.

First they argued with her, then they argued with each other, and then they appealed to her again, while William Hick made it worse by putting in remarks. Demelza, a little overwrought, waved her glass and said they should toss a coin for her. This struck Carruthers as eminently fair, only he preferred dice; but Sir Hugh grew angry and said he had no intention of gaming on a ballroom floor for any woman. All the same, he was not willing to give up the woman. Demelza suggested he should take Verity. Verity said, "Oh, Demelza," and Sir Hugh bowed to Verity and said, thank you, a later dance, certainly.

At that moment a tall man showed at the back of the others and Demelza wondered with a sinking feeling if this was a fourth claimant. Then she raised her head and saw it was indeed.

"Forgive me, sir," said Ross, pushing a way in. "You'll pardon me, sir. You'll pardon me, sir." He arrived on the edge of the ring and bowed slightly, rather coldly to Demelza. "I come to see if you were in need of anything, my dear."

Demelza got up. "I knew I'd promised this dance to someone," she said.

There was a general laugh, in which Sir Hugh did not join. He had been drinking all evening and did not at first recognize Ross, whom he saw seldom.

"Nay, sir. Nay, ma'am; this is unfair, by Heavens! It was promised to me. I tell you it was promised to me. I tell you it was promised. I'll not have it! I'm not accustomed to have my word called in question!"

Ross looked at him, at the silk ruffles of his shirt stained with splashes of wine, at his broad heavy face, hair growing in tufts in the nostrils and the ears, at the curled black wig worn low over the brow, at his dark purple coat, red silk embroidered waistcoat and silk knee breeches. He looked him up and down, for Sir Hugh, no less than the others, had had his hand in Jim's death. The fact that he had been dancing with Demelza was an affront.

"Have you promised this dance?" Ross said to Demelza.

Demelza looked up into his cold eyes, sought there for understanding and found none. Her heart turned bitter.

"Yes," she said. "Maybe I did promise this to Sir Hugh. Come along, Sir Hugh. I hardly know quite how to dance the gavotte, not properly like, but you can show me. You showed me splendid in that last country dance, Sir Hugh."

She turned and would have gone out with the baronet to join the others who were now all formed up. But Ross suddenly caught her hand.

"Nevertheless, I take this by right, so you must disappoint all your friends."

Sir Hugh had recognized him now. He opened his mouth to protest. "Damn it! it's late in the evening to show a lively interest——"

But Ross had gone, and Demelza, furious and desperately hurt, went with him.

They bowed to each other as the music began. They didn't dance at all well together.

"Perhaps," said Demelza, trembling all over, "perhaps I'd ought to have asked for an introduction seeing it's so long since we met."

"I don't doubt you have been well consoled in my absence," said Ross.

"You were not concerned to come and see whether I was or no."

"It seems that I was unwelcome when I did."

"Well, everyone wasn't so ill-mannered and neglectful as you."

"It is always possible at these places to collect a few hangers-on. There are always some such about looking for those who will give them encouragement."

Demelza said with triumphant bitterness: "No, Ross, you do me wrong! And them too! One is a baronet an' lives at Werry House. He has asked me to tea and cards. One is a clergyman who has travelled all over the continent. One is an officer in the Navy. One even is a relative of yours. Oh, no, Ross, you can't say that!"

"I can and do." He was as furious as she was. "One is a lecherous old roué whose name stinks in decent circles. One is a simpering posturing fop who will bring the church more disrepute. One is a young sailor out for a lark with any moll. They come for what they can get, they and their kind. I wonder you're not sick with their compliments."

I'll not cry, said Demelza to herself, I'll not cry. I'll not cry. I'll not cry.

They bowed to each other again.

"I detest them all," Ross said on a slightly less personal note. "These people and their stupidity. Look at their fat bellies and gouty noses, and wagging dewlaps and pouchy eyes: overfed and overclothed and overwined and overpainted. I don't understand that you find pleasure in mixing with them. No wonder Swift wrote of 'em as he did. If these are my people, then I'm ashamed to belong to them!"

They separated, and as they came together again Demelza suddenly fired back.

"Well, if you think all the stupids an' all the fat and ugly ones are in your class you're just as wrong as anyone! Because Jim had ill luck and died, an' because Jim and Jinny were good nice people you seem to think that all poor folk are as good and nice as they. Well, you're mortal wrong there, and I can tell you because I know. I've lived with 'em, which is more'n you'll ever do! There's good an' bad in all sorts and conditions, an' you'll not put the world to rights by thinking all these people here are to blame for Jim's death——"

"Yes, they are, by their selfishness and their sloth——"

"And you'll not put the world to rights neither by drinking brandy all evening an' gambling in the gambling-room and leaving me to see for myself at my first ball and then coming halfway through an' being rude to them that have tried to look after me——"

"If you behave like this you'll not come to another ball."

She faced him. "If you behave like this I'll not want to!"

They found they had both stopped dancing. They were holding up people.

He passed a hand across his face.

"Demelza," he said, "we have both drunk too much."

"Would you kindly move off the floor, sir," said a voice behind him.

"I don't want to quarrel," Demelza said with a full throat. "I have never, you know that. You can't expect me to feel the same about Jim as you do, Ross. I didn't know him hardly at all, and I didn't go to Launceston. Maybe this is commonplace for you, but it is the first time I ever been to anything. I'd be that happy if you could be happy."

"Damn the rejoicings," he said. "We should never have come."

"Please move aside, sir," said another exasperated voice. "If you wish to hold conversation do it elsewhere."

"I talk where I please," said Ross, and gave the man a look. The fellow wilted and backed away with his partner.

Demelza said in a soft voice: "Come, Ross. Dance. Show me. A step this way, isn't it, an' then a step that. I've never properly danced the gavotte, but it is nice and lively. Come, my dear, we're not dead yet, an' there's always to-morrow. Let us dance together nicely before we fall out worse."

CHAPTER XI   The ball was over but not the night. At midnight they had joined in singing patriotic songs and "God Save the King," and those belonging to Warleggan's party had left after that.

But when they reached the Warleggans' house there was little sign of anyone ready for bed. Food and drink were waiting for them: hot pasties, cakes and jellies, syllabubs and fruits, punch and wines, tea and coffee. People quickly settled down to play whist and backgammon and faro; and Sanson pestered Ross into joining him at a table of french ruff.

Demelza anxiously watched him go. The whole of the assembly had passed off without his knocking anybody down or insulting the Lord Lieutenant; but he was still in a peculiar mood.

It had been a hectic evening. The excitement had been faintly unhealthy. Oh, yes, she had enjoyed it, but her pleasure had never been free.

Nor, though the numbers were down, was she without followers here. Sir Hugh had got over his umbrage, John Treneglos had escaped from his wife and Carruthers had stuck to his guns. Verity disappeared upstairs, but when Ross left Demelza she was not allowed to do the same. Protesting, she was persuaded towards the faro table, a chair found for her, money put in her lap, advice and instruction breathed in each ear. That she knew nothing about the game carried no weight: anyone could play faro, they said; you just put money on one of the cards on the table, the banker turned up two cards of his own, and if your card when it came went on one pile, you won, and if it went on the other, you lost.

This seemed easy enough, and after wriggling in her seat to make sure that Sir Hugh didn't put his hand back on her bare shoulder, she settled meekly to lose the money she had been lent.

But instead of losing she won. Not briskly but steadily. She refused to be reckless. She would not stake more than a guinea on any card; but each time she staked she found others following her, and when the card turned up to win there were growls of triumph behind her. William Hick had popped up from somewhere, and a tall, handsome, rather loud-voiced woman called Margaret, whom Francis didn't seem to like. In the next room someone was playing a piece by Handel on the spinet.

They had lent her twenty pounds, she had taken careful note of that; and she thought if she ever got to seventy, leaving fifty for herself, she would get up with her winnings and all the kind men in the world wouldn't stop her. She had reached sixty-one when she heard William Hick say to someone in an undertone:

"Poldark is losing heavily."

"Is he? But I thought the banker had just had to pay him."

"No, I mean the other Poldark. The one playing with Sanson."

Something turned cold inside her.

She staked and lost, staked again and lost, staked hurriedly with five guineas and lost.

She got up.

"Oh, no," they protested, trying to persuade her to stay; but she would have no argument, for this time it was not personal choice but an urgent panic need to find Ross. She just had the wit to count out the thirty-four sovereigns belonging to her, and then she pushed her way through and looked about.

In the corner of the second room a crowd was round a small table, and at it were Ross and Sanson, the fat miller. She drew near them and, careless of danger to her frock, squeezed in until she could see the cards.

French ruff was played with thirty-two cards, each of the players being dealt five, and the play being as at whist except that the ace was the lowest court card. The hazard and lure of the game lay in the fact that before playing either player could discard and take up from the pack as many new cards as he chose and do this as many times as he chose, at the discretion of the nondealer.

Demelza watched for some time trying to understand the play, which was difficult for her. They played quickly and besides exchanging money at the end of each rubber they bet in the middle of nearly every hand. Ross's long lean face with its prominent jawbones showed nothing of all his drink, but there was a peculiar deep-cleft frown between his brows.

Ross had first played the game with a high French officer in a hospital in New York. They had played it for weeks on end, and he knew it inside out. He had never lost much at it, but in Sanson he had met his match. Sanson must have played it all his life and in his sleep. And he had astonishing luck to-night. Whenever Ross assembled a good hand the miller had a better. Time after time Ross thought he was safe and time after time the freak draw beat him. His luck was out and it stayed out.

When he had given drafts for two hundred pounds, which was about as much as Harris Pascoe would honour and which was all the ready money he had in the world, he stopped and sent a footman for another drink.

"I'm finished, Sanson," he said. "I do not think the luck could have stayed so much longer." Someone tittered.

"It is hard to predict," said Sanson, blinking rapidly and rubbing his white hands together. "Give me some surety if you want to continue. It is not late yet."

Ross offered his gold watch, which had belonged to his father and which he seldom wore.

Sanson took it. "Fifty guineas?"

"As you please."

Ross's deal. He turned up diamonds as trumps, and picked up the nine, ten, ace of diamonds, the knave, ten of spades.

"I propose," said Sanson.

"How many?"

"The book."

"I'll take two," said Ross. Sanson changed all his cards for five new ones, Ross threw his spades and picked up the king of hearts and the eight of spades.

"Propose," said Sanson.

Ross nodded, and they again threw, Sanson two and Ross one. He picked up the king of spades.

Sanson indicated that he was satisfied. "I'll lay for ten guineas."

"Twenty," said Ross.

"I'll take it."

They played the hand. Sanson had the king, queen, seven, eight of trumps and a small club and made four tricks to Ross's one.

"The luck of Old Nick," someone whispered near Demelza.

In a few minutes the fifty guineas was gone.

Sanson sat back and wiped a little sweat from round his fat face. He blinked rapidly at the watch.

"Well, it is a good piece," he said to a friend. "A little high-priced. I trust it keeps good time." There was a laugh.

The manservant came back with the drinks.

"Bring me a new pack of cards," Ross said.

"Yes, sir."

"What do you intend to play with?" Sanson asked, a trifle sarcastically.

"Assets I can realize," said Ross.

But Demelza knew that he meant the Wheal Leisure shares. She had been edging nearer to him, and now she abruptly leaned forward and put her thirty-four sovereigns on the table.

"I have a little loose money, Ross."

He glanced up in surprise, for he had not known she was there. First his eyes looked through her, then they looked at her, but this time they were not unfriendly. He frowned at the money.

"To please me, Ross."

The footman came with the new pack. Hearts were trumps and Sanson dealt Ross the queen, knave, seven of hearts and nine, seven of clubs.

"I propose," said Ross.

"No," said Sanson, refusing the discard. "Ten guineas again?"

He clearly had a good hand, but his refusal of the exchange meant that Ross's winnings would be doubled. It was a fair hand he had, and he nodded. It turned out that Sanson had the king, ace, ten of trumps, the king of diamonds and the king of spades. Sanson ruffed Ross's first club lead with a trump and led his king. Ross dropped his queen on it.

It was a bluff, and the bluff succeeded. Sanson thought he was void and led his ace of trumps, which Ross took with his knave. Then he made his seven of trumps and his seven of clubs.

Everyone seemed pleased, with the exception of Sanson.

For a time the luck changed, and presently Ross had nearly a hundred pounds before him. Demelza didn't speak. Then the luck veered back and Sanson picked up hand after hand which was cast-iron. The money went down and disappeared. The watchers began to thin. Somewhere in the distance a clock was striking two. For some time Ross had not been drinking. The brandy he had ordered was untouched.

Sanson wiped his hands and blinked at Ross.

"Confess you are beat," he said. "Or have you other jewellery to sell?"

"I have shares."

"No, Ross; no, Ross," whispered Demelza. "Come away! The cock will be crowing soon."

"How much are they worth?"

"Six hundred pounds."

"It will take me a little while to win all that. Would you not prefer to resume in the morning?"

"I am fresh enough."

"Ross."

"Please." He looked up at her.

She was silent. Then she saw Sanson's eyes on the ruby brooch Ross had bought her. She drew back an inch or two and instinctively put up a hand to cover it.

Ross was already dealing again.

Suddenly she put the brooch on the table beside him.

"Play for this if you must play."

Ross turned and looked at her, and Sanson stared at the brooch.

"Is it real?" he asked.

"Stay out of this, Demelza," Ross said.

"You mustn't lose the other things," she whispered. "Play with this; I give it you freely—if you must go on."

"What is it worth?" Sanson asked. "I am no judge of stones."

"About a hundred pounds," Ross said.

"Very well. I accept that. But it is late. . . ."

"Your deal."

They played, and Ross began to win. Those who had stayed to watch did not leave now. The whist players had gone to bed and the faro table at length broke up. Some of those who had been playing came over to watch. At three o'clock Ross had won back enough to cover his watch. At a quarter after three Demelza's winnings were back on his side of the table.

George Warleggan intervened. "Come, come, this won't do. Ecod,

Ross, you must have a little pity on us all. Put a closure after this hand, and then you may begin all over again to-morrow if you choose."

Ross looked up as he took a very small sip of brandy.

"I'm sorry, George. Go to bed if you want, but the outcome of this game is still too far undecided. Send your servants to bed; we can find our own way."

Sanson wiped his forehead and his hands. "Well, to tell the truth, I am overtired myself. I have enjoyed the play, but I did not challenge you to an all-night sitting. Drop it before the luck turns again."

Ross did not budge. "Play for another hour and then I will rest."

Sanson blinked. "I think our host has the first claim——"

Ross said: "And let us double all stakes bid. That should expedite a result."

Sanson said: "I think our host——"

"I am *not* content to leave this game where it stands," Ross said.

They stared at each other a moment, then Sanson shrugged his fat shoulders.

"Very well. One hour more. It is your deal."

It seemed that Sanson's advice had been good, for from that moment the luck changed again in his favour. By half-past three Ross had sixty pounds left. At a quarter to four it was gone. Sanson was sweating a good deal. Demelza felt as if she was going to be sick. There were seven watchers only now.

With half an hour to go they began to bargain for the shares in Wheal Leisure. Sanson put all sorts of obstacles in the way of accepting them as a stake. It might have been he who was losing.

Five minutes had gone in arguing, and four o'clock struck with the position unchanged. At five past four Ross picked up the king, ten, ace of trumps and two useless cards. At the first discard he picked up two kings. He bet fifty pounds on it, which meant the actual stake was a hundred. When they played it turned out that Sanson had the five remaining trumps and made the odd trick.

Demelza looked round for a chair but saw none near enough. She took a firmer grip of Ross's chair and tried to see through the mist that was in her eyes.

Ross dealt himself the seven, eight, nine of diamonds and the nine, ten of spades. With hearts trumps it was a hopeless hand.

"Propose," said the miller.

"How many?"

"One."

"I'll take the book," Ross said, and threw away all five. And then it seemed that he forgot Sanson had to draw first, for he stretched out his hand to draw at the same time. Their hands somehow got mixed up with each other, and instead of drawing more cards Ross's hand had caught Sanson's wrist. Sanson gave a grunt as Ross slowly turned his hand up. In the palm of the hand was the king of trumps.

There was a moment's silence.

Ross said: "I wonder if you will explain how you came to have a card in your hand before you drew one from the pack."

Sanson looked as if he was going to faint. "Nonsense," he said. "I had already drawn the card when you caught it."

"I rather think that was so, Ross," said George Warleggan. "If——"

"Oh, no, he had not!" Hick and Vosper broke in together.

Ross suddenly released the fat man's wrist and instead caught him by the ruffles of his shirt, pulling him out of his seat and half across the table.

"Let me see if there are any more tricks inside you."

In a moment the quiet scene had broken into confusion. The table was upset and sovereigns and guineas were rolling across the floor. Sanson was struggling on his back while Ross ripped open his shirt and pulled his coat off.

There were two playing cards in the inner pocket of his coat. That was all.

Ross got up and began to examine the coat, taking out his own bills and putting them on a chair. Sanson stood there mutely and then made a sudden rush to retrieve his coat. Ross held him off, then dropped the coat and thrust him sharply away. The man half sat in a chair, choked, got up again. Ross twisted him round and took him by the back of his shirt and the seat of his silk breeches.

"Open the window, Francis," he said.

"Listen, Ross"—George interposed his heavy figure—"we don't want any horseplay——"

But Ross stepped aside and carried the struggling miller to the french window. They went out and down the four steps. Some of the others followed but George Warleggan did not go farther than the top step.

The river was out. Under the late stars it looked like a black pit with sloping sides. As he got near the bank Sanson began to struggle harder and tried to kick himself free. They neared the edge. On the very brink he began to shout for help. Ross shook him till he stopped. Then he tensed his muscles, lifted the man off his feet, swung back and away. The effort nearly took him over the brink himself. Sanson's shouts, thin and childlike, ended in a heavy *plop*.

Ross recovered his balance and stared down. He could see nothing. He turned away and went back to the house, not looking at any of the people he met. Near the steps George caught his arm.

"Has he gone in the river?"

"He has gone where the river should be. It was not at home."

"Man, he'll suffocate in that mud!"

Ross looked at him. Their eyes met together with a peculiar glint, like the memory of an old strife.

"I am sorry for assaulting your guest and causing this commotion," Ross said. "But if you will give such fellows the protection of your roof you should arrange for a more convenient way of disposal." He went in.

Demelza had been in the bedroom ten minutes when Ross came up. She had undressed, hanging up her lovely frock in the massive mahogany wardrobe, and taken down her hair and combed it and put on her nightdress with the frill of lace under her chin. She looked about sixteen, sitting up in bed and watching him with a wary expression.

For though she understood Ross's mood she did not know how to manage it. He was beyond her to-night.

He shut the door and glanced at her, eyes so light-coloured, as they always were when he was angry. He looked at her sitting there and then looked down at something in his hand.

"I have brought your brooch," he said. He was dead-sober now, might not have touched a glass all day.

"Oh, thank you."

"You left it on the chair."

"I didn't rightly like to touch it, Ross."

He moved over and put it on the dressing table. "Thank you for the loan of it."

"Well, I—I—I didn't like to think of Wheal Leisure . . . all your planning and scheming . . . Have you got it all back?"

"What?"

"All you lost to-night."

"Oh, yes." He began to undress.

"When did you first think he was cheating, Ross?"

"I don't know. . . . When you came. No, later than that, but I wasn't sure."

"Was that why you wouldn't let up?"

"At times he didn't cheat and then I began to win. I knew if I kept on long enough he'd have to start cheating again. His hands kept getting sticky with sweat; it was my chief hope."

"What happened to him, Ross? He wasn't . . . suffocated?"

"George got two servants."

"I'm glad. Not for his sake but . . ." She began to slip out of bed.

"Where are you going?"

"To put the brooch away safe. I couldn't sleep with it lying there."

"You'll have to sleep with it lying somewhere."

"Then let it be under my pillow."

She looked tall and very young and slender in her long white cotton nightgown. She did not look like the mother of Julia.

Ross caught her elbow as she came back.

"Demelza," he said.

She stopped and looked up into his strained face, still uncertain.

"It has not been a good night for your debut into society."

"No," she said, lowering her head.

His hands went round the back of her neck and buried themselves in the mass of her hair where it curled over her shoulders. He pulled on it gently until she was again meeting his gaze.

"Those things I said to you in the dance-room."

"Yes?"

"They were not well said."

"About?"

"You had a right to the attentions of those men since I was so neglectful."

"Oh . . . but I knew why you were. It wasn't for want of knowing— or sympathizing. I was worried. They came round like a swarm o' bees. I didn't have time to think. And then when you came . . ."

She climbed back into the big curtained bed, and he sat on the edge on her side, his feet on the step. She nursed her knees and looked at him.

"And then there was Verity."

"Verity?"

She told him.

A long silence followed, one of those communicative, friendly silences which frequently fell between them.

"Oh, God," he said, "it is a wry world." He leaned back against her knees. "All this week I've wanted to strike at the air, for there was nothing more substantial to strike at. As you know. But I believe I am too tired to hate any more just at present, Demelza."

"I'm glad," she said.

After a few minutes he got into bed beside her and lay quiet, staring up at the canopy of the bed. Then he leaned across and blew out the candle.

She put her arms about him and drew his head on to her shoulder.

"This," he said, "is the first time I have been sober for four days."

It was the first time they had ever lain like this, but she did not say so.

There was no doubt next morning that the War-leggans looked with disfavour on the end of the gaming quarrel. Constraint and stiffness was marked. Ross wondered if they expected their guests to sit down and be ruined in silence.

But he had not much time for considering the matter just then, for he had to see Harris Pascoe before they left for home.

All during these days the copper company had almost been forgotten; but there was much business now to do and much to discuss. After a while the banker said nervously:

"I hear you have been in Launceston for a few days."

"So you've heard."

"It is a curious thing, you know, that I hardly ever stir from my house except now and then to walk up the hill for the good of my health—and yet all the n-news of the world comes to me. I trust you're no worse for the adventure?"

"No worse if you mean in body. Of course there is another few days for the fever to come out."

Pascoe winced slightly. "I—er—gather that your action in breaking open the gaol has not been a popular one."

"I did not expect it to be."

"Quite so. The young man died? Yes. . . . Mind you, I don't think very much will come of it in that case. The question of whether the prison was in fact fit for human habitation would naturally come up at any inquiry on your behaviour, and it would not be in the interests of the magistrates concerned to have too much publicity given to the incident. Really, you know, almost all of them are well-meaning gentry with apathy as their worse crime. Many of them rule with admirable public spirit. And they have regard enough for what the country thinks not to wish to show up badly. I think they will decide to close their ranks and ignore your part in it. That's my personal opinion for what it's worth."

Ross tapped his riding boot.

"It is p-perhaps a little unfortunate," Pascoe said, looking out of the window, "that several of your fellow shareholders on the Carnmore Copper Company should be, so to say, on the other side of the fence."

Ross looked up. "What do you mean?"

"Well, they are magistrates, are they not, and as such likely to see the matter in their own light: St. Aubyn Tresize and Alfred Barbary and the others. However that may not at all eventuate."

Ross grunted and rose. "What they don't seem ɔ see is that we shall have plenty to fight without fighting among ourselves."

Pascoe fixed his spectacles and dusted some snuff off his coat. "I was not at the ball last night, but I am told the Assembly altogether was most enjoyable. Your wife, I understand, was quite the success of the evening."

Ross looked up sharply. Pascoe was not normally a man of sarcasm. "In what way?"

The banker met his gaze in slight surprise. "In the pleasantest way, I imagine. If there is an unpleasant way of being a success I have yet to learn it."

"Oh," said Ross. "Yes. I was very much out of sorts last night. I took little notice."

"I hope it isn't any symptoms of the fever?"

"Oh, no. . . . You were saying?"

"About what?"

"About my wife."

"Oh, I was merely repeating what came my way. Several ladies remarked on her beauty. And I believe the Lord Lieutenant asked who she was."

"Oh," said Ross, trying not to show his surprise. "That is very gratifying."

Harris Pascoe went with him to the door. "You're staying with the Warleggans?"

"We could hardly refuse. I don't think we are likely to be asked again, for the news of my being concerned in the copper company can't be long in leaking out."

"No-o. And the trouble last night between yourself and Matthew Sanson will be a further strain on good feeling."

"You're certainly well informed."

Pascoe smiled. "A man called Vosper told me. But that s-sort of quarrel is soon about the town."

"There's no reason why it should be a reflection on the Warleggans. They were not even playing at the time."

"No, but he's a cousin, you know."

Ross halted. "Of the Warleggans? I didn't know."

"The old man, the grandfather—you knew he was a blacksmith? Yes, well he had three children. The daughter married a good-for-nothing fellow called Sanson, father of Matthew Sanson. The eldest child of the old man is Nicholas, George's father, and the younger son is Cary."

"Oh," said Ross, thinking it over. There was a lot to think over. "He's a miller by trade, isn't he?"

"S-so they call him," said Harris Pascoe with a peculiar expression.

They took leave of the Warleggans at one, George magnanimously coming down the steps to see them off. No word more of the fracas of the night, and Sanson was as if he had never been. They separated with laughter and thanks and various insincere promises to meet again very soon, and the five Poldarks turned their horses up Princes Street. As she was about to mount, an ostler from the Seven Stars Tavern came across to Demelza and gave her a sealed letter; but with so many people about she had only time to thrust it into the pocket of her riding coat and hope that the others hadn't noticed.

They did not leave constraint behind, for Francis had not spoken a word to his sister since last night, and while they rode bunched together no one seemed inclined to talk. But when they reached the open moors Ross and Francis rode ahead and the three girls followed in line abreast, with the two Trenwith servants and the baggage on ponies behind. So it happened that Ross and Francis had the last friendly talk they were to have for many a day; and behind them, since Verity had nothing to say, Elizabeth and Demelza spoke together as equals for the first time in their lives.

Ross and Francis, carefully avoiding the subject of Captain Blamey, talked of Matthew Sanson. Francis had not known of his relationship with the Warleggans.

"Damn me," said Francis, "what troubles me is that I have played with the skunk for the last three years. There's no question but that he has been the greatest gainer. He used to lose sometimes, but seldom to me. It gives me to wonder how much I've been cheated."

"Of most of it, I should guess. Look, Francis, I don't think this should stay as it is. I've no more to gain by pursuing it, but you have. And so must others have. I don't think you can afford to consider the Warleggans."

"We might try to squeeze some of his back winnings out of him?"

"Why not? He's a miller and swimming in money. Why should he not be made to pay?"

"I wish I had thought of it before we left; I could have sounded some of those I know will be feeling sore. I've an uncomfortable feeling that before we can do anything he will clear out of the district."

"Well, there are his mills. He can't abandon them."

"No-o."

Ross saw that Demelza and Elizabeth were talking, and the sound of their voices on the wind gave him pleasure. It would be strange and gratifying if those two women made up a friendship. He had always wanted that.

When they reached Trenwith they had to go in and take tea. And Geoffrey Charles had to be inspected as well as Julia, so it was late before Ross, carrying the crowing baby in his arms, and Demelza, edging up her horse to peer at his bundle, began the last three miles to Nampara.

"Verity has taken it bad again," Ross said. "Sitting there through tea scarcely speaking. Her expression made me uneasy. Thank God, at least, that we had no part in it."

"No, Ross," said Demelza, the letter burning in her pocket. (She had looked at it a moment at Trenwith.

MISTRESS DEMELZA [it began],

Since you brought us together this second time, I turn to you for further help at this crisis in our affairs. Francis is quite impossible; there can never be any reconciliation. Therefore Verity must choose, and choose quickly between us. I do not fear her choice but only lack the means to communicate with her and make final arangements. It is in this that I ask your help. . . .)

"No, Ross," Demelza said.

As they reached the coppice, turning into their valley, the sun came out, and they stopped a moment to look down. He said suddenly: "I dislike coming back to-day, to our house and to our land, because it's to the thought of Jinny's misery and to my failure."

She put her hand on his. "No, Ross, it can't be. We're coming back to our happiness and to our success. I'm sad for Jinny too, shall always be; but we can't let other people's misery spoil our lives. We can't, for else there'd be no happiness for anyone ever again. We can't be all tied up one with another like that, or why did God make us separate? While we've got our happiness we must enjoy it, for who knows how long it will last?"

He looked at her.

"That's all ours," she said, "and we must cherish it, Ross. Tis no good crying for the moon and wanting everyone to be so lucky as we are. I'm content an' I want you to be the same. You were once, not so long ago. Have I failed you?"

"No," he said. "You have not failed me."

She took a deep breath. "How lovely it is to see the sea after being away for more than a day."

He laughed a little—the first time since he had come home.

The wind had been blowing from the south-east for a fortnight. Sometimes the sea had been flat and green and at others full of spumy feathery breakers. But to-day a great swell had developed. They could see the long lines of breakers parading slowly in, the sun-green tops breaking far out and spreading the whole bay with white valleys of glinting foam.

As they dipped among the trees Garrick came bounding towards them, froth on his mouth and his red tongue lolling with excitement. Darkie knew him and ignored the show, but Caerhays, Demelza's new horse, did not like it a bit and there was some side-stepping and head-shaking before it all quieted down. As they restarted they saw a girl's figure running across towards the rising ground on the side. Her long black hair blew out, and she carried a bag, which she swung as she ran.

"That's Keren Daniel again," said Demelza. "Whenever she go to Sawle for anything she takes a short cut back across my garden."

"No one has told her different, I suppose. By the way, I was asked this morning if Dwight Enys was going with a woman in the neighbourhood. Have you heard any such rumour?"

"No," said Demelza, and then everything slipped into place. "Oh."

"What is it?"

"Nothing."

They reached the bridge and crossed it. Ross had the sudden impulse to meet Demelza's desire for happiness, to atone to her for what had been unpleasant in last night. Why not? Strange sometimes how easy bitter words came, how hard the kind ones.

"You've heard me speak of Harris Pascoe?"

"Your bank person?"

"Yes. He appears to be the best-informed man in the county. He had not even been to the Assembly last night yet he knew all about your success there."

"My success?" Demelza said, looking for sarcasm just as Ross had done.

"Yes; about how the ladies had said how beautiful you were and how the Lord Lieutenant had wished to know your name."

"Judas!" said Demelza, going very hot. "You're joking."

"I'm not at all."

"Whoever told him that?"

"Oh, it would be on good authority."

"Judas," said Demelza again. "I never even knew which the Lord Lieutenant was."

"So you see others were in good mood to appreciate you, even if I was not."

"Oh, Ross, I can't believe it," said Demelza, with a funny little lift in her voice. "No one could notice anything in such a crush. He was saying it to please you."

"Far from it, I assure you."

They reached the door of their house. It was open but no one was there to greet them.

"I'm . . . It seem queer to think of," she said. "It must have been your lovely dress."

"A nice frame doesn't make a nice picture."

"Phoo. . . . It's made me feel queer. I never thought to think . . ."

John Gimlett came trotting round the house, apologizing for not being there to greet them; his shining round face was good-tempered and friendly and made them feel they were welcome home. Ross was going to hand him the baby but Demelza protested and was helped down first.

She took the kicking baby from Ross and stood for a moment gathering her more comfortably into her arms. Julia at once knew who was holding her, and a grin of welcome spread across her chubby face. She crowed and put up a clenched fist. Demelza kissed the fist and examined the child's face for signs of change. Julia looked vaguely less comely than she had done thirty-six hours before. Demelza came to the view that at that age no child was tidy for long without its mother. (The ladies had said how beautiful, and the Lord Lieutenant had asked . . . "Your lovely dress it was, Ross"; but, "A nice frame doesn't make a nice picture," he had said.) Demelza had known that when Julia grew up she would be proud of her father; it had not occurred to her that she might also be proud of her mother. A splendid thought, shining like that sun on the sea. She would do all she could. Learn to be a lady, learn to grow old with grace and charm. She was only young yet, so there was still a chance to learn.

She raised her head and looked across at Ross just dismounting. Last night and the night before she had feared for him. But to-day he had got back his balance. If she could persuade him to stay at home for a little now, she thought he would gain back his content. It was up to her really to see that he did.

Julia wriggled and crowed. "Na—na—na," she said. "Do—do—buff—war—na—na," and laughed at her own absurdity.

Demelza sighed, with a sense of the complexity of life but of its personal goodness to her, and turned and carried her baby into the house.

CHAPTER XIII   Keren had been hurrying for a very good reason. She had Mark's supper, two salted pilchards for which she had paid twopence, in her bag, and she did not want to be late in cooking it. She reached home, running most of the way, burst into the cottage, began gathering sticks for lighting a fire. Mark had been doing a turn of work for Will Nanfan on his small holding to earn more money. All this week while he had been on the night core his routine had been: down the mine from ten until six in the morning, sleep from seven to twelve, hoe his own garden for an hour, then a mile's walk to Nanfan's, where he worked from two till seven. He had been getting home about half-past seven, when he would turn in for another hour or so before it was time for supper and tramping off to the mine again. Hard going but necessary, for Keren was not a good manager. She always wanted to be buying something to eat instead of contriving something. It was an attitude of mind quite foreign to her neighbours.

Down in Sawle she had stayed watching two men fight over a disputed net. Now she found she was home in good time and need not have hurried. But she did not swear at herself or inwardly rail at Mark for keeping her so tied to time—and that for another very good reason. Dwight was home to-day.

She had not seen him for nearly a week. And he was home to-day.

She cooked the supper and woke Mark and watched him eat it, pecking at things herself like a bird. She was unstable in this as in all things, choosing to half starve herself when the food did not appeal, then when something tasty came along she would eat until she could hardly move.

She sat there watching Mark get ready for the mine, with a curious hidden tenseness in her body as she had done many times before, and always with the same reason. He had been more morose of late, less pliable to her moods; sometimes she thought he was watching her. But it did not worry her, for she was confident of always being able to outwit him and she was careful not to do anything suspicious when he was about. Only on these night cores of Mark's was she really free, and up to now she had been afraid to make use of them—not afraid of discovery but afraid of Dwight's opinion of her.

The sun had gone down behind a mass of night cloud, and its setting was only to be noticed by a last flush in the sky before dark. In this room the shadows were already heavy. Keren lit a candle.

"You'd be best to save your light till tis full dark," Mark said. "What wi' candles at ninepence a pound an' one thing and another."

He was always complaining about the price of things. Did he expect her to live in the dark?

"If you'd built the house the other way round it would have kept a lot lighter in the evening," she said.

She was always complaining about the way the house faced. Did she expect him to pick it up and set it down again just as she fancied?

"Mind you bolt the door while I'm away," he said.

"But that means I've got to get up to let you in."

"Never you mind. You do as I say. I don't fancy you sleeping here alone and unwatched like you was this morning. I wonder you fancy to sleep that way yourself."

She shrugged. "None of the local folk'd dare venture here. And a beggar or a tramp wouldn't know you were away."

He got up. "Well, see you bolt it to-night."

"All right."

He picked up his things and went to the door. Before he went he glanced back at her sitting there in the light of the single candle. The light shone on her pale skin, on her pale eyelids, on her dark eyelashes, on her dark hair. Her lips were pursed and she did not look up. He was suddenly visited by a terrible spasm of love and suspicion and jealousy. There she sat, delectable, like a choice fruit. He had married her, yet the thought had been growing in him for weeks that she was really not for him.

"Keren!"

"Yes?"

"And see you don't open it to no one afore I git back."

She met his gaze: "No, Mark. I'll not open it for no one."

He went out wondering why she had taken his words so calmly, as if the thought held no surprise.

After he left she sat quite still for a long time. Then she blew out the candle and went to the door and opened it so that she could hear the bell at the mine ringing the change of core. When this came she shut the door and bolted it and lit the candle again, carrying it into her bedroom. She lay down on the bed, but there was no danger of falling asleep. Her mind was crammed with thoughts and her nerves and body atingle.

At length she sat up, combed her hair, scraped round the box to find the last of the powder, put on a shabby black cloak and tied up her hair with the scarlet kerchief Mark had won. Then she left the house. As she went she hunched her shoulders up and walked with a careful hobble, to deceive anyone who might see her.

There was a light in the Gatehouse as she had expected, in the window of his living-room. There was also a glimmer in one of the turreted windows. Bone was going to bed.

She did not knock at the door but tiptoed round among the brambles until she reached the lighted window facing up the hill. There she stopped to take off her scarf and shake out her hair. Then she tapped.

She had some time to wait, but did not knock again for she knew how good his hearing was. Suddenly the curtains were drawn back and a hand unlatched the window. She found herself looking into his face.

"Keren! What is it? Are you well?"

"Yes," she said. "I—I wanted to see you, Dwight."

He said: "Go round to the front. I'll let you in."

"No, I can manage here if you'll help."

He stretched out a hand; she grasped it and climbed nimbly into the room; he hastily shut the windows and pulled the curtains across.

A fire crackled in the grate. Two candelabras burned on the table, on which papers were spread. He was in a shabby morning gown and his hair was ruffled. He looked very young and handsome.

"Forgive me, Dwight. I—I couldn't come at any other time. Mark is on night core. I was so anxious . . ."

"Anxious?"

"Yes. For you. They told me you'd been with the fever."

His face cleared. "Oh, that. . . ."

"I knew you were home Tuesday but I couldn't get across and you didn't send me any word."

"How could I?"

"Well, you might have tried somehow before you left for Truro again."

"I did not know what work Mark was on. I don't think there was any reason to worry about me, my dear. We disinfected ourselves very thoroughly before we came home. Do you know that even my pocket-book stank after being in that gaol and had to be burned?"

"And then you say there was no danger!"

He looked at her. "Well, you are good to have worried so. Thank you. But it was dangerous to come here at this time of night."

"Why?" She met his gaze through her eyelashes. "Mark is down the mine for eight hours. And your servant is in bed."

He smiled slightly, with a hint of constraint. All the way into Truro yesterday and at times in the middle of the Assembly, Keren Daniel had been before him. He saw plain enough where their way was leading, and he was torn between two desires, to halt and to follow. Sometimes he had almost decided to take her, as he saw she wanted him to, but he knew that once begun no man on earth could predict where it would end. The thought was bulking between him and his work.

He had been grateful for the ball last night and the sudden refreshing contact with people of his own class. It was helpful to meet Elizabeth Poldark again, whom he thought the most beautiful woman he had ever seen. It had been helpful to meet Joan Pascoe and to contrast her poised, clear-skinned, clean-thoughted maidenhood with the memory of this wayward, impulsive little creature. He had come back to-day sure that this fantastic playing with fire must stop.

But faced with Keren, the choice was not so easy. Joan and the other girls were "at a distance"; they were remote, they were young ladies, they were people who made up the world. Keren was *reality*. Already he knew the taste of her lips, the melting touch of her body.

"Well," she said, as if reading his thoughts, "aren't you going to kiss me?"

"Yes," he said. "And then you must go, Keren."

She slipped her cloak on quickly and stood up to him with her hands behind her back, her attitude one of odd urgent demureness. She put up her face and half closed her eyes.

"Now," she said. "Just one."

He put his arms about her and kissed her cool lips, and she made no attempt to return his kiss. And while he was kissing her the knowledge came that he had missed this during the last week, missed it more than anything in life.

"Or a thousand," she said under her breath.

"What?" he asked.

She glanced sidelong away. "The fire's nice. Why should I go?"

Dwight knew then he was lost. And she knew too. There was nothing he could do about it. He would follow now. He would follow.

"What did you say?" he asked.

"Or a thousand. Or twenty thousand. Or a million. They're yours for the asking."

He put his hands up to her face, pressed it between his hands. There was a sudden tender vehemence in his touch.

"If I take there'll be no asking."

"Then take," she said. "Then take."

CHAPTER XIV   On Saturday the second of May in the morning, in one of the upper rooms of the Great House, there was a meeting of the three chief business members of the Warleggan family. Mr. Nicholas Warleggan, large and deliberate and hard, sat with his back to the window in a fine Sheraton armchair; Mr. George Warleggan lounged by the fireplace, tapping every now and then with his stick at the plaster ornamentations; Mr. Cary Warleggan occupied the table, looking over some papers and breathing through his nose.

Cary said: "There's little from Trevaunance. There was no official ceremony, according to Smith. At noon Sir John Trevaunance and Captain Poldark and Mr. Tonkin went down to the works, Sir John said a few words and the workmen lit up the furnaces. Then the three gentlemen went into one of the tin huts which have been set up, and drank each other's health and went home."

Mr. Warleggan said: "How is it situated, this works?"

"Very convenient. At high tide a brig can come into Trevaunance

Cove and edge right alongside the quay, and the coal is unloaded beside the furnaces."

George lowered his stick. "What are they doing for rolling and cutting?"

"At present they've come to an agreement with the venturers of Wheal Radiant for the use of their rolling and battery mill. That is about three miles away."

"Wheal Radiant," said George thoughtfully. "Wheal Radiant."

"And what of the ticketing?" asked Mr. Warleggan.

Cary rustled his papers.

"Blight tells me the meeting was very crowded. That was to be expected, for the news has got around. Things went much as planned and the Carnmore Company got no copper at all. The high prices of course pleased the mines. It all passed off very quiet."

George said: "They bought enough last time to keep them going three months. It is when they begin to run short that we shall have the fireworks."

"After the ticketing," Cary said, "Tremail discreetly sounded Martin on his loyalty to the company. However, Martin became very unpleasant and the conversation had to be broke off."

Mr. Nicholas Warleggan got up. "I don't know if you are party to this, George, but if so it is not a departure that I view with any pleasure. I have been in business now for forty years, and much if not all you have been able to do has been built on the foundations laid by me. Well, our bank, our foundry, our mills have been raised on principles of sound business and honest trading. We have that reputation and I am proud of it. By all means fight the Carnmore Copper Company with the legitimate means to hand. I have every intention of putting them out of business. But I do not think we need descend to such measures to gain our end."

Having said so much, Mr. Warleggan turned his back and stared out over the lawns and the river. Cary sorted his papers. George traced the mouldings with the point of his stick.

Cary said: "This absurd secrecy is no better than a sharp practice, contrived to mislead and confuse."

"I do not think we can hold that against them," Mr. Warleggan said ponderously. "They have as much right as we have to use agents and figureheads."

Cary breathed through his nose. "What does George say?"

George took out his lace handkerchief and flicked away a little plaster which had floated down upon his knee. "I was thinking. Isn't Jonathan Tresidder the chief shareholder in Wheal Radiant?"

"I believe so. What of it?"

"Well, does he not bank with us?"

"Yes."

"And has some money on loan. I think it could be made clear to him that he should choose which side of the fence he wishes to come down on. If he helps the Carnmore with his mill let him go elsewhere for his credit. We can't be expected to subsidize our competitors."

Cary said rather sarcastically: "And what does Nicholas think of that?"

The old man by the window clasped his hands but did not turn. "I think if it was gone about straightforwardly it could be considered a legitimate business move."

"It's certainly no worse than the way you treated the owners of the paper mills at Penryn," Cary said.

Mr. Warleggan frowned. "They were holding up all our projects. Expediency will often justify severity."

George coughed. "For my part," he said, "although I don't condemn these manœuvres of Cary's—they're too unimportant to concern us much —yet I'm inclined to agree with you, Father, that we're too big to stoop to them. Let's defeat this company by fair means."

"Fair means," said Cary.

"Well, business means. We'll have all the smelters and merchants backing us. There should be no difficulty in squeezing these interlopers out once we know who they are——"

"Exactly," said Cary.

"And we shall know, never fear. Don't tell me a secret can be kept for very long in these parts. Someone will begin to whisper to someone else. It is just a question of not being too impatient and of knowing enough not to go too far."

Cary got up. "You mean you wish these inquiries stopped?"

Mr. Warleggan did not speak, but George said:

"Well, kept within the limits of dignity. After all we shall not be ruined even if the company establishes itself."

"You seem to forget," Cary said pallidly, "that the man directing this company is the man responsible for Matthew's disgrace."

"Matthew got nothing more than he deserved," said Nicholas. "I was shocked and horrified at the whole thing."

George rose also, stretching his bullneck and picking up his stick. He ignored his father's last remark.

"I have forgot nothing, Cary," he said.

BOOK THREE

CHAPTER I   "Read me the story of the Lost Miner, Aunt Verity," Geoffrey Charles said.

"I have read it you once already."

"Well, again, please. Just like you read it last time."

Verity picked up the book and absently ruffled Geoffrey Charles's curly head. Then a pang went through her that at this time to-morrow she would not be there to read to him.

The windows of the big parlour were open, and the July sun lay across the room. Elizabeth sat embroidering a waistcoat, with dusty sun bars touching colour in her beige silk frock. Aunt Agatha, having no truck with fresh air, crouched before the small fire she insisted on their keeping and drowsed like a tired old cat, the Bible, this being Sunday, open loosely in her lap. She did not move at all, but every now and then her eyes would open sharply as if she had heard a mouse in the wainscot. Geoffrey Charles, in a velvet suit and long velvet trousers, was a weight on Verity's knees where she sat by the window in the half shadow of a lace curtain. Francis was somewhere about the farm. In the two topped beech trees across the lawn pigeons were cooing.

Verity finished the story and slid Geoffrey Charles gently to the floor.

"There is mining in his blood, Elizabeth," she said. "No other story will suit."

Elizabeth smiled without looking up.

"When he grows up conditions may have changed." Verity rose. "I do not think I will go to Evensong. I have a headache."

"It will be with sitting in the sun. You sit too much in the sun, Verity."

"I must go now and see about the wine. You can never trust Mary to look at it, for she falls into a daydream when she should not."

"I'll come with you," said Geoffrey Charles. "Let me help you, eh?"

While she was busy in the kitchen Francis came in. This summer he had been trying to help about the farm. The work somehow did not suit him; it sat bleakly on his nature. Geoffrey Charles ran towards him but, seeing the expression on his father's face, changed his mind and ran back to Verity.

Francis said: "Tabb is the only man left with any farming in him. Ellery is worse than useless. He was told to rebuild the hedge in the sheep field, and it has broke in a week. It has taken us best part of an hour to get the flock back. I'll turn the fellow off."

"Ellery has been a miner since he was nine."

"That's the whole trouble," Francis said wryly. He looked at his hands, which were caked with dirt. "We do our best for these local people, but how can you expect miners to become hedgers and ditchers overnight?"

"Are the oats undamaged?"

"Yes, thanks be. By a mercy the first sheep turned down the lane instead of up."

The oats were to be cut next week. She would not be here for it. She could hardly believe that.

"I shall not come to church this evening, Francis. I have a headache. I think it's the warm weather."

"I'm much of a mind to stay away myself," he said.

"Oh, you can't do that." She tried to hide her alarm. "They're expecting you."

"Elizabeth can go by herself. She will stand for the family well enough."

Verity bent over the boiling wine and skimmed it. "Mr. Odgers would be heartbroken. He was telling me only last week that he always chooses the shortest psalms and preaches a special sermon for Evensong to please you."

Francis went out without replying, and Verity found that her hands were trembling. Geoffrey Charles's chatter, which had broken out again when his father went, was a tinkling noise that came to her from a distance. She had chosen Sunday at four as the only time of the week when she could be sure of Francis's being out. His movements these last months had been unpredictable; to this conventional habit he had been faithful. . . .

"Auntie Verity!" cried the boy. "Auntie Verity! Why don't you?"

"I can't listen to you now, sweetheart," she said abruptly. "Please leave me alone." She tried to take hold of herself, went into the next kitchen, where Mary Bartle was sitting and spoke to her for a few minutes.

"Auntie Verity. Auntie Verity. Why aren't any of you going to church this afternoon?"

"I am not. Your father and mother will be going."

"But Father just said he was not."

"Never mind. You stay and help Mary with the wine. Be careful you don't get in her way."

"But if——"

She turned quickly from the kitchen and, instead of walking through the house, went quickly across the courtyard with its disused fountain and came in at the big hall. She ran up the stairs. It might be the last time she would see Geoffrey Charles, but there was no chance of saying good-bye.

In her bedroom she went quickly to the window. From this corner of it, by pressing her face against the glass, she could just see the drive by which Francis and Elizabeth would walk to church—if they were going.

Very faintly in the distance the bells had begun to ring. Number three was slightly cracked and Francis always said it set his teeth on edge. Francis would take ten minutes or a quarter of an hour to put on clean linen. She expected that at this moment he and Elizabeth were debating whether he should go or not. Elizabeth would want him to go. Elizabeth must make him go.

She sat there stilly on the window seat, a curious chill creeping into her body from the touch of the glass. She couldn't for a second take her eyes from that corner of the drive.

She knew exactly how the bell ringers would look, sweating there in the enclosed space of the tower. She knew how each one of the choir would look, fumbling in the pews for their psalters, exchanging whispers, talking more openly when she did not come. Mr. Odgers would be bustling about in his surplice, poor, thin, harassed little fellow. They would all miss her, not merely to-night but in the future. And surely all the people whom she visited, the sick and the crippled, and the women struggling, overburdened with their families. . . .

She felt the same about her own family. Had times been good she would have left with a much freer heart. Elizabeth was not strong, and it would mean another woman to help Mrs. Tabb. More expense when every shilling counted. And no one could do just what she had done, holding all the strings of the house economically together, keeping a tight but friendly hold.

Well, what other way was open? She couldn't expect Andrew to wait longer. She had not seen him in the three months since the ball, all word having gone through Demelza. She had already put off her flight once because of Geoffrey Charles's illness. It was almost as bad now, but leave she must or stay for ever.

Her heart gave a leap. Elizabeth was walking down the drive, tall and slender and so graceful in her silk frock and straw hat and cream parasol. Surely she could not be going alone. . . .

Francis came into view. . . .

She got up from the window. Her cheek had stuck to the glass and it tingled sharply with returning blood. She looked unsteadily round the room. She knelt and from under the bed drew out her bag. Geoffrey Charles would still be running about, but she knew how to avoid him.

With the bag she came to the door, stared back round the room. The sun was shining aslant the tall old window. She slipped quickly out and leaned back against the door trying to get her breath. Then she set off towards the back stairs.

Having given way to Elizabeth and made the effort to go to church, Francis had felt a slow change of mood. This country farmer-squire life he led left him bored and frustrated almost to death. He longed for the days he had lost. But now and then, since all things are relative, his boredom waned and he forgot his frustration. It was the more strange to-day since he had been so angry over the sheep; but the afternoon was so perfect that it left no room in a man's soul for discontent. Walking here with the sun-warmed air on his face he had come up against the fact that it was good just to be alive.

There was perhaps a certain pleasure in finding most of the congregation waiting outside for them, ready to bob or touch their hats as they came by. After grubbing about the farm all week one was curiously grateful for this buttress to one's self-esteem.

Even the informal sight of Jud Paynter sitting on one of the distant gravestones drinking a mug of ale was not to be cavilled at.

The church was warm but did not smell so strongly as usual of mildew and worm and stale breath. The thin little curate bobbing about like an earwig was not an active irritation; and Joe Permewan, rasping away at the bass viol as if it were a tree trunk, was worth liking as well as laughing at. Joe, they all knew, was no angel and got drunk Saturday nights, but he always sawed his way back to salvation on a Sunday morning.

They had said the psalms and read the lessons and echoed the prayers, and Francis had been gently dozing off to sleep when the sudden bang of the church door roused him. A new worshipper had come in.

Jud had been to France for a couple of nights and had been merrying himself on the share-out. Sobriety never turned him to his Maker, but as always when the drink was in him he felt the urge to reform. And to reform not only himself but all men. He felt the fraternal pull. This afternoon he had wandered from the kiddleys and was in fresh fields.

As Mr. Odgers gave out the psalm he came slowly down the aisle, fingering his cap and blinking in the dark. He took a seat and dropped his cap, then he bent to pick it up and knocked over the stick of old Mrs. Carkeek sitting next to him. After the clatter had died he pulled out a large red rag and began to mop his fringe.

"Some hot," he said to Mrs. Carkeek, thinking to be polite.

She took no notice but stood up and began to sing.

Everyone in fact was singing, and the people in the gallery by the chancel steps were making the most noise of all and playing instruments just like a party. Jud sat where he was, mopping himself and staring round the church. All this was very new to him. He looked on it in a detached and wavering light.

Presently the psalm was done and everybody sat down. Jud was still staring at the choir.

"What're all they women doin' up there?" he muttered, leaning over and breathing liquorously on Mrs. Carkeek.

"Sh-sh. Tis the choir," she whispered back.

"What, they, the choir? Be they nearer Heaven than we folk?"

Jud brooded a minute. He was feeling kindly but not as kindly as all that. "Mary Ann Tregaskis. What she done to be nearer Heaven than we?"

"Ssh! Ssh!" said several people around him.

He had not noticed that Mr. Odgers had come to be standing in the pulpit.

Jud blew his nose and put the rag away in his pocket. He turned his attention to Mrs. Carkeek, who was sitting primly fingering her cotton gloves.

"Ow's your old cow?" he whispered. "Calved yet, have she?"

Mrs. Carkeek seemed to find a flaw in one of the gloves and gave it all her attention.

"Reckon 'er's going to be one of the awkward ones. Reckon ye did no good by yerself, buyin' of 'er from old Uncle Ben. Slippery ole twitch, he be, and in the choir at that. . . ."

Suddenly a voice spoke loudly, as it were just above his head. It quite startled him, seeing that everyone else seemed afraid of speaking a word.

"My text is from Proverbs Twenty-three, verse Thirty-one. 'Look not thou upon the wine when it is red. At the last it stingeth like an adder and biteth like a serpent.'"

Jud raised his head and saw Mr. Odgers in a sort of wooden box with a sheaf of papers in his hands and an old pair of spectacles on his nose.

"My friends," said Mr. Odgers, looking round, "I have chosen the text for this week after due thought and anxious prayer. My reason for so doing is that on Thursday next we celebrate Sawle Feast. As you all know, this holiday has long been the occasion not merely for harmless healthy jollification but for excessive indulgence in drink. . . ."

"Earear," said Jud, not quite to himself.

Mr. Odgers broke off and looked down severely at the bald old man sitting just below him. After staring for a moment and hearing nothing more he went on:

"For excessive indulgence in drink. It is my plea this evening to the members of the congregation that on Thursday next they should set a shining example in the parish. We have to remember, dear friends, that this feast day is no time for drunkenness and debauchery; for it was instituted to commemorate the landing of our patron saint, St. Sawle, from Ireland, who came to convert the heathens of west Cornwall. It was in the fourth century that he floated over from Ireland on a mill-stone and——"

"On a what?" Jud asked.

"On a millstone," Mr. Odgers said, forgetting himself. "It is a historical fact that he landed——"

"Well, I only axed!" whispered Jud in irritation to the man behind, who had tapped him on the shoulder.

"*Sanctus Sawlus*," said Mr. Odgers, "that is the motto of our church, and it should be a motto and a precept for our daily lives. One which we bear with us as St. Sawle brought it to our shores——"

"On a millstone," muttered Jud to Mrs. Carkeek. "Who ever 'eard of a man floating on a millstone. Giss along! Tedn sense, tedn reasonable, tedn right, tedn proper, tedn true!"

"You will see that we have with us to-day," said Mr. Odgers, rashly accepting the challenge, "one who habitually looks upon the wine when it is red. So the Devil enters into him and leads him into a house of God to flaunt his wickedness in our faces——"

"'Ere," said Jud unsteadily. "I aren't no different not from them up there. What you got in the choir, eh? Naught but drunkers and whores' birds! Look at old Uncle Ben Tregeagle with 'is ringlets settin' up there all righteous. And he'd do down a poor old widow woman by sellin' 'er a cow what he know is going to misfire."

The man behind grasped his arm. "Here, you come on out."

Jud thrust him back in his seat with the flat of his hand.

"I aren't doing no harm! Tes that little owl up there as be doing the harm. 'Im an' his whores' birds. Tellin' a wicked ole yarn about a man *floating* on a millstone. . . ."

"Come along, Paynter," said Francis, who had been urged by Elizabeth. "Air your grievances outside. If you come disturbing us in church you are likely to end up in gaol."

Jud's bloodshot eyes travelled over Francis. Injured, he said: "What for d'ye turn me out, eh? I'm a fisherman now, not nobody's servant, an' I know millstones no more float than fly."

Francis took his arm. "Come along, man."

Jud detached his arm. "I'll go," he said with dignity. He added loudly: "Tes a poor murky way ye take to repentance by followin' the likes of he. Ye'll go to the furnace, sure as me name's Jud Paynter. The flesh'll sweal off of yer bones. A fine lot of dripping ye'll make. Especially old Mrs. Grubb, there, 'oo's takin' up two seats wi' her fat! And Char Nanfan in the choir expectin' of 'er third!"

Two large men began to lead him up the aisle.

"'Ullo, Mrs. Metz, buried any more husbands, 'ave ee? Why and there's Johnnie Kimber as stole a pig. And little Betty Coad. Well, well. Not wed yet, Betty? Tes 'igh time . . ."

They got him to the door. Then he shook himself free and sent out a last blast.

"Twon't always be the same as this, friends. There's doings in France, friends. There's riots and bloody murder! They've broke open the prison an' the Governor's 'ead they've stuck on a pole! There'll be bonfires for some folk here afore ever they die! I tell ee——"

The door slammed behind him and only distant shouting could be heard as he was led to the lych gate.

People slowly began to settle down again. Francis, half annoyed, half amused, picked up a couple of prayer books and returned to his pew.

"Well," said Mr. Odgers, mopping his brow, "as I was saying, quite apart from the—er—legend or—er—miracle of St. Sawle . . ."

CHAPTER II   They walked home with Mr. and Mrs. Odgers. Francis admitted the arguments of his womenfolk that, with ten children to feed, this was probably the only square meal the Odgers got in a week (and this not so immensely square as it had once been); but it did not make them any better company. He would not have minded so much if they had been less agreeable. Sometimes he twisted his own opinions just to take a contrary view and found amusement in watching Odgers's acrobatics in following. One thing the Odgers were obstinately determined not to do and that was fall out with the Poldarks.

They walked home in twos, the ladies on ahead, the gentlemen pacing behind. Oh, Lord, thought Francis, if only the man could play hazard and had money to lose.

"That fellow Paynter is going to the dogs," he said. "I wonder why my cousin got rid of him? He stood enough ill behaviour from him in the past."

"It was some scandal he spoke, so I heard. The man is a thorough-going scoundrel, sir. He deserves to be put in the stocks. I do not think the congregation ever settled down proper after he left."

Francis suppressed a smile. "I wonder what he had to say of France. Was he making it all up, I wonder?"

"There has been some story about, Mr. Poldark. My wife in the course of her parish duties had occasion to visit Mrs. Janet Trencrom —you know, the niece-by-marriage of *the* Mr. Trencrom. Mrs. Trencrom said—— Now what were her words? Maria! What was it Mrs. Trencrom told you?"

"Oh, well, Mrs. Trencrom said they were full of it in Cherbourg, but of course it will have been magnified. She said that French prison— what is it called?—was overthrown by rioters about Tuesday or Wednesday last and the Governor and many of his men slaughtered."

"I query the truth of it," Francis said, after a moment.

"I trust there is *no* truth in it," Mr. Odgers said vehemently. "Mob law is always to be deplored. That man, Paynter, for instance, is a dangerous type. He would have the houses about our ears if we gave him half a chance."

Francis said: "When there are riots in this country they are not led or incited by tipsy old men. There, Odgers, look at that field of oats. If the weather holds we shall begin to cut to-morrow."

At Trenwith Francis led the little curate out into the garden while the ladies tidied themselves. When they went into the winter parlour for supper and Mrs. Odgers's small, anxious grey eyes were glistening at the sight of all the food, Francis said:

"Where's Verity?"

"I went to her bedroom as soon as I came back, but she was not there," Elizabeth said.

Francis put his mouth against Aunt Agatha's long pointed ear.

"Have you seen Verity?"

"What? Eh?" Aunt Agatha rested on her sticks. "Verity? Out, I believe."

"Out? Why should she go out at this time?"

"Leastwise, I fancy she be. She came and kissed me an hour gone and she had on her cloak and things. I didn't gather what she said; folk mumble so. If they was learned to talk out like they was learned in my young days there'd be less trouble in the world. No mines working. I tell ye, Francis, tis a poor world for the old and aged. There's some that would go to the wall. Nay, Odgers, I tell you myself, there's little comfort in——"

"Did she say where she was going?"

"What? Verity? I tell you I could catch nothin' she said. But she left some sort of letter for you both."

"A letter?" said Elizabeth, jumping at the truth far before Francis. "Where is it?"

"Well, aren't you goin' to ask to see it? Damme, no curiosity these days. I wonder what I did with it. It was just here in my shawl." She hobbled to the table and sat down, her wrinkled old hands fumbling in the laces and folds of her clothes. Mr. Odgers waited impatiently until he too could sit down and begin on the cold fowl and the gooseberry pies.

A couple of lice were all she disturbed at first, but presently one claw came trembling out with a sealed paper between finger and thumb.

"I thought it smelt somewhat of an insult puttin' wax on a letter I was to carry," said the old lady. "Eh? What d'you say? As if I cared for Miss Verity's secrets. . . . I bring to mind well the day she was born. The winter o' fifty-nine. Twas just after the rejoicings on the takin' of Quebec, and me and your father had rid over to a bearbaiting at St. Ann's. We'd scarce got home and inside the house when——"

"Read this," said Francis, thrusting the open letter towards Elizabeth. His small features were pinched with a sudden uncontrollable anger.

Her eyes glanced swiftly over it.

I have known and loved you all my life, dear Francis [it ran], and you Elizabeth more than seven years, so I pray you will both understand the grief and loss I feel that this should be our Parting. For three months and more I have been torn two ways by loyalties and effections which lived and grew in me with equal Strength, and which in happier circumstances could have existed without conflict. That of the two I have chosen to tear up the deeper rooted and follow after a Life and destiny of my own with a man whom you distrust may seem to you the height of folly, but I pray you will not look on it as a desertion. I am to live in Falmouth now. Oh, my dears, I should have been so happy if only distence were to separate us. . . .

"Francis!" Elizabeth said. "Where are you going?"

"To see how she went—if there is time to bring her back!" He left the room with a sudden swing.

"What's to do?" asked Agatha. "What's got him? What does the note say?"

"Forgive me." Elizabeth turned to the gaping Odgers. "There is—— I am afraid there has been some misunderstanding. Do please sit down and have your supper. Don't wait for us. I am afraid we shall be a little time." She followed Francis.

The four remaining house servants were in the big kitchen. The Tabbs, just back from church, were telling the Bartles about Jud Paynter. The laughter stopped suddenly when they saw Francis.

"At what time did Miss Verity leave this house?"

"Oh, an hour and a half gone, sur," said Bartle, glancing curiously at his master's face. "Just after you'd gone church, sur."

"What horse did she take?"

"Her own, sur. Ellery went with her."

"Ellery. . . . Was she carrying anything?"

"I dunno, sur. He's back in the stables now, just giving the 'orses their fodder."

"Back . . . ?" Francis checked himself, and went swiftly out to the stables. The horses were all there. "Ellery!" he shouted. The man's startled face appeared round the door.

"Sur?"

"I understand you have been riding with Miss Verity. Is she back with you?"

"No, sur. She changed 'orses at Bargus Cross. A gentleman was waiting for her there with a spare 'orse, and she changed over to 'is and sent me back."

"What sort of gentleman?"

"Seafaring I should guess, sur. Leastwise, by his clothes . . ."

An hour and a half. They would already be beyond Truro. And they could take two or three different routes. So she had come to this. She had made up her mind to mate herself with this wife-kicking drunkard, and nothing should stop her. Blamey had the Devil's power over her. No matter what his record or his ways, he had but to whistle and she would run.

When Francis got back to the kitchen Elizabeth was there.

"No, mistress," Mary Bartle was saying. "I don't know nothing about that, mistress."

"Ellery is back without her," Francis said. "Now, Tabb; and you, Bartle; and you women; I want to hear the truth. Has Miss Verity been receiving letters through your hands?"

"No, sur. Oh, no, sur," they chorused.

"Come, let's talk it over quietly," Elizabeth suggested. "There is little we can do at present."

But Francis was bitterly careless of appearances. He knew it must all come out in a day or two. He would be the butt of the district: the man who tried to stop his sister's courting, and she calmly eloping one afternoon while he was at church.

"There must have been some contact unknown to us," he said sharply to Elizabeth. "Have any of you seen a seafaring man hanging about the grounds?"

No, they had seen nothing.

"She has been out and about visiting poor people in Sawle and Grambler, you know," Elizabeth said.

"Has anyone been calling here unknown to us?" Francis demanded. "Someone who saw Miss Verity and might have carried a message?"

No, they had seen no one.

"Mistress Poldark from Nampara has been over often enough," said Mary Bartle. "By the kitchen way——"

Mrs. Tabb trod on her toe, but it was too late. Francis stared at Mary Bartle for a moment or two, then went out, slamming the door behind him.

Elizabeth found him in the large parlour standing, hands behind back, at the window, looking over the garden.

She closed the door to let him know she was there, but he did not speak.

"We must accept the fact of her going, Francis," she said. "It is her choice. She is grown-up and a free agent. In the last resort we could never have stopped her if she had chosen to go. I could only have wished she had done it openly if she was to do it at all."

"Damn Ross!" Francis said between his teeth. "This is his doing, his and that impudent brat he married. Don't you see . . . he—he has stored this up all these years. Five years ago, knowing we disapproved, he gave them leave to meet at his house. He encouraged Verity in the teeth of all we said. He has never got over his defeat. He never liked to be the loser in anything. I wondered how Verity met this fellow again; no doubt it was at Ross's contrivance. And for these last months after my quarrel with Blamey, knowing I had broken the link again, he has been acting as agent for Blamey, keeping the skunk's interests warm and using Demelza as a postman and go-between!"

"I think you're a little hasty," Elizabeth said. "So far we don't even know that Demelza is concerned in it, let alone Ross."

"Of course," he said passionately, still not turning from the window, "you will always stand up for Ross in all things. You never imagine that Ross could do anything to our disadvantage."

"I am not standing up for anyone," Elizabeth said, a spark of anger in her voice. "But it is the merest justice not to condemn people unheard."

"The facts shout aloud for anyone with half an ear. There's no other way Blamey could have arranged her flight. She has had no post. I've seen to that. Demelza alone could not have done it, for she never knew

Blamey in the old days. Ross has been riding about all over the country-side on his damned copper concerns. What more easy than to call in at Falmouth from time to time and bear a message both ways."

"Well, there's nothing we can do about it now. She is gone. I don't know what we shall do without her. The busiest season of the year; and Geoffrey Charles will miss her terribly."

"We'll get along. Be sure of that."

"We should go back to the Odgers," Elizabeth said. "They'll think us very rude. There's nothing to do to-night, Francis."

"I want no supper just yet. They'll not mind my absence so long as they're fed themselves."

"What must I tell them?"

"The truth. It will be all over the district in a day or two anyway. Ross should be pleased."

There was a tap on the door before Elizabeth could open it.

"If you please, sir," said Mary Bartle, "Mr. Warleggan has called."

"Who?" said Francis. "Devil take it! I wonder if he has some news."

George came in, well groomed, polite, heavy in the shoulders and formidable. A rare visitor these days.

"Ah, well, I'm glad to find you have finished supper. Elizabeth, that simple dress suits you to——"

"Good God, we haven't yet begun it!" Francis said. "Have you brought news of Verity?"

"Is she away?"

"Two hours since. She has gone to that skunk Blamey!"

George glanced quickly from one to the other, sizing up their moods, not pleased by his brusque greeting. "I'm sorry. Is there anything I can do?"

"No, it's hopeless," Elizabeth said. "I have told Francis we must swallow it. He has been quite raving since. We have the Odgers here and they'll think we have all gone crazy. Forgive me, George, I must go and see if they have begun supper."

She swept past George, whose admiring glance flickered after her. Then he said: "You should know, Francis, that women can't be reasoned with. They are a headstrong sex. Let her have her bit, dear boy. If she falls at a fence it will be none of your doing."

Francis pulled at the bell. "I can't face those two agreeable sheep for supper. Your arrival on a Sunday evening was so unexpected that for a moment I hoped . . . How I hate the thought of that fellow getting his way with her after all!"

"I have spent the day at the Teagues and was feeling monstrous tired of the old lady's chatter, so I thought of an agreeable duty to perform at Trenwith. Poor Patience. There she sits on the hook, waiting for me to bite; a nice enough girl in an oncoming sort of way, but no true breeding about her. I'll swear her legs are on the short side. The woman I marry must not only have the right blood but show it."

"Well, you have come to a household that'll offer you no graces to-night, George. Oh, Mrs. Tabb, serve supper in here. Bring half of one of the boiled fowls if the Odgers have not yet picked 'em clean, and some cold ham and a pie. I tell you, George, there is that in this flight which makes me more than commonly angry."

George patted down the front of his silk flowered waistcoat. "No doubt, dear boy. I see I could not have called on a more untimely night. But since we have you so seldom in Truro these days I'm compelled to wait on you and mix duty with pleasure."

It reached Francis's taut and preoccupied mind that George was leading up to something. As his chief creditor George was in a dangerously powerful position; and feeling had not been too good between them since the gambling affray in April.

"An *agreeable* duty?"

"Well, it may be considered so. It has to do with Sanson and the matter you raised some time since."

So far neither Francis nor anyone else had got anything out of the miller. He had left Truro the day following Ross's exposure and was believed to be in London. His mills, it turned out, belonged to a company and that company to other companies.

George took out his gold-mounted snuffbox and tapped it.

"We have talked this over several times, my father and I. While there's no obligation in it, Sanson's conduct is a stain we feel rather deeply. As you know, we have no ancestors to bring us repute; we must make our own."

"Yes, yes, you are clear enough," Francis said briefly. It was seldom that George mentioned his humble beginnings.

"Well, as I told you in May, many of your bills given to Matthew Sanson have found their way into Cary's hands. He has always been somewhat the treasurer of the family, as Matthew was the black sheep, and your bills were accepted by Cary in exchange for cash advances made to Matthew."

Francis grunted. "I take that as no advantage."

"Well, yes, it is. We have decided between us as a family to cancel one half of all the drafts which came into Cary's hands from Matthew. It will not be a crushing matter, but it will be a token of our will to undo what wrong has been done. At I say, not a big thing. About twelve hundred pounds."

Francis flushed. "I can't take your charity, George."

"Charity be hanged. You may have lost the money unfairly in the first place. From our viewpoint we wish it, to re-establish our integrity. It is really nothing at all to do with you."

Mrs. Tabb came in with the supper. She set up a table by the window, put her tray on it and two chairs beside it. Francis watched her. Half his mind was still battling with the desertion of Verity, the perfidy of Ross—the other half facing this princely gesture from a man he had begun to distrust. It *was* a princely gesture and one that no stubborn pricky pride must force him to refuse.

When Mrs. Tabb had gone he said: "You mean—the money would be put to reducing my debt to you?"

"That's for you to decide. But I'd suggest one half of it should go to reducing the debt and the other half should be a cash payment."

Francis's flush deepened. "It is very handsome of you. I don't know quite what to say."

"Say nothing more about it. It's not a comfortable subject between friends, but I had to explain."

Francis dropped into his chair. "Take some supper, George. I'll open a bottle of my father's brandy after in honour of the occasion. No doubt it will loosen up my anger over Verity and make me a more easy companion. You'll stay the night?"

"Thank you," said George.

They supped.

In the winter parlour Elizabeth had just excused herself and left again. Mr. Odgers was finishing up the raspberry syllabub and Mrs. Odgers the almond cake. With only the old lady's eyes on them their manners had eased up.

"I wonder if he means to do the honest thing by her," Mrs. Odgers said. "They could not get married to-night, and you never can tell with these sailors. He may well have a Portugee wife for all she knows. What do you think, Clarence?"

"Um?" said Mr. Odgers, with his mouth full.

"Little Verity," said Aunt Agatha. "Little Verity. Imagine little Verity going off like that."

"I wonder what the feeling will be in Falmouth," said Mrs. Odgers. "Of course in a port morals are always more lax. And they may go through some marriage ceremony just to pull the wool over people's eyes. Anyway, men who kill their first wives should be forbidden ever to marry again. Don't you agree, Clarence?"

"Um," said Mr. Odgers.

"Little Verity," said Aunt Agatha. "She was always obstinate like her mother. I bring to mind when she was six or seven, the year we held the masquerade ball . . ."

In the large parlour the brandy had come.

"I can't bear these sneaking underhand dealings," Francis said bitterly. "If he had had the guts to come here and face me out maybe I should not have liked that, but I shouldn't have held him in such dead contempt." After his estrangement from George the reaction was carrying him back beyond the old intimacy. As good as in his pocket was six hundred pounds he had never thought to see again—and the same amount cut from his debts. Never could it have been more welcome than to-day. During the coming months it might just make all the difference. It meant an easing of their life and the strain of bitter economy. A grand gesture which deserved the grand recognition. Adversity showed up one's friends.

"But all along," he continued, "that has been his way. At the outset he went sneaking behind our backs and meeting the girl at Nampara—with Ross's connivance. All the time it has been this sneaking, sneaking. I've half a mind to ride to Falmouth to-morrow and flush them from their love nest."

"And no doubt you'd find he had just left for Lisbon and she with him." George tasted the brandy on his lips. "No, Francis, leave them be. It is no good putting yourself in the wrong by trying to force her to return. The harm is done. Maybe she'll soon be crying to come back."

Francis got up and began to light the candles. "Well, she shall not come back here, not if she cries for a year! Let her go to Nampara, where they have fathered this thing. Damn them, George." Francis turned, the taper showing up his angry face. "If there is one thing in this that cuts me to the root it is Ross's cursed underhand interference. Damn it, I might have expected a greater loyalty and friendship from my only cousin! What have I ever done to him that he should go behind my back in this fashion!"

"Well," said George, "I suppose you married the girl he wanted, didn't you?"

Francis stopped again and stared at him. "Oh, yes. Oh, yes . . . But that's long ago." He blew out the taper. "That was patched up long since. He is happily married himself; more happily than . . . There would be no point in feeling a grudge on that score."

George looked out on the darkening garden. The candles threw his blurred hunched shadow on the wall.

"You know Ross better than I, Francis, so I can't guide you. But many people—many people we accept on their face value have strange depths. I've found it so. It may be that Ross is one such. I can't judge, but I do know that all my own overtures towards him have met with rebuffs."

Francis came back to the table. "Aren't you on friendly terms? No, I suppose not. How have you offended him?"

"That's something I can't guess. But I do know when his mine was opened all the other venturers were for the business being put through our bank, yet he fought tooth and nail until he got them to accept Pascoe's. Then sometimes remarks he has made have been repeated to me; they were the words of a man with a secret resentment. Finally there is this wildcat scheme he has launched of some copper-smelting company, which privately is directed at us."

"Oh, I don't think exactly at you," Francis said. "Its aim is to get fairer prices for the mines."

George glanced covertly at him. "I'm not at all upset about it, for the scheme will fail through lack of money. Still, it shows an enmity towards me which I don't feel I deserve—any more than you deserve to have had this betrayal of the best interests of your family."

Francis stared down at the other man, and there was a long silence. The clock in the corner struck seven.

"I don't think the scheme need necessarily fail through lack of money," Francis said whitely. "There are a good many important interests behind it. . . ."

CHAPTER III   It was an easterly sky, and as they reached Falmouth the sun was setting like a Chinese lantern, swollen and crimson and monstrous and decorated with ridges of curly cloud. The town was a grey smudge climbing the edge of the bay.

As they went down the hill Andrew said: "Your last letter left all to me, my dear; so I trust what I have done you'll find to your liking."

"I'm willing to do whatever you say."

"The wedding is set for eleven to-morrow—at the Church of King Charles the Martyr. I took a licence from Parson Freakes yesterday morning. Just my old landlady and Captain Brigg will be there as witnesses. It will be as quiet as ever possible."

"Thank you."

"As for to-night"—Andrew cleared his throat—"I had thought at first the best would be to take a room at one of the inns. But as I went round they all seemed too shoddy to house you."

"I shall not mind."

"I misliked the thought of you being there alone with perhaps noisy and drunken men about." His blue eyes met hers. "It wasn't right."

She flushed slightly. "It wouldn't have mattered."

"So instead I'd like you to go to your new home, where Mrs. Stevens will be there to see to your needs. I'll sleep in my ship."

She said: "Forgive me if I seem dull . . . It isn't that at all. It's only the wrench of leaving the things I've loved so long."

"My dear, I know how you must feel. But we have a week before I need sail. I believe it will all seem different to you before I go."

Another silence fell. "Francis is unpredictable," she said suddenly. "In some ways, though I shall miss them so much, I wish we were further than a score of miles. It is within too-easy riding distance of some quarrelsome impulse."

"If he comes I will soon cool it for him."

"I know, Andrew. But that is above all what I don't want."

He smiled slightly. "I was very patient at the Assembly. At need I can be patient again."

Sea gulls were flying and crying. The smell of the sea was different from home, tanged with salt and seaweed and fish. The sun set before they reached the narrow main street, and the harbour was brimming with the limpid colours of the afterglow.

People, she thought, stared at them. No doubt he was a well-known figure in the town. Would the prejudice be very strong against him? If any remained, then it was her task to break it down. There could clearly be none against her.

She glanced sidelong at him for a moment, and the thought came into her head that they had met not three dozen times in all their lives. Had she things to face that she knew nothing of yet? Well, if they loved each other there was no other consideration big enough to stand beside it.

They stopped and he helped her down and they went into the porticoed house. Mrs. Stevens was at the door and greeted Verity pleasantly enough, though not without a trace of speculation and jealousy.

Verity was shown the dining-room and kitchen on the ground floor, the graceful parlour and bedroom on the first floor, the two attic bedrooms above, which were for the children when they were home, these children she had never seen. Esther, sixteen, was being educated by relatives; James, fifteen, a midshipman in the Navy. Verity had had so much opposition to face at home that she had hardly yet had time to consider the opposition she might find here.

Back in the parlour Andrew was standing looking out across the glimmering colours of the harbour. He turned as she came and stood beside him at the window. He took her hand. The gesture brought comfort.

"Which is your ship, Andrew?"

"She's well back from here, in St. Just's Pool. The tallest of the three. I doubt if you can make her out in this light."

"Oh, yes, she looks beautiful. Can I see over her sometime?"

"To-morrow if you wish." She suddenly felt his happiness. "Verity, I'll go now. I have asked Mrs. Stevens to serve your supper as soon as she can. You'll be tired from your ride and will not mind being quiet."

"Can you not stay to supper?"

He hesitated. "If you wish it."

"Please. What a lovely harbour this is! I shall be able to sit here and see all the shipping go in and out and watch for your coming home."

In a few minutes they went down into the little dining-room and ate boiled neck of mutton with capers, and raspberries and cream. An hour ago they had been very adult, making a rash gesture with strange caution, as if unable quite to free themselves of the restraints and hesitations grown with the years. But the candlelight loosed thoughts, softened doubts and discovered pride in their adventure.

They had never had a meal together before.

Net curtains were drawn across the windows, and figures crossed and recrossed them in the street outside. In the room they were a little below the level of the cobbles, and when a cart rumbled past the wheels showed up more than the driver.

They began to talk about his ship, and he told her of Lisbon, its chiming bells, the endless blazing sunlight, the unbelievable filth of the streets, the orange trees, the olive groves. Sometime she must go with him. Was she a good sailor?

She nodded eagerly, never having been to sea.

They laughed together, and a clock in the town began to strike ten. He got up.

"This is disgraceful, love. Compromising in the eyes of Mrs. Stevens, I'm sure. She'll expect us to have eaten all her cakes."

"I'm so glad you stayed," she said. "If you had gone before I should have felt very strange here alone."

His self-disciplined face was very much unguarded just then. "Last night I closed a book on my old life, Verity. To-morrow we'll open a new one. We must write it together."

"That's what I want," she said. "I'm not at all afraid."

He walked to the door, and then glanced at her still sitting at the table. He came back.

"Good night."

He bent to kiss her cheek, but she offered him her lips. They stayed so a moment; and his hand on the table came up and lay on her shoulder.

"If ill comes to you, Verity, it will not be my doing. I swear it. Good night, love."

"Good night, Andrew, my love, good night."

He broke away and left her. She heard him run upstairs for his hat and then come down again and go out. She saw him pass the window.

She stayed there for a very long time, her eyes half closed and her head resting back against the high-backed chair.

CHAPTER IV At about the time Verity was climbing the stairs with a candle to sleep in her new bed, Mark Daniel was taking up his pitch in Wheal Leisure Mine.

With him was one of the younger Martin boys, Matthew Mark, who was there to help him by carrying away the "dead" ground as he picked it and dumping it in a pit in the near-by cave. The air was so bad in here that their hempen candles would not burn properly; so that they worked in more than half darkness. The walls of the tunnel streamed with moisture and there was water and slush underfoot. But Matthew Mark thought himself lucky to work for so experienced a man for sixpence a day—or night—and he was learning fast. In another few years he would be bidding for a pitch of his own.

Mark never had much to say when he was working, but to-night he had not spoken a word. The boy did not know what was wrong and was afraid to ask. Being only just nine, he might not have understood quite what was gnawing at his companion even if he had been told.

For days now Mark had given up trying to believe there was nothing wrong. For weeks he had known in his heart but had said no to himself. The little signs had piled up, the hints from those who knew and did not dare, the sly glances; small by themselves, they had grown like snowflakes on a roof, weight to weight, until the roof crashed in.

He knew now, and he knew who.

She had been clever. He had always looked for signs of a man in the cottage but had never found any. He had tried to catch her out, but always she thought ahead of him. Her wits moved quick. The snow leopard was sharper than the black bear.

But in the wet weather of last week she had not been so clever. The ground had been so soft that even though she kept to the stony places there were marks here and there of her feet.

He dreaded this week of nightwork because it would bring him to some climax. The fear he felt in breaking out was because he could not shake his anger free from the clinging strands of his love. They still bound him; he struggled in a mesh with his grief.

The powder for blasting was needed now. He could go no farther with the pick. He said as much to Matthew and picked up his great hammer and the steel borer. With ease come from long practice he chose his place in the hard rock, drilled a deep hole in the face of the work, pulled out the borer and cleaned and dried the hole. Then he took up his case of powder and dropped powder in. Through the powder he pushed a tapering rod like an iron nail and filled up the mouth of the hole with clay, ramming it hard with his boring bar. This done, he pulled out the nail and into the thin hole threaded a hollow reed filled with powder, for a fuse.

He took off his hat, gently blew the smoky candle until it flickered into a flame and lit the reed. Then they both backed away round the first corner.

Mark counted twenty. Nothing. He counted another twenty. He counted fifty. Then he picked up his can and swore. In the darkness he had planted it against the wall and water had got into it.

"A misfire," he said.

"Have a care, Mr. Daniel," Matthew said. Blasting was the part of mining he did not like. "Give it a while."

But Mark had grunted and was already walking up to the charge. The boy followed.

As Mark drew out the reed there was a flash and a rumble and the rocks flew in his face. He put up hands to his eyes and fell back. The wall gave way.

The boy lost his head and turned and ran away, going for help. Then he checked himself and pushed his way through the choking black fumes to where Mark was trying to climb out from among the rocks.

He caught at his arm. "Mr. Daniel! Mr. Daniel!"

"Get back, boy! There's only a part gone."

But Matthew would not leave him and they groped their way to the bend in the tunnel.

Matthew blew on his candle, and in the flickering light stared at Mark. His gaunt face was black and striped with blood, his front hair and eyebrows singed.

"Your eyes, Mr. Daniel. Are they all right?"

Mark stared at the candle. "Aye; I can see." There was another roar in the tunnel as the rest of the charge went off. Black smoke billowed out and around them. "Take heed, boy, an' a warning that you always d'use the powder wi' a greaterer care."

"Your face. Thur's blood."

Mark stared down at his hands. "Tes these." His left hand was bleeding from the palm and fingers. The dampness of the powder had caused the accident but it had saved his life. He took out a dirty rag and wrapped it round his head.

"We'll wait till the fumes clear, an' then we'll see what it's brought down."

Matthew sat back on his heels and looked at the blood-streaked figure. "You did ought to see surgeon. He's proper with wounds an' things."

Mark got up sharply. "Nay. I'd not go to him if I was dying." He turned into the smoke.

They worked on for a time, but he found it hard to use his injured hand, which would not stop bleeding. His face was stinging and sore.

After an hour he said: "Reckon I'll go up to grass for a bit. You'd best come too, boy. There's no good breathin' this black air if you've no need."

Matthew followed him gladly enough. The nightwork tired him more than he would admit.

They reached the main shaft and climbed up it; the distance was nothing to Grambler and they were soon sniffing the fresh night air and hearing the rumble of the sea. There was a lovely biting sweetness in filling your lungs as you came up to grass. One or two men were about, and they clustered round Mark giving him advice.

He had come up to have a proper bandage put on and go below again. But as he stood there talking with the others and let his fingers be tied up, all the old trouble came back and he knew with angry panic that this was the moment for the test.

For a while he resisted, feeling it sprung on him too soon, that he had need to be prepared. Then he turned to Matthew and said:

"Run along home, boy. Twill be better for me not to go b'low again to-night."

When Matthew Mark was out and working he never let himself think of sleep—it didn't do—but now he was overwhelmed. It was little after midnight. A whole six extra hours in bed! He waited respectfully for a moment to walk part way home with Mark, but another gruff word sent him off in the direction of Mellin Cottages.

Mark saw him out of sight, then briefly bade good night to the other men and followed. He had told them he didn't know whether to bother Dr. Enys; but in fact his mind was quite made up. He knew just what he was going to do.

He walked quietly home. As the cottage showed up in the starlight he felt his chest grow tight. He would have prayed if he had been a praying man, for his own mistake, for Keren's trueness, for a new life of trust. He came to the door, reached out for the latch, grasped it, pressed.

The door opened.

Breathe hard now and clumsily go in; he couldn't hold his breath, it panted away as if he'd been running for his life. No stop to make a light but pass through into the bedroom. Shutters were closed, and in the dark with unhurt hand grope a way round the walls of the cottage —his cottage—to the bed. The corner, the rough blanket. Sit on the edge and hand move over bed for Keren—his Keren. She was not there.

With a deep grunt of pain he sat there knowing this was the end. His breath was in sobs. He sat and panted and sobbed. Then he got up.

Out in the night again a pause to rub fingers over his eyes, to look right and left, to sniff, to set off for Mingoose.

The Gatehouse looked in darkness. He made a circle, sizing it up. A chink of light in an upper window.

Stop and stare and try to fight down the pain. It was in his blood, beating through him. The door of the house.

And there he stopped. To hammer to be let in would give warning. Time to think before they opened. She might slip out another way. They both thought so much quicker. They'd brazen it out. This time he must have proof.

I'll wait, he thought.

He crept slowly away, his long back bent, until he was just right to watch the front door or the back.

I'll crouch here and wait.

The stars moved up the sky, climbing and turning on their endless roundabout. A gentle wind stirred and sighed among the bracken and the brake, stirred and moved and then lay down again to sleep. A cricket began to saw among the gorse, and somewhere overhead a night-hawk cried: a ghostly sound, the spirit of a long-dead miner walking sightless over his old land. Small animals stirred in the undergrowth. An owl settled on the roof top and harshly cried.

I'll wait.

Then in the east a faint yellow light showed, and there crept up into the sky the wasted slip of an old moon. It hung there sere and dry, climbed a little, and then began to set.

The door of the Gatehouse opened a few inches and Keren slipped out.

For once she was happy. Happy that this was only the first night of Mark's night core. Their way—hers and Dwight's—was still strange, touched with things which had never been in her first thoughts. Possessive and a little jealous, she found herself forced to allow a division of his loyalty. His work was his first love. She had reached him by taking an interest in his work. She held him by maintaining it.

Not that she really minded. In a way she enjoyed playing the role of sober helpmeet. Something like her old part in *Hilary Tempest*. She sometimes dreamed of herself as his wife—Mark out of the way—wholly charming in a workmanlike but feminine dress, helping Dwight in some serious strait. Her hands, she knew, would be cool and capable, her manner superbly helpful; he would be full of admiration for her afterwards; and not only he but all the gentry of the countryside. She would be talked of everywhere. She had heard all about Mistress Poldark having been a great success at the celebration ball, and quite a number of people had been riding over to see her since then. Keren could not think why.

It had gone to her head, for she'd thought fit last month to come the lady and drop a hint to Keren about being careful what she did; and Keren had resented it. Well, if she were so successful in society, Keren, as a doctor's wife, would go much further. She might not even stay a doctor's wife all her life. There was no limit to what might happen. A big, hairy elderly man, who had been over to the Poldarks one day, had met her as she crossed Nampara Combe, and he had given her more than a moment's look. When she knew he was a baronet and unmarried she'd been thankful for wearing that flimsy frock.

She ploughed through the rough undergrowth on her way back to the cottage. It had been the half after three by Dwight's clock, so there was nice time. As well not to run it too close. A mist had settled on the low ground between the two houses. She plunged into it as into a stream. Things were hung heavy with moisture; the damp touched her face and glistened on her hair. Some moonflowers showed among the scrub, and she picked one as she passed. She groped across the gully, climbed again and came out into the crystal-cool air.

So to-night as she lay naked in Dwight's arms she had encouraged him to talk: about the work of the day, about the little boy who had died of the malignant sore throat over at Marasanvose, about the results of his treatment on a woman in bed with an abscess, about his thoughts for the future. All this was like a cement to their passion. It had to be with him. She did not really mind.

The moon was setting as she reached the cottage, and dawn was blueing the east. Back the way she had come the gully was as if filled with a stream of milk. Everywhere else was clear.

She went in and turned to close the door. But as she did so a hand from outside came to press it open. "Keren."

Her heart stopped; and then it began to bang. It banged till it mounted to her head and seemed to split.

"Mark!" she whispered. "You're home early. Is anything wrong?"

"Keren . . ."

"How dare you come startling me like this! I nearly died!"

Already she was thinking ahead of him, moving to attack and defeat his attack. But this time he had more than words to go on.

"Where've you been, Keren?"

"I?" she said. "I couldn't sleep. I have had a pain. Oh, Mark, I had such a terrible pain. I cried for you. I thought perhaps you could have made me something warm to send it better. But I was all alone. I didn't know what to do. So I thought maybe a walk would help. If I'd known

you was coming home early I'd have come to the mine to meet you."
In the half-dark her sharp eyes caught sight of the bandage on his hand.
"Oh, Mark, you're hurt! There's been an accident. Let me see!"

She moved to him, and he struck her in the mouth with his burnt
hand, knocked her back across the room. She fell in a small injured
heap.

"Ye dirty liar! Ye dirty liar!" His breath was coming in sobs again.

She wept with her hurt. A strange, kittenish, girlish weeping, so far
from his own.

He moved over to her. "Ye've been wi' Enys," he said in a terrible
voice.

She raised her head. "Dirty yourself! Dirty coward! Striking a
woman. Filthy beast! Get away from me! Leave me alone. I'll have you
sent to prison, you! Get out!"

A faint light was coming in from the glimmering dawn; it fell on his
singed and blackened face. Through the screen of her hands and hair
she saw him, and at the sight she began to cry out.

"You've been wi' Enys, lying wi' Enys!" His voice climbed in great
strides.

"I've not! I've not!" she screamed. "Liar yourself! I went to see him
about my pain. He's a doctor, ain't he? You filthy brute. I was in such
pain."

Even now the quick-thoughted lie gave him pause. Above all things
he had always wanted to be fair, to do the right thing by her.

"How long was you there?"

"Oh . . . over an hour. He gave me something to take an' then
had to wait an——"

He said: "I waited more'n three."

She knew then that she must go and go quickly.

"Mark," she said desperately, "it isn't what you think. I swear before
God it isn't. If you see him he'll explain. Let's go to him. Mark, he
wouldn't leave me alone. He was always pestering me. Always and all
the time. And then when once I yielded he threatened he'd tell you if I
didn't go on. I swear it before God and my mother's memory. I hate
him, Mark! I love only you! Go kill him if you want. He deserves it,
Mark! I swear before God he took the advantage of me!"

She went on, babbling at him, throwing words at him, any words,
pebbles at a giant, her only defence. She sprayed words, keeping his
great anger away from her, twisting her brain this way and that. Then
when she saw that it was going to avail no longer she sprang like a cat
under his arm, leapt for the door.

He thrust out one great hand and caught her by the air, hauled her
screaming back into his arms.

She fought with all strength in her power, kicking, biting, scratching. He pushed her nails away from his eyes, accepting her bites as if they were no part of him. He pulled the cloth away from her throat, gripped it.

Her screaming stopped. Her eyes started tears, died, grew big. She knew there was death; but life called her, sweet life, all the sweet of youth, not yet gone. Dwight, the baronet, years of triumph, crying, dying.

She twisted and upset him and they fell against the shutter, whose flimsy catch gave way. They leaned together out of the window, she beneath him.

A summer morning. The glazing eyes of the girl he loved, the woman he hated; her face swollen now. Sickened, mad, his tears dropped on her face.

Loose his hold, but her beautiful face still stared. Cover it with a great hand, push it away, back.

Under his hand, coming from under his hand, a faint gentle click.

He fell back upon the floor of the cottage, groping, moaning upon the floor.

But she did not move.

There was no cloud in the sky. There was no wind. Birds were chirping and chattering. Of the second brood of young thrushes which Mark had watched hatch out in the stunted hawthorn tree only a timid one stayed; the others were out fluttering their feathers, shaking their heads, sharp with incentive, eyeing this strange new world.

The ribbon of milky mist still lay in the gully. It stretched down to the sea, and there were patches across the sand hills like steam from a kettle.

When light came full the sea was calm, and there seemed nothing to explain the roar in the night. The water was a pigeon's-egg blue with a dull terra-cotta haze above the horizon and a few pale carmine tips where the rising sun caught the ripples at the sand's edge.

The ugly shacks of Wheal Leisure were clear-cut, and a few men moving about among them in their drab clothes looked pink and handsome in the early light.

The mist stirred before the sun's rays, quickened with the warmth and melted and moved off to the low cliffs, where it crouched in the shade for a while before being thrust up and away.

A robin that Keren and Mark had tamed fluttered down to the open door, puffed out his little chest and hopped inside. But although the cottage was silent he did not like the silence, and after pecking here and there for a moment he hopped out. Then he saw one of his friends leaning out of the window, but she made no welcoming sound and he flew away.

The sun fell in at the cottage, strayed across the sanded floor, which was pitted and scraped with the marks of feet. A tinderbox lay among the sand, and the stump of a candle, a miner's hat beside an upturned chair.

The moonflower Keren had picked lay on the threshold. Its head had been broken in the struggle but the petals were still white and damp with a freshness that would soon begin to fade.

CHAPTER V   Ross had been dreaming that he was arguing about the smelting works with Sir John Trevaunance and the other shareholders. It was not an uncommon dream or one which went by contraries. Half his waking life was made up of defending the Carnmore Copper Company from inward fission or outside attack. For the battle was fully joined, and no one could tell which way it would go.

Nothing much was barred in this struggle. Pressure had been brought to bear on United Mines, and Richard Tonkin had been forced out of the managership. Sir John Trevaunance had a lawsuit dragging on in Swansea over his coal ships.

Ross dreamed there was a meeting at Trevaunance's home, as there was to be in a few days, and that everyone was quarrelling at once. He pounded the table again and again trying to gain a hearing. But no one would listen and the more he pounded the more they talked, until suddenly everyone fell silent and abruptly he found himself awake in the silent room and listening to the knocking on the front door.

It was quite light and the sun was falling across the half-curtained windows. The Gimletts should be up soon. He reached for his watch but as usual had forgotten to wind it. Demelza's dark hair clouded the pillow beside him, and her breathing came in a faint *tic-tic*. She was always a good sleeper; if Julia woke she would be out and about and asleep again in five minutes.

Hasty footsteps went downstairs and the knocking stopped. He slid out of bed and Demelza sat up, as usual wide-awake, as if she had never been asleep at all.

"What is it?"

"I don't know, my dear."

There was a knock on the door and Ross opened it. Somehow in such emergencies he still expected to see Jud standing there.

"If you please, sur," said Gimlett, "a boy wants to see you. Charlie

Baragwanath, who's gardener's boy over to Mingoose. He's terrible upset."

"I'll be down."

Demelza breathed a quiet sigh into the bedclothes. She had thought it something about Verity. All yesterday, lovely yesterday, of which they had spent a good part on the beach in the sun paddling their feet in the sun-warmed water, all the time she had thought of Verity. It had been Verity's day of release, for which she, Demelza, had plotted and schemed for more than a year. She had wondered and waited.

With only her eyes showing over the rim of the bedclothes she watched Ross dress and go down. She wished people would leave them alone. All she wanted was to be left alone with Ross and Julia. But people came more, especially her suitors, as Ross satirically called them. Sir Hugh Bodrugan had been several times to tea.

Ross came back. She could tell at once that something was wrong.

"What is it?"

"Hard to get sense out of the boy. I believe it is something at the mine."

She sat up. "An accident?"

"No. Go to sleep for a little. It is not much after five."

He went down again and joined the undersized boy, whose teeth were chattering as if with cold. He gave him a sip or two of brandy and they set off through the apple trees over the hill.

"Were you first there?" Ross asked.

"Aye, sur . . . I—I b'long to call that way on my way over. Not as they're always about not at this time o' year when I'm s'early; but I always b'long to go that way. I thought they was all out. An' then I seen 'er ·. . . an' then I seen 'er. . . ."

He covered his face with his hands.

"Honest, sur, I near fainted away. I near fell away on the spot."

As they neared the cottage they saw three men standing outside. Paul Daniel and Zacky Martin and Nick Vigus.

Ross said: "Is it as the boy says?"

Zacky nodded.

"Is anyone . . . inside?"

"No, sur."

"Does anyone know where Mark is?"

"No, sur."

"Have you sent for Dr. Enys?"

"Just sent, sur."

"Aye, we've sent fur he, sure 'nough," said Paul Daniel bitterly. Ross glanced at him.

"Will you come in with me, Zacky," he said.

They went to the open door together, then Ross stooped his head and went in.

She was lying on the floor covered with a blanket. The sun from the window streamed across the blanket in a golden flood.

"The boy said . . ."

"Yes . . . We moved 'er. It didn't seem decent to leave the poor creature."

Ross knelt and lifted back the blanket. She was wearing the scarlet kerchief Mark had won at the wrestling match twenty months before. He put back the blanket, rose, wiped his hands.

"Zacky, where was Mark when this happened?" He said it in an undertone, as if not to be overheard.

"He should have been down the mine, Cap'n Ross, should by rights have been coming up now. But he had an accident early on his core. Matthew Mark was home to bed before one. Nobody has seen Mark Daniel since then."

"Have you any idea where he is?"

"That I couldn't say."

"Have you sent for the parish constable?"

"Who? Old Vage? Did we oughter have done?"

"No, this is Jenkins's business. This is Mingoose Parish."

A shadow fell across the room. It was Dwight Enys. The only colour in his face was in the eyes, which seemed suffused, as in a fever. "I . . ." He glanced at Ross, then at the figure on the floor. "I came . . ."

"A damned nasty business, Dwight." Friendship made Ross turn away from the young man towards Paul Daniel, who had followed him in. "Come, we should leave Dr. Enys alone while he makes his examination."

Paul seemed ready to challenge this; but Ross had just too much authority to be set aside, and presently they were all out in the sun. Ross glanced back and saw Dwight stoop to move the cloth. His hand was trembling and he looked as if he might fall across the body in a faint.

All that day there was no word of Mark Daniel. Blackened and hurt, he had come up from the mine at midnight, and in the early hours of Monday morning had put his stamp upon unfaithfulness and deceit. Then the warm day had taken him.

So much everyone knew. For like the quiet movement of wind among grass, the whisper of Keren's deceit had spread through villages and hamlets round, and no one doubted that this had brought her death. And curiously, no one seemed to doubt the justice of the end. It

228

was the Biblical punishment. From the moment she came here she had flaunted her body at other men. One other man, and they knew Who, had fallen into her lure. Any woman with half an eye would have known that Mark Daniel was not to be cuckolded lightly. She had known the risk and had taken it, matching her sharp wits against his slow strength. For a time she had gone on and then she had made a slip and that had been the end. It might not be law but it was justice.

And the Man in the case might thank his stars he too wasn't laid across the floor with a broken neck. He might yet find himself that way if he didn't watch out. If they were in his shoes they'd get on a horse and ride twenty miles and stay away while Mark Daniel was at large. For all his scholaring he was not much more than a slip of a boy, and Daniel could snap him as easy as a twig.

There wasn't much feeling against him, as there might well have been. In the months he had been here they had grown to like him, to respect him, where they all disliked Keren. They might have risen against him as a breaker of homes; but instead they saw Keren as the temptress who had led him away. Many a wife had seen Keren look at *her* man. It wasn't the surgeon's fault, they said. But all the same they wouldn't be in *his* shoes. He'd had to go in and examine the body, and it was said that when he came out the sweat was pouring off his face.

At six that evening Ross went to see Dwight.

At first Bone would not admit him; Doctor had said in no circumstances was he to be disturbed. But Ross brushed him aside.

Dwight was sitting at a table with a pile of papers before him and a look of hopeless despair on his face. He hadn't changed his clothes since this morning and he hadn't shaved. He glanced at Ross and got up.

"Is it something important?"

"There's no news. That's what is important, Dwight. If I were you I should not stay here until nightfall. Go and spend a few days with the Pascoes."

"What for?" he asked stupidly.

"Because Mark Daniel is a dangerous man. D'you think if he chose to seek you out Bone or a few locked doors would stop him?"

Dwight put his hands to his face. "So the truth is known everywhere."

"Enough to go on. One can do nothing in private in a country district. For the time being——"

He said: "I'll never forget her face! Two hours before I'd been kissing it!"

Ross went across and poured him a glass of brandy.

"Drink this. You're lucky to be alive and we must keep you so."

"I fail to see any good reason."

Ross checked himself. "Listen, boy," he said more gently, "you must

229

take a good hold on yourself. This thing is done and can't be undone. What I wish above all is to prevent more mischief. I'm not here to judge you."

"I know," said the young man. "I know, Ross. I only judge myself."

"And that, no doubt, too harshly. Anyone sees that this tragedy has been of the girl's making. I don't know how much you came to feel for her."

Dwight broke down. "I don't know myself, Ross. I don't know. When I saw her lying there, I—I thought I had loved her."

Ross poured himself a drink. When he came back Dwight had partly recovered.

"The great thing is to get away for a time. Just for a week or so. The magistrates have issued a warrant for Mark's arrest, and the constables are out. That is all that can be done for the moment and it may be enough. But if Mark wants to evade capture I'm sure it will not be enough, because although every villager is bound by law to help in his capture, I don't believe one of them will raise a hand."

"They take his side, and rightly so."

"But not against you, Dwight. However, in a day or two other measures may be taken, and in a week Mark should be put away and it should be safe for you to return."

Dwight got up, rocking his half-empty glass.

"No, Ross! What d'you take me for! To skulk away in a safe place while the man is tracked down and then to come slinking back! I'd sooner meet him at once and take the outcome." He began to walk up and down the room. Then he came to a stop. "See it my way. On all counts I've let these people down. I came among them a stranger and a physician. I have met with nothing worse than suspicion and much that's been better than kindness. Eggs that could be ill spared pressed on me in return for some fancied favour. Little gestures of good will even from people who are Choake's people. Confidence and trust. In return I have helped to break up the life of one of their number. If I went now I should go for good, a cheat and a failure."

Ross said nothing.

"But the other way and the harder way is to see this thing out and to take my chance. Look, Ross, there is another case of sore throat at Marasanvose. There is a woman with child at Grambler who nearly died last time with the ill management of a midwife. There are four cases of miner's consumption which are improving under treatment. There are people here and there trusting on me. Well, I've betrayed them; but it would be a greater betrayal to leave now—to leave them to Thomas Choake's farmyard methods."

"I was not saying you should."

Dwight shook his head. "The other's impossible."

"Then spend a few days with us. We have a room. Bring your man."

"No. Thank you for your kindness. From to-morrow morning I go about as usual."

Ross stared at him grimly. "Then your blood be on your own head."

Dwight put his hand up to his eyes. "Keren's blood is already there."

From the Gatehouse, Ross went direct to the Daniels. They were all sitting round in the half gloom of the cottage doing nothing. They were like mourners at a wake. All the adult family was present except Beth, Paul's wife, who was sharing Keren's lonely vigil in the cottage over the hill. Despised by Keren in life, Beth could yet not bear the thought of allowing her to lie untended all through the summer evening.

Old Man Daniel was sucking his clay pipe and talking, talking. Nobody seemed to listen; the old man didn't seem to care. He was trying to talk his grief and anxiety out of himself.

"I well call to mind when I was on Lake Superior in 'sixty-nine thur were a case not mislike this'n. On Lake Superior in 'sixty-nine—or were it 'seventy?—a man runned off wi' the storekeeper's woman. I well call it to mind. But twur through no fault——"

They greeted Ross respectfully, Grannie Daniel hopping tearfully off her shaky stool and inviting him to sit down. Ross was always very polite to Grannie Daniel, and she always tried to return it in kind. He thanked her and refused, saying he wanted a word in private with Paul.

"Twur through no fault of 'is. A man runned off wi' the storekeeper's woman, an' he plucked out a spade an' went arter 'em. Just wi' a spade. Nought else but a spade."

Paul straightened up his back and quietly followed Ross out into the sun. Then he closed the door and stood a little defensively with his back against it. There were other people about, standing at the doors of their cottages and talking, but they were out of earshot. "No news of Mark?"

"No, sur."

"Have you an idea where he could be?"

"No, sur."

"I suppose Jenkins has questioned you?"

"Yes, sur. And others in Mellin. But we don't know nothing."

"Nor would you tell anything if you did know, eh?"

Paul looked at his feet. "That's as may be."

"This is a different crime from petty theft, Paul. If Mark had been caught stealing something from a shop he might be transported for it; but if he hid for a time it might be forgotten. Not so with murder."

"How do we know he done it, sur?"

231

"If he did not, why has he fled?"

Paul shrugged his big shoulders and narrowed his eyes at the declining sun.

"Perhaps I should tell you what is likely to happen, Paul. The magistrates have issued a warrant and sent out the constable. Old blacksmith Jenkins from Marasanvose will do his best and Vage from Sawle will help too. I don't think they'll be successful."

"Maybe not."

"The magistrates will then organize a search. A man hunt is a very ugly thing. It should be avoided."

Paul Daniel shifted but did not speak.

Ross said: "I have known Mark since I was a boy, Paul. I should be unhappy to think of him hunted down perhaps with dogs and later swinging on a gibbet."

" 'E'll swing on a gibbet if he give his self up," Paul said.

"Do you know where he is?"

"I don't know nothing. But I can 'ave me own ideas."

"Yes, indeed." Ross had found out what he wanted. "Listen, Paul. You know Nampara Cove? Of course. There are two caves. In one cave is a boat."

The other man looked up sharply. "Yes?"

"It is a small boat. One I use for fishing just around the coast. The oars I keep on a shelf at the back of the cave. The rowlocks are at home so that she shall not be used without my sanction."

Paul licked his lips. "Aye?"

"Aye. Also at home is a detachable mast and a pair of sails which can turn the boat into a cutter. She's a weatherly little craft, I know from experience. Not fit for ocean going when the seas are steep; but a resolute man could fare a lot worse in summer time. Now Mark is finished so far as England is concerned. But up in the north there's Ireland. And down in the south is France, where there's trouble at present. He has acquaintances in Brittany and he's made the crossing before."

"Aye?" said Paul, beginning to sweat.

"Aye," said Ross.

"An' what of the sails and the rullocks?"

"They might find their way down to the cave after dark. And a few bits of food to keep a man alive. It was just an idea."

Paul rubbed his forearm over his forehead. "Be thanked for the idea. Why, if——"

"I make one condition," Ross said, tapping him on the chest with a long forefinger. "This is a secret between two or three. Being accessory to murder is not a pretty thing. I will not have the Viguses privy to it, for Nick has a slippery way of letting things escape him when they are to the detriment of others. There are those in authority who would find a greater relish in their meals if I ran my neck into a noose. Well, I don't intend to do that, not for you nor your brother nor all the broken hearts in Mellin. So you must go careful. Zacky Martin would help you if you needed another outside your own family."

"Nay, I'll keep it to myself, sur. There's no need for others to be in on it. Twould kill the old man to see Mark swing—an' mebbe old Grannie too, though there's no guessing what she'll survive, like. But tes the disgrace of it. If so be——"

"Do you know where he is now?"

"I know where I can leave un a note; we used to play so as lads. But I reckon twill be to-morrow night 'fore anything can be done. First I've to fix a meetin', and then I've to persuade'n as tis best for all that he go. They d'say he's fair broke up with it all."

"Some have seen him then?"

Paul glanced quickly at the other man. "Aye."

"I don't think he will refuse to go if you mention his father. But make it urgent. It must be not later than to-morrow."

"Aye. I'll do that. If so be as it can be fixed for to-night I'll leave ee know. An' *thank* ee, sur. Them as don't know can't ever thank ee, but they would, fairly they would!"

Ross turned to walk back. Paul re-entered the cottage. Inside Old Man Daniel was going on just as if he had never stopped in his quavering, rusty voice, talking round and round to stop the silence from falling.

CHAPTER VI   Thoughtfully Ross walked back to Nampara. He found John Gimlett cleaning the windows of the library, for which Mrs. Gimlett had been making needlework curtains. The industry of the Gimletts, contrasting with the sloth of the Paynters, always surprised him afresh. The garden prospered. Last year Demelza had bought some hollyhock seeds, and in the windless summer they had coloured the walls of the house with their stately purples and crimsons. Julia lay in her cot in the shade of the trees and, seeing her awake, he walked across and picked her up. She crowed and laughed and clutched at his hair.

Demelza had been gardening, and Ross ran with Julia on his shoulder to meet her. She was in her white muslin dress and it gave him a queer twist of pleasure to see that she was wearing gloves. Gradually, without pretentiousness or haste, she was moving towards little refinements of habit.

She had matured this summer. The essential impish vitality of her would never alter, but it was more under her control. She had also grown to accept the startling fact that men found her worth pursuing.

Julia crowed with joy and Demelza took her from him.

"There is another tooth, Ross. See here. Put your finger just here. Is your finger clean? Yes, it will do. Now."

"Yes, indeed. She'll soon be able to bite like Garrick."

"Is there news of Mark?"

In an undertone Ross told her.

Demelza glanced at Gimlett. "Will it not be a great risk?"

"Not if it is done quick. I fancy Paul knows more than he has told me, and that Mark will come to-night."

"I am afraid for you. I should be afraid to tell anyone."

"I only hope Dwight will keep indoors until he is safe away."

"Oh, there is a letter for you from Elizabeth," Demelza said, as if she had just remembered.

She felt in her apron pocket and brought out the letter. Ross broke the seal.

DEAR ROSS [it ran],

As you may know Verity left us last night for Captain Blamey. She left while we were at Evensong and has gone with him to Falmouth. They are to be married to-day.

ELIZABETH.

Ross said: "Well, so she has done it at last! I greatly feared she might."

Demelza read the letter.

"Why should they not be happy together? It is what I have always said, it is better to take a risk than mope away all your life in dull comfort and secureness."

"Why 'As you may know'? Why should she think I would know?"

"Perhaps it is already about."

Ross pushed back the hair Julia had ruffled. It was an action which made him suddenly boyish. Yet his expression was not so.

"I do not fancy her life with Blamey. Yet you may be right in thinking she'll be happy with him. I pray she will." He released his other hand from Julia's clinging grasp. "It never rains but it pours. This means I must go to Trenwith and see them. The letter is abrupt in tone. I expect they are upset."

So it has all come, Demelza thought, and Verity by now is married to him, and I too pray they will be happy together, for if they are not I shall not be easy in my bed.

"It is less than an hour to sunset," Ross said. "I shall have to make haste." He looked at her. "I suppose you would not go and see them in my place?"

"Elizabeth and Francis? Judas, no! Oh, no, Ross. I would do a lot for you, but not that."

"I don't see that you need feel such alarm. But of course I must go. I wonder what at last brought Verity to the plunge—after all these years. I think also she might have left some letter for me."

When Ross had gone Demelza set Julia on her feet and allowed her to walk about the garden on her leading strings. She toddled here and there, crowing with delight and trying hard to get at the flowers. In the meantime Gimlett finished the windows and picked up his pail and went in, and Demelza thought her thoughts and watched the sun go down. It was not the sort of sunset one would have expected to follow the day; the sky was streaked and watery and the light faded quickly.

As the dew began to fall she picked up the child and carried her in. Gimlett had already taken in the cot and Mrs. Gimlett was lighting the candles. The Paynters' going had helped Demelza in her quest for ladyship.

She fed Julia on a bowl of bread and broth and saw her safely to sleep, and it was not till then that she realized Ross had been gone too long.

She went down the stairs and to the open front door. The fall of night had drawn a cloud across the sky, and a light cool wind moved among the trees. The weather was on the change. Over in the distance she caught the queer lap-dog bark of a moor hen.

Then she saw Ross coming through the trees.

Darkie neighed when she saw her at the door. Ross jumped off and looped the reins over the lilac tree.

"Has anyone been?"

"No. You've been a long time."

"I've seen Jenkins—also Will Nanfan, who always knows everything. Two other constables are to help Jenkins. Bring a candle, will you; I'd like to get those sails down at once."

She went with him into the library.

"The wind is rising. He must go to-night if it's at all possible. To-morrow may be too late for another reason."

"What's that, Ross?"

"Sir Hugh is one of the magistrates concerned, and he's pressing for calling in the military. Apparently she—Keren—apparently Sir Hugh had noticed her, seen her about, thought her attractive, you know what a lecherous old roué he is——"

"Yes, Ross. . . ."

"So he's taking a personal interest. Which is bad for Mark. He has another reason too."

"How is that?"

"You remember at St. Ann's last week when the Revenue man was mishandled. The authorities have sent out a troop of dragoons to-day to St. Ann's. They are to be stationed there for a time as a cautionary measure, and may make a search during their stay. Sir Hugh, as you know, is a friend of Mr. Trencrom and buys all his spirits there. It would not be unnatural to take attention from the smugglers for a day by asking help in a search for a murderer."

". . . Shall I come down to the cave with you?"

"No, I shall not be more than half an hour."

"And—Verity . . . ?"

Ross paused at the door of the library with the mast on his shoulder. "Oh . . . Verity is gone sure enough. And I have had a fantastic quarrel with Francis."

"A quarrel?" She had sensed there was something else.

"In good measure. He taxed me with having arranged this elopement and even refused to believe me when I said not. I've never been so taken aback in my life. I gave him credit for some degree of—of intelligence."

Demelza moved suddenly, as if trying to shift the cold feeling that had settled on her.

"But, my dear . . . why you?"

"Oh, they thought I had been using you as a go-between; picking up his letters somewhere and getting you to deliver them to Verity. I could have knocked him down. Anyway, we have broken for a long time. There will not be any easy patching up after what has been said."

"Oh, Ross, I'm . . . that sorry . . . I . . ."

To hide his own discomfort he said lightly: "Now stay about somewhere while I'm gone. And tell Gimlett I'm back. It will occupy him to tend on Darkie."

So in a few minutes more she was alone again. She had walked a little way along the stream with him and had watched his figure move into the dark. From this point you could hear the waves breaking in the cove.

Before she had been uneasy, a little nervy and anxious, for it was not pleasant to be helping a murderer to escape. But now her unhappiness was a different thing, solid and personal and settled firm, as if it would never move, for it touched the all-important matter of her relations with Ross. For a year she had worked untiringly for Verity's happiness, worked open-eyed, knowing that what she was doing would be condemned by Ross and doubly condemned by Francis and Elizabeth. But she had never imagined that it would cause a break between Ross and his cousin. That was something outside all sensible counting. She was desperately troubled.

So deep was she in this that she did not notice the figure coming across the lawn towards the door. She had turned in and was closing the door when a voice spoke. She stepped back behind the door so that the lantern in the hall shone out.

"Dr. Enys!"

"I hadn't thought to startle you, Mistress Poldark. . . . Is your husband in?"

Having begun to thump, Demelza's heart was not quieting yet. There was another kind of danger here.

"Not at the moment."

Her eyes took in his dishevelled look, so changed from the neat, comely, black-coated young man of ordinary times. He might have been without sleep for a week. He stood there indecisive, conscious that he had not been asked in, knowing something guarded in her attitude but mistaking the causes.

"Do you imagine he'll be long?"

"About half an hour."

He part turned away as if leaving. But there he stopped. "Perhaps you'll forgive me for intruding on you . . . ?"

"Of course."

She led the way into the parlour. There might be danger or there might not: she could not avoid it.

He stood there very stiffly. "Don't let me interfere with anything you may be doing. I don't at all wish to interrupt you."

"No," she said in a soft voice, "I was doing nothing." She went across and drew the curtains, careful to leave no nicks. "As you'll see we are late with supper, but Ross has been busy. Would you take a glass of port?"

"Thank you, I won't. I . . ." As she turned from the window he said impulsively: "You condemn me for my part in this morning's tragedy?"

She coloured a little. "How can I condemn anyone when I know such a small bit about it?"

"I shouldn't have mentioned it. But I have been thinking—thinking all to-day and speaking to no one. To-night I felt I must come out, go out somewhere. And this house was the only one . . ."

She said: "It might be dangerous to be out to-night."

"I think highly of your opinion," he said. "Yours and Ross's. It was his confidence that brought me here; if I felt I had forfeited it, it would be better to cut and go."

"I don't think you've forfeited it. But I don't think he will be pleased by you coming here to-night."

"Why?"

"I should rather not explain that."

"Do you mean you want me to go?"

"I b'lieve it would be better." She picked up a plate from the table and set it in another place.

He looked at her. "I must have some assurance of your friendship—in spite of all. Alone in the Gatehouse this evening I have come near to—near to . . ." He did not finish.

She met his eyes.

"Stay then, Dwight," she said. "Sit down and don't bother 'bout me."

He slumped in a chair, passed his hands across his face. While Demelza pottered about and went in and out of the room he talked in snatches, explaining, arguing. Two things were absent, self-pity and self-apology. He seemed to be trying to make out a case for Keren. It was as if he felt she was being harshly judged and could offer no defence. He must speak for Keren.

Then the third time she went from the room and came back he did not go on. She glanced at him and saw him sitting tense.

"What is it?"

"I thought I heard someone tapping at the window."

Demelza's heart stopped beating altogether; then she gulped it into motion again. "Oh, I know what that is. Don't you get up. I will see for it myself."

Before he could argue she went out into the hall, shutting the parlour door behind her. So it had come. As she had feared. Now of all times. Pray Ross would not be long. Just for the moment she had to handle the crisis alone.

She went to the hall door and peered out. The dim lantern light showed an empty lawn. Something moved by the lilac bush.

"Beg pardon, ma'am," said Paul Daniel.

Her glance met his; strayed beyond him.

"Captain Ross has just gone down to the cove. Is . . . anyone with you?"

He hesitated. "You know about un?"

"I know."

He gave a low whistle. A dim figure broke from the side of the house. Paul leaned behind Demelza and pulled the hall door half shut so that the light should not shine out.

Mark stood before them. His face was in the shadow but she could see the caverns of his eyes.

"Cap'n Ross is down in the cove," said Paul. "We'd best go down to 'im."

Demelza said: "Sometimes Bob Baragwanath and Bob Nanfan go fishing there at high tide."

"We'll wait by yonder apple trees," said Paul. "We'll be well able to see 'im from thur."

And well able to see anyone leave the house. "You'll be safer indoors. You'll—be safer in the library."

She pushed open the door and moved into the hall, but they drew back and whispered together. Paul said:

"Mark don't want to tie you folk up wi' this more'n he can. He'd better prefer to wait outside."

"No, Mark. It don't matter to us. Come in at once!"

Paul entered the hall and after him Mark, bending his head to get in the doorway. Demelza had just time to take in the blisters on his forehead, the stone grey of his face, the bandaged hand, before she opened the door of the bedroom which led to the library. Then as she picked up the lantern to go in there was a movement at the other side of the hall. Their eyes flickered across to Dwight Enys standing in the threshold of the parlour.

CHAPTER VII   Silence swelled in the hall, and burst.

Paul Daniel had slammed the outer door.

He stood with his back to it. Mark, gaunt and monstrous, stood quite still, the veins growing thick and knotted in his neck and hands.

She moved then, turned on them both.

"Dwight, go back into the parlour. Go back at once! Mark, d'you hear me! Mark!" Her voice didn't sound like her own.

"So tes a bloody trap," said Mark.

She stood before him, slight and seeming small. "How dare you say that! Paul, have you no sense? Take him. This way, at once."

"You bastard, you," said Mark, looking over her head.

"You should have thought of that before," said Dwight. "Before you killed her."

"Damned slimy adulterer. Tradin' on your work. Foulin' the nests o' those you pertend to help."

"You should have come for me," Dwight said, "not broken a girl who couldn't defend herself."

"Yes, by God——"

Demelza moved between them as Mark stepped forward. Blindly he tried to brush her away, but instead of that she stood her ground and hammered him on the chest with her clenched fists. His eyes flickered, lingered, came down.

"D'you realize what this means to us?" she said, breathless, her eyes blazing. "We've done nothing. We're trying to help. Help you both. You'd fight and kill each other in *our* house, on *our* land. Have you no loyalty and—and friendship that stands for anything at all! What's brought you here to-night, Mark? Mebbe not the thought to save your own skin, but to save the disgrace for your father an' his family. Twould kill him. Well, which is most important to you, your father's life or this man's? Dwight, go back into the parlour *at once!*"

Dwight said: "I can't. If Daniel wants me I must stay."

"What's 'e doing 'ere?" said Paul to the girl.

Dwight said: "Mistress Poldark tried to drive me away."

"You bastard," said Mark again.

Demelza caught him by the arm as he was about to raise it. "In here. Else we shall have the servants coming and there'll be no secret at all."

He did not move an inch under her pressure. "There'll be no secret wi' him in the know. Come outside, Enys. I'll finish you there."

"Nay." Paul had been useless so far, but now he took a hand. "There's no sense in that, Mark. I think bad of the skunk, same as you, but twill finish everything if you fight him."

"Everything's finished already."

"It *isn't!*" cried Demelza. "It *isn't*, I tell you. Don't you see! Dr. Enys can't betray you without betraying us."

Dwight hesitated, every sort of different impulse clamouring. "I won't betray anyone," he said.

Mark spat out a harsh breath. "I'd as lief trust a snake."

Paul came up to him. "It is an ill meetin', Mark; but we can't do nothin' about en. Come, old dear, we must do what Mistress Poldark say."

Dwight put his hands up to his head. "I'll not betray you, Daniel. Three wrongs don't make a right any more than two. What you did to Keren is with your conscience, as—as my ill-doing is with mine."

Paul pushed Mark slowly towards the bedroom door. Abruptly Mark shook off his arm and stopped again. His gaunt terrible face worked for a moment.

"Mebbe this ain't the time for a reckoning, Enys. But it will come, never fear."

Dwight did not raise his head.

Mark looked down at Demelza, who was still standing like a guardian angel between him and his wrath. "Nay, ma'am, I'll not stain your floor with more blood. I'd not wish hurt to this 'ouse. . . . Where d'you want for me to go?"

. . . When Ross came back Dwight was in the parlour, his head buried in his hands. Mark and Paul were in the library, Mark every now and then shaking with a spasm of anger. In the hall, between them, Demelza stood sentinel. When she saw Ross she sat down in the nearest chair and burst into tears.

"What the Devil . . . ?" said Ross.

She spoke a few disjointed words.

He put the sail down in the corner of the hall.

"My dear . . . Where are they now? And you . . ."

She shook her head and pointed.

He came over to her. "And there'll been no bloodletting? My God, I'll swear it has never been nearer. . . ."

"You may swear it in truth," Demelza said.

He put his arm about her. "Did you stop it, love? Tell me, how did you stop it?"

"Why have you brought the sail back?" she asked.

"Because there'll be no sailing yet. The swell has got up with the tide. It would overturn the boat before we ever could get her launched."

An hour before dawn they went down to the cove, following the bubble of the stream and the descending combe, with a glowworm here and there green-lit like a jewel in the dark. The tide had gone out but the swell was still heavy, rushing in and roaring at them whenever they got too near. That was the trouble with the north coast: a sea could get up without warning and then you were done.

In the first glimmerings of daybreak, with the deathly moon merging its last candlelight in the blueing east, they walked slowly back. Twenty-four hours ago there had been a terrible anger in Mark's soul, bitter and blighting and hot; now all feeling was dead. His black eyes had sunk deep into the frame of his face.

As they neared the house he said: "I'll be gettin' on my way."

Ross said: "We'll house you here till to-morrow."

"No. I'll not have ye into it more."

Ross stopped. "Listen, man. The country folk are on your side, but you'll bring trouble on them if you shelter among 'em. You'll be safe in the library. To-night may be calm enough, for no wind is up."

"That man may tell about you," said Paul Daniel.

"Who? Enys? No, you do him an injustice there."

They went on again.

"Look, mister," said Mark, "I don't concern whether I hang or fly. Nothing don't matter a snap to me now. But one thing I'm danged sure on is that I'll not skulk where I bring trouble to them as friends me. An' that's for sartin. Ef the soldiers d'come, well, let em come."

They reached the house in silence.

"You always were a stubborn mule," Ross said.

Paul said: "Now look ee here, Mark. I've the thought——"

Someone came out of the house.

"Oh, Demelza," Ross said in half irritation, "I told you to go to bed. There's no need to worry yourself, my dear."

"I've brewed a dish of tea. I thought you'd all be back about now."

They went into the parlour. By the light of a single candle Demelza poured them hot tea from a great pewter pot. The three men stood round drinking it awkwardly, the steam rising before their faces, two avoiding each other's eyes, the third staring blindly at the opposite wall. Paul warmed his hands on the cup.

Demelza said: "You can hear the roar upstairs. I thought it was no use."

"It were roarin' last night," Mark said suddenly, "when I come up from the mine. God forgive me, twas roarin' then. . . ."

There was a grim silence.

"You'll stay here to-day?" said Demelza.

Ross said: "I have already asked him but he'll not hear of it."

Demelza glanced at Mark and said no more. He was not to be argued with.

Mark lowered his cup. "I was reckoning to go down Grambler."

There was another silence. Demelza shivered.

Paul hunched his shoulders uncomfortably. "The air may be foul. You know what Grambler always was for foul air. There's easier berths than that."

"I was reckoning," said Mark, "to go down Grambler."

Ross glanced at the sky. "You'll not be there before it is light."

Demelza too glanced out of the window, at the ruin on the sky line. "What of Wheal Grace? Is there still a ladder for that?"

Ross glanced at Mark. "The ladder was sound enough six years ago. You could use a rope to be sure."

Mark said: "I was reckoning to go down Grambler."

"Oh, nonsense, man. No one could blame me for your hiding in Grace. Don't you agree, Paul?"

" 'S I reckon he'd be safe there. What do ee say, old dear? The light's growing fast. No military man would follow down there."

Mark said: "I don't like it. Tes too close to this 'ouse. Folk might suspect."

"I'll go and get you some food," Demelza said.

An hour later the day broke. It was an unhappy day for Demelza, and she had lost her good spirits.

At nine o'clock the burly Sam Jenkins mounted a pony outside his forge and rode over to Mingoose, stopping in to see Dr. Enys on the way. At fifteen minutes to ten Sir Hugh Bodrugan also arrived at Mingoose; the Rev. Mr. Faber, rector of St. Minver Church, followed. The conference lasted until eleven, then a messenger was sent to fetch Dr. Enys. At noon the meeting broke up, Sir Hugh Bodrugan riding over to Trenwith to see Mr. Francis Poldark and then going on to St. Ann's, where he met Mr. Trencrom, and they went together to see the captain of the dragoons. It was a somewhat stormy meeting, for the captain was no fool, and Sir Hugh rode home to dinner with the fine rain to cool his heated whiskery face. Thereafter some hours went by in expectant calm. At four Ross walked down to look at the sea. The gentle rain had quieted it, but there was still an ugly swell. Both low tides would be in daylight, but any time after midnight might do on the falling tide. At five word came through that the soldiers, instead of being set to the man hunt, had been searching the St. Ann's houses all afternoon and had uncovered a fine store of contraband. Ross laughed.

At six three dragoons and a civilian rode down the narrow track of Nampara Combe. Nothing like it had ever been seen before.

Demelza was the first in the house to sight them and she flew into the parlour, where Ross was sitting thinking over his quarrel with Francis.

He said: "No doubt they are making a social call."

"But why come here, Ross, why come here? D'you think someone has told on us?"

He smiled. "Go change your dress, my dear, and prepare to be the lady."

She fled out, seeing through the half-open front door that the civilian was Constable Jenkins. Upstairs she hurriedly changed to the sound of clopping hooves and the distant rattle of accoutrements. She heard them knock and be shown in; then the faint murmur of voices. Anxiously she waited, knowing how gentle Ross could be or how much the opposite. But there was no uproar.

She turned her hair here and there with a comb and patted it into place. Then she peeped behind the curtain of the window, to see that only one of the soldiers had entered. The other two, in all the splendour of black and white busbies and red coats, waited with the horses.

As she went down and reached the door there was a sudden tremendous burst of laughter. Heartened, she went in.

"Oh, my dear, this is Captain McNeil of the Scots Greys. This is my wife."

Captain McNeil looked enormous in his red and gold coat, dark gold-braided trousers and spurred shiny boots. On the table stood a huge busby and beside it a pair of yellow gauntlet gloves. He was a youngish man, plump, well groomed, with a great sandy moustache. He set down the glass he was holding and bowed over her hand military fashion. As he straightened up his keen brown eyes seemed to say: "These outlandish country squires do themselves well with their womenfolk."

"You know Constable Jenkins, I think."

They waited until Demelza had taken a chair and then sat down again.

"Captain McNeil has been describing the amenities of our inns," said Ross. "He thinks the Cornish bugs have the liveliest appetite."

The soldier gave a softer echo of his tremendous laugh.

"Nay, I wouldn't say so much as that. Perhaps it is only that there are more of 'em."

"I have offered that he should come and stay with us," said Ross. "We are not rich in comfort but neither are we rich in crawlers." (Demelza blushed slightly at Ross's use of her old word.)

"Thank ye. Thank ye kindly." Captain McNeil twisted one end of his moustache as if it was a screw that must be fastened to his face. "And for old times' sake I should be uncommon pleased to do so. It terrns out, mistress, that Captain Poldark and I were both in a summary affray on the James River in 'eighty-one. Old campaigners together as ye might say. But though here I would be near the scene of the merrder, I'm much too far from the contraband we picked up this noon, and contraband was what I was sent into this part to find, ye see." He chuckled.

"Indeed," said Demelza. (She wondered what it would feel like to be kissed by a man with a moustache like that.)

"Hrr—hmm," said Constable Jenkins diffidently. "About this murder . . ."

"Och, yes. We mustn't forget——"

"Let me fill your glass," Ross said.

"Thank ye. . . . As I was explaining to your husband, mistress, this is but a routine inquiry, as I understand he was one of the airly finders of the body. Also it is said the wanted man has been seen in this neighbourhood. . . ."

"Really," said Demelza. "I had not heard it."

"Well, so the constable says."

"It was rumoured so, ma'am," Jenkins said hastily. "We don't know where it come from."

"So I made this call to see if ye could advise me. Captain Poldark has known the man since boyhood and I thought perhaps he would have some notion of where he might be lairking."

"You might search for a year," said Ross, "and not exhaust all the rabbit holes. All the same I do not imagine Daniel will linger. I think he will make for Plymouth and join the Navy."

Captain McNeil was watching him. "Is he a good sailor?"

"I have no idea. Every man here has some of the sea in his blood."

"Now tell me, Captain Poldark: are there overmany places on this coast where a boat may be launched?"

"What, a naval boat?"

"No, no, just a small boat which would be handled by one or two men."

"In a flat sea there are half a hundred. In a steep sea there isn't one between Padstow and St. Ann's."

"And what would ye call the present?"

"To-day it is moderate, dropping a little, I fancy. It may be feasible to launch a boat from Sawle by to-morrow evening. Why do you ask?"

Captain McNeil screwed up his moustache. "Are there overmany suitable boats about whereby a man could make his escape, d'you imagine?"

"Oh, I see your point. No, not that one man could handle."

"Do ye know anyone with a suitable boat at all?"

"There are a few. I have one myself. It is kept in a cave in Nampara Cove."

"Where d'you keep the oars, sur?" ventured Constable Jenkins.

Ross got up. "Can I persuade you to stay to supper, gentlemen? I will give the order now."

The blacksmith was a little nervous at this favour, but Captain McNeil rose and declined. "One day I'll call again and we'll have a lively crack over old times. But I should appreciate the favour of being shown the cove and cliffs if ye can spare the time now. I have a notion that it would help me one way or another. If ye can shoot at two birds with the one ball as ye might say . . ."

"Well, there is no hurry," said Ross. "Try this brandy first. I trust you will be able to tell from the flavour whether or not duty has been paid on it."

The soldier broke into his great good-humoured laugh.

They chatted a while longer and then the captain took his leave of Demelza. He clicked his heels and bowed low over her hand, so that the soft whiskers of his moustache tickled her fingers. For a second he looked at her with bold admiration in his brown eyes. Then he picked up his gloves and his great busby and clanked out.

When Ross came back from showing him the cove and cliffs Demelza said:

"Phew, I'm that glad it turned out that way. And you were so good.

245

No one would have dreamed you knew anything. What a nice man. I should not mind so much being arrested by him."

"Don't underrate him," Ross said. "He's a Scotsman."

CHAPTER VIII   Heavy windless rain set in as night fell.

At ten, when the tide was nearly full, Ross went down to the cove and saw that the swell had dropped. There could not have been a more favourable night; the darkness was like extra eyelids squeezing away the thought of sight.

At midnight two men waited inside the roofless engine house of Wheal Grace. Paul Daniel, with an old felt hat, and a sack over his shoulder, Ross in a long black cloak that came to his ankles and made him look like a bat. Presently in the depths of the pit there flickered a light.

With the ceaseless drum of the rain in their ears, falling on their hats and bodies and on the long wet grass, they waited and watched.

As he neared the top the light went out. His head and shoulders showed above the rim on the shaft and he clambered out and sat a moment on his haunches. The rain drummed on the grass.

"I thought twas near morning," he said. "What of the tide?"

"It will do."

They set off down the valley to the house.

"There's money in that mine," said Mark. "To keep from going off my head—I went all over."

"Someday perhaps," said Ross.

"Copper . . . I've never seen a more keenly lode. An' silver lead."

"Where?"

"On the east face. Twill be underwater most times. . . ."

The parlour light showed brightly, but Ross made a detour and came up against the library wall. Then he groped for the door and they were inside in the darkness. There was some scraping and then a candle burned in the far corner—in the corner where Keren had acted and danced.

A meal was set on a table.

Mark said: "Tes dangering you needless." But he ate rapidly while the other two kept watch.

With the lighted parlour as a decoy, Demelza was sitting in the darkness of the bedroom above keeping watch up the valley. After the visit of the soldier Ross was taking no chances.

Very soon Mark was done. He looked terrible to-night, for his strong beard was half an inch long and the heavy rain had washed streaks down the dirt of his face.

"There's this," said Ross, putting forward a parcel of food, "and this." An old coat. "It is the best we can do. You will need all your efforts to be out of sight of the land by morning, for there's no breeze to help you."

Mark said: "If thanks would bring things for ee . . . But listen . . ."

"Tell me on the way down."

"I been thinking of my house, Reath Cottage, that I builded for she. You won't—you won't let it fall down?"

"No, Mark."

"There's stuff in the garden. That's for you, Paul. It has yielded well."

"I'll see for it," said Paul.

"And," said Mark, turning his eyes on Ross, "and there's one thing else. It's . . . You'll see she's buried proper? Not in a pauper's grave. . . . She was above that. . . ."

"I'll see to it," Ross told him.

"There's money under the bed in the cottage. It'll be enough to pay. . . . I'd like a stone. . . ."

"Yes, Mark. We'll see it's done right."

Mark picked up his things, the food, the coat.

"Keren on the stone," he said indistinctly. "She never liked Keren-happuch. Keren Daniel. Just Keren Daniel. . . ."

They set off for the cove. The rain had not put out the lights of the glowworms. The sea was quieter to-night, grumbling and hissing under the steady downpour. It was not quite so black here; the white fringe of surf was faintly phosphorescent, easing the night's dark weight. They left the stream and moved across the soft sand. They were within a few yards of the cove when Ross stopped. He put out a hand behind and drew Paul level.

"What is that?" he breathed.

Paul put down the mast and stared. He had very sharp eyes, well used to dark places. He bent a little and then straightened.

"A man."

"A soldier," said Ross. "I heard the creak of his belt."

They squatted.

"I'd best go," said Mark.

"Nay, I'll quiet him," said Paul. "They're soft enough under their tall hats."

"No killing," said Ross. "I will do it. . . ." But the elder Daniel had gone.

Ross crouched in the sand, pulling the mast towards him. Mark began to mutter under his breath. He would have given himself up.

Ross thought: McNeil has strung his men out all along the cliffs. Shooting at two birds. This way he may either pull in the murderer or some free traders. But if he's watching all points between here and St. Ann's his men will be widely spaced.

Creep forward.

A sudden sharp challenge. They rushed forward. The musket exploded, flat and loud, in the mouth of the cave. A figure sank on to the sand.

"All right," said Paul, short of breath. "But a damnation noise."

"Quick, the boat!"

Into the cave; Ross flung in the mast and the sail; Mark groped for the oars.

"I'll get them; you launch her!"

The brothers began to slide the boat through the soft sand. Twice it stuck. Then they had to drag the stirring figure of the soldier aside. Ross came with the oars, thrust them in, put his weight to the boat and it went sliding down towards the sea.

The sound of boots striking rock somewhere, and shouts. Men were coming.

"This way!" shouted a voice. "By the cave!"

Reached the sea. The fringe of surf might show them up.

"Get in!" Ross said through his teeth.

"Rullocks!" said Mark.

Ross took them from his pocket, passed them to Mark; one fell in the sand. They groped: found it: Mark was in: pushed off. A wave broke among them and swung the boat; nearly capsized; back in shallow water. Mark got the oars out.

"Now!"

The noise they were making. Men were running towards them. A musket was fired. Straighten up; waves were malevolent; shove again together! The boat suddenly came to life, floated off into the blackness. Paul fell on hands and knees in the surf, Ross caught his shoulders, hauled him to his feet. A figure came up and grasped his cloak. Ross ducked as a musket exploded in his ear. He knocked the soldier flat upon the sand. They ran along the beach. Figures were after them as they turned in towards the stream. Ross stopped short and hit at a figure running past him. The man rolled into the stream. Then he changed his course and began to climb up among the bracken that stood four feet high along the side of the combe. They could seek him all night here. Unless they could light a torch they were helpless.

He lay flat on his face for a few minutes gaining his breath, listening to men shouting and searching. Was Paul safe? He moved again. Another danger existed and must be met.

This way it was farther to Nampara. You climbed through the bracken until it gave way to open ground and patches of gorse, then you struck the west corner of the long field and, keeping in the ditch at the side of it, made your way down the hill to the back of the house.

This he did. The Gimletts had been in bed hours, so he slipped in through the kitchen, peeped into the parlour and blew the candles out, quickly mounted the stairs to his bedroom.

Demelza was by the north window but was across the room as soon as his footsteps creaked at the door.

"Are you safe?"

"Ssh! Don't wake Julia." While he told her what had happened he was pulling off his long cloak, dragging his stock from his neck.

"Soldiers! Their . . ."

He sat down suddenly. "Help me, my dear. They may call on us."

She fell on her knees and began to unlace the tall boots in the dark. "I wonder who gave you away, Ross? *Could* it have been Dwight Enys?"

"Heavens, no! Sound reasoning on the part of the—charming Mc-Neil."

"Oh, Ross, your hands!"

Ross stared closely at them. "I must have cut the knuckles when I hit someone." Then his fingers closed over Demelza's. "You're trembling, child."

"So would you be," she said. "I've been sitting up here alone in the dark; and then those shots . . ."

Her voice died as a knock came at the front door.

"Now gently, my love, gently. Take your time. That knock is not very peremptory, is it? They are not sure of themselves. We'll wait for another knock before making a light."

He stood up, gathered together the clothes he had taken off and moved to the cupboard.

"No," Demelza said, "under the cot. If you can lift it carefully I'll slip them under."

While they were doing this the knock came again, and louder.

"That should wake Gimlett," said Ross, making a light himself. "He'll think he is always being roused in the middle of the night."

There was water in the room and Demelza hurriedly poured some in a bowl. As the light of the candle grew she took up a flannel and bathed his face and hands. When Gimlett came to the door Ross was just putting on his gown.

"What is it now?"

"If you please, sur, there's a sergeant o' the soldiery askin' to see you downstairs."

"Confound it, this is a time to call! Ask him in the parlour, John. I'll be down very soon."

CHAPTER IX Mr. Odgers might have thought his pleas effective, for Sawle Feast passed barely marked. But in fact conditions preached the surest sermon.

And the soldiers still lay like a blight on the land. Everyone had been hoping for their going, but instead a contingent moved to Sawle and showed no signs of feeling themselves unwanted. They bivouacked in an open field just behind Dr. Choake's house, and to everyone's disappointment the weather cleared again and no wind blew to strip them in sleep.

Ross had spent an uncomfortable few days. Apart from the chance of trouble over Mark Daniel, there was his breach with Francis. They had never quarrelled in this way before. Even during the ups and downs of these last years Francis and he had always held each other in mutual respect. Ross was not upset at being suspected of helping Verity to elope but at being disbelieved when he denied it. It would never have occurred to him to doubt Francis's word. But it had seemed as if Francis didn't *want* to believe the denial, almost as if he was afraid to believe it. It was all inexplicable and left a nasty taste.

On the Friday, Ross had to go to Trevaunance. Richard Tonkin was to be there, and they were to go into the general accounts before the general meeting that evening. Ever since the opening of the smelting works opposition to the working of the company had been fierce. Mines had been induced to boycott them, attempts made to squeeze them from the available markets for the refined product; they had been overbid again and again at the ticketings.

But so far they had ridden the storm.

This was the first time Ross had been out since Tuesday evening, and when he reached Grambler he was not overpleased to see a tall cavalry officer coming the other way.

"Why, Captain Poldark." McNeil reined in his horse and bowed slightly. "I was on my way to see ye. Can ye spare the time to turn back for a half-hour?"

"A pleasure I have been looking forward to," Ross said, "but I have a business appointment at Trevaunance. Can you ride with me that far?"

McNeil turned his horse. "Aye, mebbe we can talk a wee bit as we go. I had intended calling on you airlier but I've been more than a little busy what with one thing and another."

"Oh, yes," said Ross, "the smugglers."

"Not only the smugglers. Ye'll remember there was the small matter of that mairderer's escape."

"D'you think he has escaped?"

Captain McNeil screwed his moustache. "Has he not! And from your cove, Captain, and in your boat!"

"Oh, that. I thought it was a brush with the free traders you'd had. The sergeant——"

"I think Sergeant Drummond left ye in no doubt as to his views."

"I judged him mistaken."

"May I ask why?"

"Well, I understand there were several men concerned. Murderers do not hunt in packs."

"No, but he had the sympathy of the neighbourhood."

They jogged along in silence.

"Well, it was a pity you did not catch one of the rascals. Were any of your troopers hurt?"

"Not as ye would say hurrt. Except in a small matter of dignity. It might have gone ill with one of the lawbreakers if he had been caught."

"Ah," said Ross. And, "Do you know much of churches, Captain? Sawle Church reminds me of one I saw in Connecticut except that it is so badly preserved."

"And then," said the officer, "there was the matter of the rowlocks. How do ye suppose they were got?"

"I should say Daniel—if it was he—stole a pair somewhere. Every man here is a fisherman in his spare time. There are always rowlocks about."

"Ye do not seem very upset at the loss of your boat, Captain Poldark."

"I am becoming philosophical," Ross said. "As one nears thirty I think it is a state of mind to be sought after. It is a protection, because one becomes more conscious of loss—loss of time, of dignity, of one's first ideals. I'm not happy to lose a good boat but sighing will not bring it back any more than yesterday's youth."

"Your attitude does you credit," McNeil said dryly. "Might I, as a man a year or so your senior offer ye a word of advice?"

"Of course."

"Be careful of the law, Captain. It is a cranky, twisty old thing and you may flout it a half dozen times. But let it once come to grips with ye, and ye will find it as hard to be loose from as a black squid. Mind you, I have a sympathy with your point of view. There's something about arrmy life that makes a man impatient of the Justice and the parish constable; I've felt it so myself; indeed I have. . . ." He gave a brief, sudden chuckle. "But that——" He stopped.

Ross said: "See those children, McNeil. It is the only beech copse round here and they are gathering the leaves and will take them home to be cooked. It is not a very nourishing dish and makes their stomachs swell."

"Yes," said the captain grimly. "I see them well."

"I confess I sometimes feel impatient of a lot of things," Ross said. "Including the parish constable and the local magistrates. But I think it dates from earlier in my life than you imagine. I joined the Fifty-second Foot to escape them."

"That's as may be. Once a rebel, always a rebel, you may say. But there are degrees of rebellion, Captain, just as there are degrees of misdemeanour, and when the parish constable comes to be supported by a troop of His Majesty's cavalry——"

"And a crack regiment at that."

"And a crack regiment, as ye say; then recklessness becomes folly and is likely to lead to bad consequences. A military man out of uniform may be no respecter of perrsons. A military man in uniform will be still less so."

They left Sawle Church behind and took the track past Trenwith. Ross said: "I feel we have a good deal in common, Captain McNeil."

"That's one way of putting it."

"Well, I have been in and out of scrapes a good part of my life, and I imagine you have been the same."

The captain laughed, and a flock of birds rose from a neighbouring field.

"I think perhaps you will agree," Ross said, "that though we may revere the law in abstract, in practice there are considerations which take a higher place."

"Such as?"

"Friendship."

They rode on in silence.

"The law would not admit that."

"Oh, I do not expect the law to admit it. I was asking you to admit it."

The Scotsman screwed in his moustache. "No, no, Captain Poldark. Oh, dear, no. You are out of uniform but I'm still in it. I'll not be manœuvred into a corrner by such moral arguments."

"But moral argument is the most potent force in the world, Captain. It was that more than force of arms which defeated us in America."

"Well, next time you must try it on my troopers. They will appreciate the change." McNeil reined in his horse. "I think we have gone far enough, Captain."

"It is another mile to Trevaunance yet."

"But farther I doubt before we reach agreement. It's time we parted. I should have appreciated an assurance that ye had taken good heed of my warning——"

"Oh, I have done that, I do assure you."

"Then there's no more need be said—this time. It may be that we shall meet again—in different circumstances I should hope."

"I shall look forward to it," Ross said. "If you are ever in these parts again consider my house at your disposal."

"Thank you." McNeil extended his hand.

Ross took off his glove and they shook hands.

"Have ye hurt your hand somewhere?" McNeil said, glancing down at the scarred knuckles.

"Yes," said Ross, "I caught it in a rabbit trap."

They saluted and separated, Ross going on his way, McNeil turning back towards Sawle. As the soldier rode away he twisted his moustache vigorously and now and again a subdued laugh shook his big frame.

The smelting works now straggled up the side of Trevaunance Quay.

A long way off it was possible to see the immense volumes of smoke from the furnaces, and on this still day it hung in the valley shutting out the sun. Here was industry with a vengeance, with great piles of coal and heaps of ashes and an unending stream of mules and men busy about the copper house and the quay.

He dismounted first beside the works to look them over.

Several reverberatory furnaces had been built, some for roasting and some for fusing the ore. The copper was roasted and then melted, whilst at intervals the waste was removed, until after twelve hours it was turned out in a molten state into a trough of water. This sudden cooling brought it to a mass of small grains, which were roasted for another twenty-four hours and again turned out, until eventually the coarse copper was run off into sand moulds to cool. This melting and refining had to take place several times before it reached a proper state of purity. The whole process averaged a fortnight. Small wonder, Ross thought, that it took three times as much coal to smelt a ton of copper as a ton of tin. And coal at fifty shillings a wey.

Although the place had been open only three months he noticed already how ill and wan many of the men were who worked there. The great heat and the fumes were too much for any but the strongest, and there was a higher sickness rate here than in the mines. A factor he had not foreseen. He had laboured long hours to b..ng this thing to pass, believing it meant prosperity for the district and perhaps salvation for the mines; but there did not seem much prosperity for the poor devils who worked here.

The fumes were blighting the vegetation in this pretty cove. The bracken was brown a month in advance of its time and the leaves of the trees were twisted and discoloured. Thoughtfully he rode up to Place House, which stood on the other side of the valley.

When he was shown in Sir John Trevaunance was still at breakfast and reading the *Spectator*.

"Ah, Poldark, take a seat. You're early. But then I'm late, what? I do not expect Tonkin for half an hour." He flipped the paper. "This is a confoundedly disturbing business, what?"

"You mean the riots in Paris?" said Ross. "A little extravagant."

Sir John put in a last mouthful of beef. "But for the King to give way to them! Ecod he must be a lily! A round or two of grapeshot is what they wanted. It says the Comte d'Artois and several others have left France. To bolt at the first grumble of thunder!"

"Well, I fancy it should keep the French occupied with their own affairs," Ross said. "England should take the hint and put her own house in order."

Sir John munched and read in silence for a while. Then he crumpled up the paper and threw it impatiently to the floor. The great boarhound by the fireplace rose and sniffed at the paper and then walked off, disliking the smell.

"That man Fox!" said the baronet. "Damme, he's a fool if ever there was one! Going out of his way to praise a rabble such as that. One would think the gates of Heaven had opened!"

Ross got up and walked over to the window. Trevaunance stared after him.

"Come, man, don't tell me you're a Whig! Your family never was, not any of 'em."

"I'm neither Whig nor Tory," Ross said.

"Well, drot it, you must be something. Who d'you vote for?"

Ross was silent again for some time and bent and patted the hound. He seldom thought these things out.

"I'm not a Whig," he said, "nor ever could belong to a party that was for ever running down its own country and praising up the virtues of some other. The very thought of it sticks in my crop."

"Hear, hear!" said Sir John, picking his teeth.

"But neither could I belong to a party which looks with complacency on the state of England as it is. So you'll see the difficulty I'm in."

"Oh, I don't think——"

"And you must not forget," Ross said, "that it is but a few months since I stormed a gaol of my own. And one which held considerably more than the six prisoners of the Bastille. It is true I didn't parade the streets of Launceston with the gaoler's head stuck on a pole, but that was not for lack of feeling like it."

"Hm!" said Sir John uncomfortably. "Hrrrm! Well, if you will excuse me, Poldark, I'll change my gown to be ready for Tonkin."

He left the room hastily and Ross continued to pat the head of the boarhound.

CHAPTER X   Demelza had been wrestling with her conscience ever since Monday evening, and when Ross left on the Friday she knew she would have no peace unless she gave way.

So after he had gone she walked over to Trenwith. She was almost as nervous as she had ever been in her life, but there was no escape. She had hoped for a letter from Verity yesterday with the *Mercury*, but none had come.

Making the mistake of most early risers, she was surprised to find that Trenwith House had an unawakened look, and when she plucked at the doorbell Mary Bartle told her that Mrs. Poldark was still in bed and that Mr. Poldark was breakfasting alone in the winter parlour.

This might suit better than she had hoped and she said:

"Could I see him, if you please?"

"I'll go and ask, ma'am, if you'll wait here."

Demelza wandered round the splendid hall, staring up at the pictures, able to take a longer view of them than she had ever done before. A strange crew, more than half of them Trenwiths, Ross said. She fancied she could detect the Poldark strain coming in, the stronger facial bones, the blue, heavy-lidded eyes, the wide mouth. Those early Trenwiths were the men with the looks, soft curling dark beards and sensitive faces, and the red-haired girl in a velvet gown of the style of William and Mary—but perhaps the Poldarks had given a new vigour. Was it they too who had brought the wild strain? Elizabeth had not been painted yet. That was a pity, in fairness Demelza had to admit it.

The house was very quiet, seemed to lack something. She suddenly realized that what it was lacking was Verity. She stood quite still and saw for the first time that she had robbed this household of its most vital personality. She had been the instrument of a theft, perpetrated on Francis and Elizabeth.

She had never looked on it that way before. All the time she had seen Verity's life as incomplete. She had looked at it from Andrew Blamey's point of view but not from Elizabeth's or Francis's. If she had thought of them at all she had considered them as clinging to Verity from selfish motives, because she was so useful to them. It

255

hadn't occurred to her that everyone in this household might in fact love Verity and feel her personal loss—not until she stood in this hall, which seemed so large and so empty to-day. She wondered how she had had the impertinence to come.

"Mr. Poldark will see ee right away," said Mary Bartle behind her.

So while Sir John Trevaunance was entertaining Ross at his breakfast table, Francis was entertaining Demelza.

He got up when she went in. Unlike Sir John he was fully dressed, in a buff-coloured morning coat with velvet lapels, a silk shirt and brown breeches. His look was not friendly.

"I'm sorry," he said shortly, "Elizabeth is not down. She breakfasts upstairs these days."

"I didn't come to see Elizabeth," Demelza answered, flushing. "I came to see you."

"Oh. In that case, please sit down."

"I don't want for you to interrupt your meal."

"It is finished."

"Oh." She sat down, but he stood, a hand on the back of his chair. "Well?"

"I have come to you to tell you something," she said. "I b'lieve you had a quarrel with Ross over Verity leaving the way she did. You thought he was at fault."

"Has he sent you here this morning?"

"No, Francis; you know he would not do that. But I—I have to clear this up, even if you hate me for it ever after. Ross had nothing to do with Verity's elopement. I know that for certain."

Francis's angry eyes met hers. "Why should I believe you when I have disbelieved him?"

"Because I can tell you who did help."

He laughed shortly. "I wonder."

"Yes, I can. For I was the one who helped, Francis, not Ross. He knew nothing about it. He didn't approve of her going any more than you did."

Francis stared at her, frowned at her, turned sharply away as if shaking her confession aside, went to the window.

"I believed it was . . . I believe it was for Verity's happiness," she stumbled on. She had intended to tell him the whole truth but her courage failed her. "After the Assembly I offered to act as—as a go-between. Captain Blamey wrote to me an' I passed the letters to Verity. She gave letters to me and I gave them to the *Mercury* man. Ross didn't know nothing at all about it."

There was silence. A clock in the room was ticking. Francis took a deep breath, then blew it out slowly on the window.

"You damned interfering . . ." He stopped.

She got up.

"Tisn't pleasant to come here and confess this. I know how you feel for me now. But I couldn't let this quarrel betwixt you and Ross go on from my fault. I didn't wish to hurt you or Elizabeth, please know that. You're right: I was interfering; but if I did wrong twas out of love for Verity, not to hurt you——"

"Get out!" he said.

She began to feel sick. She had not thought the interview would be nearly as bad as this. She had tried to repair a mistake, but it did not seem that she had done any good at all. Was his feeling for Ross any different?

"What I came for," she said, "was to take the blame. If you hate me, that's maybe what I deserve, but please don't let this be a quarrel between you and Ross. I should feel——"

He put up his hand to the catch of the window as if to open it. She saw that his hand was trembling. What was the matter with him?

"Will you go," he said, "and never enter this house again. Understand, so—so long as I live I never want you to come near Trenwith again. And Ross can stay out as well. If he will marry an ignorant trull such as you then he must take the consequences."

He had controlled his voice so hard that she could only just hear what he said. She turned and left him, went out into the hall, picked up her cloak, passed through the open doorway into the sun. There was a seat beside the wall of the house and she sat on it. She felt faint, and the ground was unsteady.

After a few minutes the breeze began to revive her. She got up and began to walk back to Nampara.

Lord Devoran was not present, being kept away by an attack of tissick. Mr. Trencrom was away also, being still privily occupied with the claims of his suffering employees—those who had had the misfortune to be found with contraband goods in their cellars and lofts.

From the beginning Ross felt there was something wrong. This was a general meeting of the shareholders and as such was not held until after dark. No general meeting had ever yet been held in daylight, since there might always be a spy about watching comings and goings.

A score had turned up. Chief item for discussion was Ray Penvenen's proposal that a rolling and cutting mill should be built at the top of the hill where his land joined Sir John's, he personally to pay half the cost, the company the other half. The project was urgent, for the venturers of Wheal Radiant had suddenly refused to renew the lease on their battery mill. Unless the company put up its own mill at once it would be forced to sell the copper solely in block ingots.

The only debatable point was the selection of site. Nevertheless Ross was for making the concession to Penvenen's *amour-propre*, for Penvenen had what was at a premium, free money. What Ross expected was opposition from Alfred Barbary. And he got it. The dreary old argument was dragged up about the north-coast shareholders' getting all the plums.

Ross listened to the wrangle but noted again that the cross-eyed Aukett sat silent, plucking at his bottom lip. A carpet manufacturer called Fox might have been turned to stone. Presently Tonkin, who made the perfect chairman, said: "I should like the opinion of some of the other shareholders."

After the usual sort of hesitation some views were given, mainly in favour of the mill near the works. Then Aukett said: "It's all very well, gentlemen, but where's our half of the money coming from, eh; that's what I'd like to know?"

Tonkin said: "Well, it was understood by the leading shareholders that additional calls might be expected and we all accepted that. The need is great. If we can't roll and beat the copper we miss nearly all our small markets. And the small markets may just turn the scale. We can't force the Government to buy our copper for the Mint, but we can expect our own friends to buy their requirements from us."

There was a murmur of agreement.

"Well, that's very well," said Aukett, squinting worse than usual in his excitement, "but I'm afraid our mine will be unable to meet any such call. Indeed, it looks as if someone will have to take over the shares I hold."

Tonkin looked at him sharply. "Whether you sell the shares is your own concern, but so long as you retain them you're in honour bound to accept the responsibilities we all jointly incurred."

"And so we'd like to," said Aukett. "But you can't get blood out of a stone. Whether we like it or not we shall have to contract out of the undertaking."

"You mean default?"

"No, there's no question of defaulting. The shares are paid up. And our good will you'll retain, but——"

"What's wrong?" said Blewett. "You told me on Tuesday that the higher prices at the last ticketing had put the Wheal Mexico venturers in better heart than they'd been for years."

"Yes," Aukett nodded. "But yesterday I had a letter from Warleggan's Bank telling me they could no longer support our loan and would we make arrangements to get it transferred elsewhere. That means——"

"You had that?" said Fox.

"That means ruin unless Pascoe's will take it over, and I have my doubts, for Pascoe's was always on the cautious side and want more security. I'm calling in at Warleggan's on my way home to see if I can persuade them to reconsider it. It's unheard of suddenly to withdraw one's credit like this——"

"Did they give any reason?" Ross asked.

"I had a very similar letter," Fox interrupted. "As you know I have been extending my business in several directions and I have drawn heavily during the last year. I went to see Mr. Nicholas Warleggan last evening and explained that a withdrawal of their facilities would mean the failure of these schemes. He was not very amenable. I believe he knew all about my interest in Carnmore and resented it. I really believe that was at the bottom of it."

"It was." Everyone looked at St. Aubyn Tresize. "My private business is not for discussion at this table, gentlemen. But money has been advanced to me during the last few years from Warleggan's Bank. They have the finest security in the world: land; but it is a security I don't propose to forfeit. If they foreclose at this stage I shall fight them—and they'll not get the land. But they will get most of my assets—including my shares in the Carnmore Copper Company."

"How the Devil have they come to know all this?" Blewett demanded nervously. "More than half of us here have some indebtedness that can be assailed."

"Someone has been talking," said a voice at the bottom.

Richard Tonkin tapped the table. "Has anyone else here had word from the Warleggans?"

There was silence.

"Not yet," said Johnson.

"Well, drot it," said Trevaunance. "You should all bank with Pascoe, as I do; then you'd not get into this mess. Get Pascoe's to take over your accounts."

"Easier said than done," Fox snapped. "Aukett's right. Pascoe's want a better security. I was with them and could not get enough free money and I changed to Warleggan's. So there's small hope of me being able to change back."

Ray Penvenen grunted impatiently. "Well, that's a matter personal to you. We can't all start confessing our private difficulties or it will smack of a Methody revival. Let's get back to this question of the mill."

At length it was agreed that the mill should be put up as a separate venture by Penvenen on the site of his own choosing. The Carnmore Company should hold only thirty per cent of the shares. Unreality had come to sit among them. Very well for Penvenen with his upcountry interests, to dismiss the matter as of no moment. Mines worked on credit, and these were not times for facing its withdrawal. Ross saw the same look on many faces. Someone has let us down. And if three names are known, why not all?

The meeting closed early. Decisions were taken, proposals went through; the name of Warleggan was no more spoken. Ross wondered how many of the decisions would be put into effect. He wondered if there was any danger of their stiff fight becoming a debacle.

When it was over he shook hands all round and was one of the first to leave. He wanted to think. He wanted to consider where the leak might have occurred. It was not until he was riding home that a very uncomfortable and disturbing thought came to him.

CHAPTER XI   Demelza was in bed but not asleep. When she spoke he gave up the attempt to undress in the dark.

"You're roosting early," he said. "I hope this is a sign of a reformed life."

Her eyes glittered unnaturally in the growing yellow light of the candle.

"Have you any news of Mark?"

"No; it's early."

"There are all sorts of rumours about France."

"Yes, I know."

"How did your meeting go?"

He told her.

She was silent after he had finished. "D'you mean it may make more difficulties for you?"

"It may."

She lay quiet then while he finished undressing, her hair coiled on the pillow. One tress of it lay on his pillow as he came to get into bed. He picked it up and squeezed it in his fingers a moment before putting it with the rest.

"Don't put out the light," she said. "I've something to tell you."

"Can't you talk in the dark?"

"Not this. The darkness is so heavy sometimes. . . . Ross, I b'lieve we should sleep sweeter without the bed hangings these warm nights."

"As you please." He put the candle beside the bed where it flung yellow fancies on the curtains at their feet.

"Have you heard anything more of Verity?" she asked.

"I've not stirred from Trevaunance Cove all day."

"Oh, Ross," she said.

"What is the matter?"

"I . . . I have been to Trenwith to-day to see Francis."

"The Devil you have! You'd get no welcome there. And certainly no news of Verity."

"It wasn't for news of Verity I went. I went to tell him he was mistaken in thinking you'd encouraged Verity to elope."

"What good would that do?"

"I didn't want that blame laid to me, that I'd caused a quarrel between you. I told him the truth: that I'd helped Verity unbeknown to you."

She lay very still and waited.

Annoyance was somewhere within him but it would not come to a head: it ran away again into channels of fatigue.

"Oh, Heavens," he said at length, wearily. "What does it matter?"

She did not move or speak. The news sank further into his understanding, set off fresh conduits of thought and feeling.

"What did he say?"

"He—he turned me out. He—he told me to get out and . . . He was so angry. I never thought . . ."

Ross said: "If he vents his ill-humour on you again . . . I could not understand his attitude to me on Monday. It seemed just as wild and unreasonable as you say——"

"No, Ross, no, Ross," she whispered urgently. "That's not right. It isn't him you should be angry with, it is me. I am in the fault. Even then I didn't tell him all."

"What did you tell him?"

"I—that I had passed on letters from Andrew Blamey and sent him letters from Verity ever since the Assembly in April."

"And what didn't you tell him?"

There was silence.

She said: "I think you will hit me, Ross."

"Indeed."

"I did as I did because I loved Verity and hated her to be unhappy."

"Well?"

She told him everything. Her secret visit to Falmouth while he was away, how she had contrived a meeting and how it had all happened.

He did not interrupt her once. She went right through to the end, faltering but determined. He listened with a curious sense of incredulity. And all the time that other suspicion was beating away. This thing was a part of it. Francis must have realized that Verity and Blamey had been deliberately brought together. Francis had suspected *him*. Francis knew all about the Carnmore Copper Company. . . .

The candle flame shivered and the light broke its pattern on the bed.

It all came round to Demelza. The thing welled up in him.

"I can't believe you did it," he said at last. "If—if anyone had told me I should have named him a liar. I'd *never* have believed it. I thought you were trustworthy and loyal."

She did not say anything.

The anger came easily now; it could not be stemmed.

"To go behind my back. *That* is what I can't stomach or—or even quite believe yet. The deceit——"

"I tried to do it openly. But you wouldn't let me."

She had betrayed him and was the cause of the greater betrayal. It all fitted into place.

"So you did it underhand, eh? Nothing mattered, no loyalty or trust, so long as you got your own way."

"It wasn't for myself. It was for Verity."

"The deceit and the lies," he said with tremendous contempt. "The continual lying for more than twelve months. We have been married no long time but I prided myself that this, this association of ours, was the one constant in my life. The one thing that would be changeless and untouchable. I should have said there was absolute trust and confidence between us. I should have staked my life on it. Demelza was true to the grain. There wasn't a flaw in her—— In this damned world——"

"Oh, Ross," she said with a sudden great sob, "you'll break my heart."

"You expect me to hit you?" he said. "That's what you can understand. A good beating and then over. But you're not a dog or a horse to be thrashed into the right ways. You're a woman, with subtler instincts of right and wrong. Loyalty is not a thing to be bought: it is freely given or withheld. Well, by God, you have chosen to withhold it . . . !"

She began to climb out of bed, blindly; was out and clung sobbing to the curtains, released them and groped round the bed. Her whole body shook as she wept.

As she reached the door he sat up. His anger would not subside.

"Demelza, come here!"

She had gone and had shut the door behind her.

He got out of bed, took up the candle and opened the door again. She was not on the stairs. He went down shedding grease, reached the parlour. She was trying to close the door but he flung it open with a crash.

She fled from him towards the farther door, but he put down the candle and caught her by the fireplace and pulled her back. She struggled in his arms, feebly, as if grief had taken her strength. He caught her hair and pulled her head back. She shook it.

"Let me go, Ross. Let me go."

He held her while the tears ran down her cheeks. Then he let her hair go and she stood quiet, crying against him.

She deserves all this and more, he thought. More, more! Let her suffer! He could well have struck her, taken a belt to her. Drunken hind and common drudge. What a foul mixture and mess!

Damn her for an impudent brat! Verity married to Blamey and all, *all* this trouble through her meddling. He could have shaken her till her teeth chattered.

But already his sense of fairness was fighting to gain a word. It was her fault in part, but not her blame. At least not the consequences. Verity married to Blamey might be the least of them. Damn Francis. Incredible betrayal! (Did he run too fast and too far? No, for it surely all fitted.)

"Come, you'll get cold," he said roughly.

She took no notice.

She had already had the quarrel with Francis. That too must have upset her, for she had been very low when he got home. Curious that that should have upset her so much.

His anger was slowly subsiding, not disappearing but finding its true level. She could not stand his tongue. What had he said? Or *how* had he said it? The Poldarks were an unpleasant lot when they were crossed. Damn Francis, for all this trouble really lay at his door: the first break between Verity and Blamey, his later obstinate refusal to reconsider his dislike. Demelza no doubt had acted for the best. The road to Hell being so paved.

But she had no right to act so, for best or worst. She had no right. She had interfered and lied to him; and although now she was desperately upset, in a day or two she would be happy and smiling again. And all the consequences would go on and on and on, echoing in this man's life and that.

She had stopped now and she broke away from him.

"I'll be all right," she said.

"Well, do not stay down here all night."

"You go on. I'll come in a little."

He left her the candle and went back to the bedroom. He lit another candle and walked over to the cot. Julia had kicked off all the bedclothes. She was lying like a Muslim worshipper, her head down and her seat in the air. He was about to cover her when Demelza came in.

"Look," he said.

She came over and gave a little gulping "Oh," when she saw the child. She swallowed and turned her over. Julia's curly brown hair was like a halo for the innocent cherubic face. Demelza went quietly away.

Ross stayed staring down at the child, and when he turned Demelza was already in bed. She was sitting well back among the curtains, and he could only see the pyramid of her knees.

Presently he got in beside her and blew out the candle and lay down. She did not move to settle for a long time. Extravagant and contrary in all things, he thought: her loyalties, her griefs. She betrays me, deceives me without a flicker out of love for Verity. Am I to blame her, who know so much about conflicting and divided loyalties?

She causes this breach between Francis and me. The enormity of it, bringing perhaps failure and ruin.

"Ross," she said suddenly, "is it as bad as all that, what I've done?"

"No more talk now."

"No, but I must know that. It didn't seem so wrong to me at the time. I knew it was deceiving you, but I thought I was doing what was best for Verity. Truly I did. Maybe it's because I don't know any better, but that's what I thought."

"I know you did," he said. "But it isn't just that. Other things have come into it."

"What other things?"

"Nothing I can tell you yet."

"I'm that sorry," she said. "I never dreamed to make trouble between you and Francis. I never *dreamed*, Ross. I'd never ha' done it if I thought that."

He sighed. "You have married into a peculiar family. You must never expect the Poldarks to behave in the most rational manner. I have long since given up expecting it. We are hasty—quite incredibly hasty, it seems—and sharp-tempered; strong in our likes and dislikes and unreasonable in them—more unreasonable than I ever guessed. Perhaps, so far as the first goes, yours is the common-sense view. If two people are fond of each other let 'em marry and work out their own salvation, ignoring the past and damning the consequences. . . ."

There was another long silence.

"But I—I still don't understand," she said. "You seem to be talking in riddles, Ross. An' I feel such a cheat and—and so horrible. . . ."

"I can't explain more now. It is impossible until I am sure. But as for what I said . . . I spoke in heat. So forget it if you can and go to sleep."

She slid an inch farther down the bed.

She blew out a long breath. "I wish—I shall not be very happy if this quarrel between you and Francis does not quickly heal."

"Then I am afraid you will be unhappy for a long time."

Silence fell and this time was not broken. But neither of them went to sleep. She was on edge after the quarrel, desperately unsatisfied and not much relieved by her tears. She felt insecure and much in the dark. She had been told of other reasons for his anger but could not guess them. She bitterly hated anything to be incomplete, especially to leave a trouble unresolved. Yet she knew she could go no further to-night. He was restless and overtired and uneasy. Thoughts ran through his head in endless procession. After a time she closed her eyes and tried to go to sleep. But he did not even try.

BOOK FOUR

CHAPTER I   On Christmas Eve Demelza opened a letter from Verity which ran as follows:

MY DEAR COUSIN DEMELZA,

Your welcome letter reached me yesterday morning and I am replying—prompt for me!—to say how pleased I am to learn all are well, with all this sickness abroad. In this Town it is very bad, two or three things rage and who has not got one takes another. However, thanks to God, we too escape, at Church on Sunday the Pews were but half filled owing to it, and afterward we called on Mrs. Daubuz the mayor's wife to condole with her on the loss of her baby son. We found her very sad but resigned, she is a fine woman.

I am glad that you have at last had news that Mark Daniel is safe in France—that is if anyone can be safe there at this present. It was a horrible thing to happen and I wish it had never been, I can sympathize with Mark but not condone his act.

We have been very busy here for a week past. The East India Fleet consisting of three fine ships and a frigate, with two Fleets from the West Indies as well as one from Oporto bound home are all come into our port except a few from the Leeward Islands, which are gone up Channel. The Harbour is a fine sight with above 200 sail of Vessels in view from our House. The Fleets are very valuable and the Town is full of Passengers from them.

Well my dear I am very happy in my new life. I think age is much how you feel, as a spinster of nearly thirty-one I felt old and sere but as a married woman I do not at all seem the same. I have put on weight since I came and get no more Catarr, perhaps it is the softer Climate which suits me, but I think that is not it. Andrew too is happy and is always whistling in the house. It is strange because no one at Trenwith ever whistled. Some things I miss terrible, some of my old work, and often I long to see the old faces, especially when Andrew is away, but so far my dear you can claim that your faith in us has not gone Awry. Bless you for all you did.

I could have wished that this Christmas time could have seen a reconsiling of us all, a real gathering of just the six of us, with of course Julia and Geoffrey Charles. That would have been good, alas I'm afraid Francis will never soften. But I know Ross will, and in the Spring when the weather improves and Ross is less busy I want you both to come over and spend a week with me. We have quite a number of friends and no one dislikes Andrew who knows him well.

My dear I am so sorry that all Ross's work seems to be coming to nought, it is too bad and such a Pity, for the industry needs all the help it can get, there are distressed tinners round here and some entered the Town last week and made a disturbance. So far it has been a terrible winter and I hope and pray with so many near starving that nothing will happen here like what has happened across the water. Try not to let Ross take this to heart as sometimes he is inclined to do, feeling that any failure is *his* failure. If the very worst comes and the smelting works closes it may be only a setback for a few years, and happier times will see a reopening. Captain Millett one of the Frigate Captains said yesterday that what we need is another war. A terrible solution, but there were others in the room to agree with him. Better Poverty than that, I say.

My only regret is that Andrew is away so much. He leaves this evening and will be gone all Christmas and into the New Year. I have thought often to go with him but he says wait until the summer when the Bay of Biscay will not be so Steep. He loves the sea devotedly but is known throughout the Service as a "driver." Always when he comes home he seems strained, as if the voyage has tried his nerves, he is easier to cross and a trifle moody. I think too he drinks a little during his time at sea, no wonder, for he needs something to sustane him, but never touches a drop while ashore. It takes me one day of his precious time at home to make him quite content, then soon he has to be up and away.

I have not met my two "children" yet. That is something of an Ordeal which may be mine about Easter, when *The Thunderer* with James Blamey on board as a cadet, is expected home. Esther Blamey, Andrew's daughter, is at boarding school and lives with his Sister near Plymouth. It may be that she will come and visit us too in the Spring. Pray for me then! I do so wish to make a home for them here and to make them welcome, if only our relationship will allow. I sometimes think I am such a poor mixer and wish I had an Easy manner, which some people have.

Our housekeeper, Mrs. Stevens was taken so ill with pains in the stomach last night that we sent for Dr. Silvey, but he said it was cramp and gave her a piece of roll Brimstone sewed in fine linen to hold near the affected part when she felt the pain. This has been a wonderful cure, but for my part I do not think she takes enough rhubarb.

I shall think of you this Christmas. I am very, very glad you gave me the courage to make my own life.

God bless and keep you both

VERITY.

CHAPTER II   Ten o'clock had struck before Ross returned that night. It was a fine night and an hour before Sawle Church choir had been up to the door singing carols. Demelza had never had much to do with religion but she still said the prayers her mother taught her, adding a postscript of her own to keep them abreast of the times; and at Christmas she had always felt an inward impulse to go to church. Something in the ancient wisdom of the story and the fey beauty of the carols tugged at her emotions; and with a suitable invitation she would have been willing to join the choir. She specially wanted to help them this evening hearing their depleted voices struggling through "Remember, O thou Man." But even her enjoyment of the two carols was a little spoiled by anxiety as to how she had best behave when they knocked on the door. She sent Jane Gimlett for the cakes she had made that afternoon and took down a couple of bottles of canary wine from Ross's cupboard.

They came in, a sheepish, blinking, uncertain lot, headed by Uncle Ben Tregeagle; ill-clad and undernourished every one, and only eight in all, for two of the choir were ill with the ulcerous sore throat and three were sick with influenza and Sue Baker had her fits. So Uncle Ben said, looking sly and foreign with his hooked nose and his long greasy black hair curling in little ringlets on his shoulders.

Demelza nervously gave them all a drink and took one herself; she would almost sooner have entertained Sir Hugh Bodrugan than these humble choristers; at least she knew where she was with him. She pressed cakes on them and refilled their glasses and when they rose to go she gave them a handful of silver—about nine shillings in all—and they crowded out into the misty moonlit night, flushed and merry and opulent. There they gathered round the lantern and gave her one more carol for luck before filing off up the valley towards Grambler.

Laughing now at her own absurdity and her success in spite of it, she went back into the parlour and began to pick out on the spinet the simple tune of "In Dulce Jubilo." Then she sat down and filled in with the other hand. She was getting good at this, though Mrs. Kemp frowned on it and said it wasn't music at all.

While she was so playing she heard Ross return. She met him at the door and at once saw how everything was.

"I've saved some pie for you," she said. "Or there's cold chicken if you want. And some nice fresh cakes and tarts."

He sat down in his chair and she helped him off with his boots.

"I had supper with Tonkin. Not a feast but enough to satisfy. A glass of rum will do and a bite or two of your cake. Have we had visitors?"

Demelza explained. "There's a letter here from Verity. It came this morning."

Ross read it slowly, puckering his eyes as if they too were tired. She put her hand on his shoulder, reading it again with him, and he put his fingers over hers.

The quarrel between them on that July evening had long been ignored but never forgotten. It had been ignored, and for that reason was still felt more by her than by him, it being her temperament to dislike anything not clear and downright. Also he had been fighting other things all these months and away more than at home. That he suspected Francis of betrayal had come to her gradually, and with it all the rest of his reasoning; so that she sometimes felt not only responsible for his quarrel with his cousin but also for the mounting difficulties of the copper company. It was not a pleasant thought and had lain heavy on her, far heavier than he knew. It was the first real shadow on their relationship and it had spoiled her happiness all this autumn. But outwardly there was no change.

"So your experiment prospers more than mine," he said. "Perhaps your instinct was the surer."

"Is there no better news for you?"

"Johnson and Tonkin and I have gone through the books item by item. Sir John has come to the view, which I think will be general among those who are left, that it is better to cut our losses than to refuse to admit defeat. There will be a final meeting after the ticketing on Monday. If the decision goes against us I will spend Tuesday helping to wind up our affairs."

"Who are for going on, do you know?"

"Tonkin of course, and Blewett and Johnson. All men of good will and no financial standing. Lord Devoran is for going on so long as he is asked for no more money. Penvenen is already considering converting his mill to other uses."

Demelza sat down beside him. "You'll have till Monday free?"

"Yes—to make merry over Christmas."

"Ross, don't get bitter. You see what Verity says."

He sighed, and the sigh turned to a yawn.

". . . She says you feel everything too deep and that is the trouble, I b'lieve. What difference will it make to our money, Ross?"

"I may have to sell some of the Wheal Leisure shares."

"Oh, no!"

"Perhaps only half—those I bought from Choake."

"But they are paying a—a dividend, d'you call it—it would be such a shame! Is Harris Pascoe not a friend of yours?"

"He's a banker, my dear. His first obligation is to his depositors."

"But he must have a pile of money heaped up in the vaults. It would be no use to him! He knows he will be safe with your promise to pay. Why, you will be able to pay him in a few years out of the div—what I said—if he will only give you time."

Ross smiled. "Well, that will all be thrashed out. I shall have to be in Truro for two days, and Pascoe has invited me to stay with him. It will be difficult for him to be too hard on a guest."

Demelza sat in gloomy silence, nursing her knees.

"I don't like it," she said at length. "It isn't fair, Ross! It is wicked an' inhuman. Have bankers got no Christian bowels? Don't they ever think, 'How should I feel if I was in debt?'"

"Come, my dear; don't you too get despondent or we shall be a pretty pair to wish each other a happy Christmas."

"Ross, could we not raise a mortgage on this house?"

"It's already raised."

"Or sell the horses and the oxen. I don't mind walking about my business or going short of some foodstuffs—it is only what I was always used to. Then there is my best silver frock and my ruby brooch. You said that was worth a hundred pounds."

He shook his head. "All told these things wouldn't discharge the debt, nor half of it. We must accept the position if it has to be."

"*Is* there a chance of going on?"

"Something will depend on the ticketing on Monday. And there is a movement on to drop the smelting but prevent the failure by becoming merchants pure and simple. I dislike face-saving."

Demelza looked at him. She wondered if she was very selfish to feel glad that in the coming year there might be fewer calls on his time. If the failure of the company meant a return to old ways then there was some recompense even in failure.

Christmas passed quietly inside Nampara and out—the calm before the storm. He had had scarcely so much leisure since the project took shape. They had worked shorthanded on the farm all through the summer to cut down expense. He had scraped to put everything into Carnmore, and now it seemed he might just as well have thrown it over the cliff.

A bitter reflection but one that had to be faced. Ever since that meeting of the company in July, Ross and his fellow shareholders had been fighting a losing battle. St. Aubyn Tresize, Aukett and Fox had all as good as resigned that day, and since then almost every week had seen a fresh casualty. Those the Warleggans could not touch directly they worked round to affect indirectly. Miners found their credit suddenly withdrawn or their coal supplies held up. Sir John was still fighting his case in Swansea. Alfred Barbary's title to some of the wharves he used in Truro and Falmouth was called in question, and litigation was pending here until he contracted out of the Carnmore. Even Ray Penvenen was not immune.

Of course it was not all the Warleggans, but it was the result of forces put in motion by them. If their grip had been complete the company could not have survived a month, but there were gaps in all their schemes. Only one third of the other copper companies were directly controlled by them, the rest were in friendly co-operation with the same ends in view.

On Boxing Day, the only windy day of the week, Ross and Demelza rode over to Werry House to visit Sir Hugh Bodrugan. Ross disliked the man but he knew Demelza had been secretly hankering to go ever since her first invitation nine months ago and he felt it right to humour her. They found Sir Hugh bottling gin, but he gave up with a good grace and ushered them into the great parlour, where Constance, Lady Bodrugan, was busy among her puppies.

She was not so rude as Ross remembered her, and received them without blasphemy. She had got used to the strange idea of her elderly stepson's having this liking for Ross Poldark's underbred wife. They took tea at a respectful distance from the greatest log fire Demelza had ever seen, and surrounded by spaniels, boarhound puppies and other breeds, whom Constance fed with cakes from the table and who made polite conversation a tenuous affair punctuated by the snaps and snarls of the disputing feeders. Every now and then a great gust of smoke would billow out from the fireplace, but the room was so high that the fog made a canopy over them and drifted away through the cracks in the ceiling. In this peculiar atmosphere Demelza sipped strong tea and tried to hear what Constance was saying about her treatment for dog's distemper; Ross, looking very tall and rather out of place on a chair too small for him, nodded his lean intelligent head and threw the ball of conversation back at Sir Hugh, who was just then leaning back scratching his ruffles and wondering what sort of a bedfellow Demelza would really make.

After tea Sir Hugh insisted on showing them the house and the stables, although by then darkness was near. They walked down draughty passages, led and followed by a groom with a horn lantern, up staircases to a great room on the first floor once elaborately decorated but now damp and mildewed, with creaking boards and cracked windows. Here the Dowager Lady kept her yellow rabbits in great boxes along one wall and bred her puppies in boxes opposite. The smell was overpowering. In the next room was a family of owls, some dormice, a sick monkey and a pair of racoons. Downstairs they went again, to a passage full of cages with thrushes, goldfinches, canary birds and Virginia nightingales. Sir Hugh squeezed her arm so often that Demelza began to wonder if this show was all a pretext for being with her in dark and draughty places. In one room, where the wind was so high that they might have been out of doors, the rear lantern went out and Sir Hugh put his short thick arm round her waist. But she slipped away with a faint rustle of silk and moved quickly up to Ross.

The stables were the best-kept part of the house, with many fine hunters and a pack of hounds, but inspection was abandoned halfway, Lady Bodrugan not being concerned for the comfort of her guests but thinking the horses would be needlessly disturbed.

So back they went to the great parlour, in which the fog had thickened since they left. Demelza had not yet learned to play whist, so they had a hand of quadrille for an hour, at which she won five shillings. Then Ross got up and said they must go before the wind grew worse. Sir Hugh, perhaps with vague hopes of further intimacies, suggested they should stay the night, but they thanked him and refused.

On the way home Demelza was rather silent, more silent than the gusty night dictated. When they got into the shelter of their own combe she said:

"It isn't always the people with the biggest house who are the most comfortable, is it, Ross?"

"Nor the best-bred who are the cleanest."

She laughed. "I did not fancy staying there the night. The wind was everywhere. And I should have dreamed of finding that old sick monkey in my bed."

"Oh, I don't think Sir Hugh is sick."

Her laughter bubbled up again, overflowed and ran with the wind.

"Serious, though," she said breathlessly, "what is the use of a big house if you cannot keep it nice? Are they short of money?"

"Not desperate. But old Sir Bob squandered most of what was not entailed."

"It must be strange to have a stepson old enough to be your father."
Little eddies of laughter still bubbled inside her. "Serious, though, Ross, would he have money to loan you to tide you over just for the present?"

"Thank you, I would rather the company was put away decently."

"Is there no one else? Would old Mr. Treneglos help? He has done well out of the mine you started for him. How much do you need to carry on a while longer?"

"A minimum of three thousand pounds."

She pursed her lips together as if to whistle. Then she said:

"But for yourself, Ross, so as not to have to sell the Wheal Leisure shares. That's what I care about most of all."

"I shall be more sure when I've talked of it with Pascoe," Ross said evasively. "In any event I would not be willing to borrow from friends."

CHAPTER III   He would not be willing to borrow from friends.
He said that to himself as he left for Truro on the Monday morning. At heart he would have agreed with Demelza, that his own happiness lay with her and little Julia and having leisure to labour on his own land and to see it grow. That was what he had thought at the beginning and nothing could alter it. He might even look back on this year as a nightmare well over and best forgotten. Yet nothing would remove the stigma of the failure, nothing would remove the sting of the Warleggan triumph.

And nothing would solve the bitter disappointment of having to part with the whole of his holdings in Wheal Leisure, which he knew was coming, though he had hidden it from Demelza. To lose that was the worst blow of all.

At the clump of firs Zacky Martin was waiting.

The pony and the horse fell naturally into step, having now made many journeys together. Ross tried to forget the business on hand and asked after Zacky's family. The Martins were a tenacious stock. Mrs. Zacky made them all drink pilchard oil during the winter and although it was foul and stank it seemed to be to their good. Jinny's three were brave, thanking you, Zacky said; and Jinny herself more better in spirits. There was a miner at Leisure called Scoble, a widow man in the thirties, lived beyond Marasanvose, no doubt Captain Poldark knew him.

"You mean Whitehead?"

"That's of him. They call him that on account of his hair. Well, he's taking an interest in Jinny, and she won't have nothing to do with him. Tisn't as she dislike him, she say, but that no one could do for Jim's place. That's well enough and as it should be, her mother say, but you've three young children to think of, and he's a nice steady feller with a little cottage, still some years to run and no children of his own. Mebbe in a year or so, Jinny say, I could consider it, but not yet for a while, twouldn't be possible. That's well enough, her mother say, but he's lonely and you're lonely, and men don't always wait and wait, for there's other girls'd be glad of the chance and they single and no family."

Ross said: "There is a lot in what Mrs. Zacky says. And no need to fear appearances. I know a clergyman in Truro called Halse who married his second wife within two months of losing his first. It is nothing unusual in the upper classes."

"I'll tell her that. It may help her to see it right. It is no good to marry a man if you dislike him; but I don't think she do; and I b'lieve it would do her good once the ice was broke."

When they reached the fork near Sawle Church they saw Dwight Enys, and Ross waved a hand and would have branched off towards the Bargus crossroads, but Dwight signalled him to stop. Zacky rode on a few paces to be out of earshot.

As Dwight came up Ross noticed how his good looks had come to have a cadaverous threat.

His place in the countryside was secure enough now; his work during the epidemics of the autumn had made sure of that. All remembered and a few still whispered behind his back, but none wished him gone. They liked him, they respected his work, they depended on him. Since the closing of Grambler many of Choake's former patients had come to Enys. Not that such work showed much return, but no one ever asked in vain. He was working off the disgrace within himself. But when not working he liked to be alone.

"You look in need of a holiday," Ross said. "I am lying to-night with the Pascoes and they would be pleased to see you."

Dwight shook his head. "It is out of the question, Ross. There is a mountain of work. If I was absent for three days I should never catch up in three months."

"You should leave Choake more to do. It is not a fair distribution, for you do a hundred poor cases and he does ten rich."

Dwight said: "I am getting along. Old Mr. Treneglos called me in last week for his gout, and you know how he distrusts our profession." The smile faded. "But what I had to tell you is not good news. It is about Mr. Francis Poldark. Had you heard? They say he is ill, also their little son."

"Oh . . . ? No. Have you seen them?"

"Dr. Choake is of course in charge. It is rumoured it is the sore throat. *Morbus strangulatorius.*"

Ross stared at him. This disease had been hanging round the district for nearly nine months. It had never been quite epidemic in the way the familiar diseases were epidemic; but it struck here and there with great rapidity and terrible results. Sometimes a whole family of children was swept off. It flared up in this village or that and then went underground again.

"Only last week," Dwight said, frowning, and as if following his thoughts, "I looked up what records there were on the matter. There was a bad outbreak in 'forty-eight. In Cornwall, that was. But since then we have been tolerably immune."

"What is the cause?"

"No one knows. Some put it down to a mephitic quality of the air, especially when near water. All our views are much in the melting pot since Cavendish proved there was both dephlogisticated and inflammable air."

"I wish you could get to see them, Dwight." Ross was thinking of Elizabeth.

The younger man shook his head. "Unless I am called in . . . Besides, I lay no claim to a cure. The results are always unpredictable. Sometimes the strong will go and the weak survive. Choake knows as much as I do."

"Don't belittle yourself." Ross hesitated, wondering whether he should obey his impulse to ride at once and see Elizabeth. It was the Christian thing to do, to forget all the old bitterness. Almost impossible with the copper company dying before his eyes. And the ticketing would not wait. He had only just time to get there.

As he was hesitating, Dr. Choake himself topped the hill out of Sawle riding towards them. . . .

"You'll pardon me," Dwight said. "This man has tried to make every sort of trouble for me. I don't wish to meet him now." He took off his hat and moved away.

Ross stood his ground until Choake was fairly up with him. The physician would have ridden by without a word if he could have got past.

"Good day to you, Dr. Choake."

Choake looked at him from under his eye-thatches.

"We'll trouble you to move aside, Mister Poldark. We are on urgent business."

"I'll not detain you. But I hear that my cousin is gravely ill."

"Gravely ill?" Choake bent his eyebrows after the departing figure of his rival. "Dear me, I should not be inclined to lend an ear to every story if I were you."

Ross said curtly: "Is it true that Francis has the malignant sore throat?"

"I isolated the symptoms yesterday. But he is on the mend."

"So soon?"

"The fever was checked in time. I emptied the stomach with fever powder and gave him strong doses of Peruvian bark. It is all a question of competent treatment. You are fully at liberty to inquire at the house." Choake moved to edge his horse past. Darkie blew through her nostrils and stamped.

"And Geoffrey Charles?"

"Not the throat at all. A mild attack of quartan fever. And the other cases in the house are the ulcerous throat, which is quite a different thing. And now good day to you, sir."

When Choake was past Ross sat a moment gazing after him. Then he turned and followed Zacky.

The ticketing was over and the feast about to begin.

Everything had gone according to plan, someone else's plan. The usual care had been taken to see that the Carnmore Copper Company did not get any of the copper. The mines did well out of it—so long as the Carnmore was in existence as a threat. As soon as Zacky ceased to put in his bids the prices would drop into the ruck again.

Ross wondered if the mines—the remaining mines—were really as powerless as the Warleggans had shown them up to be. They had not been able to stay together so they had fallen by the way. It was a dismal, sordid, disheartening business.

Ross sat down at the long dinner table with Zacky on his one hand and Captain Henshawe, representing Wheal Leisure, on his other. It wasn't until he was served that he noticed George Warleggan.

Ross had never seen him before at a ticketing dinner. He had no plain business there, for although he owned the controlling interest in a number of ventures he always acted through an agent or a manager. Strange that he had condescended, for as George grew more powerful he grew more exclusive. A brief silence had fallen on the men gathered there. They knew all about Mr. Warleggan. They knew he could make or break a good many if he chose. Then George Warleggan looked up and caught Ross's eye. He smiled briefly and raised a well-groomed hand in salute.

It was a sign for the dinner to begin.

Ross had arranged to meet Richard Tonkin at the Seven Stars Tavern before the others arrived. As he came out of the Red Lion Inn he found George Warleggan beside him. He fell into step.

"Well, Ross," he said in a friendly fashion, as if nothing had happened between them, "we see little of you in Truro these days. Margaret

Vosper was saying only last night that you had not been to our little gaming parties recently."

"Margaret Vosper?"

"Did you not know? The Cartland has been Margaret Vosper these four months, and already poor Luke is beginning to fade. I do not know what there is fatal about her, but her husbands seem unable to stand the pace. She is climbing the ladder and will marry a title before she's done."

"There is nothing fatal in her," Ross said, "except a greed for life. Greed is always a dangerous thing."

"So she sucks the life out of her lovers, eh? Well, you should know. She told me she'd once had the fancy to marry you. It would have been an interesting experiment, ecod! I imagine she would have found you a hard nut."

Ross glanced at his companion as they crossed the street. They had not met for eight months; and George, Ross thought, was becoming more and more a "figure." In his early days he had striven to hide his peculiarities, tried to become polished and bland and impersonal, aping the conventional aristocrat. Now with success and power firmly held, he was finding a new pleasure in allowing those characteristics their freedom. He had always tried to disguise his bullneck in elaborate neck-cloths; now he seemed to accentuate it slightly, walking with his head thrust forward and carrying a long stick. Once he had raised his naturally deep voice: now he was letting it go, so that the refinements of speech he had learned and clung to seemed to take on a bizarre quality. Everything about his face was big, the heavy nose, the pursed mouth, the wide eyes. Having as much money as he wanted, he lived now for power. He loved to see himself pointed out. He delighted that men should fear him.

"How is your wife?" George asked. "You do not bring her out enough. She was much remarked on at the celebration ball, and has not been seen since."

"We have no time for a social round," Ross said. "And I don't imagine we should be the more wholesome for it."

George refused to be ruffled. "Of course you will be busy. This copper-smelting project takes a good portion of your time." A pretty answer.

"That and Wheal Leisure."

"At Wheal Leisure you are fortunate in the grade of your ore and the easy drainage. One of the few mines which still offer prospects for the investor. I believe some of the shares are shortly coming on the market."

"Indeed. Whose are they?"

"I understood," said George delicately, "that they were your own." They had just reached the door of the Seven Stars, and Ross stopped and faced the other man. These two had been inimical since their school days but had never come to an outright clash. Seeds of enmity had been sown time and again but never reached fruit. It seemed that the whole weight of years was coming to bear at once.

Then George said in a cool voice but quickly: "Forgive me if I am misinformed. There was some talk of it."

The remark just turned away the edge of the response that was coming. George was not physically afraid of a rough and tumble but he could not afford the loss to his dignity. Besides, when quarrelling with a gentleman it might not end in fisticuffs even in these civilized days.

"You have been misinformed," Ross said, looking at him with his bleak pale eyes.

George humped his shoulders over his stick. "Disappointing; I am always out for a good speculation, you know. If you ever do hear of any coming on the market, let me know. I'll pay thirteen pound fifteen a share for 'em, which is more than you—more than anyone would get at present in the open market." He glanced spitefully up at the taller man.

Ross said: "I have no control over my partners. You had best approach one of them. For my part I would sooner burn the shares."

George stared across the street. "There is only one trouble with the Poldarks," he said after a moment. "They cannot take a beating."

"And only one trouble with the Warleggans," said Ross. "They never know when they are not wanted."

George's colour deepened. "But they can appreciate and remember an insult."

"Well, I trust you will remember this one." Ross turned his back and went down the steps into the tavern.

CHAPTER IV   It was afternoon before Demelza heard the bad news of Trenwith. All three of the younger Poldarks had it, said Betty Prowse, with only Aunt Agatha well, and three out of the four servants had taken it. Geoffrey Charles was near to death, they said, and no one knew which way to turn. Demelza asked for particulars, but Betty knew nothing more. Demelza went on with her baking.

But not for long. She picked up Julia, who was crawling about on the floor under her feet and carried her into the parlour. There she sat on the rug and played with the child before the fire while she wrestled with her torment.

She owed them nothing. Francis had told her never to come near the house again. Francis had betrayed them to the Warleggans. A despicable, horrible thing to do.

They would have called in others to help, perhaps some of the Teague family or one of the Tremenheere cousins from farther west. Dr. Choake would have seen to that for them. They were well able to look after themselves.

She threw the linen ball back to Julia who, having rolled on it to stop it, now forgot her mother and began to try to pull the ball apart.

There was no reason for her to call. It would look as if she were trying to curry favour and patch up the quarrel. Why should she patch it up, when Elizabeth was her rival. Elizabeth had not appeared so much in that light this last year; but she was always a danger. Once Ross saw that fair fragile loveliness . . . She was the unknown, the unattainable, the mysterious. His wife he knew would be here always, like a faithful sheep dog, no mystery, no remoteness, they slept in the same bed every night. They gained in intimacy, lost in excitement. Or that was how she felt it must be with him. No; leave well alone. She had done enough interfering.

"Ah—ah!" Demelza said. "Naughty girl. Don't tear it abroad. Throw it back to Mummy. Go to! Push with your hand. Push!"

But it was her interference which put her in an obligation deep down. If she had not contrived Verity's marriage, Verity would have been there to take charge. And if she had not so contrived Francis would never have quarrelled with Ross or betrayed them. Was it really all her fault? Sometimes she thought Ross thought so. In the night—when she woke up in the night—she felt that sense of guilt. She glanced out of the window. Two hours of daylight. The ticketing would be over. He would not be home to-night, so she could not have his advice. But she did not want his advice. She knew what she knew.

Julia was crowing on the rug as she went to the bell. But she did not pull it. She could never get used to having servants at call.

She went through to the kitchen. "Jane, I am going out for a while. I expect to be back before dark. If not, could you see to put Julia to bed? See the milk be boiled an' see she takes all her food."

"Yes, ma'am."

Demelza went upstairs for her hood and cloak.

The company had assembled in the private room of the Seven Stars. They were a depleted and a subdued party. Lord Devoran was in the chair. He was a fat dusty man dressed in snuff brown, and he had a cold in the head from leaving off his wig.

"Well, gentlemen," he said stuffily, "you have heard Mr. Johnson's statement of accounts. It is all very disappointing I aver, for the company was started in such high hopes not fourteen months ago. It has cost me a pretty penny and I suspicion most of us are a good degree poorer for our interest. But the truth is we bit off more'n we could chew, and we've got to face the fact. Some of us I know feel sore about the tactics of those who have fought us; and I can't say myself that I'm any too satisfied. But it has all been legal, so there's no redress. We just haven't the resources to carry on." Devoran paused and took a pinch of snuff.

Tonkin said: "You can form a company like this with fair enough prospects and find many people willing to invest a little. But it is altogether a different matter to find people willing to buttress up a shaky concern or to buy shares suddenly flung on the market. They see that the company is in difficulty and aren't agreeable to risk their money then."

Sir John Trevaunance said: "The company would have stood twice the chance if we had restricted it to people with unassailable credit."

Tonkin said: "You can't hold an inquiry into people's finances when they wish you well. And of course it was not thought that the exact composition of the company should ever become publicly known."

"Oh, you know what it is in these parts," Sir John remarked. "No man can keep a secret for five minutes. I do believe it is something in the air, it is moist and humid and breeds confidences."

"Well, somebody's confidences have cost us dear," said Tonkin. "I have lost my position and best part of my life's savings."

"And I am for bankruptcy," said Harry Blewett. "Wheal Maid must close this month. It is doubtful if I will stay out of prison."

"Where is Penvenen to-night?" Ross asked.

There was silence.

Sir John said: "Well, don't look at me. I am not his keeper."

"He has lost interest in the sinking ship," Tonkin said rather bitterly.

"He is more interested in his rolling mill than in the copper company," Johnson said.

"As for a *sinking* ship," Sir John said, "I think in truth the ship may be considered sunk. There is no question of desertion. When one is left struggling in the water it is but natural to make what provision one can to reach dry land."

Ross had been watching the faces of his companions. There was the barest touch of complacency about Sir John that he had not noticed before Christmas. In this venture Sir John stood to lose the most—though not proportionately the most. The great smelting furnaces stood on his land. During the company's brief life he had been the only one to receive a return for his larger investment—in the shape of port dues, increased profit from his coal ships, ground rent and other items. This change was therefore surprising. Had he during Christmas caught sight of some dry land not visible to the others?

All the time Ross had been striving to sense the mood of the other men. He had been hoping for signs of a greater resilience in some of them. But even Tonkin was resigned. Yet he was determined to make a last effort to bring them round.

"I don't altogether agree that the ship is yet sunk," he said. "I have one suggestion to make. It might just see us through the difficult months until the spring. . . ."

Trenwith House looked chill and grey. Perhaps it was only her imagination harking back to the last visit. Or perhaps it was knowing what the house now held.

She pulled at the front doorbell and fancied she heard it jangling somewhere away in the kitchens right across the inner court. The garden here was overgrown, and the lawn falling away to the stream and the pond was green and unkempt. Two curlews ran across it, dipping their tufted heads and sheering away as they saw her.

She pulled the bell again. Silence.

She tried the door. The big ring handle lifted the latch easily and the heavy door swung back with a creak.

There was nobody in the big hall. Although the tall mullioned window faced south the shadows of the winter afternoon were already heavy in the house. The rows of family pictures at the end and going up the stairs were all dark except for one. A shaft of pale light from the window fell on the portrait of the red-haired Anna-Maria Trenwith, who had been born, said Aunt Agatha, when Old Rowley was on the throne, whoever he might be. Her oval face and the fixed blue eyes stared out through the window and over the lawn.

Demelza shivered. Her finger touching the long table came away dusty. There was a herby smell. She would have done better to follow her old custom and go round the back. At that moment a door banged somewhere upstairs.

She went across to the big parlour and tapped. The door was ajar and she pushed it open. The room was empty and cold and the furniture was hung in dust sheets.

So this was the part they were not using. Only two years ago she had come to this house for the first time, when Julia was on the way, had been sick and drunk five glasses of port and sung to a lot of ladies and gentlemen she had never seen before. John Treneglos had been there, merry with wine, and Ruth his spiteful wife, and George Warleggan; and dear Verity. This house had been glittering and candlelit then, enormous and as impressive to her as a palace in a fairy tale. Since then she had seen the Warleggans' town house, the Assembly Rooms,

Werry House. She was experienced, adult and grown-up now. But she had been happier then.

She heard a footstep on the stairs and slipped back quickly into the hall.

In the half-light an old woman was tottering down them clutching anxiously at the banister. She was in faded black satin and wore a white shawl over her wig.

Demelza went quickly forward.

Aunt Agatha's ancient tremblings came to a stop. She peered at the girl, her eyes interred before their time in a mass of folds and wrinkles.

"What—eh . . . ? Is it you, Verity? Come back, have ye? And about time too——"

"No, it's Demelza." She raised her voice. "Demelza, Ross's wife. I came to inquire."

"You what? Oh, yes, tis Ross's little bud. Well, this be no time for calling. They're all sick, every last jack of them. All except me and Mary Bartle. And she be so busy attending on them that she's no time to bother with a old woman. Let me starve! I b'lieve she would! Lord damme, don't an old body need just so much attention as a young?" She clung precariously to the banister and a tear tried to trickle down her cheek, but got diverted by a wrinkle. "Tis all bad managing, and that's a fact. Everything has gone amiss since Verity left. She never ought to have left, d'you hear. Twas selfish in her to go running after that man. Her duty was to stay. Her father always said so. She'd take no notice of me. Always headstrong, she was. I bring to mind when she was but five——"

Demelza slipped past her and ran up the stairs.

She knew where the main bedrooms were, and as she turned the corner of the corridor an elderly black-haired woman came out of one of the rooms carrying a bowl of water. Demelza recognized her as Aunt Sarah Tregeagle, Uncle Ben's putative wife. She dipped a brief curtsy when she saw Demelza.

"Are they in here?"

"Yes, ma'am."

"Are you—seeing after them?"

"Well, Dr. Tommy calls me in, ma'am. But tis midwifing that belongs to be my proper work, as ye d'know. I come 'cos there was no one else. But my proper work be lying-in—or laying-out, when need be."

Her hand on the door, Demelza stared after the woman, who was slopping water on the floor in her carelessness. Everyone knew Aunt Sarah. Not the nurse for these gentlefolk. But of course there was no choice. The smell of herbs was much stronger here.

She opened the door gently and slipped in.

After the meeting of the shareholders Ross did not go straight back to the Pascoes. They did not sup till eight, and he did not want to spend an hour making polite conversation with the ladies in the parlour.

So he strolled through the back streets of the little town. Deliberately he turned his mind away from all the things which had just finished. Instead he thought about himself and his family, about his rake of a father, who had been in and out of trouble all his life, making love to one woman after another, fighting with this husband and that parent, cynical and disillusioned and sturdy to the end. He thought of Demelza and of how his estrangement from Francis sometimes seemed to come between her and him. It had no business to but it did—a sort of reservation, a bar sinister on their clear intimacy. He thought of Garrick her dog, of Julia, laughing and self-absorbed and untroubled with the perplexities of the world. He thought of Mark Daniel away in a foreign land, and wondered if he would ever bring himself to settle down there, or whether one day homesickness would lure him back into the shadow of the gibbet. He thought of the sickness at Trenwith and of Verity.

The drift of his steps had taken him out of the town and towards the river, which was full to-night and gleamed here and there with the lights of ships and the lanterns moving about the docks. There were three vessels moored alongside the wharves: two small schooners and a ship of some size for this creek, a brigantine Ross saw when he got near enough to make out the yards on her foremast. She was a nice new ship, recently painted, with brass glistening on the poop. She would draw so much water, he thought, as to make it unsafe to put in and out of here except at the high tides. That was the reason for all the bustle to-night.

He strolled on towards the trees growing low to the riverbank and then turned to come back. From here, although there was no moon, you could make out the wide gleam of the flood tide with the masts like lattices in the foreground and the winking pins of light in the black rim of the town.

As he came near the brigantine again he saw several men going aboard. Two sailors held lanterns at the top of the gangway, and as one of the men reached the deck the lantern light fell clear on his face. Ross made a half movement and then checked himself. There was nothing he could do to this man.

He walked thoughtfully on. He turned back to look once, but the men had gone below. A sailor passed.

"Are you for the *Queen Charlotte?*" Ross asked on impulse.

The sailor stopped and peered suspiciously. "Me, sur? No, sur. *Fairy Vale*. Cap'n Hodges."

"She's a fine ship, the *Queen Charlotte*," Ross said. "Is she new to these parts?"

"Oh, she's been in three or four times this year, I bla."

"Who is her master?"

"Cap'n Bray, sur. She's just off, I reckon."

"What is her cargo, do you know?"

"Grain for the most part; an' pilchards." The sailor moved on.

Ross stared at the ship a moment longer and then turned and walked back into the town.

The heavy smell of incense came from a little brazier of disinfectant herbs burning smokily in the centre of the bedroom. Demelza had found them all in the one room. Francis lay in the great mahogany bed. Geoffrey Charles was in his own small bed in the alcove. Elizabeth sat beside him.

Any resentment she might once have felt for Demelza was as nothing before relief at her coming now.

"Oh, Demelza, how kind of you! I have been in—in despair. We are in—terrible straits. How kind of you. My poor little boy. . . ."

Demelza stared at the child. Geoffrey Charles was struggling for breath, every intake sounded raw and hoarse and painful. His face was flushed and strained and his eyes only half open. There were red spots behind his ears and on the nape of his neck. One hand kept opening and shutting as he breathed.

"He—he has these paroxysms," Elizabeth muttered. "And then he spits up or vomits; there is relief then; but only for—for a time before it begins all over again."

Her voice was broken and despairing. Demelza looked at her flushed face, at the piled fair hair, at the great glistening grey eyes.

"You're ill yourself, Elizabeth. You did ought to be in bed."

"A slight fever. But not this. I can manage to keep up. Oh, my poor boy. I have prayed—and prayed. . . ."

"And Francis?"

Elizabeth coughed and swallowed with difficulty. "Is . . . a little . . . on the mend. There—there my poor dear . . . if only I could help him. We paint his throat with this Melrose; but there seems small relief. . . ."

"Who is it?" said Francis from the bed. His voice was almost unrecognizable.

"It is Demelza. She has come to help us."

There was silence.

Then Francis said slowly: "It is good of her to overlook past quarrels. . . ."

Demelza breathed out a slow breath.

"If . . . the servants had not been ill too," Elizabeth went on, "we could have made a better shift. . . . But only Mary Bartle . . . Tom Choake has persuaded Aunt Sarah . . . It is not a pretty task . . . He could find no one else."

"Don't talk any more," Demelza said. "You should be abed. Look, Elizabeth, I—I didn't know if I came to stay for a long time, for I didn't know how you was fixed——"

"But——"

"But since you need me I'll stay—so long as ever I can. But first—soon—soon I must slip home and tell Jane Gimlett and give her word for looking after Julia. Then I'll be back."

"Thank you. If only for to-night. It is such a relief to have someone to rely on. Thank you again. Do you hear, Francis, Demelza is going to see us through to-night."

The door opened and Aunt Sarah Tregeagle hobbled in with a bowl full of clean water.

"Aunt Sarah," said Demelza, "will you help me with Mrs. Poldark. She must be put to bed."

After supper at the Pascoes, when the ladies had left them and they were settling to the port, Harris Pascoe said:

"Well; and what is your news to-day?"

Ross stared at the dark wine in his glass. "We are finished. The company will be wound up to-morrow."

The banker nodded his head.

"I made a last effort to persuade them otherwise," Ross said. "For the first time in years copper has moved up instead of down. I put that to them and suggested we should try to keep together for another six months. I suggested that the furnace workers should be invited to work on a profit-sharing basis. Every mine does the same thing when it strikes bargains with tributers. I suggested we should make one last effort. A few were willing but the influential men would have none of it."

"Especially S-Sir John Trevaunance," said the banker.

"Yes. How did you know?"

"You are right about the price of copper. I had news to-day, it has risen another three pounds."

"That is six pounds in six weeks."

"But, mind you, years may pass before the metal reaches an economic level."

"How did you know Sir John would be opposed to my suggestion?"

Harris Pascoe licked his lips and looked diffident.

"Not so much opposed to your suggestion in p-particular as to a continuance in general. And then I was rather going on hearsay."

"Which is?"

"Which is that—er—Sir John, after battling against the wind for twelve months, is now preparing to sail with it. He has lost a tidy sum over this project and is anxious to recoup himself. He does not wish to see the smelting works lying idle permanently."

Ross thought of Sir John's voice that evening; he remembered Ray Penvenen's absence.

He got up. "Do you mean he is selling out to the Warleggans?"

The little banker reached for his wine.

"I think he is willing to come to some accommodation with them. Beyond that I know nothing."

"He and Penvenen are going to make a deal to cover their own losses while the rest of us go to the wall!"

"I imagine it likely," said Pascoe, "that some sort of a caretaker company will be formed, and that the Warleggans will have a representative on it."

Ross was silent, staring at the books in the cabinet.

"Tell me," he said, "this evening I thought I saw Matthew Sanson boarding a ship in the docks. Could that be possible?"

"Yes, he has been back in Truro for several months."

"He is allowed to come back here and trade as if nothing had happened? Are the Warleggans complete masters of the district?"

"No one cares sufficiently about Sanson to make a fuss. There are only four or five people whom he cheated, and they are not influential."

"And the ship he sails in?"

"Yes, that is the property of a company controlled by the Warleggans. There's the *Queen Charlotte* and the *Lady Lyson*. No doubt they're a profitable side line."

Ross said: "If I were in your shoes I should tremble for my soul. Is there anyone besides you in the town they don't own from head to toe?"

Pascoe coloured. "I like them little more than you. But you're t-taking an extreme view now. The average man in the district only knows them as rich and influential people. You know them as something more because you chose to challenge them on their own ground. I am only sorry—profoundly sorry—that you have not been more successful. If g-good will would have sufficed you would have triumphed without a doubt."

"Whereas good will did not suffice," Ross said. "What we needed was good gold."

"It was not my project," said the banker, after a moment. "I did what I could and will be the poorer for it."

"I know," Ross said. "Failure puts an edge on one's tongue." He sat down again. "Well, now comes the reckoning. Let's get it over. The company will almost clear itself; so that leaves only our personal ends to be settled. What is my indebtedness to you?"

Harris Pascoe straightened his steel spectacles. "Not a big sum—about n-nine hundred pounds or a little less. That is over and above the mortgage on your property."

Ross said: "The sale of my Wheal Leisure shares will meet most of that—together with the dividend we have just declared."

"It will rather more than meet it. By chance I heard of someone inquiring for shares of Wheal Leisure only yesterday. They offered eight hundred and twenty-five pounds for sixty shares."

"There is one other small matter," Ross said. "Harry Blewett of Wheal Maid is worse hit than I am. He fears going to prison and I don't wonder. The shares and the dividend will come to nearly a thousand and I want the extra to go to him. It's possible that with it he'll be able to keep his head up."

"Then you wish me to sell the shares at that price?"

"If it's the best you can get."

"It is better than you would receive if they were thrown on the open market. Thirteen pounds fifteen shillings a share is a good price for these days."

"Thirteen pounds . . ." The wineglass suddenly snapped in Ross's fingers and the red wine splashed over his hand.

Pascoe was standing beside him. "What is wrong? Are you ill?"

"No," said Ross. "Not at all ill. Your glass has a delicate stem. I hope it was not an heirloom."

"No. But something . . ."

Ross said: "I have decided different. I do not sell the shares."

"It was a m-man called Coke who approached me. . . ."

Ross took out a handkerchief and wiped his hand. "It was a man called Warleggan."

"Oh, no, I assure you. What makes you——"

"I don't care what nominee they chose. It is their money and they shall not have the shares."

Pascoe looked a little put out as he handed Ross another glass. "I had no idea. I s-sympathize with your feeling. But it is a good offer."

"It will not be taken," Ross said. "Not if I have to sell the house and the land. I'm sorry, Harris; you'll wait for your money whether you like it or not. You cannot force me for another month or so. Well, I'll get it before then—somehow. In the meantime, I'll keep my own mine smelling sweet if I go to gaol for it."

Mr. Notary Pearce was at home playing cribbage with his daughter when Ross was announced. Miss Pearce, a comely young woman of twenty-five who never made enough of her good looks, rose at once and excused herself, and Mr. Pearce, pushing aside the table, poked at the huge fire with his curtain rod and invited Ross to sit down.

"Well, Captain Poldark; I declare this is quite an event. Can you stay for a hand of cribbage? Playing with Grace is always a little dull, for she will not hazard a penny on the outcome."

Ross moved his chair farther from the fire.

"I need your advice and help."

"Well, my dear sir, you may have them if they are mine to give."

"I want a loan of a thousand pounds without security."

Mr. Pearce's eyebrows went up. Like the other shareholders of Wheal Leisure, he had stood aloof from the battle of the copper companies. But he knew very well which way it had gone.

"Hrr-hm. That is rather a severe proposition. *Without* security, you said? Yes, I thought so. Dear, dear."

Ross said: "I should be willing to pay a high rate of interest."

Mr. Pearce scratched himself. "*Without* security. Have you tried Cary Warleggan?"

"No," said Ross. "Nor do I intend to."

"Just so. Just so. But it will be very difficult. If you have no security, what can you offer?"

"My word."

"Yes, yes. Yes, yes. But that would really amount to a friendly accommodation. Have you approached any of your friends?"

"No. I want it to be a business arrangement. I will pay for the privilege."

"You will pay? You mean in interest? Yes . . . But the lender might be chiefly concerned for his capital. Why do you not sell your shares in Wheal Leisure if you need the money so badly?"

"Because that is what I am trying to avoid."

"Ah, yes." Mr. Pearce's plum-coloured face was not encouraging. "And your property?"

"Is already mortgaged."

"For how much?"

Ross told him.

Mr. Pearce took a pinch of snuff. "I think the Warleggans would raise that figure if you transferred the mortgage to them."

"Several times in recent years," Ross said, "the Warleggans have tried to interest themselves in my affairs. I mean to keep them out."

It was on Mr. Pearce's tongue to say that beggars could not be choosers, but he changed his mind.

"Have you thought of a second mortgage on the property? There are people—I know one or two who might be willing for the speculative risk."

"Would that bring in sufficient?"

"It might. But naturally such a risk would be a short-term one, say for twelve or twenty-four months——"

"That would be agreeable."

"—and would carry a very high interest rate. In the nature of forty per cent."

For a loan of a thousand pounds now he would have to find fourteen hundred by this time next year, in addition to his other commitments. A hopeless proposition—unless the price of copper continued to rise and Wheal Leisure struck another lode as rich as the present.

"Could you arrange such a loan?"

"I could try. It is a bad time for such things. There is no cheap money about."

"That is not cheap money."

"No, no. I quite agree. Well, I could let you know in a day or two."

"I should want to know to-morrow."

Mr. Pearce struggled out of his chair. "Dear, dear, how stiff one gets. I have been better but there is still some gouty humour lurking in my constitution. I could let you know to-morrow possibly, though it might take a week or so to get the money."

"That will do," Ross said. "I'll take that."

On Tuesday he delayed leaving the town until five in the afternoon.

He and Johnson and Tonkin and Blewett wound up the Carnmore Copper Company before dinner. Ross did not pass on Harris Pascoe's hint of yesterday. There was nothing any of them could do now to prevent Sir John's entering into some agreement with the Warleggans if he chose to. There was nothing to prevent the smelting works from coming into the hands of the Warleggans or a new company being formed to exploit their own hard work. But the company would be one of the circle, and he would see that it did not force up prices for the benefit of the mines.

Although Tonkin was not ruined, Ross felt most sorry for him, for he liked him the best and knew the quite tireless work he had put in, arguing, persuading, contriving. Fifteen months of fanatical energy had gone into it, and he looked worn out. Harry Blewett, who had been the instigator and first supporter of the idea, had pledged his last penny, and to-day was the end of everything for him. The big, dour, hard-headed Johnson stood the failure more confidently than the others; he was a better loser because he had lost less.

After it was over Ross went to see Mr. Pearce again, and learned that the money was forthcoming. He wondered if Mr. Pearce himself had advanced it. The notary was an astute man and fast becoming a warm one.

Then Ross went back to the Pascoes. The banker shook his head at the news. Such improvident borrowing was utterly against his principles. Better by far to cut your losses and start again than to plunge so deep in that there might be no getting out—merely to put off the evil day.

While he was there Ross wrote to Blewett saying he had placed two hundred and fifty pounds to his name at Pascoe's Bank. This was to be considered a five-year loan at four per cent interest. He hoped it would tide him over.

The journey home in the dark took Ross about two hours. On the way down the dark combe, just before the lights of Nampara came in sight, he overtook a cloaked figure hurrying on ahead of him.

He had been feeling bitter and depressed, but at sight of Demelza he mustered up his spirits.

"Well, my dear. You are out late. Have you been visiting again?"

"Oh, Ross," she said, "I'm that glad you're not home before me. I was afraid you would have been."

"Is anything wrong?"

"No, no. I'll tell you when we're home."

"Come. Up beside me. It will save a half mile."

She put her foot on his and he lifted her up. Darkie gave a lurch. Demelza settled down in front of him with a sudden sigh of contentment.

"You should have someone with you if you intend to be abroad after dark."

"Oh . . . it is safe enough near home."

"Don't be too sure. There is too much poverty to breed all honest men."

"Have you saved anything, Ross? Is it to go on?"

He told her.

"Oh, my dear, I'm that sorry. Sorry for you. I don't belong to know how it has all happened. . . ."

"Never mind. The fever is over. Now we must settle down."

"What fever?" she asked in a startled voice.

He patted her arm. "It was a figure of speech. Have you heard that there is illness at Trenwith, by the way? I had intended to call to-day but I was so late."

"Yes. I heard . . . yesterday."

"Did you hear how they were?"

"Yes. They are a small bit better to-day—though not yet out of danger."

The house loomed ahead of them as they crossed the stream. At the door he got down and lifted her down. Affectionately he bent his head to kiss her, but in the dark she had moved her face slightly so that his lips found only her cheek.

She turned and opened the door. "John!" she called. "We're back!"

Supper was a quiet meal. Ross was going over the events of the last few days; Demelza was unusually silent. He had told her that he had saved his holding in Wheal Leisure, but not how. That would come when repayment was nearer. Sufficient unto the day.

He wished now he had kicked George Warleggan into the gutter while there was the opportunity: George was the type that was usually careful to avoid giving an excuse. And to have the impertinence to bring Cousin Sanson back. He wondered what Francis would have to say. Francis.

"Did you say Geoffrey Charles was better also?" he asked. "The sore throat is usually hard on children."

Demelza started and went on with her supper.

"I b'lieve the worst is over."

"Well, that is some satisfaction. I shall never have room for Francis again after the trick he served us; but I would not wish that complaint on my worst enemy."

There was a long silence.

"Ross," she said, "after July I swore I would never keep a secret from you again, so you had best hear this now before it can be thought I have deceived you."

"Oh," he said, "what? Have you been to see Verity in my absence?"

"No. To Trenwith."

She watched his expression. It did not change.

"To call, you mean?"

"No . . . I went to help."

A candle was smoking but neither of them moved to snuff it.

"And did they turn you away?"

"No. I stayed all last night."

He looked across the table at her. "Why?"

"Ross, I had to. I went but to inquire, but they were in desperate straits. Francis—the fever had left him but he was prostrate. Geoffrey Charles was fit to die at any moment. Elizabeth had it too, though she would not admit it. There was three servants ill, and only Mary Bartle and Aunt Sarah Tregeagle to do anything. I helped to get Elizabeth to bed and stayed with Geoffrey Charles all night. I thought once or twice he was gone; but he brought round again and this morning was better. I came home then an' went again this afternoon. Dr. Choake says the crisis is past. Elizabeth, he says, has not took it so bad. I—I stayed so long as ever I could, but I told them I could not stay to-night. But Tabb is up again and can see to the others. They will be able to manage to-night."

He looked at her a moment. He was not a petty man, and the things that came to his lips were the things he could not say.

And, though at first he struggled to deny it, he could not in the end fail to acknowledge that the feeling moving in her had moved him no differently in the matter of Jim Carter. Could he blame her for the sort of impulse on which he had acted himself?

He could not subdue his thoughts, but honesty and the finer bonds of his affection kept him mute.

So the meal went on in silence.

At length she said: "I couldn't do any other, Ross."

"No," he said, "it was a kind and generous act. Perhaps in a fortnight I shall be in a mood to appreciate it."

They both knew what he meant but neither of them put it more clearly into words.

CHAPTER VI   A south-westerly gale broke during the night and blew for twenty hours. There was a brief quiet spell and then the wind got up again from the north, bitterly cold, and whipping rain and sleet and snow flurries before it. New Year's Day 1790, which was a Friday, dawned at the height of the gale.

They had gone to bed early as Demelza was tired. She had had a broken night the night before, Julia being fretful with teeth.

All night the wind thundered and screamed—with that thin, cold whistling scream which was a sure sign of the "norther." All night rain and hail thrashed on the windows facing the sea, and there were cloths laid along the window bottoms to catch the rain that was beaten in. It was cold even in bed with the curtains drawn, and Ross had made up a great fire in the parlour below to give a little extra heat. It was useless to light a fire in the bedroom grate, for all the smoke blew down the chimney.

Ross woke to the sound of Julia's crying. It reached very thinly to him for the wind was rampant, and he decided, as Demelza had not heard, to slip out himself and see if he could quiet the child. He sat up slowly; and then knew that Demelza was not beside him.

He parted the curtains, and the cold draught of the wind wafted upon his face. Demelza was sitting by the cot. A candle dripped and guttered on the table near. He made a little hissing sound to attract her attention, and she turned her head.

"What is it?" he asked.

"I don't rightly know, Ross. The teeth, I b'lieve."

"You will catch a consumption sitting there. Put on your gown."

"No, I am not cold."

"*She* is cold. Bring her into this bed."

Her answer was drowned by a sudden storm of hail on the window. It stopped all talk. He got out of bed, struggled into his gown and took up hers. He went over to her and put it about her shoulders. They peered down at the child.

Julia was awake but her plump little face was flushed, and when she cried her whimper seemed to end in a sudden dry cough.

"She has a fever," Ross shouted.

"I think it is a teething fever. I think . . ."

The hail stopped as suddenly as it had begun and the scream of the wind seemed like silence after it.

"It will be as well to have her with us to-night," Demelza said. She bent forward, it seemed rather clumsily to him, and picked up the child. Her dressing gown slipped off and lay on the floor.

He followed her back to the bed and they put Julia in it.

"I will just get a drink of water," she said.

He watched her go over to the jug and pour some out. She drank a little slowly, and took some more. Her shadow lurched and eddied on the wall. Suddenly he was up beside her.

"What is the matter?"

She looked at him. "I think I have caught a cold."

He put a hand on hers. Although the icy breeze was in the room her hand was hot and sweaty.

"How long have you been like this?"

"All night. I felt it coming last evening."

He stared at her. In the shadowed light he could see her face. He caught at the high frilly collar of her nightdress and pulled it back.

"Your neck is swollen," he said.

She stepped back from him and buried her face in her hands.

"My head," she whispered, "is that bad."

He had roused the Gimletts. He had carried the child and Demelza down into the parlour and wrapped them in blankets before the drowsy fire. Gimlett he had sent for Dwight. Mrs. Gimlett was making up the bed in Joshua's old room. There there was a fire grate which would not smoke, and the only window faced south; a more habitable sick-room in such a gale.

He found time to be grateful for having changed the Paynters for the Gimletts. No grudging grumbling service, no self-pitying lamentation on their own ill luck.

While he sat there talking in the parlour, talking softly to Demelza and telling her that Julia was a sturdy child and would come through quick enough, his mind was full of bitter thoughts. They flooded over him in waves, threatening to drown common sense and cool reason. He could have torn at himself in his distress. Demelza had run her head recklessly into the noose. The obligations of relationship . . .

No, not that. Although he could not see through to the source of her generous impulses, he knew it was much more than that. All these things were tied together in her heart: her share in Verity's flight, his quarrel with Francis, his quarrel with her, the failure of the copper company, her visit to the sick house of Trenwith. They could not be seen separately, and in a queer way the responsibility for her illness now seemed not only hers but his.

But he had not shown his anxiety or resentment three days ago; he could not possibly show it now. Instead he wiped her forehead and joked with her and watched over Julia, who slept now after a bout of crying.

Presently he went out to help Jane Gimlett. A fire was burning already in the downstairs bedroom, and he saw that Jane had stripped the bed upstairs to make up this one so that there should be no risk of damp. While he was helping Demelza to bed the whole house echoed and drummed, carpets flapped and pictures rattled. Then the front door was shut again and Dwight Enys was taking off his wet cloak in the hall.

He came through and Ross held a candle while he examined Demelza's throat; he timed her heart with his pulse watch, asked one or two questions, turned to the child. Demelza lay quiet in the great box bed and watched him. After a few minutes he went out into the hall for his bag, and Ross followed him.

"Well?" said Ross.

"They both have it."

"You mean the malignant sore throat?"

"The symptoms are unmistakable. Your wife's are further advanced than the baby's. Even to the pink finger ends."

Dwight would have avoided his eyes and gone back into the room but Ross stopped him.

"How bad is this going to be?"

"I don't know, Ross. Some get past the acute stage quick, but recovery is always a long job, three to six weeks."

"Oh, the length of recovery is nothing," Ross said.

Dwight patted his arm. "I know that. I know."

"The treatment?"

"There is little we can do: so much hangs on the patient. I have had some success with milk—boiled, always boiled, and allowed to cool until it is tepid. It sustains the patient. No solids. Keep them very flat, and no exertion or excitement. The heart should have the least possible work. Perhaps some spirits of sea salt painted on the throat. I do not believe in bloodletting."

"Does the crisis come soon?"

"No, no. A day or two. In the meantime be patient and have a good heart. They stand so much better a chance than the cottage people, who are half starved and usually without fire and light."

"Yes," said Ross, remembering Dwight's words two mornings before. "The results are always unpredictable," he had said. "Sometimes the strong will go and the weak survive."

CHAPTER VII   The northerly gale blew for three days more.
In the late part of New Year's Day snow began to blow in flurries before the wind, and by next morning there were drifts of it against all the hedges and walls, though the gale-swept ground was free. The pump in the yard was hung with tattered icicles like a beggar woman, and the water in the pail was frozen. The clouds were livid and low.

In the middle of the day the hail began again. It seemed hardly to fall at all but to blow flatly across the land. One felt that no glass would withstand it. Then it would rap, rap, rap a dozen times and suddenly stop and one could hear the wind like a roaring mighty beast rolling away in the distance.

To Demelza all the noise and fury was a true part of her nightmare. For two days her fever was high, and something in being in old Joshua's big box bed threw her errant mind back to the first night she had ever spent at Nampara. The years slipped off and she was a child of thirteen again, ragged, ill fed, ignorant, half cheeky, half terrified. She had been stripped and swilled under the pump and draped in a lavender-smelling shirt and put to sleep in this great bed. The weals of her father's latest thrashing were still sore on her back, her ribs ached from the kicks of the urchins of Redruth Fair. The candle smoked and guttered on the bedside table and the painted statuette of the Virgin nodded down at her from the mantelpiece. To make things worse she could not swallow, for someone had tied a cord about her throat; and there was Someone waiting behind the library door until she fell asleep and the candle went out, when they would creep in in the dark and tighten the knot.

So she must stay awake, at all costs she must stay awake. Very soon Garrick would come scratching at the window, and then she must go to open it and let him in. He would be a comfort and a protection through the night.

Sometimes people moved about the room, and often she saw Ross and Jane Gimlett and young Dr. Enys. They were there, but they were not real. Not even the child in the cot, her child, was real. They were the imagination, the dream, something to do with an impossible future, something she hoped for but had never had. The *now* lay in the guttering candle and the nodding statuette and the aching ribs and the cord round her throat and the Someone waiting behind the library door.

"Ye've slocked my dattur!" shouted Tom Carne, while she trembled in the cupboard. "What right ha' you to be seein' her back! I'll have the law on you!"

"That statuette seems to be worrying her," Ross said. "I wonder if it would be wise to move it."

She looked over the edge of the bed, out of the cupboard, down, down, to two tiny figures fighting on the floor far below her. Ross had thrown her father into the fireplace but he was getting up again. He was going to put something round her throat.

"Are ye saved?" he whispered. "Are ye saved? Sin an' fornication an' drunkenness. The Lord hath brought me out of a horrible pit of mire an' clay an' set my feet 'pon a rock. There's no more drinkings an' living in sin."

"Saved?" said Francis. "Saved from what?" And everyone tittered. They weren't laughing at Francis but at her, for trying to put on airs and pretending to be one of them when she was really only a kitchen wench dragged up in a lice-ridden cottage. Kitchen wench. Kitchen wench. . . .

"Oh," she said with a great sigh, and threw her life and her memories away, out over the edge of the bed into the sea. They fell, twirling, twisting away, growing ever smaller, smaller. Let them drown. Let them perish and die, if she could but have peace.

"Let him drown in the mud," Ross said. "Cheating at cards—let him drown."

"No, Ross, no, Ross, no!" She grasped his arm. "Save him. Else they'll say tis murder. What does it matter so long as we've got back what we lost. So long as we haven't lost Wheal Leisure. We'll be together again. That is all that counts."

She shrank from the touch of something cool on her forehead.

"It's unusual for the fever to persist so long," said Dwight. "I confess I am at a loss to know what to do."

Of course Mark had killed Keren this way. The men had not told her, but word had gone round. Against the window somehow, and then he had choked the life out of her. They were trying to do that now to her. She had been dozing and Someone had come in from the library and was just tightening the cord.

"Garrick!" she whispered. "Garrick! Here, boy! Help me now!"

"Drink this, my darling." Ross's voice came from a long way away, from the other room, from the room that was not hers, echoing out of her dreams.

"It is useless," said Dwight. "She can't swallow anything at present. In a few hours perhaps, if . . ."

Garrick was already scratching, eagerly scratching.

"Open the window!" she urged. "Open quick, afore tis . . . too . . . late."

Something large and black and shaggy bounded across the room to her, and with a gasp of joy she knew that they had done as she said. Her face and hands were licked by his rough tongue. She wept for sheer relief. But suddenly to her horror she found that the dog had somehow made a horrible mistake. Instead of knowing it was his mistress he thought she was an enemy and fastened his teeth in her throat. She struggled and fought to explain, but her voice and her breath were gone, were gone. . . .

The candle had blown out and it was cold. She shivered in the dark. Julia was crying with her teeth again, and she must get up and give her a drink of water. If only the wind was not so cold. Where was Ross? Had he not come back? He takes things so much to heart, Verity said, he takes things to heart. Well, then, I must not disappoint him this time. Deceived him once. Deceived him. I must not let him down. Clear, clear, but how might it happen? If you don't know you can't be sure.

Something with Julia and herself. But of course, Julia was sick. She had been watching by her bed all night. Francis was sick too, and Elizabeth was sick if she would only admit it. There was a horrible taste of copper in her mouth. It was those herbs they were burning. Aunt Sarah Tregeagle had come straight from carol singing to tend on them all. But where was . . .

"Ross!" she called. "Ross!"

"He's gone to sleep in his chair in the parlour, ma'am," said a woman's voice. It was not Prudie. "Do you want for me to call him? He's been without sleep these three nights."

It would not do for any of them to be asleep if her father came. He would bring all the Illuggan miners and they would set fire to the house. But he had reformed. He was a new man altogether. He had married Aunt Mary Chegwidden. How would he come this time, then? Perhaps with a choir of Methodists and they would sing outside the window. It seemed funny, and she tried to laugh but choked. And then she knew it was *not* funny, for *there* they were outside the window, there as she looked down on them, a great sea of faces. And she knew that they were hungry and wanted bread.

They were in a huge crowd stretching right up the valley and shouting. "Our rights be bread t'eat an' corn to buy at a fair an' proper price. We want corn to live by, an' corn we'll have, whether or no!"

And she realized that the only bread she could give them was her own child. . . .

Beside her was Sanson, the miller; and Verity and Andrew Blamey were talking in the corner, but they were too lost in each other to notice her. She wept in an agony of fear. For the miners were crazy for bread. In a minute they would set fire to the house.

She turned to look for Ross, and when she turned back to the window the massed, staring tiny faces were already fading behind dense ·columns of white smoke.

"Look," said Jane Gimlett, "it is snowing again."

"Snowing!" she tried to say. "Don't you see, it is not snow but smoke. The house is on fire and we shall be smothered to death!" She saw Sanson fall and then felt the smoke getting into her own breath.

Choking, she put up a hand to her throat and found that someone else's hand was already there.

On the morning of January the fourth the wind broke and it began to snow in earnest. By midday, when the fall ceased, the fields and the trees were thick and heavy with it. Branches bowed and thick floes drifted down the stream. John Gimlett splitting wood in the yard had to tug at the logs to get them apart, for the cold had bound them tight. Gimlett's nine ducks padding laboriously towards the water looked dirty and jaundiced in this purity. On Hendrawna Beach the tide was out and the great waves leaped and roared in the distance. The ice and foam and yellow scum which had covered the beach for a week was itself overlaid by the cloth of snow. Sand hills were mountain ranges, and in the distance the dark cliffs brooded over the scene, wearing their new dress like a shroud.

The hush everywhere was profound. After the fanatic ravings of the gale it was as if a blanket had fallen on the world. Nothing stirred and a dog's bark echoed round the valley. The roar of the sea was there but had somehow become lost in the silence and could only be heard by an effort of thought.

Then at two the clouds broke up and the sun came out dazzlingly brilliant, forcing a brief thaw. Branches and bushes dripped, and small avalanches of snow, already part thawed from within, began to slip down the roof. Dark stains showed on one or two of the fields, and a robin, sitting among the feathery snow of an apple branch, began to sing to the sun.

But the break had come late in the day, and soon the valley was streaked with shadow and the frost had set in again.

About four o'clock, as it was getting dark, Demelza opened her eyes and looked up at the wooden ceiling of the bed. She felt different from before, calmer and quite separate. She was no longer the child of nightmare. There was only the one reality and that was of this moment of waking to the long smooth shadows in the room, to the livid glimmering paleness of the ceiling, to the curtains drawn back from the latticed windows, to Jane Gimlett nodding sleepily in the glow of an old peat fire.

She wondered what day it was, what time of day, what kind of weather. Some noise had stopped; was it in her head or out in the world? Everything was very peaceful and unemphatic, as if she looked at it from a distance, no longer belonged to it. All life and energy was spent. Was she too spent? Where was Ross? And Julia? Had they all been ill? She was not clear on that. She would have liked to speak but somehow was afraid to try. In speaking she either broke the shell of quiet in which she lay, or stayed within it for ever. That was at the very heart of the choice. She did not know and was afraid to try. And Jud and Prudie, and her father and Verity and Francis . . . No, no, stop; that way, down that turning lay the nightmare.

Just then some of the peat fell in and caused a sharp glow and heat to fall on Jane Gimlett's face. She woke, sighed and yawned, put on more fuel. Presently she got up from her seat and came over to the bed to glance at the patient. What she saw there made her leave the room in search of Ross.

She found him slumped in his chair in the parlour staring into the fire.

They came back together and Ross went over alone to the bed.

Demelza's eyes were closed, but after a moment she seemed to feel the shadow across her face. She looked up and saw Ross. Jane Gimlett came to the bed with a candle and put it on the bedside table.

"Well, my love," said Ross.

Demelza tried to smile, and after a moment's frightened hesitancy took the risk of trying her voice.

"Well, Ross . . ."

The shell was broken. He had heard. Somehow she knew then she was going to get better.

She said something that he did not catch; he bent to hear it and again could not.

Then she said quite clearly: "Julia . . ."

"All right, my darling," he said. "But not now. To-morrow. When you're stronger. You shall see her then." He bent and kissed her forehead. "You must sleep now."

"Day?" she said.

"You've been ill a day or two," he said. "It has been snowing and is cold. Go to sleep now. Dwight is coming to see you again this evening and we want you to show improvement. Go to sleep, Demelza."

"Julia," she said.

"To-morrow. See her then, my love. Go to sleep."

Obedient, she closed her eyes and presently began to breathe more deeply and more slowly than he had seen her do for five days. He went over and stood by the window, wondering if he had done right to lie to her.

For Julia had died the night before.

CHAPTER VIII   They buried the child two days later. The weather had stayed quiet and cold and heaps of snow lay in sheltered corners about the fields and lanes. A great number of people turned out for the funeral. Six young girls dressed in white—two Martins, Paul Daniel's daughters, and two of Jim Carter's younger sisters—carried the small coffin the whole of the mile and a half to Sawle Church, and all the way along the route were people who stood silently by and then quietly fell in behind the other followers to the church. Sawle choir, uninvited, met the procession halfway, and each time the six girls stopped to rest they sang a psalm, in which the mourners joined.

Dwight Enys walked with Ross, and behind them were John Treneglos and Sir Hugh Bodrugan. Harry Blewett and Richard Tonkin had come, and Harris Pascoe had sent his eldest son. Captain and Mrs. Henshawe followed Joan Teague with one of the cousins Tremenheer. Behind them were Jud and Prudie Paynter, all the rest of the Martins and Daniels and Carters, the Viguses and the Nanfans, and then followed a great mass of ragged miners and their wives, small farmers and farm labourers, spallers, wheelwrights, fishermen. The sound of all these people singing psalms in the still, frosty air was very impressive. When they finished and before the shuffling movement of the procession began again, there was each time a brief hush when everyone heard the distant roar of the sea. In the end Mr. Odgers found he had to read the burial service before more than three hundred and fifty people, overflowing the church and standing silent in the churchyard.

It was this unexpected tribute that broke Ross up. He had hardened himself to all the rest. Not being a religious man, he had no resources to meet the loss of the child except his own resentful will. Inwardly he railed against Heaven and circumstance, but the very cruelty of the blow touched his character at its toughest and most obstinate.

That Demelza was likely to live did not in this early stage strike him as cause for thankfulness. The one loss had shocked and shaken him too much. When his mother had taken him to church as a child he had repeated a psalm which said: "To-day if ye will hear His voice, harden not your hearts." But when his mother died, even while he was crying, something within him had risen up; a barrier to shield off his weakness and tenderness and frailty. He had thought: All right, then, I've lost her and I'm alone. All right then. To-day the adult impulse followed the childish.

But the curious silent testimony of respect and affection given to-day by all these ordinary working or half-starving neighbours of his, turning out from field and farm and mine, had somehow slipped through his defences.

That night the gale blew up again from the north, and all the evening he sat with Demelza. After a collapse when they broke the news to her yesterday she was slowly regaining the lost ground. It was as if nature, bent on its own survival, had not allowed her tired brain strength to dwell on her loss. The one thing it was concerned with was preserving her body. When the serious illness was really over, when the convalescence began, then would be the testing time.

About nine Dwight came again and after he had seen Demelza they sat in the parlour for a time.

Ross was brooding, inattentive, did not seem to follow the simplest remark. He kept on repeating how sorry he was he had not asked the mourners in for food and wine after the funeral. It was the custom in this part of the world, he explained, as if Dwight did not know, to give people food to eat and wine to drink and plenty of it at a funeral. The whole countryside had turned out to-day, he couldn't get over that; he had not expected it at all and hoped they would see that with Demelza still so ill, things couldn't be done as they should have been.

Dwight thought he had been drinking. In fact he was wrong. Since the third day of their illness Ross had lost the taste. The only physical thing wrong with him was lack of sleep.

There was something mentally wrong with him, but Dwight could do nothing for that. Only time or chance or Ross himself could set things to rights there. He could find no submission in defeat. If he was to regain his balance there must be some recoil of the spring of his nature, which had been pressed back within itself unbearably.

Dwight said: "Ross, I have not said this before, but I feel I must say it sometime. It is how acutely I feel that I was not able to save—her."

Ross said: "I had not expected to see Sir Hugh to-day. He has more compassion in him than I thought."

"I feel I should have tried something else—anything. You brought me into this district. You have been a good friend all through. If I could have repaid that . . ."

"There was none from Trenwith at the funeral," said Ross. "I expect they are all still unwell."

"Oh, if they have had this they will not be out for weeks. I have seen so much of this during last summer and autumn. I wish so much . . . Choake will no doubt say it was due to some neglect on my part. He will say that he saved Geoffrey Charles——"

"Demelza saved Geoffrey Charles," Ross said, "and gave Julia in his place."

The gale buffeted tremendously against the house.

Dwight got up. "You must feel that. I'm sorry."

"God, how this wind blows!" Ross said savagely.

"Would you like me to stay to-night?"

"No. You need the sleep also and need your strength for to-morrow. I can spend all this year at recovery. Take a hot drink and then go."

Ross put a kettle on the fire and had soon mixed a jug of grog, which they drank together.

Ross said: "They were a poor lot at the funeral, Dwight. I wish I could have fed and wined them after. They needed it."

"You could not be expected to victual the better part of three villages," Dwight said patiently.

There was a tap on the door.

"Beg pardon, sir," said Jane Gimlett, "but Mistress is asking for you to come and see her."

"Is anything wrong?"

"No, sur."

When Dwight had gone Ross went into the bedroom. Demelza looked very slight and pale in the big bed. She stretched out her hand and he took it and sat on the chair beside her.

Two candles flickered on the table, and the fire smouldered and glowed in the grate. Ross tried to find something to say.

"We had a letter from Verity this forenoon. I don't know what has become of it."

"Is—she—well?"

"Seems so, yes. I will read it you when it comes to light. She was inquiring for Francis and family. She had only just heard that there was some sort of sickness in the house."

"And us?"

". . . She had not heard about us."

"You—must write, Ross. An' tell her."

"I will."

"How are they . . . Ross? Elizabeth and . . ."

"Ill, but improving." He nearly added: "Even Geoffrey Charles," but killed his bitterness. Above all, there must never be any of that. He leaned his head against the wooden side of the bed and tried to forget all that had passed in these last weeks, all the frustration and the pain, tried to think himself back to the happy days of a year ago. So they sat for a long time. The wind was backing a little, would probably blow itself out in the north-west. The fire sank lower, and now and then the candles ducked and trembled.

He moved his hand a little, and at once she caught it more firmly in hers.

"I was not leaving you," he said, "except to stir the fire."

"Let it stay, Ross. Don't go just now. Don't leave me."

"What is it?" he asked.

"I was . . . only thinking."

"What?"

"That Julia—will be lonely. She always so hated the wind."

Ross stayed beside the bed all night. He did not sleep much but dozed fitfully off and on, while the wind buffeted and screamed. Awake and asleep the same thoughts lived in his brain. Frustration and bereavement. Jim Carter and the Warleggans and Julia. Failure and loss. His father dying untended in this same room. His own return from America, his disappointment over Elizabeth and happiness with Demelza. Was all that last joy gone? Perhaps not, but it would have changed its tone, and would be edged with memories. And his own life; what did it add up to? A frenzied futile struggle ending in failure and near bankruptcy. He would be thirty in a few weeks' time. No great age, but a part of his life was ended, a phase, an epoch, a turning, and he could not see himself starting again along the same track. What had ended with this phase? Was it his youth?

How would he feel to-night if everything had happened different, if he had triumphed over the prison authorities and the Warleggans and disease and was not bereaved and beaten, lightheaded and tired to death? He would have been asleep and safe from these thoughts. Yet would the phase have ended just the same? He did not know and was too down to care. It did not seem just then that success in anything had ever been possible or that anything would ever be possible again. Failure was the end of life, all effort was dust, necessary and complete. All roads led to the bleak parapet of death.

In the cold gale of the early morning he fetched more wood, piled the fire high and then drank several glasses of neat brandy to keep out the chill. When he sat down again beside the bed the spirit seemed to set fire to his brain and he fell asleep.

He dreamed fantastic things, in which stress and conflict and the will to fight were all that meant anything: he lived over again in a few moments a concentrate of all the trouble of the last months and climbed back to wakefulness slowly, to find a grey daylight filtering through the curtains and John Gimlett bending before the fire.

"What time is it?" Ross asked in a whisper.

John turned. "About fifteen minutes before eight, sur, and there's a ship drifting in on the beach."

Ross turned and looked at Demelza. She was sleeping peacefully, her tumbled curls about the pillow; but he wished she did not look so white.

"Tes 'ardly light enough to see him proper yet, sur," whispered Gimlett. "I did but notice him when I went for the wood. I do not think any other has spied him so far."

"Eh?"

"The ship, sur. He looks a tidy size."

Ross reached for the brandy bottle and drank another glass. He was stiff and cold and his mouth was dry.

"Where away?"

"Just b'low Damsel Point. He cleared the point but he'll never get out o' the bay in this wind an' sea."

Ross's brain was still working slowly but the new brandy was having effect. There would be pickings for the miners and their families. Good luck to them.

"I b'lieve ye could see him from an upstairs window by now."

Ross got up and stretched. Then he went out of the room and listlessly climbed the stairs. The north window of their old bedroom was so thick with salt that he could see nothing at all, but when he had got it open he soon made out what Gimlett meant. A two-masted ship of fair size. She was dipping and lurching in the trough of the waves. All her sails were gone except a few strips flying in the wind, but some sort of a jury rig had been put up forward and they were trying to keep way on her. Unless she grew wings she would be on the beach soon. It was low water.

Losing interest, he was about to turn away, when something took his attention again and he stared at the ship. Then he went for his father's spyglass and steadied it against the frame of the window. It was a good glass, which his father had had in some bargain from a drunken frigate captain at Plymouth. As he peered the billowing curtains blew and flapped about his head. The wind was dropping at last.

Then he lowered the glass. The ship was the *Queen Charlotte*.

He went down. In the parlour he poured out a drink.

"John!" he called, as Gimlett went past.

"Please?"

"Get Darkie saddled."

Gimlett glanced up at his master's face. In his eyes was a light as if he had seen a vision. But not a holy one.

"Are you feeling slight, sur?"

Ross drained another glass. "Those people at the funeral, John. They should have been entertained and fed. We must see that they are this morning."

Gimlett looked at him in alarm. "Sit you down, sur. There's no need for taking on any more."

"Get Darkie at once, John."

"But——"

Ross met his glance, and Gimlett went quickly away.

In the bedroom Demelza was still quietly sleeping. He put on his cloak and hat and mounted the horse as it came to the door. Darkie had been confined and was mettlesome, could hardly be contained. In a moment they were flying off up the valley.

The first cottage of Grambler village was dark and unstirring when Ross slithered up to it. Jud and Prudie had had smuggled gin in the house and, finding no free drink outcoming from the funeral, had returned, complaining bitterly, to make a night of it on their own.

Knocking brought no response so he put his shoulders to the door and snapped the flimsy bolt. In the dark and the stink he shook someone's shoulder, recognized it as Prudie's, tried again and scored a hit.

"Gor damme," shouted Jud, quivering with self-pity, "a man's not king of his own blathering 'ouse but what folks burst in——"

"Jud," said Ross quietly, "there's a wreck."

"Eh?" Jud sat up, suddenly quiet. "Where's she struck?"

"Hendrawna Beach. Any moment now. Go rouse Grambler people and send word to Mellin and Marasanvose. I am on to Sawle."

Jud squinted in the half-light, the bald top of his head looking like another face. "Why for bring all they? They'll be thur soon enough. Now ef——"

"She's a sizable ship," Ross said. "Carrying food. There'll be pickings for all."

"Aye, but——"

"Do as I say, or I'll bolt you in here from the outside and do the job myself."

"I'll do en, Cap'n. Twas only as you might say a passing thought, like. What is she?"

Ross went out, slamming the door behind him so that the whole crazy cottage shook. A piece of dried mud fell from the roof upon Prudie's face.

"What's amiss wi' you!" She hit Jud across the head and sat up.

Jud sat there scratching inside his shirt.

"Twas some queer, that," he said. "Twas some queer, I tell ee."

"What? What's took you, wakin' at this time?"

"I was dreamin' of old Joshua," said Jud. "Thur he was as clear as spit, just like I seen un in 'seventy-seven, when he went after that little giglet at St. Ives. An' damme, ef I didn't wake up an' *thur* he was standin' beside the bed, plain as plain."

"Who?"

"Old Joshua."

"You big soft ape, he's been cold in 'is grave these six year an' more!"

"Aye, twas Cap'n Ross, really."

"Then load me, why don't ee say so!"

"Because," said Jud, "I've never seen 'im look so much like old Joshua before."

CHAPTER IX   By superb seamanship Captain Bray kept her off the beach for over an hour.

In this he was helped by the sudden lull in the storm, and once there even seemed a chance that he would fight his way clear.

But then the tide began to flow strongly and all was lost. Ross was home again just in time to see her come in.

He remembered the scene years after. Although the tide was out the sand was wet and foam-covered right up to the sand hills and the shingle. In places the cliffs were grey to the top with foam; and suds whirled in flocks between the cliffs like gulls wheeling. Along the edge of the sea proper a block rim of thirty or forty people were already come at his summons for the harvest. Riding in quickly, stern foremost, racked and tossed and half smothered by the sea, was the *Queen Charlotte*. As Ross climbed the wall the sun sprang up out of the broken black clouds fleeing to the east. A sickly unearthly yellow lit the sky, and the mountainous waves were tarnished with flecks of gold light. Then the sun was swallowed up in a tattered curtain of cloud and the light died.

She struck stern first as her captain aimed to do, but did not run in firm enough and a side wash lurching in a great pyramid across the tide broke over her and slewed her round broadside. In a few seconds she had heeled over, her decks facing the shore and the waves spouting.

Ross ran across the beach, drunkenly in the gusts; she had come ashore midway up, just this side of Leisure Cliff.

There was no chance of reaching her yet, but she was quickly being washed in. The waves had a tremendous run on them, would flood in halfway to the sand hills and then go out, leaving great glassy areas of water a half inch deep.

The men on board were trying to launch a boat. This was the worst thing, but on an incoming tide they stood no better chance by staying in the ship.

They lowered her from the well deck and set her in the water without mishap, and then, with only three or four in, a flood of water swirled round the lee side of the brigantine and swept the small boat away. The men rowed frantically to keep within the shelter, but they were as in a tide race and were borne quite clear. A wave rushed on them, and smothered in water, they were carried inshore. Then they were left behind in the trough, and the next wave turned the boat upside down and broke it to pieces.

The men on shore had given way before the tide, but as the biggest waves passed, Ross and a few others stood staring out at the wreck while the retreating water rushed past their knees trying to carry them along.

"We'll not get to un this morning," said Vigus, rubbing his hands and shivering with cold. "Tide'll break un to bits, an' we shall have the pickings on the ebb. Might just so well go home."

"I can't see one o' they men," said Zacky Martin. "I expect they've been sucked under and'll be spewed out farther downcoast."

"She'll not stand in this sea even for one tide," Ross said. "There'll be pickings soon enough."

Zacky glanced at him. There was a savagery in Ross this morning.

"Look fur yourself!" someone shouted.

An immense wave had hit the wreck and in a second a straight stiff column of spray stood two hundred feet in the air, to collapse slowly and disintegrate before the wind. Two men grasped Ross and dragged him back.

"She's going over!" he shouted.

They tried to run but could not. The wave caught them waist-high, swept them before it like straws; they were carried part way up the beach and left behind struggling in two feet of water, while the wave rushed on to spend its strength. There was just time to gain a foothold and brace themselves against the sudden rush back again. Ross wiped the water out of his eyes.

The *Queen Charlotte* could not last now. The great weight of the wave had not only carried her in; it had almost turned her bottom up, snapping off both masts and washing away all but one or two of the crew. Spars and tangles of wreckage, barrels and masts, coils of rope and sacks of corn were bobbing in the surf.

People streaming down to the scene carried axes and baskets and empty sacks. They were a spur to those who were before them and soon the shallow surf was black with people struggling to reach what they could. The tide washed in everything it could strip away. One of the crew had come ashore alive, three dead, the rest had gone.

As the morning grew and the day cleared more people came, with mules, ponies, dogs to carry away the stuff. But only a small part of the cargo was yet ashore, and there was not enough to go round. Ross made the people divide the spoils. If a barrel of pilchards came in it was broken open and doled out, a basketful to everyone who came. He was everywhere, ordering, advising, encouraging.

At ten three kegs of rum and one of brandy came in together and were at once opened. With hot spirit inside them men grew reckless and some even fought and struggled together in the water. As the tide rose, some fell back into the sand hills and lit bonfires from the wreckage and began a carouse. Newcomers plunged into the surf. Sometimes men and women were caught in the outrun of a wave and went tobogganing back into the sea. One was drowned.

At noon they were driven off most of the beach and watched the pounding of the hulk from a distance. Ross went back to Nampara, had something to eat, drank a great deal and was out again. He was gentle in reply to Demelza's questings but unmoved.

A part of the deck had given way and more sacks of corn were coming in. Frantic that these should be taken before all the corn was spoiled, many had rushed down again, and as he followed them Ross passed the successful ones coming away. A great dripping sack of flour staggered slowly up the hill and under it, sweating and red-faced, was Mrs. Zacky. Aunt Betsy Triggs led a half-starved mule, laden with baskets of pilchards and a sack of corn. Old Man Daniel helped Beth Daniel with a table and two chairs. Jope Ishbel and Whitehead Scoble dragged a dead pig. Others carried firewood, one a basket of dripping coal.

On the beach Ross found men trying to loop a rope over a piece of hatchway which the sea was carrying out again. Restless, unsatisfied, trying to forget his own hurt, he went down to join them.

By two-thirty the tide had been ebbing an hour and nearly five hundred people waited. Another hundred danced and sang around the fires on the sand hills or lay drinking above high water. Not a piece of driftwood or a broken spar lay anywhere. Rumour had whispered that the Illuggan and St. Ann's miners were coming to claim a share. This lent urgency where none was needed.

At three Ross waded out into the surf. He had been wet on and off all day, and the stinging cold of the water did not strike him now.

It was bad going out—unless the sea malevolently chose to take you—but when he judged himself far enough he dived into a wave and swam underwater. He came up to face one that nearly choked him, but after a while began to make headway. Once in the lee of the wreck he swam up and grasped the splintered spar which had once been the main mast and now stuck out towards the shore. He hauled himself up; men on shore shouted and waved soundlessly.

Not safe yet to climb to the high side of the deck. He untied the rope about his waist and hitched it to the root of the mast. A raised hand was a signal to the shore, and the rope quivered and tautened. In a few minutes there would be a score of others aboard with axes and saws.

Still astride the mast, he glanced about the ship. No sign of life. All the forecastle had given way and it was from here that the cargo had come. There would be pickings astern. He glanced to the poop. A different sight now from Truro Creek. All this week of gales and blizzard she must have been beating about in the channel and off Land's End. For once the Warleggans had met their match.

He stepped off the mast and, leaning flat on the deck, edged his way towards the poop. The door of the cabin faced him askew. It was an inch or two ajar but jammed. A trickle of water still ran from a corner of it as from the mouth of a sick old man.

He found a spar and thrust it into the door, tried to force it open. The spar splintered but the gap widened. As he got his shoulder into the opening the ship rocked with another great wave. Water flung itself into the air, high, high; as it fell the rest of the wave swirled round the ship, rising to his shoulders; he clung tight, it swirled, dragged, sucked, gave way at last. Water poured from the cabin, deluged him long after the rest had gone. He waited until this too had fallen to his waist before he forced his way in.

Something was tapping gently at his leg. Curious green gloom as if underwater. The three larboard portholes were buried deep, the starboard ones, glass smashed, looked at the sky. A table floating, a periwig, a news sheet. On the upper wall a map still hung. He looked down. The thing tapping his leg was a man's hand. The man floated face downwards, gently, submissively; the water draining out by the door had brought him over to greet Ross. For a second it gave the illusion of life.

Ross caught him by the collar and lifted his head. It was Matthew Sanson.

Wth a grunt Ross dropped the head back in the water and squeezed his way out into the air.

As the tide went out hundreds waded out and fell on the ship. With axes they burst open the hatches and dragged out the rest of the cargo. A quantity of mixed goods in the rear hatch was undamaged, and more kegs of rum were found. The deck planks were torn up, the wheel and binnacle carried off, the clothing and bits of furniture in the bunks and cabins. Jud, well gone in liquor, was saved from drowning in two feet of water, his arms clasped round the gilt figurehead. He had either mistaken her for a real woman or the gilt for real gold.

As dusk began to fall another bonfire was set up near the ship to light the scavengers on their way. The rising wind blew whorls of smoke flatly across the wet beach where it joined the fires on the sand hills.

Ross left the ship and walked home. He changed his clothes, which were stiff with half-dried salt, had a brief meal and then sat with Demelza. But the restless devil inside himself was not appeased; the pain and the fury were not gone. He went out again in the gathering windy dark.

By the light of a lantern a few of the more sober citizens were burying seven corpses at the foot of the sand hills. Ross stopped to tell them to go deep. He did not want the next spring tide uncovering them. He asked Zacky how many had been saved and was told that two had been taken to Mellin.

He climbed a little and stared down at the crowd round a bonfire. Nick Vigus had brought his flute and people were jigging to his tune. Many were drunk and lay about, too weak to walk home. The wind was bitter, and there would be illness even in this bounty.

A hand caught his arm. It was John Gimlett.

"Beg pardon, sur."

"What is it?"

"The miners, sur. From Illuggan an' St. Ann's. The first ones are comin' down the valley. I thought——"

"Are there many?"

"In their 'undreds, Bob Nanfan d'say."

"Well, get you back into the house, man, and bolt the doors. They're only coming to loot the ship."

"Aye, sur, but there's little left to loot—on the ship."

Ross rubbed his chin. "I know. But there's little left to drink either. We shall manage them."

He went down to the beach. He hoped the Illuggan miners had not spent all the daylight hours drinking by the way.

On the beach things were quieter. The bonfire sent a constant shower of sparks chasing across the sand. Just beyond the wreck the surf piled up, a pale mountainous reef in the half-dark.

Then his arm was caught a second time. Pally Rogers from Sawle.

"Look ee! What's that, sur? Isn't it a light?"

Ross stared out to sea.

"Ef that be another ship she's coming ashore too!" said Rogers. "She's too close in to do else. The Lord God ha' mercy on their souls!"

Ross suddenly caught the glint of a light beyond the surf. Then he saw a second light close beside. He began to run towards the edge of the sea.

As he neared it the foam came to meet him, detaching itself from the mass and scudding and bowling across the sand in hundreds of flakes of all sizes. He splashed into a few inches of water and stopped, peering, trying to get his breath in the wind. Rogers caught him up.

"Over thur, sur!"

Although the gale had grown again a few stars were out, and you could see well enough. A big ship, bigger than the brigantine, was coming in fast. A light forward and one amidships but no stern light. One minute she seemed right out of the water, and the next only her masts showed. There was no question of manœuvring to beach her; she was coming in anyhow as the waves threw her about.

Someone aboard had seen how near the end was, for a flare was lit—rags soaked in oil—and it flickered and flared in the wind. Dozens on the beach saw it.

She came in nearer the house than the *Queen Charlotte* and seemed to strike with scarcely a jar. Only her foremast toppling slowly showed the impact.

At the same moment the vanguard of the St. Ann's and Illuggan miners streamed on to the beach.

CHAPTER X *Pride of Madras*, an East Indiaman homeward bound with a full cargo of silks, tea, and spices, had suddenly appeared, a flying wraith in the fog of the storm, off Sennen in the forenoon of that day.

She had seemed certain to strike Gurnard's Head but the lull in the gale had just given her sea room. Then she had been seen off Godrevy, and a little later the miners of Illuggan and St. Ann's, with news of the *Queen Charlotte* wreck in their ears, had heard that a finer prize was due any minute at Gwithian or Basset's Cove.

So they had been pulled two ways, and instead of marching for Nampara had flocked into the gin shops and kiddleys of St. Ann's while scouts kept watch on the cliffs.

She had slipped right under St. Ann's Beacon unseen in the mist, and it was not until just before dusk that she had been picked up again ducking across the mouth of Sawle Cove. She must come ashore within a few miles, and the miners had followed along the cliffs and down the lanes, so that their leaders reached Hendrawna Beach at the same time as the ship.

What followed would not have been pretty in the sun of a summer afternoon. Happening as it did through a winter's night, starlit in a gale, it was full of the shadowed horror and shrill cadences of another world.

She came in so swiftly that only half a dozen of the locals knew of her until she lit the flare. Then when she struck, everyone began to run towards her. They and the newcomers converged together. Rivalry flared up in a second.

To begin they could not get near her; but the tide had still another two hours to ebb and very soon the venturesome, reckless with rum and gin, plunged through the surf. There was still one light on the ship though the waves were breaking right over her, and two sailors were able to swim ashore, one with a rope. But they could get no one interested enough to hold it, and a third sailor, washed ashore half conscious, was set upon and stripped of his shirt and breeches and left groaning naked on the sand.

Great numbers of miners were now coming, and soon the grey of the sands was black in a huge semicircle before the ship. Ross played no part in it now, either in wreck or rescue. He had edged a little away to watch, but those who saw his face saw no disapproval on it. It was as if the goad of the pain in him would leave him no respite for judgment and sanity.

Others of the crew had got ashore, but now it was the common thing to seize anything they carried, and those who resisted were stripped and roughly handled and left to crawl away as best they could. Two who drew knives were knocked unconscious.

By seven the ship was dry, and by then there were three thousand people on the beach. Barrels in which the pilchards had come ashore were set alight, and these, thick with oil, flared and smoked like giant torches. The ship was a carcase on which a myriad ants crawled. Men were everywhere, hacking with knives and axes, dragging out from the bowels of the ship the riches of the Indies. Dozens lay about the beach, drunk or senseless from a fight. The crew and eight passengers—saved at the last by Zacky Martin and Pally Rogers and a few others—broke up into two parties, the larger, led by the mate, going off into the country in search of help, the rest huddling in a group some distance from the ship, while the captain stood guard over them with a drawn sword.

With rich goods seized and fine brandy drunk, fights broke out everywhere. Smouldering feuds between one hamlet and another, one mine and the next, had come to flame. Empty bellies and empty pockets reacted alike to the temptations of the night. To the shipwrecked people it seemed that they had been cast upon the shore of a wild and savage foreign land where thousands of dark-faced men and women talking an uncouth tongue were waiting to tear them to pieces for the clothes they wore.

As the tide began to creep round the ship again Ross went aboard, swarming up by a rope that hung from her bows. He found an orgy of destruction. Men lay drunk about the deck, others fought for a roll of cloth or curtains or cases of tea, often tearing or spilling what they quarrelled over. But the saner men, aware like Ross that time was short, were labouring to clear the ship while she was still intact. Like *Queen Charlotte, Pride of Madras* lay beam on, and another tide might break her up. Lanterns were in the hold, and dozens of men were below passing up goods in a chain to the deck, where they were carried to the side and thrown or lowered to others waiting on the sand. These were all St. Ann's men, and farther forward the Illuggan men were doing the same.

Aft he found some from Grambler and Sawle tearing out the panelling in the captain's cabin. Among all the hammering and the shrill squeaks of wood, Paul Daniel slept peacefully in a corner. Ross hauled him to his feet by the collar of his jacket, but Paul only smiled and sank down again.

Jack Cobbledick nodded. "Tes all right, sur. We'll see to 'e when we d'leave."

"Another half-hour is all you can take."

Ross went on deck again. The high wind was pure and cold. He took a deep breath. Above and behind all the shouts, the laughter, the distant singing, the hammering, the scuffles and the groans, was another sound, that of the surf, coming in. It made a noise to-night like hundreds of carts rumbling over wooden bridges.

He avoided two men fighting in the scuppers, went forward and tried to rouse some of the drunks. He spoke of the tide to some of those who were working, had bare nods in exchange.

He stared over the beach. The funnels of fire and smoke from the barrels were still scattering sparks over the sand. Sections of the crowd were lit in umber and orange. Milling faces and black smoke round a dozen funeral pyres. A pagan rite. Back in the sand hills the volcanoes spumed.

He slid over the side, hand by hand down the rope. In water up to his knees.

He pushed his way through the crowd. It seemed as if normal feelings were coming to him. Circulation to a dead limb.

He looked about for the survivors. They were still huddled together just beyond the thickest of the crowd.

As he came near, two of the sailors drew knives and the captain half lifted his sword.

"Keep your distance, man! Keep clear! We'll fight."

Ross eyed them over. A score of shivering exhausted wretches; if they had no attention several might die before morning.

"I was about to offer you shelter," he said.

At the sound of his more cultured voice the captain lowered his sword. "Who are you? What do you want?"

"My name is Poldark. I have a house near here."

There was a whispered consultation. "And you offer us shelter?"

"Such as I have. A fire. Blankets. Something hot to drink."

Even now there was hesitation: they had been so used that they were afraid of treachery. And the captain had some idea of staying here the night to be able to bear his full witness to the courts. But the eight passengers overruled him.

"Very well, sir," said the captain, keeping his sword unsheathed, "if you will lead the way."

Ross inclined his head and moved off slowly across the beach. The captain fell into step beside him, the two armed sailors followed close behind and the rest straggled after.

They passed several dozen people dancing round a fire and drinking fresh-brewed tea (ex *Pride of Madras*) laced with brandy (ex *Pride of Madras*). They overtook six mules laden so heavy with rolls of cloth that their feet sank inches in the sand at every step. They skirted forty or fifty men fighting in a pack for four gold ingots.

The captain said in a voice trembling with indignation:

"Have you any control over these—these savages?"

"None whatever," Ross said.

"Is there no law in this land?"

"None which will stand before a thousand miners."

"It—it is a disgrace. A crying disgrace. Two years ago I was shipwrecked off Patagonia—and treated less barbarously."

"Perhaps the natives were better fed than we in this district."

"Fed? Food—oh, if it were food we carried and these men were starving——"

"Many have been near it for months."

"—then there might be some excuse. But it is not food. To pillage the ship, and we ourselves barely escaped with our lives! I never thought such a day could be! It is monstrous!"

"There is much in this world which is monstrous," Ross said. "Let us be thankful they were content with your shirts."

The captain glanced at him. A passing lantern showed up the taut, lean, overstrained face, the pale scar, the half-lidded eyes. The captain said no more.

As they climbed the wall at the end of the beach they saw a group of men coming towards them from Nampara House. Ross stopped and stared. Then he caught the creak of leather.

"Here is the law you were invoking."

The men came up. A dozen dismounted troopers in the charge of a sergeant. Captain McNeil and his men had been moved some months before, and these were strangers. They had marched out from Truro on hearing of the wreck of the *Queen Charlotte*.

This much the sergeant was explaining when the captain burst in with an angry flood of complaint, and soon he was surrounded by the passengers and crew, demanding summary justice. The sergeant plucked at his lip and stared across at the beach, which stirred and quickened with a wild and sinister life of its own.

"You go down there at your own risk, Sergeant," Ross said.

There was a sudden silence, followed by another babel of threat and complaint from the shipwrecked people.

"All right," said the sergeant. "Go easy. Go easy now, we'll put a stop to the looting, never you fear. We'll see no more is carried away. We'll put a stop to it."

"You would be advised to delay until daylight," Ross said. "The night will have cooled tempers. Remember the two customs officers who were killed at Gwithian last year."

"I have me orders, sir." The sergeant glanced uneasily at his small band and then again at the struggling smoky mass on the beach. "We'll see all this is put a stop to." He patted his musket.

"I warn you," Ross said, "half of them are in drink and many fighting among themselves. If you interfere they'll stop their quarrelling and turn on you. And so far it has been fists and a few sticks. But if you fire into them not half of you will come out of it alive."

The sergeant hesitated again. "Ye'd advise me to wait until first light?"

"It is your only hope."

The captain burst out again, but some of the passengers, shivering and half dead from exposure, cut him short and pleaded to be led to shelter.

Ross went on to the house, leaving the troopers still hesitant on the edge of the maelstrom. At the door of the house he stopped again.

"You'll pardon me, gentlemen, but may I ask you for quietness. My wife is just recovering from a grave illness and I do not wish to disturb her."

The chattering and muttering slowly died away to silence.

He led the way in.

CHAPTER XI   Ross woke at the first light. He had slept heavily for seven hours. The inescapable pain was still there but some emotional purging of the night had deadened its old power. It was the first time for a week he had undressed, the first full sleep he had had. He had gone up to his old room, for Demelza had seemed better last night, and Jane Gimlett had said she would sleep in the chair before the fire.

He dressed quickly, stiffly, but was quiet about it. Below him in the parlour and in the next two rooms twenty-two men were sleeping. Let them lie. All the strain of last night had brought the stiffness of the French musket wound back, and it was with a sharp limp that he went to the window. The wind was still high and the glass as thick with salt. He opened the window and stared out on Hendrawna Beach.

Dawn had just broken, and in a clear sky seven black clouds were following each other across the lightening east like seven ill-begotten sons of the storm. The tide was nearly out and both wrecks were dry. The *Queen Charlotte*, lying almost deserted, might have been an old whale cast up by the sea. Around and about the *Pride of Madras* people still milled and crawled. The sands were patchy with people, and at first he thought Leisure Cliff and those east of it had been decorated by some whim of the revellers. Then he saw that the wind had been the only reveller, and costly silks had been blown from the wreck and hung in inaccessible places all along the beach and cliffs. Goods and stores were still scattered on the sand hills and just above high-water mark, but a large part was already gone.

There had been bloodshed in the night.

Jack Cobbledick, calling in just before midnight, had told him that the troopers had gone down to the beach and tried to stand guard over the wreck. But the tide had driven them off and the wreckers had gone on with salvaging their prizes as if the soldiers had not existed. The sergeant, trying to get his way by peaceful measures, was roughly handled; and some of the soldiers fired into the air to scare the crowd. Then they had been forced off the beach step by step with about a thousand angry men following them.

A little later an Illuggan miner had been caught molesting a St. Ann's woman, and a huge fight had developed which had only been broken by the inrush of the sea threatening to carry off the booty, and not before a hundred or more men were stretched out on the beach.

Ross did not know whether the troopers had again tried to take over the wreck when the tide went back, but he thought not. It was more likely that they still kept discreet watch in the sand hills while the sergeant sent for reinforcements.

But in another six hours the ships would be nothing but hulks, every plank and stick carried away, the bones picked clean.

He closed the window, and as the rimed glass shut out the view the pang of his own personal loss returned. He had planned so much for Julia, had watched her grow from a scarcely separable entity, seen her nature unfold, the very beginning of traits and characteristics make their quaint showing. It was hardly believable that now they would never develop, that all that potential sweetness should dry up at its fount and turn to dust. Hardly believable and hardly bearable.

He slowly put on his coat and waistcoat and limped downstairs.

In the bedroom Jane Gimlett slept soundly before a fire that had gone out. Demelza was awake.

He sat beside the bed and she slipped her hand into his. It was thin and weak, but there was a returning firmness underneath.

"How are you?"

"Much, much better. I slept all the night through. Oh, Ross. Oh, my dear, I can feel the strength returning to me. In a few days more I shall be up."

"Not yet awhile."

"And did you sleep?"

"Like the——" He changed his simile. "Like one drugged."

She squeezed his hand. "An' all the folk from the ship?"

"I have not been to see."

She said: "I have never seen a real shipwreck, not in daytime. Not a proper one."

"Soon I'll carry you up to our old bedroom and you can see it all through the spyglass."

"This morning?"

"Not this morning."

"I wish it was not this time o' year," she said. "I seem to be tired for the summer."

"It will come."

There was a pause.

"I believe to-morrow will be too late to see the best of the wreck."

"Hush, or you'll wake Jane."

"Well, you could wrap me in blankets an' I should come to no harm."

He sighed and put her hand against his cheek. It was not a disconsolate sigh, for her returning life was a tonic to his soul. Whatever she suffered, whatever loss came to her, she would throw it off, for it was not in her nature to go under. Although she was the woman and he a fierce and sometimes arrogant man, hers was the stronger nature because the more pliant. That did not mean she did not feel Julia's death as deeply and as bitterly, but he saw that she would recover first. It might be because he had had all the other failures and disappointments. But chiefly it was because some element had put it in her nature to be happy. She was born so and could not change. He thanked God for it. Wherever she went and however long she lived she would be the same, lavishing interest on the things she loved and contriving for their betterment, working for and bringing up her children. . . .

Ah, there was the rub.

He found she was looking at him. He smiled.

"Have you heard of them at Trenwith?" she asked.

"Not since I told you before." He looked at her and saw that despite her loss there was no trace of bitterness in her thoughts of Elizabeth and Francis. It made him ashamed of his own.

"Did they say there was any loss among those who were in the *Pride of Madras?*"

"None of the passengers. Some of the crew."

She sighed. "Ross, I b'lieve the miners, the Illuggan and St. Ann's miners, have made a rare mess of the garden. I heard 'em tramping over it all last evening, and Jane said they had mules and donkeys with them."

"If anything is damaged it can be put to rights," Ross said.

"Was Father amongst them, did you see?"

"I saw nothing of him."

"Maybe he is reformed in that way too. Though I doubt there must have been many Methodies among those who came. I wonder what—what he will say about this. . . ."

Ross knew she was not referring to the wreck.

"Nothing that can make any difference, my dear. Nothing could have made any difference."

She nodded. "I know. Sometimes I wonder if she ever really stood any chance."

"Why?"

"I don't know, Ross. She seemed to have it so bad from the start. And she was so young. . . ."

There was a long silence.

At length Ross got up and pulled the curtain back. Even this did not wake Jane Gimlett. The sun had risen and was gilding the waving treetops in the valley.

As he came back to the bed Demelza wiped her eyes.

"I think, I believe I like you with a beard, Ross."

He put his hand up. "Well, I do not like myself. It will come off sometime to-day."

"Is it going to be a fine day, do you think?"

"Fine enough."

"I wish I could see the sun. That is the drawback to this room, there is no sun until afternoon."

"Well, so soon as you are well you shall go upstairs again."

"Ross, I should like to see our room again. Take me up, just for a few minutes, please. I believe I could walk up if I tried."

On an emotional impulse he said: "Very well: if you wish it."

He lifted her out of the bed, wrapped a blanket round her legs, two round her shoulders, picked her up. She had lost a lot of weight, but somehow the feel of her arm about his neck, the living companionable substance of her, was like a balm. Still quiet to avoid rousing Jane, he slipped out of the room, mounted the creaking stair. He carried her into their bedroom, set her down on the bed. Then he went to the window and opened one to clean a circle in the salt of the other. He shut the window and went back to the bed. Tears were streaming down her face.

"What is wrong?"

"The cot," she said. "I had forgotten the cot."

He put his arm about her and they sat quiet for a minute or two. Then he picked her up again and took her to the window and sat her in a chair.

She stared out on the scene, and with his cheek pressed against hers he stared with her. She took up a corner of the blanket and tried to stop the tears.

She said: "How pretty the cliffs look with all those streamers on 'em."

"Yes."

"Redruth Fair," she said. "The beach puts me in mind of that, the day after it is over."

"It will take some clearing, but the sea is a good scavenger."

"Ross," she said, "I should like you to make it up with Francis sometime. It would be better all round."

"Sometime."

"Sometime soon."

"Sometime soon." He had no heart to argue with her to-day.

The sun shone full upon her face, showing the thin cheeks and the pallid skin.

"When something happens," she said, "like what has just happened to us, it makes all our quarrels seem small and mean, as if we were quarrelling when we hadn't the right. Didn't we ought to find all the friendship we can?"

"If friendship is to be found."

"Yes. But didn't we ought to seek it? Can't all our quarrels be buried and forgot, so that Verity can come to visit us and we go to Trenwith and we can—can live in friendship and not hatred while there's time."

Ross was silent. "I believe yours is the only wisdom, Demelza," he said at length.

They watched the scene on the beach.

"I shan't have to finish that frock for Julia now," she said. "It was that dainty too."

"Come," he said. "You will be catching cold."

"No. I am quite warm, Ross. Let me stay a little longer in the sun."